U0358348

黑暗之心

HEART OF DARKNESS

[英] 约瑟夫·康拉德 著

李行宽 注译

上海交通大学出版社

SHANGHAI JIAO TONG UNIVERSITY PRESS

内容简介

　　黄昏的泰晤士河上，马洛向他的船员朋友们讲述了自己曾经驾驶一艘汽船，沿着非洲刚果河溯流而上，去丛林深处救援一个名叫库尔茨的传奇探险者的经历。一路上，他目睹了非洲大地荒凉原始的景象，也目睹了殖民者对黑人劳工的种种暴行；在神秘的白雾散去的时候，汽船遭遇了野人部落的突然袭击。沉默的原始丛林里，究竟掩盖着怎样不为人所知的、惊心动魄的故事？库尔茨最后的遗言，又给马洛带来了怎样的震撼？一切的答案，尽在这部《黑暗之心》。

图书在版编目（CIP）数据

　　黑暗之心 /（英）约瑟夫·康拉德（Joseph Conrad）
著；李行宽注译. --上海：上海交通大学出版社，
2024.8（2024.10重印）--（康拉德作品译评系列）. -- ISBN 978-7-313-
31423-9

　　I. I561.44

　　中国国家版本馆CIP数据核字第2024WQ2419号

黑暗之心

HEI'AN ZHI XIN

著　　者：［英］约瑟夫·康拉德　　　　注　　译：李行宽

出版发行：上海交通大学出版社　　　　地　　址：上海市番禺路951号

邮政编码：200030　　　　　　　　　电　　话：021-64071208

印　　制：上海颛辉印刷厂有限公司　　经　　销：全国新华书店

开　　本：880mm × 1230mm　1/32　　印　　张：14.375

字　　数：319千字

版　　次：2024年8月第1版　　　　　印　　次：2024年10月第2次印刷

书　　号：ISBN 978-7-313-31423-9

定　　价：66.00元

约瑟夫·康拉德 (Joseph Conrad，1857-1924)，20世纪最杰出的小说家之一。他的代表作有：航海小说《"水仙号"上的黑水手》《台风》《青春》等，丛林小说《黑暗之心》《吉姆老爷》《礁湖》等，政治小说《诺斯特罗莫》《间谍》《在西方的目光下》等。其作品极具现代主义内涵，尤其是作品中对文明本质和人性的探讨发人深思，后世的许多欧美作家深受其影响。

李志，字行宽，号场外居士。祖籍广东鹤山，生于山东青岛，现为华南地区一名普通的高校物理教师。兴趣广泛，尤爱文史。曾讲授数理逻辑、科学史，业余钻研"唐八史"，小有心得。喜爱金庸、古龙，以及杰克·伦敦、爱伦·坡。十分欣赏约瑟夫·康拉德的小说，希望未来能够一直翻译下去，让这位优秀的英文作家的作品在博雅的汉语中焕发新生。欢迎读者来信交流，邮箱：lixingkuan2024@163.com。

代　序

一个近代最伟大的境界与人格的创造者

我最爱的作家——康拉得[1]

对约瑟·康拉得（Joseph Conrad，一八五七——一九二四年）的个人历史，我知道的不多，也就不想多说什么。圣佩韦的方法——要明白一本作品须先明白那个著者——在这里是不便利用的；我根本不想批评这近代小说界中的怪杰。我只是要就我所知道的，不完全的，几乎是随便的，把他介绍一下罢了。

谁都知道，康拉得是个波兰人，原名 Teodor Jozef Konrad Korzeniowski；当十六岁的时候才仅晓得六个英国字；在写过 Lord Jim[2]（一九〇〇）以后还不懂得 cad 这个字的意思（我记得仿佛是 Arnold Bennet[3] 这么说过）。可是他竟自给乔叟，莎士比亚，狄更斯们的国家增加许多不朽的著作。这岂止是件不容

---

1. 老舍译作康拉得，此处保留。——校者注
2. 即康拉德的代表作之一《吉姆爷》。——校者注
3. 阿诺德·本涅特，英国作家。——校者注

易的事呢！从他的文字里，我们也看得出，他对于创作是多么严重热烈，字字要推敲，句句要思索；写了再改，改了还不满意；有时候甚至于绝望。他不拿写作当种游戏。"我所要成就的工作是，借着文字的力量，使你听到，使你觉到——首要的是使你看到。"是的，他的材料都在他的经验中，但是从他的作品的结构中可以窥见：他是把材料翻过来掉过去的布置排列，一切都在他的心中，而一切需要整理染制，使它们成为艺术的形式。他差不多是殉了艺术，就是这么累死的。文字上的困难使他不能不严重，不感觉艰难，可是严重到底胜过了艰难。虽然文法家与修辞家还能指出他的许多错误来，但是那些错误，即使是无可原谅的，也不足以掩遮住他的伟大。英国人若是只拿他在文法上与句子结构上的错误来取笑他，那只是英国人的藐小 [1]。他无须请求他们原谅，他应得的是感谢。

　　他是个海船上的船员船长，这也是大家都知道的。这个决定了他的作品内容。海与康拉得是分不开的。我们很可以想象到：这位海上的诗人，到处详细的观察，而后把所观察的集成多少组，像海上星星的列岛。从飘浮着一个枯枝，到那无限的大洋，他提取出他的世界，而给予一些浪漫的精气，使现实的一切都立起来，呼吸着海上的空气。Peyrol 在 *The Rover* [2] 里，把从海上劫取的金钱偷偷缝在帆布的背心里；康拉得把海上的一切偷来，装在心里。也正像 Peyrol，海陆上所能发生的奇事都不足以使他惊异；他不慌不忙的，细细品味所见到听到

---

1. 本篇错别字因老舍原文如此，不作修改。——校者注
2. 康拉得的最后一部长篇小说，中文译名为《流浪者》，皮罗尔（Peyrol）为小说主人公。——校者注

的奇闻怪事，而后极冷静的把它们逼真的描写下来；他的写实手段有时候近于残酷。可是他不只是个冷酷的观察者，他有自己的道德标准与人生哲理，在写实的背景后有个生命的解释与对于海上一切的认识。他不仅描写，他也解释；要不然，有过航海经验的固不止他一个人呀。

关于他的个人历史，我只想提出上面这两点；这都给我们一些教训："美是艰苦的"，与"诗是情感的自然流露"，常常在文学的主张上碰了头，而不愿退让。前者作到极端便把文学变成文学的推敲，而忽略了更大的企图；后者作到极端便信笔一挥即成文章，即使显出点聪明，也是华而不实的。在我们的文学遗产里，八股匠与所谓的才子便是这二者的好例证。在白话文学兴起以后，正有点像西欧的浪漫运动，一方面打破了文艺的义法与拘束，自然便在另一方面提倡灵感与情感的自然流露。这个，使浪漫运动产生了伟大的作品，也产生了随生转灭，毫无价值的作品。我们的白话文学运动显然的也吃着这个亏，大家觉得创作容易，因而就不慎重，假如不是不想努力。白话的运用在我们手里，不像文言那样准确，处处有轨可循；它还是个待炼制的东西。虽然我们用白话没有象一个波兰人用英文那么多的困难，可是我们应当，应当知道怎样的小心与努力。这个，就是我爱康拉得的一个原因；他使我明白了什么叫严重。每逢我读他的作品，我总好像看见了他，一个受着苦刑的诗人，和艺术拼命！至于材料方面，我在佩服他的时候感到自己的空虚；想象只是一股火力，经验——像金子——须是先搜集来的。无疑的，康拉得是个最有本事的说故事者。可是他似乎不敢离开海与海的势力圈。他也曾写过不完全以海为背景的故事，他的艺术在此等故事中也许更精到。可是他的名誉到底不建筑在这样的故事上。一遇到海和在南洋的冒险，他便没有敌手。我不敢说康拉得是个大思想家；他绝不是那种寓言家，先有了要宣传的哲理，而后去找与这哲理平行的故事。他是由故事，由他的记忆中的经验，找到一个结论。这结论也许是错误的，可是他的故事永远活跃的立在我们面前。于此，我们知道怎样培养我们自己的想象，怎样先去丰富我们自己的经验，而后以我们的作品来丰富别人的经验，精神的和物质的。

关于他的作品，我没都读过；就是所知道的八九本也都记不甚清了，因为那都是在七八年前读的。对于别人的著作，我也是随读随忘；但忘记的程度是不同的，我记得康拉得的人物与境地比别的作家的都多一些，都比较的清楚一些。他不但使我闭上眼就看见那在风暴里的船，与南洋各色各样的人，而且因着他的影响我才想到南洋去。他的笔上魔术使我渴想闻到那咸的海，与从海岛上浮来的花香；使我渴想亲眼看到他所写的一切。别人的小说没能使我这样。我并不想去冒险，海也不是我的爱人——我更爱山——我的梦想是一种传染，由康拉得得来的。我真的到了南洋，可是，啊！我写出了什么呢？！失望使我加倍的佩服了那《台风》与《海的镜》的作家。我看到了他所写的一部分，证明了些他的正确与逼真，可是他不准我摹仿；他是海王！

可是康拉得在把我送到南洋以前，我已经想从这位诗人偷学一些招数。在我写《二马》以前，我读了他几篇小说。他的结构方法迷惑住了我。我也想试用他的方法。这在《二马》里留下一点——只是那么一点——痕迹。我把故事的尾巴摆在第一页，而后倒退着叙说。我只学了这么一点；在倒退着叙述的部分里，我没敢再试用那忽前忽后的办法。到现在，我看出他的方法并不是顶聪明的，也不再想学他。可是在《二马》里所试学的那一点，并非没有益处。康拉得使我明白了怎样先看到最后的一页，而后再动笔写最前的一页。在他自己的作品里，我们看到：每一个小小的细节都似乎是在事前准备好，所以他的叙述法虽然显着破碎，可是他不至陷在自己所设的迷阵里。我虽然不愿说这是个有效的方法，可是也不能不承认这种预备的工夫足以使作者对故事的全体能准确的把握住，不至于把力量全用在开首，而后半落了空。自然，我没能完全把这个方法放在纸上，可是我总不肯忘记它，因而也就老忘不了康拉得。

郑西谛说我的短篇每每有传奇的气味！无论题材如何，总设法把它写成个"故事"。这话——无论他是警告我，还是夸奖我——我以为是正确的。在这一点上，还是因为我老忘不了康拉得——最会说故事的人。说真的，我不信自己在文艺创作上有个伟大的将来；至好也不过能成个下得去的故事制造者。就是连这点希冀也还只是个希冀。不过，假设这能成为事实呢，我将永忘不了康拉得的恩惠。

刚才提到康拉得的方法，那么就再接着说一点吧。

现在我已不再被康拉得的方法迷惑着。他的方法有一时的诱惑力，正如它使人有时候觉得迷乱。它的方法不过能帮助他给他的作品一些特别的味道，或者在描写心理时能增加一些恍忽迷离的现象，此外并没有多少好处，而且有时候是费力不讨好的。康拉得的伟大不寄在他那点方法上。

他在结构上惯使两个方法：第一个是按着古代说故事的老法子，故事是由口中说出的。但是在用这个方法的时候，他使一个 Marlow，或一个 Davidson 述说，可也把他自己放在里面。据我看，他满可以去掉一个，而专由一人负述说的责任；

因为两个人或两个人以上述说一个故事，述说者还得互相形容，并与故事无关，而破坏了故事的完整。况且像在 *Victory*[1] 里面，述说者 Davidson 有时不见了，而"我"——作者——也没一步不离的跟随着故事中的人物，于是只好改为直接的描写了。其实，这个故事颇可以通体用直接的描写法，"我"与 Davidson 都没有多少用处。因为用这个方法，他常常去绕弯，这是不合算的。第二个方法是他将故事的进行程序割裂，而忽前忽后的叙说。他往往先提出一个人或一件事，而后退回去解析他或它为何是这样的远因；然后再回来继续着第一次提出的人与事叙说，然后又绕回去。因此，他的故事可以由尾而头，或由中间而首尾的叙述。这个办法加重了故事的曲折，在相当的程度上也能给一些神秘的色彩。可是这样写成的故事也未必一定比由头至尾直着叙述的更有力量。像 *Youth* 和 *Typhoon*[2] 那样的直述也还是极有力量的。

在描写上，我常常怀疑康拉得是否从电影中得到许多新的方法。不管是否如此吧，他这种描写方法是可喜的。他的景物变动得很快，如电影那样的变换。在风暴中的船手用尽力量想从风浪中保住性命时；忽然康拉得的笔画出他们的家来，他们的妻室子女，他们在陆地上的情形。这样，一方面缓和了故事的紧张，使读者缓一口气；另一方面，他毫不费力的，轻松的，引出读者的泪——这群流氓似的海狗也是人哪！他们不是只在水上漂流的一群没人关心的灵魂啊。他用这个方法，把海与陆联上，把一个人的老年与青春联上，世界与生命都成了整

---

1. 康拉德晚期小说《胜利》。——校者注
2. 分别为康拉德小说《青春》和《台风》。——校者注

的。时间与空间的距离在他的笔下任意的被戏耍着。

这便更像电影了："掌舵的把桨插入水中，以硬臂用力的摇，身子前俯。水高声的碎叫；忽然那长直岸好像转了轴，树木转了个圆圈，落日的斜光象火闪照到木船的一边，把摇船的人们的细长而破散的影儿投在河上各色光浪上。那个白人转过来，向前看。船已改了方向，和河身成了直角，船头上雕刻的龙首现在正对着岸上短丛的一个缺口。"（*The Lagoon*[1]）其实呢，河岸并没有动，树木也没有动，是人把船换了方向，而觉得河身与树木都转了。这个感觉只有船上的人能感到，可是就这么写出来，使读者也身入其境的去感觉；读者由旁观者变为故事中的人物了。

无论对人物对风景，康拉德的描写能力是惊人的。他的人物，正像南洋的码头，是民族的展览会。他有东方与西方的各样人物，而且不仅仅描写了他们的面貌与服装，也把他们的志愿，习惯，道德……都写出来。自然，他的欧洲人被船与南洋给限制住，他的东方人也因与白人对照而没完全得到公平的待遇。可是在他的经验范围里，他是无敌的；而且无论如何也比 Kipling[2] 少着一点成见。

对于景物，他的严重的态度使他不仅描写，而时时加以解释。这个解释使他把人与环境打成了一片，而显出些神秘气味。就我所知道的，他的白人大概可以分为两类：成功的与失败的。所谓成功，并不是财富或事业上的，而是由责任心上所起的勇敢与沉毅。他们都不是出奇的人才，没有超人的智慧，

---

1. 康拉德小说《礁湖》。——校者注
2. 即约瑟夫·鲁德亚德·吉卜林，英国作家、诗人，1907 年获诺贝尔文学奖。

他们可是至死不放松他们的责任。他们敢和台风怒海抵抗，敢始终不离开要沉落的船，海员的道德使他们成为英雄，而大自然的残酷行为也就对他们无可如何了。他们都认识那"好而壮的海，苦咸的海。能向你耳语，能向你吼叫，能把你打得不能呼吸"。可是他们不怕。Beard 船长，Mao Whirr 船长，Allistoun 船长，都是这样的人。有这样的人，才能与海相平衡。他的景物都有灵魂，因为它们是与英雄们为友或为敌的。Beard 船长到船已烧起，不能不离开的时候才恋恋不舍的下了船，所以船的烧起来是这样的：

"在天地黑暗之间，她（船）在被血红火舌的游戏射成的一圈紫海上猛烈的烧着；在闪耀而不祥的一圈水上。一高而清亮的火苗，一极大而孤寂的火苗，从海上升起，黑烟在尖顶上继续的向天上灌注。她狂烈的烧着；悲哀而壮观象夜间烧起的葬火，四面是水，星星在上面看着。一个庄严的死来到，像给这只老船的奔忙的末日一个恩宠，一个礼物，一个报酬。把她的疲倦了的灵魂交托给星与海去看管，其动心正如看一光荣的凯旋。桅杆倒下来正在天亮之前，一刻中火星乱飞，好似给忍耐而静观的夜充满了飞火，那在海上静卧的大夜。在晨光中她仅剩了焦的空壳，带着一堆有亮的煤，还冒着烟浮动。"

类似这样的文字还能找到许多，不过有此一段已足略微窥见他怎样把浪漫的气息吹入写实里面去。他不能不这样，这被焚的老船并非独自在那里烧着，她的船员们都在远处看着呢。康拉得的景物多是带着感情的。

在那些失败者的四围，景物的力量更为显明："在康拉得，哈代，和多数以景物为主体的写家，'自然'是画中的恶人。"是的，他手中那些白人，经商的，投机的，冒险的，差不多一经失败，便无法逃出——简直可以这么说吧——"自然"给予的病态。山川的精灵似乎捉着了他们，把他们像草似的腐在那里。*Victory* 里的主角 Heyst 是"群岛的漂流者，嗜爱静寂，好几年了他满意的得到。那些岛们是很安静。它们星列着，穿着木叶的深色衣裳，在银与翠蓝的大静默里；那里，海不发一声，与天相接，成个有魔力的静寂之圈。一种含笑的睡意包覆着它们；人们就是出声也是温软而低敛的，好象怕破坏了什么护身的神咒。"Heyst 永远没逃出这个静寂的魔咒，结果是落了个必不可免的"空虚"（nothing）。

　　Nothing，常常成为康拉得的故事的结局。不管人有多么大的志愿与生力，不管行为好坏，一旦走入这个魔咒的势力圈中，便很难逃出。在这种故事中，康拉得是由个航员而变为哲学家。那些成功的人物多半是他自己的写照，爱海，爱冒险，知道困难在前而不退缩。意志与纪律有时也可以胜天。反之，对这些失败的人物，他好像是看到或听到他们的历史，而点首微笑的叹息："你们胜过不了所在的地方。"他并没有什么伟大的思想，也没想去教训人；他写的是一种情调，这情调的主音是虚幻。他的人物不尽是被环境锁住而不得不堕落的，他们有的很纯洁很高尚；可是即使这样，他们的胜利还是海阔天空的胜利，nothing。

　　由这两种人——成功的与失败的——的描写中，我们看到康拉得的两方面：一方面是白人的冒险精神与责任心，一方面是东方与西方相遇的由志愿而转入梦幻。在这两方面，"自然"都占据了重要的地位，他的景物也是人。他的伟大不在乎他认识这种人与景物的关系，而是在对这种关系中诗意的感得，与有力的表现。真的，假如他的感觉不是那么精微，假如他的表现不是那么有力，恐怕他的虚幻的神秘的世界只是些浮浅的伤感而已。他的严重不许他浮浅。像 *The Nigger of the "Narcissus"*[1] 那样的材料，假若放在 W. W. Jacobs[2] 手里，那将成为何等可笑的事呢。可是康拉得保持着他的严重，他会使那个假装病的黑水手由恐怖而真的死去。

可是这个严重态度也有它的弊病：因为太热心给予艺术的刺激，他不惜用尽方法去创作出境界与效力，于是有时候他利用那些人为的不自然的手段。我记得，他常常在人物争斗极紧张的时节利用电闪，像电影中的助成恐怖。自然，除去这小小的毛病，他无疑的是近代最伟大的境界与人格的创造者。

老　舍

载于一九三五年十一月十日

上海《文学时代》月刊创刊号

---

1. 康拉德代表作之一《"水仙号"上的黑水手》。——校者注
2. W. W. 雅各布斯，英国小说家。——校者注

译者的话

　　我生在海边，长在海边。记忆中儿时的我，曾在丽日下灿金色的沙滩上玩耍，背景是一片天海相连的湛蓝，和从远方奔涌而来，在岸边不断绽放和消逝的雪白浪花；夜晚我就枕着浪涛声睡着，这是大海温柔沉静的呼吸，也是大自然的天籁，总能令我安然入梦。

　　我的姥爷是一位海员，一生都在大海上漂泊。他的航海生涯对我产生了很大的影响。我常常回想起他讲给我的海上故事，想象着有朝一日，自己也能驾船出海，亲眼目睹茫茫碧海上壮观奇丽的景象。

　　在我的身上流淌着航海者的血液，在我的内心深处，始终回荡着大海召唤着我的声音。

　　康拉德是一位海洋小说家，他写的故事往往是以他自己真实的航海经历作为背景的。正因如此，康拉德的作品对于我具有一种天然的吸引力。年少时我甚至曾和他一样，面对着世界地图发过幻想，期待着航行到海洋最深处的无人岛上，在那里找到一处埋藏已久的远古的宝藏。

　　年岁稍长，我并未如愿出海，而是走上了科研的道路。面对卷帙浩繁的外国文献，如何尽快提升英语水平曾经一度是困扰我的难题。我想到了康拉德和他的海洋小说。而这一次，我翻开的是英文原版《黑暗之心》。

　　我的英文水平有了长足的进步。从一开始的艰涩难行，到后来渐渐舒卷流畅，再到最后全然领略文字背后蕴藏的深邃和壮美，这并不是一个轻松的过程。但是我坚持了下来。这个艰辛而又充满成就感的过程，在我看来堪比一场奥德修斯式的海上苦旅，而我最后终于也得到了期待已久的宝藏。那些曾经晦涩艰深的文字，在我的眼前演变成了一幅幅极富真实感的画卷。

　　康拉德拥有不世出的语言天赋，英语并非他的母语，他却在近二十年的海员生涯中，从最初只会六个英语单词，到最后能使用英语写下辞藻丰赡堪比莎士比亚戏剧的数十部作品。放眼世界文坛，这样的成就也是极其罕见的。《黑暗之心》正是康拉德小说中思想性和艺术价值最高的一部。在康拉德笔下，辽阔无际的大海，苍茫原始的非洲丛林，静静流淌着的刚果河，这些异域风光无比真切地呈现在读者眼前，宛如一部高清分辨率的大型纪录片，气魄雄浑而又温柔细腻。而小说中人物跌宕起伏的心理活动，他们在面对欲望和诱惑时的种种抉择，则有如外科手术刀一般，深刻而犀利地剖析了充满矛盾的人性。这部作品自始至终情绪饱满，格调高昂；在脉络清晰的故事主线中，作者穿插了大量的景物描绘和抒情性的独白，读来如江河奔泻，酣畅淋漓，有时竟至于令人心潮激荡，神魂悚栗，感受到一种来自灵魂深处的震撼。

　　例如这一段对刚果河的描绘：

　　　　我的鼻孔里充满了泥土的味道——啊！那真正是来自远古的气息。眼前的原始森林高邈而沉静，黑色的溪流上，水面不时荡起潋滟的波光。月亮给世间万物披上了一层薄薄的银纱——蔓生的荒草，淤积的泥滩，从庙宇的墙头伸出的丛丛枝桠，还有那条静静流淌的宽广的大河，全都在朦胧的月色里泛出梦幻般的光采。我曾经透过那个昏暗的门洞望向那条大河，如今她的胴体完全呈现在我的面前，雍容地舒展着，闪烁着白银似的光泽。

这段文字即使单独拿来看，也是极清丽的散文；月色下的刚果河，平静恬然，却有着一种惊心动魄的美。接下来，作者笔锋一转；置身在无边的荒野，面对着经理的爪牙对自己的咄咄盘问，主人公马洛的心中发出了这样的感慨：

　　浩瀚宇宙，万象恢宏，一切都于无声处孕育着未来的希望；而那个人却一直在我耳边絮絮聒聒地讲着他自己的盘算。天地之间，人类何其渺小，这无边的寥廓见证了我们的一言一行，却报之以完全的静默——我不知道，这对我们究竟是一种启示，还是一种威赫？我们究竟是为何来到这世上，又是为何流落到了这里？究竟是谁能赢得最后的胜利，是我们，还是那寂静的荒野？我心中有无数疑问，而这荒野只是沉默不语；也许，它根本就听不到、也不在乎我们在说些什么，它只是延伸、延伸，向着无穷的远方延伸。

康拉德借人物之口发出了人类对于宇宙时空、自身命运的永恒之问，极大地宕延了小说的思想境界，而这宕开的一笔，却又和故事的情节、人物性格和命运的塑造非常自然地贴合在一起，不得不令人叹为观止。

又如，马洛在去往刚果的法国军舰上，见到海岸边划桨的一群黑人小伙子。对这幅情景，康拉德是这样描述的：

> 划着桨的都是些黑人，你从很远的地方就能看到他们闪射着光亮的白瞳仁。他们在呼喊，在歌唱；他们身上汗落如雨，脸上肌肉扭曲得好似戴着奇异的面具——这些小伙子们！他们的每一寸筋骨和肌肉，全都在张扬着野性的活力、不竭的能量——就和岸边的海浪一样自然而真实。无须理由，他们都是本就该属于这里的自然之子。

作者在这里尽情讴歌了不受殖民者奴役的黑人原住民自然纯朴、野性张扬的生活状态，他们没有被所谓的先进文明异化，是作者眼中真正令人羡慕的"自然之子"。这一段描绘令我想起了老一辈散文家刘成章先生的《安塞腰鼓》。不同时空的中外两位作家，描绘的是不同的情景，流露的却是完全相同的对于自然勃发的生命最热烈的颂赞。

《黑暗之心》写就了一出悲剧。在小说中，借由马洛之口叙述的主线人物库尔茨，原本是对非洲抱持着善意的理想主义者，但是当他来到了非洲，面对着财富的巨大诱惑，他却最终选择了不顾一切地掳掠象牙，为此不惜挑动部落战争，甚至肆意杀人。原本圣洁的天使接受魔鬼的交易，终于堕落进黑暗深渊的故事并不鲜见，然而在康拉德笔下，人性的矛盾挣扎被大段的文字铺衍得淋漓尽致。库尔茨尽管已经堕落得无可救赎，他的身上竟还闪烁着理想主义的光辉；也正是这种始终未曾熄灭的人性之光，令他的灵魂感受到撕裂的痛苦，也赋予这个人物一种古希腊悲剧英雄的崇高之美——对自我的深刻省视令他如同烈焰焚身的赫拉克勒斯，而英雄式的自毁倾向则令他在与命运的抗争中注定走向失败。这种进退两难的选择，也许正是人类共同的道德困境。康拉德以瓦格纳歌剧般华丽而铿锵的文字，将整个故事的悲剧性渲染到极致；他的行文是那样的有气力，有深度，那样的震撼人心，没有一段文字不是充荡着呐喊般的激情，难怪康拉德自己曾说，"每完成一部作品，都有一种几乎心力耗竭之感。"仅从文学性的层面而论，《黑暗之心》的文字之美，如同骊珠昆玉，绝不逊色于索福克勒斯和莎士比亚的名篇。例如他描绘库尔茨令人赞叹的雄辩才能，文中是这样写的：

> 真正关键的是——他是一个天赋英华的人；而在他的众多才能之中，最引人瞩目且最具有真实存在感的，正是他那舌绽莲花的口才，和他口中说出的那些言语——那是一种从心所欲表达思想的才能，它能让你堕入迷惑，也能使你茅塞顿开；它能施与你最崇高的教谕，也可以让你蒙受最卑劣的熏染；那是一条律动着的光明之河，闪耀着智慧与道德；那也是满载着谎言与欺骗的肮脏浊流，从那浓墨般深沉的黑暗之心汩汩而出。

在这里，大段的排比气势夺人，华丽的辞藻璀璨夺目，几具一种英雄史诗般的质感；而在描绘库尔茨的贪欲的时候，他这样写道：

> 这样，只要他的眼睛还看得见，他就可以满心欢喜

地看着它们，因为直到他生命的最后时刻，他仍然异常喜爱他的这些宝贝。你们真应该听听他这样说，"我的象牙。"哦，是的，我亲耳听他说过。"我的未婚妻，我的象牙，我的贸易站，我的河流，我的——"一切都是属于他的。这让我不禁屏住了呼吸，似乎那荒野马上就要爆发出一阵响彻天地的隆隆大笑，笑得群星震颤，日月无光。

渺小的人类，却有着蛇吞巨象般无尽的贪婪，如果以大自然的眼光看来，实在是可发一笑。可是面对名和利的引诱，又有多少人能抑制住内心本能的欲望，而不堕入无止境的贪婪中去呢？而贪念无度之人，双手尽管攥满宝物，身死之后，还不是终归于尘土？旷野的狂笑，穿越古今，振聋发聩。

严格说来，《黑暗之心》并不是一部真正意义上的海洋小说，而更是一部反映人性的现实主义小说。康拉德是一位世界级的小说家，他的英文是非母语写作的奇迹，是一种极具高雅宏阔之美的艺术。找一个安静的角落坐下来，花上一整个下午，细细品读这部《黑暗之心》，你将会得到一种前所未有的美学体验。这场阅读之旅，注定不虚此行。

古人云，独乐乐不如众乐乐。我想把我的目之所见、心之所感，和更多的同道者一起分享，这也是我动笔翻译《黑暗之心》的缘起和初心。由于水平所限，错漏之处在所难免，敬请读者不吝批评指正，不胜感谢。

癸卯年孟秋于华师勤园

李行宽

致　谢

　　首先，感谢本书的绘图团队。团队成员包括华南师范大学的同学们和我的很多好朋友们，他们年轻、热情、才华横溢，用一幅幅精美的插画为本书增色不少。他们为此付出了很多辛劳——在繁忙的学习、工作之余，潜心研究 AI 绘图技术，并仔细推敲情节、构思意境、反复修改，力求达到比较完美的效果。他们勤奋认真、一丝不苟的精神令我敬佩，而他们的辛勤付出，我也全都看在眼里，记在心头。在此向可爱的他们一一致以最真挚的感谢：（按姓氏笔画为序）

　　王小铭、王润玲、邓竣翀、邓慧瑜、卢自由、卢泳扬、刘桂娟、刘晓靖、孙青、纪春秀、苏琪淇、李木子、李丽彦、李美慧、李珊忠、李润泽、李静舒、李蔚琳、杨珊、吴沛桐、余凌峰、余楠霞、张园、张佳铭、张舒婷、陆龙业、陈睿杰、陈嫚妮、陈霭耒、罗琳月、周婉彤、郑易淇、练世成、郝一凡、胡玥、胡章伟、胡喜丹、钟一辉、秦子豪、郭泽虹、郭政鑫、黄肖健、黄育蕾、黄恺芊、黄冠淇、黄润东、黄森、黄游游、黄熙彦、梁丹丹

　　在我们的团队中，我还要特别感谢张舒婷同学。作为团队的负责人，她展现出了很强的组织能力。她擅长与伙伴们沟通，勇于攻克技术难题，扎实肯干，任劳任怨，令我深受感动。

　　同时，我也要感谢我可敬的同事们。汪隽老师在本书刚脱稿的阶段给予了我很大的鼓励和支持。可以说，如果没有汪老师的积极奔走，也许在那个最艰难的时刻，我已经早早打消了自己的出书计划。宝儿姐（夏宝君老师）为本书的出版和宣传出谋划策，让我备受鼓舞。正是因为她的"馊主意"，囊中羞涩的我才有了众筹出书的想法，并在朋友们的大力支持和慷慨预订下，终于一步步接近和实现了那个曾经"遥不可及"的理想。

　　我还要感谢上海交通大学出版社蔡丹丹编辑。她不仅对我有知遇之恩，更在本书的编审工作中恪守职责，倾尽心力。大到丛书的出版规划，小到标点符号的修改，无不体现着她的勤勉和专业精神。不仅如此，在很多翻译问题上她也给予了我相当有价值的建议；在与她的讨论中，本书的译文质量得到了很大的提升。

　　最后，也是最重要的，感谢有缘翻阅本书的每一位读者朋友。我将会不断努力，不断提升后续作品的质量，来回报我所热爱的你们。我想，没有什么比这更能表达我最诚挚的尊重和感谢了。

李行宽

目 录
CONTENTS

一

　　河水漫涨，微风轻拂。奈利号连帆都没有抖动一下，就吃住锚链，稳稳地停泊下来。奈利号是一艘双桅巡航帆船，想要顺流而下，它只有耐心等待下一次退潮时刻的到来。

　　我们的前方是泰晤士河入海口；再往前方，就是浩渺无边的汪洋。极目远望，海天一色。波光粼粼的水面上，一艘艘驳船乘着潮水向上游驶去，棕褐色的主帆仿佛静立在高耸的帆布簇成的红色花丛里；在夕照之下，就连涂了清漆的桅杆也溢彩流光。在河岸渐渐低沉、最终隐没于海水的地方，一团薄雾静静飘浮。格雷夫森德天色阴沉，远处更是彤云密布，笼罩着这座地球上最恢宏、最伟大的城市。

　　公司董事既是船长，又是船东。当他站在船头瞭望大海的时候，我们四个人都用热切的目光从后面望着他。整条河道上，唯有这一幕最富于航海色彩。他现在简直就像个领航员，而在水手眼里，领航员就是最踏实、最可靠的人。但你一定想不到，其实他工作的地方并不是在远处夕阳映照的海湾上，而是在他身后浓云覆盖的城市里。

　　我以前曾经说过，大海就是把我们联结在一起的纽带。有了这条纽带，即使分别很久之后才重聚，我们仍能勠力同心；不仅如此，我们还能耐心聆听对方讲述过往的故事，容忍彼此观点上的迥异。那个可亲的老头儿是我们的律师，因为年高德

劲，所以拥有甲板上仅有的坐垫和毯子，现在正在上面躺着
呢。会计百无聊赖，拆了一盒多米诺骨牌垒房子玩。马洛盘着
腿坐在船尾右侧，身子倚在后桅上。他两颊深陷，脸色暗黄，
脊背却挺得笔直，充满着苦行禁欲的气息；此时他手臂下垂，
掌心向外，姿态宛如一尊神像。董事直到帆船锚稳才放了心，
他向我们几个人走过来，也在船尾坐下。我们懒洋洋地聊了几
句就无话可说了，整条船又陷入了一片寂静。我们各怀心事，
谁也没有再开口。我们耽于默想，什么也懒得做，只是出神地
凝望远方。在夕阳的余晖中，一切都是那么静谧安详——又一
天结束了。明净的水面波光闪烁，万里长空寥廓而澄澈，显得
是那样温和；就连埃塞克斯沼泽地上空的雾霭也变得好像一片
微微发亮的薄纱，舒展开几乎透明的皱褶，从岸边林木茂密的
高地上飘去，直到把低处的河岸全给掩住。唯有西边盘桓在河
道上游的乌云，似乎由于落日的来临而愠怒，变得越来越幽暗
阴深了。

终于，太阳循着一条弧线慢慢落下，原本耀眼的白光已
变成了一团无光无热的昏暗的殷红。乌云笼罩在人们的头顶，
似乎随时将给那奄奄的太阳最后一击，让它彻底熄灭。

夜幕骤然降下。余晖里宁静的泰晤士河一下子变得阒寂
深沉。这是一条古老的河流，在数不清的岁月里，它默默滋
养着两岸的居民；当白日的喧嚣化作温柔的夜色，泰晤士河
静静流淌，宽广的水域仿佛永无休止，一直延伸到世界的尽
头——这是何等的庄严与安详！我们敬仰这条河，并不是因为
眼下这短暂的、即将匆匆而逝的一天中所见到的景象，而是因
为内心深处那些闪耀着光辉、永远不可磨灭的记忆。的确，对
于一个曾经满怀着热忱和憧憬扬帆出海的人来说，只要一望见

泰晤士河的入海处，昔日的万丈豪情就会再次涌上心头。潮水涨而复落，永不停息，载着无数船帆往来其上，也载着人们无数的回忆——有的是历尽劫波，终于得以归来；有的是意气昂扬，奔赴海上战场。想想那些英格兰民族的骄傲——无论是弗朗西斯·德雷克爵士，还是约翰·弗兰克林爵士，他们每一个人都曾经从这里驶向大海。泰晤士河不会忘记他们；无论受封与否，他们都配得上称为骑士，而且真正是伟大的海上游侠。再想想那些曾经驶过泰晤士河的舰船——"金鹿号"凯旋归来，弧形舷舱里满载的奇珍甚至惊动了女王驾临，从此成为不朽的传奇；"幽冥号"和"恐怖号"为征服遥远的疆域启程远航，一去竟永无再返之日。这一个个名字就像暗夜里璀璨的宝石，即使日久年深，仍放射着不灭的光辉。泰晤士河不会忘记他们——那些劈波斩浪的舰船和勇往直前的英雄。他们从伊里斯、德特福德、格林尼治张帆而来，开始了异国探险和殖民征服的旅途；皇家巨轮和普通商船往来海上，各色人物纷纷登场，其中有民间的船长，舰队的司令；有手持委任状的东印度舰队"将军"，还有在远东贸易中浑水摸鱼的神秘"黑手"。为了追逐黄金和名望，他们顺流而下、驶入海洋，手中高举着长剑和火炬——他们执行了欧洲王权的殖民统治，同时也播撒了欧洲文明的神圣火种。人们的梦想、联邦国家的种子、大英帝国的雏形，连同着其他许多伟大的事物，随着泰晤士河的每一次潮落，汇入了无边的海洋，最终漂流到遥远而神秘的未知之境……

太阳完全沉落，黑暗笼罩了整条河道。不一会儿，岸边亮起了点点灯火。满是淤泥的河滩上，矗立在三角悬架上的查普曼灯塔发射出耀眼的光芒。夜航的船只也点亮了灯盏，它们

对于一个曾经满怀着热忱和憧憬扬帆出海的人来说，只要一望见泰晤士河的入海处，昔日的万丈豪情就会再次涌上心头。

（张舒婷　绘）

在河面上往来穿行，看上去就像一团团浮动的光晕。向西边放眼望去，泰晤士河上游的城市犹如蹲伏的巨兽，在它的上空，仍然覆盖着不祥的黑翳；白日里那团挥之不去的阴云，已化作星空下森然可怖的冷光。

　　"其实，"马洛突然开口了，"这里始终都还是地球上的一处黑暗之地。"

在我们几个人里面，只有马洛还在当水手。但是怎么说呢，他看起来和别的水手都不一样。马洛在船上过着四海为家的生活，而他的思想也放达不羁，就像一个无拘无束的漫游者。和他相比，大多数海员的生活简直都是如出一辙，乏善可陈。他们无论身在何方，总感觉自己似乎根本就没踏出家门。他们总是待在船上，船就是他们的家；而船总是漂浮在大海上，大海就是他们无边无际的王国。一条船和另一条船几乎没什么区别，大海也总还是那个老样子。每天的工作一成不变，大洋彼端的海岸、异国风情的面孔、多姿多彩而又富于变幻的生活场景，只是在他们眼前一掠而过，却无法真正地撩动他们的心弦；这倒不是因为异域事物本身蒙着什么神秘的面纱，而是因为隐藏在他们内心深处的傲慢和无知。因为对水手来说，大海才是主宰他们命运的女神，而她性格乖张，喜怒无常，和命运之神一样变幻莫测——世上还能有什么事物比大海更神秘呢？至于其他的一切，只要在结束漫长的工作之后，上岸去随便逛逛，或者狂欢痛饮一番，新大陆的秘密不就全都尽收眼底了吗？而这些秘密简直不值一提！所以海员们的故事都是一样的简陋浅显，故事的全部意义都像是藏在一个破裂的干果壳里——让人一眼就全看透了。但是马洛和他们不一样。虽然马洛也爱滔滔不绝地讲故事，但是他认为不应该像果壳包裹着果核那样，把意义塞进故事的里面去。每一段故事的意义，都应该能够自内而外发出光芒，让故事本身在意义的光轮之中呈现；这就好像被雾气晕染了的月亮往往浮现出朦胧柔和的光环一样。

这句开场白平平无奇。这正是马洛的风格，淡泊如水，语不惊人。大家就这么默默地听着，谁也懒得吭声。于是马洛继续讲了下去，讲得非常慢——

"我在想很久很久以前，罗马人初次踏上这片土地的情景……时光已经流逝了一千九百年，但是那情景还历历在目，一切就好像刚刚发生在几天前。继续回想，也许自从亚瑟王时代开始，这条河上就出现了文明之光——这光明就好像燎原的烈焰，或者是云中的闪电，而我们就生活在这电光石火的闪烁的一瞬间——但愿这道光能够一直照耀着人们，和永远不停旋转的地球一起亘古长存吧！但是黑暗笼罩的时代还恍如昨日。想象一下，假如你是一位舰队司令，指挥着那个威风凛凛的——那叫啥来着？——好像是地中海的三桨座战船吧，突然接到了北上的命令，你会是什么感受？你得迅速穿越高卢人的领地去接管一艘舰船；如果史书里的描述可信的话，那么仅用了一两个月的时间，那些堪比能工巧匠的罗马军团士兵就建造了上百条这样的战船。想象一下——你站立在这荒蛮之地，望着那铅灰色的大海，烟青色的天空——这里简直就是世界的尽头。你还看到一条和六角手风琴一样难以操弄的大船正在溯流而上，满载着各种物资、预定的货物或者别的什么东西。到处都是沙洲、沼泽、密林、野蛮人。对于一个文明人来说，这里的食物几乎全都难以下咽，如果还想来点杯中之物——那就只有泰晤士河的河水。这里没有法伦葡萄酒，没有可以登岸的码头。旷废的兵营偶尔可见，它们就像掉进草堆里的绣花针一样微不足道，被这广袤的荒野慢慢吞噬。死神悄然而至，它隐匿在空气里，潜藏在水里，蛰伏在密林里——寒冷、迷雾、风暴、瘟疫、流浪——最终归于死亡。在这里，兵士们贱如蝇蚁般一批批死去。但是你终于完成了任务，而且毋庸置疑，干得非常出色。而你也没有老想着这件事，只不过偶尔拿来吹吹牛，说自己当年曾经如何如何。当然了，敢于直面蛮荒的黑暗，就无愧为真正的男子汉。也许还有个信念一直支撑着你——如果能结识罗马的权贵，又能抗得住这蛮夷之地的险恶环境，也许有朝一日就能得到机遇的垂青——在你仰慕已久的拉文纳舰队里谋得一席之地。再想象一下，假如你是一位身披宽袍、仪表堂堂的年轻罗马公民，为了能够出人头地，打算狠狠地赌上一把；于是继那些地方官、税务官、商人之后，你也万里迢迢来到了这里。你在一片沼泽地旁边弃船登陆，步行穿过茂密的树林，直到深入腹地。在驿站里，你终于意识到自己已经被野性彻底包围——那是一种只属于荒野的神秘生命力，它是山林丛莽间的枯荣轮转，是野蛮人内心深处的血脉天性。而你永远也无法融入这种神秘之境——你生活在这不可理喻的野蛮世界里，心里充满了厌憎。这世界有着一种奇异的魅力，令你为之动容，却又恨之如仇。与日俱增的懊悔，想要逃离的渴望，深深厌恶却又无能为力，无奈顺从却更加衔怨怀恨——这些情感叠加在一起，简直会让你发疯。"

说到这里，他停顿了一下。

"请注意，"马洛继续说道，同时弯起一条胳臂向上托举，掌心朝外；他盘膝而坐，姿态正犹如开坛说法的佛陀，只不过他身上穿的是欧洲服饰，脚下也没有宝座莲台——"请注意，我们再也无法真正体会罗马人的感受了。而使我们不必重蹈覆辙的正是效率——确切来说，是我们对效率的狂热追求。说实话，这些家伙根本就没什么了不起。他们不是来殖民的；我猜测他们在这儿的统治也是稀松平常，不过如此。他们为了征服新的土地而来，作为征服者，他们从来只信奉暴力；但是拥有暴力又有什么可夸耀的呢？你的强大，只不过是因为碰巧遇到比你更弱小的对手罢了。征服者为了掠夺而掠夺，这不是别的，就是抢劫——而且是规模更大、更加残暴甚至满手血腥的抢劫——而他们对此习以为常，甚至还乐在其中。在他们看来，要对付荒蛮蒙昧的黑暗世界，暴力和杀戮就是天经地义。从肤色和我们不同的人、抑或是鼻梁比我们扁平的人手中抢走他们的家园，在大多数时候，这就是所谓的领土征服；仔细想一想，你就会发现这种事情其实并不怎么光彩。但是在征服的背后有这样一种信念，或许会成为我们唯一的救赎——注意，我说的是信念，而不是什么惺惺作态的自辩——这种信念甚至可以成为一种博大而无私的信仰，你可以树立它，景仰它，乃至献身于它……"

他的语声凝住了。一团团光焰在河面上浮动，它们颜色各异，有的湛青，有的通红，有的炽白；远远望去都十分渺小。这些光焰行进着，追逐着，时而前后超越，时而相互汇合。有时候它们相对而行，越来越近，最终在交错之际迅速分开，抑或是缓缓地彼此远离。夜色愈发浓重，在不眠的泰晤士河上，这座伟大城市的交通永不停息。我们观望着河上的景色，耐心地等待着——在潮水回落之前，我们什么事也做不了。沉默许久之后，马洛试探着又开了口，他说道："伙计们，你们应该还记得吧，我以前在内河上干过一阵子水手。"于是我们心知，在潮落之前，我们注定要坐在这里，听马洛讲一段他的亲身经历——一个难以评说、亦没有结局的故事。

"其实我也不想啰里啰唆，总是和你们聊我的个人经历，"这句话暴露了马洛的弱点，他和很多讲故事的人一样，往往并不知道自己的听众究竟最喜欢听什么；"不过，那次的经历深深地影响了我。而要理解这一点，你就得听我把整件事和盘托出——我去那里的缘由，我一路上的所见所闻，我是如何溯流而上，直到那里——最后见到了那个人的。那里是我航程所及最远的地方，那里的经历令我感到了心灵的震撼。经过这件事，我似乎茅塞顿开，把周遭所有的一切都看明白了。这件事实在是沉郁凄凉，令人叹惋；但是它也绝对称不上什么非凡的故事，甚至连清晰鲜明都算不上——真的，它没有什么鲜明的故事感。但它就像一束光照亮了我的内心，令我豁然开朗了。

"你们还记得吧，那时候我刚刚回到伦敦。差不多六年时间我都在跑东方航线——一趟印度洋，再一趟太平洋，再一趟中国海……如此这般。然后我就回来赋闲了。我无事可做，到处晃荡，经常在你们工作的时候还拉着你们扯闲篇儿，或者连个招呼也不打就闯到你们家里来了。呵，那时候我就好像肩负着什么天职似的，非要拉住你们说教一番。开始我还觉得这样挺好，可是时间一长，这种无所事事的日子就令人厌倦了。然后我就开始找船。找船这事儿，可比世界上任何工作都艰难得多了。那些船连正眼儿都不瞧我。到后来我也就心灰意冷，懒得再提找船的事儿了。

"当我还是个小男孩儿的时候，我曾经对地图十分迷恋。我常常会一连几个小时看着南美洲、非洲或是澳大利亚的地图，痴痴地想象着那光辉荣耀的探险事业。那时候，世界地图上还有很多空白，而每当我发现某一处空白的地方特别诱人（但对我来说，它们全都令人着迷），我就会伸手指着它说：'等我长大了，我一定要到那里去。'我还记得其中一个地方是北极。好吧，直到现在我也还没到过北极，而且目前也没这个打算。它对我已经没有诱惑力了。其他的地方则分布在世界各处，两个半球上都有。其中有些地方我已经去过了，而且……

算了，今天先不说这个。但是还有一个地方——那个可以说是面积最大、信息最少的一处空白——令我一直魂牵梦绕，期待着追寻。

"但其实，它很快就不再只是一片空白了。还没等我长大成人，它就已经填满了大大小小的河流湖泊，还注上了形形色色的地名。地图上那片充满了神秘、令人向往的空白消失了，小男孩儿关于荣耀的梦想也随之幻灭了。取而代之的是一片黑暗之地。但是在那地图上，有一条河流引人注目。那河流非常大，看上去就像一条伸展开来、正在休憩的巨蛇——它头枕大海，蜿蜒曲折的身躯横陈在广袤的土地上，尾部隐没于这片国土的纵深之处。当我透过商店橱窗看到那幅地图时，我的心神立刻就被它攥住了。我就像一只被蛇魔住了的小鸟，完全无法抗拒那摄魂夺魄的魔力，迷迷糊糊地沉沦其中了。然后我想起来，有一家大公司在那条河上做贸易。妈的，就它了！我心里想，他们要在那么大的内河上做生意，有一样东西是必不可少的——汽船！我为什么不去那儿弄条汽船呢？我得去那儿当个船长——我沿着舰队街往前走着，满脑子都是这个念头。那条巨蛇已经彻底迷住我了。

"要知道那可是欧洲大陆的一家联合公司，或是贸易协会什么的。但是我也有很多住在大陆上的亲戚朋友。他们说，还是在大陆的生活更便宜，而且那里的环境其实也并不差。

"说来惭愧，我开始麻烦他们帮我找门路了。这对我来说是一个全新的体验，你们知道，以往我可从来不是这样做事的。我习惯凡事靠自己，用自己的双手打开属于自己的一片天。我也不敢相信自己好像变了个人似的，但是天知道在那个时候，我一门心思只想着我必须达到目的，管他走正门还是走后门呢！于是我就跑去拜托他们。男人们嘴上说得好听，'我亲爱的老伙计'，结果却都袖手旁观。后来——你们相信吗？我竟然去找女人帮忙。我，堂堂的查理·马洛，为了得到一份工作，找女人去帮我说项。老天！但是你们知道，这全是被那个念头给逼出来的。我有个姨妈，她为人和善又有一副热心肠。她写信给我说：'那种工作一定很有意思。我会想尽办法、不遗余力地帮你的忙。你的想法真让人钦佩！我不光认识一位高官的太太，还认识一个有权有势的大人物，'等等。她已经下定决心，如果我当真想在内河汽船上当船长，她就一定要把任命书给我弄来，不达目的誓不罢休。

"就这样，我被任命为船长了——这简直是毫无悬念。而且这任命来得很快。据说是因为那家公司得到了消息，他们的一名船长在殴斗中被土人打死了。于是我的机会来了，我更急着想赶快动身了。但是直到好几个月之后，在搜寻那个船长的遗骸的时候，我才得知这场冲突的起因竟然是几只母鸡——没错，就是两只黑母鸡引发的一场误会。那位船长老兄——对了，他叫弗雷斯利文，是个丹麦人——觉得自己在这笔交易中吃了亏，于是提了一根棍子回到岸上，狠狠地抽打村长。呵，听到这事儿，我一点儿也不觉得稀奇。他们接着还告诉我说，弗雷斯利文又沉静又文雅，简直是人类中的典范。好吧，我当然也相信他是个好人。但是他已经在那里干了好几年'崇高事业'了，所以他还是觉得要做点儿什么来显示自己的威风。所以他残酷无情地毒打那个老黑人，把围观的村民都吓得胆颤心寒。然后有个人——据说是村长的儿子——在老家伙持续不断的惨叫声中终于发了狂，拿起长矛向白人戳过去了。他只是就试着戳了这么一下，结果那长矛就直接戳穿白人的肩胛骨了。

这对村民们来说无异于大祸临头，他们拔腿就跑，一转眼全都躲进树林里不见了；另一边，弗雷斯利文麾下的船员们也慌作一团，赶紧拔锚开溜了，我想，那会儿顶替船长指挥的可能是船上的轮机长吧。后来似乎也没人想去管弗雷斯利文的尸体了，直到我来到这儿接手了船长的位子——我可不能丢下他不管。但是当我终于得以亲眼见到我这位前任的时候，从他肋骨的缝隙间长出来的青草已经高得足以掩蔽他的尸骨了。他的骨头一根也没少——这家伙够玄乎的，倒毙之后竟然连野狗也没碰过他。整个村子阒无人迹，四下里一片荒凉；已经坍毁的围墙里面，破败的茅草屋也都几乎倾垮，它们发霉朽烂，门户洞开，里面黑黢黢的。一看就知道，这里发生过一场大灾难。那时候，巨大的恐惧让村民们发了疯一样地四散奔逃，无论男女老少全都奔入丛林，而且没人再敢回来。至于那两只母鸡的下落，我也不得而知，反正'文明的使者'早晚也会抓到它们。不管怎样，由于这场突如其来的光辉事件，我都还没来得及好好地企盼一番就得到了船长的任命。

"于是我立刻打点行装，忙得天昏地暗、飞沙走石。还不到四十八小时，我已经在横渡英吉利海峡，准备和老板见面签合同了。又过了几小时我就到了那个城市——也许是出于某种偏见吧，我总觉得那城市就好像一座精心粉饰过的巨大坟墓。我没费吹灰之力就找到了那家公司的总部，那是城里最高大的建筑，而且我遇见的每个人都知道它。那公司正打算建立一个海外贸易王国，借此来赚取数不清的钞票。

"那座华厦就矗立在我面前，它投下深长的阴影，笼罩着狭窄的街道。街上没什么人，沉寂得好似一座坟墓；砖石的缝隙里还长着青草。抬眼望去，只看见高楼上数不清的百叶窗。

庄严的马车拱道分列左右，巨大而沉重的双扇门半开半掩。我
从门缝里侧身进去，顺着楼梯往上走。楼梯间一尘不染，而且
毫无装饰，就像沙漠一样令人兴味索然。我推开面前的第一
扇门，看到两个女人，一胖一瘦，正坐在草垫椅子上织着黑
毛线。那个瘦一点的女人站起身，径直向我走来——一边走，
一边仍在低眉垂眼织着她的毛线！我开始考虑要不要给这位梦
游者让个路。就在这时，她停下脚步，抬头看了看我。她的穿
着简单朴素，简直和雨伞套子没什么两样。她一言不发，转身
领着我进了一间等候室。我报了姓名，然后打量了一下四周。
房间正中放着一张杉木桌，沿着墙壁摆满了样式简单的椅子。
桌子一端放着一幅很大的地图，上边五颜六色的很是亮眼，加
起来都能凑出一条彩虹了。其中最引人注目的是一大片红色，
说明那儿已经扎扎实实地干完了不少事情；蓝色的面积也相当
不小；另外还有一抹绿色，零星的橙色，在东海岸还有一小片
紫色——嘿，你看，到处都有贼厉害的文明使者在喝着贼棒的
熟啤酒了。但是这些都不是我想去的地方。我要去的是地图正
中的那片黄色区域。那条河就在那里——它宛如巨蛇，浑身散
发着致命的诱惑。这时，随着吱呀的一声，一扇门开启了一条
缝，伸出来一个脑袋——满头白发，满脸同情——显然是个秘
书先生；接着门缝里又伸出一根细手指向我勾了勾，示意我跟
他进密室里去。里面光线昏暗，正中央趴着一张沉重的写字
台；在那写字台后面，我慢慢看见了一个罩着礼服外袍的又白
又胖的东西。这就是大老板本人了。我估计他的身高还不到六
英尺，可是在他手心里却攥着不知道多少沓百万大钞。他和我
握握手，咕咕哝哝地用法语说了句旅途愉快。我想他对我的法
语还是挺满意的。

我要去的是地图正中的那片黄色区域。那条河就在那里——它宛如巨蛇，
浑身散发着致命的诱惑。

（邓慧瑜　绘）

"前后不到一分钟，我就又回到等候室，和秘书先生坐在
一起了。这位和蔼的秘书拿来几份文件让我签字，脸上满是忧
伤和怜悯。我还记得，在我签了字的众多条款中有这么一条：
不得泄露任何商业机密。这还用说吗，我当然会保守秘密的。

"我开始有点不安，你知道我向来不习惯这种阵仗，而且我感觉周遭的气氛似乎有点诡异。这简直就像是——我也不知道该怎么形容——被卷入了某种阴谋，或者是什么不太正当的事儿；因此，走出来的时候，我大大地松了一口气。在外面的房间里，那两个女人仍在一刻不停地飞针走线。更多的人陆续来到这里，那个年轻些的女人来回奔走，把他们一个一个领进去。年老的那个仍然坐在椅子上。她脚上穿着平底的布拖鞋，蹬着一个暖脚炉，腿上还蜷着一只猫。这个老女人的脸颊上有颗肉瘤，她头戴挺括的白帽，鼻尖上挂着一副银丝眼镜；我经过的时候，她从眼镜上方瞥了我一眼。被这种平静而又漠然的眼光冷冷扫过，实在是令人着恼。旁边两个青年傻乎乎地被领进去，还眉欢眼笑，一脸开心；她同样以那种洞悉一切的神态，迅速而冷漠地瞟了他们一眼。她似乎已经看透了他们，也看透了我。我不禁有些悚然——这个神秘的老女人，似乎真的是命运的某种预兆。很久以后，尽管早已远远离开了那个地方，我还时常回想起那两个女人。她们守着通往黑暗的大门，仿佛在编织尸衣似的织着黑毛线；一个不断地把人领进那未知的世界，另一个则用她那双无比冷漠的老眼打量着那一张张毫无觉察的快乐脸孔。万岁！编织黑毛线的老女人——赴死者向您致敬。被她瞅过一眼的那些人里，根本没有几个还能再见到她。

"接下来还得去体检。'手续很简单的，'秘书满怀同情地安慰我，一副恨不得替我受苦受难的样子。于是一个年轻人从楼上不知道什么地方走了下来，领我去医生那儿。他的帽檐压得很低，几乎盖住了左眉；我猜测他是个办事员，因为尽管这座楼就像死城之中的鬼屋一样静寂，但是作为一家公司，办事员总还是得有几个的吧。他衣服破旧，外套的袖子上还沾着墨水点儿，完全是不修边幅的模样；鼓鼓囊囊的大领结上边，伸出来一个狭长的下巴，看起来真像老式皮靴的靴尖儿。现在去体检还有点儿太早，于是我提议不妨去喝一杯，他一听这话马上就面露喜色。我们坐下来喝着苦艾酒的时候，他一个劲儿夸赞公司的事业多么多么好。后来我自然而然地惊叹说，既然这样好，那他为什么不去呢？他一下子冷静下来，变得相当审慎了。'借用柏拉图对弟子说过的一句话吧：虽然我看上去不太聪明，其实我可一点儿也不蠢。'他抛下这么一句话，一仰脖子喝干了杯中酒，就站了起来。

"那个老医生摸着我的脉搏，但有些心不在焉，显然脑子里在琢磨着别的什么事情。'很好，去那儿没问题，'他喃喃地说。接着他的神色变得急切，问我是否愿意让他量一下我的头围。尽管有点儿吃惊，我还是同意了，于是他拿出一个类似卡尺的东西，前前后后、左左右右地围着我的头量了一通，然后仔细地记录下来。这个老家伙个头矮小，胡子拉碴，身穿一件像是工作服的破旧衣服，脚上是一双拖鞋。我想，这不过是个人畜无害的科学怪人罢了。'为了研究科学，我经常借职务之便，测量即将出发去那儿的人的头骨，'他说。我接着问道，'然后等他们回来的时候再量一次？''噢，我再也没有见过他们。'他说，'再说了，发生变化的地方在头骨的里面呢。'他露出微笑，仿佛刚才讲的是个冷笑话。'你就快要出发了，好，很好。'他睃巡了我片刻，又在本子上记下了一笔。'你家里有人得过精神病吗？'他问道，认真的口气不像是在开玩笑。我感到十分恼火。'这个问题也是为了研究科学？''如果可以的话，'他完全不理会我的恼怒，自顾说道，'我是说，如果可以当面观察人的思想变化的话，对于科学研究当然是很有意义的。但是……'那你就是精神病专家了？'我打断了他。'每个医生都应该多少懂一点精神病学，'这个怪人神色自若地说，'我有一个小小的理论，请你们这些到那边去的先生们一定帮我验证一下。法国拥有相当广阔的海外属地，也获得了相当可观的利益。而我的研究也算是从中分了一杯羹吧。这也是我能留给后人的一点儿财富。请原谅我向你提出的这些问题，不过在我的观察样本里面，你是第一个英国人……'我赶紧告诉他说，千万不要以为英国人都像我这样。'如果我是个典型的英国人，'我说，'那么我是不会这样对您说话的。''你的话似乎另有深意啊，而且八成是个谬论，'他说着笑了起来。'记住，少晒太阳，更要少动肝火。Adieu。嗯，你们英国人是怎么说来着？Good-bye。对了，是 Good-bye。啊！Good-bye。Adieu。在热带地区，保持冷静比什么都重要。'他一边伸出食指以示告诫，一边用法语连连说道：'冷静些，再冷静些。'

"现在还得去办一件事：去和我那了不起的姨妈道别。她就像打了一场胜仗似的，神色间悠然自得。我喝了一杯高级茗茶——以后很长的日子都将喝不到这样的好茶了。房间舒适体面，和我想象中的太太们的会客室毫无二致。我们坐在壁炉边，低声交谈了许久。经过这次密谈，我才得知了整件事的内情——她向那个大人物的太太推荐了我。而且除了那位太太，她还向不知道多少达官贵人说过我的好话。在她口中，我是个才能非凡、无与伦比的人物；对这家公司来说，更是个打着灯笼都找不到的精英人才。老天！而我要去做的，只不过是指挥一条挂着廉价哨子的廉价汽船罢了。可是在她眼里，我已经是那些'先导者'当中的一员了，就好像什么'光明的使者'啦、'初等的使徒'啦。那时候，无论是书刊报纸上还是坊间闲谈里，到处都充斥着这些胡扯的鬼话；而我那了不起的姨妈，被这些胡言乱语的滔滔洪流裹挟着，已经被冲昏了头脑了。她讲来讲去都是'得让那几百万无知的野蛮人摆脱他们野蛮的状态'，到后来，说真的，她实在让我受不了了。我斗胆暗示说，那家公司的宗旨只是赚钱。

"'你忘了，亲爱的查理，路加福音说过——一分耕耘一分收获。'她神采飞扬地说。真奇怪，女人的头脑总是这么脱离现实。她们活在自己想象出来的世界里，而这样的世界别说以前没有，以后也不会有——它太天真、太美好了，如果女人们非要把它带进现实世界，那么连一天的时间都不到，它就会土崩瓦解。自从上帝创世以来，我们男人就心平气和地接受了一些不怎么美好的生活现实；而现实会彰显它的力量，把幻想的世界砸个粉碎。

"说完这句话，她拥抱了我一下，告诉我要记得穿法兰绒衣服，一定要经常给她写信，等等。然后我就告辞了。走在大街上，也不知道为什么，一种奇怪的感觉忽然涌上心头——我觉得自己也成了一个欺世盗名的骗子。要知道，我做事向来干脆利落；如果要我在二十四小时内整装完毕，出发去世界上任何一个地方，我会立刻行动起来，眼都不眨一下——别人在过马路之前还得先看一看，想一想呢。这就不对劲儿了。像我这样的人，面对那么一件平常的事情，竟会有那么一瞬间感到了悚骇——虽然我出发的决心还没有动摇。这么说吧，那一瞬间我似乎觉得，我要去的地方不是一块大陆的中心，而是那不见天日的地球中心。

"我乘坐一艘法国轮船出发了。这条船一路上把他妈的大大小小的港口都停靠了个遍。据我观察，这船唯一的目的就是往海外运送士兵和海关官员。我眺望着海岸线。站在船头，看着眼前的海岸线渐行渐近，真像在思忖着一个未解之谜。它就在前面等待着你，但却是情态各异——有的含笑相迎，有的蹙眉冷对；有的卑微渺小，有的大气磅礴；有的平淡无奇，有的充满野性——一样的沉默着，却都在向着你发出有如耳语般的诱人召唤：'来吧，快过来看看吧。'眼前这片海岸却显得没什么特色，就像一件尚未完成的作品，单调而又阴沉。最先映入眼帘的是岸边的莽莽丛林，苍翠沉郁，几成墨色；雪白的浪花为这大片的墨绿镶了一条直若刀裁的银边，沿着碧蓝的大海一直伸向远方。一团雾气渐渐弥漫开来，遮住了海面；头顶上烈日炎炎，远处的陆地却在海雾之中闪闪发亮，湿润得好似要滴出水来。银色的海浪上面渐渐浮现出一些灰蒙蒙白茫茫的东西，这儿一丛那儿一簇的，有的上面还飘着旗子——那是已有数百年历史的殖民定居点。再往远处就是渺无人烟的广袤荒野，映衬之下，那些定居点实在比针尖儿大不了多少。我们的轮船隆隆前行，靠岸，下锚，让士兵登陆；然后继续前行，把海关官员也送上岸去——在仿佛被上帝遗弃了的茫茫荒野上，孤茕地立着一个插着旗杆的铁皮小屋，他们就在那里征税；然后，也许是为了保护这些官员——再运来更多的士兵。我听说，有的人就这么淹死在海浪中了；但是好像没人真正在乎他们到底是生是死，命运如何。轮船只管把他们扔到目的地就行了，然后接着前进。日复一日，每个海岸看起来都是一个样子，好像我们根本就没有移动过；而实际上，轮船已经驶过了许多地方。那都是些海外贸易点，叫作些什么'大巴萨姆'或者'小波波'之类，而这些名字听上去更像是在幽暗的幕布前演出的某种卑劣的闹剧。作为一个普通的乘客，我终日无所事事；和同船的人也没什么话好讲，茕茕孑立，形单影只；举目四望，到处都是浓酽酽、懒洋洋的海水；每天看到的海岸都是一样的单调而又阴沉，和前一天的所见毫无区别。这一切都是那么的苍凉、凄迷、虚无缥缈，我就像置身于令人惆怅的梦幻之中，完全脱离了生活的真实。时不时传来的海浪声，好似教会兄弟的倾诉，给我带来了些许安慰；这声音如同自然的天籁，自有其存在的原因和意义。岸边偶尔开过来的一条小船，把我的思绪拉回了现实。划着桨的都是些黑人，你从很远的地方就能看到他们闪射着光亮的白瞳仁。他们在呼喊，在歌唱；他们身上汗落如雨，脸上肌肉扭曲得好似戴着奇异的面具——这些小伙子们！他们的每一寸筋骨和肌肉，全都在张扬着野性的活力、不竭的能量——就和岸边的海浪一样自然而真实。无须理由，他们都是本就该属于这里的自然之子。望着他们，我感到了莫大的安慰。一时间，我似乎觉得自己还属于那个浑然天成的世界。但我知道，往往用不了多久，突然出现的某些事情就会打破这份宁静和美好。记得有一次，我们遇上了一条在海岸边停泊的军舰。岸边连一个草棚子都没有，可是军舰却朝着丛林的方向不停地开炮。听说法国人正在这片地方进行一场战争。军舰上的旗帜像一条破布似的耷拉着，从船舷低处伸出一排六英寸口径大炮的炮口；油腻腻、黏糊糊的海水懒洋洋地涌着，一会儿把船抬起，一会儿又让它落下；随着船身的晃动，细细的桅杆也左摇右摆。天地广阔，大海无涯；而在这无比巨大的空间之中，一条小小的军舰停在那儿，只管向一片陆地开炮——这可真让人有点儿莫名其妙！嘭的一声，那六英寸的大炮又响了；一小簇火焰一下子爆开来，很快就不见了；一

他们的每一寸筋骨和肌肉，全都在张扬着野性的活力、不竭的能量，就和岸边的海浪一样自然而真实。

（邓竣翀　绘）

小团白色的烟雾慢慢消散了，一颗很小的炮弹发出了一声微弱的尖啸，然后就没事儿了。呵，你说还能发生什么事儿呢？这真有点儿像疯子行径，让人看着，只觉得又可怜又可笑。尽管军舰上的人一脸严肃地告诉我，在那儿有个看不见的地方藏着不少土著人——也就是所谓的敌人！我还是只觉得他们又可怜又可笑。

"我们把带来的信件交给军舰上的人，然后继续出发了。后来我听说在那条孤零零的军舰上发生了瘟疫，每天都会倒下三个人——可怕的高烧就这样夺去了船员们的性命。我们又去了别的一些地方，它们的名字五花八门，都很滑稽；带着土腥味的空气凝滞着，那感觉就好像在闷热的墓室里一样，死亡和贸易就在这些地方狂欢乱舞。驶向陆地的时候，那破碎的海岸和汹涌的海浪，仿佛是自然本身设下的阻挡入侵者的防线；接近河口的时候，我们又目睹了一道道奔流的死水，它们河岸腐烂成泥，河水化作浓浆，不断地冲刷、摧残着已被扭曲的红树林，使得它们在一种全然无能为力的绝望中痛苦地扭动。我们在每个地方停留的时间都很短，短到不足以留下什么特别的印象；但我总是隐隐感到一种不安。这种无以名状的压抑的感觉与日俱增，越来越沉重地压在我的心头。这就像一场梦魇中的漫长旅途，四下里鬼影憧憧、危机暗伏，令人心力交瘁。

"又过了三十多天，我才见到了那条大河的入海口。轮船在公司管理机构驻地的附近停泊下来。但是我可不能停在这里——还要航行差不多二百英里才到我工作的地方。所以一有机会，我便立即出发，向上游三十英里的一个地方赶去。

"我搭上了一艘很小的海轮。船长是个瑞典人，他见我是个同行，便邀请我到驾驶台上去。这是个瘦削的年轻人，肤色很白，脾气乖戾；他把长头发披在脑后，老是拖着脚走路。我们驶离那个小得可怜的码头的时候，他轻蔑地一扬下巴，指了指岸边的方向。'一直就住在那边？'他问道。我说：'是的。''那帮官老爷们还挺好心的，是吧？'他接着说。他讲的英语措辞准确，但是相当地尖酸刻薄。'真好笑，有些人为了一个月这点儿法郎，什么都肯干。难不成内陆那边也会是这样？'我对他说，很快我就能见着了。'很……很快？'他大声喊道。他拖着脚横跨一步，保持警觉地向前方观望。'可别想得这么容易，'他接着说，'前几天我在路边解下来一个上吊自杀的家伙，他也是个瑞典人。''上吊自杀？天啊！那是为什么呢？'我叫了起来。他仍在警觉地观察水上的情况，'谁知道呢，可能是因为这儿的太阳，也可能就是因为这个鬼地方。反正他受不了了。'

"我们终于驶入一片开阔的水域。我们看到了一片山崖，还看见岸边翻掘出来的成堆的泥土。山上有一些房子，另一些是铁皮顶棚的小屋；它们要么倚坡而建，要么建在那些挖土留下的大坑旁边。高崖上的激流不断地发出哗哗声响，回荡在这到处是人、杂乱不堪的地方。这里大半都是光着身子的黑人，好像一群群蚂蚁似的来回奔走。一段栈桥一直延伸到河中。太阳时不时迸发出一阵炽烈的强光，刺得人头晕目眩，一时间什么也看不见了。'那儿有你们公司的一个站点，'瑞典人一边说，一边指着石坡上好像军营一样联排的三间木房子。'我会让人把你的行李送上去。你说是四个箱子，对吧？好了，就这样吧。再见。'

"在一个半埋在深草里的锅炉旁边，我找到了一条通向山上的小路。每当遇到大块的岩石，这条小路就从一旁绕过去；

它还绕过了一节小型的火车货厢。这节车厢四轮朝天地仰躺在那里，还有一个轮子已经掉了，看上去就像一个死去多时的动物的尸体。再往前走，我又遇到更多的扔在那里朽坏了的机器，还有一堆生锈的铁轨。左边一片树丛下的浓荫里，似乎有些黑色的东西有气没力地动弹着。我用力眨了眨眼睛，但是这条小路太陡峭了，实在看不真切。右边传来了一阵嘟嘟的号角声，我看到一些黑人在狂奔。紧接着一阵沉闷的爆炸声，震动了脚下的大地，一股白烟从峭壁上升起，然后就没动静了。那巨石的表面似乎没有任何变化。他们在那儿修建铁路。山上的岩崖并没有妨碍他们什么；但是他们却在那里忙个不停，到处狂轰滥炸。

"身后忽然传来一阵轻微的吭唧声。我转头一看，只见六个黑人排成一列纵队，正沿着这条小路吃力地往山上挪。他们都直着身子慢慢地走着，头上顶着装满泥土的小筐，每走一步便发出一阵吭唧声。他们腰间缠着黑色的破布，末端一截短短的布头在他们身后甩来甩去，看起来就像尾巴一样。我数得清他们的每一根肋骨，他们手臂和腿上的关节好像绳子上扭结的疙瘩那样鼓了出来；每个人的脖颈上都套着铁项圈，一条铁索把他们几个连成一串。伴随着他们的脚步，铁索吭唧吭唧发出规律的撞击声。轰——！山崖上又传来一阵爆炸声，马上就让我想起了那条向着一片陆地开炮的军舰。这同样是一种充满了恶意的声音；但是就算你绞尽了脑汁从鸡蛋里面挑出骨头来，他们也无法被叫作什么'敌人'。他们被叫作罪犯；而他们触犯的是一些从天而降的无从说起的法律，就和那些从海上飞来的莫名其妙的炮弹一样，令他们全然无可奈何。他们干瘦的胸脯剧烈地起伏着，使劲儿张开的鼻孔翕动着，无神的双眼默默注视着山顶。他们从我身旁触手可及的地方经过，却谁也不曾看我一眼。这些野人承受着苦难，脸上只剩下死一般的冷漠和木然。在这群不开化的野人后边，有一个却显得与众不同。很明显，他是新势力作用下的产物——一个'开化了'的野人。这个人手里横提着一支来复枪，神情沮丧地来回踱步。他身穿制服，上边还敞着一颗纽扣；一见路边有个白人，他马上就把来复枪扛到了肩上。他这么做只是出于谨慎，因为所有的白人

这些野人承受着苦难，脸上只剩下死一般的冷漠与木然。

（张佳铭　绘）

一眼望去都长得差不多，他一时也不确定我到底是谁。很快他就松了一口气，朝我露出一个大大的、白人式的谄笑，然后迅速瞄了一眼手下的犯人们。看起来，他向我献上了他心中至高的信任和崇敬；毕竟我也是白人，也是眼下那高尚、正义的伟大事业的一分子。

"我不再继续上山，而是转身沿着左边的小路往山下走去。我想等到那些被铁链锁住的家伙们走远以后再说。你知道，我这个人可不是个没胆色的孬种，我也曾大打出手，击退来犯之敌。必要的时候我会反抗，更会进攻——进攻才是最好的反抗。我会不惜代价全力进击，如果陷入了背抵墙角的境地，哪怕是玩儿命都成。我曾见过暴力的魔鬼、贪婪的魔鬼、欲望的魔鬼，可是，老天作证！这些拿人——注意，我说的是人——当作牲畜一样随意支使的魔鬼，绝对是些强大的、贪婪之极的、红了眼的魔鬼。当我站在山坡上的时候，我已经预感到，在这片骄阳似火的土地上，我将会遇到一个装腔作势而又色厉内荏、目光短浅而又贪婪成性、当真是愚蠢到无可救药的魔鬼。这个魔鬼究竟有多么阴狠毒辣，我还得再过几个月，再走完一千多英里的路程之后才会知道。而这时，我怔怔地站在那儿，似乎已经感受到了某种警示。最后，我沿着斜路向山下走去，走向我刚才看到的那片树林。

"我绕过了山坡上的一个大坑，这个坑明显是有人故意挖的，但是它的用途是什么恐怕只有天晓得。反正它看起来不像采石或者采砂用的。它就是这么一个平白无故挖出来的坑。也许挖这个坑只是为了让罪犯们有点事儿做，算是出于一种仁慈的好意吧。反正我不知道。随后我差点跌进一条窄窄的小沟壑，这沟细得就像山坡上的一条疤痕似的。往里面一瞧，我发现那儿堆着好多排水管子——都是从海上大老远运来，原本打算用来建设居民点的。里面一根完好的管子也没有了，它们已经全给砸得稀巴烂。最后我终于来到了那片树荫下。我本来想着在这片荫凉下散散步，消磨一会儿时间；可是我刚走进那片树林，马上感到自己好像是闯入了阴森可怖的炼狱。那激流显然离这里很近。哗哗，哗哗——那一刻也不间断的、单调而又喧嚣的水流奔涌的声音在树林里那令人悲伤的寂静中回荡；这儿没有一丝微风，也没有一片摇动的树叶，天地间充斥着那激流的声音，仿佛大地向前飞奔的脚步声忽然间变得清晰可闻了。

"黑色的人形蜷伏着，躺卧着，或是坐在树丛间；他们有的倚靠着树干，有的趴在土地上，还有的一半身子暴露在阳光下，一半隐没在暗影里——这些人形呈现着各种各样的痛苦、认命或者绝望的姿态。山崖那边又传来一阵爆炸声，我感到脚下的土地发出轻微的颤动。工作还在继续。啊，工作！就在我眼前的这个地方，一些曾经帮着工作的人被留下来等待死亡。

"但是很显然，死亡的降临也不会那么快。他们不再是敌人，也不再是罪犯了，他们即将与这个苦难的尘世彻底告别——现在，他们只不过是疾病和饥饿的黑色影子，横七竖八地倒卧在青绿色的树荫里。一份份写着期限的合同，一道道合法的手续，把他们从海岸深处的各个地方弄到了这里，然后他们不得不在这无法适应的异乡，咽下从未见过的食物；直到他们生了病，再也干不动活儿了，才能得到允许，爬到这里来慢慢等死。死神正在召唤他们——如今，他们终于可以像风一样自由；但是他们也像风一样，随时都会消逝。我慢慢看清了树下一对对眼睛发出的微弱的光。后来我偶一低头，看到了近在手边的一张脸。那是一张皮包骨头的脸，软软地耷拉在脖子上，一只肩膀倚着旁边的大树；他眼皮慢慢地掀起，一对凹陷的眼珠转上来望着我，显得深邃而又空洞；眼窝深处飘忽着已经无法聚焦的一缕白光，正在渐渐地消散。那人看上去很年轻，几乎还是个孩子——不过你知道，我也不太会判断他们的年龄。面对这副情景，我一时也不知道该做什么，下意识地从口袋里摸出一块从瑞典船长那里带来的饼干，放到了他手上。他的手指慢慢收拢，攥住了那块饼干——他的眼睛不再看我，随后也不再动弹了。我发现他的脖颈上系着一小段白色毛线——这是什么意思？他是从哪儿弄来这毛线的？这是一个标记，一种装饰，一个符咒，还是一种祈愿？这东西是不是寄托了他的某种念想？总之，这一小段来自大洋彼岸的白色毛线，缠绕在他黝黑的脖子上，看上去实在有点儿骇人。

"离开那棵树不远，还有两副峰棱支离的瘦骨抱着膝盖坐在那里。其中一个把下巴支在膝盖上，呆滞的两眼望着虚空，那样子非常可怕，简直令人不敢直视；他身旁那个同样将入幽冥的兄弟则把额头搁在膝盖上，仿佛已经困倦得再也支撑不住了。剩下的人也都以各种各样的姿态，扭曲着身体倒作一片，形成一幅只有在大屠杀或者大瘟疫之后才能见到的恐怖图画。我站在那里，极度的惊惧令我几乎迈不动步。后来我看到他们当中有一个人用膝盖和双手撑起身子，四肢并用地慢慢挪动着，爬到河边喝水。他用手捧起水来喝着，然后在阳光里坐下，把两腿曲起，盘在身前。过了不一会儿，他那毛蓬蓬的头便一下子垂到胸口去了。

"我一秒钟也不想在这片树荫下多待了，于是我急匆匆向贸易站赶去。快到那片房子的时候，我遇见一个白人。他的衣着打扮出乎意料的优雅，第一眼看到他的时候，我还以为是自己眼花了。他身穿淡色的毛呢外套，高高的衣领浆洗得雪白挺括，袖口和长裤同样雪白洁净；胸前打着整齐的领带，脚下的皮靴擦得锃亮。头顶上没有戴帽子，梳理得一丝不乱的头发从中间分开，上面还涂了刨花油。他用一只宽大白皙的手掌举着一把镶着绿边儿的太阳伞，耳后别着一支钢笔。说真的，他这身打扮太让人惊叹了！

　　"我和这个神迹一般的家伙握了握手，他告诉我他是公司的会计主管，而且所有的账目都是在这个站点核算的。他出来是想溜达一会儿，可照他的话说，是为了'得到一点新鲜的空气。'我发现他讲话非常别扭，带着一股常年伏案工作的人特有的书卷气。我之所以觉得这个会计师值得一提，是因为从他的嘴里，我第一次听到了那个人的名字——而那个人的名字，如今早已和我对那段时间的记忆融为一体，密不可分。当然了，除此之外，我对这位会计师本人也满怀敬意。没错，他雪白的衣领、宽阔的袖边、一丝不乱的头发，全都令我肃然起敬。他整个人就像理发店里的假人模特儿一样精致考究，要知道，这里的一切都让人意气消沉、萎靡不振，而他却能始终保持着优雅的仪表，这真正是一身傲骨！他挺直的领子和齐楚的衬衣，全都在彰显着某种坚韧的品格。他已经在外工作将近三年了；后来我实在忍不住问他，究竟是如何把衣物打理得这么光鲜整洁的？他脸上微微一红，接着有些腼腆地说：'我在教一个土著女人做些贸易站上的事。真不容易啊！她可不情愿做这些工作。'这么看来，他的成就还真是了不得。同时，他也精心地管理他的账本，把它们一摞一摞码放得整整齐齐。

　　"可是除了这位会计师，贸易站的其他一切都和'整洁'

毫不沾边：人员混杂，东西乱放，就连房子也建得潦潦草草。一帮帮满身尘垢的黑人从这里进去出来，全都大张着两脚使着力气；于是各种工业制品、粗劣的棉布、玻璃珠和铜丝源源不断地被送进那黑暗的深处，换回来一批批珍贵的象牙。

"我还得在这个贸易站里再等上十天——这简直是遥遥无期的漫长等待。我住在院子里的一间小木屋里，可是周围实在是太嘈杂了，为了图个清静，有时候我不得不跑到那个会计师的办公室里去。他的办公室是用木条横着拼起来的，而且拼接得十分粗糙；当他伏在高高的办公桌上工作的时候，透过那些缝隙射进来的阳光，就在他全身上下印满了一道道明暗相间的条纹。而且，你根本用不着打开那宽大的百叶窗就可以看得到外面。屋子里非常闷热，肥大的苍蝇可怕地嗡嗡叫着，它们不叮人，但是会到处瞎飞乱撞。我一般都直接坐在地板上，而那位会计师则衣冠楚楚，有时还喷点香水；他就这样端坐在高高的凳子上，手中的笔不停地写啊写的。有时候他也站起来活动一下。后来有个病人被送进这间办公室，那人恹恹无力地躺在一张带轮子的矮床上，据说原先是个在内陆做贸易的代理人。会计师神色间显得有些烦恼，但是态度依然温和。'这病人的呻吟，'他说，'会扰乱我的注意力。气候本就有些难挨，如果再没法集中注意力的话，想要记账不出差错，真是太难了。'

"有一天，他头也不抬地对我说：'等你深入内陆以后，肯定会遇见库尔茨先生的。'我疑惑地问他库尔茨先生是谁，他说那是一位高级代理人。这回答让我有点儿失望。看到我的神情，他放下手中的笔，缓缓说道：'他是个非常出色的人物。'一再追问之下，我得知库尔茨先生正掌管着一个贸易站——一个非常重要的站点，位于那边一个真正的象牙产地，在'那个地方的尽头。那个贸易站的象牙产量抵得过其他所有贸易站的总和……'说完他又拿起笔来。矮床上的病人已经连呻吟的力气都没有了。办公室里一片死寂,只有苍蝇在嗡嗡嗡地叫。

"外面忽然传来一阵嘈杂的人语声和沉重的脚步声,随着这声音越来越响,一支运输队进来了。在木板搭起来的办公室外面,开锅似的突然爆出一阵七嘴八舌的粗蛮的土话——所有的野人搬运工都在争相嚷嚷着什么。在这一片混乱的噪声之中,依稀能够分辨出总代理人那沉痛哀悼的声音:'算了吧,已经没救了。'这一天之中,他已经满含热泪地说出这句话不止二十次了。会计师慢慢站起身来,'这吵闹声多可怕。'他说着便向屋子那头轻轻走过去,看了看那个病人,接着走回来对我说:'他可是听不见了。''什么!他已经死了吗?'我不禁吓了一跳。'不,还没死呢。'他若无其事地说。然后他朝着院子里传来吵闹声的方向一扬头,说道:'在你生怕把账记错的时候,你没法儿不痛恨这些野人——简直要恨死他们了。'他沉思了一会儿。'你见到库尔茨先生的时候,'他说,'请代我告诉他,这里的一切——'他朝着院子瞥了一眼,'一切都非常令人满意。我不想给他写信,因为我们的邮差一把信件拿到总站去,你就永远想不到你的信会落到什么人手里。'他用温和而又期待的眼神注视了我一会儿。'哦,他前程远大,不可限量,'他接着说,'用不了多久他就会成为公司管理层的一个大人物。上面的人——我指的是欧洲的董事会,你懂的——有意提拔他。'

"他又埋头工作了。外面的吵闹声已经平息,我也准备回去了。刚走到门口,我却一下子顿住了脚步——在不绝于耳的苍蝇嗡嗡声中,将要被送回家去的代理人毫无知觉,直挺挺地

将要被送回家去的代理人毫无知觉，直挺挺地躺在那儿；旁边那位，一心扑在账簿上，正在把一笔笔完美的交易变成完美的账目。

（张佳铭　绘）

躺在那儿；旁边那位，一心扑在账簿上，正在把一笔笔完美的交易变成完美的账目；而就在台阶下面不到五十英尺的地方，我看到了那片死亡之林寂静的树梢。

“第二天我终于离开了那个贸易站。我和一支六十人组成的运输队一起出发，开始了一段二百英里的徒步之旅。

“这段行程实在没什么好说的。茫茫的荒野中有很多被人踩出来的小路，这儿一条那儿一条的，它们纵横交错，形成了一张大网——有的穿过茂密的深草，有的穿过焚烧过的焦土，有的穿过低矮的灌木丛；它们依着地势，勾画出一条条蜿蜒起伏的曲线：向下深入寒气逼人的裂谷，再一路攀缘向上，翻越炙热欲燃的岩丘。抬眼远望，连一个人、一间屋子也看不见，四下里除了荒凉，还是荒凉。这里的人们很早以前就全都跑光了。你想想，如果有一天，在迪尔和格雷夫森德郊外的小路上，突然冒出一大群神秘的黑鬼，带着各种可怕的武器到处抓人，强迫英国佬给他们搬运沉重的货物；我想根本用不了多久，那一带所有的村庄和农场就会变得空无一人。但是眼下这个地方，不仅人影儿不见一个，就连屋子也不见一间。不过，我也曾路过几个废弃了的村子。在那里，一片片塌倒了的茅草墙乱七八糟的，看上去就像小孩做的玩意儿，让人觉着幼稚得可怜。日复一日，六十双光脚板在我身后噼噼啪啪地拖拉着走着，每双脚板都承载着六十磅的重荷。扎营，做饭，睡觉，拔营，出发。日复一日。有时候，一个正扛着重载的脚夫会忽然倒下，于是他就这样在路旁的深草中安息。天空和大地都沉默无声，陪伴他的只有一个已经喝空了的葫芦和一根他曾经用过的长棍。也许在某个宁静的夜晚，远处会传来一阵颤动的鼓声，时而低沉徘徊，时而高亢激昂；那鼓皮的颤动似乎有着穿透灵魂的力量，从夜色中凄迷的饮泣，渐渐弥漫成雷鸣般的回响，充满整个天地。这原始而又奇异的声音，仿佛是一种倾诉，也仿佛在暗示着什么——也许和基督教国家的钟声有着同样深切的含义。有一回，我遇见一个白人带着一些高瘦的桑给巴尔人组成的武装护卫队在路边扎了营。这个白人身穿制服，却也不系扣子，就这么敞胸露怀，看上去热情好客，喜气洋洋——更别提他那一身酒气了。他宣称自己正在进行'道路清理'。说实话，我可没看见什么道路，自然也谈不上什么道路清理；可是当我刚往前走出三英里，我就被一具中年黑人的尸体结结实实地绊了一跤——尸体的额头上，赫然是一个枪窟窿！原来，这就是所谓'一劳永逸地清理了道路'。我还有一个白人同伴，他人倒也不坏，可就是一身赘肉，而且经常在离树荫和水源还很远的时候，一下子就他妈的晕倒在酷热的山坡上了。你想想，你得举着自己的上衣给他当遮阳伞，等着他慢慢地醒过来，这得有多么地让人心烦。有一次我忍不住问他，到底是干什么跑到这儿来了。他对我的问题嗤之以鼻：'当然是搞钱了，你以为还能是什么？'没多久，他又发起烧来，我们只好弄来一根木杠子，下边挂着一个吊床把他抬着走。因为他体重二百好几十磅，为这事儿，我和那些脚夫不知道争吵过多少回。他们发着牢骚，没人愿意上前，到了半夜就想连着货物一起开溜——简直是要造反了。因此有一天晚上，我打着各种手势发表了一场英文演说。在我面前的六十双眼睛显然全都看明白了我这一堆手势是什么意思，于是第二天早晨我又让人抬起那个吊床走在队伍前面了。一切都很正常。但是一小时之后我却发现，那位老兄已经连人带吊床被扔在灌木丛里了。我目瞪口呆地看着眼前的一切：人躺在地上哼哼唧唧，吊床和毯子扔在一边，简直是一片狼藉。那位老兄已经出离愤怒了——掉下来的木杠子把他的鼻子蹭去了一大块皮。他急切地要我处死几个人以示惩戒，但是那些脚夫早已经跑得连影子都看不见了。这时我想起了那个老医生说过的话：'如果可以当面观察人的思想变化的话，对于科学研究当然是很有意义的。'我感到我这个人就要开始对科学的发展产生意义了。可是现在说这些还有什么用呢！十五天之后，我终于又看到了那条大河。于是我鼓起劲儿来，一簸一簸地朝着总站跑过去。总站建在一个被树丛环绕着的死水湾旁边，一边拦着一堆'色味俱佳'的烂泥沼，另外三边则围着不可思议的草篱笆；中间一个没人管的破洞就是总站那堂而皇之的大门。这个演活剧似的鬼地方你只要瞧上一眼，就会知道在这管事儿的一定是个不会管事儿的混蛋。几个手拿长棍的白人从房子那边循声过来，他们都懒洋洋的，对我看一眼，然后又溜达着回到不知道什么地方去了。只有一个黑胡子壮汉，一听我自报家门，马上激动地对着我滔滔不绝、绘声绘色但却语无伦次地描述着说——我的那条汽船已经沉到河底了。我顿时五雷轰顶。什么？怎么搞的？为什么？！哦，一切'都挺好的，''经理本人'当时就在那儿。一切都照章操作，完全没问题。'每个人的表现都棒极了！他们全都棒极了！'——我听着都蒙了——'你现在，马上，'他仍在口沫横飞，'就得去见我们经理！他正等着！'

"我一时间还想象不到这条沉船究竟意味着什么。我想我现在应该已经完全知道了。但就算是现在，一想起来这件事，我还好像在做梦似的——这简直愚蠢至极，完全不像人干的事儿。真的是蠢到家了。可是在当时，我只不过觉得，自己遇上了一件非常恼人的麻烦事。我的汽船就这么沉了。两天前，他们忽然急匆匆地要开船到上游去，经理上了船，安排了一个自告奋勇的家伙充当船长。结果汽船开出去还不到三个小时，船底就被礁石撕开了一条大口子，然后就在靠近南岸的地方沉下去了。我想，这一下我连船都没有了，这儿还有我什么事呢？呵，事实上我要做的事可多了去了——我得把自己麾下的这个大家伙从河里捞上来。第二天我就紧锣密鼓地开始干活了。把沉船打捞出水，再把船体一块块搬到站上，然后再进行修理，前后需要好几个月的时间。

"我和经理第一次见面的情景，真是一言难尽。那天早晨我已经步行了二十多英里的路，可是他竟然都没让我坐下。他的外表看上去十分普通，无论是相貌肤色，还是神态声音，全都没什么特点；他不算高也不算矮，身材也很一般。他长着一双蓝眼睛，很常见的那种；但那眼神却是相当冰冷，当他向你投过来一瞥的时候，真让人有一种被利刃剖开的错觉。奇怪的是，尽管目光犀利，他整个人的态度却又不凉不热，就像一盆温吞水似的。除此之外，他的嘴唇上总是噙着一丝似笑非笑的表情，那表情很难形容，它总是隐约地浮现在他的嘴角，有时候浅淡得几乎令人难以觉察。我说不清楚，但是我到现在还记得他那个样子。这是一种无意识的表情，可能算是一种微笑吧，每当他说完几句什么话的时候，那笑容就会忽然一下子变深。就这样，他讲完一段话就勾一勾嘴角，好像给这段话贴了张封条，使得他讲的哪怕最简单的一句话也变得高深莫测起来。他就是个普通的交易员，从很年轻的时候就在这里做事。仅此而已。尽管大家都服从他，但是大家对他既不爱戴，也不惧怕，甚至连尊敬都谈不上。他只会让人觉得不自在。对了，就是这个词儿：不自在。倒也不是明显的不信任，但就是让人不自在。仅此而已。你无法想象这么样一个机构……呃，一帮子人，还能谈得上什么做事效率。他没有组织能力，缺乏进取心，甚至没法让手下的人各安其职。总站给他弄成现在这副糟糕的样子，本身就足够说明问题了。他要知识没知识，要才能没才能，但最后还是坐上了经理的位子——为什么？也许就因为他从来不生病……三年一个任期，他都干了三个任期了……

众人病恹恹，唯独他健康。而强健的体格本身就是一种优势。当他回家休假时，他总是花天酒地，得意洋洋——虽然他不是水手，但是这副做派和上了岸的水手没什么两样。只要随便和他聊几句你就会发现，他这个人没有任何创见，只会例行公事。仅此而已。但是他有一点非常厉害，那就是：你根本不知道这世上到底有什么东西能降得住他。而他自己也守口如瓶，无懈可击。他既没有优点，也没有弱点，也许，其实他整个人都是个中空的皮囊，里边什么也没有——但是谁也无法证实这个猜测，因为你可没法在这儿进行外科检查。有一次，好几种热带病一起袭来，几乎把站上所有的代理人都撂倒了。这时有人听他说，'来这儿的人根本就不该带着肚肠。'说完他又用那诡秘的微笑把这句话封印起来，仿佛这是一扇由他看守着的通往黑暗的大门；你似乎感觉窥到了些什么，但是他马上就把那门关闭了。吃饭的时候，那些白人总是为了排座次而争执不休。他一怒之下，命人特制了一张巨大的圆桌，再命人盖一间屋子，专门用来放这张桌子。于是这里就成了总站的饭厅。他坐在哪儿，哪儿就是首席，剩下的位子全都是末席——这下谁也不用争了。你能看得出来，他对自己的权威坚信不疑。他既不是彬彬有礼，也不是粗暴蛮横，他只是不动声色。他纵容他的'听差'——来自海边什么地方的一个脑满肠肥的年轻黑人——当着他的面，用一种近乎寻衅的无礼态度对待他手下的那些白人。

　　"一见到我，他就开始侃侃而谈。他说我在路上耽搁了太久，让他都等不及了。所以他只好自己先干起来了。上游的那些贸易站需要补充给养。而运输任务一次又一次地被耽搁下来，所以现在他也不知道那些人是死是活，情况怎么样，等

他对自己的权威坚信不疑——他坐在哪儿，哪儿就是首席，剩下的位子
全都是末席。

（梁丹丹、张舒婷　绘）

等。他也不听我讲话，只顾自己喋喋不休。他手里不停地把
玩着一根火漆棍，嘴里翻来覆去地说现在的情况‘非常严重，
非常严重’。他又说，有一个非常重要的贸易站也似乎情况不
妙，那里的负责人——库尔茨先生，据说生了病。他希望那些
话不是真的，因为库尔茨先生是个……我感到非常疲惫，也非
常烦躁。绞死那个他妈的库尔茨吧，我心里想。我直接打断

他的话，我说我刚上岸的时候就已经听说过库尔茨的大名了。'噢！这么说来，就连下游的人也在谈论他。'他喃喃自语道。然后他又开始讲个没完，一再告诉我，库尔茨先生是他手下最好的代理人，是一个非凡的人物，对整个公司都意义重大；所以我得理解他为什么如此焦虑。他说他现在'非常、非常地不安'。这我当然看得出来。他坐在椅子里不停地扭动着屁股，如坐针毡；然后突然大喊一声'啊，库尔茨先生！'——激动得一下子把手里的火漆棍都给掰断了。这个意外好像把他自己也吓了一跳。接下来，他说他想知道'得花多长时间才能……'我又一次截住了他的话。你想想，我当时饥肠辘辘，他还一直让我站着，我心里窝的火就快要冒出来了。'我怎么知道？'我说，'那个沉船我连一眼还都没看过呢——怎么着也得几个月吧。'在我看来，这场谈话就是一堆彻头彻尾的废话。'几个月啊，'他说，'那好，咱就说三个月吧，然后就可以航行了。对，三个月的时间，这件事儿应该办得成的。'谈话一结束，我立刻头也不回地离开了他的屋子（他住着一间单独的土坯房，那房子外面还修了个阳台），嘴里还低声痛骂着这个饶舌的白痴。那时我确实当他是个白痴，但是后来我收回了这句话——因为他对'办这件事儿'所需要的时间，估计得竟是相当精确；当我明白过来的时候，我真的是浑身发凉。

"第二天我就立刻投入工作了。这么说吧，借着工作，我就不必理睬站上的事了。我觉得只有这样我才能紧紧抓住真实的生活，弥补这段时间给我带来的空虚感。可是，既然人在这儿，有时候总会不得不看到些什么；于是我就看到站上的那些人头顶着太阳，漫无目的地在院子里四处溜达。我不禁问自己，这帮人到底在搞什么？他们手里拿着一根可笑的长棍子，这儿逛逛那儿转转，活像一群失去了信仰的朝圣者，在一个破烂的草篱笆里边鬼迷心窍了。从这些人絮絮的低语和轻声的喟叹中，时不时飘来'象牙'这个词儿，简直就好像某种虔诚的祷告似的。一股贪婪而又愚昧的气息透过这个词儿在空气里飘荡，犹如死去的躯体在发出阵阵尸臭，熏人欲呕。老天！我一辈子都没见过如此荒诞的情景。我向贸易站的外边望去，忽然感到一阵颤栗——那寂静的荒野浩荡无边，而且不可战胜，就像人世间永恒的罪恶和真理一样；它只是沉默着，包围着大地上这一丁点人工开辟出来的地方，耐心地等待着这场疯狂侵略结束的时刻。

"唉，那几个月简直是……算了，不说也罢。反正是什么事儿都有。一天晚上，一间堆满了印花布、棉布、玻璃珠子和各种乌七八糟的东西的草棚子突然着火了。这场大火来得那么突然，就好像大地突然裂开嘴来喷出一股复仇的火焰，要把这堆破烂货统统焚成灰烬。当时我正站在那条被拆卸了的汽船旁边安静地抽着烟，然后我就看见火光中的那些人影，都高举着两手胡窜乱跳，跟些个活宝似的；那个黑胡子壮汉手里抱着一只铁皮桶朝河边一溜小跑，一看见我，又连声说每个人'都表现得棒极了！他们全都棒极了！'他从河里舀起了大约一升水，匆匆忙忙又跑了回去。这时候我注意到，他的水桶底下破了一个大洞。

"我缓步朝那边走去。慌张什么？你瞧，整个草棚子就像一盒点着了的火柴，烧得可带劲儿了。这打从一开始就根本没法救。火焰蹿得老高，谁也不敢上前，眼睁睁看着一样样东西全都着了火——然后接连不断地倾塌。草棚子转眼间就变成了

一堆闪烁着火花的灰烬。不远处，他们正在鞭打一个黑人。他
们说这场火是他引起来的；谁知道呢，也许真的是这样吧，可
是这黑人被他们打得惨叫连连，听着都瘆人。后来，我看到他
在一片小树荫下面坐了好几天，他非常虚弱，挣扎着想缓过一
口气；然后他站起身子走了出去——沉默的荒野就这样把他也
揽入了怀抱。我从黑暗中慢慢向那堆余烬走过去，忽然发现
前面有两个人，正在那儿窃窃私语。我听到他们提起库尔茨
的名字，然后又听到这样一句话，'得利用这场大火，好好做
点文章。'那两人当中有一个，赫然正是经理。于是我和他打
了声招呼，'晚上好。''以前见过这种事吗——嗯？真让人难
以置信，'他一边说着，一边慢慢走开了。另一个人仍站在那
里。那人是个高级代理人，很年轻，颇有点绅士派头；他留着
一小撮八字胡，长着一只鹰钩鼻子。那人话不多，和别的代理
人也不怎么打交道，大家都说他是经理派来搞监视的密探。我
以前也没和他说过几句话，但是这回却攀谈起来了。我们边说
边走，慢慢溜达着离开了那堆仍在嘶嘶作响的灰烬。他邀我去
他的住处，于是我跟着他来到了总站的主楼。他划亮一根火
柴，在跳动的火光下，我发现这个年轻的贵族不但拥有一只镶
着银边的镜匣，而且还独自享用着一整根蜡烛。这在当时，按
说只有经理才有权使用蜡烛。土墙上覆着一张当地土著的草
席，还挂着一大堆战利品：长矛、非洲梭镖、盾牌和各式刀
剑。我听人说，委派给这个家伙的差事是烧砖；但是整个站上
连一块碎砖的影子也没有，而他在这儿已经待了一年多了——
什么也没干，就在等着。看样子是因为缺了点什么，所以他才
没法烧砖，具体我也不知道——也许是因为没有稻草？不管怎
样，在当地肯定是找不到稻草的，而且也不太可能从欧洲给他

送稻草来，所以我也搞不清他到底在等什么。也许他在等的是某种奇特的创世神迹吧！而他们——所有这些将近二十个朝圣者——远涉重洋来到这里，全都在等待着什么；要我说，就从他们的'工作'态度来看，待在这里也算不上什么不顺心的事儿，虽然他们唯一在做的事情就是生病。他们用一些愚蠢的伎俩，搞一些尔虞我诈、背后攻讦的把戏来消磨时间。贸易站里到处弥漫着一股阴谋诡计的气味；不过，倒也没有当真发生过什么事情。这实在是让人感觉很魔幻，就和这里其他的一切同样虚无缥缈——公司的慈善宣传是个假幌子、每个人讲话都是在瞎扯淡、管理制度似有实无、工作也只是在装装样子。在这里，唯一真实的想法就是怎样把一个象牙产地的贸易站搞到手。只要能在那儿当上负责人，就可以坐享提成了。所有的阴谋诡计、诽谤中伤、仇视怨恨，全都是为了争夺这份美差。但你若是想要他们稍稍动一下小指头干点儿实实在在的工作——哦，那可不成。我的天啊！世上竟会有这种事儿——有的人可以盗马，而别人连看一眼马嚼子都不行。盗马的尽管大摇大摆把马牵走。很好，没问题。然后他还可以骑到马上遛几圈。但是如果别人瞟了一眼马嚼子，那些哪怕是最仁慈的圣徒都会立刻火冒三丈、暴跳如雷。

"我起先并不知道他为什么对我如此热情。但是聊着聊着，我忽然意识到这个家伙别有用心——原来他是想从我嘴里打探消息。他总是会把话题引到欧洲，提到他觉得我可能认识的一些人；比如他会循循善诱地问我，我在那座坟墓似的城市里都认识些什么人呀，等等诸如此类的问题。他的一双小眼睛像云母片那样闪闪发亮，里面充满了好奇和渴望——尽管他也在竭力装出一副矜持的样子。一开始我还真有点吃惊，但很快，我的好奇心也上来了，我倒要看看他究竟想从我这里挖到些什么。因为我真是想不出，我身上能有什么东西值得他如此费心思。看着他那副机关算尽的样子，真是挺有趣的——因为对他们钻营的那些东西，我全然是冷眼旁观；而在我的头脑里，除了那条破汽船的事儿以外，也别无他物。后来，他显然以为我故意不讲实话，简直是无耻之尤。他生气了。为了掩饰自己的

画中人是一个女子，她身披斗篷，手执火炬——火炬在熊熊燃烧，她的双眼却是蒙着的。

（陈睿杰　绘）

恼怒，他打了个哈欠。于是我站起身来。刚走到门口，我看到门板上挂着一幅很小的油画，画中人是一个女子，她身披斗篷，手执火炬——火炬在熊熊燃烧，她的双眼却是蒙着的。画面的背景非常阴沉，几乎是一片漆黑。画中女子仪态庄严，可是那火焰映在她脸上的光影却显得阴森而诡异，似乎是某种不祥之兆。

"我伫立在画像前凝视着，他彬彬有礼地站在一旁，手里握着一个半品脱的香槟酒瓶（其中的酒已经被当作安神药喝光了），瓶中插着那支蜡烛。我问起这画的来历，他说这是一年多以前，库尔茨先生在总站这里画的——当时他正在等着什么交通工具来载他回到那边的贸易站去。'请你一定要告诉我，'我说，'这位库尔茨先生到底是什么人？'

"'他是内陆贸易站的站长，'他移开视线，简短地回答说。'真是多谢你了，'我笑了起来。'我还知道你是总站负责做砖的。这些事人人皆知，不是吗？'他沉默了一会儿，最后还是开口了。'他是一位奇才，'他说，'他是慈悲、科学和进步的使者，天知道他可能还有着别的什么使命。我们要有……'他忽然提高了声音，大声吟诵道：'为了更好地指引欧洲交付给我们的事业，也就是说，我们要有更高的智慧、更广泛的同情心和矢志不移的目标。''这话谁说的？'我问道。'他们都这么说，'他回答，'有的人还给写成了文章。所以他就到这里来了。但是他与众不同——这一点你当然知道。''我当然知道？——你这是什么意思？'我惊讶地打断了他的话。但是他没理我，'是呵！今天他是最好的贸易站的站长，明年他就会当上副经理，再过两年他就是……我敢说，你一定知道再过两年他将被提拔成什么。你属于新的那一派——道德派。当年特地把他派到这儿来的那些人现在又推荐了你。你就别再不承认了。我的一双眼睛可是全都看见了。'听到这里我恍然大悟，原来这个年轻人知晓了我亲爱的姨妈那些高官朋友的态度，这才上演了今天晚上这出人意料的一幕剧。我差点忍不住要笑出声来。'你看过公司的机密邮件吗？'我问他，这问题让他哑口无言，不知怎样回答才好。太解气了。'等到库尔茨先生，'我神情严肃地继续说，'当了总经理，而你还敢这么做，那你就等着瞧吧。'

"他冷不丁就把蜡烛吹灭，于是我们一起走出了房间。月亮已经升起来了。几条黑色的人影在那里蔫头耷脑地来回走着，往那堆灰烬上泼水，发出一阵嗤嗤声；月光下，灰堆上腾起一股股白色的烟气，受了刑的黑人在附近什么地方痛苦地呻吟着。'瞧这畜生闯了多大的祸！'那个黑胡子壮汉说着朝我们走过来。他精力旺盛，好像从来都不会疲倦似的。'他这是自找的。犯了规矩就该惩罚，惩罚就是狠狠地揍！绝不手软，绝不手软。这是唯一的办法，好保证我们以后不再有火灾。我刚才还跟经理这么说来着……'这时他看到了我的那位同伴，立刻就把后半截话咽了下去，低眉顺眼地垂下了头。'您还没睡吗，'他十分关切地问道，一脸谄媚讨好的样子：'这很正常，这很正常。哈！危险——往往会令人不安。'一说完他就从我们眼前消失了。我径直朝河边走去，那位伙伴则一直跟着我。我听见他压低声音从牙缝里迸出一句，'全是一帮笨蛋——都给我去他妈的吧。'那些朝圣者三三两两聚在一起，指手画脚地在讨论着什么。有几个人手里仍然拎着长棍子——你要说他们抱着棍子睡觉我都信。篱笆外面，重重叠叠的树木在月光的映照下仿佛无数幽幽的鬼影；透过那婆娑树影的摇曳，透过那萧条院落里凄凉的低响，大地的沉默深深地沁入了我的心底——连同着它的神秘、它的伟岸，以及它生命中那隐秘的一面——那些曾经发生过的令人动容的故事。受伤的黑人在不远处低声呻吟着，突然间发出一声沉重的悲叹；我听不下去，立刻转身走开了。这时一只手伸过来挽住了我的胳膊。'我亲爱的先生，'那位伙伴说道，'我不希望别人误解我的意思，尤其不想被您误会。因为在我有幸见到库尔茨先生之前，您将会早早地见到他。我不想库尔茨先生对我这个人有什么错误的印象……'

"我就任他一直说下去。这个纸糊的梅菲斯特，我觉得我只要伸出一根手指就可以把他捅穿，然后看到他的肚囊里边除了一点儿稀屎之外空空如也。你们也看出来了吧？这家伙计划着要在经理手下一步一步往上爬，当上个副经理。我还看得出来，那个库尔茨的到来使他们两个都有些进退失措。他急促地不停解释着，而我也根本不去打断他。我把肩膀倚在我的破船上，那条船已经被拖到了山坡上，就像某种巨大的水生动物的尸体那样躺在那里。我的鼻孔里充满了泥土的味道——啊！那真正是来自远古的气息。眼前的原始森林高邈而沉静，黑色的溪流上，水面不时荡起激潋的波光。月亮给世间万物披上了一层薄薄的银纱——蔓生的荒草，淤积的泥滩，从庙宇的墙头伸出的丛丛枝桠，还有那条静静流淌的宽广的大河，全都在朦胧的月色里泛出梦幻般的光采。我曾经透过那个昏暗的门洞望向那条大河，如今她的胴体完全呈现在我的面前，雍容地舒展着，闪烁着白银似的光泽。浩瀚宇宙，万象恢宏，一切都于无声处孕育着未来的希望；而那个人却一直在我耳边絮絮聒聒地讲着他自己的盘算。天地之间，人类何其渺小，这无边的寥廓见证了我们的一言一行，却报之以完全的静默——我不知道，这对我们究竟是一种启示，还是一种威赫？我们究竟是为何来到这世上，又是为何流落到了这里？究竟是谁能赢得最后的胜利，是我们，还是那寂静的荒野？我心中有无数疑问，而这荒野只是沉默不语；也许，它根本就听不到、也不在乎我们在说些什么，它只是延伸、延伸，向着无穷的远方延伸。那里面究竟都有些什么东西？我看到了从那里运出来的一些象牙，我还听说库尔茨先生也在那儿。关于那地方我已经听说得够多了——但是天知道，这些只言片语，根本无法在我脑海中构筑起什么鲜明的形象。这就好比有人告诉我说，那儿住着一位天使或者一个魔鬼。我对此只能半信半疑，就像你们听说在遥远的外空住着火星人一样。我认识一个苏格兰的船帆工人，他曾经斩钉截铁地对我说，火星上面住着人。如果你接着问他那些人长什么样子？怎么行动的？他就会露出窘迫的神色，小声咕哝着说'他们都是四肢着地，爬着走的。'如果你忍不住微微一笑，他就会大发雷霆，要和你干上一架——尽管他已经是个六十多岁的老头子了。我可绝不会为了这个库尔茨去跟人干架，但是我为了他却几乎撒谎了。你知道我向来对撒谎深恶痛绝，简直无法容忍。这倒不是由于我比别人更正直，而仅仅是因为谎言会让我感到恐怖——谎言往往会散发出死亡的味道。世上没有比死亡更恐怖的事了，我更是压根儿就不愿意想到它。一想到死亡是万物的终结，我就好像吞了一口腐肉那样又恶心又难受。这也许是天性使然吧。好吧，我几乎撒谎了——我让那个年轻的傻瓜尽管去想象我在欧洲有着多么大的靠山。从我对他装腔作势的那一刻起，我也就和那些走火入魔的朝圣者没什么两样了。当时我只是简单地想着，这样做多少算是帮了'库尔茨'一点忙。可是你也知道，那时候的'库尔茨'对于我只不过是一个抽象的名字而已——我还没亲眼见过这个人呢。你想想，那个名叫'库尔茨'的人，你们见过他吗？了解他的经历吗？知道关于他的任何事吗？你一定会连连摇头。你对他一无所知，而我也完全一样。我只是在徒劳地描绘着一个虚幻缥缈的梦境。梦里的感受总是难以言喻的——你在黑暗里

我曾经透过那个昏暗的门洞望向那条大河，如今她的胴体完全呈现在我的面前，雍容地舒展着，闪烁着白银似的光泽。

（张佳铭　绘）

辗转挣扎、魂惊胆战，周围的一切都令你感到荒谬、惊异和迷茫；你似乎被什么不可思议的东西紧紧地攫住了——而那种不可思议的东西，就是梦的本质……"

说到这里，马洛沉默了一会儿。

"……不，不可能说得出的。生活的感受同样难以言喻。我们都生活在人生中的某一个阶段，而每个阶段都有其自身的现实和意义——那种幽微玄妙而又无所不在的意义，就是生活的本质——但是谁也无法说得出。我们总是孤独地生活，一如我们只能孤独地入梦……"

他又停了下来，似乎在思索着什么，然后接着说道——

"伙计们，你们现在回头来看这些事，自然能比那时的我看得更清楚些。你们了解我，就会知道那时的我……"

夜色漆黑如墨，我们这几个听故事的人已经几乎看不清彼此了。马洛独坐一旁，身影更是完全隐没在黑暗里；似乎已经有很久很久，只有他的声音在我们耳畔悠悠回响。大家全都沉默着，一言不发。也许他们都睡着了，可是我却异常清醒。我静静地聆听着，循着马洛口中的每一句话，每一个字，细细咀嚼着这个故事；我几乎产生了一种错觉，这娓娓讲述的声音并不是出自马洛之口，而是随着那沉郁的晚风，从泰晤士河的夜色深处，自己飘荡而来的——我想从中寻到一点线索，弄明白到底是什么——让这个故事在我的心底勾起了一丝淡淡的悲愁。

"……是的——我让他一直讲下去，"马洛又接着说，"关于我背后到底有什么靠山的这个问题，他爱怎么想就怎么想吧。所以我就笑而不语，由着他猜。可事实上，我什么靠山也没有！在我的背后，只有我正用肩膀倚着的那条又破又旧的沉船。而他却在大谈特谈什么'做人就是要有远大的志向,''如果一个人能来这里,你该知道他可不是来赏月的。'库尔茨先生是个'全能的天才',但是即使是天才,想要顺利地开展工作,也得有'称手的工具——也就是聪明人'的帮忙。他的职责是做砖,可是他一块砖也不做,啊哈!那是因为某种不可违抗的物理定律碍着他的事了——这我完全知道;而他乐意给那位经理做秘书活儿,那是因为'任何有理性的人,都不会毫无理由地拒绝来自上司的信任。'话说到这儿,我还能有什么不明白的? 这一切我简直太明白了。那么我想要的是什么? 老天! 我想要的只有铆钉、铆钉——有了铆钉我才能继续工作,才能把船上的大洞给补上。我需要铆钉! 在海岸那边有成箱成箱的铆钉,它们摞成一座座小山,箱子都给撑开了,撒得到处都是! 在山坡上那个贸易站的院子里,你只要一抬脚就会踢到一个扔在地上的铆钉。有的铆钉都滚落到那片死亡之林里去了。如果你愿意弯腰去捡,你很快就可以用铆钉装满你所有的口袋——可是在这个真正需要铆钉的地方,却连一颗铆钉都没有。我们有大小合适的钢板,但是没有铆钉,怎么把它们给接上去? 每星期,那个黑人信差都会独自出发,他肩上扛着邮包、手里拿着棍子,从我们这个总站到海岸那边去;而海岸那边的运输队,每星期也会往我们这里送好几次货——让人一看就吓一跳的磷光闪闪的印花布、一分钱一大堆的玻璃球、印着让人眼花缭乱的斑斑点点花纹的棉布手绢,等等——可就是没有铆钉。而只要三个脚夫,就可以运来能让汽船重新下水的全部铆钉。

"他絮絮地向我吐露了不少秘密,我却没有什么消息给他投桃报李。我想,也许是这种漠然的态度最终惹恼了他。他一字一句地警告我说，他既不怕上帝，也不怕魔鬼，更不会怕一个区区凡人耍花招。我说这我当然明白，但是我真的只想要那么一些铆钉——如果库尔茨先生了解当下的状况，那么他真正想要的也不过就是这些铆钉。现在不是每星期都会往海岸那边送信吗……'我亲爱的先生，'他几乎喊了起来，'我写的信全都是经理口授的。'这我不管，我只要铆钉。总会有办法解决的——他不是自称聪明人吗？于是他脸色丕变，一下子就冷若冰霜；话锋一转，却跟我谈起河马来。他问我，睡在那汽船上（我一直夜以继日地抢修船只）会不会时常被吵醒。因为那儿有一头烦人的老河马，一到夜里它就爬上岸来，在总站这一带四处游荡。站里的朝圣者们常常倾巢出动，他们带着所有的来复枪，恨不得把枪里所有的子弹都倾泻到那老河马的身上。有的人甚至通宵达旦守在那里，专等着它出现。然而这一切都是白费力气。'那头畜生有神灵护体，'他说，'但是在这个地方，神灵只会庇佑野兽，而不是人类——你听懂我的意思了吗？在这里的人，谁也没有什么护身符。'他站在那儿，月光照在他的脸上——有一瞬间我看到，他精致的鹰钩鼻子几不可察地扭曲了一下，眼中却精光闪烁，一眨也不眨。然后他简短地向我道了声晚安，就走开了。在我想来，这一番诘问令他心烦意乱，他已经理屈词穷，无从推脱了。于是我一扫前几天的阴霾，心中又燃起了希望。总算摆脱了这个家伙，我心情大好，轻快地走向我那位'有势力的朋友'——我的'靠山'——那条残破扭曲、几乎被撞废了的廉价汽船。我爬上船去，脚下的甲板立刻哐啷哐啷地响起来，就好像你沿着街沟边走边踢亨特利·帕尔玛牌饼干的空罐子的声音一样。这艘船造得很不结实，外形也谈不上美观，但是我已经为它付出了那么多的辛勤劳动，我便爱上它了。对我来说，它比任何一个有势力的朋友都更加管用。它使我有机会出来转一转，看看自己到底能做成什么事。当然了，我并不喜欢工作。我更喜欢无所事事地闲逛，脑子里只想着那些便宜的好事儿。我不喜欢工作——没有人喜欢。可是我喜欢工作赋予我们的东西：那个发现自我的机会。那是一个真实的自我，只属于你，无关他人——而他人也永远不会了解。他们只看得到你愿意展示出来的表象，却总也无法触及那隐藏于表象之下的真谛。

"我看见船尾的甲板上坐着一个人，两腿悬在泥滩上面荡来荡去。对于这一幕，我一点儿也不会大惊小怪。你知道，我倒情愿和站上的那几个技工交朋友，而那些朝圣者自然是对他们不屑一顾的——大概就是因为他们的言行有些粗鄙吧。眼前这个人是工长，他干的是造锅炉的行当，手艺也非常好。他身材又高又瘦，脸色发黄，一双眼睛炯炯有神。他看上去有些忧郁，头顶就像手掌心那样光秃秃的；他所有的头发似乎都一齐聚拢到了下巴上，然后在这个新地方欣欣向荣地生长起来，越来越长——一直拖到了腰间。他是个鳏夫，家中有六个还没成年的孩子（为了能来这里，他把孩子们托付给他的一个姊妹照料）。他平生最大的爱好就是养鸽子、放鸽子。他不但热衷此道，而且还是个大行家。他一谈起鸽子就滔滔不绝，完全停不下来。他经常一放工就从工棚那儿跑来找我，跟我聊他的孩子、他的鸽子；工作的时候，因为他得从泥滩上爬到汽船底下去，他总是用一大块白餐巾似的包袱皮先把胡子给包起来。那块包袱皮是专门用来包胡子的，它两边各有一个圆环，可以挂在耳朵上。到了傍晚，你就会看到他蹲在河沟的岸边仔仔细细地清洗那块包袱皮，然后郑重其事地把它摊在树丛上晾干。

"我在他后背上猛拍了一巴掌，喊着说：'我们就要有铆钉啦！'他一骨碌爬起来，叫道：'不会吧！铆钉！'仿佛他根本不敢相信自己的耳朵。然后他压低嗓门：'你——嗯？'也不知道为什么，我俩那时候乐不可支，简直如醉如狂。我把一根手指竖在嘴边，神秘地点了点头。'真有你的！'他大声喊道，同时一只手举过头顶，手指一捻'叭'的一声脆响，脚下就迈开了舞步。我也跟着跳起了快步舞。我们就这样在铁皮甲板上胡蹦乱跳起来。船身发出惊人的哐当哐当声，接着，河沟对面的原始森林传来一阵阵巨大的回声，滚雷般回荡在沉睡的贸易站的上空。这声音肯定把那些睡在茅屋里的朝圣者们惊醒了。经理住处的门廊映着灯光，出现了一条黑色的人影，随即又消失了；过了片刻，那门廊也在黑暗中消失不见了。我们停住了脚，于是被我们的脚步声驱走的宁静，又从大地的各个角落重新汇聚了起来。那茂密丛林好似巍峨的城墙，错落参差的干、纵横交叠的枝、苍翠纷繁的叶、锦团绣簇的花、披离蒙茸的蔓，密密匝匝地纠缠成一大片，岿然不动地耸立着；在月光下望去，那丛林就好像无数植物涌起了滔滔巨浪，浪头越积越高，翻卷的浪峰好似乌云压顶，随时要向这边的河流倾覆而下；这无声的生命似乎要发动一场狂暴的淹袭，好把我们这些人——这些微不足道的渺小生物——一下子冲荡个干净。但是那丛林并没有动。远处突然传来一阵水花飞溅的声音，接着是巨大而沉闷的喷鼻声，仿佛有一条远古的鱼龙正在那条大河里享受月光浴。'不管怎么说，'那个锅炉工心平气和地说，'凭什么我们就不能有铆钉呢？'是啊，凭什么？凭什么不让我们得到铆钉——我实在想不出任何理由。'三星期之内铆钉就会来啦，'我信心满满地说。

"可是铆钉并没有来。铆钉没来，意想不到的访客却纷至沓来，把这里袭扰得一团糟。在接下来的三个星期里，他们一批接一批陆续来到，每一批都由一个白人领头。那白人高坐在驴背上，脚蹬皮靴，衣饰光鲜，时不时向着左右那些围观惊叹的朝圣者们点头致意。一群脸色疲惫的黑人乱哄哄地跟在驴屁股后边，每个人脚上都磨起了大泡；于是大大小小的帐篷、野营凳、铁皮盒子、白色衣箱和黄布包裹转眼间堆满了一院子。这突如其来的混乱场面，让这个本就神秘兮兮的贸易站更加令人捉摸不透了。这些人前后一共来了五批。他们活像是洗劫了无数服装店和食品店之后仓皇逃窜到了这里；看着他们那副可笑的样子，你简直会以为，接下来他们就要把这些掳掠来的赃物拖到野地里去平分了。当然了，这些东西并不是什么赃物，满地狼藉的状况倒也无可厚非；只是那些人的蠢样总让我忍不住联想到强盗分赃。

"这一帮狂热分子自称是黄金之国探险队，我相信他们也一定发过誓不吐露机密。但是他们说起话来就像一伙不入流的海盗——飞扬跋扈却又毫无见识、爱财如命却又胆小如鼠、心狠手辣却又贪生怕死。这帮家伙完全没有什么坚定的目标，更没有一点儿卓越的远见，而他们似乎也根本不知道，无胆无识之辈是不可能在这世上干成什么事业的。他们唯一的欲望就是攫走这片土地上所有的财富，除此之外绝没有什么高尚的道义可言——这就和夜半撬开保险柜的窃贼没什么两样。至于这一'崇高事业'的经费从何而来，我也不得而知，但是那帮人的头目正是我们经理的叔父。

"从外表看，他的样子就像个生意冷清的屠户，惺忪蒙眬的眼睛里透露着一丝阴险。他用两条短腿托着上边那个那肥硕

从外表看，他的样子就像个生意冷清的屠户，惺忪蒙眬的眼睛里透露着一丝阴险。

（郭政鑫、李丽彦　绘）

的肚囊，神态不可一世；当他手下那帮人好似一群老鼠在贸易站里四处滋扰的时候，他却谁也不搭理，只跟自己的侄子说话。你可以看到这叔侄俩整天到处溜达，两个脑袋黏在一起窃窃地说个没完。

　　"我已经完全不再为铆钉的事伤脑筋了。让我区区一个人去应付这种荒唐事儿，我可没那么大的本事。不管了，去他妈的！——让他们自己看着办吧。我现在有了大把的时间，爱想什么想什么；于是我有时不免就会想到那个库尔茨。但是我对他这个人并不多么感兴趣。真的，没什么兴趣。尽管如此，我还是很想看看，这个人带着他那些崇高的理想来到这里，究竟能不能爬到那个最高的位子上去；如果爬上去了，他又会在这里干出些什么。"

二

"一天傍晚，我正仰面躺在汽船的甲板上，忽然听到有人说话，声音越来越近——原来是那对叔侄正沿着河边散步。于是我仍又把头枕回胳膊上。就在我迷迷糊糊快要睡着了的时候，却听到一阵话语声直似近在耳畔，那声音说道：'我就像个天真的孩子一样，绝对没有害人之心；但我也受不了总让别人牵着鼻子走。我到底还算不算是经理了？他们居然命令我把他送到那儿。这真是让人难以置信。'……我意识到这两个人正站在河岸上我的汽船前头，恰好就在我的脑袋底下。我没有动，也压根儿就不想动——我睡意正浓呢。'确实令人不快，'叔父压着喉咙咕哝着。'是他自己要求上头派他去那儿的，'经理接着说，'他无非就是想显摆自己的能耐；而我也就因此接到了上头的命令。你瞧瞧，这个人还真是神通广大。这不是太可怕了吗？'他们两个都深有同感，认为此人的出现实在可怕，然后又叽叽咕咕地讲了一堆让人摸不着头脑的话：'借势成事——就一个人——董事会——掌握局面'——这些莫名其妙的词句不断地飘过来，渐渐驱走我的睡意，所以当那位叔父再次开口的时候，我已经几乎完全清醒了。他说：'这里的气候会帮你解决掉这个麻烦。他自己一个人在那边吗？''是的，'经理回答说，'他打发助手顺流而下送了个字条给我，上面竟写着这样的话："让这个笨蛋家伙赶紧离开这里吧，也不必麻烦你再送这种人过来了。我宁可一个人做事，也不想和你派过来的人待在一起。"这是一年多以前的事了。你能想象竟会有这么狂妄自大的人吗！''之后情况如何？'那叔父瓮声瓮气地问道。'象牙，'侄子咬牙切齿地说，'大批的象牙——都是头等货——源源不断地从他那里运过来。真让人烦透了。''除了象牙还有什么？'粗重低沉的声音又问。'发货单，'那回答来得又快又狠，就好像从经理口中飙出的一梭子弹。然后是一阵沉默。他们说的是库尔茨。

"这时我已经完全清醒了，但是我仍然保持着那个放松的姿势，躺在那里一动不动——我也完全没必要动弹。'那么大老远那些象牙是怎么运过来的？'老的那个闷声咆哮，显然已经怒火中烧；小的那个就解释说，象牙是由一队独木船送过来的，负责押运的是库尔茨手下一个印欧混血的英国籍职员。当时库尔茨的贸易站里，货物已经全部运出，而补给也已经消耗殆尽，所以他原本是打算亲自运送象牙前来的；不曾想，在走了三百英里的路程之后，他却突然改变了主意——他上了一条很小的独木船，让四个船夫划着，掉头返航了。于是只剩下那个混血职员继续顺流而下，送来了象牙。这迥异常人的行径让那叔侄俩也大为惊诧，他们百思不得其解，为什么库尔茨要这样做？至于我，却仿佛第一次真正见到了库尔茨。虽然只是匆匆一瞥，他的形象却在我脑海中异常鲜明地浮现出来：一个白人乘在独木船上，四个野蛮人奋力划着桨；那孤独的白人就这样沿着逆流渐行渐远，把公司总站、衣食补给、或许还有对家乡故土的眷恋——全部都抛到了身后；他把目光投向了那荒野的深处，向着他那个一无所有的荒凉的贸易站决然而去，直到他的身影从河上消逝。我也无从知晓，为什么库尔茨要这样做。也许，他只不过是个工作狂，一心一意地扑在他的事业上？我不知道。库尔茨的名字，在那叔侄俩的对话中一次也没有出现过；在他们口中，他只是'那个人'。而那个在我的想象中，一定是抱着巨大的勇气完成了这次艰难旅程的恪尽职守的混血职员，则每每被那叔侄俩蔑称为'那个混蛋'。'那个混蛋'曾报告说'那个人'害过一次重病——到现在还没有完全康复……在我下边说话的两个人向远处走开了几步，然后便在离船不远的地方来回踱着。我的耳边不时飘过来一些零碎的字句：'军队的驻地——医生——两百英里——现在只剩他一个了——不可避免的耽搁——九个月——还没有消息——一些奇怪的风言风语'。后来他们又向我这边走过来，经理口中正说着：'据我所知，没人能从那些土著人手里搞来象牙，除了散货贩子里头那个瘟神似的家伙。'他们现在谈论的又是谁呢？从他们的只言片语中，我猜想这个人大概是在库尔茨的辖区里做贸易的，而且他的活动并没有经过这位经理的许可。'除非绞死这个家伙以儆效尤，否则我们永远都摆脱不了这种不公平的竞争，'他说。'说得没错，'那叔父低沉地回应道，'绞死他！这有什么不行的？在这个地方什么事情——我说的是任何事情——都可以干。不管他是什么人，只要到了这个地方——你懂我的意思——他都不能威胁你的地位。我为什么这么说？因为你受得了这里的气候——你总是比他们活得长。真正的威胁来自欧洲；所以在离开欧洲之前我已经在想办法把——'他们两个走开了几步，压低声音耳语片刻，然后才又放开了嗓门。'这一连串出乎意料的耽搁不是我的错。我已经尽力了。'那个胖家伙一声长叹，'我心里也十分难过。''还有他那些蛊惑人心的胡说八道，'另一个接着说，'他在这儿的时候差点把我给烦死了。他说，"每个贸易站都应该像道路上的一盏明灯，指引着我们迈向更美好的前景；我们的站点不应该仅仅是个贸易中心，更要担起人道主义、改善生活和施行教化的责任来。"你听听——那头蠢驴！而且他竟然还想当经理！想得倒美，那可是——'那语声突然哽在了喉咙里，他已经出离愤怒了。这时我下意识地抬了抬头，竟然一下子看见了他们——他们离我那么近，现在正在我身子下边。我只要张口一啐，就可以把唾沫星子吐到他们的帽子上。他们两个低着头，眼睛垂向脚下的地面，好似已经陷入了沉思一般。经理只管拈着一根细树枝在自己腿上一个劲儿地掸来掸去，那位老于谋算的叔父则若无其事地抬起头来：'你这趟出来一直都还好吧？''谁？我？'经理冷不丁一惊，这才如梦初醒。'哦！简直就是神灵保佑——神灵保佑。但是别的那些人——哦，我的天哪！全都生病了。他们还都死得特别快，我简直都来不及把他们送出这个地方——真是让人难以置信！''嗯哼。正是这样，'那叔父嘎声道，'啊，年轻人，相信这一切吧——记着，你得相信这一切。'我看见他伸出龟鳍般粗短的胳臂张开来，那姿势，仿佛要把眼前的森林、溪流、江河和大地统统揽为己有——他似乎要在这映着夕阳余晖的大地面前，用这样一种包藏祸心的可怕姿态，向那潜伏着的死神、蠢蠢欲动的魔鬼和那深不见底的黑暗之心，发出邪恶的召唤。这情形实在是太过于骇异，我禁不住一跃而起，转头望向身后的森林，好像这恶念的昭示真的会引出什么不祥之物来。你知道，有时候人是会一下子变得这么神经质的。然而什么也没有发生。在那两人面前，高耸的丛林静默无声；它只是抱着一种阴沉沉的耐心，等待着这荒诞的侵袭以某种方式慢慢走向终结。

他们离我那么近，现在正在我身子下边。我只要张口一啐，就可以把唾沫星子吐到他们的帽子上。

（王润玲、郑易淇　绘）

"这两人突然同时爆出一阵粗口——我觉得，这纯粹是为了掩饰他们自己内心深处的恐惧。然后这两人装作根本没看见我，转身向贸易站走去了。在斜斜的夕阳下，他们倾着身子，肩并肩地一起往前走着，好似要把那滑稽的一长一短两条影子吃力地拖上山去；而那拖在他们背后的两条黑影，在高高的草丛上慢慢滑过，却不曾压弯哪怕一片草叶。

"几天后，黄金之国探险队终于踏进了那片一直在耐心等待着他们的荒野。就好像潜水员没入平静的海面那样，他们的身影消失在了无边的原野里。很久以后才传来消息——所有的驴子都死掉了。至于那些并不比驴子更高贵的两足动物，我也不知道他们究竟下场如何。不过毋庸置疑，他们一定会像我们所有人一样，得到自己最终应有的归宿。我没工夫去打听。一想到可能很快就见得到库尔茨了，我的心情竟有些激动起来。当然了，我所谓的'很快'只是相对而言。从我们离开那条溪流整整两个月后，我们才到了库尔茨贸易站下边的河岸。

"沿着那条河溯流而上，仿佛时光倒转，让我们回到了鸿蒙初开的原始世界；那时候大地上草木丛生，参天的巨树就是俯瞰众生的君王。河面上空荡荡的，除了我们再也杳无人迹；两岸的丛林翳翳郁郁，简直密不透风，一切都笼罩在沉沉的寂静之中。温暖的空气黏糊糊、懒洋洋的，似乎随时就要凝滞不动了。在白晃晃的骄阳底下，任何活动都毫无乐趣可言。漫长的河道蜿蜒向前，沿途荒无人烟；河水静静地流向远方，直到消逝在一片丛林荫蔽的黑暗之中。银光粼粼的沙岸上，河马和鳄鱼一起慵懒地晒着太阳。继续行去，河道越发开阔，林木葳蕤的岛屿星罗棋布；在这宽广的水面上，你就像沙漠中的旅人一样，完全辨不清方向。你急于找到那条能带你逃出生天的主航道，但是一整天下来，你却发现自己只是被困在沙洲和浅滩之间左冲右撞。这里简直有如一场梦魇，一个魔咒，把你和曾经熟悉的一切事物永远地隔绝开来——那过去的世界遥不可及，仿佛已经隐入了另一个渺远的时空。有时候你明明忙得无暇分神，忽然间，往事却回到了你的心头；但是那过去的记忆纷乱喧嚣，有如梦中破碎的片段，在你正全神贯注地应对这奇幻般的现实世界——万籁俱寂，满目尽是苍莽的丛林和汪洋的河水——的时候，不期而至地浮现在你的眼前。而生命中的这种平静，绝不是真正意义上的平静。在这宁静的背后，往往有一种不可抗拒的强大力量正在酝酿着某种阴深难测的企图。它用一种风雨欲来的神情默默注视着你，在暗处伺机而动。后来我渐渐习惯了，就对它视而不见了——我也没那个闲工夫总是提心吊胆。我必须一直振作精神，判断哪里才是真正的深水航道；我得根据经验——当然更多的时候是靠直觉——来辨别哪里是林莽掩蔽下的河岸；我得警惕那些潜藏在水底的暗礁；为了不让剧烈跳动的心脏从嗓子眼儿里飞出去，我还得学会及时咬紧牙关——我的汽船好几次死里逃生，堪堪避开一截不知打哪儿冒出水面的可恶的老树桩；如果躲避不及的话，不光这铁皮盒子一样的廉价汽船会被开膛破肚，就连船上那些朝圣者们都得统统被送进河里喂鱼。除此之外，我还得留意看着哪儿有合适的枯树，好在晚上砍回来供第二天烧锅炉用。当你不得不疲于奔命地应付各种杂事儿的时候，你的注意力就会被眼前这些鸡毛蒜皮牵绊住，而现实——我说的是真正的现实——反倒是无暇顾及了。幸而那内在的真实永远还在那里，还是那样。真是谢天谢地！但我总是能够感受到它的存在；在我手忙脚乱地搞那套猴把戏的时候，我总是能感到它用那种神秘而平静的目光注视着我，就好像它也在注视着你们一样。你们这些家伙不也都在各自的钢丝绳上卖力表演吗，只为了——那是怎么说的来着？——两分半钱就给翻一个跟斗……"

"说话尽量客气点，马洛。"一个粗嗓门抱怨起来。于是我知道了，除我之外，至少还有一个醒着的人在倾听这个故事。

"不好意思。哦对了，还得再加上一阵肉痛才能凑够你应得的价钱。不过话说回来，只要你那套猴把戏耍得好，钱多钱少又有什么大不了的？你们的把戏都耍得挺好，而我耍得也不赖——第一次出航我就保住了那条汽船，总算没让它沉下去。现在一想起这事儿，我还觉得简直是个奇迹。想想看——蒙上你的眼睛，让你在坑坑洼洼的道路上开货车——你觉得怎么样？说实话，那一趟航行，我一路上都冷汗淋漓，紧张得浑身打颤。毕竟对一个船员来说，那玩意儿那就该一直漂在水面上才像话；要是在你的一番操作下把船底给划穿了，那你简直就是犯下了不可饶恕的罪行。别人听不见那一记心跳，但是你自己知道——是吧？嘭的一声就好像直捣在你心脏中间的一记重拳——那滋味足以让你终生难忘。它会成为你永远甩脱不掉的记忆，即使多少年过去，它也会突然出现在你的梦里，然后你会在黑夜里猛然惊醒，翻来覆去地回想着它，浑身一会儿火辣辣地发烧，一会儿又冰凉凉地淌汗。我也不打算和你们吹牛皮，说我的船一直都在水面上漂得好好的。它曾经不止一次搁浅在岸边，然后二十个食人生番围着它铆足了劲儿推；他们艰难地跋涉着，在它的四周溅起一阵阵水花。还好我们在路上招了这么一批生番上船。他们都是好样的——那些生番——每一个都能坚守岗位，任劳任怨。我不仅乐意和他们共事，甚至还对他们心怀感激。再说了，根据我的观察，这些食人生番并没有吃掉他们的同伴；他们带着好些河马肉当作干粮。没多久那些肉就开始腐烂发臭了，结果，荒蛮之地的神秘气息全都变成了阵阵扑鼻的恶臭。呸呸！我现在还闻得到那股臭味儿。和我一起航行的除了经理，还有三四个手提棍子的朝圣者——他们在我的船上安然无恙，连一根头发都没掉。有时候我们会路过一个倚河而建的贸易站，于是你会望见一群白人从那些看上去一吹就倒的茅草屋里争先恐后地朝我们跑过来；这些'沦落天涯'的白人惊喜交加地向我们大打手势，表示欢迎——那情景却让我感到说不出的怪异，我觉得那群人就好像一伙囚徒，被什么符咒给封印在那里了。接着，'象牙'这个词儿又会在空气中回荡一阵子——直到我们的汽船继续启程。我们又回到了那无边的阒寂之中，驶过渺无人烟的水道，绕过风平浪静的河湾，沿着蜿蜒迂回的河流，穿过夹岸耸峙的群山——沿途只有船尾螺旋桨那沉重的击水声在空谷里回响。一片又一片的树木向远方绵延，无边无际，遮天蔽日；在它们脚下，我们那条满身尘垢的小汽船紧贴着河岸缓慢地逆流而上，就好像一只在巍峨的廊柱下沿着台阶缓缓爬行的小甲虫。这幅图景让你觉得自己非常渺小，简直怅然若失；但是这种感觉也并不会让你完全灰心丧气，因为即使再怎么渺小，那只脏兮兮的小甲虫仍然在努力地向前爬着——它所做的也正符合你对它的期待。我不知道那些朝圣者期待着它去往何方，不过我敢打赌，他们一定希望它爬到那个能让他们大捞一笔的地方去。但是对我来说，它正在爬向库尔茨——这才是它唯一真正的目的地。而当船上的蒸汽管开始漏气的时候，我们也就爬得越发缓慢了。那条大河好似一幅无穷无尽的画卷，迎着我们向前眺望的目光徐徐展开，又在我们身后遥远的地方缓缓合拢；那情景，仿佛两岸的森林正悠然横越过水面，最后合抱在一起，挡住了我们的归途。我们就这样渐渐深入，不断地接近那黑暗的中心。那里非常宁静。夜里，有时候在丛林的深幕后面会响起一阵阵鼓声，咚隆隆地一直传到上游很远的地方；那隐约的鼓声经久不息，在我们头顶上空盘旋回荡，直到东方天际露出第一缕曙光。那彻夜的鼓声究竟意味着什么，是战争，还是和平？抑或是某种祈祷？我们谁也说不清。黎明之前总是凄冷而又静寂；伐木工仍在酣睡，他们的篝火却已近熄灭；这时，即使是树枝折断的噼啪声也会让你猛地一惊。我们都成了在史前地球上漫游的行者，而这片洪荒之地，看上去全然是另一个陌生的星球。我们尽可以狂想一番——这份丰饶的遗产与灾祸和诅咒相伴而来，而我们就是接受这遗产的第一批人类；只有付出极深的苦痛和极大的辛劳，我们才能够消弭其中的诅咒，真正拥抱这丰厚的遗产。但是事实上，我们并不是'第一批人'——刚刚艰难地转过一个河湾，我们眼前突然出现了一大片芦苇墙和尖尖的茅草屋顶；在静静低垂着的浓荫下，数不清的黝黑人影在那里手舞足蹈——他们的身体在摇动，在旋转；一双双手在鼓掌，一只只脚在踩地；伴随着肢体的扭动，他们口中发出呼啸和呐喊，黑白分明的眼睛顾盼流连。岸边的黑色人潮在汹涌，而我们的汽船就沿着这不可思议的狂乱景象缓缓前行。这些史前人类究竟是在诅咒我们，还是在向我们祈祷？或者说，他们是在欢迎我们？——谁也不知道。我们完全无法理解发生在周围的这一切，于是我们好像幽灵一般悄无声息地滑了过去；正如神志清醒的人面对疯人院里的一场狂欢鼓噪那样，我们心中既充满了惊讶，也在暗暗害怕。我们无法理解，是因为我们已经和他们天差地别；我们只是不经意间闯入了人类最初那黑暗蒙昧

这些史前人类究竟是在诅咒我们，还是在向我们祈祷？或者说，他们是在欢迎我们？——谁也不知道。

（张舒婷 绘）

的年代——那年代已经太过久远，早已被我们遗忘；对我们而言，它几乎没有留下任何痕迹——也没有留下任何记忆。

"这片大地怪诞离奇，简直不似人间。我们都看惯了那些在镣铐的束缚下完全驯服的野蛮人，但是在这儿，你眼前的一切都在无拘无束地尽情张扬着野性。你会觉得，既然这里不似人间，那么这些人是不是也——不，你错了。他们可并非没有人性。是啊，你看，最糟糕的事儿发生了——你开始怀疑，莫非他们其实也是有人性的？呵，慢慢地你就会陷入这种怀疑了。他们又叫又吼，又蹦又跳；挥舞着手臂，旋转着身体，做出各种可怕的鬼脸；但是真正令你热血沸腾的是这种想法——想到他们也和你我一样具有人性；想到我们的远祖也曾经这样狂野而又热情地吼叫。这情景丑陋吗？没错，实在是够丑的；但是如果你是个真正有勇气的人，你就会自己承认，那无所顾忌的野蛮喧嚣，竟然也在你的心中引起了一丝共鸣；你会隐约感到，尽管离创世之初的黑暗时代已经非常遥远，你却似乎听懂了那野性的声音里包含着的某种意义。是啊，怎么会听不懂呢？人类的思想分明是能够驾驭一切的——古今未来、宇宙万物，全部都包容在人类的思想之中。但那思想里边究竟有些什么？欢乐、恐惧、忧愁、热忱、勇气、愤怒——谁能数得清呢——但却唯独没有真实——那褪去了时间的外衣的真实。让那些傻子们张口结舌、惊慌失措去吧，真正的人不但能够听懂，而且还可以坦然地站在一旁观看——只要他也能和那些河岸上的舞者一样真实而纯粹。他必须以真正的自我——内心深处那与生俱来的力量——去拥抱那份真实。在这儿，讲原则、谈主义是行不通的；再多的财富、再美的华服，也只不过是一块漂亮的遮羞布——只需要用力一扯，它们就会随风飞散。在这儿，你真正需要的是一种坚定成熟的信念。那凶悍的吼叫正是他们向我发出的邀请——难道不是吗？那很好，我不但听懂了，而且接受了；于是我也要发出自己的声音，那就是我要说出来的话语——无论我说的是对是错，反正我绝不会噤口不言。当然了，一个胆小怯懦而又情趣高雅的傻子是永远不会说错话的。谁在那儿嘟嘟囔囔？你是想问我为什么不跑到岸上去，和他们一起大叫大跳吗？是啊，我确实没去。你说什么？因为我情趣高雅？呸，去他妈的高雅。我只是没时间。大把的时间都花在那条破汽船上了——就是这么回事。我得用白铅粉和撕成长条的羊毛毯子跟别人一起把到处漏气的蒸汽管子紧紧包住；我得随时关注航向、避开水里的树桩，好歹也得让这个铁皮盒子能继续往前开。这么明显的事情，你用不着多么聪明也能看得出来。每过一会儿我就得过去看看担任锅炉工的那个野人。这个野人比他的同胞开化了不少，他已经会自己烧立式锅炉了。他工作的地方在我下边，说实话，一看到他我就会忍不住在心里感慨，就好像你看到一条狗模仿人类穿上了马裤、戴上了插着羽毛的帽子、还把两条后腿直立起来走路那样的滑稽。我们对这个相当不错的家伙进行了几个月的训练，所以他能够壮起胆子，眯着眼睛仔细去看蒸汽压力表和水位指示表——这个可怜的野人小伙子，他的牙齿被锉刀挫尖了，羊毛似的鬈发剪成了相当古怪的样式，两颊上还各有三个装饰性的疤痕。原本他也应该在河岸上和他们一起手舞足蹈的，而现在他却学了很多先进的知识，在这里不辞辛苦地劳作——就像一个被神奇的巫术驱使着的奴隶。他能帮着做事，是因为我们教给了他一些东西；而我们实际上是这样对他说的——如果那个透明玩意儿里边没水了，藏在锅炉里的魔鬼就会口渴难耐；它会勃然大怒，然后发起可怕的报复。所以他汗流浃背地干个不停，一边往炉膛里添火，一边面带惊惧地不断观察着那根玻璃管（他还用破布临时做了一个护身符系在胳膊上，又贴着下嘴唇横穿了一根磨得光溜溜的骨头，大小和一块手表差不多）。就这样，那片林木掩映的河岸从我们身边缓缓地滑过去，那一阵短暂的喧嚣也被我们渐渐抛到了身后。接下来又是绵延无尽的寂静——我们不停地爬啊，爬啊，一直爬向库尔茨所在的地方。但是河里的树桩越来越多，河水也越来越浅，一路上险象环生，危机四伏；而那锅炉里边也似乎真的藏着一个脸色越来越阴沉的魔鬼，于是我和那个野人锅炉工都忙得顾不上胆战心惊、也没时间去胡思乱想了。

"在距离上游的内陆贸易站大约五十英里的地方，我们偶然发现了一间芦苇棚屋。屋子门口孤零零地斜插着一根旗杆，上面挂着几缕随风飘荡的碎布条——也许这曾经是一面什么旗帜，但如今已经破旧难辨了。旁边还整整齐齐地摞着一堆木柴。这可真是出乎意料，于是我们就上了岸。在那堆木柴上头，我们发现了一块薄薄的木板，上边有几行已经模糊了的铅笔字迹；仔细辨认了一番，原来那木板上写的是：'柴火留给你们，快点来。靠近时须警惕。'下面还有个签名，已经完全无法辨识了。但那绝对不是库尔茨——这个签名可比'库尔茨'要长得多。'快点来。'来什么地方？来上游那里吗？'靠近时须警惕。'我们来的时候可没怎么警惕呀！那么这个警告应该不是指这里，因为我们完全是在到了这里之后才得到它的。一定是上游出了什么事情。但会是什么事呢——有多严重？这可把我们问住了。于是我们对着这个密电码似的愚蠢留言发了一通牢骚。茂密的丛林缄默不语，而且它还遮住了我们的视线，让我们无法看得更远。棚屋门口挂着一条红色的斜纹布帘子，风一吹，这条破敝的布帘子就迎着我们翻飞起来，那哗哗的声响就像是在哀伤地倾诉着什么。屋子里已是破败不堪，但我们还能看得出来，不久前这里曾经住过一个白人。里面留着一张简陋的桌子——也就是用两根桩子支着的一块木板；在不起眼的角落里还堆着一堆破烂儿。我在门边捡起了一本书。书的封面已经没有了，书页也被翻得脏兮兮、松蓬蓬的；但是书脊却用白棉线很珍重地重新装订过，而且那白棉线看上去还十分干净。这可真是个非同寻常的发现！书名是《航海术提挈》，作者叫作陶森还是陶松——反正差不多就是这么个名字吧。他是皇家海军的一位船长。这本书读起来相当枯燥，附有好些原理图解和令人生畏的数字表格，而且还是六十

仔细辨认了一番，原来那木板上写的是："柴火留给你们，快点来。靠近时须警惕。"

（郑易淇　绘）

年前出版的。我极尽小心地拈起了这件令人惊叹的老古董，好像一不留神它就会在我手中散佚了似的。在这本书里，那个陶森或者陶松十分认真地探讨了船上的锚链和吊索的极限拉力，还有其他一些类似的问题。这实在不是一本特别引人入胜的书；但是只要略略一翻，你就会发现作者意图明朗，态度恳切，他在非常用心地教给你一些正确的操作方法。这样一想，即使在非专业的读者眼里，这些穿越了几十年时光的平凡书页也能焕发出绚丽的光彩。这位朴实的老水手和他那些关于锚链和绞盘的理论，令我一时间忘记了外面的丛林和那些朝圣者，全然沉浸在一种无以言喻的美妙感觉之中——我居然在这个地方邂逅了无可辩驳的可贵的真实。这里会有这样一本书，本身已经够让人感到惊奇的了；谁知道更神奇的事还在后面——书页边沿的空白处用铅笔写着许多读书笔记。我简直不能相信自己的眼睛！那笔记竟然全是密码！没错，看上去很像是密码。谁能想到竟会有这么一个人，把这样的一本专业书带到这个在地图上都找不到的地方来，不但仔细地研读，还记下了笔记——用的还是密码！这事儿实在有点太玄乎了。

　　"我好像隐隐约约听到一阵让人心烦的嘈杂声。后来我终于抬起头来，发现那堆木柴已经不见了，而经理正站在河边朝我大声叫喊；那些朝圣者也在跟着他一起喊。我只好把那本书塞进衣服口袋里。实话跟你说，要我把它放下，简直就好像把我从知心老友的家里强拉出去一样。

　　"我发动了那台蹩脚的破引擎，汽船又向前驶去。'这肯定就是那个晦气的散货贩子了——那个敢在我地盘上搞事的家伙。'经理大声说着，同时回过头去，恶狠狠地看着我们刚刚离开的那个地方。'他一定是个英国人，'我说。'如果不识相的话，就算他是个英国人也免不了得碰上点儿麻烦，'经理阴沉沉地低声说。于是我故作天真地回敬道，在这个世上谁都免不了得碰上点儿麻烦。

"前面的水流越发湍急，汽船在水中好像已经奄奄一息了，只有船尾的螺旋桨还在有气没力地拍打着。我不得不踮起脚来，屏息凝神地倾听船桨下一次的拍打声，因为说真的，我感觉这条可怜的破船随时有可能要完蛋——就好像你看着快要咽气的人在回光返照一样。但是那船仍在慢慢地往前爬。有时候，我会盯住前边不远处的一棵树作为标记，盘算着我们又向着库尔茨前进了多少距离；可是每次还没等到跟前，我就已经找不着它了。眼睛那么长时间地总是盯着同一个东西瞧，即使是最有耐心的人也受不了。此时这位经理却表现得泰然自若，完全一副听之任之的姿态。我心急如焚，每多待一刻都是莫大的折磨；我在心里暗暗思忖，到底要不要去和库尔茨坦白地谈一谈呢？但是无论决定谈或不谈，其实我自己早就知道，和盘托出——保持沉默——抑或是采取别的任何行动，都只不过是在白费力气罢了。一个人知道什么或者不知道什么又有什么打紧呢？谁当经理又与我何干呢？有时候人就是这样，一闪念间就顿然醒悟了。这件事的本质深深地隐藏在它的表象之下，我既无从了解，也将无力干涉。

"第二天太阳快要落山的时候，我们估计大约还有八英里就能到达库尔茨的贸易站了。我想要一鼓作气，马上赶完这段路；但是经理却一脸严肃地对我说，越往上游越是危险，而现在天色已晚，因此最明智的做法就是原地停泊，等到明天早晨再出发。他还提醒我说，如果还记得那句警告：'靠近时须警惕'，那么我们就应该在天光大亮之时前往那个贸易站——而不是在夜色里披星戴月地赶去。这理由还真是冠冕堂皇。八英里的路程意味着我们的汽船还要继续航行三个小时；而我也确实看到了，在那段河道的上游有一些令人生疑的水纹。尽管如此，我还是对这又一夜的耽搁感到说不出的恼火，虽然我也知道自己并不占理——好几个月的时间都过去了，何必非得计较这区区一个晚上呢？既然我们的船上木柴充足，又被告知要谨慎，于是我就把船开到河中心停了下来。那里的河道既窄且直，河岸又高，很像是铁路的路堑。夕阳尚未沉下，幽暗的暮霭便已降临河上；河水平稳而急速地流动着，两岸的丛林却仿佛凝固了似的，一丝动静也没有。那些缠挂着藤蔓的葱郁的大树，那些生气蓬勃的茂盛的灌木，甚至连那最细小的柔枝、最娇嫩的叶芽，好像全都已经化成了石头。这情景，与其说万物都沉在宁静的睡梦中，倒不如说更像是所有的魂灵都出了窍，地面上只剩下了一大堆呆呆的空壳。四下里哪怕连最细微的一丝声音都没有。你茫然地环顾四周，不由得怀疑自己是不是变成了聋子——接着黑夜突然降临，你顿时又变成了瞎子。凌晨三点钟左右，有条大鱼突然跃出水面；寂静之中骤然响起的巨大溅水声简直堪比一记重炮，惊得我一下子跳了起来。太阳升起以后，河上到处弥漫着温暖潮湿的白雾，让我们如堕暮夜之中，完全看不清周围的一切。那一大片白雾稠稠地把你包裹起来；它既不飘荡，也不流动，简直就像某种凝固起来的有形物质一样。到了大概八九点钟，好像一只看不见的手刷地拉开了百叶窗，这片白雾转瞬间消散得干干净净。连绵不绝的参天大树、无边无际的茂密丛莽，又重新回到了我们的视野；我们还看到太阳好似一个发光的小球，高悬在丛林的上空——一切都安详地沉浸在静谧之中——然后不经意间，我们发现那白色的百叶窗又悄然降下，就像沿着涂满润滑油的导槽一滑而落那样的自然随性。我连忙下令把正在往回收的锚链再放出去。锚链在水下发出低沉的轧轧声，可还没等我们放完，蓦然间一声凄厉的号叫划破长空——这声音仿佛从那无尽的荒凉深处拖着长长的尾音奔袭而来，在我们身边白雾漫天的空气里盘旋激荡。号叫声停止了。继而是一阵戾气冲天的狂嚣，夹杂着野人混乱癫狂的鼓噪，几乎要把我们的耳膜震破。这一切都让人猝不及防，我只感觉自己的头发根根直竖，简直都要把帽子给顶起来了。我不知道别人作何反应，但是在我听来，那狂肆而又凄怆的嚎叫声来得那么突然，而且似乎是从四面八方同时发作，我真以为是我们周围的白雾骤然一齐尖叫起来了。蓦地又从什么地方爆发出一阵令人完全无法忍受的刺耳的尖啸，把这场噩梦般的狂飙推上了最高潮——然后一切戛然而止。我们全都肝胆俱裂，一个个维持着原先的姿势僵在那儿，好像一群呆头鹅似的。不知过了多久，我们还竖着耳朵，向着那同样恐怖、同样令人无法忍受的寂静使劲儿倾听。'我的上帝！这是什么意思呀——'一个朝圣者在我身旁结结巴巴地说。这家伙又矮又胖，长着赭色的头发和红色的连鬓胡子，穿着系松紧带的靴子，粉色睡衣的裤管塞在袜子里头。另外两个，大张着嘴巴呆立了足足一分钟，随后一个激灵窜进一间小仓房里去，接着又以同样鬼使神差的步伐冲了出来，站在那儿瞪着眼睛，恐惧地四处张望，手里端着'随时可以开火'的温彻斯特步枪。现在我们视野之中就只有自己所在的这条汽船，而它的轮廓也影影绰绰，好像下一秒钟就要融进雾里了；我们还能勉强看到汽船周围大约两英尺宽的一带河水，同样灰惨惨雾蒙蒙的——此外便什么也看不见了。在这一片白色的迷障里，我们尽管睁圆了双眼，竖直了耳朵，外面的世界却仍然声影全无；整个宇宙似乎都已经荡然无存，没有留下半点儿声息，也没有留下半点儿印痕。

"我往船头跑去，喝令立刻收紧锚链，做好准备，一有情况马上起锚开船。'他们会进攻吗？'一个声音战战兢兢地小声问。'我们都会在这场大雾里被宰掉的，'另一个声音喃喃着说。这几个人紧张得脸孔抽搐，两手簌簌地抖个不停，连眼睛都忘了眨了。面对这个意外，船上那些白人和黑人的表现大相径庭；如果你给他们来做个对比的话，那可真是意味深长。船上的黑人和我们一样从未涉足过这片流域——他们的家乡离这儿也就是八百英里吧。白人们不仅是心慌意乱；他们被这一阵凶恶的吼叫声吓破了胆，全都变成了一副失魂落魄的鬼样子。而那些黑人，他们只是微露警觉，脸上很自然地浮现出一种颇感兴趣的表情；他们始终面不改色，其中有一两个在往回拉扯锚链的时候甚至还在咧着嘴笑。他们简短地低声交谈了几句，对这件事似乎已经找到了满意的解释。他们的头领此时正站在我的身边，他是个膀大腰圆的年轻黑人，身披一件深蓝色带流苏的长衣，举止端严；他的鼻孔硕大无比，束起的头发巧妙地结成一个个油光发亮的小圆环。'啊哈！'为了表示友好，我主动向他打了个招呼。'抓住他们，'他厉声说道，眼里嗜血的红光越来越盛，锋利的尖齿闪闪发亮——'抓住他们，然后交给我们。''交给你们，干吗？'我问道，'你想把他们怎么样？''吃掉！'他简短地回答，然后探身用手肘撑在栏杆上。他向远方眺望着，凛冽的目光仿佛能够刺透浓雾；在他的脸上，则是一种深沉的、若有所思的神情。要不是我当时忽然想到他和他的同伴们都已经饿极了的话，那会儿我绝对会

被吓个半死；因为至少在最近的这一个月，他们肯定是越来越
饥饿难忍了。他们的雇用期是六个月（我想他们当中大概谁
也没有清楚的时间概念，而我们在过去无数的年代里也是一
样；可以说，他们仍然徘徊在创世之初——在这方面，他们并
没有从先辈那里传承下来的经验）。当然了，既然当初在河道
下游根据某条可笑的法律和他们订立了文书，那他们就得干满
六个月；至于在这六个月里他们靠吃什么活着，压根儿就没
人想过。没错，他们刚来的时候身上都带着些臭烘烘的河马
肉；但是那些食物也撑不了多久，更何况在一场惊心动魄的冲
突中，朝圣者们把几乎一大半的河马肉都给扔到河里去了。看
上去倒很像是专横跋扈的欺压；可这实际上只是一场正当防
卫。想想看，如果你无论是醒着还是睡着，甚至连吃饭的时候
都被那臭不可当的气味紧紧包围，那你的小命简直是岌岌可
危——因为你随时有可能被那股味儿熏死。另外，他们每星期
发给黑人三根铜丝当作报酬，每根铜丝大约九英寸那么长；按
照白人的想法，那些黑人可以拿着铜丝当钱使，到河岸边的村
子里去买东西吃。你就看吧，这个办法行得通才怪。一路上要
么没有村子，要么被村民视为敌寇，要么那位经理根本就不让
靠岸——至于他的理由嘛，多少总有点儿让人费解。说到经理
自己，他也和我们一样天天吃罐头；但是他的餐桌上时不时还
会摆上一头老公羊。所以，除非黑人们能把铜丝直接吞下肚去
当饭吃，或者把铜丝弯成圈套去捉鱼，否则我实在看不出，这
份慷慨的薪水对他们到底能有什么用。不过我得承认，每次的
工资都付得十分及时，这倒还有点儿言出必行的大贸易公司派
头。那么黑人们到底还能拿什么东西填肚子呢？我看见他们手
中仅有的食物——那样子简直没法吃——是几块脏兮兮的深紫

色的东西，有点像烤得半生不熟的面团。他们把这东西裹在树叶里，饿得受不了就拿出来啃一块；但是他们每次只会啃一小口，那副浅尝辄止的样子，与其说当真是在为了生存而吃饭，倒不如说仅仅是做了个吃饭的架势而已。那焚心噬骨的饥饿，为什么没有把他们变成扑向我们的恶鬼？——论人数双方是三十比五——他们满可以痛痛快快地饱餐一顿。我至今一想起来，还觉得很是不可思议。他们都是高大魁梧的男人，个个孔武有力，做起事来往往也是干脆利索，不计后果；尽管他们原本富有光泽的皮肤黯淡了许多，肌肉也不比先前的硬实，但是他们仍然拥有不可小觑的胆气和力量。所以我想一定是什么原因在抑制着他们；一定是人性中的某种秘密在发挥作用，阻止了这可怕的想象变为现实。我承认，那时候我确实相信过不了多久，自己就会变成他们的盘中餐；但是我对他们越来越感兴趣，倒也不完全是因为这个——这么说吧，我正在以一种全新的眼光审视这件事——你瞧，那些朝圣者看上去都病恹恹的，一点儿也不好吃；而我希望（说实话，那时候我真是这样想的）我自己的样子不会是那么的——怎么说呢？——那么的——让人一看就倒胃口。这种虚荣心当然是够荒唐的，但是那段时间我整天都好似梦游一般恍恍惚惚，所以脑子里冒出什么古怪的想法都不足为奇。那会儿我好像还有点发烧；但是谁知道呢，就算是你自己的身体，你也不可能总是对它了如指掌。我经常'发点儿低烧'，或者时不时染点儿别的小恙——这片荒野顽皮地伸出爪子挠你一下，在它迟早凶相毕露地扑向你之前，它要先戏弄你一番，消磨消磨时间。没错，我看着那些黑人，就好像你们看着一个受刑者那样；我好奇地观察着，当他们在肉体上经受着来自生理需求的残酷考验时，他们

会想怎么解决，会有什么冲动；哪些事情他们干得出来，哪些
事情他们干不出来。忍耐！这是何等的忍耐呵！这到底是出于
迷信、厌恶、耐心或者恐惧——还是出于某种原始的道义？但
是，任何恐惧也经不住饥饿的冲击；多么强大的耐心也无法抵
消饥饿的痛苦；在饥饿面前，根本就不存在对于食物的厌恶；
至于什么迷信和信仰，还有什么所谓的原则，则更是轻如鸿
毛，一文不值。你们知不知道，那长时间饥饿的可怕折磨、它
所带来的使人发疯的痛苦、它所勾引起的阴森的思想，和那每
分每秒都仿佛置身炼狱一般的煎熬，到底是一种什么滋味？我
可是知道的。和饥饿斗争，你得握紧双拳，咬碎牙根，迸出身
体里的全部力量才行。而那些人间惨事——痛失至亲、遭人羞
辱、抑或是肉身与灵魂的毁灭——比起这种日复一日的饥饿
来，都根本算不上什么了。听起来是不是挺可悲的？但事实的
确如此。而那些黑人，根本无须顾忌任何世俗的理由。忍耐！
我倒还不如指望一条在战场的尸堆里潜行觅食的鬣狗忍得住不
去大快朵颐呢。然而事实就摆在我眼前——这个事实令我百思
不得其解，它就像从大海深处浮起的泡沫，就像深不见底的幽
潭表面的一丝涟漪；每当我想起它的时候，我总觉得它比任何
谜题都要神秘的多，甚至远胜于从那隔着重重白雾的河岸边传
来，在我们身边回荡着的野蛮狂嚣中所隐藏着的那种无以言喻
的、奇异而又充满绝望的悲凉之声。

"两个朝圣者正急促地低声争论着该往哪边靠岸。'左边。'
'不，不，那怎么行？右边，当然是右边。''看来事情很严
重，'从我身后传来了经理的声音，'要是库尔茨先生在我们到
达之前有个什么闪失，那留下我孤零零的，岂不是要伤心死
了。'我看了他一眼。我觉得他在说这话的时候，态度之恳切，

我向船头跑去，喝令立即收紧锚链，做好准备，一有情况马上起锚开船。

（陈睿杰 绘）

语气之真诚，简直无懈可击。他就是那种总是要把表面文章完全扯足的人，这也就是属于他的忍耐。但是，当他咕哝着说要赶快启航的时候，我连理都懒得理他。我明白，他也明白，这时候开船是完全不可能的。一旦真的从河底拔起锚来，我们的船马上就会失去航向，变成断了线的风筝。到那时候，谁也不敢保证船会开到什么地方去——也许是往上游开，也许是往下游开，也许是一直往岸边横着开——这也得等到我们撞到这一边或者那一边的河岸上才知道——然后我们一时半会儿也搞不清撞上去的河岸到底是哪一边。所以我当然不会开船。我可不想把船给撞毁。你根本想不出一个比这里更要命、更容易发生船难的地方。无论是不是马上被淹死，反正我们肯定会以这样或者那样的方式命丧当场。'我准许你冒一切风险继续前进，'他沉默了一阵，然后这样说。'我拒绝冒任何风险，'我直截了当地回答。我的拒绝正在他意料之中，但是我的口气可能让他颇感意外。'那好吧，我必须遵从你的意见，因为你是船长，'他用一种特别客气的语调说。我向他稍微侧了一下身子以示感谢，然后望向那片茫茫的白雾。这雾还要持续多久呢？唉，简直没有比这更徒劳无功的瞭望了。想要找到正在荒凉的乱树丛中掠取象牙的库尔茨，真是谈何容易。他就好像一个被施了魔法、沉睡在神话古堡中的公主，谁想要接近他，非得历尽千难万险不可。'依你看他们会进攻吗？'经理这次用一种知己般亲密的口气问道。

"我认为他们不会，这里面有几个显而易见的理由：其一，雾实在太大了。只要他们乘着独木舟离开河岸，他们肯定会在雾里迷失方向，这就和我们一拔锚就会迷航完全一样；其二，据我判断，河岸的丛林太过茂密，完全阻挡住了我们的视线——然而在那里面却有许多双眼睛，正在紧紧地盯着我们。尽管河边的丛林密不透风，但是后面低矮的灌木丛却显然稀疏得多。就在刚才浓雾暂时消散的时候，我巡视了整条河道，都没有看到任何独木舟的影子——当然更没有什么迫近我们汽船的敌人了。而真正让我确信他们无意攻击的，却是刚才从河岸边传来的那一阵喧嚣——或者说，是那种声音带给我的感觉。我听得出来，那其中并没有宣战式的腾腾杀气。尽管那不期而来的狂嚣是那么粗野，又那么悍烈，但是听着却让人不自禁地感到一股悲凉。不知为何，我们这条汽船的出现，使那些野人的心中充满了无限哀伤。我解释说，若说有什么危险的话，那只能是因为我们触及了一种突然迸发出来的深沉情感。即使是极度的忧伤，最后往往也会以最激烈的形式宣泄出来；虽然在更多的时候，我们看到的只是一种深深压抑着的沉默……

　　"哈！真该让你们瞧瞧那些朝圣者目瞪口呆的模样！我发表了一番郑重其事的演说，可是他们却不敢报以嗤笑，更不敢反唇相讥；我可以断定，他们全都以为我疯了——也许是被吓疯的。亲爱的伙计们，光发愁是没有用的；继续瞭望？没错，你就想想我正像猫儿盯着耗子似的一眼不眨地盯着浓雾，竭力想找出一丝消散的迹象。但是当时我们就像被埋在了几英里深的棉花堆里，眼睛已经完全派不上任何用场；而这浓雾也恰和棉花堆一样，让人感到一种窒息般的温暖，简直就要透不过气来。话说回来，我刚才的那番演讲，尽管听来好似有些离奇，却绝对符合事实。虽然我们后来总把这件事说成是一场攻击，但实际上，他们只不过是想试着把我们轰走。他们的行动远不是什么攻击——甚至也不是一般意义上的防御。那只是在一种走投无路的绝望之下被迫采取的行动，他们唯一的目的只是自卫。

　　"我估摸着，雾散了以后，大约过了两个小时，事情才开始有了进展。转机出现在距离库尔茨的贸易站大约还有一英里半的地方。当时我们费尽力气，终于磕磕绊绊地绕过了河湾；

于是我看到了一个河心岛。那个岛非常小，充其量是个野草丛生的圆形沙丘。开始的时候，我以为河中只有这么一个岛屿。可是在我们更深地进入那段河道以后，我却发现那小岛只是一条狭长沙洲的开端；在它后面，是沿着河中心一直往前延伸的一连串小沙洲。它们刚好没于水面之下，好似一溜颜色黯淡、若隐若现的影子，让我不禁联想到隐伏在皮肤之下、纵贯于躯干中央的脊椎骨。按理说，这时我们既可以从沙洲的右边走，也可以从沙洲的左边走。当然了，我对两边河道的情况都一无所知。两边的河岸看起来都完全一样，水深似乎也差不多；但是因为有人曾告诉我，那个贸易站坐落在河的西岸，于是我自然而然地驶入了西边的河道。

"刚一进入那条河道，我就发现它比我原先的估计要狭窄得多。我们左手边是那条绵延不断的细长沙洲，右手边则是高峻陡峭的河岸，上面长满了茂盛的灌木；灌木之上，则是高耸的密林。河道上空垂覆着厚密的枝叶；时不时会有粗大的树枝从远处直伸过来，横亘在河面上。那时早已是下午的光景，太阳渐渐西斜，沉郁的丛林默然耸立着，在水面上投下一片宽广的阴影。我们就在这阴影中缓缓地逆流而上——你简直想象不到有多慢。我朝一侧用力打舵，让汽船尽量贴近岸边行驶——因为测深杆告诉我，靠近河岸边的水最深。

"一个正默默忍耐着饥饿的黑人船员在我下边的船头处测量着水深。我们的汽船就好像一条铺了甲板的驳船，甲板上面还有两间柚木小屋，门窗俱全。锅炉在船头，机器在船尾；几根柱子支撑起一张轻便的顶棚，罩住了整个船身。一根烟囱穿过顶棚直伸到外面。烟囱的前边有一间用薄木板搭成的小船舱，那就是驾驶室了。那里面有一张躺椅、两个折叠凳、一张

小桌子和驾船的舵轮。墙角倚着一支装满子弹的马蒂尼·亨利
式来复枪。驾驶室前方有一扇宽大的门，两侧各有一扇宽敞的
百叶窗。当然了，所有的门窗都成天敞开着。白天我就坐在顶
棚的最前边；到了晚上，我就睡在那张躺椅上，而且经常也睡
不好。船上的舵手是一个身强力壮的黑人，他来自海岸边的某
个部落，是那位不幸的前任船长一手训练出来的。他的耳朵上
挂着一对夸张的铜耳环，一大块蓝色包布从腰一直裹到脚踝，
脸上总是一副自命不凡的神态。他实在是我生平仅见的那种最
不靠谱的傻瓜。当你在他身边时，他掌起舵来架势十足，看上
去简直无所不能；而当你一走开，他马上就慌了手脚，完全不
知所措了。不出一分钟，就不是他在操纵汽船，而是这条蹩脚
的破汽船在摆布他了。

　　"我低头看着测深杆，发现每测探一次水位就下降一点，
不由得忧心忡忡。而这时，我却看到船头的测水员突然停下了
手里的工作，直挺挺地躺在了甲板上，甚至连手中的测深杆
都没给我捞回船上来——他一只手攥着那杆子，任它漂曳在
水中，载浮载沉。与此同时，我也瞥见那个在我下面的锅炉
工，猛地在炉膛前边抱头坐下了。我大感惊异。但是来不及细
想，我就得迅速凝神盯紧前方的水面，因为河道上又出现了一
个大树桩。许多细小的棍子从四面八方向我们飞来，简直铺天
盖地；它们有的从我眼皮底下嗖嗖飞过，有的掉落在我脚下，
有的砰砰地撞在我身后驾驶室的墙上。而就在这期间，无论是
河上、岸边还是丛林里，到处都是一片安静——简直安静得吓
人。我只能听到螺旋桨沉重的拍水声和那些细棍子撞到东西的
噼啪声。我们使出浑身解数勉强躲开了那个树桩。这时我才意
识到，那些细棍子竟然是箭！天啊，有人正朝我们放箭！我赶

快跑进驾驶室，想把正对着河岸的那扇百叶窗关上。那个笨蛋
舵手，此时正紧紧抓着轮辐，两个膝盖抬得老高，一边使劲蹬
着脚，一边咬牙咧嘴，活像一匹被缰绳勒紧了脖子的马。这个
没药救的蠢货！汽船晃晃悠悠地漂了过去，眼看着已经离河岸
不到十英尺了。我必须探出身子去拉动那沉重的百叶窗；就在
这时，我的眼中突然映入了一张人脸——那张脸隐藏在与我视
线完全平齐的树林之中，正用恶狠狠的眼神死死地盯着我。接
着，仿佛蒙眼的布罩突然被揭开，我一下子看清了眼前的景
象——在那枝蔓纠缠的幽暗丛林里，到处是裸露的胸膛、手
臂、腿脚和闪动着怒芒的眼睛。啊，丛莽之中竟然满是人！他
们的肢体随着每一次动作，闪烁着古铜色的光泽。树枝不停地
摇动着，发出飒飒的声响，一支支箭就从那里飞出来——我唰
的一声关上了百叶窗。'稳住舵，照直往前开！'我向舵手喝
道。他挺着脖颈，一动不动地昂着头，脸一直朝着前方；但
是他的眼神却游移不定，两脚止不住地一会儿抬起一会儿放
下，嘴角还流出了些许白沫来。'你最好镇静些！'我忍不住
大发雷霆。让他不要慌张，倒还不如命令狂风中的树枝不许乱
摇呢！我冲出驾驶室。从我下边的铁皮甲板上传来一阵杂沓的
脚步声，许多人的叫喊声乱成一片；一个声音尖叫道，'你就
不能往回开吗？'我发觉前方水面上有一道 V 字形的水纹。什
么？又一个树桩！空中箭如飞蝗，数不清的箭矢纷纷掉落在我
脚边；朝圣者们已经端起温彻斯特步枪开火了，但是他们的还
击只不过是把铅弹往树丛中胡喷一通而已。霎时间，一大团活
见鬼的硝烟从枪管里冒出来，慢慢往前飘去。我望着那烟雾破
口大骂。托他们的福，我既看不见水纹，也看不见树桩了。我
站在驾驶室的门边，眯起眼睛紧盯着水面；而就在此时，箭矢

仍如暴雨般向我们袭来。箭头上可能淬了毒药，但是看上去好像就连一只猫也射不死。那片丛林开始嚎叫起来，声音撼天动地；我们船上的伐木工也扯开嗓门，回以冲锋陷阵般的呐喊。更不用说就在我身后不断爆响的来复枪声，简直要把我的耳朵震聋了。我转头瞥了一眼，然后一个箭步冲向舵轮——我的驾驶室里正充斥着乱七八糟的声音和一片浓白的硝烟。那个笨到家的黑人，为了要拉开窗子发射马蒂尼·亨利来复枪，早就把舵轮丢下不管了。他正站在完全洞开着的百叶窗前面，瞪眼往外张望；我大声喊着要他退回来，同时匆匆一扭舵轮，拉回了正在急转的汽船。到了这份儿上，就算我想往回开，也已经没有了周旋的余地。前方的树桩就在那团该死的烟雾下面，离我们越来越近，片刻也容不得耽搁。我当下转舵，把船朝着岸边径直开去——我知道那里的水更深。

"河岸边都是郁郁葱葱的树丛，披离的枝叶从我们头顶高处垂下。汽船缓缓地闯了过去，所经之处枝折叶落，四下纷扬。这时，甲板上的几支来复枪几乎同时哑了火——他们的子弹打光了。我早就料到了会这样。耳畔突然间传来嗖的一声，我急忙向后一仰，眼前只见一道箭光穿堂而过，它从驾驶室的一边窗口飞进来，又从另一边飞了出去。舵手一边挥舞着手里那支没了子弹的来复枪，一边发疯似的朝着岸边大喊大叫；我从他身旁望过去，隐约看到岸边一些奔跑的人影，他们弓着身子向前纵跃疾奔，速度之快，简直是迅如飞鸟——原本还是清晰的人形，转眼化作一道残影，再一转眼已经消失不见——蓦然间，一个巨大的物体径直扑上百叶窗，来复枪几乎立刻就顺着船舷掉进了河里，舵手迅速向后退了几步，扭头看了我一眼——那眼神似曾相识却又异乎寻常，好像有千言万语想要诉

说——然后他就向我的脚下扑倒了。他的额头重重磕在舵轮上
又反弹了一下，一根好似藤条的长棍子啪啦甩过去打翻了一个
小折叠凳。那情景，就好像他从岸上什么人手里夺过了这条棍
子，却因为用力过猛一下子摔倒了。此时，那片硝烟已经散
去，我们也总算是安然躲过了那个树桩。我向前望去，心想再
航行大约一百码就可以扭转舵轮，让汽船远离河岸了；可还没
等这个念头转完，我忽然感到脚下又暖又湿，连忙低头去看。
只见舵手翻倒在地上仰面躺着，两眼直勾勾地瞪着我，双手还
紧紧地握着那根棍子。那棍子其实是一支长矛的木柄，不知道
是从窗口掷进来的还是戳进来的，正扎在他肋骨下面的侧腰
上。矛尖在他的身体上洞开了一个可怕的伤口，深深地埋入了
血肉之中。我的鞋子里已经灌满了黏腻腻的血。舵轮底下，一
大摊血淤积在地上，闪射着暗红色的幽光。甲板上再次枪声大
作，他焦灼地注视着我，眼睛里闪烁着一种奇异的光采；他的
双手仍然紧握着那长矛不肯放松，就好像攥着一件什么宝物，
唯恐被我夺去似的。我好不容易才从那张不肯瞑目的脸上移开
了视线，强迫自己专注于驾船。我腾出一只手往头顶上边摸索
着，终于拽住了那根拉汽笛的绳子，立刻一下接一下地猛拉汽
笛。汽船发出长长的尖啸，顿时压住了那片愤怒嘈杂的喊杀
声；接着，从密林深处传来一声悠远而又凄厉的哀号，带着无
法言喻的悲哀的战栗，在长空里徘徊激荡——那音调里充满了
忧伤、恐惧和心死般的悲凉，仿佛已经濒临无底的深渊，失去
了留连在这个世界上的最后一缕希望。丛林中骤然陷入了一片
混乱，箭雨停了下来，只有零星的几支箭尖鸣着飞了出去——
然后一切重归静寂。于是船尾螺旋桨那懒洋洋的单调的击水声
又回到了我的耳边。正在我向右打满舵的时候，那个身穿粉色

蓦然间，一个巨大的物体径直扑上了百叶窗。

（张佳铭　绘）

睡衣的朝圣者突然出现在门口，他的脸颊由于激动和亢奋涨得通红，拖着官腔说道：'经理派我前来，让你——'话犹未尽，他就惊呼起来：'哦，仁慈的上帝啊！'然后怔怔地望着地上那个奄奄一息的人。

　　"我们两个白人站在他的身旁，他那满是惶惑的眼睛里闪动着光，定定地望向我们；看着他那探询的眼神，我觉得他似乎马上就要用一种我们听得懂的语言，向我们吐出他心中的疑问来。但是他至死也没有说出一个字；他连手指头也没有抬动一下，甚至连些许的抽搐都没有。他只是在濒死的最后一刻，深深地皱了一下眉头，似乎是在回应一个我们无法看见的幻象，抑或是一声我们无法听到的低语；而那拧扭的双眉，使得他那张黑色的死面显现出一种若有所思的阴沉表情，透着一股说不出的狰狞和怪异。他那充满困惑的目光逐渐黯淡了，最后只余下一片玻璃似的空茫。'你能掌舵吗？'我急切地问那个朝圣者。他迟疑着答不出话来，但是我不由分说一把攥住了他的胳膊，于是他马上明白，无论他回答是或否他都必须要给我掌舵了。说实话，我那时满脑子只想赶紧换掉自己的鞋袜，多等一秒钟都受不了。'他就这么死了，'那家伙喃喃低语着，似乎心中有万分感慨。'毫无疑问，而且已经死透了，'我一边说，一边发疯似的扯着鞋带。顺便说一句，那时候我深信库尔茨先生恐怕也已经遭了毒手了。

"这个念头萦绕在我的脑海中，挥之不去。我陷入了深深的失落和懊丧之中，那种感觉，就好像我忽然发现，原来自己一直在奋力追寻的东西终究只是一团泡影。如果说我不远万里跋涉到此的唯一目的就是为了和库尔茨先生谈几句话，那么我现在的心情简直懊恼得无以复加。咦，谈几句话？——我脱下一只鞋抛进河里，心里回味着刚刚那一闪念，突然意识到其实这才是我一直以来最期待的事——能够和库尔茨先生谈一次话。我奇怪地发现，自己从来没有想过他会做什么，而是一直在想象着他会说什么。我心里从未想过'啊，我再也见不到他了，'或者'我再也不能和他握手了，'我只是在心里不断地对自己说，'我将永远也听不到他的谈话了，'就好像'库尔茨先生'只不过是一个能对着我侃侃而谈的声音而已。当然，我并非觉得他只是一个空虚的符号，没有什么生动的形象，也没有什么具体的行为。我绝不是这样想的。不是早就有很多人，或是嫉妒或是艳羡地告诉我，库尔茨先生一直在搜集、交换、骗取和盗窃象牙，而且他弄到手的象牙比其他所有代理人加在一起的还要多吗？但是这些都不是最关键的。真正关键的是——他是一个天赋英华的人；而在他的众多才能之中，最引人瞩目且最具有真实存在感的，正是他那舌绽莲花的口才，和他口中说出的那些言语——那是一种从心所欲表达思想的才能，它能让你堕入迷惑，也能使你茅塞顿开；它能施予你最崇高的教谕，也可以让你蒙受最卑劣的熏染；那是一条律动着的光明之河，闪耀着智慧与道德；那也是满载着谎言与欺骗的肮脏浊流，从那浓墨般深沉的黑暗之心汩汩而出。

"我脱下另一只鞋用力一抛，它在空中划过一道弧线，然后就落到河心深处的水神或者水鬼那里去了。我心里想，'天哪！一切全完了。我们终究是来晚了；一支长矛、一副弓箭或者一根木棒，已经使他命归黄泉——他那天纵的才华也随之消逝了。我将再也无法听到他的谈话了！'——这种强烈的悲哀在我胸中激起千万道震荡，令我从灵魂深处迸发出阵阵颤栗；那种感觉，绝不逊于丛林野人的凄厉嚎叫中蕴含着的那种悲伤和绝望。即使是迷失了生活的目标，抑或是被剥夺了信仰，我也不会像现在这样，只感到无边的孤独与凄凉……是谁在那里粗声叹气，好似有什么话要讲？什么，荒唐？是呵，你觉得荒唐。我的上帝呀！难道一个人就不能——来，再给我一点烟叶。"……

他停了下来，四周又陷入了一片沉沉的寂静。接着，一根火柴划着了，火光里映出了马洛瘦削的脸——那张脸上写满了沧桑和疲倦，双颊凹陷，眼皮松弛，甚至已经有了明显的皱纹。但是他的神情相当专注；当他使劲嘬着烟斗的时候，随着那微小的火光一明一灭，他的面容也在黑夜里时隐时现。火柴慢慢熄灭了。

"荒唐！"他突然大声说。"给人讲点儿什么，最怕的就是这个……你们安安稳稳地坐在船上，整日往返于出发地和目的地之间，过着踏踏实实的日子，就好像系着两个锚的大船一样；这边街角有一家肉铺，那边街角站着个警察，你们要什么有什么——呱呱叫的好胃口，不高也不低的正常体温——听见了吗？一年到头体温都正常。然后你们给我说，荒唐！让荒唐——见他妈的鬼去吧！荒唐！我亲爱的伙计们，对于一个由于过度激动而刚把一双新鞋扔进河里的人，你们还能指望他怎么样呢！现在回想起来，连我自己都非常惊讶，我当时竟然没有痛哭一场。坚毅刚强一直是我引以为傲的长处，但是一想到自己永远失去了聆听天才的库尔茨演讲的宝贵机会，我就完全抑制不住内心的痛楚。当然，现在我知道自己弄错了。那个千载难逢的机遇仍在等着我。哦，是的。我不但聆听了，而且听到的足够不少了。而且我之前的想法倒也是对的。'一个声音'，是的，他确实也只不过是一个声音罢了。我倾听着库尔茨侃侃而谈，或者说，我倾听着他的声音——还有别的人的声音；说起来，其实所有的人物都只不过是一些声音罢了。那些声音，连同那段时间里的记忆，全都在我脑中萦绕不去；它们是那样的没有真实感，就像水中月、镜中花，就像一场人声鼎沸的狂欢之后渐渐低沉的余响——除了愚蠢、残忍、肮脏、野蛮和赤裸裸的卑鄙下流，没有任何意义可言。这个人只不过是个声音，那个人也只不过是个声音，甚至就连那个年轻的女人——现在也只不过是个——"

他一下子顿住了，然后沉默了很久。

"最后，我不得不用一句谎言埋葬了他那天才的鬼魂，"他突然又开口讲了下去。"年轻女人！什么？我刚才说到女人了吗？哦，她和这个故事没有关系——完全是个局外人。她们——我是说女人们——都应该和这种事无关——她们都应该是局外人。我们必须保护她们，让她们一直活在她们自己的美好世界中，免得让男人的世界变得更糟。哦，绝不能把她牵扯进来。如果库尔茨先生从坟墓里走出来，你们还会听到他这样念叨着：'我的未婚妻。'这样你们就会明白，她还是冰清玉洁的，完全没有受到牵连。我还记得库尔茨先生那高耸的前颅！他们说，有的人还能再长出头发来，但是这个——呵——这个样本，却光秃秃的，十分惹眼，再也没能长出一根头发。那顽皮的荒野曾经拍打过他的头，你们瞧，这头颅就变得好像光溜溜的球那样了——一个象牙球；荒野还曾经抚摸过他，然后——看哪！他很快就委顿了；但那荒野还是不肯放过他，它俘虏了他，钟爱他，拥抱他；它钻进他的脉管，啮噬他的血肉，通过这种不可思议的邪恶仪式拉他入伙，直到连他的灵魂也完全归它所有。那荒野宠着他，纵着他，他就是茫茫荒原上的天之骄子了。因为象牙吗？我想是的。成堆的象牙，成垛的象牙，那间破旧的土坯房都快要被象牙给撑破了。你就这样想吧，在那片国土上，无论天上地下都再也找不到一根象牙了——所有的象牙全都已经被他搜刮殆尽。'大多数都是些化石，'经理曾经带着轻蔑的神气这样说过。其实，那象牙和我一样，并不怎么算得上是化石；但是因为它们是从地底下给掘出来的，所以就被他们叫作化石。看来那些黑人确实把一部分象牙埋入了地下——但是很显然，因为他们埋得还不够深，所以最终也没能挽回天才的库尔茨先生的命运。我们的汽船里装满了象牙，就连甲板上也堆了许多。这样只要他的眼睛还看得见，他就可以满心欢喜地看着它们，因为直到他生命的最后时刻，他仍然异常喜爱他的这些宝贝。你们真应该听听他这样说，'我的象牙。'哦，是的，我亲耳听他说过。'我的未婚妻，我的象牙，我的贸易站，我的河流，我的——'一切都是属于他的。这让我不禁屏住了呼吸，似乎那荒野马上就要爆发出一阵响彻天地的隆隆大笑，笑得群星震颤，日月无光。一切都是属于他的——好吧，你就姑且听之。重要的是你得知道，他究竟是属于谁的，到底有多少黑暗的势力在争夺对他的所有权。一念及此，顿时让人毛骨悚然；这件事已经超出了你的认知，而且就算知晓了真相，也绝不会对你有什么好处。好吧，实话告诉你——在这片大陆的众多魔鬼之中，他的地位高高在上。而你对此是无法理解的。你怎能理解得了呢？——你们脚下踩着坚实的人行道，周围都是些彬彬有礼的邻居——虽然他们也会拜高踩低，慕强凌弱；你们仪态优雅地穿梭于肉铺和警察之间，对流言蜚语、绞刑架和疯人院天然地怀有深深的恐惧。你们如何能够想象，如果一个人能够抛弃一切牵绊、真正自由地行走，那么他会流浪到何等原始而又奇异的国度呢？他完全追随自己的意志行走着，一路上是那样的荒凉——连一个警察的影子也没有；一路上又是那样的寂静——绝没有好心的邻人在旁边小声提醒，要他注意什么公众舆论。这些细节微不足道，却造成了天壤之别。因为当这一切全都不复存在的时候，仍然在约束着你的，就只剩下你与生俱来的天性，和坚守信念的那份力量。当然，如果你大愚若智，反倒不会出岔子——你甚至蠢得都不知道自己正在遭受黑暗势力的攻击。依我看，从来就没有一个傻瓜拿自己的灵魂和魔鬼做过交易；要么是因为傻瓜太愚蠢，要么是因为魔鬼太精明——谁知道到底是哪一种情况呢？要不然你就是个非凡的高洁之人，除了来自上天的意象和声音，你对俗尘中的一切都视而不见，听而不闻。这样一来，地球对你而言只不过是个踏足之地而已——但是这究竟是福是祸呢？我也不敢妄言。而我们这些凡夫俗子、芸芸众生，既不是前面所说的蠢蛋，也不是后面所说的圣人。地球是我们辗转生存的地方，在这里，我们得学会忍耐各种也许并不那么美好的景象、声音，还有气味——哦，我的上帝！比如说死河马肉的那种臭味——而且还不能被它们侵染身心。你看到了吗？你得完全依靠自己的力量和信念，去默默地承受这一切，把所有的肉身的痛苦和思想的彷徨，若无其事地、深深地埋藏在心底——这就是最无私的奉献；是的，你并不是为了一己私利，而是在为了那无人知晓的事业鞠躬尽瘁。这场历程真可谓是千难万险，惊心动魄。注意，我这样说并不是想要找托辞，或者想要解释什么。我只是在为了——为了——库尔茨先生，或者说为了库尔茨先生那不甘的幽魂，自说自话地做一番剖白。这个来自黑暗深处无名之地的天才的幽魂，在它归于虚无之前，曾经是那样的信赖我，使我感到莫大的荣幸。这也许是因为它能够对我讲英语。库尔茨早年曾在英国受过教育，而且他也这样爽直地说过——他的同情总是与正义同在。他的母亲拥有一半英国血统，他的父亲拥有一半法国血统，追溯起来，可以说在库尔茨的身上汇聚了整个欧洲的血脉。后来我还听说，'肃清野蛮习俗国际协会'曾委托他写一份报告，用来当作该协会以后的工作指南。他显然是最合适的人选，而且这份报告他也已经写了出来。我见到过，而且还仔细拜读了。这篇文章意气潇洒，宏谈阔论，处处洋溢着动人的才华——只是措辞有些太高调了，我觉得。他居然挤出时间来写了满满十七页！不过，这一定是在他——怎么说呢，在他精神失常之前——写出来的，他还因此常常得去主持一些什么'夜半舞会'，而且在舞会结束时还有一些令人羞于启齿的仪式。根据我从不同的人口中陆陆续续拼凑出来的情形，我不得不承认，这些舞会和仪式，全都是奉献给他的——你们听懂了吗？——全都是献给库尔茨先生一个人的。但是不可否认，那确实是一部得意之作。只是那部作品的开篇，在我已然知晓了他的全部命运之后再回头来看，却是一语成谶，令人心惊。他开宗明义地写道，我们白人，就目前已经达到的发展水平来说，'必然要以某种超自然的形象出现在他们（野蛮人）的眼前——我们须带着神明般的伟力降临到他们身边。'等等；'只要我们愿意，我们就能以高掌远跖的气魄和铁一样的手腕去改造他们的世界，成就无量功德。'等等。从这一理论出发，他开始慷慨陈词，警言譬喻层出不穷，尽情展现着论辩的才能；他那璀璨的言辞晃花了我的眼，也打动了我的心，令我深深折服。报告的结论部分更是大气磅礴。虽然我没法逐字复述出来，但是它留给我的印象异常深刻——那是一种前所未有的浩然之气，一种庄严而又博大的慈悲胸怀。我激动得浑身战栗，热血沸腾。这就是雄辩的力量——每一个字都力透纸背，雷霆万钧，仿佛要从那纸页上喷薄出无尽的光芒和热力，化作熊熊燃烧的烈焰。整部报告裹挟着激越的情感一挥而就；而似乎是为了不打断这酣畅淋漓的抒发，报告中并没有一个字涉及实际运作中的问题。我一直翻到最后一页，才在最下边找到了一句附记，似乎可以看作是一种如何处理实际问题的说明；而那行字显然是在很久以后才加上去的，笔迹零乱潦草，让人觉得那只执笔的手似乎一直在颤抖。这句附记非常简短，但是在他饱蘸着利他主义的情感发出那些感人肺腑的呼吁之后，这最后的一句话却仿佛晴空里的一道霹雳，用可怕的电光瞬间照亮了一切，狠狠地灼伤了我的眼睛——'把这些畜生统统消灭掉！'奇怪的是，这句一语道破天机的附记，后来似乎被他全然忘掉了。因为后来，当他的神智稍微清醒些的时候，他一再请求我一定要保存好'我的小册子'（他是这样称它的），因为毫无疑问，这本小册子对他将来的事业仍然大有好处。我对他的一切都了如指掌，而且到了后来，我还得保全他身后的声名。对此我算是尽心竭力了。因为如何评判他最后的那段日子，全在我的一念之间；我握着无可辩驳的权力，可以把他——如果我愿意的话——一劳永逸地抛进时间的垃圾堆，让他和那些'人类文明的死猫烂狗'——那些只能永远沉默的弱小者一起，化作历史的尘埃。但是你知道，我不能这样做。他是不会被人忘记的。褒也好，贬也罢，他总归是一个非比寻常的人物。他拥有不可思议的能力，让那些蒙昧的野蛮人要么畏惧他，要么崇拜他，最后全都围绕着他，向他献上顶礼膜拜的巫祝之舞；他能震慑那些朝圣者，让他们虚弱渺小的灵魂在疑惧不安中瑟瑟发抖；而且他还收获了一个忠心耿耿的朋友，于是在这世上，至少有一个既不愚昧、也未曾沾染利己主义的心灵憧憬他，仰慕他，甘愿为他的才华而倾倒。是的，我忘不了他；但是我也无法说服自己去相信，为了找到他，真的就值得让那条鲜活的生命付出血的代价。我非常想念那个死去的舵手——甚至当他的尸体还躺在驾驶室里的时候，我就感到了失去他的痛苦。也许你们觉得我这样哀悼一个野人未免荒谬，因为他只不过是众多黑人之中微不足道的一个，就好像撒哈拉之中的一粒沙；可是你们没有看到，好几个月的时间里，他是怎样任劳任怨地帮助我。他干了不少工作，一直在为那条船掌舵。他是一个好助手——一件称手的工具。我们两个结成了伙伴。他为我掌舵——所以我就得关照他。我曾因为他的力不胜任而忧心忡忡，这样就在我们之间形

他拥有不可思议的能力，让那些蒙昧的野蛮人要么畏惧他，要么崇拜他，最后全都围绕着他，向他献上顶礼膜拜的巫祝之舞。

（张舒婷、张佳铭　绘）

成了一条微妙的纽带；而我却只是在这纽带突然断裂之时，才恍然感悟到它的存在。直到今天，他在受伤后向我投来的那种充满信赖和依恋的深沉目光，还时常清晰地浮现在我的眼前——那仿佛是一个无比崇高的时刻；那一刻我们心心相通，确认了彼此之间牵连着来自远古的共同血脉。

"可怜的傻瓜！他真不该靠近那扇百叶窗。他没有自制力，完全控制不了自己——这简直和库尔茨先生毫无两样——就像一株只能随着狂风东摇西摆的树。我刚换上一双干净拖鞋，就开始把他往外拖；当然我先是拔出了扎在他腰侧的那根长矛——我承认，我是紧闭着双眼拔的。他的两个脚踵拖曳在地上，在经过驾驶室低矮的门槛时一齐弹跳了下；我把他的肩膀紧紧地抵在胸前，使出浑身的力气从背后抱住他。哦！他可真沉，沉极了；我觉得他简直比世界上任何人都更沉。接着我就毫不犹豫地把他推下船去。滚滚的水流立刻夺走了他，仿佛他只不过是一捆稻草；我看见他的尸体在河水中翻滚了两下，然后就永远地失去了踪影。经理和那些朝圣者们都向驾驶室聚拢过来，他们站在棚子底下的甲板上，好像一群激动的麻雀在那儿叽喳个不停；有的人还在愤愤地嘀咕着，说我转眼间就把尸体处理完毕，简直是毫无人性，冷酷无情。我倒想请问他们，把那尸体在船上多留一时片刻，究竟目的为何？哈，也许他们还想给它涂上防腐的香膏吧。然而从底下的甲板上，传来了另一些人不怀好意的窃窃私语。那些伐木工同样对这件事愤愤不平，而且他们的理由似乎更充分——尽管我承认，这理由本身无论如何都是不可接受的。哦，绝对不可接受！我早已下定决心，如果我那死去的舵手注定要沦为食物，那也只能让他去喂鱼。他活着的时候是个次等的舵手，如今他死了，倒很可能变成了上等的诱惑，说不定还会惹出一场轩然大波。再说当时我还着急回去掌舵，因为我看得出来，那个穿粉色睡衣的家伙在这一行上是个一窍不通的蠢货。

"那简单的葬礼一结束，我马上就抓住了舵轮。汽船稳稳地在河流的正中央半速前进，我一面驾船，一面倾听着我身边的谈话。他们已经放弃了库尔茨，也放弃了那个贸易站；库尔茨已经死了，贸易站也已经被烧掉了——等等。那个红头发的朝圣者，或许是想到我们至少已为可怜的库尔茨报了仇，激动得简直不知所以。'喂！我们可算把丛林里的那些野人全给杀了个干净。一场了不起的胜利！嗯？你们说是不是？来呀，说说呀！'这个嗜血的小可怜虫口沫横飞地说着，竟还兴奋得跳起舞来了。可是就在刚才，他还差点被那舵手的伤口吓晕过去！我忍不住接口说道，'没错，你们可算是放出了一大团了不起的烟雾。'当时一看见丛林顶梢上枝叶纷飞的情景，我就知道，他们射出去的子弹几乎全都打偏了。你只有把枪托抵在肩上，眯起眼睛瞄准，才有可能击中目标；但是这帮家伙却把枪顶在胯上，闭着眼睛乱放一气。至于那些野人为何突然撤退，我坚信——而且后来也证明我是对的——完全是因为那长而尖厉的汽笛声。我的这番话令他们勃然大怒；他们马上忘掉了库尔茨，全冲着我喊叫起来，七嘴八舌地表示抗议。

"经理站在舵轮边，压低了声音用很殷切的口吻对我说，我们必须离这里越远越好，天黑以前无论如何也得开回下游去。正在这时，我突然看到远处的河边有一块空地，隐约有些房子的轮廓。'那是什么？'我问道。他讶异地看过去，随即拍了一下手，惊呼道：'是贸易站！'于是我立刻打舵，让船贴向岸边驶过去。

"汽船仍保持半速前行。我从望远镜里看到一处山坡，坡上一株灌木也没有，只有零零落落的几棵树。一座狭长的破屋半掩在山顶的深草中，尖耸的屋顶上露着许多大窟窿，远望去好似一张张骏黑的大嘴；屋子后面全都是乱草和树林。四周没有围墙，也没有篱笆，但显然以前曾经是有过的——因为屋子旁边还有排成一行的六七根细木桩。那些木桩削得相当粗糙，但是每根桩子顶上都装饰着一个雕刻出来的圆球。桩子之间的栏杆，或者说扶手之类的东西，全都已经消失不见了。这山顶的小屋就坐落在群山的襟抱之中，环望着茫茫的林海。河岸上一片空旷，视野非常开阔；于是我看到一个白人站在水边。他头戴一顶车轮那么大的帽子，不停地挥舞着双臂向我们打招呼。我仔细地观察着那一大片树林，发现丛莽间有动静——到处都有正在快速移动的人影。我完全相信自己的眼睛。我小心地把船开过去，然后关闭引擎，让汽船顺着水流漂过去。岸上那个人开始喊叫，催促我们赶快登岸。'我们刚刚受到了攻击！'经理大声喊道。'我知道——我知道。没事儿！'那个人大声回答，那样子简直是欣喜若狂。'快过来吧！没问题的。我非常高兴！'

"他那副表情让我感觉似曾相识——就像是曾经在什么地方见到过的一个滑稽形象。在驾船靠近岸边的时候，我一直在暗自琢磨，'这家伙到底像个什么来着？'突然间我想起来了，他正像是戏剧里扮演的小丑。他身上的衣服原来也许是用棕色荷兰布做的，但是现在已经缀满了补丁——那些补丁个个色彩鲜艳，红的、蓝的、黄的，特别亮眼——你就看吧，他后背上有补丁，胸前有补丁，手肘和膝盖上也有补丁；他的上衣镶着彩色的滚边，裤脚上也绣着大红色的条纹。灿烂的阳光照耀着

于是我看到一个白人站在水边。他头戴一顶车轮那么大的帽子，不停地挥舞着双臂向我们打招呼。

（陈睿杰　绘）

他，使他看上去干净整洁，欢乐洋溢；同时你也能看清楚，他身上所有那些补丁都补得多么漂亮。他肤色白皙，胡子也刮得干干净净，看上去颇有些孩子气。他的面貌平平无奇，晒脱了皮的鼻子上边，眨着一双并不算大的蓝眼睛。他那纯真的面庞时而微笑着，显得十分快乐；时而又皱起眉头，好似有什么隐忧。悲与喜在他的脸上交替闪现，宛如那风云变幻的平原时阴时晴。'要当心，船长！'他朝我大喊，'昨天晚上这里刚打进去一个树桩。'什么？又一个树桩！我承认我当时什么脏话都骂出来了。我差点儿把我那条破汽船给捅上个窟窿，让这一趟美妙的旅程就此完蛋大吉。岸上的小丑朝我扬了扬他的狮子鼻，'你是英国人？'他满面笑容地问道。'你呢？'我手握着舵轮向他喊。看到我的表情，他脸上的笑容消失了；他摇了摇头，似乎在对我的失望表示抱歉。然后他又欢快起来。'没关系！'他喊道，好像在给我打气。'我们没有来晚吧？'我问道。'他就在那边，'他回答说，把头朝着山坡那边一扬，脸色蓦地又阴沉下来。他的神情就像秋日的天空一样变化无常，一会儿阴霾满布，一会儿又晴空朗朗。

"经理在那些武装到牙齿的朝圣者们的簇拥下，走进那所房子里面去了。这时，那家伙也跳上船来了。'喂，我可不喜欢这种欢迎方式。那些土人还都藏在林子里面吧，'我对他说。他则一个劲儿地向我保证，他们绝没有恶意。'他们全都头脑简单，'他补充说，'啊，我可是真的盼望着你们来。我一直想办法不让那些土人靠近这里。''但是你说过他们没有恶意，'我叫了起来。'哦，他们绝不会伤害你们的，'他说；然后在我的瞪视下，他又改口说，'好吧，话也不能说得太满。'然后他四下一望，活泼地说，'我的天哪，你的驾驶室也该好好打扫一下啰！'紧接着他又奉劝我，一定得让锅炉里随时有充足的蒸汽，这样的话一旦遇到麻烦，就可以马上拉响汽笛。'汽笛的一声尖叫可比所有的来复枪都更管用。那些土人全都头脑简单，'他重复说。他就这样连珠炮似的说个不停，我简直完全插不进嘴去。他似乎是太久不曾和别人说话了，所以现在要抓住机会说个尽兴；而且他还真的大笑着表示，实际情况正是如此。'难道你不跟库尔茨先生谈话吗？'我问道。'你永远不能跟他谈话——你只能听他讲话，'他用无比尊崇的口气大声说。'不过现在——'他摆了摆手，眼神一下子黯淡下来，似乎整个人都意气消沉了。可是过了一会儿，这只泄了气的皮球又自己鼓胀了起来；他一跃而起，紧紧攥住我的双手，一边不停地摇晃着，一边放炮似的急促地说：'水手兄弟……我的荣幸……真高兴……介绍一下我自己……俄国人……大主教的儿子……坦波夫政府……什么？烟草！啊哈，还是英国烟草！太棒了！这才是好哥们儿。你问我抽不抽烟？嘿，天底下哪有不抽烟的水手。'

"抽过一袋烟后，他终于平静下来。慢慢地我了解到，他早年就自己辍了学，跟着一条俄国船出过海；后来又从船上跑掉了；然后在英国船上干过一阵子；现在终于跟他的主教父亲和解了。他把这事儿详详细细地说给我听。'不过话说回来，一个人趁着年轻，总该出去见见世面，积累见闻，增长经验，开阔自己的眼界。''就在这儿？'我打断了他的话。'这你可说不准！就是在这儿我才遇上了库尔茨先生，'他嗔怪了我一句，然后孩子气地板起了脸。于是我再不提起这个话题了。据他说，他曾说服海边的一个荷兰贸易站供给他物资装备，随后就轻松愉快地一头扎进丛林，深入到荒野的腹心地带去了；他就像个天真懵懂的孩童一样，从来就没考虑过自己将会遇到什么危险。他沿着这条大河独自游荡了将近两年，可以说完全是与世隔绝了。'其实我可没有看上去那么年轻。我都已经二十五岁了，'他说。'一开始，老范休顿总是叫我赶紧快滚，'他兴高采烈地讲着自己的故事，'但是我缠上他了。我今天谈，明天谈，谈得他晕头转向；他真怕我再谈下去，连他那条心爱的小狗都要受不了我了。于是他只好给了我一些不值钱的东西和几条枪，并且告诉我说，他这辈子都不想再看见我了。老范休顿——那个荷兰人，真是有一副好心肠。去年我让人捎给他一包象牙，这样等我将来回去的时候，他就没法再骂我是什么小贼啦。我希望他这会儿已经收到那些象牙了。至于别的事儿，我全都不在乎。我还在下游给你们准备了一垛木头。那儿有我以前住过的房子。你们瞧见了吗？'

"于是我摸出那本陶森的书还给他。他那副样子简直是忍不住要来吻我，但他还是克制住了激动的情绪。'这是我落下的唯一一本书。我还以为再也找不回来了呢，'他一边说，一边不胜欢喜地望着那本书。'如果你孤身一人到处流浪，谁知道会遭遇多少意外的麻烦。有时候你的小木船可能会突然翻了，有时候不小心惹怒了那些土人，你又得赶紧抱头逃窜。'他翻动着手里的书页。'这些都是你用俄文写的笔记吗？'我问道。他点了点头。'我还以为它们是密码呢，'我说。他闻言大笑不已。接着他的神情又变得严肃起来，'为了不让那些土人过来，我可真费了不少力气，'他说。'他们想杀死你吗？'我问。'哦，不！'他大声说，那样子有些欲言又止。'那他们为什么攻击我们？'我追问道。他犹豫了一会儿，然后有点儿忸怩地说：'他们不想让他走。''不想让他走？'我好奇地问道。他神秘地点了一下头，仿佛其中充满了某种不可言传的智慧。'让我来告诉你吧，'他终于大声说道，'正是这个人让我大开眼界。'他张开双臂，睁圆了他那双蓝色的小眼睛，用晶莹闪亮的目光直视着我。"

三

　　"我愕然地看着他，一时竟回不过神来。那人就站在我的面前，穿着一身花花绿绿的衣服，好像一个刚从滑稽剧团里逃跑出来的丑角儿，那样的热情洋溢，又那样的荒诞离奇。他的存在本身就是一个匪夷所思的奇迹，就像一个活生生的海市蜃楼。你无法相信自己的眼睛。他是一个不解之谜。你无论如何也想象不出来，他是怎样活下来的，又是怎样一路走到这荒蛮远僻之地的？时至今日他怎还会依然活着，要知道稍有差池，那荒野立刻就会张开大口将他吞噬。'我只不过往前走一点，'他说，'然后再往前走一点——不知不觉间就走了那么远，远得我自己都找不到回去的路了。没关系，反正有的是时间。我能应付得来。你赶快把库尔茨先生带走——要赶快——我告诉你。'他那斑驳褴褛的衣衫、穷困潦倒的窘相、孤苦伶仃的处境，还有那无所建树的漫长漂泊带给他的落寞神情，全都掩不住他身上那股蓬勃的朝气——那是一种只属于年轻人的青春活力。日复一日，年复一年，他一直都过着朝不保夕的日子，在死亡的边缘挣扎辗转；但是他仍然意气昂扬地迎接来自荒野的挑战，既不瞻前，也不顾后，无忧无虑地活过每一天。他简直就像是拥有金刚不坏之身，而实际上他也不过是仗着自己年轻力壮，初生牛犊不怕虎罢了。我几乎仰慕起他来——或者说更像是嫉妒。青春的朝气引领着他向前进，也保护着他，使他一路上安然无恙。他对这片荒野一无所求，他来到这里，只有一个目的——驰骋在广阔的天地之间，尽情呼吸自由的空气；而他也只有一个任务——活下去，并且冒着最大的危险、忍受着最大的困苦继续前进。如果说世上曾有人超越了对现实利益的算计和谋求，真正焕发着纯粹而热烈的冒险主义精神，那必定是眼前这个人无疑。他身上穿着缀满补丁的衣衫，心中却跳动着温暖明亮的火焰——我真是忍不住要羡慕他。这热情的火焰似乎燃尽了一切自私的情感，甚至当他正在亲口向你讲述的时候，你也几乎忘记那就是他——就是站在你眼前的这个人——曾经忍受了那么多的坎坷艰难。但是他对于库尔茨的那种近乎崇拜的忠诚，我却很是不以为然。我觉得他并没有深思熟虑过。库尔茨闯进了他的生活，他便觉得一切都是命中注定，便义无反顾地向他献出了满腔热忱。可是在我看来，那却是他生平遭际的最大的凶险。

"仿佛是一场无法逃避的宿命，他们两个相遇了。他们就像两条小船，在无风的海上漂荡，彼此越靠越近，终于紧紧地挨到了一起。我想，库尔茨先生需要一个倾听者。因为在树林里宿营的时候，他们曾经彻夜长谈。当然更有可能的情况是，库尔茨先生自己从日落讲到天明。'我们无话不谈，'他说；回想起当时的情景，他心醉神驰。'我竟忘记了世界上还有睡眠这种事！一整夜的时光流逝了；可是在我觉得，我们才谈了不到一个小时。我们什么都谈！无所不谈！……啊，当然也谈到了爱。''什么？他竟对你讲到爱情！'我说。我差点笑了起来。'不是你所想的那样，'他激动地大声说，'那是更崇高、更博大的爱。他让我懂得了许多事情——开阔了我的眼界。'

也许，库尔茨先生需要一个倾听者。因为在树林里宿营的时候，他们曾经彻夜长谈。

（陈睿杰　绘）

"他再次高扬起双臂。我们那时站在甲板上，那群野人伐木工的头领正在不远处踱着步，这时也转过头来，用他那深沉疲倦，但仍炯炯有神的眼睛望着他。我环顾着四周。不知道为什么，我从未如此强烈地感受到，那片土地、那条河流、那苍莽的丛林和耀眼的天穹，竟是那样的深不见底，令人绝望；理性的光芒照不透这无边的黑暗，而它对人类的苦难也冷漠无情，绝没有丝毫的垂怜。'看来，从那以后，你就和他结伴同行啰？'我说。

"事实恰恰相反。由于这样那样的原因，他们的联系也时不时中断。他不无骄傲地告诉我说，库尔茨害过两次大病，都是在他的照料下才转危为安；他的眼里闪动着熠熠的神采，似乎觉得这种经历就堪比什么英雄传奇了。但是大多数时候，库尔茨总是独自一人到处闯荡，深入到遥远的丛林腹地中去。'事情经常是这样的：我来到这站上，然后还得再等上好长一段日子他才回来，'他说。'啊，等待也是值得的！——有时候是。''他在外边都干些什么？是勘探地形，还是为了别的？'我问。'哦，是的，当然，'他发现了许多村庄，还发现了一个湖泊——他也不晓得那些地方的具体方位，打听得太多没准会惹祸的——然而他探险的主要目的还是寻找象牙。'但是那时候，他手里已经没有能交换象牙的货物了，'我反驳道。'可是那时候他手里还有不少子弹呀，'他回答说，然后别开了视线。'那么，打开天窗说亮话，他就是到那些村子里去抢劫了？'他点了点头。'当然了，他干这事儿也不是单枪匹马。'接着，他低声嘀咕了几句关于那个湖泊附近的村落的情况。'库尔茨让那个部落里的人为他做事，是吗？'我试探着问道。他有些局促不安起来。'他们都非常崇拜他，'他说。他这句话的口气实在有些异样，这让我不禁用探究的目光去打量他。一说到库尔茨他就半吞半吐，似乎内心深处充满了矛盾，又急着想谈而又不敢多谈；这种态度可真是耐人寻味。这个人似乎已经无处不在，他占据了他的生活，支配了他的思想，左右着他的情绪。'你还能希望是怎么样呢？'他忍不住冲口而出，'要知道，他是带着雷霆和闪电降临到他们中间的——这样的事物他们从来都没有见到过——他们都被吓坏了。他有如神明一般赫赫生威，主掌着他们的生杀之权。你绝不能像评判一个普通人那样，去评判库尔茨先生。不行，不行，绝对不行！现在——好吧，就让你知道知道——我也不怕说给你听。有一天，他还想一枪把我也打死呢——但是就算这样，我也不想对他妄加评判。'打死你？'我叫了起来，'为什么呢？''是这样的，我有一小包象牙，是附近村子的村长送给我的。因为我经常帮着他们打猎。是啊，他看上了那包象牙，什么道理也不肯听。他扬言说，要是我不肯把那些象牙给他，并且从此以后滚出他的地盘，他就会一枪打死我；他完全可以那样做，而且也很乐意那样做，因为在这世上他高兴杀谁就杀谁，什么也阻止不了他。事实也确实如此。我就把象牙给他了。我不在乎！但是我没有滚。不，不行，我不能离开他。当然我也变得更加小心翼翼了，直到过了一段时间之后，我们才重归于好。那时他又害了第二场病。从那以后，我再不碰象牙了，可是我不在乎。他大部分时间都住在湖畔的那些村子里。他回到河边来的时候，有时候对我和颜悦色，有时候呢，我就不得不谨言慎行，小心从事。这个人什么罪都受过。他对这里的一切都深恶痛绝，可不知怎么就是没法脱身。我一有机会总是恳求他，趁现在还来得及，赶紧离开这里；我甚至还说，我愿意和他一起回去。他有时说好，可结果却仍然待在这里不肯走；然后又出发去找象牙了，一连几个星期都不回来。一到了那些土人中间，他就浑然忘我了——他已经不是从前的样子了——你能听得懂吗？'天哪！那他是不是疯了，'我说。他马上愤慨地打断我，库尔茨先生是不可能疯的。倘若我听到他讲话，哪怕是两天之前的讲话，我也绝不敢如此轻率地妄下论断。在我们谈话期间，我举起望远镜观察了河岸边的情况，巡视着那所房子的背后，以及视野之中所有的树林。我知道那密林里有人暗藏其中，山顶上的破房子里面也有人——可是到处都阒无声息；一念及此，我不由得心中怵栗。眼前的一切都是那样的平静，我简直无法想象其中竟发生过这样惊心动魄的故事。我似乎觉得，这些事情并不是面前的这个人用言语讲给我听的，而是他那欲说还休的神态、凄凉愁郁的感慨、无可奈何的耸肩和最后那不无遗憾的一声长叹，让这些画面在我的脑海中一幕一幕浮现出来的……树林默默地耸立着，一丝动静也没有；它们无悲无喜，好似一副沉重的面具，又好似监狱里一扇紧闭着的门——它们怀藏着无数秘密，仿佛在耐心地等待着什么；但它们全都寂然无声。这是一种令人莫敢仰视的沉静。俄国人继续对我说，直到最近，库尔茨先生才回到河边这里，身后跟着那个湖畔部落的所有佣兵。他已经有好几个月杳无音信了——我想他也许是在忙着登上神坛——然后就这样出人意料地回来了。看他那架势，显然打算要到对岸或者下游去进行一场洗劫。他对象牙的欲望已经越来越贪婪，全然压倒了他的那些——怎么说呢——那些不求功利的理想和抱负。但是他的身体已经撑不住了。'我听说他病倒在那里没人照顾，就跑去看他——趁机再劝劝他。'那个俄国人说。'哦，他的情况很糟，非常糟。'于是我把望远镜转向那所房子。那里看不到任何生命活动的迹象，只有那满是破洞的屋顶，还有那长长的泥巴墙，张开着三个大小不同的方形窗孔，从深草中探出头来张望。透过望远镜看去，这一切仿佛都触手可及。接着我又一转望远镜，没料想，那早已腐朽无存的篱笆墙剩下的木桩一下子跃进了我的视野。还记得吗，我曾经远远望见那些桩子顶上的球形柱头；当时我就十分惊讶——这里的环境如此荒凉萧索，

竟然还有人愿意费心劳神，弄出来这些格格不入的装饰？现在
那些圆球近在咫尺了——而我甫一看清它的样子，立刻本能地
把头往后一仰，就好像要躲开迎面挥来的一记重拳似的；接着
我攥紧手里的望远镜，一根桩子一根桩子地仔细看过去，终于
明白自己起初竟完全弄错了。那些'圆球'并不是美丽的装

直到最近，库尔茨先生才回到河边这里，身后跟着那个湖畔部落的所有
佣兵。

（纪春秀、黄育蕾　绘）

饰，而是恐怖的象征——它们的含义呼之欲出，却又让你难以置信；它们只是安静地放在那里，就足以刺得你目眩神昏，从脊髓深处都止不住地冒出寒气来——它们会让看到这一幕的人心惊肉跳，思潮起伏；也会让盘旋觅食的秃鹫欢欣不已，从高空里直扑而下；但是它们最终还是做了那些肯耐心地沿着木桩往顶上爬去的蚂蚁的食粮。这些放在桩子顶上的人头，要不是因为全都面朝着房子那边，一定会带给你更强烈的视觉冲击，让你在睡梦中也难以忘怀。其中只有一个人头，也就是我最初看清的那一个，是面朝着我这边的。我其实并没有如你们想象的那般害怕。我当时往后一仰，也只是由于始料不及罢了。你知道的，我本以为那些都是雕刻出来的木球。于是我调转望远镜，特意又对准了那第一个人头——他仍旧挂在那里——深黑、干瘪、眼睛紧闭着——仿佛已经在那个木桩顶上沉沉地睡着了。从他那已经皱缩的嘴唇里露出一线白色的牙齿；他在微笑，不停地笑，好像在笑这永无止尽的睡眠中一场同样没完没了的滑稽的梦。

　　"我可不是在向你们泄露什么商业秘密。事实上，那位经理后来说过，库尔茨先生的做法把那一带的生意全给毁了。我不想评论他的话，但是我真的希望你们能够理解，把风干的人头挂在门口绝不是什么生财之道。它们只能证明库尔茨先生无法控制自己那些五花八门的欲望。在他身上缺乏某种东西——尽管微不足道，但却极其必要；你瞧，他尽可以宏论滔滔、吐出华丽的辞藻，但是这种东西的重要性，他却一点儿也意识不到。好吧，我也不确定他自己是否知道这一点；我想他最后应该是知道了——可惜那时已经太晚了。但是那荒野早就发现了他的弱点，而且对他那无尽的饕餮给予了可怕的报复。我想那荒野曾附在他的耳边轻声低语，让他恍然发现了一个完全陌生的自己——那是在他与这巨大的荒凉世界对话之前，从来都未曾想到过的事情——而这致命的诱惑令他根本无法抗拒。那动人的耳语蛊惑着他，在他的躯体里弥漫成一阵阵巨大的回响，直到他逐渐失去了自我而完全听命于它，变成了一个空心人……我放下望远镜，眼前那近得仿佛能够与我贴面交谈的人头倏然而去，消失在了遥不可及的远方。

　　"那位库尔茨先生的崇拜者现在有点垂头丧气了。他小声嗫嚅着分辩道，他不敢把那些——我们且叫它象征吧——从桩子上拿下来。他并不害怕那些土著；只要库尔茨先生不发话，他们就不敢乱动。在那些土人心中，他的地位至高无上。他们的帐篷围绕着他的住处，他们的首领每天都要向他问安。他们甚至爬在地上……'别说了，我对他们拜谒库尔茨先生的那套仪式不感兴趣，'我喊了起来。说来奇怪，我突然间觉得，这种细节竟比那些正在库尔茨先生的窗户底下慢慢晒干的人头更让人难以忍受。那些木桩和人头，毕竟也不过是一种野蛮的景象罢了；而此刻我却好像置身于一个暗无天日的地方，陷入了难以揣测的恐怖之中——在那里，简单直接的野蛮行径反倒成了一种实在的安慰，可以堂而皇之地暴露于光天化日之下了。那个年轻人惊异地看着我。我想他也没有料到，库尔茨先生并不是我崇拜的偶像。他忘记了我那时还没有听到过哪怕一句库尔茨先生的美妙独白——关于什么来着？是了，关于爱，正义，以及端正的品行——或者是与这些光明的事物相反的一切。说到那'爬在地上'的荒唐仪式，这个年轻人和那些黑暗世界的野蛮人根本就没什么两样，他的灵魂也早已卑微地匍匐在库尔茨脚下了。我不知道那些头颅怎么来的，他说：这全都是谋逆者的人头。我不禁放声大笑起来，震得他浑身一颤。谋逆者！接下来还会冒出什么样的新称呼呢？有人把他们叫做敌人，叫做罪犯，叫做劳工——现在他们又成了谋逆者了。而那些挂在桩子顶上的大逆不道的人头，在我看来个个都是面目温驯的。'你不会知道，这样的生活是如何淬炼出一个像库尔茨先生这样的人，'库尔茨的最后一个门徒大声说。'没错。而且还淬炼出来了你，是不是？'我说。'我，我……我是个头脑简单的人。我没有什么伟大的思想。我也不想索取别人的任何东西。你怎么能拿我去比……？'他激动得再也说不下去，整个人几乎崩溃了。'我怎么也想不通，'他哽咽着，'我尽了最大的力气帮他活到现在，这已经够了。我没有参与这些事。我真没用。在这里，好几个月都找不到一滴药水，或者是一口可以喂给病人吃的食物了。那些可耻的人已经把他抛弃了，把一个这样的人，一个这么有思想的人给抛弃了。可耻啊！可耻！我——我——已经接连十个晚上没有合眼了……'

"他的悲诉渐渐消失在宁静的暮色中。在我们谈话的时候，树林那深长的影子已经漫过了那破败的茅屋和那一排象征性的木桩，漫到了山脚下。一切都笼罩在阴暗之中，只有河岸边的我们仍站在明亮的阳光里。我们眼前的这片河面平静安详，闪烁着粼粼的波光；上游和下游的河湾却都已沉入黑暗的夜幕里了。岸上一个人影也没有。丛林里一片寂静。

"那栋破房子的转角处突然出现一伙人，简直就好像从地底下一下子冒出来了似的。他们相互紧挨在一起，在齐腰深的野草丛中往前跋涉；队伍中间的几个人抬着一副临时搭成的担架。突然间，在那空旷的原野上，一声尖厉的长啸划破了原本宁静的夜空——就像一支响箭直插向大地的心脏。仿佛是在魔法的召唤下，一群群野人从那幽暗阴深的丛林里不断地奔涌而出，很快就占满了那片空地；他们全都赤裸着身体，手里拿着长矛、弓箭和盾牌，姿态野蛮，目露凶光。一时间，树林里枝摇叶晃，飒飒有声，连地上的野草也跟着乱舞起来。很快一切又重归寂静。所有人都屏息凝神，连空气也似乎凝固了。

"'现在，要是他不为我们说几句话，我们就全完了，'站在我旁边的俄国人说。抬着担架的那伙人也好似突然化成了石头，一动不动地僵在了原地。他们离河边的汽船还有一半路程。我看见担架上的那个人坐起来，他身材瘦长，干枯的手臂高高探起，都高过了那些抬着他的人的肩头。'让我们祈祷，这个能把人类的博爱谈得天花乱坠的家伙，这次能找出个实在一点的理由来饶我们一命吧，'我说。眼下这命悬一线的荒谬局面令我深恶痛绝，又倍感耻辱；但是既然落到了这个残暴的魔鬼手中，我也只能无可奈何。我听不到他们在远处的对话，可是透过望远镜，我看到他那瘦削的胳膊威严地高举着，下颚一张一阖；那个将死的幽灵，两只眼睛深陷在几乎干枯的眼窝里，阴森森地闪着光；他那骷髅般的头颅痉挛似的点了一下，看起来相当怪异。库尔茨——库尔茨——这在德文中是'短'的意思——对吧？是的，从生到死，这名字正如他曾在这世上短暂拥有过的一切；只除了他那颀长的身材——他看起来至少有七英尺那么高。他身上盖着的被单滑落了，于是他的身体就好像从一条裹尸布中蓦地暴露了出来，显得既可怜又可怖。我能看到他的两排胸肋不停起伏，他那皮包骨的胳膊不停挥舞。那情景，真仿佛是一具用腐朽的象牙雕刻出来的活死人的偶像，正在向一群肃然静立的、闪烁着黑亮光泽的铜俑，挥动着他的枯手发出威胁。我看见他张大了嘴——这让他显露出

那情景，真仿佛是一具用腐朽的象牙雕刻出来的活死人的偶像，正在向一群肃然静立的、闪烁着黑亮光泽的铜俑，挥动着他的枯手发出威胁。

（张舒婷、张佳铭　绘）

一副无与伦比的贪婪神态，仿佛他正想一口吞掉所有的空气，所有的土地，以及所有站在他面前的人。我隐约听到一阵低沉的声音从他那里传来，那一定是他正在竭力嘶喊。突然间他仰天倒了下去。于是那担架又抬起来了，摇摇晃晃地往前走。几乎与此同时，我发现那一大群野人也悄然撤退了，转眼已杳无踪迹。这就好像刚才忽然将他们吐出来的那片森林，现在又用一口长气把他们全都吸了回去似的。

"几个朝圣者跟在担架后面，手里提着他的武器——两条霰弹枪、一支重型来复枪和一把轻型左轮卡宾枪——这便是那位可怜的天神朱庇特的雷霆和闪电了。经理走在他旁边，弯下腰去对他轻声说了句什么。他们把他放在一间小舱房里——你知道，那里窄得仅能容得下一张床和一两个小凳子。我们给他带来了积存已久的书信，于是撕开的信封和摊开的信纸便铺得满床都是了。他伸出一只虚弱无力的手在那些纸张中摸索着。他脸色憔悴，神情却恬静安详，目光灼灼如炬。我非常吃惊——那可真不像是沉疴已久的样子。他似乎根本没什么病痛。这个枯瘦的人影看起来心满意足，沉静平和，仿佛人世间的种种甘苦，他都已品尝够了。

"他哆哆嗦嗦地拿起一封信，望着我的眼睛说，'我很高兴。'有人给他写信谈到了我。那些推荐我的信又出现在了这里。他的声音是那么清晰，那么有力；然而他讲话的时候毫不费劲，似乎连嘴唇都不曾动过。我再一次吃惊了——就是那个声音！就是那个声音！那声音肃穆，深沉，荡涤人心；而那个人本身却几乎连喘息的力气都没有了。但是无论如何，他还有着足够强大的力量；即便已是强弩之末，他也足以拖上我们所有的人一起堕入地狱。很快我就会讲到这件事了。

"经理一声不响地来到门口。我马上走出房间，然后他把我身后的帘子放了下来。那俄国人正紧紧地盯着河边，朝圣者们都好奇地看着他。我沿着他的视线向岸边望去。

"在远处阴暗的树林边缘，依稀可见几条黑色的人影向前疾奔。河边有两个深棕色皮肤的人站在夕阳下；他们戴着样式奇异的斑纹兽皮头饰，手握长矛，姿态威武，就像两座武士塑

落日余晖里，一个浑身散发着野性气息、妆饰张扬而华丽的女人，正有如一个神秘的幽灵在河畔徘徊。

（陈睿杰　绘）

像似的伫立在那里纹丝不动。落日余晖里，一个浑身散发着野性气息、妆饰张扬而华丽的女人，正有如一个神秘的幽灵在河畔徘徊。

"她身披缀着流苏的斑斓长衣，昂然地踩着河边的泥土缓缓踱步，满身佩戴着的野蛮人的装饰品叮当作响，闪闪发光。她高高地扬着头，头上的发式看上去好像一顶帽盔；她缠着及膝的铜裹腿，手臂上套着金黄的铜钏，深棕色的脸上画着一个大红点，脖子上戴着无数条玻璃球串成的项链；她浑身挂满了许多奇异的物件，有各种各样的符咒，还有巫师的献礼，简直数也数不清。她每踏出一步那些东西都会熠熠发光，不停地摇响。她全身上下的配饰很可能价值好几根象牙。她显得既野蛮又高贵，既狂肆又威严；她的步伐缓慢而沉重，仿佛正在决然地走向一场悲壮的仪式。时空凝滞，万籁俱寂。在这片悲伤的宁静之中，那无边的荒野，那孕育着丰饶而神秘的生命的巨大身躯，似乎正在用沉思的神情凝视着她——宛如正在凝视着自己那同样艰晦而又热烈的灵魂。

"她走到汽船前方，面朝着我们停下了脚步。她那长长的影子直拖到河水边。她的脸上流露出一种悲伤而狂烈的神情，交织着难以压抑的哀恨和无处呼告的痛苦，甚至还有犹疑和恐惧——一个苍凉的结局在等待着她，她似乎已决意奔赴，可终究还是心余力绌，踟蹰难前。但她只是站在那儿，静静地注视着我们。她就像那神秘难测的荒野一样，似乎在沉默地思索着某种不为人知的意图。整整一分钟过去了，她终于向前迈出了一步——随着是一阵轻微的叮当声响，黄灿灿的金属光芒闪亮，缀着流苏的衣袂也随风飘扬——而她却像忽然失去了勇气似的，再次顿住了脚步。我身边的年轻人向她发出一声低吼。

朝圣者们在我身后议论纷纷。她望着我们，几乎目不转睛——仿佛她已将自己的全部生命都倾注在了这一刻的凝视之中。突然间她张开光裸的双臂，笔直地高举过头顶，似乎有一种无法遏止的冲动在驱使着她，要她向苍天发出呼唤。就在这时，迅速弥漫过来的阴影遮蔽了大地，遮蔽了河谷，把那汽船也拢入到它阴暗的怀抱里了。顷刻间，无边的寂静笼罩了一切。

"她慢慢转过身，沿着河岸走进了左边的丛林。她仅仅向着我们回眸一望，随后便消失在了那片昏暗茂密的丛林里。

"'如果她提出要上船来，我想我真的会朝她开枪的，'那个满身补丁的家伙仍然紧张不已。'最近这两个星期，我每天都拼命阻止她，不让她走进那所房子里面去。有一天她还是进去了，就因为我从库房里拣了些碎布头来补衣服，她就借机向我大吵起来。我也不是那么好惹的。至少我那会儿肯定是回嘴了，于是她就好像发疯似的对着库尔茨狂喊了足足一个小时，还时不时用手指点着我。我也听不懂那个部落的土话。好在那天库尔茨大概是病得太难受，没精神搭理她，要不然天知道该怎么收场呢。我真是不明白……不明白。不说啦——反正这些事儿我也搞不懂。啊，算了，一切都已经过去了。'

"这时，我听见帘子后面传来库尔茨低沉的声音：'把我带回去？——其实你只是想把那些象牙带回去吧！快别再说这些话了。哈，你竟会救我。为什么？因为你说——我必须得救你啊，你现在扰乱了我的计划啊。恶心！恶心！哼，我是病了，但是还没病到如你所愿的那种地步。其实什么都无所谓。只是我还没实现我的抱负——我一定会卷土重来的。我得让你们都看看，这里究竟能变成什么样的一番天地。你，还有你那些鸡肠狗肚的蠢主意——你们才是在扰乱我的计划。我一定会

回来的。我……'

"经理走了出来。他伸手揽住我的肩膀把我带到一边，显出一副非常宠信我的模样。'他的状态不好，很不好。他把别人都想得太坏了，'他说。他觉得说完这句话必须得叹息一番，结果顾此失彼，忘记了继续装出那副悲哀的样子。'我们对他已经是仁至义尽了——对吧？所以我也不怕实话实说，库尔茨先生对公司已经是弊大于利了。他不明白，采取强硬手段的时机还不成熟。谨慎些，再谨慎些——这才是我的原则。我们现在还是得谨慎行事。一段时间之内，我们都没法在这儿开展工作了。瞧瞧他干的好事！总而言之，我们的贸易事业蒙受了损失。当然，我不否认他弄到了相当多的象牙——虽然大部分都是化石。我们必须把这批象牙救出去，不惜一切代价——可是你看看我们目前的处境多么危险——为什么会弄成这样？还不全是拜他所赐——因为他的方法不稳妥。''你把这个，'我望着河岸说，'叫作"不稳妥的方法?"''这还用问，'他几乎暴跳起来，'你敢说不是吗？'……'这根本就谈不上什么方法，'过了一会儿，我才喃喃地说。'一点儿也不错，'他立刻转怒为喜。'我早就知道他会蛮干。他这个人完全不懂得审时度势。我有责任向有关方面汇报这一情况。''哦，'我说，'那家伙——他叫什么名字来着？——那个负责做砖的，他会替你写一份娓娓动听的报告的。'他大为惊愕，半晌说不出话来。我感觉自己从未呼吸过如此肮脏龌龊的空气，于是我便在精神上投向了库尔茨来寻求解脱——真的是为了寻求一种解脱。'无论如何，在我心里，库尔茨先生都是一个非常了不起的人物，'我一字一顿地说。他很是吃惊，继而冷厉地瞥了我一眼，语调平静地说，'他曾经是。'然后就背过身去不理睬我了。我就此失了宠。我知道自己已经被划为库尔茨的同伙了，和他一样笃信那种时机还不成熟的方法；而且我这个人也是'不稳妥'的。啊！如果一个人敢于自己选择去堕入哪一个噩梦，他就算得上是条汉子了。

"但是我真正投向的是那片荒野，而非库尔茨。说到库尔茨先生，我不得不承认，他一只脚已经踏进坟墓了。有那么一刻，我甚至觉得自己也被埋进了一座巨大的坟墓之中，那里包藏着无数不可告人的阴暗秘密。在那里，我的鼻端充斥着潮湿的泥土气息，无法承受的重负压迫着我的心口；腐败和堕落无处不在，我看不见它们，却听得到它们得意洋洋的笑声；黑暗沉沉有如无尽的长夜，透不进哪怕一线光明……那个俄国人在我肩膀上轻轻拍了一下。我听见他嗫嚅着，吞吞吐吐地说着什么'水手兄弟——不能瞒你——会给库尔茨先生的名誉抹黑的一些事儿。'我等着他说下去。很显然，在他看来，库尔茨先生和坟墓什么的还不沾边；我简直怀疑他眼中的库尔茨先生就好似神仙一样长生不老。'好啦！'我终于忍不住催他，'快说出来吧。我恰好也是库尔茨先生的一个朋友——差不多算是吧。'

"他一本正经地向我反复声明，要不是因为我俩'是同行'，他一定会让这些事儿烂在自己肚子里，才不会去管什么后果呢。'他怀疑这些白人对他虎视眈眈，不怀好意，似乎要——''你猜对了，'我说。我想起了之前无意中听到的那场谈话。'那个经理认为你真该被绞死。'这句话起初只让我觉得好笑，而他甫一听到，却立刻警惕起来。'那我还是走为上策，'他十分认真地说，'我留在这里也帮不上库尔茨什么忙了，而他们很快就会找到借口对付我。谁能阻止他们呢？啊，离这儿三百英里的地方有个军营。''如果要我说,'我告诉他,'要是你在附近有什么野人朋友的话,你最好还是赶快去找他们。''朋友很多,'他说,'他们都是些头脑简单的人——而且你也知道,我对他们也从无索求。'他站在那里咬了咬嘴唇,又说:'我也不希望这些白人遭遇什么不幸,但是你知道我最在意的是库尔茨先生的名声——而你是我的水手兄弟,所以——'过了一会儿,我对他说,'放心吧。'当时我也不知道自己这句话究竟有几分真,但是我还是对他说,'有我在,库尔茨先生的名声就不会受到损害。'

"于是他压低声音对我说,正是库尔茨亲自下令进攻汽船的。'有时候,一想到那些人将要带他离开这里,他就会变得烦恶暴躁——那个时候他的情绪又发作了。但是我不太明白这些事。我是个头脑简单的人。他想着这样就会把你们吓走——你们就会以为他死了,以后都不会再来找他了。我没有办法阻止他。唉,最近这一个月,我的日子可真难熬啊。''知道了,放心吧,'我说,'他现在已经没事了。''是的——是的,'他喃喃着,显然心里仍有几分犹疑。'谢谢你,'我说,'我会多加留意的。''但是记得别声张——嗯?'他连忙叮嘱了我一句。'那会对他的名声很不利,倘若这儿的什么人——'我郑重地向他保证,我一定谨言慎行。'离这儿不远有一条小船和三个黑人朋友在等我。我得走了。你能不能给我几发马蒂尼·亨利来复枪的子弹?'我说可以,然后就给了他——当然是私底下悄悄地给他的。他对我眨眨眼,然后自己伸手从我兜里抓了一大把烟丝。'只有咱们当水手的才知道——你懂的——顶呱呱的英国烟。'他走到驾驶室的门口又转过身来。'我说,你有没有多余的鞋子给我一双?'他抬起一只脚,'你

瞧。'他的赤脚上只用几根打着结的绳子好像草鞋似的绑了两
个鞋底。我翻出了一双旧鞋,他赞赏地看了一眼就塞在左腋底
下了。他的一只口袋(鲜红色的)鼓鼓囊囊地装满了子弹,另
一只口袋(深蓝色的)露出了那本'陶森的探索',等等。他
似乎颇为满意,觉得自己已经装备精良,完全可以去和那荒野
进行下一场较量了。'啊,我将再也、再也遇不到这样的一个
人了。你真该听听他朗诵的诗歌——而且他告诉我,这都是他
自己写的。诗歌啊!'回想起那些愉快的往事,他神情振奋,
连眼珠子都在闪闪发亮。'哦,他让我大开了眼界!''再见
了!'我说。他和我握了握手,然后就消失在茫茫夜色中了。

他似乎颇为满意,觉得自己已经装备精良,完全可以去和那荒野进行下
一场较量了。

(陈睿杰、张舒婷　绘)

有时候我不禁疑惑，自己是否真的见到过他呢？——是否真的有可能遇见过这样一个奇人！……

"当晚午夜刚过，我忽然醒来。除了头顶几点星光闪烁，整个天地都被巨大的黑幕沉沉地包裹着。他警告的话语在我的脑海里回响；在这暗夜之中，那危险的暗示似乎也变得愈发真实迫人，于是我再也坐不住，索性起身四处查看一番。山顶上燃着一大堆篝火，火光忽明忽暗地映着贸易站仓库歪斜的一角。一个公司代理人带着我们雇佣的几个黑人在放哨，他们全副武装，寸步不离地看守着那些象牙。然而在那森林深处，峥嵘的山峰犹如黑色巨擘，无数红色的微光在起伏的峰峦间明灭闪烁——那显然是库尔茨的信徒们在他们的扎营地燃起的篝火。此刻，他们也正怀着不安的心情彻夜守望。一面大鼓发出单调的咚咚声，使夜空中充满了沉闷的轰响和经久不息的震颤。在那黑如漆、密如墙的丛林后面，许多人正各自吟唱着一些怪异的咒语；这持续不断的吟诵声就像嗡嗡离巢的蜂群一样萦绕在我耳畔，对我那本就不太清醒的头脑产生了一种奇特的催眠作用。当时我似乎是倚在船边的栏杆上，昏昏沉沉地堕入了梦乡。后来，一阵突然迸发的狂啸，仿佛一种被压抑已久的神秘愤怒如洪水决堤般一倾而出，又如万里晴空骤然炸响的一声惊雷，令我昏沉恍惚的神智刹那间通亮清明，如梦初醒。凄厉的长啸戛然而止，而那低沉的嗡嗡声却仍在继续着。那是一种能够听得到的寂静，如同轻风的抚慰，令人感到心神安宁。我不经意地瞥了一眼那间小小的舱房。屋里的灯盏依然亮着，可是库尔茨却不见了。

"如果我那时相信自己的眼睛，我一定会当场惊叫起来。但是我根本就不相信这是真的——这简直太不可思议了。事实上，我那时被这种无形无质、全然抽象的恐怖骇得魂飞天外，连浑身的力气似乎都被一下子抽空了——尽管眼下并没有任何明显迫近的危险。一种极其强烈的情绪瞬间席卷了我，那就好像——应该如何形容它呢？——那是一种突如其来的精神打击，就好像有人把一件狰狞怪诞、令人从灵魂深处感到无比憎恶和抗拒的东西，猝不及防地塞到了我的手上。当然了，这种剧烈的情绪转瞬即逝，随之而来的就是那种众所周知的普通的危机感，我似乎已经预见到了一系列致命的危险——一场近在眼前的突袭，一场你死我活的搏杀，或者别的什么类似的情形——相比之下，对这些具体状况的预测倒让我乐于接受，而且使我逐渐平静下来。实际上，很快我就恢复了镇定，因而并没有大声告警。

"甲板上，一个代理人裹着一件系扣的长外套，正在离我不到三英尺远的一把椅子上面呼呼大睡。刚才的那一阵叫嚣声并没有把他吵醒，他还在轻轻地打着鼾；我也不去惊扰他的好梦，自己悄悄跳到了岸上。我没有出卖库尔茨先生——上天让我永远不能出卖他——命中注定我必须忠于我所选择的噩梦。我迫不及待地想要和这幽灵来一场单独的较量。直到今天我仍然不知道，自己为什么会那样满心妒忌，不愿与任何人分享那个夜里旷古绝今的黑暗一刻。

"一踏上河岸，我就有了发现——深草丛中有一道挺宽的压痕。我还记得我当时很得意地对自己说：'他没法走路——他是在地上爬着往前挪的。我就快要抓住他了。'荒草沾满了露水，湿漉漉的。我紧攥双拳，大步向前疾行。我当时似乎还想象着自己正扑倒在他身上，按着他一顿痛揍。似乎是这样的吧，现在我也说不清了。那时候，我脑子里走马灯似的转了许多愚蠢的念头。那个腿上卧着一只猫、手中织着黑毛线的老女人也闯进了我的脑海——真是难以想象，在这样一件壮举的另一端，竟然如此不合时宜地坐着那样一个人。我还看到那些朝圣者站成一排，他们把温彻斯特步枪顶在胯上，向半空中不停地倾泻着铅弹。我心想，我也许永远都回不到那条汽船上了，我想象着自己孤身一人、手无寸铁地被遗弃在丛林里，直到须发苍苍，老死在无人知晓的荒野中——总之尽是些这类乱七八糟的念头。我还记得，我把那咚咚的鼓声错当成了自己的心跳，而且还颇感欣慰——因为它的声音又规律又平稳。

"我沿着草丛里的痕迹紧追不舍——有时候也停下脚步，倾听周围的动静。夜色清朗，天空一片深蓝，星光和草叶上的露珠相映生辉；抬眼望去，四周都是些静静伫立着的黑影。我觉得我看到了前方有什么东西在蠕动。那个晚上，我莫名其妙地对任何事都觉得胸有成竹。于是我绕过了草地上的痕迹，绕开去跑了大半个圆圈（我确信自己当时一边跑，一边止不住地暗自发笑），这样我就可以跑到那个蠕动着的东西前面——如果我没有看错的话。我在包抄库尔茨，就像在玩一场小孩子之间的游戏。

"我迎面撞在了他的身上。要不是他先听到我的脚步声，而且及时站了起来，我很可能就被他一下子绊倒了。他瘦长的身形摇摇晃晃地站在那里，显得苍白而又模糊，就好像从地底下冒出来的一股烟雾，朦朦胧胧、无声无息地飘在我面前。我身后的树丛深处隐约现出一些火光，还传来许多人低声说话的声音。我刚才非常机智地截住了他；可是当我真正挡在他面前的时候，我才好像幡然醒悟了过来，意识到自己已经陷入了何等危险的境地。危机迫在眼前。要是他叫喊出声怎么办？尽管他已经连站都站不稳了，可是在他的声音里却还蕴藏着相当大的能量。'走开——赶快躲起来，'他用那种低沉有力的声音说。那声音真让我有些胆寒。我朝后边瞥了一眼，发现最近的一堆篝火离我们还不到三十码。一条黑色的人影站立起来，黝黑的长腿迈开步子，修长的胳膊来回摆动，在那些火光之间行走着。那条人影的头顶上有两只角——也许是羚羊角。毫无疑问，这个人不是术士就是巫师；在我看来，他的样子就像鬼怪一样骇人。'你知道自己在做什么吗？'我低声说。'完全知道，'他提高嗓门说出了这短短一句话——那声音在我听来似乎很遥远，却又很响亮，就好像是从话筒之中传出来的一声呼喊。我心中暗想，如果在这里吵嚷起来，那我们就全完了。很显然，现在并不是用拳头解决问题的好时机；更何况，我也根本不可能狠下心去殴打这个风烛飘摇的可怜人——这个四处流浪、饱经磨难的幽灵。'这一去，你就不再是你了，'我说——'永远不再是原来的你了。'你知道，有时候人是会情急智生的。我这句话完全击中了他的内心。虽然事实上，他那时候早就已经迷失了自我，彻底沦丧得无药可救了；但是从我说出这句话的那一刻起，我们就成了一生一世的知己——我们相知相惜的感情甚至跨越了生死的界限，比一生一世更加长久——一直绵延到时间的尽头。

"'我还有很多宏伟的计划，'他犹豫着喃喃低语。'我知道，'我说，'但是你如果喊出声来，我就用这个砸烂你的头——'我四下一瞧，却发现地上既没有木棍也没有石块。于是我改口说，'我就一把掐死你。''我的伟大事业才刚刚开始，'他的话似是分辩又似是恳求，其中充满了期待、感伤以及强烈的不甘，顿时让我觉得整个身体连血都冷透了。'可是现在，全都因为这个卑鄙愚蠢的小人——''无论如何，你在欧洲已被奉为英雄。'我斩钉截铁地告诉他。你们知道，我当然并不想真的掐死他——实际上，那样做也根本没有任何好处。我只是极力想要打破那道魔咒——那来自荒野的巨大而无声的蛊惑；似乎正是那诱人的魔咒，唤醒了他早已遗落在记忆深处的野蛮本性，让他重新记起了过去曾经饱餍的那种恣肆的激情，从而把他拉入了荒野那无情的怀抱。我相信，正是这魔咒驱使着他一路向前，来到森林边，走进原始的丛莽中；驱使着他奔向了那闪烁着篝火、回荡着隆隆鼓声和奇异的嗡嗡诵祷声的地方——正是这魔咒诱出了他灵魂中最狂纵的一面，让他胸中的欲念无限地膨胀，膨胀——直到天地不容，神怒人怨。你看到了吗，当时我面临的最大的危险并不是吃上一记闷棍——当然了，被袭击的危险无时不在——而是我正在试图说服一个心如铁石的人。无论是用至善的上帝来感召，还是用至恶的魔鬼来恐吓，都全然无法打动他的心。我甚至不得不和那些黑人一样，唯有向他祈求——向他那崇高、孤傲而又无比堕落的灵魂发出祈求。我深知，在这世上他早已无所畏惧，在他眼中既没有头上的青天，也没有脚下的地狱；他已经看透一切，超脱了尘世。他早就把脚下踏着的大地给一脚踢开了。这个可恶的家伙！他把整个大地都踢成碎片了。他已经游离于这个世界之外，就算是在他面前的我，此刻也不知道究竟是飘在空中，还是立在地上。我一直在絮絮地复述我们之间都说了些什么——重复着我们讲过的一些话语——可那又有什么用呢？那都是些普普通通的日常言语而已——每天醒来我们都使用这些熟悉而又模糊的声音彼此交流。但是这些声音究竟意味着什么？在我看来，在这些话语的背后隐匿着可怕的暗示，有如迷梦中恍惚之所闻、惊魇中癫狂之所呓。灵魂！如果说有人真正曾经与一个灵魂搏斗过，那就是我。但我绝不是在与一个疯人争执。信不信由你，他的心智全然清醒冷静——是的，他的眼中只有他自己，他对自我的高度关注已经达到了匪夷所思的境地，但他仍是清醒的；而我唯一的机会就在于此——那时我无法当场结果他的性命，因为那肯定会发出响声，惊动旁

无论是用至善的上帝来感召，还是用至恶的魔鬼来恐吓，都全然无法打动他的心。我甚至不得不和那些黑人一样，唯有向他祈求——向他那崇高、孤傲而又无比堕落的灵魂发出祈求。

（郑易淇　绘）

人。可是他的灵魂却已经疯了。由于长时间孤独地待在荒野中，它已经彻底看透了它自己。天哪！我告诉你们，它确实是疯了。也许这就是我命中的孽缘吧——我不得不去经历这一场严酷的考验，窥见他灵魂深处的隐秘。他临终时喊出的那句肺腑之言胜过任何雄辩，足以让你心中对于整个人类的信念瞬间崩塌。他也在和自己作斗争——这一切我全都听在耳中，看在眼里。一个不知道节制、失去了信仰、也根本无所畏惧的不可思议的灵魂，在那一刻卸下了它所有的神秘外衣，赤裸裸地悬呈在我面前——它甚至仍在徒劳地和自己搏斗着，至死方休。我倒始终还能保持着清醒的头脑；可是，当我最后让他躺回到那张长榻上时，我擦了擦额头，两条腿瑟瑟地抖个不停，仿佛刚才下山时背上负荷了千钧的重载。而事实上，我只不过是搀扶着他，让他枯瘦的胳膊搭在我的肩颈上罢了；而且他的体重已经和一个孩子相差无几了。

　　"第二天中午时分，我们起航离开了那儿。我一直都清楚地知道，在那树木的帷幕后面隐藏着无数野人；此时他们如洪水般从树林中涌了出来，顷刻间，河岸边的空地上，附近的山坡上，到处都布满了古铜色的、呼吸起伏着的赤裸身躯。汽船继续向前开了一会儿，然后向下游掉转头来——上千双眼睛都紧盯着这个噼噼啪啪打着水转身的凶猛水怪，看着它用可怕的尾巴拍打着河水，向半空中喷吐出一团又一团的黑烟。在靠近河边的人群前面站着三个人，他们全身从头到脚都涂满了鲜艳的红色泥土，正急促地迈着大步走来走去。当我们的船又开到他们跟前的时候，他们面朝着河水用力跺脚，摇晃着艳红色的身体，不停地点着他们戴了兽角的头；他们朝着这个可怕的水怪挥舞着一束黑色的羽毛，还有一张拖着尾巴的肮脏斑驳的兽皮——那样子就好像一只干瘪的葫芦；他们隔一会儿就齐声喊出一连串奇特的声音，根本不像是任何人类的语言；而那从他们身后的人群中发出、间或被猛然打断的低沉的喃喃声，则像是在用某种邪异的祈祷来对他们做着回应。

"我们把库尔茨抬进了驾驶室，那里空气更新鲜些。他躺在长椅上，透过打开的百叶窗凝望着外面。只见人群如潮水般刷然分开，那个顶着头盔般的发式、面颊棕黄的女人快步走出，来到了河岸上。她伸出双手，大声喊了几句什么，于是那狂野的人群马上响应着她，爆发出一阵音节清晰、节奏急促、让人几乎透不过气的齐声嘶吼。

"'你听得懂他们在喊什么吗？'我问道。

"他仍是越过我望着窗外，炽热的目光充满怀恋，脸上露出怅惘与憎恨交织的神情。他没有回答，可是我看见一丝微笑，一丝含意不明的微笑，浮现在他那已经没有血色的嘴唇上；过了片刻，那嘴唇痉挛似的抽动了一下。'我会听不懂？'他喘着气慢慢说。而这寥寥的几个字，竟像是某种超自然的力量从他的心里面生生撕扯出来的。

"我拉了一下汽笛的拉绳。我之所以这样做，是因为我看到甲板上那些朝圣者们都已经拿出枪来，摆开架势，准备好好取乐一番了。这一声突如其来的尖啸在岸边那雁翼形的队伍中激起了一阵骚动，令他们不能自已地恐慌起来。'别拉！别把他们给吓跑了呀！'甲板上有人很不高兴地朝我大喊。我充耳不闻，一下接一下地猛拉汽笛。人群散乱了，他们开始逃跑；他们有的跳了起来，有的蹲下身子，有的到处乱窜，都竭力想要躲开那伴随着一声声巨嚣临空而来的恐怖。身上涂满红泥的三个人，脸朝下直挺挺地趴在河岸边，就好像已经被枪打死了似的。只有那个野蛮而又高贵的女人没有退缩；她跟在汽船后面，隔着那条阴沉地闪着波光的河流，悲哀地向我们举起了赤裸的双臂。

"这时，甲板上的那帮蠢材开始了他们无聊的取乐。硝烟弥漫开来。我的眼前蒙上了一片惨白，什么也看不见了。

"褐色的浊流从那黑暗之心急速地流出来，以两倍于来时的速度载着我们冲向入海口；库尔茨的生命也在迅速流失，就好像退落的潮水从他的心口汩汩流出，消逝在无情的时间之海。那位经理神色平静，他现在已经高枕无忧了；他用一种意味深长而又心满意足的眼神瞥了我们两人一眼：这件'事情'已经如他所愿那样地了结了。我知道，用不了多久我就会变成'不稳妥的方法'的唯一拥趸了。朝圣者们也对我冷眼相向，我已经被他们——权且这么说吧——看作与这个死人是一伙的了。说来奇怪，我心里竟也默认了这种始料未及的伙伴关系；在被这些卑鄙而又贪婪的魑魅魍魉侵袭的黑暗土地上，我选择了这个强加给我的噩梦。

"库尔茨开始对我讲话。是这个声音！就是这个声音！这声音一直在深沉地回响，直到他生命的最后一刻。他曾经用宏伟华丽的辩才掩盖了自己内心的黑暗和荒芜，而现在，虽然他已不再拥有这种雄辩的激情，但是他的声音依旧响亮。啊，他的灵魂在挣扎！如今，他那疲惫衰竭的头脑已经如同繁华凋零之后凄凉的废墟，萦绕着种种幽灵般的幻象——然而他雄辩的才华仍放射着不可磨灭的崇高光辉，让那些财富的幻影、名望的幻影全都卑微地遮隐在这光芒之下，有如黯淡的群星追随着太阳旋转。我的未婚妻、我的贸易站、我的事业、我的理想——他偶尔会带着高尚的情感谈起这些话题。原先那个库尔茨的幽魂时常回来探望如今这个缠绵病榻的库尔茨——他单薄而又羸弱，只剩下一副空荡荡的皮囊；而这皮囊也即将迎来它最后的命运，被埋葬到这片原始大地的一个土丘之中。这个幽魂对于它所曾洞悉的神秘世界抱着复杂的情感，其中交织着最疯狂的爱与最彻骨的恨；这极致的爱与恨相执不下，争斗不休——它们都想要占有这个灵魂——这个饱尝了原始的激情、渴望着浮华的名声、醉心于虚假的荣耀、谋求着徒有其表的成功与权势的灵魂。

"有时候他天真单纯得就像个孩子，简直让人可笑。他梦想着到一个未名之地成就一番伟业；而当他从这荒蛮的地方归来之时，列国的王侯都在火车站上迎候他的凯旋。'你要让他们看到，你能够为他们带来无穷的财富；这样他们就会对你心悦诚服，不吝赞赏，'他这样对我说。'当然了，你还得不忘初心——善良的初心——并且始终如一。'一段段河道，如出一辙；一个个河湾，大同小异。这古老的河流和岸边葱郁了几个世纪的原始森林，从我们的船边滑过；它们平静地注视着这个来自另一个世界的肮脏碎片，这个带来了变革、征服、贸易、屠戮和福音的先驱。我手握船舵，观察着前方。'把窗户关上，'有一天库尔茨忽然说，'看着外面的情景，实在让我受不了。'我照做了。船舱里一阵沉默。'等着吧，总有一天，我还会让你在我面前颤栗的！'他朝着那片看不见的荒野放声大喊。

"我们半途抛锚了——我早料到会这样——于是不得不停靠在一个小岛上进行修理。这场耽搁破天荒地让库尔茨的信心产生了动摇。有一天早晨，他给了我一包文件和一张照片——这些东西全用一根鞋带捆在一起。'替我保管它们，'他说，

'那个卑鄙的蠢材（他指的是经理），要是我看不见，他一定会翻遍我的箱子。'那天下午我又去看他。他闭着眼睛仰面躺着，我就一声不响地退了出来。这时我听到他喃喃地说，'活要活得光明磊落，死，死要死得……'我静静地听着。但是里面再没有声音了。他是在睡梦中排练一场演说吗？还是在重复着报纸上的一段文章呢？他过去一直在为报纸撰稿，而且还打算继续写下去，'为了向人们宣扬我的思想，这是一种责任。'

"他本身就是一种黑暗，任何人也无法看透他。我望着他，就像俯视着一个躺在深崖绝壁之下的人，那里是光明永不降临的所在。但是我并没有多少时间去照顾他。因为我正帮着轮机工拆卸漏水的气缸，扳直弯曲了的连接轴，或者干些其他类似的活儿。我每天都像是生活在水深火热的炼狱里，满眼都是我痛恨的那些东西——铁锈，锯末，螺帽，螺栓，扳手，锤子，棘轮钻——而它们也不听我使唤。幸好船上带上了个小小的锻铁炉，我便去照管它；我被困在这堆破铜烂铁里面，整天忙得疲惫不堪——除非两条腿抖得站不住了，才能歇一会儿。

"一天傍晚，我举着蜡烛走进驾驶室，听见他用微微颤抖的声音说，'我正躺在这片黑暗之中，等待着死亡。'我不禁吃了一惊。我把蜡烛举到他眼前大约一英尺的地方，强使自己低声回答道，'哦，快别胡说了！'我俯身去看他；下一秒钟，我呆呆地站在那儿，就好像身体一下子被木楔钉住了似的。

"我从来没有见到过任何情景，能够比拟当时在他脸上浮现的种种变化；我真希望自己永远不会再见到这样的情景。啊，我不是心生恻隐了，而是被他脸上的表情深深地吸引住了。就好像蒙着的面纱忽然被人揭去，在他那象牙般苍白的脸上，高傲沉郁、刚毅从容、恐惧畏缩的神情交错闪现，最终汇成了一种万念俱灰的极度绝望。他是不是在这个大彻大悟的神圣时刻，细细地重温了过去那充满了欲望、诱惑和沉沦的生活？他似乎是对着眼前的某个阴影，抑或是某个幻象，用尽气力发出了两声细若游丝的呼喊；他喊道——

"'可怕！可怕啊！'

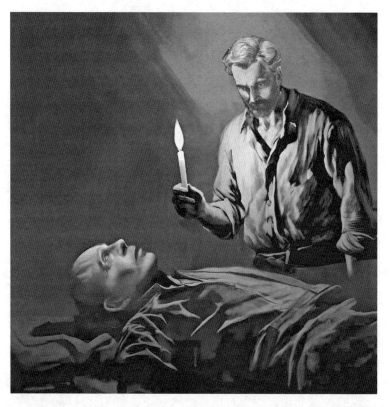

他似乎是对着眼前的某个阴影，抑或是某个幻象，用尽气力发出了两声细若游丝的呼喊；他喊道——"可怕！可怕啊！"

（张舒婷　绘）

"我吹灭蜡烛，离开了那个房间。朝圣者们正在餐室里吃晚饭，我也在经理对面的位置坐下。他抬起头向我投来询问的眼光，我装作没看见，不予理会。他身子往后一靠，神色平静；在他脸上又露出了那种独特的微笑，掩藏着他心底里深不可测的卑鄙。小苍蝇如雨点般不断地飞来，它们聚集在灯上和桌布上，落到我们的脸上和手上。突然，经理的听差把他那傲慢的黑脑袋从门缝里伸进来，用一种刺耳的轻蔑口气说：

"'库尔茨先生——他死啦。'

"朝圣者们全都冲出去看了。我连头都没抬一下，继续吃着我的晚饭。我知道，他们一定都认为我冷酷无情，毫无人性。我仍一动不动地坐在那儿，可是我已经吃不下什么了。餐室里有一盏灯——它意味着光明，你们明白吗——而在那外边，则到处遍布着可怕的黑暗。我再也没有走近那个卓异不凡的人；他的灵魂已经为自己在这个世界上的全部经历下了论断。那个声音已经永远消逝了。那么他还留下了什么呢？啊，我当然知道。第二天，那些朝圣者们就把那样东西埋进了涌流着黄泉的泥穴里。

"那个时候，他们也几乎埋葬了我。

"然而，如你所见，那时我并没有追随库尔茨而去。我没有。我继续活着，活下来直到做完那场噩梦，这样才能再一次向库尔茨表达我的忠诚。这就是命运啊，我的命运！呵，人生是个多么滑稽可笑的玩意儿——无情的逻辑做出了种种神秘的安排，而最后的一切终究却只是镜花水月，过眼云烟。你从中得到了什么？最多也就是看清了你自己——而且已为时太晚——你收获的只不过是绵绵无尽的悔憾。我也曾和死神较量过，而那简直就是你能想象得到的最枯燥乏味的角斗了——周围笼罩着一片渺渺茫茫的灰暗，你的脚下无处托足，你的身畔空无一物；既无人观战，也无人呐喊；那里根本没有什么荣耀可言，你既没有强烈的求胜欲，也没有太多对于失败的恐惧；在这样一种不温不火、充满疑惑的病态氛围里，你不怎么相信自己代表的就是正义，更不相信你的对手会安什么好心。如果说这就是至高的智慧，那么生命这个未解的谜题，一定比我们所想象的更为宏大和神秘。我几乎就要藉着这个最后的机会说出我的论断了；可是在张开口的那一刻，我才羞愧地发现自己竟无话可说。就是因为这个原因，我才认定库尔茨是个了不起的人物。他有自己的话要说。而且他已经说出来了。我也曾从生死的边缘向彼岸窥视过，所以我比其他任何人更能懂得，他那凝视的目光意味着什么。那目光已经看不见蜡烛燃烧的火焰，但却宽广得足以包纳整个宇宙，锐利得足以穿透所有在黑暗中跳动着的心。他总结了一切——并且给出了论断：'可怕啊！'他确实是个非同一般的人物。归根结底，这一句话道出了他内心深处的信念。它坦率而又坚定；它轻若息吹，却激荡着叛逆和反抗的强音；它揭开了真相的一线面纱，却让人骇然窥见了一张狰狞可怖的面孔——那是欲望和憎恨的奇异结合。然而，在我脑海中最清晰的记忆，并不是我自己曾经濒临的绝境——在一片悠悠荡荡的灰色幻景之中，肉身在痛苦地叫嚣；而魂灵却仿佛飘忽其上，带着一种漫不经心的冷蔑，俯瞰着世间万物如烟云般倏然而逝——甚至连痛苦本身也一同归于寂灭。不！我似乎亲身体验过的，完全是他那时濒临的绝境。是的，他已经迈出了他最后的一步，他已经跨过了那道生死的边界；而我却得以在稍窥彼岸之后，收回了自己犹豫不决的脚步。也许，我们之间最大的差别就在于此；也许，一切的智慧、一切的真理、一切的诚挚，全都凝聚在我们迈入幽冥世界时那微不可察的一瞬间。也许真的就是这样啊！我常想，到了那个时刻，我的总结不应该仅是一句无谓的鄙薄。他的呼喊显然更好——好得多。那是掷地有声的判决，是人间道义的胜利——它是用无数次失败、难以言说的恐惧和阴暗堕落的缩足作为代价换来的。但那到底是一种胜利！这就是我将永远忠于库尔茨的原因——我将超越时光的流逝和死亡的阻遏，永生永世追随于他。甚至在很久以后，当我的耳畔再次响起他的声音——不是他曾亲口对我说过的话语，而是他那水晶般清澈、高崖般巍峨的灵魂用他恣肆的雄辩在我心中激起的阵阵波澜——我仍然对他怀抱着至死不渝的忠诚。

"是的，他们没有埋掉我。尽管我带着一种不寒而栗的惊异隐约地记起，有那么一段时日，我就像穿行在一个既无希望也无欲求、空洞而又恍惚的世界中。我发现自己又回到了那个坟墓般的城市，满怀憎厌地看着人们行色匆匆地穿过大街小巷，只为了骗取彼此的些许钱财；他们饕餮着俗鄙的饭食，狂饮着肮脏的啤酒，做着些毫无意义的愚蠢的美梦。他们就好像一群入侵者，时常闯进来干扰我的思想。对我来说，他们的生活充满了令人愤慨的虚伪，他们根本就不了解生命真正的意义，因为我确信他们不可能知道我所知道的那些事情。他们在绝对的安全保障之下忙着各自的生计，他们的言行神态也殊无可道之处；然而在我眼里，他们就好像一头头蠢猪，站在巨大的危险面前还浑然不知，洋洋得意，简直是愚钝得令人发指。我并不想走过去教训他们几句，但是面对着这些自命不凡的蠢猪，我却实在忍不住想要纵声大笑。我敢说，我当时的身体状况并不太好。我跟跟跄跄地奔走在大街上——要办的事儿太多了——我还得努力牵扯着嘴角，在那些非常可敬的上流人物面前保持微笑。我不是在为自己的言行找借口——但是那会儿我的体温几乎就没有正常过。我亲爱的姨妈嘱咐我要'养养元气'，但是她好像完全搞错了状况。我并不需要养什么元气，反倒是我的想象力正在渴求着慰藉。我一直保存着库尔茨给我的那些信件，不知道该拿它们怎么办。他的母亲不久前逝世了，据说生前一直是由他的未婚妻在病床前照料的。有一天，一个脸颊刮得精光、戴一副金丝眼镜的男人前来拜访我。这个人官味十足地问了我许多问题；一开始他还拐弯抹角，后来则不失礼貌地强硬起来，向我逼问一些所谓'文件'的下落。他的话并没有让我觉得吃惊，先前我就已经为这事和经理吵过两回了。我拒绝把那个包裹交给他，哪怕是最小的一张纸片也不行；对这个戴眼镜的人，我也是同样的态度。他的脸色变得越来越阴森，最后凶神恶煞地告诉我说公司有权掌握关于自己'领地'的一切情报。他说，'由于库尔茨先生的卓越才能，以及他所涉足的地方的恶劣环境，他对于那片未经探索的无名之地必然有着非常全面而又独到的了解。因此——'我明确地告诉他，库尔茨先生所知道的，无论多么广泛，都和商业贸易或者公司管理不相干。接着，他又把科学研究搬出来当幌子。'那将是一个无法估量的损失，如果……'等等，等等。我把那份关于'肃清野蛮习俗'的报告交给他；当然，写在最后那一页的附记早已被我撕去了。他迫不及待地一把抓了过去，但看完后却一脸轻蔑，对它嗤之以鼻。'我们想要得到的东西可不是这个，'他说。'那你也别想得到其他东西了，'我说，'剩下的全都是私人信件。'他嘴里威胁着说什么'那就等着法庭见'，悻悻地走了；我从此再也没有见到过他。刚过了两天，又一个人来找我，自称是库尔茨的表兄。他急切地对我说，他想知道他这位亲爱的表弟临终时的详细情形。他在不经意间向我说起，库尔茨原本曾是一位了不起的音乐家。'以他的天资，他本可以取得辉煌的成就。'那个人说。他灰色的长头发披在油腻的外套领子上，我想，他准是一位管风琴手。我没有理由怀疑他的话；可是直到今天我也说不清楚库尔茨的职业到底是什么，或者他到底有没有过固定的职业——他最大的才能又是什么。我曾经认为他是个经常给报纸写写文章的画家，又或者是一个擅长绘画的报刊记者——可是，甚至他的这位表兄（这家伙和我谈话的时候一直吸着鼻烟）也无法确切地告诉我，他过去究竟是干什么的。他是一位无所不能的天才——在这一点上我完全同意那位老伙计的意见。说到这里，他拿出一块很大的棉布手绢用力擤了一下鼻子，然后就颤巍巍地向我告辞了，顺便带走了一些家信和无关紧要的便函。最后，一个非常想要知道他那位'亲爱的同事'的生逢遭际的记者也来了。这位客人告诉我，库尔茨真正从事的工作，应该说是'为大众发声'的政治活动。他长着一对笔直的浓眉，又粗又硬的头发剃得很短，眼镜用一条宽带子拴着；他一时谈得兴起，竟把他的看法也向我一股脑全倒出来了。他说，库尔茨在写作上还欠点火候——'可是天哪，那个人的口才是多么的好啊！多少大众集会都被他煽动得群情激昂。他有信念——你看出来了吗？——他有坚定的信念。他能让自己相信任何事情——这世上的任何事情。他要是参加极端的党派，一定会成了不起的领袖。''哪个党派？'我问道。'任何党派都成，'那人回答说，'他是一个——一个——极端主义者。'难道我不也是这样以为的吗？于是我表示同意。他忽然心血来潮，好奇地问我知不知道'到底是什么力量诱惑了他，让他跑到那个地方去的？''我知道的，'我说着就把那份著名的报告递给他，希望他——如果觉得合适的话——就拿去发表。他迅速通览了全文，嘴里还低声诵读着。最后他说'这东西能行。'然后拿着这份战利品快步离开了。

"这样一来，我手里就只剩下薄薄的一小叠信件和那姑娘的一张肖像照了。我觉得她很美——我的意思是，她脸上的神情很美。我知道光线的明暗可以制造某种错觉；但是现在我觉得，无论如何处理光线或者调整姿态，都不可能仅仅凭借技术，而在画面上呈现出如她这般流露着自然和纯真的面容。她仿佛已经准备好聆听——她敞开了心扉，献出了真诚，甚至愿意自我牺牲。我决定去找她，把她的照片和那些信件亲手交还给她。由于好奇吗？是的；可也许还夹杂着别的一些情感。库尔茨曾经拥有的一切——他的灵魂，他的肉体，他的贸易站，他的计划，他的象牙，他的事业——全都已经从我的手上交了出去。现在，剩下的只有对他的记忆和他的未婚妻了——我愿意把这些也交出去，交给过去——我要亲手将他留给我的一切，全都交付给我们共同的最终命运，那就是——'遗忘'。我无意为自己辩解。我并不清楚自己想要的到底是什么。或许是一种下意识的忠诚引发的冲动，又或许是隐藏在人类天性中的某种荒谬的使命感。我不知道。我也说不清。但我还是去了。

"我原以为，对他的记忆就像是堆积在每个人生命中的对其他逝者的记忆一样——只不过是那些幽魂在人间最后的短暂时刻，在我们脑海中留下的混沌模糊的映像罢了。然而，当我走过那条有如洒扫过的墓园甬道一样肃穆幽静的小巷，穿过街道两边耸峙的楼宇，站在那扇高大沉重的门前时，我却看到了一个幻影——我看见他坐在担架上，贪婪地张大着嘴，好像要把整个地球，连同地球上所有的人类，一口全都吞下去。那一刻，他仿佛又在我面前活了过来，和过去一样栩栩如生——那是一个无餍地追求着浮华的外表、探索着可怕的现实的幽魂，一个比黑夜更加黑暗的影子，雍容尔雅地披着雄辩那瑰丽的外衣。这个幻影好像跟着我一同走进了那座华厦——随之而来的，还有那担架，那些抬着担架的幢幢鬼影，那些对他唯命是从的崇拜者汇聚成的狂野人群，那昏暗的丛林，幽深的河湾之间那段闪烁着波光的河道，以及夜色里咚咚的鼓声——那均匀而又低沉的节奏，就像是心脏的搏动——那是征服了一切的黑暗之心在跳动。这是荒野最终获胜的时刻；在这场复仇的狂暴冲荡之中，我仿佛正在孤独地战斗——为了拯救另一个不幸的灵魂，我唯有独自承受来自荒野的一切。我想起了他在那里对我说的话。在那个遥远的地方，在那富于忍耐的丛林里，那些头上戴着角的身影在火光的映照下蠢蠢欲动；他断断续续的话语又重新回响在我的耳畔，它们简洁得令人害怕，隐含着不祥的预兆。我想起了他哀痛的祈求，卑劣的威胁，他的永不知足的邪恶欲望，还有他灵魂中的虚鄙、痛苦和暴风雨般激荡着的愤怒。后来，我好像又看到了他沉静、倦怠的样子。有一天，他强打起精神对我说，'现在你看到的这些象牙，实际上都是我的。公司没有给过我一分钱。我自己一个人过着刀口舐血的日子，真正是九死一生，才把它们收集起来的。不过，恐怕他们还是会把这些象牙据为己有。唔，这事儿很棘手。你认为我应该怎么办——反抗吗？嗯？我想要的仅仅是公道而已。'……他只不过想要个公道而已——仅仅是讨个公道。站在二楼的一扇红木门前，我按响了门铃。当我等待的时候，他仿佛就从那玻璃般光亮的门板里凝望着我——他的目光无限宽广而又深邃邈远，好似要拥抱整个宇宙——同时也谴责和憎恨着世间的一切。我又听到了他那时耳语般微弱的呼喊，'可怕！可怕啊！'

"黄昏缓缓降临。我在一间高大的会客厅里等待着。三扇长长的落地窗直插穿顶，如同三根蒙着帷幔的巨大的廊柱，隐隐透出暗淡的天光。房间里的陈设渐渐变得轮廓朦胧，只有镀金的桌腿和椅背在熠熠闪烁，显露出它们弯曲的线条。高高的大理石壁炉泛着肃穆的冷白。一架大钢琴沉重庄严地立在角落，平整的表面闪着黑锃锃的亮泽，看上去就像是一口打磨过的阴沉的石棺。一扇高大的门打开——又关上了。我站了起来。

"她走向前来，一袭黑衣，面色苍白，从黑暗中飘了过来。她仍在服丧。距他去世已经一年多了，死讯传来也已经一年多了；但是她似乎要永远铭记着他，永远为他服丧下去。她握住了我的双手，轻轻地说：'我早就听说你会来。'我发现她已不再那么年轻——我是说她不再像个小姑娘了。她已经完全成熟了，这种成熟足以容纳忠贞、信仰和一切苦难。房间里似乎更昏暗了；这个郁云密布的黄昏，好像已经把所有凄凉黯淡的光都投在了她的额头上。她淡金色的头发，苍白的脸庞，纯净的眉宇，仿佛都被一个灰暗的光环笼罩着；而她那双深黑色的眼睛正透过那光环望着我。她的目光坦率，深沉；她既相信着自己，也信任着他人。她高昂着悲伤的脸，就像是为那悲伤而骄傲，仿佛她要说，'我——只有我，才知道怎样以配得上他的方式来悼念他。'可是还没等到我们的握手结束，她的脸上就流露出了难以自抑的哀伤，摧肝断肠。于是我便知道，时间也无法动摇她的感情——即使岁月流逝，沧海桑田，她的忠

贞只属于他。对她来说，他永远死在昨天。哦，天哪！她给我
带来了如此强烈的震撼，以至于我似乎也感到，他就是在昨天
才死去——不，他就是在这一刻才死去。我在这个瞬间同时看
到了她和他——他的死亡和她的哀伤——我看见了她在他临终
那一刻的哀伤。你们理解吗？我看见了，我也听见了——他们
两个人生死相随，永不分开。她曾经悲叹着说，'可是我活了
下来。'而这时，我那谛听着的耳朵似乎清楚地听到了他的声
音；在她痛不欲生的绝望悲诉中，我听到了他的那一句论断，
那轻若耳语的永恒的诅咒。我手足无措了，我不禁自问，我究
竟到这里来干什么？我心中升起一股恐慌，仿佛我无意中闯进
了一个充满了非人的残酷和荒唐的神秘之地。她示意我坐下。
我们俩都坐了下来。我把那包东西轻轻地放在桌子上，她把她
的手放在了上面……在悲哀的气氛中沉默了一会，她终于低声
说道，'您很了解他吧？'

"'在那种地方，我们很快就混熟了，'我说。'我对他的
了解，不亚于你所能想象的世上任何知己挚友。'

"'那么您也一定会崇拜他，'她说。'凡是了解他的人，都
不可能不崇拜他。不是吗？'

"'他是个很了不起的人，'我迟疑地说。她用恳求的目光
直直地望定我，似乎在期待着从我口中吐出更多关于他的话
语；于是我只得继续说下去，'所以了解他的人不可能不——'

"'爱他，'她迫不及待地替我把话说完。这使我不禁骇
然，一时间竟说不出话来。'太对了！太对了！可是您想一想，
谁也不会比我更了解他！他已经把自己最宝贵的信任，全部毫
无保留地交给了我。我最懂他。'

"'你最懂他，'我下意识地重复着她的话。我想，也许真的

是那样。我们每说一句话，房间里也变得愈发昏暗，只有她那光洁白皙的额头，仍然被那永不熄灭的信仰和爱的光辉所照亮。

"'您是他生前的朋友，'她接着说。'您是他的朋友，'她稍微提高了声音重复着说，'既然他把这东西交给您，并请您来见我，那您就一定是他的朋友。我觉得，有些话我可以说给您听——啊！我一定要把它们说出来。因为您是听到过他的临终遗言的人，所以我想让您知道——让您知道我是配得上他的……我这样说并不是因为我骄傲自负……啊，但是没错！我确实无比骄傲、无比自豪——我比世界上的任何人都更了解他——他也曾亲口对我这样说过。可是自从他的母亲去世后，这个世上就再也没有一个人——没有一个人——可以——可以——'

"我默默地听着。房间里越来越暗了。我甚至不敢肯定他交给我的这包东西有没有弄错；我很怀疑他想让我保管的其实是另一包信件，也就是在他死后，我看见经理在灯下细细检查的那些。那女人一直在絮絮地说着；她深信我对她怀有着同情，这使她的痛苦得到了些许安慰——她不停地向我倾诉，仿佛一个干渴已久的人不停地啜饮。我听说，她和库尔茨订婚的事，她的家人都不赞成。因为库尔茨没什么钱，又或者因为别的什么事情。说真的，我并不知道是不是他的一生都过得很清苦。这使我有理由相信，就是为了不再过这样的日子，为了能吐气扬眉，他才下定决心跑到那个地方去的。

"'……只要有幸听过他的话语，谁能不为之倾倒呢？'她说，'他总是能唤起人们心中最美好的情感，让人们归心于他。'她目光灼灼地望着我，'这是伟人才能拥有的天赋啊。'她就这样一直不断地说下去。伴随着她低吟般的话语声，我的

她不停地向我倾诉，仿佛一个干渴已久的人不停地啜饮。

（卢自由　绘）

耳畔似乎又响起了那些声音，我所曾听到过的那些充满了神秘、凄凉和悲愁的声音——河水奔流的汩汩声，风吹过树林的飒飒声，人群祈祷的嗡嗡声，远方传来的奇异呼喊的缥缈的回声，以及从那永恒的黑暗之中飘荡而来的低沉的耳语声。'但是您听到过他的话语啊！您是知道的！'她大声说。

"'是的，我知道，'我的心中涌上一种几乎是绝望的感觉，但我还是向着她所怀抱的坚定信念低下了头，向着那在黑暗中闪耀着光辉的、伟大而可怕的救赎幻象低下了头。在那压倒一切的黑暗之中，我无力保护她——甚至也无力保护自己。

"'对我而言，这是多么巨大的损失啊——不，应该是对我们而言！'她非常慷慨地纠正了自己的话，接着她又喃喃地说，'对于整个世界而言，也是如此。'借着黄昏的最后一抹微光，我看见她的眼睛晶莹闪烁，饱含泪水——那是她强忍着才没有滚落的泪水。

"'我曾经是多么快乐——多么幸运——多么骄傲，'她继续说，'我太幸运了。在那一小段时光里我太过幸福了。但是现在，一切都随他而去——终我一生，我将永无欢乐。'

"她站了起来，她淡黄色的头发仿佛汇聚了夕阳所有的光辉，泛出金子般的光芒。我也站起身来。

"'而所有的这一切，'她继续悲伤地说下去，'他所有的承诺，所有的才华，还有他浩瀚的思想、高贵的心灵，全都荡然无存了——他什么也没有留下——除了回忆。您和我——'

"'我们会永远记住他的，'我毫不犹豫地说。

"'不！'她叫道，'这一切不可能就这么消失了——像他那样的人不可能就这么白白牺牲，什么都没有留下——除了留给我们的无尽悲哀。您知道他曾经有过多么宏伟的计划，那些计划我也知道——或许我并不完全理解——可是还有别的人知道。一定会有些什么东西留下来。至少，他的话语还活在我们心间。'

"'他的话语将会永世流传，'我说。

"'还有他所树立的榜样，'她低声自语道。'人们都景仰他——他的一言一行，都闪耀着美德的光辉。他的榜样——'

"'是的，'我说，'还有他所树立的榜样。没错，他的榜

样。我把这一点给忘了。'

"'可是我没有忘。我不能——我不能相信——即使现在也不能。我不能相信，我永远再也见不到他了，任何人都再也见不到他了，永远，永远，永远见不到他了。'

"她伸出双臂，仿佛要挽留一个渐渐远去的身影；狭窄的窗前，天色愈来愈暗——她迎着这黯淡的天光伸开双臂，最后把苍白的双手紧紧地绞在一起。永远见不到他！可我那时却清清楚楚地看见了他。在我的有生之年，我将永远看见这个能言善辩的幽灵。我也将永远看见她，这个悲伤的、似曾相识的身影——她让我想起了另一个悲伤的女人，那个女人浑身挂满毫无灵验的咒符，在那地狱般幽暗的河流的熠熠波光之上，伸出了她褐色的赤裸的双臂。她突然用很轻的声音说，'他虽死犹生，永垂不朽。'

"'他的结局，'我说，一股难以言喻的愤怒在我胸中翻江倒海，'无论从哪个方面来看，都完全对得住他这一生。'

"'但那个时候，我没能陪伴在他身边，'她喃喃地说。一种无限的怜悯之情油然而生，平息了我的愤怒。

"'我们都已经尽力了——'我低声对她说。

"'啊，我比世上任何人——比他的母亲，甚至比他自己，都更加地信赖着他啊。他需要我！需要我！他的每一声叹息，每一句话，每一个手势，每一个眼神，我都会视如珍宝啊。'

"我感到心头一阵冰凉。'请别这样，'我勉强压住了声音说。

"'请原谅我。我——我已经默默无声地悲伤了这么久——完全一个人沉默着……您曾经和他在一起——直到最后吧？我想得到他那时多么的孤独，他身边没有一个人，能够像我这样

地理解他。也许都没有一个人听到他的话……'

"'在他最后的时刻,'我颤抖着说,'我听到了他临终的话……'我忽然惊惧起来,不敢说下去了。

"'请为我重复一遍,'她用一种令人心碎的声音低沉地说。'我需要——我需要——有点东西——给我点什么——让我靠着它活下去。'

"我几乎忍不住要在她面前狂喊起来。'难道你真的没有听见吗?'黄昏的幽暗正在我们四周用不绝于耳的低语重复着那两句话,就像风暴来临前第一缕轻微的风声——这声音愈来愈大,愈来愈响,几乎要震碎我的耳膜,撼动整个大地。'可怕!可怕啊!'

"'他最后的话——我要靠着它活下去,'她坚持要我说出来。'您难道不明白我爱他——我爱他——我爱他!'

"我用尽全身的气力,慢慢地说出了一句话。

"'他在最后说的是——你的名字。'

"我听到了一声轻微的叹息;接着,我的心几乎停止了跳动——一声欣喜若狂而又凄厉可怖的叫喊,一声交织着无比的胜利喜悦和无以名状的痛苦的叫喊——让我的心脏完全停止了跳动。

"'我早就知道——我一直坚信一定会是这样!'她早就知道。她一直坚信。我听到她终于哭出声来;她用双手捂着脸哭泣。我似乎感到,不等我逃出这里,这房子就会轰然倒塌,天也会塌下来压到我的头上。然而什么也没有发生。天可不会因为这么一点小事就塌下来。我很想知道,倘若我把库尔茨应得的那点儿公道还给他,天是否还会塌下来?他不是说他想要的只不过是公道吗?但是我给不了他。我也不能告诉她。那样未免太黑暗了——实在是太黑暗了……"

马洛讲完了。他远远地坐在一旁，身影模糊，一声不响，姿势宛如一尊打坐冥想的菩萨。一时间，谁也没有动。"潮水早就退了，我们得抓紧时间，"船长突然说。我抬起头来。远处的海面上横亘着一片乌云，这条通往世界尽头的平静的大河，正在黑云笼罩的天穹下阴沉沉地流动着——仿佛要一直流进那浩荡无垠的黑暗之心。

这条通往世界尽头的平静的大河，正在黑云笼罩的天穹下阴沉沉地流动着——仿佛要一直流进那浩荡无垠的黑暗之心。

（李木子　绘）

译后记

在本书接近付梓之际，传来了一则令人振奋的消息，"2024 年 6 月 25 日 14 时 07 分，嫦娥六号返回器准确着陆于内蒙古四子王旗预定区域，标志着嫦娥六号探月任务圆满完成。这是中国航天的一次历史性创举，不仅成功实现了探测器月背着陆，而且实现了人类首次从月球背面采集月壤返回地球的宏愿。"

和所有挚爱祖国的中华儿女一样，此时此刻，我心中的激动和自豪难以言表。事实上，不仅仅是在这样的历史性时刻；每当我从报章上或是手机客户端看到我们的国家在各个领域取得成就的报道，哪怕只是一点点的进步，我也会不胜欣喜。

年少时，我曾在家中的书架上翻看过一本泛黄的《老残游记》。书中的情节我现在已不大记得，只还能想起作者是清末时人，题中的"老残"之名，意在感叹国家凋敝、民族衰微，"棋局已残，吾人将老，宁不悲乎！"小说开篇的一个场景留给了我极深刻的印象。老残在午后一梦中，望见海上行来一艘大船；海中巨浪如山，那船在浪上颠扑飘摇，处境十分危急，可是船上众人除了少数人竭力打舵欲挽狂澜，其余人却只是各行其是，有凶暴聚敛的，有高谈阔论的，也有只管独善其身的。最后那大船眼见着就将沉入海里。这隐喻的是彼时内外交困的中国。但是无论在任何时代，一个国家或者一个民族，都有如一条大船在风浪不息的海上航行，稍有不慎，就会落入险地；只有船上的人们同舟共济，每个人都像真正的海员那样坚守自己的岗位，各司其职，各尽其力，这条大船才能永不沉没，永远向前。

中学的历史课上，老师让我们背诵《南京条约》《马关条约》。说实话，那些凄惨的文字简直不忍卒睹，何况背诵？我想，只有努力学习，努力奋斗，才能让这些历史永远只是历史。

在北京读博期间，中日发生了钓鱼岛争端。有一阵子，周围的空气中似乎隐隐漫起了战争将近的硝烟味。我听着身边同学们不无忧虑的谈论，继续埋头修改我的代码。我想，如果国家需要，我可以马上改去研究强场，只要能够为守卫我们的国土尽一份绵薄之力。

正如顾炎武所说，"国家兴亡，匹夫有责"。

我在理论物理方面做的是基础性的研究，也许近几十年内也看不到大规模的理论应用成果。但是基础研究是科学大厦的根基，为了让这个根基更加牢固，我情愿一直做一个"修补匠"。

翻译康拉德的作品是我的乐趣所在。康拉德称得上是"文学家中的哲学家"；如果说理论物理是在对自然法则做"思想实验"，那么康拉德就是在对人性、对人类的心灵秘境做"思想实验"。康拉德的创造力令我惊叹。我羡慕、敬仰那些在文学上成就了伟业的人们，比如中国的鲁迅、朱自清、金庸，比如外国的杰克·伦敦、爱伦·坡、F. S. 菲茨杰拉德。真正优秀的文学作品都是民族精神的不朽丰碑，是闪耀在人类历史的天空的群星。但是创造力难以望其项背的我，目前只能以"翻译家算得上半个文学家"这句话来勉励自己，在翻译的道路上披荆斩棘，踽踽而行。在大学教书的这些年，我欣慰地看到，中国的年轻一代是带着一种前所未有的民族自信成长起来的，他们眼界开阔，学识丰富，创造力极强。如果我的译文能够引起他们的思考、激发他们的创作，擘画出中国巨轮破浪远航的史诗，那么我也算是尽了自己的"匹夫之责"了。

最后，再次向中国航天致以敬意，向在各行各业勤恳耕耘、默默奉献的人们致以敬意！

甲辰年季夏于华师勤园
李行宽

黑暗之心

HEART OF DARKNESS

评注

[英] 约瑟夫·康拉德　著

李行宽　注译

上海交通大学出版社
SHANGHAI JIAO TONG UNIVERSITY PRESS

本书配套学习资源，包含原版小说的重点单词、词组的详尽注释。扫描下方二维码，免费下载。

查普曼灯塔的真实照片（黄雁　供图）

目 录
CONTENTS

I

The Nellie, a cruising yawl, swung to her anchor without a flutter of the sails, and was at rest. <u>The flood had made, the wind was nearly calm</u>[1], and being bound down the river, <u>the only thing</u>

---

1. The flood...nearly calm：关于这里的翻译，一般来说可以按照英文原文的句序，先说到"帆船稳稳地停住"，再说"潮水上涨，风也几乎停息"。但是仔细推敲，不如两句话颠倒翻译为好。这是为了照顾汉语的行文习惯，在汉语表达中，文章或者演讲的开篇，往往先点明时令和风物，再开始进入叙事。例如苏轼在《前赤壁赋》中开篇写道"壬戌之秋，七月既望，苏子与客泛舟游于赤壁之下。"这是先点明时令再叙事；之后写道"清风徐来，水波不兴。举酒属客，诵明月之诗，歌窈窕之章。"这是先描绘景色后叙事。现代作家也擅用这种开篇形式，譬如在处女作《苍穹神剑》的开头，古龙初次落笔就这样写道："江南春早，草长莺飞。斜阳三月，夜间仍有萧索之意。"而后才引入到故事人物的出场。又如金庸在收官之作《鹿鼎记》开篇写道："北风如刀，满地冰霜。江南近海滨的一条大路上，一队清兵手执刀枪，押着七辆囚车，冲风冒寒，向北而行。"除了英汉之间句序的差别之外，两种语言形式也有不同。英语一般来说不拘于句式，而汉语中多用四字格叠句，具有一种平衡和谐之美。因此这里开篇翻译为"河水漫涨，风止浪平。奈利号连帆都没有抖动一下，就吃住锚链，稳稳地停泊下来。"此处虽为表达上的细节，但是只有用心体悟，于细节处多留意，才能保证文学作品翻译既准确，又优美，如许渊冲所说"缔造出一位忠诚的美人"。倘若失去了文学性，即使翻译得再字字如实，也已"奈何明珠变鱼目"，失去了文学作品的题中应有之义。当然，凡事过犹不及，翻译也是如此。直译和意译作为两种不可或缺的手段，应酌情配合使用，不能往任何一个方向上走极端。天马行空的意译偏离了原文，当然不可取；而不加思考和变通的直译则犹如庄子所笑的"邯郸学步"："未得其能而又失却故行，直匍匐而归耳。"

for it was to come to and wait for the turn of the tide².

The sea-reach of the Thames stretched before us like the beginning of an interminable waterway. In the offing the sea and the sky were welded together without a joint³, and in the luminous space the tanned sails of the barges drifting up with the tide⁴ seemed to stand still in red clusters of canvas sharply peaked, with gleams of varnished sprits. A haze rested on the low

---

2. the only...the tide：这里牵涉到泰晤士河水文情况的背景知识。泰晤士河每日潮汐涨落超过 20 英寸（也就是 50.8 厘米），由于伦敦地势低洼，涨潮的时候海水会倒灌回流。了解了这个情况，这句话的意思就很清晰了。奈利号是一艘准备出海的帆船，它的目标是下游的泰晤士河入海口；现在是涨潮期，海水正在往上游涌入，因而水流的方向与奈利号的行驶方向是相反的。作为常识，我们都知道顺风顺水有利于行船。此时无风、逆水，所以奈利号只能停船等待，等到入夜退潮之时再开船，就可以让驶向大海的水流顺势把船带往下游（这个过程简单来说，就是：落潮——出海；涨潮——回伦敦）。wait for the turn of the tide 就是等待落潮的意思。

3. In the offing...without a joint：如果译为"远处碧海蓝天，水乳交融，看不出丝毫接合痕迹"，意思是对的。其实通过读这个句子，大家脑海中都会映出同样一幅意象鲜明的图画，但是我觉得，由于中英文表达差异，英文中的"接合"意群取其意而弃其形为好，故译为"极目远望，水天一色。"在此就文采问题稍作讨论。文，通"纹"；就如同古人在青铜器上雕镂出繁复的云兽纹以求美观一样，多以修辞为载体的文采也使得一部文学作品在其思想价值之外，更附上一层不可或缺的美学价值。然而，"文采"的表现因语言的不同而不同，并无绝对的定法可循。因此，在语言转换的过程中，在保持作者原意不变的条件下，译文有所变通是必然之事；而正因为有所变通、有所创造，才使得译文有可能在美学价值上超越原文，有"吐纳珠玉，舒卷风云"之气象。

4. drifting up with the tide：随着潮水向上游漂去。结合上一段关于泰晤士河水文的注释，可以想象出这样一幅情景：泰晤士河正在涨潮，海水不断涌向上游；奈利号和那些将要出海的船只受到潮水的阻遏，只好停船歇息，等待潮落；而那些从海上归来的驳船则正好乘着涌入内河的海潮，轻松省力地回家去。

shores that ran out to sea in vanishing flatness. The air was dark above Gravesend[5], and farther back still seemed condensed into a mournful gloom, brooding motionless over the biggest, and the greatest, town[6] on earth.

The Director of Companies[7] was our captain and our host. We four affectionately watched his back as he stood in the bows looking to seaward. On the whole river there was nothing that looked half so nautical[8]. He resembled a pilot, which to a seaman is trustworthiness personified. It was difficult to realize his work was not out there in the luminous estuary, but behind him, within the brooding gloom.

———————————

5. Gravesend：英国港口，位于肯特郡西北部，泰晤士河南岸。这里的地名很可能含有一层隐喻。grave 的意思是"坟墓"，send 意思是"送去"，合在一起可以理解为"送往坟墓"。因为下文多次将非洲大陆比喻为尚未被文明之光照耀的"黑暗之地"（或者说，整个非洲都笼罩着殖民者入侵的阴影，因而成为"黑暗之地"），那里荒凉野蛮，疾病丛生，小说主人公库尔茨和其他很多贸易代理人都是感染了热带疾病死在那里的。从河口出海前往非洲殖民地，就等于踏上了九死一生的险途，因此地名"Gravesend"也就有了这样一种启示的意味。

6. town：这里的 town 应该是指伦敦。由于伦敦距离 Gravesend 不到四十公里，因此结合"Gravesend 的更远处"和"地球上最恢宏、最伟大的城市"这两个信息，既可以得出判断。

7. The Director of Companies：出于文化背景的考虑，我将此处的 Director 翻译成"董事"而非"主任"，以体现那个时代远洋"贸易"公司的气质。我觉得文学作品的翻译，虽然在表达上要符合汉语读者的习惯，充分发挥汉语的表达优势，但是在文化气质的传递上则应尽量贴紧原文，不失其本来风貌。

8. there was...so nautical：直译为"没有任何情景，能够及得上（眼前这幅情景的）海洋气息的一半"。注意英文句型的表达，类似于"双重否定表肯定"，事实上表强调。整句建议译为："整条河道上，唯有这一幕最富于航海色彩"。

Between us there was, as I have already said somewhere, the bond[9] of the sea. Besides holding our hearts together through long periods of separation, it had the effect of making us tolerant of each other's yarns[10]—and even convictions. The Lawyer—the best of old fellows[11]—had, because of his many years and many virtues[12], the only cushion on deck, and was lying on the only rug. The

---

9. bond：作为名词主要有两层含义："债券"；"联系"。这里的意思是"纽带；联系"。the bond of sea 也就是"大海这一纽带"的意思。直译为"在我们之间，我之前也说过，有着海洋的纽带"。出于可读性的考虑，这里我做了一点调整，译为"我以前曾经说过，大海就是把我们联结在一起的纽带"。这里的翻译涉及两个方面，一是句序的适当调整；二是对"海洋的纽带"这一表达的化译。其实严复所言"信、达、雅"，我个人总结其实就是"共感性"，即让不同语言背景的读者得到尽可能相同的阅读体验。

10. yarn："纱线，纺线"；这里指的是"（冗长的）故事；（信口开河的）奇谈"。两个词义之间有着奇妙的隐喻联系，从人口中吐出的絮絮不停的话语就好像纺织机上连绵不断的纺线。因为海员们长期漂泊海上的工作性质，他们有很多时间可以聊天，彼此讲述见闻和感想。这种滔滔不绝的讲述，就是"yarns"。

11. the best of old fellows：old fellow 指的是"老伙计；年纪较大的朋友或熟人，通常用于表示亲切和尊重"，加上 the best of，亲近之意则更加明显。这里不妨译作"那个可亲的老头儿"，将作者对这个人物的好感表达出来。事实上，前面提到的公司董事、这里提到的老头儿（他是船上的律师）和下句提到的会计，都只是马洛讲述刚果河故事的听众，并非主要人物，因而一带而过。但是作者寥寥几笔，仍然把这些戏份不多的"打酱油角色"描绘得宛在眼前。

12. virtues：意思是"美德，长处"。这句话里的"many years and many virtues"被译为"年高德劭"，事实上，"many years"在英文中包含两种可能的含义，一是这位律师年纪很大，在人间已经度过了许多年；二是这位律师资历很老了，他在公司工作（或者说在船上服役）已经好多年了。译为"年高德劭"，兼顾了文采和可读性，但是英文中的第二种隐含意思却找不到了。当然这是非常微妙的细节问题。有的译本译作"资历深厚"，似乎又隐去了英文中的第一重意味。读者如有佳译，欢迎来信探讨。

Accountant had brought out already a box of dominoes, and was toying architecturally[13] with the bones. Marlow sat cross-legged right aft, leaning against the mizzen-mast. He had sunken cheeks, a yellow complexion, a straight back, an ascetic aspect, and, with his arms dropped, the palms of hands outwards, resembled an idol. The director, satisfied the anchor had good hold, made his way aft and sat down amongst us. We exchanged a few words lazily. Afterwards there was silence on board the yacht. For some reason or other we did not begin that game of dominoes[14]. We felt meditative, and fit for nothing but placid staring. The day

---

13. toy architecturally：toy 常用作名词，意思是"玩具，小人物"，这里用作动词，意思是"漫不经心地摆弄"，architecturally 是"关于建筑地"，整句的意思就是"会计在用骨牌搭房子"，可见船上的人们在等待潮落的这段时间里都无所事事，甚至穷极无聊。注意，这句话里出现的 dominos 和 bones 是同样的意思，都是"多米诺骨牌"，因为骨牌恰如其名，最初都是用兽骨制成的。

14. For some reason...game of dominoes：这句英文有双重含义，但是联系上下文，只有一重意义可取。本句字面上意为"出于某种原因 / 不知怎的，我们没有开始玩那种多米诺游戏。"理解的关键在于"that game of dominoes"，由于上文出现过"会计拿着多米诺骨牌在玩"的情景，因而很容易译为"我们没有玩起多米诺骨牌来"。这样的译法，看似忠于原文，事实上可能曲解了英文原意。事实上，"多米诺骨牌游戏"在这一句里是顺接上文来比喻"聊天，对话"，因为聊天就是"一个人引起一个话题，然后大家一句接一句地一直说下去"。只有这样理解，上下文才能文脉通畅——我们懒懒地聊了几句；然后船上就陷入了一片沉默；不知怎的我们并没有继续聊下去；我们都沉默着各自沉思，除了呆呆出神，别的什么也不想干——每一句的意义都衔接通顺。英文中以"多米诺游戏"比喻"连续不停地聊天"，但是译为"我们谁也没有再开口"，这一比喻就在中文里丢失了。殊为可惜，但也是无奈之举。这里只是行文中的微末细节，忽略不计倒也说得通。但若遇到影响情节进展或者展示作者思想的重点关窍处，那就必须以加注或其他的形式点明，在作者和读者之间做清晰的沟通。

was ending in a serenity of still and exquisite brilliance. The water shone pacifically; the sky, without a speck, was a benign immensity of unstained light; the very mist on the Essex marsh was like a gauzy and radiant fabric, hung from the wooded rises inland, and draping the low shores in diaphanous folds. Only the gloom to the west, brooding over the upper reaches, became more sombre every minute, as if angered by the approach of the sun.

And at last, in its curved and imperceptible fall, the sun sank low, and from glowing white changed to a dull red without rays and without heat, as if[15] about to go out suddenly, stricken to death by the touch of that gloom brooding over a crowd of men.

Forthwith a change came over the waters, and the serenity became less brilliant but more profound. The old river in its broad reach rested unruffled at the decline of day, after ages of good service done to the race that peopled its banks[16], spread out in the tranquil dignity of a waterway leading to the uttermost ends of the earth[17].

---

15. as if 句：go out suddenly 和 stricken to death 这二者意义上属于"同义复现"，指的同样都是"太阳的突然熄灭"。而太阳的熄灭是在一瞬间发生的，就好像与天边的乌云瞬间相接、"一触即死"似的。直译为"像突然熄灭一般，撞死在那片人群头顶上的乌云里"，虽意思是准确的，但是照搬英文的表达，在汉语中有时可能会显得滑稽。这是由于两种语言的思维逻辑和表达习惯的差异造成的，这也是译者必须通过变通来架设桥梁、实现"共感性"的地方，万不能以"直译"为名而推脱劳力。

16. the race that peopled its banks：people 在这里是动词，意为"居住于"。race 作名词有"种族、民族、一群人"的意思，这里译为"两岸的居民"比较合适。

17. The old river...of the earth：这段文字的翻译很有趣，就好像做理论物理推演一样，要严格把握逻辑的严密性。首先理解准确原文；然后，（转下页）

We looked at the venerable stream not in the vivid flush of a short day that comes and departs for ever, but in the august light of abiding memories. And indeed nothing is easier for a man who has, as the phrase goes, "followed the sea" with reverence and affection, than to evoke the great spirit of the past upon the lower reaches of the Thames. The tidal current runs to and fro in its unceasing[18] service, crowded with memories of men and ships it had borne to the rest of home or to the battles of the sea. It had known and served all the men[19] of whom the nation is proud, from

---

（接上页）将一层层意思逻辑捋顺，再根据中文的思维习惯重新组织；最后按照中文语序准确流畅地进行表述，并兼顾文采，实现原文和译文的"共感性"。事实上，这里整个段落都是抒情性的，作者曾在泰晤士河上遥望大海，怀想着大英帝国的黄金岁月——那是一个被无数扬帆出海的舰船和富有冒险精神的殖民开拓者所定义的时代；一个英伦三岛雄霸全球，号称"日不落帝国"的时代。因此这一段文字就如同交响乐的华彩乐章，极富歌咏性和感染力。相应地，中文译文须在意义准确的基础上，达到和原文同样宏阔壮美的境界。当然，这里不讨论康拉德立场的政治性。康拉德作为英人，怀恋所谓的"帝国荣光"也无可厚非。而这一段讴颂，更像是在英帝国江河日下之际一曲无奈的挽歌——无论康拉德本人是否意识得到，20 世纪初的英国已经踏上了没落的不归路，西方国家对于殖民地的赤裸裸的侵占行径也都将随着时代的进步画上句号。留给旧欧洲的，只有感伤的喟叹和一片迷惘的精神荒原。

18. unceasing：不停的，不断的。unceasing service 在这里指的是泰晤士河的河水川流不息，一直在为人们永不停歇地服务。我认为，翻译这里的 service 最好将"服务"两字隐去。英文好使用抽象词，汉语好使用具象词，此为表达习惯使然，无关优劣。

19. It had known and served all the men：注意，这一段有三处排比句，达到了"一唱三叹，回环隽永"的效果。这里是第一处，"泰晤士河记得那些人"；接下来第二处，"泰晤士河记得那些船"；最后第三处，"泰晤士河记得那些人和那些船"。这里只是简言概括，实际译文经过艺术处理，当然并不是这样。

Sir Francis Drake[20] to Sir John Franklin[21], knights all, titled and untitled—the great knights—errant of the sea. It had borne all the ships whose names are like jewels flashing in the night of time, from the Golden Hind returning with her rotund flanks full of treasure, to be visited by the Queen's Highness and thus pass out of the gigantic tale, to the Erebus[22] and Terror[23], bound on other conquests—and that never returned. It had known the ships and the men[24]. They had sailed from Deptford, from Greenwich, from

---

20. Sir Francis Drake：这里的 Sir 不能翻译为 "先生"。Sir 在这里是对贵族之下、平民阶层之上的社会精英的一种尊称，尤其特指由于重要功绩而受到女王或国王封赐的称号，一般译为 "爵士" 或者 "勋爵"。例如英国海盗头目弗朗西斯·德雷克由于屡次洗劫西班牙船队，于 1581 年被伊丽莎白一世封爵，故应称为 "弗朗西斯·德雷克爵士"。"金鹿号" 是弗朗西斯·德雷克海盗船队的旗舰，他于 1577 年至 1579 年驾 "金鹿号" 完成了继麦哲伦之后的第二次环球航行，当然德雷克的主要目的是打劫西班牙商船。两年多的航行中，德雷克从西班牙人手中抢劫了数以吨计的黄金白银，令伊丽莎白一世喜出望外，亲自登船犒赏。

21. Sir John Franklin：约翰·弗兰克林爵士作为北极航线的探索者而被世人铭记，"幽冥号" 和 "恐怖号" 就是弗兰克林船长于 1845 年出发前往北极地区所带的船队。但是很不幸，船队湮没在极地的风雪中，再也没能返航。船队遇难的原因和经过扑朔迷离，成为一百多年来人们不断探索的话题。2014年，"幽冥号" 在加拿大被发现，但是对船上遗物和船只漂流路线的分析，非但没能解开之前的诸多疑问，反而为这场恐怖的船难蒙上了更多疑云。这个著名的历史事件被 AMC 制作公司拍成剧集《极地恶灵》(The Terror) 并于 2018 年播出。

22. Erebus：厄瑞玻斯，希腊神话中的混沌之神卡俄斯之子，永久黑暗的化身。这里是指约翰·弗兰克林爵士北极远征队中的 "幽冥号"。沉船遗骸于2014 年在加拿大被发现。

23. Terror：约翰·弗兰克林爵士北极远征队中的 "恐怖号"，于 2016 年被发现于加拿大威廉国王岛西南岸恐怖湾水下 24 米深处。

24. It had known the ships and the men：前述三重排比句中的第三处。

Erith—the adventurers and the settlers; kings' ships and the ships of men on 'Change; captains, admirals, the dark "interlopers" of the Eastern trade, and the commissioned "generals" of East India fleets. Hunters for gold or pursuers of fame, they all had gone out on that stream, bearing the sword, and often the torch, messengers of the might within the land, bearers of a spark from the sacred fire. What greatness had not floated on the ebb of that river into the mystery of an unknown earth!...The dreams of men, the seed of commonwealths, the germs of empires[25].

The sun set; the dusk fell on the stream, and lights began to appear along the shore. The Chapman light house[26], a three-legged[27] thing erect on a mud-flat, shone strongly. Lights of ships moved in the fairway—a great stir of lights going up and going down. And farther west on the upper reaches the place of the monstrous town was still marked ominously on the sky, a brooding gloom in sunshine, a lurid glare under the stars.

"And this also," said Marlow[28] suddenly, "has been one of the

---

25. What greatness...of empires：这个句子如果按照英文的语序直译，中文则会显得有些别扭。建议将句序倒过来翻译为好。

26. Chapman light house：查普曼灯塔是曾经矗立于泰晤士河入海口的一座灯塔。对于乘船出海的人来说，查普曼灯塔是泰晤士河道上的最后一座地标。1957 年，已经开始坍驰的查普曼灯塔被拆除。

27. three-legged：意为"三条腿的"，此处译为"矗立在三角悬架上的"。根据历史图片（参见文前插图）来看，查普曼灯塔是由钢架支撑建在河面上的，从某个角度看过去，钢架就好像三条腿似的。

28. Marlow：前文描写过马洛的外貌，而这里是马洛第一次开口讲话。在后面整部小说里，马洛将作为目击者和讲述者，向我们呈现那个（转下页）

dark places of the earth[29]."

    He was the only man of us who still "followed the sea." <u>The worst that could be said of him was that he did not represent his class</u>[30]. He was a seaman, but he was a wanderer, too, while most seamen lead, if one may so express it, a <u>sedentary</u>[31] life. Their minds are of the <u>stay-at-home order</u>[32], and their home is always with them—the ship; and so is their country—the sea. One ship

---

（接上页）著名的刚果河上的故事（这里我用"著名"是因为康拉德这部《黑暗之心》影响了后世许多小说、诗歌和电影的创作）。而事实上，"马洛"也是康拉德小说中的一个"著名的"讲话人，有好几部小说的故事都是通过马洛之口讲出来的，例如《青春》《吉姆老爷》和《机缘》。

29. has been...the earth：如果说"黑暗之地"指的是"原始蒙昧、未经开化的地方"，那么马洛在下文中所讲的关于罗马入侵英国的故事就可以验证这一点。那时候英国尚未被文明之光照耀，还是一片"黑暗之地"。但是，这里的时态是现在完成时，不是一般过去时，也不是过去完成时。为什么会这样呢？难道已经成了日不落帝国的英国仍然是"黑暗之地"吗？我的理解是，在小说的开篇，康拉德反复提到伦敦上空"阴云笼罩"，和这里的"黑暗之地"一样，构成了一个隐喻：英国向海外殖民地输出了很多殖民者，不少殖民者在非洲或者别的地方干着帝国主义的侵略压迫的勾当，让当地人民蒙受了种种苦难。对被压迫者而言，他们就是"阴霾"，就是"黑暗"。所以伦敦城在马洛眼里，也仍然还是一处"黑暗之地"。

30. The worst that...his class：直译为"要讲坏话么，我们最多也只能说他不代表自己的阶级。"的话，虽然字面上无误，但不能有效传达出作者真正的意思。结合上下文，这句话其实是说：马洛作为海员无可挑剔；如果非要说他哪里不好，那也只能说他和别的海员不大一样。class 在这里指的是"海员这么一类人"。

31. sedentary：久坐不动的，不迁徙的。这里指的是海员们都过着一种千篇一律、单调乏味的生活；引申的含义是，就连他们的头脑和思想也一同变得简单刻板、庸庸碌碌。

32. of the stay-at-home order：意思是"（别的海员的）行事方式就好像和待在家里的时候一样，根本就不思改变"。

is very much like another, and the sea is always the same. In the immutability of their surroundings the foreign shores, the foreign faces, the changing immensity of life, glide past, veiled not by a sense of mystery but by a slightly disdainful ignorance; for there is nothing mysterious to a seaman unless it be the sea itself, which is the mistress of his existence[33] and as inscrutable[34] as Destiny[35]. For the rest, after his hours of work, a casual stroll or a casual spree on shore suffices[36] to unfold for him the secret of a whole continent, and generally he finds the secret not worth knowing. The yarns of seamen have a direct simplicity[37], the whole meaning of which

---

33. the mistress of his existence：existence 意为"存在"，这里指的是"活着；留有一条命在"。这里是说，船员们的身家性命被大海这个"女主人"所掌控着。昔日的航海都是以性命为赌注的冒险，船员一旦出海，就相当于把自己的性命交到了喜怒难测的大海的手里。

34. inscrutable：不可理解的；无法预测的。这里是说大海凶险叵测，是一个性情古怪的"女主人"。上一秒万里晴空，下一秒就可能风暴骤起。上文提到的约翰·富兰克林远征队（"幽冥号"和"恐怖号"），就是由于不幸遭遇寒冰期，使得本应顺利完成的北极航线勘测之旅，变成了全部人员殒命于风雪之中的一场船难。

35. Destiny：这里使用大写，指的是"命运之神"。俗话说"天有不测风云，人有旦夕祸福"，就是指命运的诡谲多变。这里是说海之女神和命运之神一样，都性情难测，令船员们且敬且畏。

36. suffices：A suffices to do B 意为"要做到 B 这件事，有了 A 就足够了"。这句的意思是说，海员们觉得，如果想要了解遥远的大陆都有什么秘密，只要上岸随便走走或者找个酒馆狂欢痛饮一番，这就足够了。这说明和马洛比起来，其他很多海员相对见识浅薄。

37. simplicity：简单；朴素；无知。这里是说其他海员也爱讲故事，但是他们由于自身的见识相对浅陋，讲出来的故事也就情节简单乏味，意义单调直白，谈不上什么发人深思的效果。

lies within the shell of a cracked nut[38]. But Marlow was not typical (if his propensity[39] to spin yarns[40] be excepted[41]), and to him the meaning of an episode was not inside like a kernel but outside, enveloping the tale which brought it out only as a glow brings out a haze, in the likeness of one of these misty halos that sometimes are made visible by the spectral illumination of moonshine.

His remark did not seem at all surprising. It was just like Marlow. It was accepted in silence. No one took the trouble to grunt even; and presently he said, very slow —

"I was thinking of very old times, when the Romans first came here, nineteen hundred years ago — the other day[42]...Light came out

---

38. within the shell of a cracked nut："in a nutshell" 是一个习惯用法，意为"概括来说；简而言之"。2001 年，英国物理学家史蒂芬·霍金出版《果壳中的宇宙》，原标题即为"The Universe in A Nutshell"，意为"概说宇宙"。康拉德在这里化用"in a nutshell"的喻体，以"果核"比喻故事的意义，以"果壳"比喻故事本身，用"破裂的果壳"来比喻有的船员所讲的故事是多么的浅显粗陋，经不起推敲。译之道，千变万化，如流水不居，因势就形，难有定法。例如上文中康拉德以"多米诺骨牌游戏"比喻船员们一句接一句的连续不断的对话，就不宜直译；而此处"破裂的果壳"的比喻，则新鲜有趣，这就跟《果壳中的宇宙》一样，直译反而使译文生机盎然。

39. propensity：倾向性；习性；癖好。这里指的是马洛也和别的海员一样，倾向于滔滔不绝地讲故事。这也是在为后文做铺垫，因为全书所有的故事，都是马洛在等待潮落的几个小时里，一直不停地对同船的人讲出来的。

40. spin yarns：原意是"纺纱线"，这里是指滔滔不绝地讲故事。

41. (if his propensity to spin yarns be excepted)：康拉德常以括号的形式在文中进行补充说明，多数时候译文遵从原文，也同样采用括号形式译出；但是在这里，我已将括号中的内容提取出来，有机融入行文中了。这样可以使读者获得更流畅的阅读体验。

42. I was thinking...the other day：这句话有两种理解，要枢在于"the other day"。小说主体都是假借马洛之口讲述出来的，因此行文既有（转下页）

of this river since—you say Knights[43]? Yes; but it is like a running blaze on a plain, like a flash of lightning in the clouds[44]. We live in the flicker—may it last as long as the old earth keeps rolling[45]!

（接上页）书面语的特点，又夹杂着口语特征。在这里两者都体现得十分明显。口语特点就是经常出现倒装或补充，因此可以把 the other day 理解为补充说明的时间状语，即，"The other day, I was thinking of..."这样一来也就是说，"前几天我一直在想，罗马人初次到来的时候如何如何"。但是我在译文中没有采取这种理解，我认为这种理解是有偏差的。另一种，也就是我认为正确的理解是，把"nineteen hundred years ago—the other day"看作一处联系紧密的意义模块，后者是前者的同位语。也就是说，康拉德意在表达"沧海桑田，千百年犹如一瞬间"，也就是说"罗马人第一次来到这里"的时间状语，既是"一千九百年前"，也是"几天前"。当然后者是作者头脑中对于时间概念的抽象的压缩，因为他将"一千九百年"放在一个更大的时间尺度之下了。对比后文，可以印证这一理解。

43. Light came out...you say Knights：light 在这里是与下文中 darkness 相对应的概念，darkness 指的是黑暗时代，也就是英格兰民族还处于原始蒙昧的状态的时代；light 则指的是文明之光，标志着从荒蛮走向开化的转折。这里又再次体现了口语特征：句序随意；穿插问答。马洛在思考着说明是何时照临到泰晤士河上的，也就是在探讨英格兰民族是何时开始有了自己的文明的？也许是马洛的一个听众回答了他——自从 Knights 开始（英格兰就有了自己的历史和文明）。这里如果把 Knights 直接译为"骑士们"，我觉得似乎不妥。这里 Knights 使用了大写，说明是特指；特指哪些骑士呢？就是 King Arthur and His Knights——亚瑟王和他的圆桌骑士。亚瑟王是英格兰传说中的国王，圆桌骑士团的首领，一位近乎神话般的传奇人物。他代表着英国历史和文明的开端。因此这里其实是说"自从亚瑟王时代开始，这条河上就出现了文明之光"。

44. Yes; but it is...in the clouds：结合下一句可以看出，这里是以燎原之火和云中闪电比喻文明之光的璀璨和短暂。它的出现照亮了黑暗，但是一旦熄灭（无论是人类这个种族肉身的消亡还是理性的消亡），黑暗又将重新降临。

45. We live in...keeps rolling：这句话是说，我们所生存的年代正是人类文明之光闪耀的年代；虽然不知道这光芒究竟还能照耀人类到几时，但还是祈愿着，只要地球还在旋转，人类就会长存，而文明之光也不会熄灭。

But darkness was here yesterday[46]. Imagine the feelings of a commander of a fine—what d'ye call 'em?—trireme[47] in the Mediterranean, ordered suddenly to the north; run overland across the Gauls in a hurry; put in charge of one of these craft the legionaries—a wonderful lot of handy men they must have been, too—used to build, apparently by the hundred, in a month or two, if we may believe what we read. Imagine him here—the very end of the world, a sea the colour of lead, a sky the colour of smoke, a kind of ship about as rigid as a concertina—and going up this river with stores, or orders, or what you like. Sand-banks, marshes, forests, savages,—precious little to eat fit for[48] a civilized man, nothing but Thames water to drink. No Falernian wine[49] here, no going ashore. Here and there a military camp lost in a wilderness, like a needle in a bundle of hay[50]—cold, fog, tempests, disease,

---

46. But darkness was here yesterday：这句话把意境又拉回到这一段开头所提到的英国的黑暗时代，和下文罗马人登陆英伦的场景做了很好的衔接。

47. trireme：三桨座战船源于古代地中海文明，是腓尼基人、希腊人和罗马人常用于近海的战船。顾名思义，三桨座战船在两层甲板上有三排交错的桨手。

48. fit for：适于，合适。这句话是说在黑暗时代的英国，几乎没有什么东西能令文明人觉得可以下咽；少数能吃的东西就显得弥足珍贵。也有一种可能的情况是，precious little 只是强调"少"的程度之甚，并非含有"珍贵"之意。

49. Falernian wine：Falernian 是一个古老的英文单词，指的是一种产自意大利 Falernian 山区的葡萄酒，这里音译为"法伦葡萄酒"。它颜色深红，口感醇厚，常用于古罗马贵族饮宴的场合，因而在历史上被视为一种高贵的饮料，在西方文学和影视作品中经常提及。

50. like a needle in a bundle of hay：look for a needle in a haystack 是英语俗语，意为"大海捞针"。这里康拉德化用"草堆里的绣花针"这一形象的比喻，来说明罗马兵营和无边的荒野相比是多么微不足道，人力在大自然面前显得多么渺小。译文中也直接体现了这一比喻。顺便一提，bundle 这个词也出现在拓扑物理中，表达"类似草堆"的概念，例如 fibre bundle（纤维丛）。

exile, and death—death skulking in the air, in the water, in the bush. They must have been dying like flies here. Oh, yes—he did it[51]. Did it very well, too, no doubt, and without thinking much about it either, except afterwards to brag of what he had gone through in his time, perhaps. They were men enough to face the darkness[52]. And perhaps he was cheered by keeping his eye on[53] a chance of promotion to the fleet at Ravenna[54] by-and-by, if he had good friends in Rome and survived the awful climate[55]. Or think of a decent young citizen in a toga[56]—perhaps too much dice[57],

---

51. Oh, yes—he did it：这里是说这位罗马舰队指挥官克服了在英国这片荒蛮之地的种种艰难，成功地完成了他的任务。

52. They were...face the darkness：这里是说罗马军官和他的士兵都是真正的勇士，因为他们敢于离开舒适的文明环境，涉足这片未经开发的原始混沌的不列颠岛。"men"在这里活用作形容词，意思是"具有男子汉气概的"，即"他们都是真正的男子汉"。

53. keeping his eyes on：意思是"紧紧盯着"，这里是指这位罗马军官一直以升职到拉文纳舰队作为他的目标。

54. Ravenna：拉文纳是古代罗马的海港和重要的海军基地，现属意大利。公元前 49 年凯撒曾由此地进军罗马。

55. survived the awful climate：意思是抗住不列颠岛的恶劣环境，最终存活下来。

56. toga：古罗马人身披的宽袍。

57. too much dice：dice 意为"骰子"。这句话的理解有多种，包括"玩骰子玩腻了""大概是赌骰子输得够呛""（为了更好的前途，而）甘愿豪赌；孤注一掷"。后文中有"to mend his fortunes"，结合起来看的话，mend his fortunes 可能指的是这个年轻人赌博输掉了很多钱，所以要去不列颠豪赌一把，看看能不能赚钱还债；也可能指的是这个年轻人不满足于自己的出身或者社会地位，想通过不列颠的冒险来扭转命运，达到自己期待的人生目标。这些理解应该都是可以的。我这里译为"打算狠狠地赌上一把"。因为从当时世界文明中心之一的罗马来到原始蒙昧的不列颠岛，本身就是一种豪赌行为。这里可能是影射小说真正的主人公库尔茨从欧洲去往非洲的行为。

you know—coming out here in the train of [58] some prefect, or tax-gatherer, or trader even, to mend his fortunes. Land in a swamp, march through the woods, and in some inland post feel the savagery, the utter savagery, had closed round him—all that mysterious life of the wilderness that stirs [59] in the forest, in the jungles, in the hearts of wild men. There's no initiation [60] either into such mysteries. He has to live in the midst of the incomprehensible, which is also detestable. And it has a fascination, too, that goes to work upon him. The fascination of the abomination—you know, imagine the growing regrets, the longing to escape, the powerless disgust, the surrender, the hate [61]."

---

58. in the train of："in the train of"是一个习惯用法，意为"接着；继"。所以在这里的意思不但与"火车"毫无关系（一想便知，罗马时代当然没有火车），而且也不是"跟着什么人一起"。这里并非在说"这个罗马年轻人是跟着市长、收税员或商人一起同行而来的"，而是说这个年轻人是"继那些市长、收税员或商人之后"才来到了英国的。罗马建立殖民地，首先派驻军事人员，在当地建立威慑；然后派驻政府官员，在当地建立统治；然后才是税务人员、商人等前去开展贸易赚钱，最后才吸纳各种社会人员来冒险。从小说后文也可以看出来，后来欧洲人去往非洲建立殖民地的时候，也是这样的步骤。对于罗马或欧洲殖民者的本国政府而言，殖民地就是他们的税收来源，殖民统治是他们用来聚敛财富的手段。

59. stir：颤动；激发。这里指的是森林丛莽和野蛮人的蓬勃昂扬的生命力。

60. initiation：入门，初学；入会，入会仪式。这里指的是融入荒蛮之中去，逐渐解开那些荒野生活的谜。

61. 关于本段，有两个整体性的说明。第一，本段讲了两个马洛想象中的从文明来到蛮荒的冒险故事，主角分别是罗马军官和罗马公民。英文原文的主语都是 he，都是"想象一下，他将如何如何"；而译文中没有使用第三人称，而是使用了第二人称"你"，变为"想象一下，你将如何如何"，我认为这样更符合汉语口语中假设情境的表达，更令读者有身临其境之感。第二，读完整部小说后，读者也许会发现这两个故事其实都是在影射以主人公（转下页）

He paused.

"Mind," he began again, lifting one arm from the elbow, the palm of the hand outwards, so that, with his legs folded before him, he had the pose of a Buddha preaching in European clothes and without a lotus-flower[62]— "Mind, none of us would feel exactly like this. What saves us is efficiency—the devotion to efficiency[63]. But these chaps were not much account, really[64]. They were no colonists[65]; their administration[66] was merely a

---

（接上页）库尔茨为代表的欧洲殖民者——他们抛弃了文明社会的舒适生活投身荒野，其目标也是获得地位和财富，改变自己的命运；他们对于荒野的态度也是爱恨交织，就和文中形容的一样："这世界有着一种奇异的魅力，令你为之动容，却又恨之如仇。与日俱增的懊悔，想要逃离的渴望，深深厌恶却又无能为力，无奈顺从却更加衔怨怀恨——这些情感叠加在一起，简直会让你发疯。"破折号后面的是根据作者可能要表达的情绪做的适当延伸，也是为了汉语行文中在段落末尾能有一种稳重的结束感。

62. lotus-flower：莲花。这里指的是佛陀的宝座莲台。结合下文马洛所说的"那里的经历令我感到了心灵的震撼。经过这件事，我似乎茅塞顿开，把周遭所有的一切都看明白了"可以看出，这里描写马洛讲故事时候的神情姿态好似正在布道说法的佛陀，就是为了表明这一经历对马洛产生的巨大的心灵震撼，令他看透了一切，整个人的气质也因此改变了。

63. the devotion to efficiency：devotion 意为"奉献，热衷，虔诚追求"，efficiency 意为"效率"。这里指的是欧洲进入工业革命时代之后，各行各业的人们都在疯狂追求效率——也就是工业化大生产，因而革新了生产力和社会面貌，与罗马时代已经不可同日而语了。而资本主义和帝国主义的掠夺方式，也使现代的殖民者可以更加高效地管理和压榨殖民地人民。

64. But these...really：chap 意为"伙计们"，这里指千年前来到英国的罗马征服者。account 意为"重要性"，这里明显是对罗马人进行贬损，说他们也没什么了不起，并没有在已经敞开了大门的不列颠岛上真正有所作为。

65. colonist：殖民主义者，殖民者。在康拉德同时代人的眼中，"殖民者"可能并不完全是个贬义词。也许在他们看来，如果殖民者能够给当地带来光明和进步，那还是一件值得称道的事。

66. administration：行政机构，这里指的是罗马在英国设立的殖民政府。

squeeze[67], and nothing more, I suspect. They were conquerors, and for that you want only brute force—nothing to boast of, when you have it, since your strength is just an accident arising from the weakness of others[68]. They grabbed what they could get for the sake of what was to be got[69]. It was just robbery with violence, aggravated murder on a great scale[70], and men going at it blind[71]— as is very proper for those who tackle a darkness[72]. The conquest

---

67. squeeze：这里有两种理解，一是"挤出来的少量事物"，意为罗马当局并不真的重视不列颠岛，在当地设立的管理机构只不过是七拼八凑出来的，因而谈不上什么行政效率和力度；二是"挤压，榨汁，敲诈勒索"，意为罗马当局所谓的行政只不过是在压榨不列颠人。但是结合上一句"They were no colonists;"我认为取第一种意思的可能性更大。

68. since your...of others：A arise from B 意为"B 是引发了 A 的原因"。这里的意思是，"征服者的强大只不过是个偶然事件，因为他们碰巧遇到了弱小的对手罢了"，表达了康拉德对于暴力征服者的鄙视和嘲弄。

69. They grabbed...to be got：what was to be got 意为"征服者想要得到的东西"，for the sake of 意为"为了……的原因"，全句不妨译为"他们为了掠夺而掠夺"。

70. on a great scale：大规模的。这一句说的是暴力征服者的行径，事实上就是一场规模更大、手段更残暴的入室抢劫罢了，同样表达了康拉德对于暴力征服者的鄙视和嘲弄。

71. going at it blind：go at it 意为"全力以赴地做事"，blind 则是形容他们不问是非、不管不顾地蛮干一通。

72. as is...a darkness：as 代指上一句的"征服者盲目地投身于这场大规模的抢劫"，全句意为，"对于那些正在征服荒蛮之地的人看来，这种盲目的大规模抢劫没有任何不妥。他们觉得这样做完全是合理的。"康拉德在这里嘲弄了这种自以为是的强盗逻辑。想想八国联军洗劫北京的情景，在他们的强盗行径背后正是这种强盗逻辑。《黑暗之心》初稿完成于 1899 年，八国联军侵华发生于 1900 年，两相对照，发人深思。而即使在当今世界，某些国家作为盎撒思想文化继承者，披着自由民主的外衣，但是其内心深处也未尝不是仍然信奉这一逻辑。

of the earth, which mostly means the taking it away from those who have a different complexion or slightly flatter noses[73] than ourselves, is not a pretty thing when you look into it too much. What redeems it is the idea only. An idea at the back of it; not a sentimental pretence[74] but an idea; and an unselfish belief in the idea—something you can set up, and bow down before, and offer a sacrifice to...[75]"

He broke off. Flames glided in the river, small green flames, red flames, white flames, pursuing, overtaking, joining, crossing each other—then separating slowly or hastily[76]. The traffic of

---

73. slightly flatter noses：稍微有点扁平的鼻子。这个句子里的"肤色和我们不同的人、鼻梁比我们扁平的人"，这里是指代非洲或者亚洲遭受侵略的国家的人民。

74. sentimental pretence：sentimental 意为"多愁善感的"，这里应该贬义化，意为"忸怩作态的，惺惺作态的"。pretence 意为"借口，托词"，这里指的是"自我辩护，狡辩"。

75. What redeems...a sacrifice to：在批判了殖民征服者的强盗行径之后，这一句提出了一种救赎的信念。尽管这种信念被说得十分高尚——甚至值得人们鞠躬和献祭，但是康拉德并没有明确说明这种信念究竟为何；甚至在读完小说全文之后也找不到明确的答案。联系上文猜测一下的话，这种信念也许是：摒弃强者理应欺压弱者的霸权主义观念，要把真正的文明成果带到相对落后的地区，实现世界各民族的共同进步。如果确实如此的话，那么可以说，康拉德的思想超越了他的民族和他的时代。

76. Flames glided...or hastily：这里是描绘泰晤士河上的夜航船，船上的灯火颜色各异，一条条船只在河上往来穿梭。如果译为："团团火焰在河水上漂动，极小的绿色的火焰、红色的火焰、白色的火焰，彼此追逐着，赶上去，合在一起，彼此交叉而过——然后又或慢或快地分开"，准则准矣，文采欠佳。英文往往重视思想深度，而在词汇上不事雕琢，带有盎撒文化的"硬朗"气质，常常出现形容词罗列，或者动词罗列。然而中文却以"博雅"著称，思想与文采并重，因而不可以直译为名照搬英文，有损作品的文学性。

the great city went on in the deepening night upon the sleepless river[77]. We looked on, waiting patiently—there was nothing else to do till the end of the flood; but it was only after a long silence, when he said, in a hesitating voice, "I suppose you fellows remember I did once turn fresh-water sailor[78] for a bit," that we knew we were fated, before the ebb began to run, to hear about one of Marlow's inconclusive[79] experiences.

"I don't want to bother you much with what happened to me personally," he began, showing in this remark the weakness of many tellers of tales who seem so often unaware of what their audience would like best to hear; "yet to understand the effect of it on me you ought to know how I got out there, what I saw, how I went up that river to the place where I first met the poor chap. It was the farthest point of navigation and the culminating[80] point

---

77. The traffic...sleepless river：这一句作为泰晤士河景色描绘的结束句，亦需要在表达上具有深沉厚重之感，这里直译为"在这愈来愈浓的夜色中，这个伟大城市的交通一直仍在这彻底不眠的河水上进行着"略显不妥，达不到"共感性"要求，其主要问题是没有根据汉语的表达习惯进行合理断句，使译文显得有些臃肿。英文是"树状结构"，汉语是"竹节结构"，译者作为两种语言的熟练使用者，应对中英文的基本区别有所把握。故而为保持深沉厚重的感觉，这里我译为"夜色愈发浓重，在不眠的泰晤士河上，这座伟大城市的交通永不停息。"

78. turn fresh-water sailor：变成了 / 当过内河的水手。淡水河即内河，船员的工作有远洋船员和内河船员之分。小说的主人公马洛两种工作都做过。

79. inconclusive：这个词有两层含义，一是"事情没有结局"，二是"事情难以定性"。这里我译为"一个难以评说、亦没有结局的故事"，虽把两层意思都译出来了，但我对自己的这句译文也不甚满意，如有佳译，欢迎来信探讨。

80. culminating：达到顶点的。这里是指"达到最高潮的时刻"。

of my experience. It seemed somehow to throw a kind of light on[81] everything about me—and into my thoughts. It was sombre enough, too—and pitiful—not extraordinary[82] in any way[83]—not very clear either. No, not very clear. And yet it seemed to throw a kind of light.

"I had then, as you remember, just returned to London after a lot of Indian Ocean, Pacific, China Seas—a regular dose of the East—six years or so, and I was loafing about, hindering you fellows in your work and invading your homes, just as though I had got a heavenly mission to civilize you[84]. It was very fine for a time, but after a bit I did get tired of resting. Then I began to look for a ship—I should think the hardest work on earth[85]. But the ships wouldn't even look at me. And I got tired of that game, too.

"Now when I was a little chap I had a passion for maps. I would look for hours at South America, or Africa, or Australia,

---

81. throw a kind of light on：类似的表达有 "shed light on sth"，是在科研论文中经常用到的。字面含义是 "把光亮投到……上"，也就是 "让……能够被人们看清楚"，即 "阐明，使清晰明白" 之意。

82. extraordinary：非凡的，卓越的，令人惊奇的。这里的意思是，马洛将要讲述的这段经历并非什么令人惊叹的传奇故事，它没有类似《双城记》或者《基督山伯爵》那样一波三折、引人入胜的故事情节。

83. in any way：无论以任何方式。这里是表示强调，说明无论从哪方面来看，马洛的故事都算不上什么伟大的传奇。

84. as though...civilize you：这里是说马洛很喜欢和人聊天讲故事，向别人灌输自己的观点。

85. I should...on earth：根据上下文，这里的逻辑结构是 "I should think (of looking for a ship as) the hardest work on earth"，所以译为 "找船这事儿，可比世界上任何工作都艰难得多了。" 表现出马洛稍微带些抱怨的口气。

and lose myself in all the glories of exploration[86]. At that time there were many blank spaces on the earth, and when I saw one that looked particularly inviting on a map (but they all look that) I would put my finger on it and say, 'When I grow up I will go there.' The North Pole was one of these places, I remember. Well, I haven't been there yet, and shall not try now. The glamour's off[87]. Other places were scattered about the hemispheres[88]. I have been in some of them, and...well, we won't talk about that. But there was one yet—the biggest, the most blank, so to speak—that I had a hankering after[89].

"True, by this time it was not a blank space any more. It had got filled since my boyhood with rivers and lakes and names[90]. It had ceased to be a blank space of delightful mystery—a white

---

86. all the glories of exploration：意为"探险事业的全部荣耀"。在康拉德生活的十九世纪，航海探险在欧洲国家蔚为风气，孩子们也不免受到影响，对于扬帆出海、探索新的疆域充满了憧憬。

87. The glamour's off: glamour 意为"吸引力，魅力"。off 在这里意为"萧条的，不再运转的，消失了的"。也就是说，北极探险对于马洛已经失去了诱惑力。这里看似闲话，实际上和康拉德自己所感受的时事紧密相关。康拉德幼时正是北极探险风行一时的年代，在他成年之后，北极探险的热潮已然过去（比较大的一部分原因是上述幽冥号和恐怖号的船难）。因此这句话还有一种理解，那就是"人们对北极的探险已经不再热衷了。"

88. hemispheres：半球。这里用了复数，事实上指代整个地球。

89. I had a hankering after: hankering 意为"渴望，向往"，after 如同"chase after"或者"run after"中一样，含有一种不断追寻而不放弃（紧追不舍）的意味。

90. It had...and names：地图上的空白处在几年时间内就填满了河流湖泊和它们的名字，这说明欧洲的殖民开拓者已经染指了非洲越来越多的地方。

patch for a boy to dream gloriously over[91]. It had become a place of darkness[92]. But there was in it one river especially, a mighty big river, that you could see on the map, resembling an immense snake uncoiled[93], with its head in the sea, its body at rest curving afar over a vast country, and its tail lost in the depths of the land[94]. And as I looked at the map of it in a shop-window, it fascinated me as a snake would a bird—a silly little bird[95]. Then I remembered there was a big concern[96], a Company for trade on that river. Dash it all[97]! I thought to myself, they can't trade without using some kind of craft on that lot of fresh water—steamboats[98]! Why shouldn't I

---

91. over：意为"结束，完了"。这里是说随着地图上那片空白的消失，小男孩关于探险和荣耀的梦想也画上了句号，幻灭了。

92. It had...of darkness：这里可能有两层意思，一是由于众多地名密密麻麻地填满了地图，这片区域的颜色已经变得很深了；二是地图的日益完备意味着欧洲殖民者已经侵入了这片土地，从后文可知，殖民者在这里奴役人民、掠夺资源，把这片原本自由的土地变成了黑暗的人间地狱。

93. uncoiled：coil 意为"卷缠，盘绕"，通过添加前缀和后缀，uncoiled 的意思就是"不再卷缠的，伸展开来的"。

94. with its head...the depths of the land：这里是书中第一次对故事的发生地——刚果河进行描述。作者以马洛的视角展现了非洲地图上刚果河的雄姿。译文需要体现原文的宏大气魄。

95. it fascinated...little bird：这句的意思是"它就像蛇迷住小鸟那样迷住了我——我就好像那只不由自主的小鸟"。silly 在这里不是"愚蠢的"，而是"失去理智的，呆住了的，傻愣愣的"意思。

96. concern：意为"康采恩"，指的是"相关利益共同体""大型企业集团"，是一种规模庞大而复杂的资本主义垄断组织形式。来源于德语 Konzern。

97. Dash it all：俚语，意为"见鬼了，真该死"。这里可能是一种强化语气的表达，表示瞬间下定决心，哪怕孤注一掷也要去做某事。

98. steamboat：汽船。通过后文可知，这里的汽船指的是烧锅炉驱动的蒸汽轮船。

try to get charge of one? I went on along Fleet Street[99], but could not shake off the idea. The snake had charmed me.

"You understand it was a Continental concern[100], that Trading society; but I have a lot of relations[101] living on the Continent, because it's cheap and not so nasty as it looks, they say.

"I am sorry to own[102] I began to worry them[103]. This was already a fresh departure[104] for me. I was not used to get[105] things that way, you know. I always went my own road and on my own legs where I had a mind to go[106]. I wouldn't have believed it of

---

99. Fleet Street：舰队街是英国伦敦市内一条著名的街道，依邻近的舰队河命名。这里是几家著名报馆的所在地，通常也指代英国新闻业的中心。

100. a Continental concern：欧洲大陆的一家大公司。结合下文，这家大陆公司的总部很可能是在法国。原因有三，一是穿越英吉利海峡之后距离法国较近；二是马洛去公司总部面试的时候，老板和体检的医生都对他讲过法语；三是马洛获得船长任命前往非洲履职的时候，乘坐的是一艘法国轮船。

101. relations：这里指的是亲朋好友。

102. own：承认为某事负全责。这里意即"不好意思，我得坦白地告诉你们，……"

103. worry them：worry 在这里不是常见的"使担心"的意思，而是"烦扰，使不得安宁"之意，是说马洛开始拜托大陆上的亲友，帮他在那家公司里谋个船长职位。

104. a fresh departure：departure 意为"出发"，这里指的是"经历，经验"。也就是说，托人求职对于马洛来说，是一件前所未有之事。以前的他从未这样做过。

105. get：这里似是康拉德的笔误。be used to doing 是"习惯于做某事"，因而这里使用 getting 可能才是作者原意。be used to do 意为"被用来做某事"。get things that way 意为"以那种方式来做事"，这里是说，马洛很不习惯以那种"走后门"的方式来实现自己的目的。

106. I always...to go：这里涉及直译和意译的不同选择。有的译本译为："我总是用自己的腿，走自己的路，去自己想去的地方。"这里 （转下页）

myself[107]; but, then—you see—I felt somehow I must get there by hook or by crook[108]. So I worried them. The men said 'My dear fellow,' and did nothing. Then—would you believe it?—I tried the women. I, Charlie Marlow, set the women to work[109]—to get a job. Heavens! Well, you see, the notion drove me[110]. I had an aunt, a dear enthusiastic soul[111]. She wrote: 'It[112] will be delightful. I am ready to do anything, anything for you. It is a glorious idea. I know

---

（接上页）"用自己的腿走到自己想去的地方"是英语习惯的比喻，直译也无可厚非。但是相应的意义，在汉语中习惯的比喻，往往是"用自己的双手打开一片天。"两者皆可，见仁见智。

107. I wouldn't...of myself：这里是说连马洛自己也不敢相信，自己竟然变成了依靠"走后门"来达到目的的人。

108. by hook or by crook：英语习语，意为"不择手段，无论如何"。hook 意为"钩子"，crook 意为"曲柄杖"，意义相近，韵脚相同。也就是说有钩子用钩子，没有钩子用曲柄杖代替也行，无论手段如何，达成目的才是最重要的。

109. work：这里指的是"跑腿，游说，四下活动"。

110. the notion drove me：notion 在这里意思是"一时的念头，突发的奇想"，drive 则意为"驱使，迫使"。

111. enthusiastic soul：enthusiastic 意为"热心的，热情的"，soul 意为"灵魂，精华，"在这里是 an aunt 的同位语，代指"人"。例如，"Many poor souls have perished trying to discover the perplexing secret." 这里 souls 指的就是人，"许多不幸的人在试图揭开这个秘密的过程中遇难了。"soul 指代人往往含有抛除性别、年龄、身份地位等外在因素而抽象出来的一个个在上帝面前平等的灵魂的含义。

112. It：在英语翻译中，找到代词指代的准确的对象往往十分重要。在这里，it 可能有两种理解，一是指代"为马洛跑关系找工作"这件事，那么马洛姨妈的意思就是"帮你做事不辛苦，很乐意效劳"。二是指代信件上文中可能提到的"去非洲内河开汽船"这件事，那么马洛姨妈的意思就是"那种工作一定很有意思"。由于下文很快出现了 it is a glorious idea，她称赞马洛的想法好极了，其中 it 指代的是"开汽船"，因而我采用了第二种理解。

the wife of a very high personage in the Administration[113], and also a man who has lots of influence with,' etc. She was determined to make no end of fuss[114] to get me appointed skipper of a river steamboat[115], if such was my fancy.

"I got my appointment—of course; and I got it very quick. It appears the Company had received news that one of their captains had been killed in a scuffle with the natives. This was my chance, and it made me the more anxious to go. It was only months and months afterwards, when I made the attempt to[116] recover what was left of the body[117], that I heard the original quarrel[118] arose from a misunderstanding about some hens. Yes, two black hens. Fresleven—that was the fellow's name, a Dane—thought himself

---

113. Administration：这里用的大写，一是可能指 "政府当局"，二是可能指 "公司高层"。

114. make no end of fuss：make a fuss 意为 "小题大做，大惊小怪"，在这里加上 no end of，事实上是习惯表达的一种灵活化用，意为 "不停地忙来忙去"，也就是说马洛姨妈将 "不遗余力"，想尽一切办法来帮忙。这指一种夸张和强调的语气。

115. get me...river steamboat：get me appointed (as)... 意为 "使我被任命为……；让我得到……的职位"。skipper 意为 "队长，船长"。river steamboat 意为 "内河上的汽船"。

116. made the attempt to：试图，尝试去做某事。这里是说马洛继任船长之后，曾去寻找和收敛前任船长的尸骨。这也许是公司派给他的任务，也可能是死者家属的拜托，或者是马洛自身责任感的驱使。但是由于已经过去了很长时间，他也不确定是否还能找得到那些遗骨，所以只能说是一种尝试。

117. recover...the body：what was left of the body 和下文中的 remains 同义复现，都是指前任船长的遗骨。

118. the original quarrel：意为 "最初的争吵"，也就是指冲突的起因。

wronged somehow in the bargain[119], so he went ashore[120] and started to hammer the chief of the village with a stick. Oh, it didn't surprise me in the least to hear this[121], and at the same time to be told that Fresleven was the gentlest, quietest creature[122] that ever walked on two legs. No doubt he was; but he had been a couple of years already out there engaged in the noble cause[123], you know, and he probably felt the need at last of asserting his self-respect[124] in some way. Therefore he whacked the old nigger[125] mercilessly, while a big crowd of his people watched him, thunderstruck, till some man—I was told the chief's son—in desperation at

---

119. bargain：这里指的是"交易"，指的是那个丹麦船长向当地村民买两只母鸡的事。

120. went ashore：上岸，踏上陆地。指的是丹麦船长下船回到村子里，去找当地人的麻烦。

121. it didn't...to hear this：意为"听到这件事，我丝毫也没有感到惊讶"，这说明欧洲殖民者在非洲气焰嚣张，他们随意迫害当地人民已经是马洛见惯了的事了。

122. creature：生物，动物。结合下文"两条腿走路的"，可知这里指的是"人，人类"。这个词带点宗教意味。基督教认为，世界是上帝创造的，人也是上帝创造出来的产物。

123. engaged in the noble cause：从事高尚的事业。这里指的是欧洲人以"为非洲带来光明和进步"为幌子，行压迫和掠夺之实。这一段讲述了马洛的前任船长的故事，充分体现了康拉德写作的特征。他把对受苦难者的悲悯和对压迫者的讽刺，以及对现实的无奈和清醒的认识，化作犀利辛辣的"黑色幽默"付诸笔端，使读者倍加感受到这个世界的荒谬。

124. asserting his self-respect：assert 意为"维护，坚持"，self-respect 意为"自尊心"，这里指的是个人权威。这里是说丹麦船长决心给村民们一点颜色瞧瞧，以逞自己作为殖民者的威风。

125. nigger：对黑人的蔑称。这里借用了丹麦船长的口气以表示对殖民者的讽刺。

hearing the old chap yell, made a tentative jab[126] with a spear at the white man—and of course it went quite easy between the shoulder-blades[127]. Then the whole population cleared into the forest, expecting all kinds of calamities[128] to happen, while, on the other hand, the steamer Fresleven commanded left also in a bad panic[129], in charge of the engineer, I believe. Afterwards nobody seemed to trouble much about[130] Fresleven's remains, till I got out and stepped into his shoes[131]. I couldn't let it rest[132], though; but when an opportunity offered at last[133] to meet my

---

126. made a tentative jab：试探着戳了一下。这里的 tentative 表现了村长儿子的纠结心理，他既仇恨殖民者，不忍父亲遭受这样的毒打，又深知殖民者拥有坚船利炮，反抗的后果可能是村民们无法承受的。因而虽然他为了维护父亲拿起长矛向丹麦船长刺了过去，但是这悲愤的一刺却是纠结犹豫的，是更具有威吓和自卫性质的，而非下定决心想要杀死对方。

127. of course...shoulder-blades：shoulder-blade 意为"肩胛骨"。从这句话可以看出白人殖民者虽然倚仗火器的威力横行无忌，但是和黑人相比体格羸弱，不堪一击。村长儿子很可能只是示威一下，他也没有想到白人竟然这么容易杀，竟一下子就被长矛穿体而过、倒地而死。

128. calamities：灾难。这里指的是村民想象中欧洲殖民者会用火枪大炮之类对他们进行疯狂的报复。

129. in a bad panic：极度恐惧，一片慌乱。这里是说，欧洲殖民者其实色厉内荏，事实上他们一遇到反击就自乱阵脚，慌不择路地开船逃命去了。

130. trouble much about：为……十分操心。这里是说殖民者们匆忙撤退之后，似乎就没人关心还留在村子里的丹麦船长的尸体了。

131. stepped into his shoes：意为"设身处地；步了后尘"，这里是说马洛接了前任的位置，成了新的船长。

132. let it rest：指的是让前任的尸体就这么留在岸上，放任不管。

133. When...at last：意为"直到最后（亲眼见到前任船长）的那一刻"，使用 opportunity 和 offer，是为了令读者感受到这项搜寻工作其实成功的机会十分渺茫，最终能够找到前任船长也是运气使然了。

predecessor, the grass growing through his ribs[134] was tall enough to hide his bones. They were all there. The supernatural being[135] had not been touched after he fell. And the village was deserted[136], the huts[137] gaped black[138], rotting, all askew within the fallen enclosures. A calamity had come to it, sure enough. The people had vanished. Mad terror had scattered them, men, women, and children, through the bush, and they had never returned. What became of the hens[139] I don't know either. I should think the cause of progress[140] got them, anyhow. However, through this glorious affair[141] I got my appointment, before I had fairly begun to hope

---

134. through his ribs：从他的肋骨间。可见时间已经过去了很久，马洛找到的已经只是一副骨架了。

135. the supernatural being：直译为"超自然的人物"或者"神奇的人物"的话，意思是对的。这里是说前任船长的骨头居然还很完整地留在原地，在非洲丛林这样一个遍布猛兽和秃鹫的地方，真是让人觉得不可思议。这也从侧面反映出村子里的人全部逃走以后，村子里有多么荒凉。自然不会有人敢回来收尸，而且连狗都没有啃食过船长的尸体。这里体现出作者一种讽刺的口吻——殖民者在非洲做尽坏事，人憎狗嫌。另外，到现在已经出现了三种对"人"的代称，分别是 soul，creature 和 being，这也体现了英文善用丰富的词汇进行同义复现的行文特征。

136. was deserted：被抛弃了，被舍弃了。这里是说村民们背井离乡逃难去了，村庄就这样被荒弃了。

137. hut：简陋的小屋，棚屋。专卖披萨的连锁餐馆必胜客的英文就是 Pizza Hut，直译为"披萨小屋"。这里指的是非洲人居住的简陋草屋。

138. gaped black：意思是"张着黑洞洞的大嘴"。这里是形容破烂的草屋门窗朽坏，好似大张着嘴一样露出黑洞洞的内部。

139. What...the hens：指的是引发这场灾难的那两只母鸡的结局。

140. the cause of progress："进步的事业"，这里是讽刺殖民者的虚伪和残暴。

141. this glorious affair："这桩光荣的事件"，同样是表达了作者的讽刺。

for it[142].

"I flew around like mad to get ready, and before forty-eight hours I was crossing the Channel[143] to show myself to my employers, and sign the contract. In a very few hours I arrived in a city that always makes me think of a whited sepulchre[144]. Prejudice

---

142. before...hope for it：意为"在我还没有开始真正企盼得到任命之前"，说明拜前任船长惹出的这场乱子所赐，对马洛的任命来得很快，甚至马洛还没开始焦急等待、翘首企盼，就被告知自己已经继任船长了。这同样是作者的讽刺笔法。

143. crossing the Channel：这里的 channel 用的大写，其实指的是 the English Channel，英吉利海峡。康拉德行文有这样的特点，就是尽管读者都知道他笔下的 the river，the Channel 等等指的是什么，但是他往往不把这些地理或历史事物的全名写出来，而是隐去名称，进行模糊化处理。这也许因为这些事物对他的英语读者而言都耳熟能详，无须多说；也可能是作者想要给小说中的时空营造某种超现实的感觉。我个人认为，遇到这种情况，译者在完全拿得准的情况下，可以适当增补康拉德刻意隐去的信息；因为这些事物对于中文读者也许并不像英文读者那样"耳熟能详、心领神会"，因此弥填其中的信息差也应是译者分内之事。当然，这样做也许会打破作者"营造超现实氛围"的意图。

144. a whited sepulchre：这一个英语习惯表达，意为"伪君子，伪善者，口是心非的人"。直译为"粉刷过的坟墓"。康拉德善用象征手法，在他笔下，一个事物往往具有多重象征意义，例如本书题目中的 darkness，就象征了非洲大陆；蒙昧晦暗的非洲丛林；混沌未开的落后状态；神秘与未知之境；人类的懵懂迷惘；殖民者内心的贪婪与文明外衣下的野蛮等等。从地图上可以看到，刚果河好像一个半圆弧围住一片近似圆形的刚果盆地，而刚果盆地被称为"非洲的心脏"，原因之一就是因为它正好位于非洲大陆的正中心。非洲旧时人称"黑非洲"，这就构成了本书题目 Heart of Darkness 的表面意象。在这里，a whited sepulchre 兼具"坟墓"和"伪善者"的两重含义。就第一层意义而言，第一，这座城市朴素安静，外观上好似坟墓；第二，不明内情的青年抱着探险和开拓的梦想来到这里，然后被送到"黑非洲"，几乎全都一去不回，埋骨异乡；他们在那个洞悉他们命运的老女人的眼中已经和死人无异，因而这里可以说就是他们的坟墓；第三，这个城市中的大多数人（例如大老板和他的职员；他们代表了欧洲殖民者）都是极度自私的（转下页）

no doubt[145]. I had no difficulty in finding the Company's offices. It was the biggest thing in the town, and everybody I met was full of it[146]. They were going to run an over-sea empire[147], and make no

---

（接上页）利己主义者，他们的眼中只有金钱，他们做的一切事情都是孜孜求钱，为此不惜屠杀非洲的人民和非洲的大象；他们没有什么善良的人性和真实的情感，更罔论远大的理想，因而在康拉德看来，这些人活着也只是一具具行尸走肉，浑身散发着金钱和腐肉的臭气。所以这里就是一座"坟墓之城""死者之城"。就第二层意义而言，"伪善者"则更着重揭露了殖民者用谎言粉饰自己的行径。他们明明像是强盗和暴徒一样给非洲带去了无尽的灾难，而在他们的口中和笔下，自己却成了"光明的使徒""进步的使者"，是为蒙昧的非洲带来先进文明的充满了爱和使命感的先驱。这也解释了为什么马洛在出发前就有所预感似的充满疑虑，而在他真正目睹了发生在非洲的种种暴行之后，在目睹了人性中的极善与极恶相撞所迸发出的烈焰之后，成了故事开篇那样一个看透了人世间的种种虚伪，满面沧桑而又心怀悲悯的醒悟者。

145. Prejudice no doubt：这句和上句衔接紧密，其实是作者为了上句带贬义的比喻打圆场。和之前说过的可以确认无疑的泰晤士河、英吉利海峡不同，上句提到的城市具体是哪一个，这里无法确定；但是如果推测一下的话，很有可能是巴黎。康拉德原籍俄属波兰，他是成年以后才入籍英国的，但是他的思想行为都非常典型的英国化了，包括从文中可以看出的英国对于欧洲大陆的某种心理优越感。雨果的《巴黎圣母院》在 19 世纪就已极具声名，康拉德早年在法国读书时很可能也读过。《巴黎圣母院》中的弗雷洛副主教，道貌岸然却满肚子邪恶的欲望，正影射了那些佛口蛇心的欧洲殖民者。因而上条注释中的 a whited sepulchre，似乎也有可能是这位《巴黎圣母院》中的主人公。这一推测是否如实，也许只有康拉德本人才知道了。但是 a whited sepulchre 无疑是一句不怎么友好的评语，考虑到潜在的法国读者的感受，康拉德确实有必要紧接一句打个圆场。

146. was full of it：结合上下文可以想象，这里的"full of it"是指"滔滔不绝，口若悬河"，也就是说，马洛在打听公司总部的路径的时候，他问到的每一个路人都会滔滔不绝地告诉他该如何如何走，这从侧面反映出这家公司可谓家喻户晓，盛名远扬；城里的人没有一个不对它非常熟悉的。

147. run an over-sea empire：字面意思是"营建一个海外帝国"，但还是译为"海外贸易王国"为好，因为这家法国公司明显只是一家贸易公司，即使它富可敌国，它也并没有在海外建立起真正可以称之为"帝国"的军事和行政统治。

end of coin[148] by trade.

"A narrow and deserted street in deep shadow, high houses, innumerable windows with venetian blinds, a dead silence, grass sprouting between the stones, imposing carriage archways right and left, immense double doors standing ponderously ajar. I slipped through[149] one of these cracks[150], went up a swept and ungarnished staircase[151], as arid as a desert, and opened the first door I came to. Two women, one fat and the other slim, sat on straw-bottomed chairs, knitting black wool[152]. The slim one got up and walked straight at me—still knitting with downcast eyes—and only just as I began to think of getting out of her way, as you would for a somnambulist, stood still, and looked up. Her

---

148. make no end of coin：赚取数不清的钞票。前文中出现过 make no end of fuss，可见康拉德对于 make no end of 这个用法还是比较偏爱的。

149. slipped through：（从缝隙里）溜进去。这里是说马洛从门缝里进去，巍峨沉重的大门有一种让人显得很渺小的感觉。

150. cracks：缝隙，裂缝。这里和上文的 ajar 相呼应。因为大门是半开的（ajar），所以就会有门缝（cracks）。

151. a swept and ungarnished staircase：swept 是动词 sweep 的过去分词做形容词，意为"打扫过了的"。ungarnished 由 garnish 变化而来，意为"未经装饰的；无装饰的"。staircase 在这里意为"楼梯间"。一般来说，大公司的楼梯间会有绘画或者植物之类的装饰，显得富有生机活力；但是这里却光秃秃的什么也没有。上面的情景描绘都是在印证马洛对这座城市的整体印象：一座坟墓之城。

152. knitting black wool：编织着黑色毛线。这句中"两个女人，一胖一瘦，椅子上垫着草垫，手里织着黑毛线"，从人物到陈设都简单朴素，毫无生机。再往下读其实可以发现，这两个负责接待的女人就好像守墓人一样，经过了她们办理的手续，包括马洛在内的很多求职者就被送往了非洲之心的刚果盆地——一个"死亡和贸易在一起狂欢乱舞"的黑暗之地。

dress was as plain as an umbrella-cover[153], and she turned round without a word and preceded me into[154] a waiting-room. I gave my name, and looked about. Deal table[155] in the middle, plain chairs all round the walls, on one end a large shining map, marked with all the colours of a rainbow[156]. There was a vast amount of red—good to see at any time[157], because one knows that some real work is done in there[158], a deuce of[159] a lot of blue, a little green,

153. as plain as an umbrella-cover：plain 意为"无装饰的；单色的；朴素的"，umbrella-cover 是雨伞套子（试比较：bookcover 是书套；书皮）。这里的意思是，瘦女人的衣裙朴素得好像一只雨伞套子；她的衣服毫无装饰性，只不过是把人装在里边而已。这段文字不断描写这座"坟墓之城"是如何单调朴素，此处的描写也与前后文保持了一致。这种无处不在的"单调朴素"正符合人们对"坟墓"的印象。

154. preceded me into：precede 意为"在前领路"，这里是说瘦女人作为前台接待，领着马洛到等候室去。

155. Deal table：deal 在这里作形容词，意为"冷杉木制的"。

156. marked with...of a rainbow：这里是形容地图上标注着各种鲜亮的颜色，看上去十分惹眼。

157. good to see at any time：意思是"一看到就会让人高兴"。这里并不是说明他们认为红色是喜庆的颜色，西方文化中基本上没有"红色＝喜庆"的概念；而是说因为地图上红色标记的意思是"那里的贸易网络已经完全建设好了"，而工作上的进展总是令人愉快的。只不过，这里所谓的"工作"其实是殖民掠夺。当然还有另一种可能，"good to see"意思是"引人注目的，总是能让人一眼就看见的"。

158. some real work is done in there：在那里已经扎扎实实地完成了不少工作。

159. a deuce of：这里应该不是一个很正式的英语用法，根据上下文推测，a deuce of 在这里的作用可能只是加强语气。deuce 是一个俚语中的脏词，例如，What the deuce！真他妈见鬼！或者另一种可能，a deuce of 在这里的意思是"平分秋色的"，也就是说和红色的面积相比，蓝色的面积也相当不小，两者几乎一样大。

smears[160] of orange, and, on the East Coast, a purple patch, to show where the jolly pioneers of progress drink the jolly lager-beer[161]. However, I wasn't going into any of these. I was going into the yellow. Dead in the centre. And the river was there—fascinating—deadly—like a snake[162]. Ough! A door opened, a white-haired secretarial head, but wearing a compassionate expression[163], appeared, and a skinny forefinger beckoned me

160. smear：涂抹上去的一点污渍。这说明橙色的面积并不大。

161. where the...jolly lager-beer：pioneers of progress 意为"进步事业的先驱"，指的是那些从欧洲去往非洲的殖民开拓者。lager-beer 意为"熟啤酒"。熟啤酒是把鲜啤酒经过巴氏灭菌法处理而成的，保质期可长达 90 天以上，便于运输。非洲当地可能不产啤酒，殖民者喝的酒都是从欧洲千里迢迢运过去的，因而只能是保质期长的熟啤酒。这句里边出现了两次 jolly（愉快的），表现出"进步事业"蒸蒸日上、"文明使者"喜气洋洋的氛围，这是康拉德对殖民侵略的一种辛辣讽刺。为了表现出原文 jolly 这个词的强调性的复现，译为"到处都有贼厉害的文明使者在喝着贼棒的熟啤酒了"，这在意义上也和上文"地图好像五颜六色的彩虹"形成了呼应。另外，jolly lager-beer 似乎也在仿拟 Jolly Rogers（海盗旗；骷髅旗），揭露"文明使者"就像海盗一样具有侵略和掠夺的本性。

162. And the river...like a snake：the river 在这里指的是刚果河，也就是前文中描述的马洛小时候看过的地图以及成年后在舰队街看到的地图上的那条大河。这次他在等待工作面试，面对着眼前会议室桌子上的非洲地图，马洛即将实现多年来的夙愿，前往非洲亲眼目睹刚果河的雄姿了。激动的心情可以想见。fascinating 说明那条大河是多么的迷人，而 deadly，则说明那里充满了危险，很有可能丧命于斯，有去无回。这就像 snake 一样——想想希腊神话中的蛇发女妖美杜莎（Medusa），她的眼睛充满了邪恶的魅力，让人不知不觉沉沦其中，然后被变成石头。类似的神话还有《奥德赛》中的海妖塞壬（Siren）和海涅诗歌中的高崖上美丽的女妖罗累莱——她们和这里的刚果河一样，都是 fascinating 和 deadly 的化身。

163. wearing a...expression：wear 的意思可以是"穿着（什么衣服）"，或者是"带着（什么表情）"。compassionate 意为"同情的，怜悯的"。这里是指秘书脸上带着怜悯的神情看着马洛。

into the sanctuary[164]. Its light was dim, and a heavy writing-desk squatted[165] in the middle. From behind that structure came out an impression of pale plumpness in a frock-coat[166]. The great man himself. He was five feet six, I should judge, and had his grip on the handle-end of ever so many millions[167]. He shook hands, I fancy, murmured vaguely, was satisfied with my French. Bon Voyage[168].

"In about forty-five seconds[169] I found myself again in the waiting-room with the compassionate secretary, who, full of desolation and sympathy, made me sign some document. I

---

164. a skinny...the sanctuary: skinny 意为"极瘦的，皮包骨的"，forefinger 意为"食指"，beckoned me into 意为"把我召唤到（什么地方去）"，sanctuary 意为"庇护所，圣殿，圣堂"，因为大老板的办公室不是什么人都可以随便进的，那里有一种权威和隐私性，因而称为 sanctuary。这句话的意思是"秘书用一根瘦瘦的手指示意我跟他进到大老板的办公室里"。

165. squatted: 蹲坐；占据空间。这里和 heavy 相呼应，说明写字台又大又重，很占地方。下句中的 structure 也是对"写字台"的同义复现。

166. came out...in a frock-coat: come out 意为"出现；显露"。因为马洛从会议室进到昏暗的老板办公室，肯定需要一点时间来适应光线，所以老板的样子是慢慢浮现出来，逐渐被马洛看清的。come out an impression 这一表达用得十分形象。老板的样子就是"pale plumpness in a frock-coat"，苍白、肥硕、身穿双排扣的长礼服。pale plumpness 体现了英文善用抽象词汇的特点。但是翻译的时候，英文中的抽象词往往需要译为具体词。

167. had his grip...many millions: grip 意为"掌握之中；手心里"，这句话十分形象地表现了大老板是多么的有钱。而这些钱，都是通过掠夺非洲的财富以及剥削马洛这样的员工而获得的。

168. Bon Voyage: 法语，意为"一路顺风；旅途愉快"。

169. about forty-five seconds: 大约四十五秒。这里是说明马洛和大老板见面时间很短。大老板忙着挣钱，日理万机，自然不会留给马洛更多的会面时间。译为"前后不到一分钟"似乎更加通顺。

believe I undertook amongst other things not to disclose any trade secrets[170]. Well, I am not going to.

"I began to feel slightly uneasy. You know I am not used to such ceremonies[171], and there was something ominous in the atmosphere. It was just as though I had been let into some conspiracy—I don't know—something not quite right[172]; and I was glad to get out. In the outer room the two women knitted black wool feverishly. People were arriving, and the younger one was walking back and forth introducing them. The old one sat on her chair. Her flat cloth slippers were propped up[173] on a foot-warmer, and a cat reposed on her lap. She wore a starched white affair on her head, had a wart on one cheek, and silver-rimmed spectacles hung on the tip of her nose. She glanced at me above the glasses. The swift and indifferent placidity[174] of that look troubled me[175].

---

170. trade secrets：商业秘密。按说雇佣合同中签署保密条款属于常规操作，但是马洛从非洲回来之后才知道，所谓"商业机密"，其实就是殖民者在非洲进行掠夺和杀戮的事实。公司当然是不允许这种事情被公之于众的。

171. I am not used to such ceremonies：意思是"我不习惯这种仪式性、流程性的事情"。这说明马洛个性耿直，相比起繁文缛节的手续或者仪式，他更喜欢做实实在在的事情。

172. something not quite right：不太正当的事情。这和上面的 conspiracy 意思差不多，都是指这家公司诱骗人们去非洲做坏事。

173. propped up：prop up 意为"支撑；支持；鼓励"，这里是指那个老女人用脚蹬着暖炉的动作。

174. placidity：平稳；安静；神色不动的样子。这里是指老女人瞥向马洛的眼光里波澜不惊，不带一丝感情。

175. troubled me：这里可以理解为，老女人那平静而冷漠的一瞥令马洛感到不舒服，或者是不安、困惑。总之马洛不喜欢她的这个眼神，而且对这个眼神的含义心中不安。

Two youths with foolish and cheery countenances[176] were being piloted[177] over, and she threw at them the same quick glance of unconcerned wisdom[178]. She seemed to know all about them and about me, too. An eerie feeling came over me. She seemed uncanny and fateful. Often far away there I thought of these two, guarding the door of Darkness, knitting black wool as for a warm pall[179], one introducing, introducing continuously to the unknown, the other scrutinizing the cheery and foolish faces with unconcerned old eyes. Ave! Old knitter of black wool. Morituri te salutant[180]. Not many of those she looked at ever saw her again—not half, by a long way[181].

---

176. with foolish and cheery countenances：懵懂无知、一脸欢喜的样子。countenances 意为"面容；表情"。这里是说那些被带进去面试、签合同的人对自己的命运一无所知，他们以为自己找到了好工作，马上可以赚大钱了，自然非常开心。

177. pilot：意为"带领；指引"。和上文 precede 是同义复现。都是指那个年轻些的瘦女人走在前边领路，把马洛和别的求职者带进密室里去给大老板过目。

178. unconcerned wisdom：wisdom 意为"智慧"，说明老女人完全知道去非洲工作意味着什么；unconcerned 意为"不关心的"，意思是她知晓这些人的命运，但是她漠不关心，缄口不言。

179. pall：裹尸布；棺材罩。在这里，两个女人编织黑毛线的情景被赋予了一种隐喻意义——她们在编织裹尸布，好像在准备为马洛和那些求职者送葬。

180. Ave!Old knitter of black wool. Morituri te salutant：这句是拉丁文，传说是古罗马的角斗士在上阵之前向凯撒致意所用的口号："Ave Caesar, Morituri te salutant!"意为"恺撒万岁！我们这些将死之人向您致敬！"这里套用了这个句型，把"凯撒"换成了"编织黑毛线的老女人"，是在对"老女人"这个代表了命运的强大和吊诡的意象发出感叹，嘲讽公司诱骗年轻人去非洲送死的荒谬现实。

181. by a long way：意思是"远远不到（一半）"。这也是在暗指很多人去了非洲就回不来了。

"There was yet a visit to the doctor. 'A simple formality,' assured me the secretary, <u>with an air of taking an immense part in all my sorrows</u>¹⁸². Accordingly a young chap wearing his hat over the left eyebrow, some clerk I suppose—there must have been clerks in the business, though the house was <u>as still as a house in a city of the dead</u>¹⁸³—came from somewhere up-stairs, and <u>led me forth</u>¹⁸⁴. He was shabby and careless, with inkstains on the sleeves of his jacket, and his cravat was large and <u>billowy</u>¹⁸⁵, under <u>a chin shaped like the toe of an old boot</u>¹⁸⁶. It was a little too early for the doctor, so I proposed a drink, and thereupon he <u>developed a vein of joviality</u>¹⁸⁷. As we sat over our vermouths he glorified the Company's business, and <u>by and by</u> I expressed casually my

---

182. with an air...my sorrows：with an air of 意为"带着一种……的气氛；一副……的样子"。taking an immense part in all my sorrows 就是说，他好像恨不得把我的苦难分走一大部分；对我的不幸遭遇感同身受的样子。这里译为"一副恨不得替我受苦受难的样子"。

183. as still as a house in a city of the dead：这句话意为"就好像死城之中的一座寂静的房屋"。still 意为"静止不动的；（画面）定格的"。

184. led me forth：直译是"领我往前走"。因为上文提到"接下来要去体检"，所以为了通顺，这里译为"领我去医生那儿"。

185. billowy：汹涌的；巨浪似的。这里指的是"领结鼓鼓囊囊的"，显然也是在说明这个办事员不修边幅的样子。

186. a chin...old boot："好像老式皮靴的靴尖儿那样形状的下巴"，结合下文，可能是在暗示这个办事员是个虚伪的利己主义者。康拉德经常通过外貌描写影射人物的性格特征。

187. developed a vein of joviality：这里似乎应该是 a veil of，即"一层薄薄的……；一丝……"的意思。a veil of joviality 就是"一丝愉快的表情"。develop 意为"产生出；露出"。

surprise at[188] him not going out there. He became very cool and collected[189] all at once. 'I am not such a fool as I look[190], quoth Plato to his disciples[191],' he said sententiously, emptied his glass with great resolution[192], and we rose.

"The old doctor felt my pulse, evidently thinking of something else the while. 'Good, good for there,' he mumbled, and then with a certain eagerness asked me whether I would let him measure my head. Rather surprised, I said Yes, when he produced a thing like calipers and got the dimensions back and front and every way, taking notes carefully. He was an unshaven little man in a threadbare coat like a gaberdine, with his feet in slippers, and I thought him a harmless fool. 'I always ask leave[193], in the interests

---

188. by and by...surprise at：这里很有意思，可以看出正直的马洛也有精明和搞笑的一面。办事员一个劲儿吹捧公司的业绩有多么好，马洛不动声色，顺着他的话头，自然而然地惊叹道"哇，这么棒，能挣这么多钱，那你怎么不去呢？"直击要害，顿时让对方无处遁形。

189. cool and collected：冷静和审慎。collected 和 composed 一样，都是指"镇静的，毫不慌乱的"。保持大脑能够有条不紊地处理信息，就是"镇静、审慎"。这里是说办事员尽管鼓动别人去冒险，说得天花乱坠，无比狂热；但是如果要让他自己去，他就非常冷静，慎之又慎了。

190. I am not such a fool as I look：意为"我可不像我看起来那样的蠢"。这句话的出处我没有查到，也许是因为有人笑话柏拉图是个大块头，他才会说出这句话。

191. quoth Plato to his disciples：quoth 意思是"说"，是个古词。disciples 意为"弟子；门徒"。柏拉图是古希腊著名的哲学家。

192. emptied his glass with great resolution：empty 是动词，意为"喝光"；with great resolution 意为"以一种巨大的决心"，在这里也就是"把杯中酒一饮而尽"。

193. ask leave：常见的用法是"请假"。而这里实际上是 ask leave to measure...，也就是"征得同意，来测量（马洛等人的头围）"。

of science, to measure the crania of those going out there,' he said. 'And when they come back, too?' I asked. 'Oh, I never see them,' he remarked; 'and, moreover, the changes take place inside[194], you know.' He smiled, as if at some quiet joke. 'So you are going out there. Famous. Interesting, too.' He gave me a searching glance, and made another note. 'Ever any madness in your family?' he asked, in a matter-of-fact tone. I felt very annoyed. 'Is that question in the interests of science, too?' 'It would be,' he said, without taking notice of my irritation[195], 'interesting for science to watch the mental changes of individuals, on the spot, but...' 'Are you an alienist?' I interrupted. 'Every doctor should be— a little,' answered that original, imperturbably. 'I have a little theory which you messieurs[196] who go out there must help me to prove. This is my share in the advantages my country shall reap from the possession of such a magnificent dependency[197]. The

---

194. the changes take place inside：“变化发生在头骨里边”。这句话暗示了，去往非洲的人在目睹了那里的黑暗景象之后，他们的思想都会受到冲击而发生变化。事实上马洛就是如此。

195. without taking notice of my irritation：irritation 意为“恼怒；生气”，这里是说马洛已经相当火大，但是医生对此却没有注意到，或者是根本就没想理会。

196. messieur：（用于法国人名前）先生。

197. reap from...magnificent dependency：possession 意为“占有；拥有”，magnificent 意为“宏伟壮丽的”，dependency 意为“属国；属地”。这里是说法国能够从它所占有的广阔属地那里收割利益，而且获利颇丰；而借此之便，这位法国医生也可以从中分得一点属于他的利益——也就是借机观察他的体检对象，从而进行科学研究。这段里面描写的法国医生还是很令人敬佩的，他所追求的不是什么个人利益，而是想要通过科学研究为全人类（转下页）

mere wealth I leave to others[198]. Pardon my questions, but you are the first Englishman coming under my observation[199]...' I hastened to assure him I was not in the least typical[200]. 'If I were,' said I, 'I wouldn't be talking like this with you.'[201] 'What you say is rather profound, and probably erroneous[202],' he said, with a laugh.

（接上页）留下一些知识财富。所以马洛一开始对他出言不逊，后来醒悟过来之后也就向他"道歉"了，而这位医生也非常睿智而又和善地回复了他，还对他谆谆叮嘱，显出医者仁心。

198. The mere wealth I leave to others：医生这句话是说，他的研究成果就是他能够为人们留下的一点儿财富。

199. the first...my observation：这句话说明，以往来参加入职体检的可能都是法国人，而马洛是他"观察"（这里是医学研究的术语，指对样本的观察，也就是上文中的测量头围和询问问题等）的第一个英国人。这也说明当时刚果是法国属地，英国人去那里的还不多。

200. I hastened...least typical：这里也很有意思，"我赶紧向他保证说，我绝对不是什么典型的英国人"。在这里马洛已经看出来这位医生不是个无礼的怪人，实际上是个值得敬佩的人，而他刚才因为恼火，对医生出言不逊；又听说自己是第一个来这里的英国人，因此生怕自己刚才的言行给英国人的形象抹了黑，所以赶紧补救一下，说自己只不过是英国人中的"刺儿头"而已，真正典型的英国人是不会像自己刚才那样没礼貌的。

201. 'If I were,' said I, 'I wouldn't be talking like this with you.'：这里是上一条注释的延伸。马洛说，如果他是个真正典型的英国人，刚才一定不会用那样没礼貌的口气和医生说话。这也是他在为刚才的事打圆场，努力挽回英国人的形象。

202. What you...probably erroneous：这句话体现了医生的睿智、幽默和宽容。What you say is rather profound 说明医生已经看透了马洛的言外之意，完全明白马洛说"自己不是典型的英国人"的用意；probably erroneous 则说明医生知道，即使是真正典型的英国人，刚才也会被自己的话激怒，做出针锋相对的回应的，因此他说马洛的话"八成是个谬误"，是不对的。而且在整个过程中，马洛的情绪起伏很大，而医生一直很从容，也很宽和，无论马洛说什么他都没有生气，还为马洛的非洲之行提出建议，显得非常有气度。

'Avoid irritation more than exposure to the sun.[203] Adieu[204]. How do you English say, eh? Good-bye. Ah! Good-bye.Adieu. In the tropics one must before everything keep calm[205].' ...He lifted a warning forefinger.... 'Du calme, du calme[206].'

"One thing more remained to do—say good-bye to my excellent aunt. I found her triumphant. I had a cup of tea—the last decent cup of tea for many days[207]—and in a room that most soothingly looked just as you would expect a lady's drawing-room to look[208], we had a long quiet chat by the fireside. In the course of these confidences[209] it became quite plain to me I had been represented to the wife of the high dignitary[210], and goodness knows to how many more people besides, as an exceptional and

---

203. Avoid irritation...to the sun：和暴晒相比，更要注意的是别动气。

204. Adieu：法语词，意为"再见；再会"。

205. In the tropics...keep calm：意思是"在热带地区，保持冷静比什么都重要"。而马洛显然没能按照医生叮嘱的那样去做。在刚果河上所目睹所经历的一切，都无法令马洛无动于衷，"保持冷静"。

206. Du calme：这是一句法语，意思就是 keep calm。

207. the last...many days：意思是"在很长的时间里，这将是我喝得到的最后一杯好茶了"，这说明马洛在非洲的生活将会非常艰苦，物质匮乏。

208. in a room...drawing-room to look：a room that most soothingly looked 意为"看上去令人感到再舒适不过的房间"，后面的 just as 则进一步解释了，"完全就像你期待中的女士的客厅的样子"。这说明马洛的姨妈生活优渥，能结识很多大人物、为马洛弄到船长职位也就在情理之中了。

209. confidences：这里不是常用的词义"信心"，而更是"机密；知心话"的含义，指的是马洛和姨妈低声密谈的那些话。

210. dignitary：高官；显要人物。这里很可能指的是那家大公司的高层管理者，比如之后会提到的"（公司）欧洲董事会"的成员。

gifted creature[211]—a piece of good fortune for the Company[212]—a man you don't get hold of every day[213]. Good heavens! and I was going to take charge of a two-penny-half-penny river-steamboat with a penny whistle attached![214] It appeared, however, I was also one of the Workers, with a capital[215]—you know. Something like an emissary of light, something like a lower sort of apostle. There had been a lot of such rot let loose in print and talk[216] just about that time, and the excellent woman, living right in the rush

---

211. as an exceptional and gifted creature：这里写得很有趣。马洛的姨妈到处向人推荐他，把他吹得天花乱坠，而马洛通过这次密谈得知后，颇有点哭笑不得。这句话的意思是"作为一个卓越而富有才华的人"，是姨妈夸赞马洛的话。

212. a piece of good fortune for the Company：意思是"对于那家公司来说，是一件相当有价值的财富"。fortune 在这里意为"财富；财产"，比喻对公司来说很有价值的人才。

213. a man you don't get hold of every day：意思是"一个不是天天都能找得到的人才"，译为"一个打着灯笼也找不到的人才"。这也是一种幽默说法。

214. a two-penny-half-penny...whistle attached：意思是"一条安装着廉价汽笛的廉价汽船"。a penny 和 two-penny-half-penny，都是用夸张手法形容马洛将要掌管的汽船其实根本不值几个钱，说明马洛自己觉得自己并不是姨妈说的那种"了不得的精英人物"。

215. Workers, with a capital：意为"真正带大写的 Worker"，具体的理解有几种，一是"公司的重要工作人员"，二是类似 miracle worker 那样，能够在艰苦的环境中创造奇迹的人；他们具有奉献精神和使命感，蒙上天的感召去拯救世人，可能具有一定的宗教意味。结合下文，第二种理解似乎更准确。

216. a lot of such rot let loose in print and talk：rot 在这里不是常见的词义"腐败"，而是"胡说；废话"的意思。let loose 意为"放纵；释放；使自由"。in print 意思是"在书刊里面（充斥着这种胡扯的话）"，in talk 的意思是"在人们的闲谈里（也充斥着这些胡话）"。这里表达了作者对当时那种时代风气的讽刺。

of all that humbug[217], got carried off her feet[218]. She talked about
'weaning those ignorant millions from their horrid ways,'[219] till,
upon my word, she made me quite uncomfortable. I ventured to
hint that[220] the Company was run for profit[221].

"'You forget, dear Charlie, that the labourer is worthy of his
hire[222],' she said, brightly. It's queer how out of touch with truth

---

217. living right in the rush of all that humbug：rush 意为"激流"，humbug 意
为"谎话"。这里事实上是一个比喻，是说马洛的姨妈生活在那个时代，报
纸上看到的、耳边听到的全是那些"要为野蛮之地带去光明和进步"之类的
鬼话，她耳濡目染，也就随波逐流，就好像被那些鬼话所形成的洪流裹挟在
里面一样。

218. got carried off her feet：这里接着上句的比喻，意思是"在那股洪流里，
马洛的姨妈被冲得立足不定，已经完全被裹在其中不知道东南西北了"。也
就是说，他的姨妈已经完全被那些鬼话洗脑了。

219. weaning those...horrid ways：这句话说明马洛姨妈的口吻已经和当时书
刊报纸上的宣传完全一样了，要"让几百万无知的野蛮人戒掉他们那些可怕
的生活方式"。wean 意为"断奶"，也就是"戒掉对……的依赖"。

220. I ventured to hint that：意思是"我斗胆向她暗示说"，说明马洛已经无
法忍受姨妈高调的说教，又不得不保持礼貌，因而试着插上一句话，委婉地
表达一下自己的反对意见。

221. was run for profit：意为"经营的目的是获取利润"。这是马洛暗示的话，
他想让姨妈知道，人们去非洲并不是为了什么博爱的人道主义，而只是因为
非洲资源富饶，去那里可以赚到钱。

222. the labourer is worthy of his hire：出自《新约·路加福音》第十章第七
节，意思包括"一分耕耘一分收获""种什么因得什么果""为人出力该得到
报酬"等。这里有可能是说，姨妈以此回答马洛的"他们只是为了赚钱"的
话，她认为，只要"文明的使者"帮助野蛮人摆脱了野蛮的生活方式，让黑
暗大陆也得到了光明和进步，那么，即使赚到钱也无可厚非，因为他们的劳
动值得他们的报酬。这说明马洛姨妈并没有看到事情的本质，也没有意识到
殖民剥削的残酷性。

women are[223]. They live in a world of their own, and there has never been anything like it, and never can be. It is too beautiful altogether, and if they were to set it up[224] it would go to pieces before the first sunset[225]. Some confounded[226] fact we men have been living contentedly[227] with ever since the day of creation[228] would start up and knock the whole thing over[229].

---

223. It's queer...women are：这里是说姨妈完全不明真相，把去非洲这件事想得又光彩辉煌、又轻松愉快，马洛对此表示无语。out of touch with truth 意为"脱离现实；不接地气"。

224. if they were to set it up：意思是"如果女人们想要把想象中的美好世界搬到现实里面的话"。

225. it would...first sunset：意思是"那么这个理想化的世界不用等到第一天的太阳落山，就会分崩离析了"。这说明理想化的世界根本不可能变成现实，至少当时不能。比如说"欧洲人和非洲人一起手拉手唱歌跳舞，他们互相关爱，其乐融融"这样的画面，在那时是无法实现的。

226. confounded：意为"困惑的；讨厌的；该死的"。这里指的是真正的生活中的那些事实——例如无情的统治秩序、残酷的压迫剥削、饥饿、贫困甚至死亡等等。这些事实会令马洛姨妈那样的温室娇花感到困惑和厌恶，是一些"不怎么美好的事情"；但是，这才是现实。

227. contentedly：满足地；安心地。这里译为"心平气和地"，意思是说，现实既然如此，除了接受它并努力适应它，还能怎么样呢？天真的幻想没有用，咒骂和抱怨也没有用，投入其中，在奋斗中求生就是了。马洛他们就是这样做的。

228. ever since the day of creation：这里的意思是，自从这个世界被创造出来的那一天开始，它就不是一个完美的世界。想象一下，地球在宇宙中时刻都有被射线辐射、被天体撞击的风险；寒冰期和小行星撞击造成好几次生物大灭绝；人类的始祖要忍受酷暑、寒冷、饥饿、疾病、自然灾害，还有毒蛇和猛兽的威胁；在冷酷的资本主义社会，很多英国工人食不果腹，海外殖民地的人民也遭受着酷虐的盘剥。在现实中，苦难无处不在，以前如此，以后也还会这样——这也许就是康拉德对此的认识。

229. knock the whole thing over：意思是"把这个想象中的美好世界给打翻"。

"After this I got embraced, told to wear flannel, be sure to write often, and so on—and I left. In the street—I don't know why—a queer feeling came to me that I was an imposter[230]. Odd thing that I, who used to clear out for any part of the world at twenty-four hours' notice[231], with less thought than most men give to the crossing of a street[232], had a moment—I won't say of hesitation, but of startled pause, before this commonplace affair. The best way I can explain it to you is by saying that, for a second or two, I felt as though, instead of going to the centre of a continent, I were about to set off for the centre of the earth[233].

"I left in a French steamer, and she called in every blamed port they have out there[234], for, as far as I could see, the sole purpose of landing soldiers and custom-house officers. I watched

---

230. imposter：骗子。这里指的是那些嘴上说着要为非洲带去光明和进步，实际上却在非洲掳掠财富、压迫人民的那些殖民者。

231. clear out...hours' notice：这里是形容马洛之前做事干脆果断的风格——哪怕是通知他第二天就要出发去任何地方，他都会马上做好一切准备，绝不会拖泥带水，更不会胡思乱想。这是在铺垫，好与下文做对比。

232. the crossing of a street：过马路。这句话是说大多数人在过马路之前都要先看一看，想一想；而马洛在即将出海的时候都毫不犹豫。这是在用夸张的对比手法，强调马洛行事果断。

233. set off...of the earth：这里是说马洛对非洲之行有一种预感；那种感觉和以前出海的经验不一样。"出发去往地球的核心"，那就不是令人期待的，而是令人恐怖的了。这也预示了马洛将在非洲见到未曾想象过的黑暗图景。

234. she called...out there：call in 在这里意为"船只归港"，这句的意思是这艘法国轮船每遇到一个港口就要停靠过去。blamed 是一句加重语气的抱怨，表现了马洛对于漫长旅程的难以忍耐。而轮船每到一个港口都会放下士兵和收税官，这也从侧面说明法国的海外殖民地相当广阔。也许 every blamed port 还有一种表现马洛对于法国"竟有这么多殖民地"的感叹意味。

the coast. Watching a coast as it slips by the ship is like thinking about an enigma. There it is before you — smiling, frowning, inviting, grand, mean, insipid, or savage, and always mute[235] with an air of whispering[236], 'Come and find out.' This one was almost featureless, as if still in the making, with an aspect of monotonous grimness[237]. The edge of a colossal jungle, so dark-green as to be almost black, fringed with white surf, ran straight, like a ruled line, far, far away along a blue sea whose glitter was blurred by a creeping mist. The sun was fierce, the land seemed to glisten and drip with steam. Here and there greyish-whitish specks showed up clustered inside the white surf, with a flag flying above them perhaps. Settlements some centuries old, and still no bigger than pinheads on the untouched expanse of their background. We pounded along[238], stopped, landed soldiers; went on, landed custom-house clerks to levy toll in what looked like a God-forsaken wilderness[239], with a tin shed and a flag-pole

---

235. mute：沉默不语的。这句话里康拉德一连用了七个形容词来描摹形形色色的海岸，而形容词罗列也是康拉德的写作特色之一。还是那句话，不可以"直译"为名省却人工，译文需要思考和打磨，需要符合中文的阅读习惯并表现出和英文相对等的气势。

236. with an air of whispering：带着一种似乎要对人耳语的神气。

237. an aspect...grimness：an aspect of 指的是事物呈现某一方面的特征。monotonous grimness 意为"单调阴沉"。

238. pound along：pound 在这里是"轰隆轰隆地（前进）"的意思，along 则是指船只慢慢地侧身靠岸。据我乘船的体会，这两个词的描绘可谓精当。

239. a God-forsaken wilderness：forsaken 意为"被抛弃了的"，由动词 forsake 的过去分词变化而来。"仿佛被上帝遗弃了的茫茫荒野"，极言这片土地之孤寂荒凉。

lost in it[240]; landed more soldiers—to take care of the custom-house clerks, presumably. Some, I heard, got drowned in the surf[241]; but whether they did or not, nobody seemed particularly to care. They were just flung out there, and on we went. Every day the coast looked the same, as though we had not moved; but we passed various places—trading places—with names like Gran' Bassam, Little Popo; names that seemed to belong to some sordid farce acted in front of a sinister back-cloth[242]. The idleness of a passenger, my isolation amongst all these men with whom I had no point of contact, the oily and languid sea, the uniform sombreness of the coast, seemed to keep me away from the truth of things, within the toil of a mournful and

---

240. a tin shed and a flag-pole lost in it：代词 it 在这里指的是 "荒野"，a tin shed and a flag-pole 应该是指代官员们的 "收税站"，旗杆代表了政府行政权力。lost in it 体现了荒野之广袤和棚屋之渺小；两下对比，自然生出一种凄凉迷茫的感叹。

241. got drowned in the surf：drown 意为 "淹没，淹死"，这里是说 "淹死在海浪中"。这一笔看似漫不经心，事实上写出了海外殖民也是风险极高的一件事，一旦乘船出海去往未经开发的殖民地，则前途迷惘，人命轻贱，无法活着回到欧洲是常有的事。此前作者提到的地名 "Gravesend"（送往坟墓）和拉丁文的 "万岁！编织黑毛线的老女人——赴死者向您致敬"，也与此处遥相呼应。

242. a sinister back-cloth：back-cloth 意为 "背景幕布"，sinister 意为 "邪恶的，不怀好意的"，这里 "幽暗狰狞的幕布" 指的是无边无际的荒野。正如杰克·伦敦在 White Fang 中所说（当然他指的是北国冰封的荒原），"荒原从来不喜欢运动，生命对于它是一种唐突；因为生命是运动的，而荒原是永远企图消灭运动的。" 在这里，荒野也好像布下了陷阱、张开了大口，随时准备吞噬从 "文明社会" 来到这里活动的人；而欧洲人不断地为了追逐利益来到这里 "做贸易"，有的赚到钱，有的死在这里，就好像在 "荒野" 这片幽深的幕布上演出一幕幕 "活剧"。

senseless delusion[243]. The voice of the surf heard now and then was a positive pleasure, like the speech of a brother[244]. It was something natural, that had its reason, that had a meaning. Now and then a boat from the shore gave one a momentary contact with reality[245]. It was paddled by black fellows. You could see from afar the white of their eyeballs[246] glistening. They shouted, sang; their bodies streamed with perspiration; they had faces like grotesque masks[247]—these chaps; but they had bone, muscle, a wild vitality, an intense energy of movement, that was as natural

---

243. keep me...senseless delusion：the truth of things 指的是真实而积极的生活，也许充满忙碌，但是会让人心里感到踏实。但是船上的旅客长时间无所事事，已经脱离了这种积极进取的生活。the toil of...delusion 的意思是"耽于迷茫的苦思、一个劲儿地胡思乱想"，mournful and senseless 则说明这种幻梦般的思想既令人悲伤惆怅，又毫无意义。

244. the speech of a brother：在教会中，大家都崇敬上帝，互相之间称为"兄弟姐妹"。我曾在青岛的教堂参加过主日礼拜，其中有一个环节就是教会中的兄弟姐妹通过演说的形式，分享自己的生活经历和心路历程。这种诉说都是充满了真情实感的。因而这里翻译成"教会兄弟的倾诉"来形容令马洛感受到真实的海浪声。

245. gave one...with reality：a momentary contact 意为"暂时的接触"。这里是说，马洛在望见自岸边划来的小船的那一刻，才觉得自己不是活在一个虚无缥缈的幻梦之中，才觉得自己还是可以偶尔触摸到真实的生活场景的。可见在船上漂泊的漫长旅途已经快把马洛逼疯了，他渴望看到一些真实的生活化的场景，也渴望自己能够尽早到岸，重新投入到昂扬进取的生活和工作中去。

246. the white of their eyeballs：这里指的是眼珠中发亮的部分。黑人的眼睛黑白分明，又和皮肤的黑色有着明显的映衬，所以远远望去白得发亮，十分醒目。译成"闪射着光亮的白瞳仁"则是为了中文的通顺和谐。若译为"白得发亮的眼珠"则似乎不妥，因为眼珠当然不可能是白色的。

247. grotesque masks：古怪的面具。这里是形容黑人小伙子由于拼命使出了全身的力气，在脸上呈现出一种咬牙瞪眼的扭曲表情。

and true as the surf along their coast[248]. They wanted no excuse for being there[249]. They were a great comfort[250] to look at. For a time I would feel I belonged still to a world of straightforward facts[251]; but the feeling would not last long. Something would turn up to scare it away[252]. Once, I remember, we came upon a man-of-war anchored off the coast. There wasn't even a shed there, and she was shelling the bush. It appears the French had one of their wars going on thereabouts. Her ensign dropped limp like a rag[253]; the muzzles of the long six-inch guns stuck out all over

248. as natural...their coast：意为"就和岸边的海浪一样自然而真实"，指的是这些黑人小伙子充满了力量与和谐的美感，他们是自然的造物，在他们身上毫无险诈和矫饰，这一点是马洛十分欣赏的。

249. They wanted...being there：这些黑人出现在这里，无须任何理由。因为他们就生长在这里，这里就是他们的天然的家园。对照来看，欧洲殖民者都是需要政府许可或登记才来到这里的，他们非但不会把这里视作家园，反而还会毫无顾忌地进行破坏和掠夺。

250. a great comfort：意为"一种莫大的安慰"。因为马洛崇尚真善美，而这些黑人小伙子正是这种"真实"的化身。因而对于这种原住民辛勤劳作的场景，马洛是非常乐见的。而下文中提到的代表了"假恶丑"的殖民入侵，则是马洛辛辣讽刺的对象。

251. a world of straightforward facts：这里也指的是一个真实而自然、没有尔虞我诈的世界。

252. Something...scare it away：意为"有的东西会冒出来把它吓跑"，这是在说真实而自然的世界也无比脆弱，殖民者和他们的军舰一到来，就可以轻易地将这个浑然天成的世界给破坏掉，让它从此不复存在。

253. Her ensign...a rag: ensign 意为"船上的旗帜"，limp 意为"无精打采的"，rag 意为"破布"。也就是说"船上的旗子就好像破布片一样耷拉着"。这里一是说明非洲气候炎热，空气凝滞，几乎没有风；二是说明船上的侵略者也没有什么高昂的士气，他们没有正义的目的，也不适应热带的气候，还不敢轻易地上岸去，只能在军舰上随着海水漂荡，时不时炮轰一下岸上的丛林来完成任务。

the low hull[254]; the greasy, slimy swell[255] swung her up lazily and let her down, swaying her thin masts. In the empty immensity of earth, sky, and water, there she was, incomprehensible, firing into a continent[256]. Pop, would go one of the six-inch guns; a small flame would dart and vanish, a little white smoke would disappear, a tiny projectile would give a feeble screech[257]—and nothing happened. Nothing could happen. There was a touch of insanity in the proceeding[258], a sense of lugubrious drollery[259] in the sight; and it was not dissipated by[260] somebody on board assuring me earnestly[261]

---

254. the muzzles...low hull：muzzle 意为 "炮口"，hull 意为 "船体"。从这句话的 "船舷低处伸出一排六英寸口径大炮的炮口"，可以想见对于非洲当地人来说，侵略者的坚船利炮是何等威压。

255. the greasy, slimy swell：意思是 "油腻腻、懒洋洋的海水"。这里的 slimy swell 和后面的 swell、sway 构成了 "头韵"，即一组词都是以 s 打头，从视觉上和发音上形象地描绘出一幅海水缓缓涌动的景象。

256. In the...a continent：这句话的意思是，宽广的天地原本容得下所有人和睦相处，互不侵犯；而那条军舰停靠在岸边，轰隆隆地只管向着眼前的陆地开炮，这种蛮横的侵略行径让人无法理解。

257. a feeble screech：意为 "一声微弱的尖啸"。这里也是康拉德的讽刺笔法，有意把一场殖民侵略战争写得好似一场荒谬的闹剧。

258. a touch...proceeding：a touch of 意为 "稍许有点儿"，insanity 意为 "精神错乱"，proceeding 意为 "发生的一连串事情"。这句话意思是说，这一连串事情都显得有点儿像疯子行径。这也是在讽刺那些侵略者。

259. lugubrious drollery：意为 "悲哀的滑稽剧"，可以译为 "显得又可怜又可笑"。这也是对侵略行径的辛辣讽刺。

260. it was not dissipated by：若译为 "但那并不能改变我的感受" 或者 "但这也不能消除我的那种感觉"，意思是对的。但是为了中文的行文顺畅，可以将这一层意思化入到上下文的表达之中，比直接说出来显得更为自然。

261. earnestly：信誓旦旦地，言之凿凿地。刻画了侵略者自以为是的可笑神态。

there was a camp of natives[262]—he called them enemies!—hidden out of sight somewhere.

"We gave her her letters (I heard the men in that lonely ship were dying of fever at the rate of three a day) and went on. We called at some more places with farcical names, where the merry dance of death and trade[263] goes on in a still and earthy atmosphere as of an overheated catacomb[264]; all along the formless coast[265] bordered by dangerous surf[266], as if Nature herself[267] had tried to

---

262. a camp of natives：指的是住在岸边某个地方的一些（可能是同一个部落的）土著人。

263. the merry dance of death and trade：这是一个充满了黑色幽默，但也让人感到荒诞和悲凉的比喻。"死亡和贸易在一起愉快地跳舞"，就是说在这些地方，欧洲人为了赚钱，万里迢迢地跑来做贸易，但是其中很多人都感染了热带病或者在丛林中遭遇危险，很快就死在这里了。死亡和贸易这两件事几乎每天都在这里此起彼伏地上演，马洛会不断听说"某某来了""某某死了"，就好像死亡和贸易抱在一起跳着热烈的贴面舞一样。

264. in a still...overheated catacomb：earthy 意为"泥土的"，catacomb 意为"地下墓穴；墓室；墓道"。这里是说非洲就好像一座闷热的墓室一样，空气里充满着泥土的气味，而且几乎连一丝风也没有。这说明非洲气候炎热，条件恶劣。

265. the formless coast：这里说海岸线"几乎没有形状"，意思是海岸没有人工建设的码头，呈现自然破碎的状态，甚至有可能密布着暗礁；这对于船只来说当然是很危险的（这就是人们要在沿海建设港口的意义，为了船只的出入更加安全便捷。这也和人们要建设飞机场的道理是一样的）。

266. bordered by dangerous surf：接上条，光是破碎的海岸线还不算完，相伴出现的还有危险的海浪——可能有漩涡，有暗流等等，船只在这里一不小心就可能遭遇危险。

267. Nature herself：大自然本身。这里是将自然环境人格化、拟人化，上边提到的充满危险的海岸和海浪，好像就是这位自然女神亲手设下的防线，目的是阻挡殖民者的入侵。

ward off intruders; in and out of rivers, streams of death in life, whose banks were rotting into mud, whose waters, thickened into slime, invaded the contorted mangroves[268], that seemed to writhe at us[269] in the extremity of an impotent despair[270]. Nowhere did we stop long enough to get a particularized impression, but the general sense of[271] vague and oppressive wonder grew upon me. It was like a weary pilgrimage[272] amongst hints for nightmares[273].

"It was upward of thirty days before I saw the mouth of the big river[274]. We anchored off the seat of the government. But my work would not begin till some two hundred miles farther on. So as soon as I could I made a start for a place thirty miles higher up.

---

268. invaded the contorted mangroves：（污浊的河水）冲刷着扭曲了的红树林。mangrove 意为"红树林"，红树林群落主要生活在以赤道为中心的热带及亚热带淤泥深厚的海滩上，在海陆交界的潮间带形成壮观的海上森林；在潮起潮落的过程中，红树林会经受水流不断的冲刷。

269. writhe at us：向着我们扭动；在我们面前扭动。这里是说水流冲刷下的红树林，呈现出一种痛苦扭曲的姿态。

270. in the extremity of an impotent despair：处于一种无能为力、极度绝望的状态。这是说红树林只能任凭潮水冲刷和折磨，它们的命运完全不由自主。这似乎是一个隐喻，"红树林"可能暗指非洲的劳苦人民，在殖民者面前，他们也全然无能为力，任由宰割。

271. the general sense of：这里是说马洛心中一直有一种感觉，即，"我总是感到……"

272. a weary pilgrimage：一场无比漫长、令人身心疲惫的朝圣之旅。pilgrimage 意为"朝拜；朝圣；人生旅途"。

273. hints for nightmares：梦魇般的暗示；不祥之兆。这都是在暗示马洛到了非洲腹地之后将会见到的黑暗景象。

274. the mouth of the big river：刚果河的河口。注意，在康拉德笔下，一次也没有出现"刚果河"的名称，他总是用 the river 或者 the big river 来称呼它，这种对地名的刻意隐去，可能是为了营造一种"梦境的现实"。

"I had my passage on a little sea-going steamer. Her captain[275] was a Swede[276], and knowing me for a seaman, invited me on the bridge. He was a young man, lean, fair, and morose, with lanky hair and a shuffling gait. As we left the miserable little wharf[277], he tossed his head contemptuously at the shore[278]. 'Been living there?' he asked. I said, 'Yes.' 'Fine lot these government chaps—are they not?' he went on, speaking English with great precision and considerable bitterness. 'It is funny what some people will do for a few francs a month.[279] I wonder what becomes of that kind when it goes upcountry?[280]' I said to him I expected to

---

275. captain：船长。注意这里用的是 her captain。在英文里，提到运载工具，尤其是船的时候，往往将其拟人化为女性，指代的时候往往也用 she 或者 her。

276. Swede：瑞典人。在这里提一句，在小说里，马洛是英国人，他的前任船长是丹麦人，这里的小海轮的船长是瑞典人，年轻探险者是俄国人，他的物资是荷兰人提供的，马洛公司老板是法国人，而主线人物库尔茨的名字来自德语，他本人则是英法混血，而且他的成长过程遍历了整个欧洲。也就是说，这部小说里的贸易者和殖民者形象，是汇聚了几乎所有欧洲国家的一个群像。这一点意味深长。

277. the miserable little wharf：wharf 意为"码头；停泊处"，miserable 这里是强调码头小得可怜。可以想见，那时非洲的基础设施都建得比较简陋。

278. tossed his head contemptuously at the shore：toss 在这里意为"猛甩（头）"，就是用甩头这个动作，轻蔑地（contemptuously）指了一下岸边。

279. It is funny...a month.：这句话就体现了瑞典船长讲话很尖刻。这也从侧面反映出马洛他们其实也是公司剥削的对象，他们领到的微薄薪水和他们付出的辛苦不成正比。这里的 some people 似乎不太可能指的是黑人雇佣工，因为这里说的工资是法郎，而后文中将提到，黑人领到的工资是铜丝。

280. I wonder...goes upcountry?：这句话可能的隐含信息是，在非洲沿海条件还不算太艰苦的地方，公司员工的待遇不怎么样；由于越往腹地深入就会面临越大的危险，那么腹地（刚果河上游）的那些员工的待遇会不会因此好一点？或者说还仍然是同样工资微薄的状况？

see that soon. 'So-o-o!'[281] he exclaimed. He shuffled athwart[282], keeping one eye ahead vigilantly. 'Don't be too sure,' he continued. 'The other day I took up a man who hanged himself on the road. He was a Swede, too.' 'Hanged himself! Why, in God's name?' I cried. He kept on looking out watchfully. 'Who knows? The sun too much for him, or the country perhaps[283].'

"At last we opened a reach. A rocky cliff appeared, mounds of turned-up earth by the shore, houses on a hill, others with iron roofs, amongst a waste of excavations, or hanging to the declivity[284]. A continuous noise of the rapids above hovered over[285] this scene of inhabited devastation[286]. A lot of people, mostly

---

281. 'So-o-o!':这是瑞典船长情不自禁喊出来的一句话，看上去不是个完整的单词，应该是在重复马洛刚刚说的 soon 那个词。因为瑞典船长觉得马洛讲话的口气太轻松、太乐观了，因而重复他的话来表示惊讶和嘲弄。理解成拖着长音的"so"似乎不如"soon"更能解释得通。

282. shuffled athwart：拖着脚横跨了一步。想象一下，这是一艘很小的海轮，可能驾驶室的空间也非常狭窄，因此人在里边无法大踏步行走；船长需要操作各种仪表，那就经常一步拖到这边打舵，一步拖到那边读数；时间长了就形成了拖着脚走路的习惯。

283. The sun...country perhaps：too much 意为"忍受不了；超出了忍耐的限度"，这里是猜测路边的瑞典人上吊的原因——也许是太阳（也就是说无法适应非洲炎热的气候）；也许是 the country，也就是这个地方本身让他完全受不了了。

284. hanging to the declivity：（房子）建在倾斜的山坡上。declivity 意为"下坡；倾斜"，注意这里也是英文抽象词翻译成中文具体词。

285. hovered over：在上空盘旋。这里是说激流的声音来自山崖高处，也就是说，是从人们的头顶上传来的。

286. this scene of inhabited devastation：这里描写了马洛眼前看到的一幕。这里明显是一片工地，到处是人（inhabited），而且被搞得一片狼藉（devastation）。

black and naked, moved about like ants. A jetty projected into the river. A blinding sunlight drowned all this at times in a sudden recrudescence of glare[287]. 'There's your Company's station,' said the Swede, pointing to three wooden barrack-like structures on the rocky slope. 'I will send your things up. Four boxes did you say? So. Farewell.'

"I came upon a boiler wallowing[288] in the grass, then found a path leading up the hill. It turned aside for the boulders[289], and also for an undersized railway-truck[290] lying there on its back with its wheels in the air. One was off[291]. The thing looked as dead as the carcass of some animal[292]. I came upon more pieces of decaying machinery, a stack of rusty rails. To the left a clump of trees made a shady spot, where dark things seemed to stir feebly[293]. I

---

287. drowned...recrudescence of glare：时不时用一阵突然迸发出来的强光把这一切都淹没了（让人眼前什么也看不见了）。recrudescence 意为"再次出现；再次迸发"。

288. wallowing：原意是"在泥坑里打滚；沉陷在泥坑里"，这里是指锅炉被深埋在草丛里。

289. turned aside for the boulders：turn aside 意为"闪开；避开；转换方向"，boulder 意为"大块的石头"。这里是说这条小路绕过了很多大岩石。

290. an undersized railway-truck：undersized 意为"比一般的尺寸小的"，这里是说小路除了绕过岩石，还绕过了一个小型的铁路货车车厢。

291. One was off：off 意为"脱落了"，这里是说车厢的一个轮子已经掉了。

292. looked as...some animal：as dead as 是说车厢"一动不动"，carcass 意为"较大的动物的尸体"，比喻废弃了的车厢静静地躺在地上的样子。

293. dark things seemed to stir feebly：意为"好像有一些黑色的东西在微弱地蠕动着"。在这里作者卖了个关子，马洛也看不清那些黑色的东西到底是什么。读到下一段谜底就揭开了。这将是马洛在非洲见到的最具有视觉冲击力的黑暗图景之一。

blinked[294], the path was steep[295]. A horn[296] tooted to the right, and I saw the black people run. A heavy and dull detonation shook the ground, a puff of smoke came out of the cliff, and that was all. No change appeared on the face of the rock. They were building a railway. The cliff was not in the way or anything[297]; but this objectless blasting was all the work going on[298].

"A slight clinking[299] behind me made me turn my head. Six black men advanced in a file, toiling up the path. They walked erect and slow, balancing small baskets full of earth on their heads, and the clink kept time with their footsteps. Black rags were wound round their loins, and the short ends behind waggled to and fro like tails. I could see every rib, the joints of their limbs

---

294. blink：眨眼。这里是说马洛努力想看清那些东西到底是什么。

295. steep：陡峭的。因为山路太陡峭，所以马洛看不清楚下边的情形。

296. horn：号角声。这可能是工地上的黑人用来发信号的，以便在（修建铁路的）劳动中协调配合。

297. The cliff was not in the way or anything：那座山崖并没有挡住（修建铁路的）道路，也没有从任何方面对他们造成妨碍。

298. this objectless...going on：这句的意思是说，那些人在工地上忙得热火朝天，而他们所做的全部工作就是在那里毫无目的的狂轰滥炸。这里作者的意思是，殖民者指挥黑人炸山崖是无谓之举，纯属为了搞破坏而搞破坏。这也是康拉德常用的讽刺手法。（但是我猜测，有可能白人炸那块山崖是为了获得石料，倒也不是无事生非，乱搞破坏。）

299. A slight clinking：一阵轻微的叮当声。clink 意为"发出叮当声"。这里是指那些黑人劳工身上戴着锁链，走路的时候锁链撞击发出的声音。说成"叮当声"似乎有点悦耳的意思，但是奴役的锁链显然不会发出令人愉悦的声音。这是语言色彩的问题。而译成"哐啷声"则似乎不够 slight。所以这里译作"吭啷声"。

were like knots in a rope; each had an iron collar on his neck, and all were connected together with a chain whose bights swung between them, rhythmically clinking. Another report from the cliff made me think suddenly of that ship of war[300] I had seen firing into a continent[301]. It was the same kind of ominous voice[302]; but these men could by no stretch of imagination be called enemies[303]. They were called criminals, and the outraged law, like the bursting shells, had come to them, an insoluble mystery from the sea[304]. All their meagre breasts panted together[305], the violently dilated

---

300. ship of war：军舰；战舰。这里指的是上文说过的那条在非洲海岸上不停开炮的法国军舰。这也是西方殖民者的一贯手法，先用坚船利炮开路，然后迫使当地人民屈从于他们的淫威之下，接受他们的统治和剥削。

301. firing into a continent：向着一片陆地开火。这说明这并不是一场对等的战争，完全就是殖民者在炫耀武力。

302. ominous voice：ominous 意为"预兆的，不吉利的"，这里是说马洛在山下听到的爆炸声就和法国军舰轰击的炮声一样，对于非洲人民而言，这都是预示着灾难降临的声音。

303. these men...called enemies：stretch of imagination 意为"极力发挥想象力"，stretch 是使劲儿抻长的意思。这里是说那些非洲黑人，就算你绞尽脑汁去找他们的不是，你也无法把"敌人"这个帽子扣到他们的头上。因为他们只是在自己的家园里和平地生活，对欧洲人完全构不成任何威胁。

304. the outraged...from the sea：从这里可以看出那些被定为"罪犯"而受到苦役惩罚的黑人劳工，事实上完全是无辜的。那些"被触犯了"的法律（the outraged law）都是殖民者的欲加之罪，对于黑人来说，那都是从天而降的灾祸；他们明明什么也没做，就成了要服苦役的罪犯，就好像他们明明什么也没做，法国的军舰就要来炮轰他们，而且还振振有词地说他们是"敌人"。非洲的人们对此完全是无可奈何。

305. their meagre breasts panted together：meagre 意为"瘦弱的"，pant 是动词，意为"气喘吁吁"。这些已经很消瘦的黑人劳工都被累得直喘气，你可以看到他们的胸膛都在一起一伏，好像风箱一样。这说明黑人被压榨得十分悲惨。

nostrils quivered[306], the eyes stared stonily uphill[307]. They passed me within six inches[308], without a glance[309], with that complete, deathlike indifference of unhappy savages[310]. Behind this raw matter[311] one of the reclaimed[312], the product of the new forces at work[313], strolled despondently[314], carrying a rifle by its middle. He

---

306. the violently dilated nostrils quivered：dilated 意思是"膨胀的；扩大的"，nostrils 是"鼻孔"，quivered 是"颤抖"，这里也是在形象地描绘黑人劳工的凄惨形象。他们在炎热的气候里干着沉重的体力活，他们把鼻孔使劲张开，不断开合着想要获取更多的一点空气。

307. the eyes stared stonily uphill：stare uphill 是"望向山顶"，stonily 意为"冷漠无神地，好像变成了石头一样"。身上的负载是如此沉重，通往山顶的道路又是如此漫长，苦难的劳役日复一日没有尽头。那些黑人劳工已经疲惫到木然，这是一种生不如死的状态。

308. passed me within six inches：6 英寸大约是 15 厘米。这个距离算得上"擦肩而过"了。这是因为小路十分狭窄。

309. without a glance：擦肩而过却连一眼都不看，这说明黑人劳工已经被折磨得完全没有正常人应有的表现了。

310. with that...unhappy savages：承受着苦难的野蛮人（unhappy savages）的那种生无可恋的漠然（complete indifference）和死一样的麻木（indifference）。和上文中在海上划船的生机勃勃的黑人小伙子相比，这里的黑人劳工已经被折磨成了行尸走肉。

311. this raw matter：意为"原材料；生的东西"，也就是指"未曾开化的野蛮人"，这些虽然被迫从事苦役，但是内心深处不曾屈服于殖民者的黑人劳工。

312. the reclaimed：原意是"被开垦过的（土地）"，这里指的是已经屈服于殖民者，接受了西方"文明"，甘于为白人做走狗的黑人。

313. the product of the new forces at work：意为"正在起作用的新的力量的产物"，这里 the new forces 指的是入侵非洲的西方殖民势力。在他们的作用下，有的黑人选择了屈膝合作，接受他们的游戏规则，欺压自己的同胞。

314. strolled despondently：沮丧地来回踱步。这是说黑人劳工已经累得几乎走不动了，作为监工的黑人担心任务不能按时完成，干着急却也没办法。

had a uniform jacket with one button off[315], and seeing a white man on the path, hoisted his weapon to his shoulder with alacrity[316]. This was simple prudence, white men being so much alike at a distance[317] that he could not tell who I might be[318]. He was speedily reassured[319], and with a large, white, rascally grin[320], and a glance at his charge[321], seemed to take me into partnership in his exalted trust[322]. After all, I also was a part of the great cause of these high

---

315. with one button off：敞着一颗扣子（或者扣子掉了，不修边幅的样子）。身穿制服，说明这个黑人已经被殖民者收编了；敞着扣子，则说明气候炎热，即使他不干体力活，也已经热得要解开扣子。那么那些扛着重物的黑人劳工的感受可想而知。

316. hoisted his...with alacrity：hoist 意为"提上去"，with alacrity 意为"欣然地；愉快、迅速地接受或执行某事"，这里的黑人监工一看到马洛这个白人，马上就把来复枪扛到了肩膀上，表示尊敬。

317. being so much alike at a distance：从远处看全都长得很像。可能是黑人觉得白人都长得差不多一个样，反之亦然。

318. he could not tell who I might be：黑人监工没法迅速确认马洛究竟是谁，也许他觉得有可能是自己的白人上司来检查工作进度，所以出于谨慎先表示一下尊敬总没错。

319. He was speedily reassured：当黑人监工看清了马洛的脸，他很快就放心了。因为马洛当然并不是他的上司。

320. with a large, white, rascally grin：rascally grin 意为"下流的诡笑"，这里的用词反映了马洛对黑人监工的厌恶。关于 white 有两种理解，一是监工咧开嘴的笑容露出一口白牙，二是监工的神情动作都有意无意模仿白人，这里的笑容看上去也有点白人的味道。

321. a glance at his charge：his charge 指的是"他手下掌管的人"。这里是监工迅速瞄了一眼那些劳工，眼神里是警告"你们都给我老实一点"的那种意味。

322. take me into partnership in his exalted trust：意思是"他那崇高的信赖中也有我的一份"，就是说他尊敬那些殖民的白人，而马洛因为是白人，所以也因此得到他的尊敬。

and just proceedings[323].

"Instead of going up, I turned and descended to the left. My idea was to let that chain-gang[324] get out of sight[325] before I climbed the hill. You know I am[326] not particularly tender; I've had to[327] strike and to fend off. I've had to resist and to attack sometimes—that's only one way of resisting—without counting the exact cost, according to the demands of such sort of life as I had blundered

---

323. the great cause of these high and just proceedings：眼下正在进行着的那高尚、正义的伟大事业。指的是殖民者对非洲土地的开发和掠夺。

324. chain-gang：戴着锁链的那帮人。指的是刚刚和马洛擦肩而过的那些黑人劳工。

325. get out of sight：走出（马洛）的视线范围以外。也就是说，马洛不想和他们一路同行，一起爬上山；他想等那些劳工走远以后再上山，到建在石坡上的自己公司的贸易站去。至于原因，结合上下文猜测，可能是他觉得那些黑人劳工遭受着非人的虐待，生不如死，有可能暴起发难，拽一个白人当垫背的；也可能是马洛既然救不了那些黑人，又不忍眼睁睁地一路看着他们受苦受难，所以就干脆躲开，眼不见为净。马洛具有正义感，也认识到了资本主义和殖民主义的残暴不公，但是他并不是一个真正敢于斗争的反抗者。

326. You know I am：注意这里的时态变化。英文中的时态其实携带很多信息。马洛在叙述中整体使用一般过去时，因为他在讲述自己过去的一段经历；但是在这里，他向奈利号上的船员朋友们说"你们知道，我是个怎样怎样的人"，这是在描述他本人的性格特征，这是过去、现在、未来都一以贯之的，所以这里使用了一般现在时，表示一种状态的恒常性。本段中的时态变化有三次，这是在其他段落里不常见的。

327. I've had to：这里又是一次时态变化，使用了现在完成时，表示到目前为止马洛曾经做过的事。他曾经打斗过，也曾经自卫过，这呼应了上边的 not tender，说明他并不是个软柿子。他之所以这样向船员朋友们解释自己，是不想让他们嘲笑自己——哦马洛是个胆小鬼，他连和黑人一起上山都不敢。

into[328]. I've seen the devil of violence, and the devil of greed, and the devil of hot desire; but, by all the stars! these were strong, lusty, red-eyed devils[329], that swayed and drove men—men, I tell you[330]. But as I stood[331] on this hillside, I foresaw that in the blinding sunshine of that land I would become acquainted with[332] a flabby, pretending, weak-eyed devil of a rapacious and pitiless folly[333].

---

328. according to...blundered into：blundered into 意为"一下子跌入（某种糟糕的境况）"。这里马洛是说，如果自己陷入了某种糟糕的境地，那么为了摆脱这种状况，那就没有他不敢做的事。比如说被人围攻，需要用刀砍出一条血路才能脱困，那么好吧，他就将毫不犹豫地一路砍杀出去。这里都是马洛在为自己看到黑人劳工之后立刻转身下山的行为做辩解。

329. strong, lusty, red-eyed devils：意思是"强大的、贪婪之极的红了眼的魔鬼"。这里说的是驱使那些黑人劳工的白人殖民者。他们仗着武力，压榨出黑人的最后一滴血汗来满足自己对金钱的欲望，其贪婪和残忍，确实令马洛以前见过的那些"魔鬼"全都自愧不如。

330. swayed and drove men—men, I tell you：sway 意为"影响；支配"。drive 意为"驱使；奴役"。这里是强调那些魔鬼们好像对待牲畜那样随意支使的是人——是活生生的人。他们不把人当人，确实是"恶魔"无疑了。

331. But as I stood：这里是一般过去时，说明马洛又在叙述他在刚果河上的那段过去的经历了。本段到这里出现了一般过去时、一般现在时和现在完成时三种事态，可以看出马洛叙述的视角在切换。对英文时态具有一定的敏感性可以帮助我们更清晰地理解原文。

332. would become acquainted with：这里是过去将来时，是站在过去的时间点上往前看。be acquainted with 意为"结识"。

333. a flabby...pitiless folly：意思是"一个装腔作势而又色厉内荏、目光短浅而又贪婪成性、当真是愚蠢到无可救药的魔鬼"。后文中将出现一个重要角色——刚果河贸易总站的经理，他是全文灵魂人物——库尔茨先生的死对头。如果说库尔茨代表了一个理想主义者的堕落，那么这个经理就从来没有堕落过，因为他是一个彻头彻尾的邪恶、贪婪和庸俗的化身，一个集资本主义和殖民主义的所有罪恶于一身的人物。这里是第一次对经理这个角色进行出场预告，从那一堆形容词可以看出作者对这个人物的态度。

How insidious he could be, too, I was only to find out several months later and a thousand miles farther. For a moment I stood appalled, as though by a warning[334]. Finally I descended the hill, obliquely, towards the trees I had seen.

"I avoided a vast artificial hole somebody had been digging on the slope, the purpose of which I found it impossible to divine[335]. It wasn't a quarry or a sandpit, anyhow. It was just a hole. It might have been connected with the philanthropic desire[336] of giving the criminals something to do. I don't know. Then I nearly fell into a very narrow ravine, almost no more than a scar in the hillside. I discovered that a lot of imported drainage-pipes for the settlement had been tumbled in there. There wasn't one that was not broken[337]. It was a wanton smash-up. At last I

---

334. as though by a warning：这里是说通过看到这些被当作役使的黑人劳工，马洛预感到接下来可能还会有更黑暗的图景在等待着他。或者说是预示着经理这个最大的"魔鬼"将在刚果河上游等待着他。

335. impossible to divine：divine 意为"占卜；猜测"。这里是说马洛无法猜到（为什么有人挖了这个大坑）。

336. been connected with the philanthropic desire：意思是"与某种博爱的愿望有关"，也就是说，马洛猜测挖这个大坑的目的也许是出于某种好心。这同样是一句讽刺，和上文中的"他们到处毫无目的地狂轰滥炸"一样，都是在讽刺殖民者在非洲肆意妄为。

337. There wasn't one that was not broken：双重否定表肯定，"没有一个是好的"，那就是说那些排水管全都坏了。这里并没有明显的线索来解释这个场景。我猜测，也许是排水管规格不合适，也许是定居点改建到别处了，总之排水管就用不上了。但是欧洲人宁可砸坏扔掉，也不想让非洲人捡走。这说明殖民者根本不像他们在欧洲宣传的那样，是要把光明和进步带到非洲来的。也有可能，这些东西是黑人劳工暴力反抗殖民者的证明，这也许解释了为什么马洛对一同上山的黑人心怀忌惮。

got under the trees. My purpose was to stroll into the shade for a moment[338]; but no sooner within than it seemed to me[339] I had stepped into the gloomy circle of some Inferno[340]. The rapids[341] were near, and an uninterrupted, uniform, headlong, rushing noise filled the mournful stillness of the grove, where not a breath stirred, not a leaf moved[342], with a mysterious sound[343]—as though the tearing pace of the launched earth had suddenly become audible[344].

---

338. stroll into the shade for a moment：意思是"在树荫下散一会儿步；溜达一会儿"，这是马洛想要躲开那些黑人劳工的方法，也就是先找个地方消磨一会儿时间，等他们走远了再上山。非洲气候炎热，骄阳似火，当然是找个树荫躲一会儿太阳比较好。

339. no sooner within than it seemed to me：这里是说，马洛一踏进到那片树荫里，马上就感觉到不对劲了。

340. stepped into the gloomy circle of some Inferno：马洛觉得自己就好像一下子闯进了阴森的地狱。Inferno 意为"炼狱；阴间"。这里用的大写形式。

341. The rapids：即上文中提到的"高崖上的激流"。

342. the mournful...a leaf moved：树林里是一片令人悲伤的寂静，那里没有一丝风声，也没有一片摇动的树叶。stir 意为"搅动；动弹"，是指空气流动（或者人的呼吸）带起的一丝风。

343. with a mysterious sound：这里接上文，是说"an...noise filled the stillness with a mysterious sound"，也就是那道激流在树林里的一片寂静之中发出的哗哗声就好像一种神秘的声响。

344. as though...become audible：这里是解释为什么激流的声音好似神秘的声响，因为它就像是大地飞奔向前的脚步声（也就是地球飞速转动的声音——"坐地日行八万里"的速度。当然了，这种声音是不存在的，这是康拉德一种艺术化的想象），一下子在马洛的耳边变得清晰可闻。这里用的是反衬的手法，就是为了描写树林里有多么寂静，就用激流的声音作反衬。有点类似中国古诗里的"蝉噪林愈静，鸟鸣山更幽"。只不过这里反衬出来的寂静，是来自一种好像阴森的地狱一样可怖的画面。下一段马上就会讲到了。

"Black shapes[345] crouched, lay, sat between the trees leaning against the trunks, clinging to the earth, half coming out, half effaced within the dim light, in all the attitudes of pain, abandonment, and despair[346]. Another mine on the cliff went off, followed by a slight shudder of the soil under my feet. The work was going on. The work! And this was the place where some of the helpers[347] had withdrawn to die[348].

"They were dying slowly—it was very clear. They were not enemies, they were not criminals, they were nothing earthly now[349]—nothing but black shadows of disease and starvation, lying confusedly in the greenish gloom[350]. Brought from all the

---

345. Black shapes: 黑色的人形。这里指的是在树荫下等死的黑人。他们已经没有了正常人的生机活力，全都奄奄一息，只不过还剩下个人形的躯壳而已。

346. in all...and despair: attitude 意为"态度"，这里指的是那些黑色人形呈现的姿态。他们的姿态各种各样，但全都是痛苦、认命和绝望。

347. the helpers: 即"the helpers of the work"，也就是那些从事苦役、帮助殖民者进行土地开发的黑人劳工。

348. withdrawn to die: withdraw 意为"撤退；退出"，这里是指那些奄奄一息的劳工被扔在这里等死。这里的 withdraw 使用了主动形态，可能是劳工们觉得命不久矣，然后主动爬到这里来的。但是他们为殖民者出了力，殖民者却并没有救治他们，而是毫不在乎地放任他们死亡，所以说他们是"被抛弃"的。

349. they were nothing earthly now: 意为"他们此刻已不是任何人间之物"。earthly 是指"人间的；尘世的"。这句是说，这些人都是将死之人，人间的一切对他们而言都不再有任何关系。罪犯的身份也好，敌人的身份也好，食物、住所、劳动、工资等等，对他们都不再有任何意义。殖民者也无法再胁迫他们或者役使他们了。

350. lying confusedly in the greenish gloom: confusedly 意为"一片混乱的；浑浑噩噩的"。这里是说那些人横七竖八地在树荫下倒成一片；或者是说他们的状态是浑浑噩噩的，他们不知道究竟是什么原因把他们害到这般地步，而且对自己的命运既不挣扎也不反抗，稀里糊涂地就这么接受了。

recesses of the coast in all the legality of time contracts, lost in uncongenial surroundings, <u>fed on unfamiliar food</u>[351], they sickened, became inefficient, and were then allowed to <u>crawl away and rest</u>[352]. <u>These moribund shapes</u>[353] <u>were free as air—and nearly as thin</u>[354]. I began to <u>distinguish the gleam of the eyes</u>[355] under the trees. Then, glancing down, I saw a face near my hand. The black bones reclined at full length with one shoulder against the tree, and slowly the eyelids rose and the sunken eyes looked up at me, enormous and vacant, a kind of blind, white flicker in the depths

---

351. fed on unfamiliar food：吃着不习惯的食物。fed 这个被动形式说明他们没有选择食物的权力，殖民者给什么他们就只能吃什么。可以想象，通过压榨他们来赚取利润的殖民者当然不会那么好心，能让他们吃得饱吃得好。

352. crawl away and rest：爬走去休息。这里 rest 有两层含义，一是"休息"，也就是不用再干活了；二是"死亡"，也就是"永远安息"的意思。

353. These moribund shapes：moribund 意为"垂死的"，这里和上文的 black shapes，black shadows of disease and starvation 等都是同义复现。这里为了上下文衔接通畅，把名词"这些垂死的形体"译为短句"死神正在召唤他们"。

354. were free as air—and nearly as thin：这一句写得十分悲凉。这些黑人一直在白人的桎梏下像牛马一样做着苦力，不得自由。只要他们还有一点力气，就要干活。如今他们快死了，已经被压榨完了最后一滴膏血，终于可以自由地休息了（were free as air）。但是如今他们也已气若游丝，随时会咽下最后一口气（and nearly as thin as air）。一个优秀的作家，一定要有创造性地运用语言的能力。不仅是这里的句子，事实上在整部《黑暗之心》里面，我们都看到了康拉德对于语言文字的高超的驾驭能力。因而他笔下的场景总是富于戏剧性且打动人心，他借人物之口发出的议论总是深邃、透彻，激荡着读者的心灵。这一点令人敬佩。

355. distinguish the gleam of the eyes：分辨那些眼睛发出的微光。这是说马洛开始仔细地去打量树下那些不幸的黑人了。也可能是马洛刚从明亮的阳光下进到树荫里，眼睛慢慢适应了昏暗的光线，开始看得清楚了。

of the orbs, which died out slowly[356]. The man seemed young—almost a boy[357]—but you know with them it's hard to tell. I found nothing else to do but to offer[358] him one of my good Swede's ship's biscuits[359] I had in my pocket. The fingers closed slowly on it and held—there was no other movement and no other glance[360]. He had tied a bit of white worsted round his neck—Why? Where did he get it? Was it a badge—an ornament—a charm—a propitiatory act? Was there any idea at all connected with it? It looked startling round his black neck, this bit of white thread from beyond the seas.

"Near the same tree two more bundles of acute angles[361] sat

---

356. a kind...died out slowly：flicker 意为 "闪烁摇曳的光"，orbs 意为 "眼球；眼窝"，died out 意为 "消失；熄灭"。这里描写了黑人劳工将死的状态，眼窝深处的一缕已经无法视物的白光，正在渐渐消散。

357. almost a boy：几乎还是个孩子。这里也是在揭露殖民者的暴行，他们连年纪很小的黑人也不放过。

358. I found nothing else to do but to offer：可见马洛还是比较善良正直的，这些人的生命已经无法挽救，他也帮不上什么忙，但是他还是想多少对他们有点善意的表示。

359. my good Swede's ship's biscuits：这里 good 意为 "好心的"，但是似乎不译出来也可以，因为英文中经常在人称前加上这种修饰词，我觉得只是一种语言习惯而已，而且中文语境中没有对应的含义。

360. The fingers...no other glance：这里很明显在暗示，这个黑人就这样死在了马洛的眼前。顺便一提，下一句中出现的缠绕在这个黑人脖子上的白毛线，除了营造一种令马洛不解的诡异感，似乎也在说明一个事实，那就是在殖民之初，有的黑人部落收集白人不要的东西，比如子弹壳、扣子以及衣服上的饰物之类。因为他们见识过白人武器的力量，他们认为那是某种神力，因而他们觉得白人的物品也附有神力，可以收集来做护身符之用。

361. two more bundles of acute angles：还有两副峰棱的瘦骨。意思是马洛又看到两个待死的黑人劳工。

with their legs drawn up[362]. One, <u>with his chin propped on his knees[363]</u>, stared at nothing, in an intolerable and appalling manner: <u>his brother phantom[364]</u> <u>rested its forehead[365]</u>, as if <u>overcome with a great weariness[366]</u>; and all about others were scattered in every pose of contorted collapse, as in some picture of a massacre or a pestilence. While I stood horror-struck, one of these creatures <u>rose to his hands and knees[367]</u>, and went off on all-fours towards the river to drink. He lapped out of his hand, then sat up in the sunlight, crossing his shins in front of him, and after a time let his woolly head fall on his <u>breastbone[368]</u>.

"I didn't want any more loitering in the shade, and I made haste towards the station. When near the buildings I met a white

---

362. sat with their legs drawn up：draw up 一般指"草拟；吊起"，这里指的是"蜷起腿来抱着膝盖"的那种姿势。这是一种缩起身体来自我保护的姿势，说明人已经很虚弱。

363. with his chin propped on his knees：prop 意为"支撑；倚靠"，这里是指把下巴支在膝盖上的姿势。

364. his brother phantom：phantom 意为"幽灵；鬼魂"，指的是将死的人；brother 则是指这两个黑人劳工中的另一个。白人看黑人的种族长得都差不多，所以用 brother 称之，也有"同伴"的意味。

365. rested its forehead：放着他的额头。前边讲过，两个人的姿势都是抱膝而坐，那么这里的姿势就是 rested its forehead on his knees。这其实是抱着膝盖、把头埋在两腿间的动作，是一种自我保护的意味更强的动作。

366. overcome with a great weariness：意思是"被极度的疲倦给压垮了"。这里 overcome 是过去分词形式，表被动，前边省略了 he was。

367. rose to his hands and knees：用手和膝盖支撑起身体。这其实是准备要爬行的姿势。

368. breastbone：胸骨。头垂到胸骨上，说明人已经没有生命迹象了。

man, in such an unexpected elegance of get-up[369] that in the first moment I took him for a sort of vision[370]. I saw a high starched collar[371], white cuffs, a light alpaca jacket[372], snowy trousers, a clean necktie, and varnished boots. No hat. Hair parted, brushed, oiled[373], under a green-lined parasol[374] held in a big white hand. He was amazing[375], and had a penholder behind his ear.

"I shook hands with this miracle[376], and I learned he was the Company's chief accountant, and that all the book-keeping was done at this station. He had come out for a moment, he said, to get a breath of fresh air. The expression sounded wonderfully odd[377], with its suggestion of sedentary desk-life[378]. I wouldn't

---

369. in such an unexpected elegance of get-up：意思是"他的衣着打扮出乎意料的优雅"。get-up 在这里的意思可能是"挺括的衣服；很有精神的外表"。

370. I took him for a sort of vision：我把他当成了某个幻象。也就是说，马洛看到这里竟然有一个衣着如此整洁潇洒的白人，几乎不相信自己的眼睛，还以为是自己眼花了。

371. a high starched collar：高高的、浆洗过的衣领（显得有型有款）。

372. a light alpaca jacket：淡色的毛呢外套。alpaca 意为"羊驼；羊驼呢"。

373. Hair parted, brushed, oiled：头发分向两边，梳理过，还涂了发油。

374. a green-lined parasol：镶着绿边儿的太阳伞。

375. amazing：令人惊叹的。这里的白人会计师一身整洁时髦的装扮，和上文中那些死于饥饿、疾病和疲惫的黑人形成了鲜明的对比。

376. this miracle：这个奇迹（似的人物）。这里是指这位衣冠楚楚的会计师。在非洲这样炎热的地方，别人都热得敞胸露怀，而他却能一丝不苟地保持着仪表，实在是个奇迹。

377. The expression sounded wonderfully odd：会计师讲话的措辞听起来非常别扭。

378. with its suggestion of sedentary desk-life：suggestion 意为"联想；暗示"，sedentary 意为"久坐不动的"。这里是说，你听到会计师那些文绉绉的用词，就会感觉他一定是常年伏案工作的人。

have mentioned the fellow to you[379] at all, only it was from his
lips that I first heard the name of the man who is so indissolubly
connected with the memories of that time[380]. Moreover, I respected
the fellow[381]. Yes; I respected his collars, his vast cuffs, his
brushed hair[382]. His appearance was certainly that of a hairdresser's
dummy; but in the great demoralization of the land[383] he kept up
his appearance. That's backbone. His starched collars and got-
up shirt-fronts were achievements of character. He had been out

---

379. mentioned the fellow to you：向你们提到这个人。马洛的意思是，要不
是从这个会计师口中第一次听到了库尔茨先生的名字，那么我也许就不会向
你们提起他了。

380. the man...of that time：意思是 "这个人（库尔茨）和马洛关于那段时间
（刚果河之旅）的记忆已经密不可分地联系在了一起"。也就是说，马洛一提
起自己的刚果河之旅，就会想到库尔茨。

381. respected the fellow：我尊敬这个家伙。意思是会计师整洁的衣着体现了
他的坚韧品格（或者说态度），这种品格令马洛十分敬佩。（确实，哪怕是在
温带的夏季，也不是人人都能做到仍然整洁端庄的。）

382. I respected...brushed hair：这里是以具体事物做说明。会计师的品格体现
在他的挺括的领子、宽大的袖口、梳理得一丝不乱的头发等等这些马洛的眼
睛看得到的细节上。

383. in the great demoralization of the land：demoralization 意为 "堕落；意气
消沉；士气低落"，这里同样是要把英文抽象词译出它的具体意思来。这句
话是说在炎热的非洲，一切都令人萎靡不振，人们也很难像在欧洲那样注重
自己的仪表。马伯庸在《长安的荔枝》里也有类似的一段很有意思的描述。
长安的官员去岭南会见当地的长官，为了仪表端庄威严，连夜赶制了一套新
的官服，第二天衣冠楚楚地来到衙门参加会见。广东气候炎热，长安官员外
表光鲜，内里热得汗流浃背，一番辛苦那就不用说了。结果一看到当地长
官，居然是随便搭着个大汗衫，敞胸露怀，摇着蒲扇，再一看所有广东官员
都是这样一身凉快的打扮。广东官员奉劝他入乡随俗，这里这么热，大家还
是都不拘小节算了吧。气候的威力确实不可小觑。

nearly three years; and, later, I could not help asking him how he managed to sport such linen. He had just the faintest blush, and said modestly[384], 'I've been teaching one of the native women about the station. It was difficult. She had a distaste for the work[385].' Thus this man had verily accomplished something. And he was devoted to his books[386], which were in apple-pie order.

"Everything else in the station was in a muddle—heads, things, buildings[387]. Strings of dusty niggers with splay feet[388] arrived and departed[389]; a stream of manufactured goods, rubbishy cottons, beads, and brass-wire sent into the depths of darkness[390],

---

384. modestly：谦逊低调地；羞怯腼腆地；程度不高的。结合上句的 blush（脸红），这里的词义选择似乎是"腼腆"比"谦虚"更好些。

385. She had a distaste for the work：她不喜欢这些工作。distaste 意为"反感"。这里似乎是说，土著女人认为浆衣服、擦靴子这种事情完全是毫无必要的，衣物能穿就行，整这些没用的虚饰做什么？因而很受不了。

386. was devoted to his books：对他的账本非常尽职尽责。be devoted to 意为"专注于；致力于；献身于"，books 在这里特指会计账簿。

387. heads, things, buildings：人员，货物，建筑物。这些全都是一片混乱的状态。注意这里的 heads 更有可能是指"人员"，而不是指"领导"。

388. Strings of dusty niggers with splay feet：一队队大张着两脚、风尘仆仆的黑人。splay feet 意为"八字脚的"，那么"八字脚"到底是什么意思呢？想象一下，搬运工一起扛抬重物的时候，是会采用一种两腿分开、两脚朝外的姿势，以便身体发力的。所以这里很可能是在描述黑人搬运工全身用力的一种姿态。

389. arrived and departed：来来去去。搬运工不断地进去出来，这里说明贸易站很繁忙，欧洲人和当地黑人之间的交易热火朝天。

390. sent into the depths of darkness：被送进那黑暗的深处。这里是说欧洲人带来的不值钱的棉布玻璃珠之类的玩意儿，被卖给了居住在原始丛林深处的那些黑人部落。

and in return came a precious trickle of ivory[391].

"I had to wait in the station for ten days—an eternity[392]. I lived in a hut in the yard[393], but to be out of the chaos[394] I would sometimes get into the accountant's office. It was built of horizontal planks, and so badly put together that, as he bent over his high desk, he was barred from neck to heels with narrow strips of sunlight[395]. There was no need to open the big shutter to see[396]. It was hot there, too; big flies buzzed fiendishly, and did not sting, but stabbed. I sat generally on the floor, while, of faultless

---

391. came a precious trickle of ivory：换回了一批珍贵的象牙。这里有两个信息点，一是，殖民者用劣质的工业制品交换宝贵的象牙，这种交易可能是基于欺骗，也可能是基于胁迫，总之，白人是在利用黑人，让他们充当自己捕杀大象的猎手；二是，工业品用的词是 a stream of（像水流一样），而象牙用的词是 a trickle of（像涓涓细流一样），从两个词的对比也可以看出，不值钱的工业品是被大量倾销的，而象牙却是珍贵难得的。这种交易的不平等也就显而易见了。

392. for ten days—an eternity：又是十天的等待，这对马洛而言简直是永无尽头的折磨。说明马洛很期待尽快赶到自己的工作地点，他觉得耗费在路途上的时间太长了。

393. in a hut in the yard：马洛临时住在贸易站院子里的一个小棚屋里。

394. to be out of the chaos：为了从那片嘈杂混乱之中脱身。这是因为贸易站里搬运工来来往往地搬货物，十分吵闹，马洛不想一直待在那里，有时候就躲出去图个清静。

395. he was...strips of sunlight：因为木条拼成的会计师的办公室很粗糙，木条之间并不是衔接得毫无缝隙；阳光从木条之间射进来，在会计师身上从头到脚都印上一道道的条纹。

396. no need to open the big shutter to see：如果你想看看外面，你根本都用不着打开那扇宽大的百叶窗。这也说明木条之间缝隙很大，房屋的建设相当潦草。

appearance (and even slightly scented[397]), perching on a high stool, he wrote, he wrote. Sometimes he stood up for exercise. When a truckle-bed with a sick man (some invalid agent[398] from upcountry) was put in there, he exhibited a gentle annoyance[399]. 'The groans of this sick person,' he said, 'distract my attention[400]. And without that[401] it is extremely difficult to guard against clerical errors in this climate.'

"One day he remarked, without lifting his head[402], 'In the

---

397. even slightly scented：这里有两种理解，一是"甚至还洒了点香水"，二是由于衣物洗晒得十分干净，有一种"太阳味儿"——"甚至微微带着衣香"。但是似乎"衣香（鬓影）"这种词汇对男人不太合适，所以在此选择第一种理解来翻译。事实上第二种理解的可能性也很大。

398. some invalid agent：某个病倒了的代理人。这里描写的躺在轮床上的代理人是个打酱油角色，对他的描写是为了让读者先行了解一下丛林深处条件艰苦，贸易代理人在那里生病乃至死亡都是常事，为后文做铺垫。invalid 在这里意为"病弱的"。

399. exhibited a gentle annoyance：这里说明会计师温文尔雅，即使表达不满的时候，也是态度温和、礼貌克制。annoyance 意为"烦恼；气恼"。这里事实上也有一种对比的效果。会计师看上去是个有学识、有风度的人，但是后文可以看出，他对于同胞的生命和黑人的生命，都表现出一种令人瞠目的从容的冷漠。实际上这也可以说是资本主义制度下的产物，那时候人们追逐金钱、渴望成功，对身外之物孜孜以求，可是却失去了人性中最基本的善良和对生命的敬畏。

400. distract my attention：会分散我的注意力。这里是会计师抱怨的话，可以看出两点，一是他的措辞确实带点书卷气（从后面的对话中还可以继续看出来）；二是反映了他冷漠的内心，他对生病的同胞并没有什么关怀，只觉得呻吟声影响了自己的工作。作者对人物特征的把握始终很准确。

401. that：翻译中应注意代词的指代对象。这里 that 指的是"attention（注意力；专注）"。意思是"没有 attention，我就没法好好工作"。

402. without lifting his head：头也不抬地。这里是说会计师一边低头工作，一边随口向马洛说了句话。这也可见会计师一直"沉迷工作不能自拔"的状态。

interior you will no doubt meet Mr. Kurtz.' On my asking[403] who Mr. Kurtz was, he said he was a first-class agent[404]; and seeing my disappointment[405] at this information, he added slowly, laying down his pen[406], 'He is a very remarkable person.' Further questions elicited from him that[407] Mr. Kurtz was at present in charge of a trading-post, a very important one, in the true ivory-country[408], at 'the very bottom of there[409]. Sends in as much ivory as all the others put together...' He began to write again. The sick man was too ill to groan[410]. The flies

---

403. On my asking：on 在这里也常使用 upon 代替，意思一样，即"在我询问之下""应着问题（而回答）"。

404. a first-class agent：first-class 有"优秀的；第一流的"这种词义，但是在这里，结合下文对公司人员职位的描述，可以知道这里的 first-class 是马洛公司对贸易代理人的一种等级划分，意思是"一等代理人"或者"高级代理人"。

405. disappointment：意为"失望；沮丧"。这里也有两种理解，一是马洛可能预期这会是一个什么样的传奇人物，结果一听只是一位公司贸易代表，所以失望；二是马洛希望听到的不仅仅是库尔茨的职位，而是这究竟是个什么样的贸易代表，为什么值得一提；他觉得会计师的回答给出的信息不够充分，所以失望。

406. he added slowly, laying down his pen：这里写出了会计师的神态。他见马洛对自己的回答不以为然，或者说并没有把自己口中的"库尔茨先生"多么当回事，因此神色也变得认真了起来，放下笔，用缓慢的语气向马洛强调库尔茨先生的优秀。

407. Further questions elicited from him that：elicited 意为"引出"。这里是说马洛跟着又追问了几个问题，才从会计师口中引出了进一步的回答，得到了关于库尔茨先生的更多的信息。

408. in the true ivory-country：在一个真正的象牙之国。也就是说库尔茨先生的站点在非洲腹地真正出产象牙的地方。

409. the very bottom of there：在那里的最深处。也就是说库尔茨先生所在的地方是欧洲人当时所能探索的最深入非洲的地方。

410. was too ill to groan：（推床上的）代理人已经病得连呻吟声都发不出来了。

buzzed in a great peace[411].

"Suddenly there was a growing murmur of voices and a great tramping of feet. A caravan had come in. A violent babble of uncouth sounds[412] burst out on the other side of the planks. All the carriers were speaking together, and in the midst of the uproar the lamentable voice of the chief agent was heard 'giving it up' tearfully for the twentieth time that day[413]....He rose slowly. 'What a frightful row[414],' he said. He crossed the room gently to look

---

411. in a great peace：病人不再呻吟，会计师和马洛也停止了对话，办公室里就陷入一片寂静了。苍蝇的嗡嗡声只会让这里更加显得寂静。参见上文"蝉噪林愈静，鸟鸣山更幽"。这里似乎也在暗示，生病的代理人已经快要死了，因为"沉寂"和"苍蝇"也都是具有暗示性的事物。在后文中，库尔茨先生死去的时候，也出现了"苍蝇"这一意象。

412. A violent babble of uncouth sounds：babble 意为"胡言乱语；让人听不懂的话"，uncouth 意为"粗野的"。这里都是在描述黑人搬运工用他们的部落语言（在白人听来当然就是一些 get 不到任何意义的粗蛮的呼喊乱叫）在激动地争相说着什么。想想看，一队黑人搬运工之中突然有一个人倒下，他的同伴一定会围上来，有的说"啊，某某死了！"有的说"赶紧给他水！抬到树荫下说不定还有救！"有的会义愤填膺地向白人监工抗议说："都是因为你不让我们休息还顶着太阳走这么远，我就说一定会出事吧！"等等之类的话，这些七嘴八舌的话语混杂在一起，就形成了 a violent babble of uncouth sounds。

413. the lamentable...that day：lamentable 意为"哀伤的；悲恸的"，tearfully 意为"含泪的；眼泪汪汪的"。这句话携带了很多信息。一是，倒下的搬运工肯定死了，因为总代理人（或者是站长）说"giving it up"（算了吧，没救了；放开那具尸体吧），他用的是 it 这个词；二是，运输队每天来来往往，每天都会有很多搬运工死掉，就像这句话说的"for the twentieth time that day"，光是马洛目睹的这一天，总代理人就已经说出这句话不下二十次了；三是，白人殖民者相当虚伪，在他们眼中，黑人的命贱如蝼蚁，他们根本不在乎搬运工的死活，但是还要惺惺作态，掉着鳄鱼眼泪说"把它放下吧"。

414. What a frightful row：多么可怕（烦人）的吵闹声啊。这里可以看出会计师对死去的黑人搬运工也没有一丝同情。他只觉得外面的吵闹声和身边那个代理人的呻吟声一样，又影响自己工作了。

at the sick man, and returning, said to me, 'He does not hear[415].'
'What! Dead?' I asked, startled[416]. 'No, not yet,' he answered,
with great composure[417]. Then, alluding with a toss of the head
to[418] the tumult in the station-yard, 'When one has got to make
correct entries, one comes to hate those savages—hate them to
the death[419].' He remained thoughtful for a moment. 'When you
see Mr. Kurtz' he went on, 'tell him from me that everything
here'—he glanced at the deck[420]—'is very satisfactory[421]. I don't
like to write to him—with those messengers of ours you never

---

415. He does not hear：这个会计师的脑回路相当清奇。他居然羡慕（或者嫉妒）那个昏过去的病人听不见外面的吵闹声，不会受到任何影响。可见会计师的内心冷漠到了何种地步。

416. startled：马洛把会计师说的"他倒好，一点儿也听不见了"理解成那个病人死了，所以吓了一跳。马洛和会计师的脑回路不一样，马洛还是有人性的。

417. with great composure：不动声色，从容自若。这里的神态描写，包括上一句台词"not yet"，都说明会计师对别人的生死全不在意。

418. alluding with a toss of the head to：allude to 意为"暗指"，a toss of the head 意为"用甩头的动作来示意"，都表现了会计师那种浑不在乎，又带着轻蔑和厌恶的态度。

419. hate them to the death：恨透了他们了。这里是说会计师对黑人搬运工相当不满，因为他们的吵闹声打扰了自己工作。至于吵闹声背后的原因是一条生命的离去，会计师是完全不会去想、也根本不在乎的。

420. glanced at the deck：瞥了一眼院子。deck 意为"（屋后供休息的）平台"，这里可能指的是办公室外面的场院，也就是搬运工们正在吵吵嚷嚷的地方。

421. satisfactory：令人满意的。这一段中，作者通过神态、动作、语言，鲜明地刻画了会计师的形象。他精致（衣服整洁）、一丝不苟（总是埋头工作、精心记账）、冷漠（对于别人的苦难毫不同情）、精明且善于算计（贸易站里明明是一团乱麻，他却告诉库尔茨先生"一切都很好"；他让马洛带口信而不是写信，是为了不让信件落入经理手中，也就是说，他想瞒过经理，和库尔茨先生私下建立良好的关系。他这样做，是因为他认为库尔茨先生极有可能被提拔并取代现在的经理。可见，为了自己的前途，会计师也是费尽了心思）。

know who may get hold of your letter—at that Central Station[422].'
He stared at me[423] for a moment with his mild, bulging eyes[424].
'Oh, he will go far, very far[425],' he began again. 'He will be a
somebody in the Administration before long. They, above—the
Council in Europe, you know—mean him to be.'

"He turned to his work. The noise outside had ceased, and
presently in going out I stopped at the door. In the steady buzz
of flies[426] the homeward-bound agent was lying finished and
insensible[427]; the other, bent over his books, was making correct
entries of perfectly correct transactions[428]; and fifty feet below the

---

422. Central Station：中央贸易站；总站。这里是马洛真正工作的地方，也是掌管着"公司"在刚果河流域的所有贸易站点的"经理"的驻地。

423. stared at me：注视着我；盯着我看。这里是说会计师试图用眼神试探马洛这个人是否可靠。

424. with his mild, bulging eyes：用温和、期待的眼神。bulging 意为"鼓起的；隆起的；眼球突出的"。这里是形容会计师全神贯注地紧盯着马洛，从内心里期待着马洛能够为自己办好这件事的样子。

425. he will go far, very far：意思是会计师认为，库尔茨的仕途不可限量，他将沿着站长、经理乃至欧洲董事会成员这样一条光明大道，一路升迁到非常高的位置上。

426. the steady buzz of flies：苍蝇的嗡嗡声一刻也不停止。这说明不断有苍蝇飞来围绕着那位失去了知觉的代理人。苍蝇和秃鹫都是对死亡的气味非常敏感的动物，这位代理人很有可能已经死了。

427. was lying finished and insensible：直挺挺地躺着，毫无知觉。这里的 finished 既表示那个代理人的工作生涯结束了，也可以说他的生命也将结束了，总之就是已经"完蛋了"。insensible 意为"昏迷的；无知觉的"。

428. was making...correct transactions：正在把完美的交易记录成完美的账目。注意英文中出现了两次 correct，译文也尽量应体现这种重复性的强调语气。另外，perfectly correct transactions 也在暗指，欧洲人用不值钱的工业垃圾换走了非洲珍贵的象牙，这桩交易是多么的划算和完美。

doorstep[429] I could see the still tree-tops of the grove of death[430].

"Next day I left that station at last, with a caravan of sixty men, for a two-hundred-mile tramp[431].

"No use telling you much about that. Paths, paths, everywhere; a stamped-in network of paths spreading over the empty land, through the long grass, through burnt grass, through thickets, down and up chilly ravines, up and down stony hills ablaze with heat; and a solitude, a solitude, nobody, not a hut. The population had cleared out a long time ago. Well, if a lot of mysterious niggers armed with all kinds of fearful weapons[432] suddenly took to travelling on the road between Deal and Gravesend[433], catching the

---

429. fifty feet below the doorstep：在台阶下面不到 50 英尺的地方。因为贸易站建在山坡上，所以"死亡之林"在他们下边。

430. the still tree-tops of the grove of death：死亡之林的静止的树梢。grove 意为"树丛；小树林"，still 意为"静止不动的"，体现出那片树林的散发着死亡气息的寂静感。这里是用马洛眼中的一幅定格画面，把一心工作的会计师（资本和殖民主义的代表）与垂死的代理人和黑人劳工做鲜明的对比，让读者直观地看到欧洲人在非洲的"进步事业"是多么的荒谬和残酷，把人全都变成了非人。

431. a two-hundred-mile tramp：一段长达 200 英里的徒步旅程。200 英里约等于 321 公里。tramp 意为"长途步行；长途跋涉"。

432. a lot of...fearful weapons：这里是马洛做的一个假设，让欧洲人设身处地，体会那种被侵略的滋味。想象一下，一群拿着各种可怕的武器的神秘黑人突然出现在欧洲，抓捕那些还过着原始生活的白人乡巴佬，那么白人的反应一定也会和真实情况中的黑人一样，被吓得四散奔逃。

433. between Deal and Gravesend：这里仍是作者在打比方，如果强大而神秘的黑人出现在英国的 Deal 和 Gravesend 这些城市的郊区的道路上，事情会变得怎么样。译文中这两个地名都使用了音译，事实上，Deal 还有"交易"的意思，Gravesend 也可以理解为"送往坟墓"，但是这两个地名的隐喻意义，在译文中无法呈现出来。

yokels right and left to carry heavy loads for them, I fancy every farm and cottage thereabouts would get empty very soon[434]. Only here the dwellings[435] were gone, too. Still I passed through several abandoned villages. There's something pathetically childish in the ruins of grass walls[436]. Day after day, with the stamp and shuffle of sixty pair of bare feet behind me, each pair under a 60-lb. load[437]. Camp, cook, sleep, strike camp, march. Now and then a carrier dead in harness, at rest in the long grass near the path, with an empty water-gourd and his long staff lying by his side. A great silence around and above[438]. Perhaps on some quiet night the tremor of far-off drums, sinking, swelling, a tremor vast, faint;

---

434. every farm...very soon：于是（英国的）每个农场和村庄都会很快人去屋空。大家都被吓跑了，不敢再回来。这种想象和真实发生在非洲的事情完全一致。

435. dwellings：民居；住所。也就是说，唯一和马洛脑海中想象的场景不一样的是，白人乡巴佬逃走后，他们遗弃的地方还会留下原来的房屋；而眼前的非洲，却连房屋也没剩下，什么都不见了。

436. There's...grass walls：看着那些坍塌了的茅草墙，你会感觉到它们全都透着一股可悲的幼稚。pathetically 意为"可怜地；悲哀地"，childish 意为"幼稚的；孩子气的"，ruins 意为"遗迹；废墟"，作名词通常使用复数形式。这里似乎是解释了为什么非洲土著人逃走后只留下一大片荒野，而很少见房屋。因为他们的房屋都是茅草做的，一旦没有人住，很快就会倾塌，然后和荒野里的草丛融为一体，了无痕迹地消失了。

437. each pair under a 60-lb. load：每双脚板（每个搬运工）上面都压着 60 磅的重物。lb. 意为"磅"（源自拉丁语 libra，约等于 454 克），60 磅约等于 27 公斤。想一想扛着 50 多斤的货物在非洲的荒野里徒步行进 321 公里，这不是一般人能承受的。而这却是黑人搬运工的日常。

438. A great silence around and above：周围的人们都（累得、麻木得）不想吭声，四周的荒野、头顶的苍天也是一片寂静，毫无表示。这说明搬运工命如蝼蚁，他们的死就好像一滴水融入大海那样的无声无息。

a sound weird, appealing, suggestive, and wild[439] — and perhaps with as profound a meaning as the sound of bells in a Christian country[440]. Once a white man in an unbuttoned uniform, camping on the path with an armed escort of lank Zanzibaris[441], very hospitable and festive — not to say drunk[442]. Was looking after the

---

439. the tremor...and wild：这一句不宜字对字直译，因为英汉两种语言之间的差异，直译成"远处鼓声的震颤，一会儿低沉，一会儿高亢；那震颤声有时巨大，有时微弱；那是一种怪异、有所呼吁、有所暗示的野性的声音"，读起来似乎没什么文学性。虽然在英文的行文中，这样写是没有问题的，甚至还可以通过形容词对比性的罗列，起到了一种时强时弱有如鼓声起伏的音响效果，但是中文最好还是在透彻理解的基础上，用比较有文采的方式重新组织和表达。文学作品的翻译，我认为应该以"感受对等"为标准，也就是说，原文读者和译文读者应该能够通过对同一段文字的阅读，得到相同的感受和体验。如果读完之后，英文读者的感受是"恢宏大气"，而译文读者的感受是"不知所云"，那就似乎不可取了。另外注意，这句话省略了谓语动词，这也是文学化语言的特征之一。

440. perhaps with...Christian country：这里很可能是用基督教国家"报丧的钟声"来暗示，马洛晚上听到的非洲鼓声是在为他们的黑人同胞寄托一种哀思。事实上这也有可能是马洛主观的想法，他的感情往往会影响他看待客观事物的眼光。整部《黑暗之心》几乎完全是马洛一个人的独白，所以叙述中带有主观色彩也是无可厚非的。莎士比亚戏剧也是这样，在人物抒情性的独白里，苍天、大地、世间的一切，都在围绕着人物的命运和感情而旋转，甚至那些只是客观存在的事物也能与他们同喜同悲。文学作品打动人心的力量，很大程度上也来源于此。

441. an armed escort of lank Zanzibaris：这里的 escort 可以理解为"护卫队"，也可以理解为"护卫者"。也就是说，这里的 Zanzibaris（桑给巴尔人）是一个人（保镖）还是一群人（卫队），不太好确定。Lank（瘦高的）可能是特定的一个桑给巴尔人的特征，也可能是桑给巴尔人这个非洲部族的整体特征。桑给巴尔人居住于非洲东部，1964 年成立桑给巴尔人民共和国；同年与坦噶尼喀共和国合并，成了今天的坦桑尼亚联合共和国。

442. not to say drunk：not to say 在这里可以理解为"and（更加上）"，意思是"更别提（他还喝醉了）""更不用说还有（一身酒气）"。drunk 和上文的 hospitable、festive 一样，都是形容这个带着武装护卫的白人是处于什么样的状态的。

upkeep of the road, he declared. Can't say I saw any road or any upkeep, unless the body of a middle-aged negro, with a bullet-hole in the forehead[443], upon which I absolutely stumbled three miles farther on[444], may be considered as a permanent improvement. I had a white companion, too, not a bad chap, but rather too fleshy and with the exasperating habit of fainting on the hot hillsides[445], miles away from the least bit of shade and water[446]. Annoying, you know, to hold your own coat like a parasol over a man's head while he is coming to. I couldn't help asking him once what he meant by coming there at all[447]. 'To make money, of course. What

---

443. with a bullet-hole in the forehead：前额有个弹孔。既然是弹孔，那么凶手是谁就不言而喻了。

444. upon which...farther on：stumble 意为"遇见；绊倒"，absolutely 意为"绝对地"，即"literally speaking"，说明马洛不是仅仅"看见了那具尸体"，而是真真正正地被那具尸体绊了一跤。three miles farther on 意为"前方三英里处"。马洛和这个带着武装护卫的白人迎面相遇，那白人喷着酒气兴奋地说他在"保养 / 清理道路"，估计听到这句话，马洛一开始并不明白什么意思。可是往前刚走出 3 英里，那具额头上暴露着弹孔的尸体就让马洛一下子明白了——在刚才的来路上，白人在那里枪杀了中年黑人! 所以他才会乘着酒兴向马洛炫耀自己在"清理道路"。这是殖民者在非洲草菅人命的又一次例证。

445. with the...hot hillsides：马洛的同伴肥胖不耐热，一到炽热的山坡上就会昏过去。这个习惯对于马洛来说简直 exasperating（不胜其烦；非常恼火）。

446. miles away...and water：距离树荫和水源还很远（的时候）。the least bit of 表示强调，miles away 可能是夸张，这些词汇都表现出马洛的恼火和无可奈何。同伴动不动就昏倒在前不着村后不着店的地方，整个队伍在烈日下无法行进，换谁也受不了。

447. what he meant by coming there at all：马洛问他的同伴，到底是干嘛跑到这儿来了。意思是，马洛认为他又肥胖又羸弱，根本不适合来到非洲这样的地方。来非洲的前提条件至少得是身体强健，而不是动不动就昏倒，拖累别人。

do you think?' he said, scornfully. Then he got fever, and had to be carried in a hammock slung under a pole. As he <u>weighed sixteen stone</u>[448] I had no end of rows with the carriers. They jibbed, ran away, sneaked off with their loads in the night—quite a mutiny. So, one evening, I made a speech in English with gestures, not one of which was lost to the sixty pairs of eyes before me, and the next morning I started the hammock off in front all right. An hour afterwards I came upon <u>the whole concern wrecked in a bush</u>[449]—man, hammock, groans, blankets, <u>horrors</u>[450]. The heavy pole had skinned his poor nose. <u>He was very anxious for me to kill somebody</u>[451], but there wasn't the shadow of a carrier near. I remembered the old doctor— 'It would be interesting for science to watch <u>the mental changes of individuals</u>[452], on the spot.' I felt I

---

448. weighed sixteen stone：stone 为重量单位"英石"，16 英石约为 100 千克。译文中所有重量单位都统一为英文中最常见的"磅"。马洛同伴体重 200 多斤，难怪黑人脚夫对他避之唯恐不及。

449. the whole concern wrecked in a bush：concern 在这里的意思是"一整套装置"，也就是用那一套杆子、吊索和吊床抬着的马洛同伴。wrecked 意为"被毁坏，砸烂在地上"。这是说，马洛看见他的同伴已经被黑人脚夫扔在灌木丛里不管了。

450. man, hammock, groans, blankets, horrors：这一些名词罗列很符合英文的行文，讲的就是马洛所听见的和所看见的，但是字对字直译，不符合中文阅读习惯，最好在翻译的时候稍加变通。

451. He was very anxious for me to kill somebody：这里的 somebody 是指黑人脚夫，就是说，马洛同伴非常愤怒，他要马洛随便抓个人过来杀了给他出气。

452. the mental changes of individuals：人的思想变化。这里是一种"黑色幽默"，把马洛看到那一地狼藉的时候猝不及防、张口结舌的样子说成是 the mental changes。

was becoming scientifically interesting[453]. However, all that is to no purpose[454]. On the fifteenth day I came in sight of the big river again, and hobbled into the Central Station. It was on a back water surrounded by scrub and forest, with a pretty border of smelly mud on one side, and on the three others enclosed by a crazy fence of rushes. A neglected gap was all the gate it had, and the first glance at the place was enough to let you see the flabby devil was running that show[455]. White men with long staves in their hands appeared languidly from amongst the buildings, strolling up to take a look at me, and then retired out of sight somewhere. One of them, a stout, excitable chap with black moustaches[456], informed me with great volubility and many digressions, as soon as I told him who I was, that my steamer was at the bottom of the river[457].

---

453. I felt I was becoming scientifically interesting：马洛觉得，按照那个法国医生的说法，"观察人的思想变化"可以促进科学研究，那么现在他被眼前的情景一记重击，思想正在急速变化，正是法国医生梦想得到的"观察样本"，他已经要开始对科学的进步产生意义、变得很有科学价值了。这实际上是马洛自我解嘲的话。面对这种突发情况，除了发几句牢骚，他还能怎么办呢？

454. to no purpose：马洛自己也知道，发牢骚也于事无补，根本就没有用（to no purpose）。

455. the first glance...running that show：这是一句辛辣的讽刺，讽刺对象正是后文的重要人物——经理。flabby 意为"松弛的；软弱的"，这里是说经理根本就不会管事儿，他没有建立起一种坚强有力的领导。所以总站那副松垮破烂的样子在马洛眼里就好像一场闹剧一样。

456. a stout, excitable chap with black moustaches：一个留着黑胡子，强壮的、容易激动的家伙。这个人物后面还有戏份。他手段残暴但又没什么头脑，属于经理手下的打手一类的角色。

457. my steamer was at the bottom of the river：我的船已经沉到河底了。马洛应聘的职位就是船长，他跋山涉水来到这里准备驾船，刚到总站，就被告知船沉了。马洛内心估计也是飘过无数个问号和惊叹号。

I was thunderstruck. What, how, why? Oh, it was 'all right.' The 'manager himself' was there. All quite correct. 'Everybody had behaved splendidly[458]! splendidly!' — 'you must,' he said in agitation, 'go and see the general manager at once. He is waiting!'

"I did not see the real significance of that wreck[459] at once. I fancy I see it now, but I am not sure—not at all. Certainly the affair was too stupid—when I think of it—to be altogether natural[460]. Still...[461] But at the moment it presented itself simply as a confounded nuisance[462]. The steamer was sunk. They had started two days before in a sudden hurry up the river with the manager on board, in charge of some volunteer skipper, and before they had been out three hours they tore the bottom out of her on stones[463], and she san near the south bank. I asked myself what I was to do

---

458. behaved splendidly：表现得棒极了。这明显是在推脱责任。既然表现得棒极了，为什么船会沉了？

459. the real significance of that wreck：那条沉船真正的意义是什么；究竟意味着什么。马洛是船长，船沉了，对他来说意味着要捞船、修船等等麻烦。还有，这起沉船可能是经理的阴谋，经理要借此拖延对库尔茨的救援。

460. was too...altogether natural：too stupid to be natural 意思是"蠢得简直不像当真能发生的事情"，或者说，马洛也考虑过这起沉船事故简直蠢到了家，莫非不是自然发生的事情，而是人为的？ altogether 表示强调语气，when I think of it 是插入语。

461. Still...：表示直到如今，直到在泰晤士河上讲述这个故事的时候（马洛仍然觉得沉船这件事儿简直如梦似幻，令人百思不得其解）。

462. it presented itself simply as a confounded nuisance：刚得知这件事情的时候，我还仅仅觉得它是一件令人讨厌的麻烦事。confounded 意为"困惑的；糊涂的；讨厌的"，nuisance 意为"麻烦事；妨害行为"。

463. tore the bottom out of her on stones：在石头上把船底划开了一个大口子。注意英文中常用女性"她"代指船。

there, now my boat was lost. As a matter of fact, I had plenty to do in fishing my command out of the river.[464] I had to set about it the very next day. That, and the repairs[465] when I brought the pieces to the station, took some months.

"My first interview with the manager was curious[466]. He did not ask me to sit down after my twenty-mile walk that morning.[467] He was commonplace in complexion, in features, in manners, and in voice. He was of middle size and of ordinary build. His eyes, of the usual blue, were perhaps remarkably cold, and he certainly could make his glance fall on one as trenchant and heavy as an axe[468]. But even at these times the rest of his person seemed to disclaim the intention.[469] Otherwise there was only[470]

---

464. I had plenty...out of the river: fish 在这里是动词, 意为 "搜寻; 捞出来"。my command 意为 "归我指挥的那条船"。所以尽管船沉了, 作为船长的马洛还是有许多事情要做, 甚至比正常情况下更忙了。

465. That, and the repairs: 这里的意思是 "捞船和修船"。that 指的是 "fishing the boat out of the river"。

466. curious: 这里的意思不是 "好奇的", 而是 "不寻常的; 古怪的"。经理是个阴险小人, 而马洛善良正直, 两个人从第一次见面就彼此看不顺眼。

467. He did...that morning: 马洛远道而来, 经理见到他竟然都没让他坐下说话。实际上, 这可能是经理的一种驭人之术, 见面先给对方马威, 以树立自己的权势。

468. make his...as an axe: (经理) 把目光投到别人身上, 那目光又锋利, 又沉重, 就好像一把斧子一样。

469. But even...the intention: 但是即使在这些时候 (经理用利斧一样的眼光瞥人的时候), 他身体其他部分的动作却又似乎显得没什么攻击性, 和他凌厉的眼神很不协调。这说明经理既性情阴险, 又色厉内荏。

470. Otherwise there was only: 除此之外, 值得一提的就是 (经理那种高深莫测的笑容了)。这说明经理狠厉的眼神、诡秘的笑容, 都让马洛留下了深刻的印象。

an indefinable, faint expression of his lips, something stealthy — a smile — not a smile — I remember it, but I can't explain[471]. It was unconscious, this smile was, though just after he had said something it got intensified for an instant[472]. It came at the end of his speeches like a seal applied on the words to make the meaning of the commonest phrase appear absolutely inscrutable.[473] He was a common trader, from his youth up employed in these parts — nothing more. He was obeyed[474], yet he inspired neither love nor fear, nor even respect. He inspired uneasiness.[475] That was it! Uneasiness. Not a definite mistrust — just uneasiness — nothing more. You have no idea how effective such a...a...faculty[476] can

---

471. an indefinable...can't explain：这里很细致地描述了经理那种似笑非笑、高深莫测的表情（类似一种皮笑肉不笑的样子）。这种表情让马洛有一种很不舒服的感觉。

472. it got intensified for an instant：（每当经理说完几句话的时候）那种笑容就会一下子变深。可以想象出来，这确实是一种透露着阴险狡诈的表情。

473. It came at...absolutely inscrutable：这里有一个比喻，经理在每次说完话之后，嘴角上就扯出一个假笑，这就好像写完一段话就盖一个章一样；这个笑容会让最简单的一句话也变得令人捉摸不定，浮想联翩——莫非他还有什么言外之意吗？ inscrutable 意为"神秘的；不可理解的"。

474. He was obeyed：译文中可以将被动式变为主动式，把"他被人遵从"转换成"大家都服从他"。

475. he inspired...inspired uneasiness：意思是"他所引起的不是爱戴、惧怕，甚至也不是尊敬；他引起的是别人的不安"。这里是描述经理的行事风格，说明他并不是一个合格的领导者。译文中将"他引起别人的（什么感受）"颠倒译为"大家对他（如何看待）"。

476. such a...a...faculty：这里是马洛叙述中的自然停顿，说明马洛一边说话，一边在搜寻合适的词汇，来形容经理所管理的这个机构。两次停顿说明马洛选用 faculty 这个词是很勉强的，因而译为"这么样一个机构……呃，（转下页）

be. He had no genius for organizing, for initiative, <u>or for order</u>
<u>even</u>[477]. <u>That was evident in such things as the deplorable state</u>
<u>of the station.</u>[478] He had no learning, and no intelligence. <u>His</u>
<u>position had come to him</u>[479]—why? Perhaps because he was never
ill...He had <u>served three terms of three years</u>[480] out there...Because
triumphant health in the general rout of constitutions is a kind
of power in itself.[481] When he went home on leave he rioted on
a large scale—pompously. <u>Jack ashore—with a difference—</u>
<u>in externals only.</u>[482] This one could gather from his casual talk.
He originated nothing, he could keep the routine going—that's

---

（接上页）一帮子人"，传达出马洛对经理和他那些一盘散沙一样的手下的鄙视之情。马洛觉得他们根本称不上是一个"有序运转、有行动力的机构"，只不过就是一帮子人（为了搞象牙的目的）凑在了一起罢了。

477. or for order even：这里是说经理既没有组织能力，也没有创新能力（进取的意志），甚至连 order 都做不好。这里的 order 可以理解为"安排秩序；让事情有条理；让人员各安其职"或者"发号施令"。结合下文，我选择第一种理解。

478. That was...the station：总站这副糟糕的样子，就是经理毫无领导力的证明。

479. His position had come to him：经理这个位子是自动落到了他的头上的。因为他资历最老，别的竞争者都病了或者死了，所以只好让他当。

480. served three terms of three years：三年一个任期，他已经干了三个任期。经理在刚果河上已经工作了九年，他比这里的任何人都更有资历。

481. Because triumphant...power in itself：意为"在这样一个人都生病的地方，能够一直保持健康，这本身就是一种力量"。这也是经理能爬上这个位子的原因。甚至在后文中，强健的体魄也成了经理和库尔茨的决战中的胜负手——库尔茨病死了，经理自然而然又成了胜利者。

482. Jack ashore—with a difference—in externals only：这里是说经理一回到欧洲就狂欢纵饮，这种做派就好像回到岸上的水手一样。他和水手的区别也就只是身份和外表不同罢了，本质上都是浅薄无知。Jack 在这里是用最普通的英语人名指代水手。

all. But he was great. He was great by this little thing that it was impossible to tell what could control such a man.[483] He never gave that secret away[484]. Perhaps there was nothing within him.[485] Such a suspicion made one pause—for out there there were no external checks.[486] Once when various tropical diseases had laid low almost every 'agent' in the station, he was heard to say, 'Men who come out here should have no entrails.'[487] He sealed the utterance with that smile of his[488], as though it had been a door opening into a darkness

---

483. But he was...such a man：这里是说经理的厉害之处，就在于那么一个点——你根本不知道究竟他怕的是什么。也就是说，经理似乎是毫无弱点，无懈可击的。谁也抓不到任何把柄能够制得住他。

484. gave that secret away：究竟经理怕的是什么，他自己当然绝不会吐露。这有点类似武侠片里的"命门"，经理的"命门"在哪里，他肯定不会让别人知道。

485. Perhaps there was nothing within him：也许他的身体里空无一物，所以他才既没有优点，也没有弱点。

486. Such a suspicion...external checks：这种猜测会把人吓一跳，也把人难住了——在非洲可没有什么 X 射线之类的外科检查，可以证明经理到底是不是个"空心人"。

487. Men who come out here should have no entrails：这是经理的话，"来这儿的人根本就不该带着肚肠"。entrails 意为"内脏；（物体的）内部"。这句话的意思，一是验证了上文说的经理可能是个"空心人"，他根本就"没有肚肠"；二是说明非洲条件恶劣（细菌、病毒、寄生虫等等），一般人的体质来这儿真的受不住（除了经理这个天选之子），可能只是喝口水就得了热带病上吐下泻了，谁让他"带着肚肠"呢；三是 entrails 也可能比喻一个人内心真实的情感。经理是个"空心人"，他满口谎话、不干实事，是"虚伪"的代名词，在他身上，你看不到任何真情实感，只有贪婪、阴险和狡诈。之所以马洛最后会在精神上倒向库尔茨，那是因为库尔茨尽管事实上也是堕落了，但是他的身上还有着属于人类的真实的感情。

488. sealed the utterance with that smile of his：说完这句话，经理又用他一贯的那种笑容为这句话盖了个章 / 把这句话封印起来 / 作为这句话的结束。utterance 意为"发声；言语"。

he had in his keeping[489]. You fancied you had seen things—but the seal was on[490]. When annoyed at meal-times by the constant quarrels of the white men about precedence[491], he ordered an immense round table to be made[492], for which a special house had to be built. This was the station's mess-room. Where he sat was the first place—the rest were nowhere.[493] One felt this to be his unalterable conviction.[494] He was neither civil nor uncivil. He was quiet. He allowed his 'boy'—an overfed[495] young negro from the coast—to treat the white men, under his very eyes, with provoking

---

489. a door...his keeping: 这里用"通往黑暗的大门",比喻经理黑暗的内心。他满肚子害人的阴谋诡计,但是他谨慎地把守着自己的秘密,绝不让别人看出来。

490. but the seal was on: 但是印章已经盖上了。意思是那扇"通往黑暗的大门"关闭了,也就是说,经理已经闭上嘴,他不会再往下说了。

491. annoyed at...about precedence: 吃饭的时候,那些白人为了 precedence（地位高低;优先权）不停地吵闹,经理对此十分恼火。

492. ordered an...be made: order sth to be done 表达了一种发号施令的意思,"命令某物被做出来"。这里是说经理下令制作了一张巨型圆桌。

493. Where he...were nowhere: 只有经理坐的位置是上座,其他的位置全都不值一提。这说明在经理的观念中,只有他是掌权者,其他任何人也不能触碰他的权威。

494. One felt...unalterable conviction: 谁都看得出来,在经理心里"唯我独尊",这是他坚信不疑的立场,绝不容许任何挑战。

495. overfed: 被过度喂食的;肥头大耳的。这里隐含着一个对比。从海岸边弄来的黑人很多都成了劳工,他们遭受着疾病和饥饿的折磨,很多人都被饿死了。这个"经理的听差"也是来自海岸地带的黑人,但是和那些同胞的命运不同,他在经理这里吃香喝辣,被养得脑满肠肥。因为他甘愿做了经理的走狗——他和殖民者合作了。

insolence.[496]

"He began to speak as soon as he saw me. I had been very long on the road. He could not wait. Had to start without me[497]. The up-river stations[498] had to be relieved[499]. There had been so many delays[500] already that he did not know who was dead and who was alive, and how they got on[501]—and so on, and so on. He

---

496. to treat...provoking insolence：就在经理的眼皮底下，那个被养得脑满肠肥的黑人"跟班"可以肆无忌惮地挑衅白人。这说明那个"跟班"就好像一条被豢养的狗，在主人的纵容甚至授意下大声吠叫，以显示主人不可一世的权威。provoking 意为"挑衅的；激怒他人的"，insolence 意为"无礼；傲慢"。

497. I had been...start without me：这里是转述经理的话。他说马洛在路上的时间太长了，他因为等不及，所以只好自己开船出去了。这说明经理在暗暗地把沉船的责任推卸给马洛。我们知道，马洛从得到任命的那天开始就马不停蹄地赶往工作地点，所以他在路上花费的时间完全在正常期限以内。很有可能，经理估算时间觉得马洛快要到了，所以策划并实施了这起沉船事件。但是刚果河的水文情况很复杂，最深处达到 230 米（超过很多海湾的海水深度），河心水流速度远超两侧流速（水速差很大），甚至有时还会掀起高达数米的巨浪。难道经理为了搞沉这条船，竟会自己去冒生命危险？所以马洛说"这起沉船的意义究竟为何，实在让人想不通"。也许这也正应了前文的评语，经理是个"装腔作势而又色厉内荏，目光短浅而又贪婪成性，当真是愚蠢到无可救药的魔鬼"。

498. The up-river stations：河道上游的贸易站。这里主要指的是库尔茨的内陆贸易站。

499. to be relieved：得到救济；得到救援。上游的贸易站已经没有了食品和货物，正急需总站提供物质支援。

500. so many delays：这说明总站早就接到上游的求援信息，但是救援行动却一次次耽搁、一次次推迟。这肯定会导致上游的状况越来越岌岌可危。

501. how they got on：他们过得怎么样。这里是指库尔茨他们（在缺衣少食的情况下）的生存状况。

paid no attention to my explanations[502], and, playing with a stick of sealing-wax[503], repeated several times that the situation was 'very grave, very grave.'[504] There were rumours that a very important station was in jeopardy, and its chief, Mr. Kurtz[505], was ill. Hoped it was not true[506]. Mr. Kurtz was...I felt weary and irritable. Hang Kurtz, I thought.[507] I interrupted[508] him by saying I had heard of

---

502. paid no attention to my explanations：经理根本不给马洛解释的机会（他只顾自己讲话，不让马洛讲话）。经理这样做可能有两个原因，一是在推卸责任的时候掩盖他自己的心虚（因为马洛完全没做错任何事），二是用这种无礼的态度和对谈话主动权的把控，显示自己不容置疑的权威。

503. playing with a stick of sealing-wax：经理和马洛说话的时候，手里还把玩着物件。这自然也是展示一种居高临下的态度。sealing-wax 意为"封蜡；火漆"。注意经理手中的这件东西。火漆棍是用来封缄信件的，也是当时常见的办公用品。但是这里特别提到"经理把玩着火漆棍"，似乎在暗示总站的人（以经理为首）经常私拆欧洲和非洲之间往来的信件（前文会计师提到过，后文也有一次案例）。

504. the situation was 'very grave, very grave'：经理说"（上游的）情况现在非常严重，非常严重"。看似忧心忡忡，实则口是心非。

505. its chief, Mr. Kurtz：那里的站长库尔茨先生。

506. Hoped it was not true：这一段里有很多转述，包括这一句"希望（那些传言）不是真的"。

507. I felt weary and irritable. Hang Kurtz, I thought：马洛这时候又累又饿，还一直站着，经理却和他"库尔茨长、库尔茨短"地滔滔不绝，这让马洛越来越窝火，烦躁得无以复加——让那个库尔茨去死吧！马洛肯定会这样想。据说在明末，天启帝沉迷做木工，魏忠贤就经常在天启帝正专心致志、兴致勃勃地做木工的时候拿来一些奏章，问他那些国家事务该怎么处理。天启帝就会很不耐烦，说"你自己看着处理好了，别再问我了！"于是魏忠贤就这样慢慢把国家权力攫取到了自己手中。这两幅情景，似乎有点相似之处。他们都是先制造一个特定的情绪氛围，然后再把某个人或者某件事放进去，起到一种用情绪误导对方判断力的效果。irritable 意为"易怒的；烦躁的"。

508. interrupt：打断。打断经理说话，这说明马洛此时已经很有情绪了。

Mr. Kurtz on the coast.[509] 'Ah! So they talk of him down there,' he murmured to himself. Then he began again, assuring me Mr. Kurtz was the best agent he had, an exceptional man, of the greatest importance to the Company; therefore I could understand his anxiety. He was, he said, 'very, very uneasy.' Certainly he fidgeted on his chair a good deal[510], exclaimed, 'Ah, Mr. Kurtz!' broke the stick of sealing-wax and seemed dumbfounded[511] by the accident. Next thing he wanted to know 'how long it would take to'...I interrupted him again. Being hungry, you know, and kept on my feet too. I was getting savage. 'How can I tell?' I said. 'I haven't even seen the wreck yet—some months, no doubt.' All this talk seemed to me so futile[512]. 'Some months,' he said. 'Well, let us say three months before we can make a start. Yes. That ought to do the affair.[513]' I flung out of his hut (he lived all alone in a clay hut with a sort of verandah) muttering

---

509. I had...the coast：在海边（也就是在刚果河下游）的时候，马洛已经听说过库尔茨的大名了（会计师对他说的）。

510. Certainly he fidgeted on his chair a good deal：Certainly 是顺接上文，意为"这我当然看得出来"。fidget 意为"坐立不安；烦躁不安：因焦虑、紧张或无聊而不停地做小动作"。

511. dumbfounded：意为"目瞪口呆的，惊讶得说不出话的"。经理一直在马洛面前卖力表演（明明希望库尔茨最好赶快死掉，可是还表现出一副非常担忧的样子），但是似乎这表演有点过火了。

512. futile：徒劳的，无用的。这说明经理他们不干实事，只会动嘴皮子。马洛认为和经理的这场对话（conversation）全都是废话（nonsense），而在现代英语中有一个词"nonversation"，意为"完全无用的对话"，比较有意思。

513. Yes. That ought to do the affair：the affair 意为"那件事儿"，马洛当时肯定以为这是指"修船；出发前的准备工作"。事实上，the affair 指的是"拖死库尔茨"，这才是经理头脑里真正考虑的问题。三个月拖死库尔茨，经理认为时间够了。

to myself my opinion of him. He was a chattering idiot. Afterwards I took it back[514] when it was borne in upon me startlingly with what extreme nicety he had estimated the time requisite for the 'affair.'[515]

"I went to work the next day, turning, so to speak, my back on that station[516]. In that way only it seemed to me I could keep my hold on the redeeming facts of life[517]. Still, one must look about sometimes; and then I saw this station, these men strolling aimlessly about in the sunshine of the yard. I asked

---

514. Afterwards I took it back：后来我收回了这句话。意思是，后来马洛对经理刮目相看，原来经理绝不是什么"饶舌的白痴"，而是一个精明审慎、极具手段的魔鬼。

515. when it was...the 'affair'：意思是"他对干这件事儿所需要的时间，估计得竟是相当精确；当我明白过来的时候，我真的是浑身发凉"。在后文的情节里，当经理一行最终赶到库尔茨面前的时候，库尔茨已经病重不治了。经理成功地拖死了自己最大的对手，他对于时间的计算实在是相当精确（如果到达上游的时候库尔茨已经死了，经理可能会被董事会问责"救援不力"；如果库尔茨病得还不重，等他康复了又会成为经理的威胁。接回一个病重将死的库尔茨，对于经理来说是最有利的）。经理的手段，也令马洛不寒而栗。"bear in upon"意为"密切相关；产生影响；留下印象等"，相关的用法还有 bear in mind，意为"记在心里"。所以"when it was borne in upon me"在这里的意思是"当我明白过来的时候"。extreme nicety 意为"极度精准"。注意，因为整部小说是马洛事后的讲述，所以时间线偶尔会向前或者向后跳动；在这里，时间线明显向后跳动了。

516. turning, so to...that station：turn my back on 意为"转过身去背对着；不理睬"，是说马洛实在不想再看见总站上经理那帮人的嘴脸了。so to speak 是插入语。

517. In that...facts of life：keep my hold on 意为"紧紧抓住"，redeeming 意为"补偿的；弥补的"。这句话是倒装结构，正常语序应为"it seemed to me only in that way..."，倒装是为了强调"only in that way"，也就是说，只有努力工作，才能让马洛感到心里踏实；这似乎是唯一的方式，可以让马洛觉得自己正在弥补之前在旅途中虚度的时光，从而"紧紧地抓住真实的生活"。

myself sometimes <u>what it all meant</u>[518]. <u>They wandered here and there with their absurd long staves in their hands</u>[519], <u>like a lot of faithless pilgrims bewitched inside a rotten fence</u>[520]. <u>The word 'ivory' rang in the air, was whispered, was sighed</u>[521]. You would think they were praying to it. <u>A taint of imbecile rapacity blew through it all, like a whiff from some corpse</u>[522]. By Jove! I've

518. what it all meant：这是马洛心中的疑问，"（经理夸夸其谈，公司人浮于事，员工们到处闲逛溜达）这一切究竟意义何在？"

519. They wandered...their hands：这里是描述总站上的那些白人无所事事的样子。他们东逛逛西瞧瞧，手里提着可笑的长棍子（这是要在贸易站的院子里捉蛇吗？）。也这侧面说明经理"没法让手下人各安其职"。

520. like a lot...rotten fence：译为"活像一群失去了信仰的朝圣者，在一个破烂的草篱笆里边鬼迷心窍了"。pilgrim 意为"朝圣者；旅行者"，这里指的是贸易站里的白人员工。他们万里迢迢地从欧洲来到非洲（对应"旅行者"的意思），心中本应该抱有崇高的理想（"为非洲带来光明"，对应"朝圣者"的意思，这个词有一种甘愿为宗教献身的意味；而 faithless pilgrims 可能是指，他们要"朝"的"圣"，原本就不是什么高尚的理想，而是象牙和金钱），但是他们却无所事事，成天在这个 rotten fence（破烂的草篱笆，指的是修建得十分潦草的贸易总站）里边到处乱转（因为外面的荒野到处潜伏着危险，他们轻易也不敢出去），活像被 bewitched（鬼迷心窍了；被下了咒了）。他们是被什么东西迷了心窍，因而在这个远离欧洲的破烂地方转来转去呢？答案就是象牙。在这里，象牙意味着财富。

521. The word 'ivory'...was sighed："象牙"这个词儿在空气里飘荡，朝圣者们在低语，在叹息，从他们嘴里冒出来的词儿没有别的，全是"象牙"。这确实是一副鬼迷了心窍的样子，他们对象牙虔诚祈祷、顶礼膜拜，几乎已经具有一种宗教式的狂热了。

522. A taint...some corpse：A taint of 意为"一种气味"，imbecile rapacity 意为"愚蠢的贪婪"，blew 是 blow 的过去式，意为"风的鼓荡；吹拂"，whiff 意为"一股气味"，corpse 意为"尸体"。这句的意思是，"朝圣者"口中念叨的"象牙"这个词儿，整个散发着一股贪婪而又愚昧的气息，就好像从某个尸体上飘过来的尸臭味儿一样。这里的"尸臭味"，一是形容朝圣者令人作呕的嘴脸，二是在暗示，"象牙"是从大象的尸体上弄到的，财富的背后，是累累尸骨。

never seen anything so unreal in my life[523]. And outside, the silent wilderness surrounding this cleared speck on the earth[524] struck me as something great and invincible, like evil or truth[525], waiting patiently for the passing away of this fantastic invasion[526].

"Oh, these months! Well, never mind. Various things happened. One evening a grass shed full of calico, cotton prints, beads, and I don't know what else, burst into a blaze so suddenly that you would have thought the earth had opened to let an

---

523. By Jove!...my life：这里是马洛的感叹，他觉得这些鬼迷心窍的朝圣者的样子，实在是太如魔似幻了，完全没有一点真实的感觉。马洛认为真正的生活，就是踏踏实实地做事，通过努力的付出得到应有的报酬，而不是像这个总站这样，"朝圣者"们一点儿实际的工作也不干，却天天梦想着弄到象牙，一夜暴富。读完小说我们会发现，汽船是马洛修好并驾驶的，危机是马洛发现并化解的，大批的象牙是库尔茨亲手弄到的，但是最后把全部象牙据为己有、发了大财的，却是经理和他的"朝圣者"们。这一切都令人感到无比荒谬。

524. the silent...the earth：意思是，从大地的视角来看，这人工开辟出来的一丁点地方（指经理的贸易总站），正被沉默着的无边的荒野所包围。这里是一种对比，显示了自然的伟力；相比之下，人力是何等的渺小。

525. struck me...evil or truth：意思是，那寂静的荒野令我感到悚栗，它是那样的浩浩荡荡、不可战胜，就好像罪恶或者真理一样。宇宙中，真理万古长存；人世间，罪恶也不可遏止——作者用这些代表了永恒存在的抽象的事物，来比喻占据着永恒的（对人类而言）时间和空间的寂静荒野，这样恢宏博大的联想和直接打破了抽象和具象藩篱的如椽之笔，令人印象深刻。

526. waiting patiently...fantastic invasion：这里是说，那些在这里疯狂侵略、攫取象牙的欧洲殖民者，在浩浩无边的荒野面前，就好像一个个跳梁小丑一样。他们尽管演出种种荒谬的闹剧，但是在沉默而又极具耐心的大自然看来，这场闹剧终将迎来结束的时刻（最终他们很可能都会死在荒野里）。

avenging fire consume all that trash[527]. I was smoking my pipe[528] quietly by my dismantled steamer, and saw them all cutting capers in the light[529], with their arms lifted high, when the stout man with moustaches[530] came tearing down to the river, a tin pail in his hand, assured me that everybody was 'behaving splendidly, splendidly,' dipped about a quart of water[531] and tore back again. I noticed there was a hole in the bottom of his pail[532].

---

527. the earth...that trash：好像大地裂开了缝隙，放出来一股复仇的火焰，好把那些垃圾统统吞噬掉 / 烧光。这里是作者的讽刺笔法，殖民者倾销工业垃圾的行径是如此让人痛恨，以至于连非洲的大地都要给予他们报复了，要用火焰烧掉他们运来的这些破烂货。

528. smoking my pipe：抽着烟。马洛在后文提到，"哪有不抽烟的水手"。据说，雪莱和拜伦这对诗坛好友曾结识过一位武装民船的船长特里劳尼。雪莱十分钦佩这位曾经当过海盗的船长，甚至也想到他的船上去做一名水手。特里劳尼给了他这样的回答："不抽烟、不骂人的人是当不成水手的。"水手生活艰苦，他们要忍受高强度的工作，还要经常搏击海上的风浪，因而他们往往是作风粗犷，不拘小节。pipe 意为"烟斗"。

529. cutting capers in the light：caper 意为"跳跃；胡闹；滑稽怪诞的行为"，cut capers 或者 cut a caper 意为"蹦蹦跳跳；出洋相"。in the light 指的是"在火光中"。这句是说火光中映出了那些朝圣者们的身影，他们面对大火都惊慌失措，胡蹦乱窜，洋相百出。

530. the stout man with moustaches：那个黑胡子壮汉，即经理手下的一个打手角色。每当捅出了大篓子，他总是会说"每个人都表现得棒极了！"来推卸责任或者邀功。

531. dipped about a quart of water：夸脱（液体单位，英制中约为 1.14 升）。dip 在这里指"舀（水）；蘸（水）"，含有一种浅尝辄止的意味。一升水就是大约两瓶矿泉水的量，可见他根本没有全力舀水，把桶装满。这个贸易站的人做事都是在装样子。

532. I noticed...his pail：这里的讽刺意味就很浓厚了。黑胡子壮汉本来就没有装满一桶水，更何况桶底还有一个洞。跑回去水也该漏光了。可想而知，那样能救火吗？他们根本就不是在认真做事。

"I strolled up. There was no hurry. You see the thing had gone off like a box of matches. It had been hopeless from the very first[533]. The flame had leaped high, driven everybody back[534], lighted up everything—and collapsed[535]. The shed was already a heap of embers glowing fiercely. A nigger was being beaten near by. They said he had caused the fire in some way; be that as it may, he was screeching most horribly. I saw him, later, for several days, sitting in a bit of shade looking very sick and trying to recover himself[536]; afterwards he arose and went out—and the wilderness without a sound took him into its bosom again[537]. As I approached the glow from the dark I found myself at the back of two men, talking. I heard the name of Kurtz pronounced, then the words, 'take advantage of this unfortunate accident.'[538] One of the men was the manager. I wished him a good evening. 'Did

---

533. had been hopeless from the very first：（这场火）从一开始就没有能够扑灭的希望。棉花这样的易燃物着火是很难扑救的。

534. driven everybody back：（火焰那灼人的热度）逼得每个人都直往后退。

535. lighted up everything—and collapsed：所有的东西都着起火来，最后（草棚子）被烧得垮塌了。

536. recover himself：这里应该不是"想要康复"，因为黑人被打得受了重伤，几乎没可能康复了。这里的意思可能是"挣扎着想要缓过一口气"。因为他想要拼着最后一丝力气站起来，走出去，离开这个贸易站。他不想死在这里。

537. the wilderness...bosom again：荒野默默地把他揽入了自己的怀抱。黑人来自荒野，到贸易站做工，将死之时又独自走回了荒野，有种"回归尘土"的意味。这也暗示黑人最后是死了。这是殖民者草菅人命的又一次例证。这里也是一次时间线的向后跳荡。相比起"倒叙"，这种叙述手法或者可以称之为"超叙"。

538. take advantage of this unfortunate accident：利用这次不幸的事故（做点文章；弄点手脚）。这里不知道经理又想要干什么坏事了。

you ever see anything like it—eh? it is incredible,' he said, and walked off. The other man remained. He was a first-class agent, young, gentlemanly, a bit reserved, with a forked little beard and a hooked nose. He was stand-offish with the other agents, and they on their side said he was the manager's spy upon them. As to me, I had hardly ever spoken to him before. We got into talk, and by and by we strolled away from the hissing ruins. Then he asked me to his room, which was in the main building of the station. He struck a match, and I perceived that this young aristocrat[539] had not only a silver-mounted dressing-case but also a whole candle all to himself. Just at that time the manager was the only man supposed to have any right to candles[540]. Native mats covered the clay walls; a collection of spears, assegais, shields, knives was hung up in trophies[541]. The business intrusted to this fellow was the making of bricks—so I had been informed; but there wasn't a fragment of a brick[542] anywhere in the station, and he had been

---

539. this young aristocrat: 这个年轻的贵族。这里当然不是说这个人是真正的贵族，而是说他拥有镜匣、蜡烛等等当时的奢侈用品，他在总站过着优裕的生活，简直好像贵族一样。

540. supposed to have any right to candles：（只有经理是）被认为有权使用蜡烛（的人）。

541. a collection...in trophies：a collection of 意为"一系列；一组"，这里是说墙上挂着琳琅满目的战利品，包括 spears（长矛），assegais（非洲梭镖），shields（盾牌）和 knives（刀剑）等等。这反映出这个"年轻的贵族"有收集的癖好，为后文他收藏了一幅库尔茨先生的画作做铺垫。

542. a fragment of a brick：一块砖头的碎片。这里是说这个家伙的职责是烧砖，但是站上却连一块碎砖的影子也看不见，说明他根本就没做自己的工作。

there more than a year—waiting. It seems he could not make bricks without something, I don't know what—straw maybe.[543] Anyway, it could not be found there and as it was not likely to be sent from Europe, it did not appear clear to me what he was waiting for. An act of special creation perhaps.[544] However, they were all waiting—all the sixteen or twenty pilgrims of them[545]—for something; and upon my word it did not seem an uncongenial occupation, from the way they took it[546], though the only thing that ever came to them was disease[547]—as far as I could see. They beguiled the time by back-biting and intriguing against each other in a foolish kind of way. There was an air of plotting about that station, but nothing came of it, of course.[548]

---

543. It seems...straw maybe：这里使用讽刺的口气猜测他为什么不烧砖的原因——也许是因为这里没有稻草（烧砖的原料或者燃料）。

544. what he...creation perhaps：（我不知道）他到底在等什么——也许是在等什么创世神迹？这里是一种辛辣的讽刺。那个人（也许是因为没有稻草）不去烧砖，那么自然就不会有砖；他在站上悠哉悠哉地等，这样等一万年也还是没有砖——除非等来一个创世神迹，就好像《创世纪》里说的那样，"上帝说：要有光！于是就有了光"。

545. all the sixteen or twenty pilgrims of them：我觉得这里不必译成"十六个或者二十个朝圣者"，译成"将近二十个朝圣者"就可以了。这里只是马洛随口报的大概数字，这种随意的口气体现了马洛对他们的蔑视。

546. it did not...they took it：从他们的"工作状态"来看，这份工作倒也算不上不合心意。也就是说，这些朝圣者们在这里吊儿郎当地闲混日子，如果这也算在"工作"，那么这份"工作"倒也还不错。

547. the only...was disease：他们遇到的唯一的麻烦事（他们做的唯一的"工作"）就是生病。

548. There was...of course：译为"贸易站里到处弥漫着一股阴谋诡计的气味，不过，倒也没有当真发生什么事情"。an air of 意为"一种（什么样的）氛围"。

It was as unreal[549] as everything else — as the philanthropic pretence of the whole concern[550], as their talk, as their government[551], as their show of work. The only real feeling was a desire to get appointed to a trading-post where ivory was to be had[552], so that they could earn percentages. They intrigued and slandered and hated each other only on that account — but as to effectually lifting a little finger — oh, no.[553] By heavens! there is something after all in the world allowing one man to steal a horse while another must not look at a halter.[554] Steal a horse straight out. Very well. He

---

549. unreal：意为"不真实；很虚幻；荒谬"。马洛认为，用自己的劳动实现自己的价值，就是真实的生活；而经理和朝圣者只想着坑害他人、不劳而获，这就很荒唐。

550. the philanthropic pretence of the whole concern：philanthropic pretence 意为"慈善的伪装"，concern 这里指的是这家大公司。

551. their government：这里指的是公司的管理制度、管理机构。

552. a trading-post where ivory was to be had：一个能够弄得到象牙的贸易站。

553. as to effectually lifting a little finger — oh, no：这里是说，如果让朝圣者们真正去做哪怕一点点工作，他们也一定会摇头拒绝。

554. there is something...at a halter：世上竟会有这种事，有的人可以盗马，而别人连看一眼马嚼子（露出一点盗马的想法）都不行。halter 意为"马缰绳；笼头"，是牵马的工具。这里和中文里的谚语"只许州官放火，不许百姓点灯"意思非常接近，都是形容有的人搞双重标准，自己可以大摇大摆地干坏事，可是绝不允许别人干；如果别人露出一点可疑的意图，他们马上就会暴怒起来。这段话来自一个英文谚语：One may steal a horse while another may not look over the hedge（理解一：甲可以盗马，然而乙却连往篱笆上看一眼都不行。似乎也有"窃钩者诛；窃国者诸侯"的意思。理解二：甲一心想要得到马，乙却完全对马毫无欲望，不屑一顾。这有点类似"庄子腐鼠"（来自《庄子·秋水》）的典故——夫鹓鶵，发于南海，而飞于北海；非梧桐不止，非练实不食，非醴泉不饮。于是鸱得腐鼠，鹓鶵过之，仰而视之曰："吓！"

has done it. Perhaps he can ride.[555] But there is a way of looking at a halter that would provoke the most charitable of saints into a kick.[556]

"I had no idea why he wanted to be sociable, but as we chatted in there it suddenly occurred to me the fellow was trying to get at something—in fact, pumping me. He alluded constantly to Europe, to the people I was supposed to know there—putting leading questions as to my acquaintances in the sepulchral city, and so on. His little eyes glittered[557] like mica discs—with curiosity—though he tried to keep up a bit of superciliousness. At first I was astonished, but very soon I became awfully curious to see what he would find out from me. I couldn't possibly imagine what I had in me to make it worth his while. It was very pretty to see how he baffled himself, for in truth my body was full only of chills[558], and my head had nothing in it but that wretched steamboat business[559].

---

555. Steal a horse...he can ride：这里是描述盗马的人大摇大摆地干坏事，气焰嚣张。

556. But there is...into a kick：这里是说，盗马的人如果看见别人在瞟马嚼子，他就会以为别人也想要盗马，于是他就会立刻火冒三丈、暴跳如雷——尽管他平时装得好像圣徒一样的仁慈。也就是说，如果他怀疑有人要动自己的奶酪，那么他马上会卸下仁善的伪装，露出自己贪婪残暴的本性。这里也让我想到一句话："人们最关心的，往往是自己的利益，和他人的道德"。

557. glitter：闪闪发光。这里是形容经理爪牙的眼睛里充满期待，想从马洛口中套出话来的样子。

558. my body was full only of chills：我浑身上下冒着一股冷气。这里是说朝圣者们都为了象牙而疯癫狂热，但是马洛却冷眼旁观，丝毫不为所动。

559. my head...steamboat business：我的头脑里除了那条破汽船的事儿以外，也别无他物。相比之下，马洛眼前那个人却满脑子钻营，他费尽心思地想从马洛这里打探消息，好让自己能往上爬。

It was evident he took me for a perfectly shameless prevaricator[560]. At last he got angry, and, to conceal a movement of furious annoyance, he yawned. I rose[561]. Then I noticed a small sketch in oils, on a panel, representing a woman, draped[562] and blindfolded[563], carrying a lighted torch[564]. The background was sombre[565]—almost black. The movement of the woman was stately[566], and the effect of the torchlight on the face was sinister[567].

---

560. took me for a perfectly shameless prevaricator：他把我当成了一个恬不知耻、完全是在搪塞他的人。prevaricator 意为"说话搪塞的人；说话支吾的人"。

561. I rose：马洛站了起来，准备出门，因为对方打哈欠明显是在下逐客令，所以马洛就准备离开这里了。

562. drape：这里可能是披着斗篷，也可能是披着头巾，也可能是长裙曳地。或者也有一种可能，"身披长衣"是非洲部落地位较高的人的装扮，库尔茨在绘画中将未婚妻的形象和非洲部落贵族女性的形象糅合在一起，暗示库尔茨把一个在部落里地位较高的黑人女性当作了他远在欧洲的未婚妻的替代品（后文中有提及这个黑人女性的存在）。这也许是非洲版的《风中奇缘》（这位黑人女性类似印第安公主波卡洪塔斯）。

563. blindfolded：蒙着眼睛。事实上，这幅画是库尔茨所画，画中女子很可能是他的未婚妻。库尔茨在非洲丛林犯下了残暴的罪行，但是他的未婚妻对此毫不知情，因此她的眼睛是蒙着的——她无法看到真相。

564. a lighted torch：一支熊熊燃烧的火炬。这里似乎在暗喻，库尔茨的未婚妻以为他会为非洲带去光明；或者说，在库尔茨黑暗的内心里，他的纯洁善良的未婚妻是唯一的光明。

565. sombre：阴郁的；昏暗的。画中昏暗的背景，似乎在隐喻非洲蒙昧的荒野。

566. stately：庄严的。这里似乎在隐喻库尔茨的未婚妻一直为他守贞，她是庄严而又圣洁的。

567. the effect of the torchlight on the face was sinister：火炬映在她脸上的光影，却显得有些狰狞邪恶。这里也是在隐喻库尔茨和他的未婚妻将要遭遇的悲剧命运。

"It arrested me[568], and he stood by civilly, holding an empty half-pint champagne bottle[569] (medical comforts) with the candle stuck in it. To my question he said Mr. Kurtz had painted this—in this very station more than a year ago—while waiting for means to go to his trading post. 'Tell me, pray[570],' said I, 'who is this Mr. Kurtz?'

"'The chief of the Inner Station,' he answered in a short tone, looking away. 'Much obliged,' I said, laughing. 'And you are the brickmaker of the Central Station. Every one knows that.'[571] He was silent for a while. 'He is a prodigy,' he said at last. 'He is an emissary of pity and science and progress, and devil knows what else[572]. We want,' he began to declaim suddenly, 'for the guidance of the cause intrusted to us by Europe, so to speak,

568. It arrested me：指的是这幅油画吸引了马洛的注意力。

569. half-pint champagne bottle：半品脱的香槟酒瓶。pint 意为"品脱"（液量单位，约等于半升）。半品脱差不多就是一支小矿泉水瓶的量。

570. pray：表示一种拜托、请求的语气。这里是说马洛已经对库尔茨产生了兴趣，他很想知道库尔茨到底是个什么样的人。在《黑暗之心》前半部分的叙述里，库尔茨有点类似希区柯克的电影《蝴蝶梦》中的丽贝卡，或者金庸小说《碧血剑》中的金蛇郎君夏雪宜；他们并没有在观众或读者眼前直接出现，他们的故事都是通过其他人物的叙述而被观众或读者得知的。但是他们对故事中其他角色的影响却又无处不在，他们事实上也是故事中的主要人物，甚至灵魂人物。

571. 'And you...knows that.'：这里是一种类比反讽。马洛当然知道库尔茨是内陆贸易站的站长，就好像马洛知道眼前这个人是负责做砖的一样。这种回答完全没有信息量，这个人只是在用"人人皆知"的情况来搪塞马洛。

572. devil knows what else：天知道库尔茨先生除了要带来仁慈、科学和进步，他还能带来些别的什么。这句话又似称颂，又似讽刺，反映出这个人对库尔茨先生的钦佩、妒忌和忌惮。

higher intelligence, wide sympathies, a singleness of purpose.'
'Who says that?' I asked. 'Lots of them,' he replied. 'Some
even write that; and so he comes here, a special being, as you
ought to know[573].' 'Why ought I to know?[574]' I interrupted, really
surprised. He paid no attention[575]. 'Yes. Today he is chief of the
best station, next year he will be assistant-manager, two years more
and...but I dare-say you know what he will be in two years' time.
You are of the new gang—the gang of virtue[576]. The same people
who sent him specially also recommended you.[577] Oh, don't say no.

---

573. as you ought to know：这句话隐含的意思是，这个人认为马洛和库尔茨
都是"道德派"的高管派到这里来的，他和库尔茨很可能就是一伙的，所以
库尔茨过去的经历和升迁的前景，马洛肯定都知道。这是一句试探马洛的
话。前面他对马洛询问库尔茨先生是什么人的问题顾左右而言他，也是在防
备马洛明知故问、试探自己。他认为马洛是个城府很深、扮猪吃虎的小人。
很明显，这个人才是真正的小人，他在以小人之心度君子之腹。

574. Why ought I to know?：马洛显然还没跟上眼前这个人的脑回路，他完全
不知道对方这句话是什么意思。

575. He paid no attention：这个人不回答马洛的问话，说明他心里对"马洛
明知故问的态度"嗤之以鼻，他可能在想："你真行，话都说到这个分儿上
了你还装。看我马上就揭你老底。"这一段都是两个人的言语交锋，在这个
过程中，谁是君子，谁是小人，全都一览无余地展现出来了。

576. the gang of virtue：道德派；美德派。看来，这家公司的领导者们说不定
分成两派，一派主张要帮助非洲实现进步，颇有些道德上的理想；另一派主
张去非洲就是为了搞钱而已，没必要弄什么别的噱头。

577. The same...recommended you：库尔茨是经理那帮人最为忌惮的，而经
理他们得知马洛和库尔茨一样，也是"道德派"推荐来的，因此对马洛的态
度就很微妙。这也解释了经理为什么第一次见面要给马洛下马威，还要在他
面前表演一副担心库尔茨的样子；同时也解释了眼前这个人对马洛又是猜忌
愤恨、又是拉拢巴结的首鼠两端的态度。顺便多说一句，小说中很多细节都
是前后呼应的，可谓"草蛇灰线，伏脉千里"。这里的情节铺垫了（转下页）

I've my own eyes to trust.[578]' Light dawned upon me.[579] My dear aunt's influential acquaintances were producing an unexpected effect upon that young man[580]. I nearly burst into a laugh[581]. 'Do you read the Company's confidential correspondence?[582]' I asked. He hadn't a word to say.[583] It was great fun.[584] 'When Mr. Kurtz,'

（接上页）后文中库尔茨看到信件之后，对马洛产生的信任之情。库尔茨曾经想过 kill them all（他手下有完全听命于他的野人部落，所以他事实上只要一句话就可以把经理一行全杀光），因为他实在不愿意落在经理手里；如果在最后关头不是他对马洛这个人的信任占了上风，经理一行人很可能无法活着走出丛林。

578. I've my own eyes to trust：我相信自己的眼睛（所看到的）。意思是这个人（通过私拆信件的卑鄙手段）看到了欧洲总部和库尔茨的通信，他认为这就是马洛和库尔茨有关联的铁证。也正是这句无心的话暴露了他。

579. Light dawned upon me：这里是说好像一束光照亮了黑暗，马洛顿时完全明白过来。会计师曾经提过"只要你的信件一被拿到总站，你就永远不知道会落到什么人手里"，很显然，正是眼前这个人（还有经理）。他名义上是做砖的，实际上是经理的心腹，并且为经理管理和起草信件。只要是经过他手的信件，他都私拆查看过了，所以他才会知道很多本不该他知道的消息。

580. producing an unexpected effect upon that young man：对这个年轻人产生了出乎意料的效果。意思是，正因为这个年轻人得知了公司高管的态度，所以他对马洛的态度才会那么地出人意料、耐人寻味。在这里，最好也能将抽象的英文翻译成具象化的中文。

581. burst into a laugh：忍不住要笑出声来。马洛恍然大悟之后，觉得眼前这个人的小人嘴脸非常可笑，于是后面他决定将计就计，顺着这个人的意思和他演下去，吓唬 / 震慑他一下。

582. Do you read...correspondence?：你看过公司的机密邮件吗？这里是马洛直接戳穿这个人做过的坏事，截断他的退路。confidential 意为"机密的；保密的"，correspondence 意为"信件；往来通信"。

583. He hadn't a word to say：这个人被马洛一记重锤敲得哑口无言。马洛的问题十分厉害，他肯定也不是，否定也不是。但是答不出话就已经等于承认了。

584. It was great fun：戏弄眼前这个小人，让马洛觉得十分有趣 / 解气。

I continued, severely, 'is General Manager, you won't have the opportunity.'[585]

"He blew the candle out[586] suddenly, and we went outside. The moon had risen. Black figures strolled about listlessly, pouring water on the glow, whence proceeded a sound of hissing; steam ascended in the moonlight, the beaten nigger groaned somewhere. 'What a row the brute makes!'[587] said the indefatigable man with the moustaches[588], appearing near us. 'Serve him right. Transgression—punishment—bang! Pitiless, pitiless. That's the only way[589]. This will prevent all conflagrations for the future. I was just telling the manager...'[590] He noticed my companion,

---

585. 'When Mr. Kurtz,' I continued, severely, 'is General Manager, you won't have the opportunity.'：这里是马洛将计就计，震慑这个小人。他不是认为马洛和库尔茨一伙吗，马洛就用默认他的这个想法，还严肃地告诉他"等库尔茨先生当上了总经理，你就没机会这么干（指私拆信件）了。"马洛这句话里满含着告诫甚至威胁的意味。severely 意为"非常严肃地；严厉地"。

586. blew the candle out：吹灭蜡烛。动词原形是 blow out。这里是说经理爪牙在马洛面前碰了一鼻子灰，又没法直接发作，因而借着吹蜡烛表示心里的不忿。

587. 'What a row the brute makes!'：row 意为"喧闹声；吵嚷声"，brute 意为"粗野的人；牲畜"。这里有两种理解，一是"这个黑人捅出了多大的乱子"，指的是那场让贸易站陷入一片混乱的火灾；二是"这个黑人可真能吵"，指的是鞭打的时候黑人大声惨叫。brute 在这里是对黑人的贬称。

588. the indefatigable man with the moustaches：指的是那个精力旺盛的黑胡子壮汉。indefatigable 意为"不知疲倦的"。

589. Transgression...the only way：这句话说明了黑胡子壮汉是个称职的打手，他为虎作伥，对待黑人劳工十分凶狠。transgression 意为"违反（规矩）；僭越；犯罪"。

590. I was just telling the manager：这说明黑胡子壮汉在经理面前邀功、表现自己；他虽然很残暴，但是脑子明显不够用，所以也就只能做个打手，当不成经理的心腹。

and became crestfallen all at once[591]. 'Not in bed yet,' he said, with a kind of servile heartiness; 'it's so natural. Ha! Danger— agitation[592].' He vanished. I went on to the riverside, and the other followed me. I heard a scathing murmur at my ear, 'Heap of muffs—go to[593].' The pilgrims could be seen in knots gesticulating, discussing. Several had still their staves in their hands. I verily believe they took these sticks to bed with them. Beyond the fence the forest stood up spectrally in the moonlight, and through that dim stir, through the faint sounds of that lamentable courtyard, the silence of the land went home to one's very heart[594]—its mystery, its greatness, the amazing reality of

---

591. became crestfallen all at once：立刻（从刚才的志得意满）变得垂头丧气了。crestfallen 意为"垂头丧气的；气馁的"，源出于鸟类斗败了就会垂下（fall）自己的羽冠（crest）这一现象。中文中类似的表达有"好像一只斗败了的公鸡""霜打的茄子——蔫了"等。魔鬼里边也是有等级的，黑胡子壮汉在经理面前自我表现的行为，肯定会让那个私拆信件的经理心腹不满，所以他一看到马洛身边还站着经理心腹，立刻就蔫了下来；他不敢继续炫耀自己，而且赶紧低三下四地讨好经理心腹。

592. agitation：意为"焦虑不安"。这里是黑胡子壮汉下意识地说出"您还没睡吗"之后，赶紧忙不迭地自己帮经理心腹找台阶下——"因为晚上发生了这么危险的事，所以您觉得不安、睡不着（这完全是很正常的）。"这里用几个简单的词汇表达意思，说明黑胡子壮汉惧怕眼前这个人，他既有点语无伦次，也根本不敢多说话。

593. Heap of muffs—go to：这里是经理心腹的一句骂人话，完整形式可能是"Heap of muffs—go to hell"。这是他骂黑胡子壮汉的话，或者也是借机指桑骂槐，发泄刚才在马洛那里吃了瘪的不忿。muff 在这里的意思是"笨蛋"。

594. went home to one's very heart：（大地的沉默）直达人的心底。went home to 相当于 found its way to，意为"进入；到达"。这里是说，马洛深深地感受到了大地的沉默。人世间无论发生多么冤屈、多么悲惨的事情，大地都是永远地保持着缄默。

its concealed life[595]. The hurt nigger moaned feebly somewhere near by, and then fetched a deep sigh that made me mend my pace away from there. I felt a hand introducing itself under my arm[596]. 'My dear sir,' said the fellow, 'I don't want to be misunderstood, and especially by you, who will see Mr. Kurtz long before I can have that pleasure. I wouldn't like him to get a false idea of my disposition[597]....'

"I let him run on, this papier-mache Mephistopheles[598], and it seemed to me that if I tried I could poke my forefinger through him[599], and would find nothing inside but a little loose

---

595. the amazing reality of its concealed life：有的事情发生过，还能留得下痕迹，甚至被世人记住；有的事情发生过，却没有留下任何痕迹，永远地在大地上消失了。这就是"大地的生命中隐秘的那一面"。但是，在那些湮灭于时空之中、不为人知的故事里面，有很多都是惊心动魄，令人感叹的；而且，它们都确实曾经真切地存在过。例如，马洛亲眼见证的这个故事——贸易站突发大火，一个黑人成了替罪羊；他受到了残酷的鞭打，最后因此而死去。像这样浸透着黑人的冤屈和血泪的故事，却注定无人知晓，最后化作了大地那隐秘的生命的一部分。

596. a hand introducing itself under my arm：一只手探到了我的胳膊底下。这里是经理心腹主动伸手挽住了马洛的胳膊，向他示好。

597. get a false idea of my disposition：对我的性情产生错误的看法。disposition意为"性情；品性"。这里是经理心腹在颇费心思地讨好马洛，希望他不要向库尔茨先生说自己的坏话。

598. this papier-mache Mephistopheles：可能是法语，意为"这个纸糊的梅菲斯特"，即"色厉内荏、外强中干的魔鬼/阴险邪恶之人"的意思。Mephistopheles是歌德所著《浮士德》中的魔鬼的名字。

599. I could poke my forefinger through him：只要伸出一根手指，就可以捅穿他。这是说经理心腹的虚伪言行很容易被人一眼看穿，马洛就识破了他的真实目的；或者是说这些魔鬼看似厉害，其实不堪一击，只要稍加反击，就会令他们惊慌失措，自乱阵脚。poke意为"戳；刺；捅"。

dirt[600], maybe. He, don't you see, had been planning to be assistant-manager by and by under the present man, and I could see that the coming of that Kurtz had upset them both not a little. He talked precipitately, and I did not try to stop him. I had my shoulders against the wreck of my steamer, hauled up on the slope like a carcass of some big river animal. The smell of mud, of primeval mud, by Jove! was in my nostrils, the high stillness of primeval forest[601] was before my eyes; there were shiny patches on the black creek. The moon had spread over everything a thin layer of silver—over the rank grass, over the mud, upon the wall of matted vegetation standing higher than the wall of a temple, over the great river I could see through a sombre gap[602] glittering, glittering, as it flowed broadly by without a murmur. All this was great, expectant, mute, while the man jabbered about himself[603]. I wondered whether the stillness on the face of the immensity looking at us two[604] were

---

600. find nothing inside but a little loose dirt：这里是说这些 "色厉内荏的魔鬼" 肚子里面没别的，只有一些肮脏的、不可告人的卑鄙目的。或者是说这些人不学无术，没有真正的才干。loose dirt 意为 "松散的泥土；稀稀拉拉的脏东西"，这里指的是各种拉踩钻营的心思。

601. the high stillness of primeval forest：指的是 "高耸的、寂静的原始森林"。注意，英文善用抽象词，中文善用具体词。

602. see through a sombre gap：这里可能是说马洛曾经从总站的院子里，透过那个昏暗的、破洞似的大门，远远望见刚果河。

603. jabbered about himself：喋喋不休地说着他自己。这里指的是经理心腹生怕马洛到库尔茨面前说自己的坏话，所以一个劲儿地为自己分辩。jabber 意为 "急促（或激动）而含混不清地说"。

604. the immensity looking at us two：正在注视着我们两个人的那无边浩荡（的荒野）。这里是把荒野人格化。两个人站在荒野之中，仿佛正被荒野沉默地注视着；他们的一言一行，全都落在荒野的眼中。中文里也有 "天知地知，你知我知" 的表达，同样是将 "天地" 人格化。

meant as an appeal or as a menace. What were we who had strayed in here? Could we handle that dumb thing[605], or would it handle us? I felt how big, how confoundedly big[606], was that thing that couldn't talk, and perhaps was deaf as well[607]. What was in there? I could see a little ivory coming out from there, and I had heard Mr. Kurtz was in there. I had heard enough about it, too—God knows! Yet somehow it didn't bring any image with it[608]—no more than if I had been told an angel or a fiend was in there. I believed it in the same way one of you might believe there are inhabitants in the planet Mars[609]. I knew once a Scotch sailmaker who was certain, dead sure, there were people in Mars. If you asked him for some idea how they looked and behaved, he would get shy and mutter something about 'walking on all-fours[610].' If you as much as smiled[611], he

---

605. that dumb thing：那个喑哑的东西。指的是永远沉默的荒野。

606. how confoundedly big：（荒野）如此巨大，大得让人头脑发昏，目瞪口呆。表示一种令人震惊、令人绝望的无边的浩荡。

607. that thing...as well：那个喑哑的、或许还耳聋的东西。既聋又哑，是说荒野不仅对人世间的一切都沉默无语，或许它也根本就听不见人们在说什么、想什么。

608. it didn't bring any image with it：意思是，在广阔的荒野的里面，在那黑暗的深处，究竟是什么样的情形？尽管马洛看到了象牙，也听说了库尔茨的名字，但是他仍然想象不到那里面真实的样子。

609. the planet Mars：火星。19 世纪末、20 世纪初，人们还对火星充满了各种奇幻的想象。

610. mutter something about 'walking on all-fours.'：小声嘀咕着说什么"他们都是四肢着地，爬着走的"。mutter 意为"嘀咕；嘟囔"，all-fours 指的是四肢。人类对外星人的想象，往往还是脱离不开自身的现实。

611. as much as smiled：（听了船帆工人的话）如果你敢笑 / 忍不住笑。因为他对外星人的想象力确实是比较匮乏。

would—though a man of sixty—offer to fight you. I would not
have <u>gone so far as to fight for Kurtz</u>[612], but I went for him near
enough to a lie. You know I hate, detest, and can't bear a lie, not
because I am straighter than the rest of us, but simply because
it appalls me. There is a taint of death, a <u>flavour of mortality</u>[613]
in lies—which is exactly what I hate and detest in the world—
what I want to forget. It makes me miserable and sick, like biting
something rotten would do. Temperament, I suppose. Well, I went
near enough to it by letting the young fool there <u>believe anything
he liked to imagine</u>[614] as to my influence in Europe. I became in
an instant as <u>much of a pretence as</u>[615] the rest of the bewitched
pilgrims. This simply because I had a notion it somehow would
<u>be of help to that Kurtz</u>[616] whom at the time I did not see—you
understand. He was just a word for me. I did not see <u>the man in the
name</u>[617] any more than you do. Do you see him? Do you see the

---

612. gone so far as to fight for Kurtz：我可不会像他那么离谱，为了个虚无缥缈的"库尔茨"就和人打架。

613. a flavour of mortality：和"死亡的味道"是同义复现，这里是用排比来强化语气。mortality 意为"终有一死；死亡"。

614. believe anything he liked to imagine：让（经理心腹）尽管去天马行空地想象（马洛在欧洲有着多么大的靠山），而且越想越真，越想越怕。

615. as much of a pretence as：这是说在马洛默认（自己有靠山）、误导经理心腹的那个时候，他事实上也是在装腔作势，撒了谎；他在那个时候也和那些满口假话的朝圣者们一样了。

616. be of help to that Kurtz：帮了那个库尔茨一点忙。

617. the man in the name：叫作那个名字的人。指的是"叫作库尔茨的那个人"。因为马洛和他还不曾谋面，马洛对他的了解，只不过是一个符号式的名字而已。

story? Do you see anything? It seems to me I am trying to tell you a dream—making a vain attempt, because no relation of a dream can convey the dream-sensation, that commingling of absurdity, surprise, and bewilderment in a tremor of struggling revolt, that notion of being captured by the incredible which is of the very essence of dreams...."

He was silent for a while.

"...No, it is impossible; it is impossible to convey the life-sensation[618] of any given epoch of one's existence[619]—that which makes its truth, its meaning—its subtle and penetrating essence[620]. It is impossible. We live, as we dream—alone...."

He paused again as if reflecting, then added:

"Of course in this you fellows see more than I could then. You see me, whom you know...."

It had become so pitch dark that we listeners could hardly see one another. For a long time already he, sitting apart, had been no more to us than a voice[621]. There was not a word from anybody. The others might have been asleep, but I was awake. I listened,

---

618. convey the life-sensation: 说出生活的感受。

619. any given epoch of one's existence: 人生中的某个特定的时期，比如幼年期、青春期、中年期、老年期。epoch 意为 "时代"，existence 意为 "存在；生存；生活"。

620. its subtle and penetrating essence: its 指代的是 one's existence，这里是 "生活的那种微妙而又深刻的本质"。

621. been no more to us than a voice: 对于我们来说，他只不过就是个声音。这里是说故事的听众在黑暗中都完全看不清马洛的身影，他们只能听到马洛讲述的声音。

I listened on the watch for the sentence, for the word, that would give me the clue to the faint uneasiness inspired by this narrative[622] that seemed to shape itself without human lips[623] in the heavy night-air of the river.

"...Yes—I let him run on," Marlow began again, "and think what he pleased about[624] the powers that were behind me. I did! And there was nothing behind me! There was nothing but that wretched, old, mangled steamboat I was leaning against, while he talked fluently about 'the necessity for every man to get on[625].' 'And when one comes out here, you conceive, it is not to gaze at the moon[626].' Mr. Kurtz was a 'universal genius,' but even a genius would find it easier to work with 'adequate tools—intelligent men.' He did not make bricks—why, there was a physical impossibility in the way[627]—as I was well aware; and

---

622. the faint uneasiness inspired by this narrative：马洛的故事在"我"的心里引起的那种淡淡的忧愁。uneasiness 意为"不安；担忧"，narrative 意为"叙述；讲述"。

623. shape itself without human lips：（在漆黑的夜里，这个故事）似乎不是从人的口中讲述出来的，而是它自己（从黑暗中）形成的/飘来的。这里是形容这个故事在这样一种讲述的背景下，深深地打动了"我"的心。

624. think what he pleased about：让他（对马洛的靠山）爱怎么想就怎么想。

625. the necessity for every man to get on：意思是"往上爬对每个人来说都是必要的"，或者"每个人都必须努力升职"。

626. And when...at the moon："你知道，人们来这里可不是为了看月亮的"。这说明经理心腹来到非洲的目的十分明确，就是要捞到更高的地位和更多的金钱。

627. a physical impossibility in the way：一种物理上的不可抗力挡了他的路。意思是，经理心腹之所以不做砖，是因为某种解决不了的情况让他没办法做砖，比如"没有稻草——没法做砖"。这明显是一种推脱之词。

if he did secretarial work[628] for the manager, it was because 'no sensible man rejects wantonly the confidence of his superiors[629].' Did I see it? I saw it. What more did I want? What I really wanted was rivets[630], by heaven! Rivets. To get on with the work—to stop the hole. Rivets I wanted. There were cases of them down at the coast—cases—piled up—burst—split! You kicked a loose rivet at every second step in that station-yard on the hillside. Rivets had rolled into the grove of death. You could fill your pockets with rivets for the trouble of stooping down—and there wasn't one rivet to be found where it was wanted[631]. We had plates that would do[632], but nothing to fasten them with. And every week the messenger, a lone negro, letter-bag on shoulder and staff in hand,

---

628. secretarial work：秘书工作。这里是说，经理心腹振振有词地说自己没法做砖，又振振有词地解释自己为什么要为经理做秘书工作。这说明他推脱需要付出艰苦努力的实际工作，转而攀附上级、谋求升迁。

629. no sensible...his superiors："任何一个有理性的人都不会浪费这么好的机会，轻率地拒绝来自上司的信任。"sensible 意为"理智的"，wantonly 意为"轻率地；放纵地"。

630. rivet：铆钉。马洛维修汽船需要铆钉，而经理和他的心腹爪牙暗中使绊子，拖拉着就是不让马洛得到铆钉。这种做法针对的显然是库尔茨，因为没有铆钉，汽船就没法重新下水，就没法去上游开展救援。这也是经理在拖拉时间，等待他认为合适的时机（马洛在日以继夜地进行抢修工作，照这样的工作速度，经理很快就得必须出发了。所以他要给马洛制造麻烦，拖延进度。等到差不多拖死了库尔茨，才会把铆钉给马洛。经理——而不是马洛——才是节奏的掌控者、游戏的大玩家）。

631. where it was wanted：在需要它们的地方。意思是下游的贸易站有的是铆钉，可是在总站，马洛正在维修汽船的地方，却连一个铆钉也找不到。

632. plates that would do：（马洛有）合适的钢板。修补汽船需要钢板和铆钉，马洛有钢板，但是却没有固定钢板的铆钉。所以汽船当然修不好。

left our station for the coast[633]. And several times a week a coast caravan came in with trade goods—ghastly glazed calico that made you shudder only to look at it, glass beads value about a penny a quart[634], confounded spotted cotton handkerchiefs. And no rivets. Three carriers could have brought all that was wanted to set that steamboat afloat.

"He was becoming confidential[635] now, but I fancy my unresponsive[636] attitude must have exasperated[637] him at last, for he judged it necessary to inform me[638] he feared neither God nor devil, let alone any mere man[639]. I said I could see that very well,

---

633. left our station for the coast：离开（经理的）总站，到（会计师的）海边贸易站去。

634. glass beads value about a penny a quart：一分钱一大堆的玻璃珠子。quart 是容量单位，大约为一升。

635. becoming confidential：这里是说，经理心腹为了换取马洛的信任和"马洛手里的秘密"，不仅态度热络，而且开始告诉他一些自己知道的秘密。confidential 在这里意为"（言谈举止）神秘的；委以机密的"。

636. unresponsive：意为"无反应的；无动于衷的"。这里是说尽管马洛看出了对方的心思，但是他行得正、坐得直，自然没有什么阴暗的秘密可以拿来和对方分享。这种"投桃不报李"的态度，在经理心腹看来就是 unresponsive。

637. exasperated：意为"激怒；使恼怒"。经理心腹想和马洛"以心换心"，结果自己送出去很多机密，而从马洛嘴里却什么也撬不出来，很可能他会觉得自己被马洛耍了，因而恼羞成怒。

638. he judged it necessary to inform me：经理心腹觉得有必要威胁马洛，让他知道自己不是好要的。

639. he feared...mere man：这是经理心腹威胁马洛的话，意思是他连鬼神都不怕（或者说就算是公司的大人物来给马洛撑腰，他也不怕），更不会怕区区一个马洛和他作对。

but what I wanted was a certain quantity of rivets — and rivets were what really Mr. Kurtz wanted, if he had only known it. Now letters went to the coast every week.... 'My dear sir,' he cried, 'I write from dictation[640].' I demanded rivets. There was a way — for an intelligent man[641]. He changed his manner; became very cold, and suddenly began to talk about a hippopotamus[642]; wondered whether sleeping on board the steamer (I stuck to my salvage night and day) I wasn't disturbed. There was an old hippo that had the bad habit of getting out on the bank and roaming at night over the station grounds. The pilgrims used to turn out in a body and empty every rifle they could lay hands on[643] at him. Some even had sat up o' nights for him. All this energy was wasted[644], though. 'That animal has a charmed life[645],' he said; 'but you can say this only of brutes in this country. No man — you apprehend

---

640. from dictation：通过口授（来写信）。这里是经理心腹推卸责任给经理，或者是为自己找理由推脱。

641. for an intelligent man：对于聪明人来说（总是会有办法的）。这里是马洛借用经理心腹之前的话来反将一军。

642. hippopotamus：河马。这里是经理心腹发现马洛不跟自己分享秘密，而且一直逼自己拿出铆钉，他已经认定马洛是和库尔茨一伙、而且是要和自己作对的敌人，因此态度大变，用河马的故事来警告马洛"小心自己的性命"，或者是"连库尔茨也性命难保（你马洛又算个什么）"。

643. empty every rifle they could lay hands on：把他们能拿得到的所有的来复枪的子弹全部打光。这说明朝圣者们对那头老河马"急欲杀之而后快"。

644. All this energy was wasted：所有的精力都被浪费了。意思是朝圣者们的一番折腾全是徒劳无功，他们最后也没能杀死那头老河马。

645. has a charmed life：（老河马的）性命受到神灵的保佑。

me?—no man here bears a charmed life[646].' He stood there for a moment in the moonlight with his delicate hooked nose set a little askew[647], and his mica eyes glittering without a wink[648], then, with a curt Good-night[649], he strode off. I could see he was disturbed and considerably puzzled[650], which made me feel more hopeful than I had been for days. It was a great comfort to turn from that chap to my influential friend, the battered, twisted, ruined, tin-pot steamboat[651]. I clambered on board. She rang under my feet like an empty Huntley & Palmer biscuit-tin[652] kicked along a gutter; she was nothing so solid in make, and rather less pretty in shape,

---

646. no man here bears a charmed life：这里的人，谁也没有什么护身符。意思是说，在这里死个人是常有的事，所以如果马洛或者库尔茨不跟他们合作，那就要当心自己的性命。

647. his delicate hooked nose set a little askew：他精致的鹰钩鼻子稍微地扭曲了一下。"精致的鹰钩鼻子"暗示经理心腹是个利己主义者，"几不可察地扭曲／抽动了一下"则是一种发狠的表情，说明经理心腹正在威胁马洛。

648. his mica eyes glittering without a wink：他云母片似的闪闪发亮的眼睛一眨也不眨。这是一种狠狠瞪视的目光，也表示了一种威压和胁迫。

649. a curt Good-night：简短地道了声晚安。这说明经理心腹已经和马洛摊了牌，再也没什么话好讲了。

650. was disturbed and considerably puzzled：（经理心腹）心烦意乱，已经自乱阵脚了。这是马洛的想法，他以为自己的一番逼问（讨要铆钉）已经起作用了。其实不然。

651. my influential...tin-pot steamboat：这里是说，其实那条可怜的破汽船才是马洛真正的依靠——所谓的"有势力的朋友"。battered 意为"破旧的；弄垮了的"，twisted 意为"扭曲的"，tin-pot 意为"铁皮盒子"（比喻不值钱的汽船）。

652. Huntley & Palmer biscuit-tin：亨特利·帕尔玛牌饼干的空罐子。这里是类比马洛那条铁皮盒子一样简陋的破汽船，因为两者都不结实，一摆弄都会发出咣啷咣啷的声响。

but I had expended enough hard work on her to make me love her. No influential friend would have served me better. She had given me a chance to come out a bit — to find out what I could do. No, I don't like work. I had rather laze about and think of all the fine things that can be done. I don't like work — no man does — but I like what is in the work — the chance to find yourself. Your own reality — for yourself, not for others — what no other man can ever know. They can only see the mere show, and never can tell what it really means.

"I was not surprised to see somebody sitting aft, on the deck, with his legs dangling over the mud. You see I rather <u>chummed with the few mechanics</u>[653] there were in that station, whom the other pilgrims naturally despised — on account of their imperfect manners, I suppose. This was the foreman — <u>a boiler-maker by trade</u>[654] — a good worker. He was a lank, bony, yellow-faced man, with big intense eyes. His aspect was worried, and his head was <u>as bald as the palm of my hand</u>[655]; but his hair <u>in falling seemed to have stuck to his chin</u>[656], and had prospered in the new locality, for his beard hung down to his waist. He was a widower with six young children (he had left them in charge of a sister of his to

653. chummed with the few mechanics：和那几个技工交朋友。chum 意为"结为密友"。

654. a boiler-maker by trade：按专业／行当来划分，（他是个）锅炉匠。

655. as bald as the palm of my hand：就好像我的手掌心那样光秃秃的。这里是形容锅炉匠的光头。

656. in falling seemed to have stuck to his chin：这里的描述很有意思。因为锅炉匠是个光头，但又长着一把大胡子，马洛就想象着他的头发全都从头顶上掉下来，掉到了他的下巴上，然后在他的下巴上安了新家，欣欣向荣地生长起来了。

come out there), and the passion of his life was pigeon-flying[657]. He was an enthusiast and a connoisseur. He would rave about pigeons. After work hours he used sometimes to come over from his hut for a talk about his children and his pigeons; at work, when he had to crawl in the mud under the bottom of the steamboat, he would tie up that beard of his[658] in a kind of white serviette he brought for the purpose. It had loops to go over his ears. In the evening he could be seen squatted on the bank rinsing that wrapper[659] in the creek with great care, then spreading it solemnly on a bush to dry.

"I slapped him on the back[660] and shouted, 'We shall have rivets!' He scrambled to his feet[661] exclaiming, 'No! Rivets!' [662]

---

657. pigeon-flying：放飞鸽子。养鸽人都知道，放飞的鸽子都要是自己一手养育和训练出来的。养鸽子和放鸽子有很多乐趣，也有很多学问。著名作家老舍先生曾经写过一篇散文《小动物们（鸽）》，将养鸽人的热情与甘苦写得十分生动，读来妙趣横生，引人入胜。

658. tie up that beard of his：把他的胡子拢成一束（包起来）。tie up 意为"绑起来"，这里指的是用布包起来。

659. wrapper：包装纸；包装材料。这里所指的是包胡子用的布。

660. slapped him on the back：一巴掌拍在他的后背上。这个动作表现了马洛和锅炉工交情很好。

661. scrambled to his feet：一骨碌爬了起来。scramble 在这里意为"手脚并用地迅速（爬起；站起）"，而不是"手忙脚乱；攀登；争抢"。这个词在研究量子混沌的时候也会出现，用于描述信息从有序到完全混乱的过程，即 information scrambling；翟荟老师曾经讲过 scrambling 的意思就是"（像搅鸡蛋那样）摊开；弄混；使信息不复本来的面貌"。注意，掌握一个单词并不仅仅是从词典上查出它所有的字面意思就可以了，真正的掌握是指通过大量阅读和深刻体会，在头脑里抽象出词义的精髓（我称之为"元意义"）；这样才能够在不同的语境中结合上下文准确识别具体词义（我称之为"衍生义"）。

662. 'No! Rivets!'："不会吧！有铆钉啦！"这里有"Are you kidding me"的意思，表示对于意外的好消息简直难以置信。

as though he couldn't believe his ears. Then in a low voice, 'You...eh?' I don't know why we behaved like lunatics. I <u>put my finger to the side of my nose</u>[663] and nodded mysteriously. 'Good for you!' he cried, snapped his fingers above his head, <u>lifting one foot</u>[664]. I tried a <u>jig</u>[665]. We capered on the iron deck. <u>A frightful clatter</u>[666] came out of that hulk, and the virgin forest on the other bank of the creek sent it back in a thundering roll upon the sleeping station. It must have made some of the pilgrims sit up in their hovels. A dark figure obscured the lighted doorway of the manager's hut, vanished, then, a second or so after, the doorway itself vanished, too. We stopped, and the silence driven away by the stamping of our feet <u>flowed back again from the recesses of the land</u>[667]. The great wall of vegetation, an exuberant and entangled mass of trunks, branches, leaves, boughs, festoons, motionless in the moonlight, was like a <u>rioting invasion of soundless life</u>[668], a

---

663. put my finger to the side of my nose：中文中更习惯表达为"把手指竖在嘴边"，表示让对方噤声的意思。

664. lifting one foot：抬起了一只脚。这里指的是跳起舞来。

665. jig：吉格舞。吉格舞是英国的一种传统民间舞蹈，通常是单人即兴表演，舞步轻快活泼。

666. A frightful clatter：一阵惊人的哐啷哐啷声。clatter 意为"哗啦声；喧闹声"。frightful 说明劣质的船体几乎承受不住大的震动。

667. flowed back again from the recesses of the land：从大地的各个角落 / 大地的深处汇聚了回来。这里是一个暗喻，（携带声音的气流）就好像水流一样，会被驱走，也可以涌流回来。

668. a rioting invasion of soundless life：无声的生命（指的是植物）发动的狂暴的侵袭。rioting 意为"暴乱的"，invasion 意为"侵略；入侵"。

rolling wave of plants, piled up, crested, ready to topple over the creek, to sweep every little man of us out of his little existence[669]. And it moved not. A deadened burst of mighty splashes and snorts reached us from afar, as though an icthyosaurus[670] had been taking a bath of glitter in the great river. 'After all,' said the boiler-maker in a reasonable tone, 'why shouldn't we get the rivets?' Why not, indeed! I did not know of any reason why we shouldn't. 'They'll come in three weeks,' I said confidently.

"But they didn't. Instead of rivets there came an invasion, an infliction, a visitation[671]. It came in sections during the next three weeks, each section headed by a donkey carrying a white man in new clothes and tan shoes, bowing from that elevation[672] right and left to the impressed pilgrims. A quarrelsome band of footsore sulky niggers[673] trod on the heels of the donkey; a lot of tents, camp-stools, tin boxes, white cases, brown bales would be shot

---

669. sweep every little man of us out of his little existence：把每一个渺小的人类都呼啦卷走，让他们从此不复存在。这里也是一种带有感情色彩的想象，作者把茂密的丛林想象成一股强大的复仇力量，它似乎想要把眼前这些渺小而又贪婪的人类（欧洲殖民者）一下子全部冲荡干净，还非洲一片净土。

670. icthyosaurus：鱼龙（恐龙的一种）。这里似乎暗示的是那头老河马。

671. an invasion, an infliction, a visitation：侵略、袭扰和探视。这些在英文中用抽象词表述的事物需要译成中文里的具体词。

672. bowing from that elevation：从高处（指驴背上）额首 / 弯腰俯身。bow意为"鞠躬；点头"。

673. footsore sulky niggers：两脚酸痛、脸色阴沉的黑人。这是形容黑人长途跋涉之后疲惫不堪的样子。白人骑着驴，而黑人扛着东西步行，他们的状态肯定会大不一样。footsore 意为"（因走远路而）脚酸的；脚痛的"，sulky 意为"生着闷气的；脸色难看的"。

down in the courtyard, and the air of mystery would deepen a little over the muddle of the station. Five such instalments came, with their absurd air of disorderly flight with the loot of innumerable outfit shops and provision stores, that, one would think, they were lugging, after a raid, into the wilderness for equitable division. It was <u>an inextricable mess of things</u>[674] <u>decent in themselves</u>[675] but that human folly made look like <u>the spoils of thieving</u>[676].

"This devoted band called itself <u>the Eldorado Exploring Expedition</u>[677], and I believe they were sworn to secrecy. Their talk, however, was the talk of <u>sordid buccaneers</u>[678]: it was reckless without hardihood, greedy without audacity, and cruel without

---

674. an inextricable mess of things：一种不可避免的东西混乱的状况。这里是说（在旅途中刚到驿站的时候）把刚卸下来的东西乱堆一气，是一种很正常、也无可厚非的情形。任何人在这种情况下免不了都是如此。inextricable 意为"逃脱不掉的；解不开的"。mess 意为"杂乱；混乱局面"。

675. decent in themselves：这里是说这些胡乱堆放的东西，本身来路很正。它们都是清白的，并不是什么赃物。decent 意为"体面的；正经的"。

676. the spoils of thieving：偷来的贼赃。spoil 意为"赃物；战利品"。这句是说，那些东西本身是正路子来的，堆成那个乱样子也无可厚非，只不过那些人的蠢样（他们就像海盗一样飞扬跋扈、满脸贼相）才让马洛总觉得这幅情景就好像强盗刚洗劫完商店、准备开始分赃似的。

677. the Eldorado Exploring Expedition：黄金之国探险队。Eldorado 来自西班牙文，原意是"理想黄金国；富庶之乡"。Exploring Expedition 意为"探险远征队"。

678. sordid buccaneers：肮脏的海盗。sordid 意为"肮脏的；卑鄙的"，buccaneer 意为"海盗"。buccaneer 在法语中写作 boucanier，最初指的是喜欢露天烧烤生肉的人。后来演变为"猎人"。17 世纪，有不少法国人在当时的西班牙殖民地加勒比海地区进行打猎等活动；西班牙人将他们驱逐出去之后，一些法国人转而做了海盗，于是 buccaneer 就有了"海盗"的意思。

courage; there was not an atom of foresight or of serious intention[679] in the whole batch of them, and they did not seem aware these things are wanted for the work of the world[680]. To tear treasure out of the bowels of the land[681] was their desire, with no more moral purpose at the back of it than there is in burglars breaking into a safe[682]. Who paid the expenses of the noble enterprise[683] I don't know; but the uncle of our manager was leader of that lot.

"In exterior he resembled a butcher in a poor neighbourhood[684], and his eyes had a look of sleepy cunning[685]. He carried his fat paunch with ostentation on his short legs, and during the time his gang infested the station[686] spoke to no one but his nephew. You

---

679. not an atom of foresight or of serious intention：没有一丁点儿远见，也没有一丁点儿严肃的目的。not an atom of 是夸张的手法，用 "连一个原子也没有" 来表达 "一点也没有"。

680. these things are wanted for the work of the world：如果想要在世上当真做出一番事业，那么这些东西（卓越的远见、坚定的目标、非凡的勇气等等）是必不可少的。

681. tear treasure out of the bowels of the land：从这片土地上压榨出财富来。bowels 意为 "肠子；内脏"，这里用作比喻，指的是 "这片土地的深处"。

682. with no more...a safe：在它（指的是这帮人从非洲的土地上攫取财富的行为）的背后，根本就没什么道德可言；相比起撬开保险柜的窃贼，这帮人（在道德上）也好不到哪里去。

683. the noble enterprise：这一高尚的事业。指的是所谓的 "探险事业"——也就是从非洲的土地上掠夺财富。

684. resembled a butcher in a poor neighbourhood：好像一个贫困社区的屠夫。resemble 意为 "像；类似"。

685. a look of sleepy cunning：一种昏昏欲睡中透着阴险狡诈的样子。cunning 意为 "狡猾；诡诈"。

686. infested the station：在贸易站里到处出没。infest 意为 "（虫鼠等）为患的；大批滋生的；出没；遍布"。

could see these two roaming about all day long with their heads close together in an everlasting confab[687].

"I had given up worrying myself about the rivets. One's capacity for that kind of folly is more limited than you would suppose[688]. I said Hang! —and let things slide. I had plenty of time for meditation, and now and then I would give some thought to Kurtz. I wasn't very interested in him. No. Still, I was curious to see whether this man, who had come out equipped with moral ideas of some sort[689], would climb to the top[690] after all and how he would set about his work when there[691]."

---

687. in an everlasting confab：总是不停地谈话。confab 意为"交谈"。

688. One's capacity...would suppose：一个人应付这种蠢事的能力，比你所认为的更加有限。意思就是"你其实根本没法和那样的蠢事较劲；你可没那么厉害，能应付得了那样的蠢事"。另一种可能的理解是，"一个人对那些蠢材的忍耐是很有限的"。

689. equipped with moral ideas of some sort：怀揣着那些道德理想。equipped with 意为"装备着；带着"。

690. climb to the top：爬到顶上去，在这里指的是"当上经理"。

691. when there：等他坐上了那个位子的时候。

II

"One evening as I was lying flat on the deck of my steamboat, I heard voices approaching—and there were the nephew and the uncle strolling along the bank. I laid my head on my arm again, and had nearly lost myself in a doze, when somebody said in my ear, as it were[692]: 'I am as harmless as a little child, but I don't like to be dictated to. Am I the manager—or am I not? I was ordered to send him there. It's incredible.' ...I became aware that the two were standing on the shore alongside the forepart of the steamboat, just below my head. I did not move; it did not occur to me to move[693]: I was sleepy. 'It is unpleasant,' grunted the uncle. 'He has asked the Administration to be sent there,' said the other, 'with the idea of showing what he could do; and I was instructed accordingly[694]. Look at the influence that man must have. Is it not

---

692. as it were: 这里是错位语序，正常语序可能是"when somebody said as it were (said) in my ear"，意思是"有什么人的话语声直似近在耳畔"。

693. it did not occur to me to move: 我就没想过要动弹。一是马洛睡意正浓，二是他也没必要弄出动静，给自己找麻烦。

694. was instructed accordingly: 相应地接到了上级的命令。这里是说经理认为库尔茨能量很大，可以左右公司的领导层按照他的意思，向经理发号施令。be instructed 意为"接到指示"。

frightful[695]?' They both agreed it was frightful, then made several bizarre remarks: 'Make rain and fine weather[696]—one man—the Council—by the nose[697]'—bits of absurd sentences that got the better of my drowsiness[698], so that I had pretty near the whole of my wits[699] about me when the uncle said, 'The climate may do away with this difficulty for you. Is he alone there?' 'Yes,' answered the manager; 'he sent his assistant down the river with a note to me in these terms: "Clear this poor devil out of the country[700], and don't bother sending more of that sort. I had rather be alone than have the kind of men you can dispose of with me." It was more than a year ago. Can you imagine such impudence!' 'Anything since then?' asked the other hoarsely. 'Ivory,' jerked

---

695. frightful：可怕的；惊人的。这里说明经理一伙对库尔茨摸不着底，因而十分忌惮。

696. Make rain and fine weather：可能的意思是"翻云覆雨"或者"借势成事"，就是说，经理他们要制造各种情况以便自己能够掌控局势；他们可以 make rain（制造麻烦，让事情变得紧张），也可以 make fine weather（提供助力，让形势变得缓和）。另一种理解，这是经理他们在说库尔茨可以呼风唤雨，能量大得可怕。

697. by the nose：牵着鼻子走；完全控制（他人）。可能的意思是，欧洲董事会远在天边，鞭长莫及，因而可能会受到经理一面之词的蒙蔽，被他"牵着鼻子走"。或者说，是经理他们认为库尔茨有能力左右董事会的决定。

698. got the better of my drowsiness：战胜了／驱走了我的睡意。get the better of 意为"占上风"。这里是说马洛开始留心经理叔侄的谈话了。

699. I had pretty near the whole of my wits："我的神智已经几乎全都到位了"，意思是"我已经差不多完全清醒了"。

700. Clear this poor devil out of the country：让这个笨蛋家伙赶紧离开这里吧。clear 在这里意为"赶走；送出境"，country 在这里指的是非洲腹地的这片区域。

the nephew; 'lots of it—prime sort—lots—most annoying, from him.' 'And with that?' questioned the heavy rumble[701]. 'Invoice,' was the reply fired out[702], so to speak. Then silence. They had been talking about Kurtz.

"I was broad awake by this time, but, lying perfectly at ease[703], remained still, having no inducement to change my position. 'How did that ivory come all this way?' growled the elder man, who seemed very vexed. The other explained that it had come with a fleet of canoes in charge of an English half-caste clerk Kurtz had with him; that Kurtz had apparently intended to return himself, the station being by that time bare of goods and stores[704], but after coming three hundred miles, had suddenly decided to go back, which he started to do alone in a small dugout with four paddlers[705], leaving the half-caste to continue down the river with the ivory. The two fellows there seemed astounded at anybody

---

701. questioned the heavy rumble：这里是倒装语序，正常顺序是 "the heavy rumble questioned"。

702. was the reply fired out：这里是倒装语序，正常顺序是 "the reply was fired out"。be fired out 意为 "被发射出来的"，这里是形容经理的话就像发射出来的子弹一样又快又狠。

703. lying perfectly at ease：完全放松地躺着。at ease 意为 "一种感觉舒适、放松的状态"，例如军事训练中 "稍息" 的口令即 "stand at ease"。

704. bare of goods and stores：既没有食物，也没有货物了。be bare of 意为 "没有；别无长物"，bare 是 "光秃秃" 的意思。

705. a small dugout with four paddlers：四人划桨的一条很小的独木船。dugout 意为 "独木船"，来自 dig out，因为独木船都是用一大块木头挖出来船形的。paddlers 意为 "划桨者"。

attempting such a thing[706]. They were at a loss for an adequate motive[707]. As to me, I seemed to see Kurtz for the first time. It was a distinct glimpse: the dugout, four paddling savages, and the lone white man turning his back suddenly on the headquarters, on relief, on thoughts of home — perhaps; setting his face towards the depths of the wilderness, towards his empty and desolate station[708]. I did not know the motive. Perhaps he was just simply a fine fellow who stuck to his work for its own sake[709]. His name, you understand, had not been pronounced[710] once. He was 'that man.' The half-caste, who, as far as I could see, had conducted a difficult trip with great prudence and pluck, was invariably alluded to as 'that scoundrel.'[711] The 'scoundrel' had reported that the 'man'

---

706. attempting such a thing：竟然会这么干。这里是说经理叔侄对于库尔茨决定掉头返回内陆贸易站这件事相当吃惊，因为那时候库尔茨的贸易站已经一无所有了。在这种情况下，绝大多数人都会选择回到经理那里去补充给养。

707. at a loss for an adequate motive：意思是，经理叔侄俩想破脑袋，也没法为库尔茨的行为找到一个合理的动机。他们百思不得其解。

708. his empty and desolate station：他那一无所有的、荒凉凋敝的贸易站。desolate 意为"荒凉的；孤独的"。

709. stuck to his work for its own sake：为了拼命工作而拼命工作。for its own sake 意为"为了它本身；表示做某事是因为喜欢或认为有价值，而不是为了其他目的"。

710. been pronounced：（他的名字）被说出来。这里是说经理叔侄一次也没有在对话中直接道出库尔茨的名字，而都是用"那个人"代替。

711. was invariably alluded to as 'that scoundrel.'：一直被用"那个混蛋"来指代。invariably 意为"始终如一地；一贯地"，scoundrel 意为"恶棍；流氓"。

had been very ill—had recovered imperfectly....The two below me moved away then a few paces, and strolled back and forth at some little distance. I heard: 'Military post[712]—doctor—two hundred miles—quite alone now—unavoidable delays[713]—nine months—no news—strange rumours.' They approached again, just as the manager was saying, 'No one, as far as I know, unless a species of wandering trader—a pestilential fellow, snapping ivory from the natives.' Who was it they were talking about now? I gathered in snatches that this was some man supposed to be in Kurtz's district, and of whom the manager did not approve[714]. 'We will not be free from unfair competition till one of these fellows is hanged for an example,' he said. 'Certainly,' grunted the other; 'get him hanged! Why not? Anything—anything can be done in this country. That's what I say; nobody here, you understand, here, can endanger your position[715]. And why? You stand the climate—you outlast them all. The danger is in Europe; but there before I

---

712. Military post：军事哨所；军事基地；军队驻地。从这里的只言片语可以大概拼凑出一些信息，就是经理叔侄认为库尔茨现在距离军队驻地和医疗站都很远，因而得不到弹药补充和医疗条件，这是正中他们下怀的。库尔茨生了病，却没有医生和药物，时间拖延下去，情况就会越发对经理有利。

713. unavoidable delays：不可避免的延误。这里似乎可以看出，沉船事件很可能与经理有关。

714. approve：approve 意为"赞成；批准"或者"喜欢；赞赏"。由于 approve 的多义性，这里也有两种理解。一是那个散货贩子的活动"没有得到经理的许可"，即经理的权威受到了挑衅；二是"经理对那个散货贩子很不欣赏"，即经理很讨厌那个人。我觉得两种理解都是对的。

715. endanger your position：危及你的地位。这里是指经理叔父不允许任何人（尤其是库尔茨）将经理取而代之。

left I took care to[716] — ' They moved off and whispered, then their voices rose again. 'The extraordinary series of delays is not my fault. I did my best.' The fat man sighed[717]. 'Very sad.' 'And the pestiferous absurdity of his talk,' continued the other; 'he bothered me enough when he was here. "Each station should be like a beacon on the road towards better things, a centre for trade of course, but also for humanizing, improving, instructing." Conceive you — that ass! And he wants to be manager! No, it's — ' Here he got choked by excessive indignation[718], and I lifted my head the least bit. I was surprised to see how near they were — right under me. I could have spat[719] upon their hats. They were looking on the ground, absorbed in thought. The manager was switching[720] his leg with a slender twig: his sagacious[721] relative lifted his head.

---

716. took care to：留意着（做了某事）。这里指的是经理叔父已经留了心，临行前特意在欧洲做了一番对经理有利的安排。

717. sighed：叹息；发出一声长叹。这句的 the fat man 指的是经理叔父，他用心狠毒，又惺惺作态。从这里可以看出，这个经理叔父领头的"黄金之国探险队"似乎也是欧洲总部派去寻找库尔茨的（或者至少其中一项任务是寻找库尔茨）。

718. got choked by excessive indignation：由于过度的愤怒而说不下去了。经理一直善于伪装，而这里是他为数不多的一次真情流露。他最在乎的东西，就是自己经理的位子，因为这个职位意味着象牙贸易中最大的一份抽成。indignation 意为"愤慨；愤愤不平"。

719. spat：spit 的过去式，意为"吐口水"。这里表现了马洛对他们暗地里搞阴谋算计的鄙视。

720. switch：在这里意为"用枝条击打，轻拂"。这个动作表现了经理的阴谋被无意间撞破后，紧张、尴尬又讪讪地不知道该干什么好的样子。

721. sagacious：睿智的；聪慧的；有远见的。这里明显是反讽，说明经理叔父是一个比经理更有道行的魔鬼。

'You have been well since you came out this time?' he asked. The other gave a start. 'Who? I? Oh! Like a charm—like a charm. But the rest—oh, my goodness! All sick. They die so quick, too, that I haven't the time to send them out of the country—it's incredible!' 'Hm'm. Just so,' grunted the uncle. 'Ah! my boy, trust to this[722]— I say, trust to this.' I saw him extend his short flipper of an arm[723] for a gesture that took in the forest, the creek, the mud, the river— seemed to beckon with a dishonouring flourish before the sunlit face of the land a treacherous appeal to the lurking death, to the hidden evil, to the profound darkness of its heart. It was so startling that I leaped to my feet and looked back at the edge of the forest, as though I had expected an answer of some sort to that black display of confidence. You know the foolish notions that come to one sometimes[724]. The high stillness confronted these two figures with its ominous patience, waiting for the passing away of a fantastic invasion.

"They swore aloud together—out of sheer fright, I believe— then pretending not to know anything of my existence, turned back to the station. The sun was low; and leaning forward side by side,

722. trust to this：相信这一切吧。这里可能是经理叔父借着经理的话来威胁马洛，"要相信这里的人（如果不听话，就会）死得特别快"。

723. extend his short flipper of an arm：伸开他短鳍似的胳膊。flipper 意为"鳍状肢"，这里是比喻经理叔父又粗又短的胳臂。译为"（海龟的）龟鳍"，一是把"鳍状肢"更加具体化，二是比较符合前文对经理叔父身材的描述，"两条短腿托着个大肚囊"，想象一下，这种身材正如海龟一样，中间很大而四肢短小。

724. the foolish notions that come to one sometimes：人有时候会免不了产生一些愚蠢的想法。这里指的是马洛被惊得盯住身后的森林，似乎感觉到会有真正的魔鬼被这两个披着人皮的魔鬼从黑暗深处召唤出来。

they seemed to be tugging painfully uphill their two ridiculous shadows of unequal length, that trailed behind them slowly over the tall grass without bending a single blade[725].

"In a few days the Eldorado Expedition went into the patient wilderness, that closed upon it as the sea closes over a diver[726]. Long afterwards the news came that all the donkeys were dead. I know nothing as to the fate of the less valuable animals[727]. They, no doubt, like the rest of us, found what they deserved[728]. I did not inquire. I was then rather excited at the prospect of meeting Kurtz very soon. When I say very soon I mean it comparatively. It was just two months from the day we left the creek when we came to

---

725. without bending a single blade：却不曾压弯哪怕一片草叶。blade 意为"刀刃；（草的）叶片"。这一段以讽刺的手法揭露了经理侄佺色厉内荏的本质，也预示着经理侄父谋害他人的坏主意最后并没有实现。他们内心的邪恶就好像他们拖在身后的影子，尽管无比黑暗，但却是又无力又可笑——就连一片草叶也压不弯。

726. closed upon it as the sea closes over a diver：就好像大海吞没潜水员一样，（荒野）吞了它（指的是黄金之国探险队）。这里形象地描写了渺小的人类进入到无边的巨物（荒野或大海）之中的情形。

727. the fate of the less valuable animals：那些比驴子还不值钱的动物的命运。这里指的是黄金之国探险队的命运。荒野里潜藏的危险无处不在，任何人进去都凶多吉少。黄金之国探险队很可能在荒野里全军覆没了。用 the less valuable animals（还不如驴子值钱的动物）来指代经理侄父带领的探险队，是一种辛辣的讽刺笔法，因为他们狠毒卑鄙，所以简直不配称之为人。这里如果直译为"不如驴子值钱的动物"，当然没有问题；但是我觉得，为了读者能够毫无疑义地看出作者的讽刺，而不误以为真的是什么"动物"，译成"而至于那些并不比驴子更高贵的两足动物，我也不知道他们究竟下场如何"可能更清楚一些。

728. what they deserved：得到应有的命运；死得其所。deserve 意为"值得；应受"，既可以搭配"值得赞扬"，也可以搭配"应受惩罚"。

the bank below Kurtz's station.

"Going up that river was like traveling back to the earliest beginnings of the world, when vegetation rioted on the earth and the big trees were kings. An empty stream, a great silence, an impenetrable forest[729]. The air was warm, thick, heavy, sluggish[730]. There was no joy in the brilliance of sunshine. The long stretches of the waterway ran on, deserted, into the gloom of overshadowed distances. On silvery sand-banks hippos and alligators sunned themselves side by side. The broadening waters flowed through a mob of wooded islands; you lost your way on that river as you would in a desert, and butted all day long against shoals, trying to find the channel, till you thought yourself bewitched and cut off for ever from everything you had known once—somewhere—far away—in another existence perhaps[731]. There were moments when

---

729. An empty...impenetrable forest：直译为"一条空荡荡的河流，一片巨大的寂静，一片密不透风的森林"，似乎稍欠文学性。英语行文中类似这样的罗列句式，我觉得最好以文学的语言来表达原意，例此处译为"河面上空荡荡的，除了我们再也杳无人迹；两岸的丛林翁翁郁郁，简直密不透风，一切都笼罩在沉沉的寂静之中。"

730. warm, thick, heavy, sluggish：翻译方法同上，从"温暖、厚实、沉重、呆滞"化译为"温暖的空气黏乎乎、懒洋洋的，似乎随时就要凝滞不动了"。sluggish 意为"缓慢的；懒洋洋的"。这里是形容热带地区气候炎热，似乎连空气也滞重黏稠，让人难以呼吸。

731. cut off for...existence perhaps：你曾经熟悉的一切都（被咒语）与你分隔开来了，你曾经熟悉的那个世界好像已经到了一个非常遥远的地方，到了另一个时空。康拉德有很多文字相当抽象，但又十分深刻，值得细细咀嚼品味，滋味无穷。就像古人所说，"读书百遍，其义乃见"。《黑暗之心》全篇都是高度凝练的思想和文字，遇到一时不懂的地方，可以慢下来，花点时间，"读书百遍"，定会茅塞顿开。

one's past came back to one, as it will sometimes when you have not a moment to spare for yourself; but it came in the shape of an unrestful and noisy dream, remembered with wonder amongst the overwhelming realities of this strange world of plants, and water, and silence. And this stillness of life did not in the least resemble a peace[732]. It was the stillness of an implacable force brooding over an inscrutable intention[733]. It looked at you with a vengeful aspect[734]. I got used to it afterwards; I did not see it any more; I had no time. I had to keep guessing at the channel; I had to discern, mostly by inspiration, the signs of hidden banks; I watched for sunken stones; I was learning to clap my teeth smartly before my heart flew out[735], when I shaved by a fluke some infernal sly old

---

732. resemble a peace: 看上去好像一种平静。这里的意思是，马洛在刚果河上的航行看似一派平静，但其实危机潜伏（主要是来自自然界的危险），暗流汹涌（船上的经理是个阴谋家），因此绝非真正意义上的"平静无事"。推而广之，有时候普通人的平静的生活中也会酝酿着某种危机，就像中国古人所说的"祸兮福之所倚，福兮祸之所伏"。每个人的生命都是一场历险，每一个宁静的日子，都未必仍会有宁静相续。

733. an implacable...inscrutable intention:（在宁静表象的背后，似乎有）一种不可抗拒的力量在酝酿着某种阴深难测的企图。这句话也道出了人生的艰险不易——所谓"天有不测风云"是也。implacable 意为"不能安抚的；不能缓和的"，brood over 意为"孤独地沉思；酝酿"，inscrutable 意为"神秘的；不可理解的"。

734. with a vengeful aspect:（那种不可抗拒的力量在平静之中）带着一种仇深似海似的神情（注视着你）。译为"它用一种风雨欲来的神情默默注视着你，在暗处伺机而动"。人类在命运面前总是无比渺小；命运之诡谲正如风云之变幻，谁也无法说得清。

735. clap my teeth smartly before my heart flew out: 紧紧咬住牙关，以免心脏从腔子里飞出来。从这里可见在刚果河上驾船令马洛极度紧张，他必须全神贯注、咬紧牙关，才能避开河水中潜藏的种种危险，保证航行的安全。（转下页）

snag that would have ripped the life out of the tin-pot steamboat[736] and drowned all the pilgrims; I had to keep a lookout for the signs of dead wood we could cut up in the night for next day's steaming. When you have to attend to things of that sort, to the mere incidents of the surface[737], the reality—the reality, I tell you—fades[738]. The inner truth is hidden[739]—luckily, luckily. But I felt it all the same; I felt often its mysterious stillness watching me at my monkey tricks[740], just as it watches you fellows performing on your respective tight-

---

（接上页）clap 意为"拍手"，这里是拟声词，意思是"咔哒一声咬住（牙齿）"，smartly 意为"剧痛地；痛苦地"，flew out 即 fly out，意为"飞出去"。这里的描述很形象，甚至（如果不厚道地评价的话）还有点有趣——心脏紧张得正要飞出去（腔子里-嘴里-体外），马洛就咔哒一声闭住了牙齿（于是心脏只好又被咽回到腔子里头）。

736. ripped the life out of the tin-pot steamboat：把这个锡盒子似的廉价汽船开膛破肚，让里面的东西（比如船上载着的经理和那些朝圣者）全漏出来。rip 意为"撕裂；划破；迅速扯开"。

737. the mere incidents of the surface：（浮在生活的）表面上的那些不得不优先处理的琐碎事儿。这里指的是马洛眼下必须要全力应对的种种杂务——观察水道，操船掌舵，躲避障碍物，寻找木柴等等。

738. fade：销声匿迹了；隐藏起来了。也就是说，真正的现实反而令马洛无法顾及了。所谓 reality（真正的现实），可能指的是这趟航行的任务——寻找库尔茨。或者大一点说，是马洛想要通过工作认清自己的价值。或者再大一点，就是人生在世，为了什么而活着。

739. The inner truth is hidden：那内在的真实只不过是暂时隐藏起来了。就是说，即使马洛现在手忙脚乱地做着船上的各种杂务，忙得顾不上思考自己为什么要在这个地方干这些事儿，但是他仍在自己生活的正常轨道上运行着，生活的真实的意义仍然还在那里，还是那样，没有变化（比如航行的任务还是寻找库尔茨，马洛还是在工作中实现自己的价值，等等）。

740. my monkey tricks：我的那套猴把戏。这里指的是马洛用自己操船掌舵的专业技能在不停地忙活着工作。这里是一种自嘲的口气。

ropes for — what is it? half-a-crown a tumble[741] — ”

“Try to be civil, Marlow,” growled a voice, and I knew there was at least one listener awake besides myself.

“I beg your pardon. I forgot the heartache which makes up the rest of the price[742]. And indeed what does the price matter, if the trick be well done[743]? You do your tricks very well. And I didn’t

---

741. you fellows...a tumble：这里是马洛推己及人的一番话。每个人每天都在为了生活而奔波，处理着各种不得不做的琐事，但是生活的本质意义是相对稳定的，即使你一时感受不到，你实际上也是走在生活的既定道路上。马洛是这样，他的船员朋友们也一样。为了生活，马洛每天要发挥自己的专业技能，手忙脚乱地驾驶汽船（就好像耍猴戏一样），他的船员朋友们也一样，用他们各自的专业技能，在“各自的钢丝绳上表演着各自的把戏（比如船长、轮机长、舵手等等不同的分工）”，而他们的这番辛苦的表演，为的是什么呢？为的就是那一点可怜的工资。船员们只要半个克朗就给跑一趟船，这就和“要猴只要两分半钱就给翻一个筋斗”完全是一样的。马洛道破了人们为衣食而工作的辛酸现实，但是他的这句实话却又让他的船员朋友们多少有点儿听着刺耳——正如林宥嘉在歌曲里唱的，“人生已经如此艰难，有些事情就不要拆穿”。crown 意为“克朗”，是英国旧时货币，1 克朗等于 5 先令。tumble 意为“翻跟头”。

742. the heartache...of the price：意为“凑够你应得的价钱的那一阵心痛”。这句话的意思是，比如说你的工作本应值得一个月 100 块钱，可是老板只给一个月 70 块钱（老板可能还会说，“钱就给这么多，还有好多人等着要这份工作，你爱干不干”）。那么 “the rest of the price” 的 30 块钱，就只能用你的心痛 / 肉疼来补上了（也就是说，尽管愤愤不平 / 心里难受，你也只好咽下这口气，接受老板的条件）。在这里，面对听者的抗议，马洛先回答“不好意思”，然后接着说出这句更刺耳的话，一是说明马洛直言敢道，二是说明船员们事实上的遭遇比“两分半钱翻一个筋斗”更心酸，因为这可怜的两分半钱是被老板压了价的。相比起他的船员朋友，马洛无疑更加清醒，也更加犀利。

743. what does...well done：意为“只要你的猴把戏耍得好（工作干得好），那点儿价钱也就无所谓了 / 不跟老板计较了”。从这里我们可以看到马洛是个正直、富有责任感的人。虽然他很清楚地知道老板在压榨自己，但是既然按照老板的条件接受了工作，他就会认真负责地把自己的工作干好，绝不会像经理和朝圣者们那样偷懒耍滑。

do badly either, since I managed not to sink that steamboat on my first trip. It's a wonder to me yet. Imagine <u>a blindfolded man set to drive a van over a bad road</u>[744]. I sweated and shivered over that business considerably, I can tell you. After all, for a seaman, to scrape the bottom of the thing that's supposed to float all the time under his care is the unpardonable sin. No one may know of it, but you never forget <u>the thump</u>[745]—eh? A blow on the very heart. You remember it, you dream of it, you wake up at night and think of it—years after—and go hot and cold all over. I don't pretend to say that steamboat floated all the time. More than once she had to wade for a bit, with twenty <u>cannibals</u>[746] splashing around and pushing. We had enlisted some of these chaps on the way for a crew. Fine fellows—cannibals—in their place. They were men one could work with, and I am grateful to them. And, after all, they did not eat each other before my face: they had brought along a provision of hippo-meat which went rotten, and made the mystery of the wilderness stink in my nostrils. Phoo! I can sniff it now. I had the manager on board and three or four pilgrims with

---

744. a blindfolded...bad road：这里是一个比喻，"一个蒙着眼睛的人在糟糕的道路上开货车"的情形，就和马洛在没有地图（蒙着眼睛）又暗礁密布（道路糟糕）的刚果河上驾驶汽船（开货车）一样，都是充满了危险的旅途，让人汗流浃背、战战兢兢。blindfolded 意为"被蒙上眼睛的"，be set to do 意为"被设定为做某事；安排去做某事"，van 意为"小货车；面包车"。

745. the thump：那一记重击。在这里一是指船底触礁的一声沉重的闷响，二是指意识到事情不对的船长重重的一记心跳。

746. cannibal：同类相食的动物；食人生番。这里指的是蒙昧原始的非洲野人。

their staves—all complete[747]. Sometimes we came upon a station close by the bank, clinging to the skirts of the unknown, and the white men rushing out of a tumble-down hovel, with great gestures of joy and surprise and welcome, seemed very strange—had the appearance of being held there captive by a spell[748]. The word ivory would ring in the air for a while—and on we went again into the silence, along empty reaches, round the still bends, between the high walls of our winding way, reverberating in hollow claps[749] the ponderous beat of the stern-wheel[750]. Trees, trees, millions of trees, massive, immense, running up high; and at their foot, hugging the bank against the stream, crept the little begrimed[751]

---

747. all complete：（在马洛的船上，经理和朝圣者们）全都安然无恙。这里隐含着一个对比，经理他们第一次开着汽船出去就把船弄沉了，而马洛开船则一直平平安安，这说明马洛是有能力且态度认真地对待工作，而经理他们却是恰恰相反。

748. by a spell：意为"被某种咒语"。把这些人迷惑住了并困在这个荒蛮之地的"咒语"，不是别的，正是象牙。"象牙"这个词儿又会在空气中回荡一阵子，就是说他们又开始讨论象牙；比如说，岸上无名之地的白人可能会朝汽船大喊："你们是运送象牙的吗？""你们弄到了多少象牙？"船上的朝圣者也会互相谈论"岸上的那帮家伙们能弄到象牙吗？""我看他们好像也没弄到多少象牙"之类。他们满脑子象牙，都好像中了"象牙"的魔咒了。

749. reverberating in hollow claps："作为一种沉闷的拍击声而不断回响"。reverberate 意为"回响；反弹"，hollow 意为"（声音）沉闷回荡的；空洞的"，clap 意为"拍手；击掌；发出碰撞声"，这里指的是螺旋桨拍击水面的声音。

750. the ponderous beat of the stern-wheel：船尾螺旋桨那沉重的击水声。ponderous 意为"笨重的；沉闷的"，stern-wheel 意为"尾轮；安装在船尾的螺旋桨（用于推动船只前进）"。

751. begrimed：污秽的；肮脏的。这里倒没有什么贬义，应该只是说"烧锅炉的蒸汽船本身会被烟灰弄得脏兮兮的"而已。

steamboat, like a sluggish beetle crawling on the floor of a lofty portico[752]. It made you feel very small, very lost, and yet it was not altogether depressing[753], that feeling. After all, if you were small, the grimy beetle crawled on—which was just what you wanted it to do. Where the pilgrims imagined it crawled to I don't know. To some place where they expected to get something[754]. I bet! For me it crawled towards Kurtz—exclusively; but when the steam-pipes started leaking[755] we crawled very slow. The reaches opened before us and closed behind, as if the forest had stepped leisurely across the water[756] to bar the way for our return. We penetrated deeper and deeper into the heart of darkness. It was very quiet there. At night sometimes the roll of drums behind the curtain of trees would run up the river and remain sustained faintly, as if hovering in the air high over our heads, till the first break of day. Whether it meant war, peace, or prayer we could not tell. The dawns were heralded by the descent of a chill stillness; the wood-cutters[757] slept, their

---

752. a sluggish beetle crawling on the floor of a lofty portico：一只在巍峨的廊柱下贴着地面缓缓爬行的小甲虫。sluggish 意为 "缓慢的；懒洋洋的"，crawl 意为 "爬行；缓慢移动"，portico 意为 "有圆柱的门廊；柱廊"。

753. depressing：令人沮丧的。

754. where they expected to get something：那个能让他们捞得到东西的地方。something 在这里暗指象牙和财富。

755. leak：渗漏。蒸汽管道会漏气，这也说明汽船确实很廉价。

756. stepped leisurely across the water：悠然跨过河面。这里是形容回首远望，两岸的树林似乎又合拢起来，挡住了河面。

757. wood-cutters：伐木工。马洛他们的汽船在出发时招聘了一批黑人上船帮工，白人以铜丝作为工资，让黑人们在船上干一些伐木、烧锅炉、测水深、掌舵等工作，主要以体力活为主。

fires burned low; the snapping of a twig would make you start. We were wanderers on a prehistoric earth, on an earth that wore the aspect of an unknown planet[758]. We could have fancied ourselves the first of men taking possession of an accursed inheritance[759], to be subdued[760] at the cost of profound anguish and of excessive toil[761]. But suddenly, as we struggled round a bend[762], there would be a glimpse of rush walls, of peaked grass-roofs, a burst of yells, a whirl of black limbs, a mass of hands clapping of feet stamping, of bodies swaying, of eyes rolling, under the droop of heavy and motionless foliage. The steamer toiled along slowly on the edge of a black and incomprehensible frenzy. The prehistoric man was cursing us, praying to us, welcoming us—who could tell? We

---

758. wore the aspect of an unknown planet：带着一副未知行星的面貌；看上去就好像一个陌生的星球。

759. taking possession of an accursed inheritance：接收这份被诅咒的遗产。这里是说非洲大地的面貌仿佛史前星球，如此荒蛮又如此陌生，在这片土地上蕴藏着无尽的资源和财富，可以说是这个星球赠给我们的一份丰饶的遗产；但是与这份遗产相伴而来的，还有酷烈的气候，潜藏的瘟疫，毒蛇，猛兽，沼泽，湍流等等致命的危险——这就是来自这片土地的诅咒。take possession of 意为"拥有；占有"，accursed 意为"被诅咒的；可憎的"，inheritance 意为"继承物；遗产"。

760. subdue：抑制；镇压；制服。这里指的是"消除非洲大地上的这些诅咒"。

761. at the cost...excessive toil：以极深的苦痛和极大的辛劳为代价。这里是说，想要真正拥抱非洲广袤的资源而消弭其中的诅咒（比如说兴修铁路，建设城市，普及疫苗等），人们必须付出极大的痛苦（有的人会在开发的过程中死去）和极大的辛劳（开发的过程本身就意味着巨大的工作量）。at the cost of 意为"以……为代价"，anguish 意为"极度痛苦"，toil 意为"（长时间地）苦干；（体力上的）苦工"。

762. struggled round a bend：艰难地转过一个河湾。struggle 说的是汽船转弯的时候，船长必须全神贯注地努力进行各种操作的样子。

were cut off from the comprehension of our surroundings[763]; we glided past like phantoms[764], wondering and secretly appalled[765], as sane men[766] would be before an enthusiastic outbreak in a madhouse[767]. We could not understand because we were too far[768] and could not remember because we were travelling in the night of first ages[769], of those ages that are gone, leaving hardly a sign — and no memories.

"The earth seemed unearthly. We are accustomed to look upon the shackled form of a conquered monster[770], but there — there you could look at a thing monstrous and free. It was unearthly, and the men were — No, they were not inhuman. Well,

---

763. were cut...our surroundings：我们完全无法理解周围的环境 / 与环境格格不入。也就是说，黑人们的呼叫和舞蹈，是那些白人所无法理解的。

764. glided past like phantoms：像幽灵一样滑过。这里是说，白人因为不能理解黑人行为的含义，所以无法与黑人交流；他们只好一声不响地开着汽船从这舞蹈着的黑色人群眼前滑走。

765. secretly appalled：心里暗暗地恐惧。无法交流必然会引起恐惧和戒备。

766. sane men：神智正常的人。白人认为自己是正常人，而他们所无法理解的黑人，自然就好像"疯人"（insane men）一样。

767. an enthusiastic outbreak in a madhouse：疯人院里的狂欢鼓噪。

768. too far：这里应该不是说汽船距离岸边太远，由于看不清而无法理解。这里的 too far 是抽象含义，意思是"天差地别"，汽船上的白人和原始部落的黑人之间有着不可逾越的鸿沟，相互之间无法理解；这是由于不同的地理条件和历史文化所造成的。

769. the night of first ages：人类最初那黑暗蒙昧的年代。这一段最后的几句话被直接引用，成为 2005 年彼得·杰克逊导演的电影《金刚》里的一段旁白。

770. the shackled form of a conquered monster：被降伏了的怪物那戴着镣铐的形象。这里指的是顺从于白人命令的野蛮人，或者是丛林里被开垦出来的土地等。monster 在这里的意思是"充满了非洲野性的事物（或人）"。

you know, that was the worst of it—this suspicion of their not being inhuman[771]. It would come slowly to one[772]. They howled and leaped[773], and spun, and made horrid faces; but what thrilled you was just the thought of their humanity—like yours—the thought of your remote kinship with this wild and passionate uproar[774]. Ugly[775]. Yes, it was ugly enough; but if you were man enough you

---

771. this suspicion of their not being inhuman：怀疑他们并非没有人性，即，产生出"莫非他们也是有人性的"这种怀疑。这里是说，第一眼看到非洲部落黑人们的野蛮舞蹈，白人的第一反应就会是"啊，他们根本就不像人。他们就好像动物一样。他们只有野性，没有人性"。这种武断的看法也暗含着白人的种族优越感。但是一个真正具有平等心和公正态度的白人，会慢慢地通过黑人的舞蹈和他们的呼叫中所包含的丰富意蕴，与他们产生共鸣，体会到他们的喜怒哀乐，意识到他们也有着人类的智慧和感情——他们也有人性。这种"莫非他们也有人性"的怀疑，颠覆了大多数傲慢的白人对于黑人近乎偏见的认知，因此作者用 that was the worst of it 来表达自己对于那些傲慢无知的白人的讽刺。任何种族都是不分优劣的，黑人中有能力优秀且见识远卓的人，白人中也有愚蠢无能、贪婪懦弱的人。

772. It would come slowly to one：英译汉很重要的一点是弄清楚代词的指代对象。这里的 it 指代的是 this suspicion，也就是说，"慢慢地，你就会产生这种怀疑了"。

773. leap：跳跃。顺便说一句，英文词汇丰富，很多意义相近的词可以粗略划归同一个语义场中，但是具体来看它们又有着细微的不同，需要在使用中加以注意。例如表示"跳跃"，就有 jump、leap、hop、skip 等。

774. your remote...passionate uproar：你的远祖（你在原始时代的远亲）也曾这样狂野而又热情地吼叫。这里是说，白人和黑人都来自共同的远祖，在原始时代，他们共同的祖先就是这样野性昂扬、热情坦率（但是现代的白人，随着所谓"文明的进步"，很多人都变得优雅而又虚伪）。uproar 意为"骚乱；喧嚣"，可以指一片混乱的景象，也可以指一片混乱的声音。

775. Ugly：真丑陋。这是自恃优雅、实则虚伪的白人见到非洲舞蹈的第一反应，可以想象得出他们用鼻子不屑地哼出"Ugly"的样子。而这个词恰恰反映出他们自己内心的 Ugly——傲慢，无知，虚伪，丑陋。这里也是作者的一种讽刺笔法。

would admit to yourself that there was in you just the faintest trace of a response to the terrible frankness of that noise, <u>a dim suspicion of there being a meaning in it</u>[776] which you—you so remote from the night of first ages—could comprehend. And why not? <u>The mind of man is capable of anything</u>[777]—because everything is in it, all the past as well as all the future. What was there after all? Joy, fear, sorrow, devotion, valour, rage—who can tell?—but truth—truth stripped of its cloak of time[778]. <u>Let the fool gape and shudder</u>[779]—the <u>man</u>[780] knows, and can <u>look on without a wink</u>[781].

---

776. a dim suspicion of there being a meaning in it: 对于"那吼叫声中能有什么意义吗"这个问题的<u>一丝</u>怀疑。化译为"你似乎听懂了那野性的声音里所包含的某种意义"。

777. The mind of man is capable of anything: 人类的思想是无所不能的／是能够驾驭一切的。意思是，怎会有什么东西是人类的思想所不能理解的呢？那看似野蛮的非洲舞蹈，怎可能真的是什么完全让人无法理解的事物？（如果非要说"无法理解"，那也只是那些傲慢无知的白人在"矫情"罢了）

778. truth stripped of its cloak of time: 那褪去了时间的外衣的真实。这里指的是人类真实自然的情感宣泄，比如说那热情而又喧嚣的非洲舞蹈。马洛所目睹的散发着原始气息的黑人舞蹈，正是黑人们内心的情感流露，它代表着真实；而那些"优雅精致"的白人，如果褪去时间的外衣，让他们也回到祖先的原始时代，他们也会和眼前的黑人一样，跳着狂野奔放的舞蹈，发出直抒胸臆的吼叫。但是由于"时间的外衣"，他们的这份真实已经被重重包裹，几乎完全看不到了。

779. Let the fool gape and shudder: 让那些傻子们张口结舌、惊慌失措去吧。the fool 在这里指的是那些优雅精致、傲慢自负，实际上愚蠢无知、虚伪做作的白人。面对那些狂野奔放的黑人，他们只会失惊倒怪，用藐视的口气和"ugly"的评价来显示自己的"高贵"。

780. the man: 真正的人。这里的 the man 和上句的 the fool 相对，指的是内心真实而纯粹的、真正的人。

781. look on without a wink: 坦然从容地旁观。without a wink 意为"不眨眼睛；坦然地"，和上文 gape and shudder（目瞪口呆、浑身打战）形成鲜明的对比。

But he must at least be as much of a man as these on the shore[782]. He must meet that truth with his own true stuff[783] —with his own inborn strength[784]. Principles won't do[785]. Acquisitions[786], clothes, pretty rags—rags that would fly off at the first good shake. No; you want a deliberate belief. An appeal to me in this fiendish row[787] —is there? Very well; I hear; I admit, but I have a voice[788], too, and for good or evil mine is the speech that cannot be silenced[789]. Of course, a fool, what with sheer fright and fine

---

782. be as much of a man as these on the shore：和那些河岸上的舞者一样，是一个内心真实而纯粹的、真正的人。

783. his own true stuff：他的真实的内心；真实的自我。

784. his own inborn strength：他（内心深处）那与生俱来的力量。

785. Principles won't do：（想要真正理解并欣赏黑人舞蹈中的那种原始的力量和真实的美）用什么原则啊、主义啊，是行不通的。因为 Principles 也是人类后天搞出来的东西，而不是人类与生俱来的真实内在——比如人性中最朴素的真善美。

786. acquisition：获取的财富；习得的知识。这些东西也都是后天通过一些手段才取得的。

787. An appeal to me in this fiendish row：在这可怕的吼声里面，含着一种对我的呼吁／召唤。这里是说，黑人那原始的呼喊和歌唱，在马洛听来极富动人的力量，令他深受感染；他似乎觉得他们的吼声是一种召唤，一种邀请，他们在邀他一起加入这醅畅淋漓的呼喊中来，或者想要让他对这呼喊有所回应。联系下文，将此句化译为"那凶悍的吼叫正是他们向我发出的邀请"。

788. I have a voice：我也要发出自己的声音。这里马洛的 voice 是对黑人的 fiendish row 的回应，也就是说马洛要发表自己对黑人的这种 fiendish row 的看法。

789. mine is the speech that cannot be silenced：mine 指的是 my voice。这句的意思是"我的话绝不能不说出来"。这里有两种理解，一是"谁也夺不走我发言的权利"，二是"我自己一定要说出来，我绝不能让自己缄默不言"。结合下文，第二种理解可能是对的。

sentiments, is always safe. Who's that grunting? You wonder I didn't go ashore for a howl and a dance? Well, no—I didn't. Fine sentiments, you say? <u>Fine sentiments, be hanged</u>[790]! I had no time. I had to mess about with white-lead and strips of woolen blanket helping to put bandages on those leaky steam-pipes—I tell you. I had to watch the steering, and circumvent those snags, and get the tin-pot along by hook or by crook. There <u>was surface-truth enough</u>[791] in these things to save a wiser man. And between whiles I had to look after the savage who was fireman. He was <u>an improved specimen</u>[792]; he could fire up a vertical boiler. He was there below me, and, upon my word, to look at him was as edifying as seeing a dog in a parody of breeches and a feather hat, walking on his hind-legs. A few months of training had done for that really fine chap. He squinted at the steam-gauge and at the water-gauge with an evident effort of intrepidity—and he had filed teeth, too, the poor devil, and the wool of his pate shaved into queer patterns, and three ornamental scars on each of his cheeks.

---

790. Fine sentiments, be hanged：船员朋友猜测马洛既然这么欣赏黑人的歌舞但是自己却又不去和他们一起唱跳，莫非是由于马洛其实也高雅精致（嘴上说得好听，其实心里也还是有种优越感）？这种猜测或者玩笑话令马洛深感不忿，于是回答道"去他妈的高雅"，表示自己绝不是口是心非的人。

791. was surface-truth enough：（这事情）足够明显的。surface-truth 在这里是形容词，意为"只不过像表面的事实那样简单明了"。这里是解释马洛为什么没时间（因而没有上岸去唱歌跳舞），因为他太忙了，船上的工作很多——就这么简单。

792. an improved specimen：一个经过教化改良的样本；一个开化了不少的野人。specimen 意为"样品；标本"，这里指的是"野人当中的一个"。

He ought to have been clapping his hands and stamping his feet on the bank[793], instead of which he was hard at work, a thrall to strange witchcraft[794], full of improving knowledge. He was useful because he had been instructed; and what he knew was this—that should the water in that transparent thing disappear, the evil spirit inside the boiler[795] would get angry through the greatness of his thirst, and take a terrible vengeance. So he sweated and fired up and watched the glass fearfully (with an impromptu charm, made of rags, tied to his arm, and a piece of polished bone, as big as a watch, stuck flatways through his lower lip), while the wooded banks slipped past us slowly, the short noise was left behind, the interminable miles of silence—and we crept on, towards Kurtz. But the snags were thick, the water was treacherous and shallow, the boiler seemed indeed to have a sulky devil in it[796], and thus neither that fireman nor I had any time to peer into our

---

793. clapping his...on the bank：在河岸上拍手跺脚。这里是说如果黑人小伙子不是被马洛他们招聘上船工作，他现在很可能还过着原始部落的生活。

794. a thrall to strange witchcraft：被奇异的巫术所控制的奴隶，指的是黑人小伙子在按照科学原理做着他周而复始的烧锅炉工作。thrall 在这里意为"奴隶"。

795. the evil spirit inside the boiler：锅炉里的那个魔鬼。因为野人的头脑里没有知识基础，所以马洛他们无法通过科学原理教他怎样看管锅炉，所以就编了个故事来让他学会操作。如果锅炉里的水烧干了，锅炉就会干烧甚至爆炸，马洛他们就说这是"因为锅炉里有一个魔鬼，它口渴了就会发怒，所以那个透明玩意儿里面没水了可绝对不行"。

796. have a sulky devil in it：（锅炉）里面有一个脸色越来越阴沉的魔鬼，也就是说水位指示表的水一旦变少，野人司炉工就会想象着锅炉里面的魔鬼脸色阴沉，即将发怒。

creepy thoughts[797].

"Some fifty miles below the Inner Station we came upon a hut of reeds, an inclined and melancholy pole[798], with the unrecognizable tatters of what had been a flag of some sort flying from it, and a neatly stacked wood-pile. This was unexpected. We came to the bank, and on the stack of firewood found a flat piece of board with some faded pencil-writing on it. When deciphered it said: 'Wood for you. Hurry up. Approach cautiously.' There was a signature, but it was illegible—not Kurtz—a much longer word[799]. 'Hurry up.' Where? Up the river? 'Approach cautiously.' We had not done so. But the warning could not have been meant for[800] the place where it could be only found after approach.

---

797. peer into our creepy thoughts：窥视心中的恐惧 / 那些可怕的想法。指的是心里时不时会闪过一些可怕的念头，比如说野人司炉工会想到锅炉里的魔鬼，马洛会想到一旦触礁，汽船就会沉没，等等。这说明每个人都在全神贯注地努力工作，没时间去胡思乱想那些心中恐惧的事情了。

798. an inclined and melancholy pole：一根斜斜插着的孤独的旗杆。melancholy意为"多愁善感的；令人悲哀的"，但是中文里似乎无法和"旗杆"搭配（"忧郁的旗杆"这种表达不常见），因此译为"孤独的"；其中"悲哀、忧伤"的意味，是通过整个句子发散出来的。

799. a much longer word：这里是说，木板上的签名虽然辨认不出，但肯定不是 Kurtz，因为这个签名明显要比 Kurtz 长得多。读到后文我们就会知道，这是一个俄国人的名字，俄语人名一般都比较长。

800. been meant for：一般意为"命中注定"，这里是"意味着；指的是"的意思。就是说，马洛他们猜测 "Approach cautiously" 这句警告到底指的是approach 什么地方。如果指的是当下这个地方，那么马洛他们已经站在这里了，来时他们也没有"当心"过，而且他们不仅 approach 了而且都 reach 了才看到警告，那么这句警告已经毫无意义了。所以马洛推测一定不是指的当下这里。那么是靠近哪里要当心呢？马洛觉得可能是指上游的贸易站。

Something was wrong above. But what—and how much? That was the question. We commented adversely[801] upon the imbecility of that telegraphic style. The bush around said nothing, and would not let us look very far, either. A torn curtain of red twill hung in the doorway of the hut, and flapped sadly[802] in our faces. The dwelling was dismantled; but we could see a white man had lived there not very long ago. There remained a rude table—a plank on two posts; a heap of rubbish reposed in a dark corner, and by the door I picked up a book. It had lost its covers, and the pages had been thumbed into a state of extremely dirty softness; but the back had been lovingly stitched afresh with white cotton thread, which looked clean yet. It was an extraordinary find. Its title was, An Inquiry into some Points of Seamanship[803], by a man Towser, Towson—some such name—Master in his Majesty's Navy[804].

---

801. commented adversely：用负面的语言评论。这里是说马路他们对着这个语焉不详、让人摸不着头脑的警示牌发了一通牢骚。

802. flapped sadly：悲伤地拍动着。这里和上文的 melancholy pole 一样，都是直接将人物的感情附着在客观事物上，翻译的时候将两者拆开来可能更符合汉语表达习惯。

803. An Inquiry...Seamanship：意思是"航海术要领的探索 / 航海术指要（旨要）"，译为《航海术提挈》，是为了营造一种历史时代感，呼应文中所说"这本书是六十年前出版的"。

804. Master in his Majesty's Navy：皇家海军的船长。Master 在这里指的是"船长"。his Majesty 意味着小说中那位陶森船长的活跃时期的统治者是"英国国王"而非"英国女王"。顺便一提，康拉德（生卒年：1857—1924）主要生活在维多利亚女王（1837-1901 在位）、爱德华七世（1901—1910 在位）和乔治五世（1910—1936 在位）时代，《黑暗之心》成书年代为 1899—1902 年，正在 her Majesty 转换为 his Majesty 期间。这可能对作者在小说中的选词有一定影响。

The matter looked dreary reading enough, with illustrative diagrams and repulsive tables of figures, and the copy was sixty years old. I handled this amazing antiquity with the greatest possible tenderness, lest it should dissolve in my hands. Within, Towson or Towser was inquiring earnestly into the breaking strain of ships' chains and tackle, and other such matters. Not a very enthralling book; but at the first glance you could see there a singleness of intention, an honest concern for the right way of going to work, which made these humble pages, thought out so many years ago, luminous with another than a professional light. The simple old sailor, with his talk of chains and purchases, made me forget the jungle and the pilgrims in a delicious sensation of having come upon something unmistakably real[805]. Such a book being there was wonderful enough; but still more astounding were the notes pencilled in the margin, and plainly referring to the text. I couldn't believe my eyes! They were in cipher! Yes, it looked like cipher. Fancy a man lugging with him a book of that description into this nowhere and studying it—and making notes—in cipher at that! It was an extravagant mystery.

"I had been dimly aware for some time of a worrying noise, and when I lifted my eyes I saw the wood-pile was gone, and the manager, aided by all the pilgrims, was shouting at me from the riverside. I slipped the book into my pocket. I assure you to leave

---

805. come upon something unmistakably real：遇到了具有如此无可辩驳的真实性的东西。正直的马洛热爱真善美的东西，尤其是"真"——真正的知识和踏实的工作，都代表了"真"。

off reading was like tearing myself away[806] from the shelter of an old and solid friendship[807].

"I started the lame engine ahead. 'It must be this miserable trader[808] — this intruder,' exclaimed the manager, looking back malevolently at the place we had left. 'He must be English,' I said. 'It will not save him from getting into trouble[809] if he is not careful,' muttered the manager darkly. I observed with assumed innocence[810] that no man was safe from trouble in this world.

"The current was more rapid now, the steamer seemed at her last gasp, the stern-wheel flopped languidly, and I caught myself listening on tiptoe[811] for the next beat of the boat, for in sober truth I expected the wretched thing to give up every moment. It was like watching the last flickers of a life. But still we crawled[812]. Sometimes I would pick out a tree a little way ahead to measure

---

806. tearing myself away：把我拉出去；勉强离开；强迫自己离开某个地方或某个人。tear 在这里意为"撕扯；强拉"。

807. the shelter of an old and solid friendship：知心老友的家。这里的英文含义其实很抽象，中文则以具象化的语言对应之。

808. this miserable trader：那个晦气的（象牙）贩子。miserable 意为"糟糕的；使人痛苦的；乖戾的"。

809. save him from getting into trouble：让他免遭麻烦。save 在这里意为"免于"。

810. observed with assumed innocence：装出一副天真的样子说。observe 在这里意为"说话；评论"，assumed 意为"假装的"，innocence 意为"天真；单纯"。

811. caught myself listening on tiptoe：（我）发现自己正在跷着脚尖仔细倾听（船桨还有没有下一次的拍水声）。tiptoe 意为"脚尖"。

812. crawl：爬行；缓慢前进。这里写汽船前进得很慢，是因为马洛他们正在逆流而上，受到很大的水的阻力。

our progress towards Kurtz by, but I lost it invariably before we got abreast. To keep the eyes so long on one thing was too much for human patience[813]. The manager displayed a beautiful resignation[814]. I fretted and fumed and took to arguing with myself whether or no I would talk openly with Kurtz; but before I could come to any conclusion it occurred to me that my speech or my silence, indeed any action of mine, would be a mere futility. What did it matter what any one knew or ignored? What did it matter who was manager? One gets sometimes such a flash of insight. The essentials of this affair lay deep under the surface[815], beyond my reach[816], and beyond my power of meddling[817].

"Towards the evening of the second day we judged ourselves about eight miles from Kurtz's station. I wanted to push on; but the manager looked grave, and told me the navigation up there

---

813. was too much for human patience: 对于人类的耐心来说是一件很过分的事。这里是说马洛的汽船航行得非常慢，他经常盯着前边的一棵树作为参照物，看自己又前进了多少；可是船速实在太慢了，他不得不很长时间都在盯着那棵树，任何人的耐心也受不了这么漫长的煎熬。最后常是还不到跟前马洛就放弃盯着了，于是也就再找不到那棵树了。

814. displayed a beautiful resignation: 以优雅的风度放手不管 / 退居幕后 / 听天由命了。这里是说经理根本就不为船的速度操心，一副事不关己的悠闲样子。resignation 原意为"辞职"，在这里意为"听任；由着它去"。

815. lay deep under the surface: 深藏在表象之下。这里是说，经理和库尔茨争斗的核心问题，或者说那种你死我活的残酷本质，别人是不会知道的，而且从这趟平平无奇的旅途本身也看不出端倪。

816. beyond my reach: （马洛）无从知道；无从插手。

817. beyond my power of meddling: （马洛）也无法干涉。meddle 意为"管闲事；干预他人之事"。

was so dangerous that it would be advisable, the sun being very low already, to wait where we were till next morning. Moreover, he pointed out that if the warning to approach cautiously were to be followed, we must approach in daylight—not at dusk or in the dark. This was sensible enough. Eight miles meant nearly three hours' steaming for us, and I could also see suspicious ripples[818] at the upper end of the reach. Nevertheless, I was annoyed beyond expression at the delay, and most unreasonably, too, since one night more could not matter much after so many months. As we had plenty of wood, and caution was the word[819], I brought up in the middle of the stream. The reach was narrow, straight, with high sides like a railway cutting. The dusk came gliding into it long before the sun had set. The current ran smooth and swift, but a dumb immobility sat on the banks. The living trees, lashed together by the creepers and every living bush of the undergrowth, might have been changed into stone, even to the slenderest twig, to the lightest leaf. It was not sleep—it seemed unnatural, like a state of trance. Not the faintest sound of any kind could be heard. You looked on amazed, and began to suspect yourself of being deaf—then the night came suddenly, and struck you blind[820] as

---

818. suspicious ripples：可疑的水纹。如果水下有障碍物，水面的波纹就会有所不同。

819. caution was the word：由于谨慎的缘故。或者说，由于那句警告里（approach cautiously）提到 caution 的缘故，所以（马洛就在河道中央停下船）。

820. struck you blind：让你一下子什么也看不见了。strike 表示瞬间变黑这种突如其来的感觉。

well. About three in the morning some large fish leaped, and the loud splash made me jump as though a gun had been fired. When the sun rose there was a white fog, very warm and clammy, and more blinding than the night. It did not shift or drive; it was just there, standing all round you like something solid. At eight or nine, perhaps, it lifted as a shutter lifts. We had a glimpse of the towering multitude of trees, of the immense matted jungle, with the blazing little ball of the sun hanging over it—all perfectly still—and then the white shutter came down again, smoothly, as if sliding in greased grooves. I ordered the chain, which we had begun to heave in[821], to be paid out[822] again. Before it stopped running with a muffled rattle[823], a cry, a very loud cry, as of infinite desolation, soared slowly in the opaque air. It ceased. A complaining clamour, modulated in savage discords, filled our ears. The sheer unexpectedness of it made my hair stir under my cap. I don't know how it struck the others: to me it seemed as though the mist itself had screamed[824], so suddenly, and apparently from all sides at once, did this tumultuous and mournful uproar arise. It culminated in a hurried outbreak of almost intolerably excessive shrieking, which

821. heave in：拉回；收回（锚链）。收锚是准备开船。

822. be paid out：这里指的是"放（锚）"。放锚是准备停泊。

823. a muffled rattle：沉闷的喀喀声。这里可能指的是锚链放好之后，从水下传来拉直瞬间一抖的声音。也可能是放锚的时候锚链在水下抖动的声音。muffled 意为"沉闷的；压抑的；听不清的"，rattle 意为"喀喀作响；嘎啦嘎啦地响"。

824. as though the mist itself had screamed：简直就像浓雾本身在发出尖叫。scream 意为"尖声叫喊"。

stopped short, leaving us stiffened in a variety of silly attitudes[825], and obstinately listening to the nearly as appalling and excessive silence. 'Good God! What is the meaning—' stammered at my elbow one of the pilgrims—a little fat man, with sandy hair and red whiskers, who wore sidespring boots, and pink pyjamas tucked into his socks. Two others remained open-mouthed a while minute, then dashed into the little cabin, to rush out incontinently and stand darting scared glances, with Winchesters[826] at 'ready'[827] in their hands. What we could see was just the steamer we were on, her outlines blurred as though she had been on the point of dissolving[828], and a misty strip of water, perhaps two feet broad, around her—and that was all. The rest of the world was nowhere, as far as our eyes and ears were concerned. Just nowhere. Gone, disappeared; swept off without leaving a whisper or a shadow behind.

"I went forward, and ordered the chain to be hauled in short[829], so as to be ready to trip the anchor[830] and move the steamboat at

---

825. stiffened in a variety of silly attitudes：以各种愚蠢的姿势僵在那儿，呆若木鸡。attitude 在这里意为"姿势"。

826. Winchesters：温彻斯特步枪。

827. at 'ready'：准备好了；上好膛了。这里重复 ready，似乎是在仿拟朝圣者的对话，他们尽管端着武器却仍充满恐惧，可能会相视互问"Ready？Ready？"以求获得一种安全感。

828. on the point of dissolving：就将要融化了似的。这里是说汽船被浓雾包围，轮廓越来越让人看不清了，好像就快要和雾气融为一体了。

829. the chain to be hauled in short：立刻收紧锚链。haul in 意为"拖进；用力拉或拖动某物使其靠近或进入；收（锚链）"，short 在这里可能是副词，意为"（把锚链）拉短；（把锚链）收紧"。

830. trip the anchor：这里是航海术语，意为"起锚"。

once if necessary. 'Will they attack?' whispered an awed voice. 'We will be all butchered in this fog,' murmured another. The faces twitched with the strain, the hands trembled slightly, the eyes forgot to wink. It was very curious to see the contrast of expressions[831] of the white men and of the black fellows of our crew, who were as much strangers to that part of the river as we[832], though their homes were only eight hundred miles away[833]. The whites, of course greatly discomposed, had besides[834] a curious look of being painfully shocked by such an outrageous row. The others[835] had an alert, naturally interested expression; but their faces were essentially quiet, even those of the one or two who grinned as they hauled at the chain. Several exchanged short, grunting phrases, which seemed to settle the matter to their satisfaction[836]. Their headman, a young, broad-chested black, severely[837] draped[838] in

---

831. the contrast of expressions：对比一下（黑人和白人）的表情。

832. as much strangers to that part of the river as we：和我们一样，对那片流域并不熟悉。

833. only eight hundred miles away：（船上那些黑人们的家乡）离这儿也不过就是八百英里吧。这是一种故意以轻描淡写的口气来给读者留下更深刻的印象的写作手法。

834. besides：在这里表示"而且；（除此之外）还有"，表示一种递进的意味。

835. the others：其他那些人。指的是船上除了白人以外的那些黑人。

836. settle the matter to their satisfaction：为这件事情找到了令他们满意的解释（他们似乎就已经弄明白这是怎么一回事了）。

837. severely：严肃地；郑重地。这里可能是形容黑人头领身披长衣的样子很是端庄威严。

838. drape：大块的布披垂着的样子。非洲部落的首领人物，似乎都有在身上披布的习惯，以显示地位崇高。

dark-blue fringed cloths, with fierce nostrils and his hair all done up artfully in oily ringlets[839], stood near me. 'Aha!' I said, just for good fellowship's sake. 'Catch 'im,' he snapped, with a bloodshot widening of his eyes[840] and a flash of sharp teeth[841] — 'catch' im. Give 'im to us.' 'To you, eh?' I asked; 'what would you do with them?' 'Eat 'im!' he said curtly, and, leaning his elbow on the rail, looked out into the fog in a dignified and profoundly pensive attitude. I would no doubt have been properly horrified, had it not occurred to me that[842] he and his chaps must be very hungry: that they must have been growing increasingly hungry for at least this month past. They had been engaged for six months (I don't think a single one of them had any clear idea of time, as we at the end of countless ages[843] have. They still belonged to the beginnings of time — had no inherited experience to teach them

---

839. done up artfully in oily ringlets：（头发）给弄成一个个油亮的小发卷，精心地束了起来。do up 意为 "包扎；束起"，artfully 意为 "巧妙地"，ringlets 意为 "卷发；小圈卷；自然卷曲或人为卷曲的一小束头发"。

840. a bloodshot widening of his eyes：充血发红的眼睛越睁越大。这里是形容黑人头领想要 "择人而噬" 的欲望越来越强。

841. a flash of sharp teeth：锋利的牙齿闪着寒光。有的部落黑人有磨尖牙齿的习俗。这里也是在形容黑人头领由于饥饿，对于食物（可能是浓雾中的岸上的黑人，他的同类）越来越渴望的样子。

842. had it not occurred to me that：这里是 if 的虚拟条件句，省略 if 并将 had 提到句首倒装。

843. at the end of countless ages：站在无数年代的后面。这里指的是在过去的无数年代里（蒙昧的原始时期），我们也没什么时间的概念。但是蒙昧的年代已经过去了，我们这些后来者已经开启了文明，懂得衡量时间、记录历史、预测未来了。

as it were[844]), and of course, as long as there was a piece of paper written over[845] in accordance with some farcical law or other made down the river[846], it didn't enter anybody's head[847] to trouble how they would live. Certainly they had brought with them some rotten hippo-meat, which couldn't have lasted very long, anyway, even if the pilgrims hadn't, in the midst of a shocking hullabaloo, thrown a considerable quantity of it overboard[848]. It looked like a high-handed proceeding; but it was really a case of legitimate self-defence. You can't breathe dead hippo waking, sleeping, and eating[849], and at the same time keep your precarious grip on existence[850].

---

844. as it were：意为"可以说是；似乎；好像"。这是一个插入语，其正常的位置可能应该是在整句话的最前边，即 As it were they still belonged to... 意思是"可以说，他们似乎仍徘徊在创世之初的那些蒙昧年代"。

845. a piece of paper written over：一张已经写好了字的纸。这里指的是经理和黑人们白纸黑字地签好了在船上工作的合同。over 在这里可能是含有"（写）完了；（写）好了"的含义。

846. some farcical law or other made down the river：在刚果河下游那里（指的是白人在非洲最初的据点，比如河道下游的贸易总站）制定的某些可笑的法律或者别的什么东西（规则、契约之类）。这是白人在武力保障之下强行为非洲人民制定的游戏规则，其荒谬性在于，这些规则都是完全不平等的。farcical 意为"滑稽的；闹剧的；引人发笑的"。

847. didn't enter anybody's head：（这件事）没有出现在任何人的脑子里。也就是说谁也没去想过这件事；它完全被忽视了。

848. thrown a considerable quantity of it overboard：把相当多的（河马肉）都扔到河里去了。overboard 意为"向船外"。

849. breathe dead hippo waking, sleeping, and eating：在醒着、睡着，甚至吃饭的时候都闻着死河马（的气味）。

850. keep your precarious grip on existence：岌岌可危地紧紧抓住生命；挣扎求存。precarious 意为"摇摇欲坠的，不稳固的；（局势）不确定的，危险的"。

Besides that, they had given them every week three pieces of brass wire[851], each about nine inches[852] long; and the theory was[853] they were to buy their provisions with that currency in riverside villages. You can see how that worked[854]. There were either no villages, or the people were hostile, or the director, who like the rest of us fed out of tins, with an occasional old he-goat thrown in[855], didn't want to stop the steamer for some more or less recondite reason[856]. So, unless they swallowed the wire itself, or

---

851. brass wire：铜丝。这是殖民贸易公司发给黑人的报酬的形式。

852. inch：英寸。

853. the theory was：（白人的）理论是（黑人可以用铜丝自己去买吃的）；按照白人的想法/说法。这里用 theory 这个词表达马洛的讽刺，因为这个想法在理论上很美妙，但是现实中几乎不可行。这也导致了黑人船员在船上辛苦工作的同时，还要忍饥挨饿。

854. You can see how that worked：你就看吧，这事儿到底能搞成什么样。这里是马洛讽刺的语气。

855. with an occasional old he-goat thrown in：时不时就有一头老公羊出现在（经理的餐桌上）。thrown in 意为"作为额外的补充物添加"。he-goat 是公羊的意思，这是一种习惯用法和构词法。罗马城市的象征——青铜雕塑《母狼》（现藏于意大利罗马市政博物馆），其英文名就是 she-wolf。这里似乎也能看出为什么经理总是熬得住热带的气候身体健康，因为他总是吃最好的，生活条件比其他人优越得多。

856. for some more or less recondite reason：出于某些令人费解的理由。这里是指经理不让黑人船员上岸去买吃的，而他的理由也都是很牵强地编出来搪塞人的，没什么说服力。猜测一下，经理之所以不让停船，真实的原因可能是：第一，岸上的丛林都是未知之地，危险潜伏；二是，万一在岸上得到了关于库尔茨的消息，对于经理来说就会很棘手——去救的话不情愿；不去救的话有可能会被公司高层责怪。最好的办法就是，汽船慢慢地拖着时间航行，在河上转了一圈什么踪迹也没发现，然后平平安安回去交差即可。recondite 意为"深奥的；隐秘的"。

made loops of it to snare the fishes with, I don't see what good their extravagant salary could be to them. I must say it was paid with a regularity worthy of a large and honourable trading company[857]. For the rest, the only thing to eat—though it didn't look eatable in the least—I saw in their possession was a few lumps of some stuff like half-cooked dough, of a dirty lavender colour, they kept wrapped in leaves, and now and then swallowed a piece of, but so small that it seemed done more for the looks of the thing than for any serious purpose of sustenance[858]. Why in the name of all the gnawing devils of hunger[859] they didn't go for us—they were thirty to five[860]—and have a good tuck-in for once, amazes[861] me now when

857. a regularity...trading company：（作为报酬的铜丝的）每每按时给付和这家信誉良好的大贸易公司的身份很相符合。regularity 意为"有规律的事物"，这里指的是每当到了该付工资的时候就付工资，worthy of 意为"值得；配得上"，honourable 意为"声誉好的；体面的"。

858. it seemed...of sustenance：在这里，it 可能指代的是"they swallowed a piece of that stuff"，the thing 可能是指"eating"，也就是说，他们"吞下一小口面团"这件事似乎只是在做个吃饭的样子而已，而不是当真为了生存这个严肃的目的（而吃饭）。也就是说，黑人船员的食物少得可怜，他们不得不严格控制每次的分量，以尽力支撑更长一点时间。

859. in the name...of hunger：以"饥饿"这个折磨着他们的魔鬼的名义。即由于过度饥饿的原因（而吃掉船上的白人）。gnawing 意为"反复啃咬的；令人痛苦的"。

860. thirty to five：三十比五。黑人船员有三十人，白人有马洛、经理和三个朝圣者，共五人。双方人数悬殊。

861. amazes：这里注意两点，一是 amazes 的主语是前边的"Why in the name of all the gnawing devils of hunger they didn't go for us"，主语和谓语之间有两段插入语；二是注意时态，通篇基本都是一般过去时，这里的时间线跳到了马洛正在奈利号上的实时叙述上，谈的是马洛说话当时的心理感受，因此用的是一般现在时。

I think of it. They were big powerful men, with not much capacity to weigh the consequences, with courage, with strength, even yet, though their skins were no longer glossy and their muscles no longer hard. And I saw that something restraining, one of those human secrets that baffle probability, had come into play there. I looked at them with a swift quickening of interest—not because it occurred to me I might be eaten by them before very long, though I own to you that just then I perceived—in a new light, as it were—how unwholesome the pilgrims looked[862], and I hoped, yes, I positively hoped, that my aspect[863] was not so—what shall I say?—so—unappetizing: a touch of fantastic vanity[864] which fitted well with the dream-sensation[865] that pervaded all my days at that time. Perhaps I had a little fever, too. One can't live with one's finger everlastingly on one's pulse[866]. I had often 'a little fever,'

---

862. I perceived...pilgrims looked：可以说，那时候我以一种全新的眼光，意识到那些朝圣者们看上去是多么的不健康（即"健康食品"的那种健康）/不可口。马洛看待同类竟然使用了"是否可口"这样的评价标准，这个视角确实是从未有过的新颖。

863. my aspect：我的外表；我的样子（从是否可口的角度来审视）。

864. a touch of fantastic vanity：这点儿荒唐的虚荣心。

865. fitted well with the dream-sensation：（这种荒唐的虚荣心）和（那段时间我一直沉浸其中的）恍惚如梦的感受正好相称。fitted well with 意为"与……相配得很好"。

866. One can't...on one's pulse：直译为"一个人不可能永远用手指按着脉搏过日子"。这句话化用了一个习惯用语，即"keep one's finger on the pulse of..."（意为"掌握……的脉搏；掌握……的最新情况；对……充分了解"）。这里应该没有"把脉"的意思，因为把脉的习惯属于中医而非西医。这里的意思可能是"人没法总是对自己的身体状况了如指掌"。

or a little touch of other things⁸⁶⁷—the playful paw-strokes of the wilderness⁸⁶⁸, the preliminary trifling before the more serious onslaught which came in due course. Yes; I looked at them as you would on any human being, with a curiosity of their impulses, motives, capacities, weaknesses, when brought to the test of an inexorable physical necessity⁸⁶⁹. Restraint! What possible restraint? Was it superstition, disgust, patience, fear—or some kind of primitive honour? No fear can stand up to hunger, no patience can wear it out, disgust simply does not exist where hunger is; and as to superstition, beliefs, and what you may call principles, they are less than chaff in a breeze⁸⁷⁰. Don't you know the devilry of lingering starvation, its exasperating torment, its black thoughts⁸⁷¹, its sombre and brooding ferocity? Well, I do. It takes a man all his inborn strength to fight hunger properly. It's really easier to face

---

867. a little touch of other things：这里的意思是"除了发烧之外，还会染上点儿别的什么疾病"。

868. the playful paw-strokes of the wilderness：（时不时染点儿小恙就像是）这片荒野在开玩笑似的用爪子挠拨着你。这里似乎是隐隐把荒野比喻成一只顽皮的猫，把殖民者比喻成老鼠。猫在吃老鼠之前，总是会先拨弄它一番；等到玩够了，才会把老鼠一口吞掉。

869. brought to the test of an inexorable physical necessity：被置于来自生理需求的残酷无情的考验之下。inexorable 意为"无情的；不可阻止的"，physical necessity 意为"生理必需品；人们为了维持生命所必须具备的物质条件"，在这里指的是食物。

870. they are less than chaff in a breeze：比微风中的一把谷皮还要轻飘。意译为"轻如鸿毛，一文不值"。

871. black thoughts：阴暗的想法。这里描写了人在极度饥饿下的感受和思想，看过《少年派的奇幻漂流》也许能有所体会。

bereavement, dishonour, and the perdition of one's soul—than this kind of prolonged hunger. Sad, but true. And these chaps, too, had no earthly reason for any kind of scruple. Restraint! I would just as soon have <u>expected restraint</u>[872] from a hyena prowling amongst the corpses of a battlefield. <u>But there was the fact facing me</u>[873]— the fact dazzling, to be seen, like the foam on the depths of the sea, like a ripple on an unfathomable enigma, a mystery greater—when I thought of it—than the curious, inexplicable note of desperate grief in this savage clamour that had swept by us on the river-bank, behind the blind whiteness of the fog.

"Two pilgrims were quarrelling in hurried whispers as to which bank. 'Left.' 'no, no; how can you? Right, right, of course.' 'It is very serious,' said the manager's voice behind me; 'I would be desolated if anything should happen to Mr. Kurtz before we came up.' I looked at him, and <u>had not the slightest doubt</u>[874] he was sincere. He was just the kind of man who would wish to <u>preserve appearances</u>[875]. That was his restraint. But when he muttered something about going on at once, I did not even take the trouble to answer him. I knew, and he knew, that it was

---

872. expected restraint：指望（从鬣狗那里）看到忍耐。这里是说鬣狗是不可能会忍耐的。

873. But there was the fact facing me：但是事实就摆在眼前。这里是说，尽管马洛觉得黑人船员没有任何理由忍耐着焚心噬骨的饥饿而不去把船上的白人吃掉，但事实就是事实——黑人并没有扑向马洛他们。

874. had not the slightest doubt：绝无一丝怀疑。这里是说经理演技逼真，你从外表是绝不可能看出一丝他的真实想法的。这里也是在刻画经理的虚伪。

875. preserve appearances：维持表面；保全面子。即"伪装到完美"。

impossible. Were we to let go our hold of the bottom[876], we would be absolutely in the air—in space[877]. We wouldn't be able to tell where we were going to—whether up or down stream, or across—till we fetched against one bank or the other—and then we wouldn't know at first which it was. Of course I made no move[878]. I had no mind for a smash-up. You couldn't imagine a more deadly place for a shipwreck[879]. Whether we drowned at once or not, we were sure to perish speedily in one way or another. 'I authorize you to take all the risks[880],' he said, after a short silence. 'I refuse to take any[881],' I said shortly; which was just the answer he expected, though its tone[882]

---

876. Were we to let go our hold of the bottom：一旦我们从河底拔起锚来。这里也是虚拟条件句的倒装省略。let go our hold of 意思是"松开手不再抓住（河底）"，即"（从河底）拔起锚来"。

877. be absolutely in the air—in space：绝对就会飘到空中——甚至飘进太空。这句话是用夸张的语气，写出在不辨方向的浓雾里拔锚的后果。一旦拔锚，汽船将会完全开始乱漂，没人会知道它将漂到哪里去。

878. made no move：没有动。这里是指马洛没有开船。

879. couldn't imagine a more deadly place for a shipwreck：这里有两种理解，一是，"你根本想不出一个比这里更容易发生船难的致命地方"，强调这里容易发生撞船事故；二是，"你根本想不出一个在撞船之后比这里更容易致命的地方"，强调一旦在这里撞船，这里二百米深的河水、湍流、鳄鱼等等潜藏的危险，一定会使落水者葬身于此。第二种理解可能更加准确。不过这两处理解差异比较细微，翻译的时候可以不必太较真。

880. authorize you to take all the risks：授权／批准你冒一切风险（拔锚开船）。这里经理是要"把戏演到底"。正如黑人船员要"把饥饿进行到底"一样，经理也要"把演戏进行到底"。他们都在各自的痛苦中忍耐着。

881. refuse to take any：拒绝冒任何风险。马洛才不管经理是否演戏，作为船长，他必须要谨慎决断，为乘客的安全负责。

882. tone：语气；口气。这里是说马洛完全不给面子地直接拒绝，是经理没想到的。经理没想到手下竟然敢对自己这么"硬气"。

might have surprised him. 'Well, I must defer to your judgment. You are captain,' he said with marked civility. I turned my shoulder to him in sign of my appreciation, and looked into the fog. How long would it last? It was <u>the most hopeless lookout</u>[883]. The approach to this Kurtz grubbing for ivory in the wretched bush was <u>beset</u>[884] by as many dangers as though he had been an enchanted princess sleeping in a fabulous castle. 'Will they attack, do you think?' asked the manager, <u>in a confidential tone</u>[885].

"I did not think they would attack, for several obvious reasons. The thick fog was one. If they left the bank in their canoes they would get lost in it, <u>as we would be</u>[886] if we attempted to move. Still, I had also <u>judged the jungle of both banks quite impenetrable</u>[887]—<u>and yet</u>[888] eyes were in it, eyes that had seen

---

883. the most hopeless lookout：最无助 / 徒劳 / 令人绝望的瞭望。对船长来说，晴空朗朗、风平浪静是他们最希望看到的画面；风雨交加、巨浪滔天也只会激起他们的斗志。但是周围雾气弥漫、不辨东西，这就只能让船长束手无策了。

884. beset：充满……的；被包围的；被烦扰的。这里是说寻找库尔茨的旅途上充满了 / 遍布着各种危险。

885. in a confidential tone：用一种非常信任 / 亲密 / 知己般的口气。这里反映出经理阴险反复的性格，他为达目的能屈能伸，对马洛也是有时打压，有时拉拢。confidential 在这里意为"受信任的；委以机密的；神秘的"。

886. as we would be：完整形式是"as we would be lost in it (the thick fog)"。

887. judged the...quite impenetrable：我认为（尽管）两岸的丛林太过茂密（所以目光无法穿透，也就是说马洛他们看不到里面的情形）。impenetrable 意为"不可进入的；无法看透的"。

888. and yet：意为"然而"，表示转折。这里是说"尽管我们看不到丛林里的野人（因为丛林太密），但是那些野人却可以看得到我们"。

us. The riverside bushes were certainly very thick; but the undergrowth behind was evidently penetrable[889]. However, during the short lift[890] I had seen no canoes anywhere in the reach — certainly not abreast of the steamer. But what made the idea of attack inconceivable to me[891] was the nature of the noise — of the cries we had heard. They had not the fierce character boding immediate hostile intention[892]. Unexpected, wild, and violent as they had been, they had given me an irresistible impression of sorrow. The glimpse of the steamboat[893] had for some reason filled those savages with unrestrained grief. The danger, if any, I expounded, was from our proximity to a great human passion let loose. Even extreme grief may ultimately vent itself in violence — but more generally takes the form of apathy[894]....

"You should have seen the pilgrims stare! They had no heart

---

889. was evidently penetrable：却明显比较稀疏（目光可以透过；可以容人穿行）。

890. the short lift：雾气消散的那短暂的一段时间里。

891. what made...inconceivable to me：让我确信他们无意攻击的原因是……。inconceivable 意为"无法想象的；难以置信的"。

892. the fierce...hostile intention：象征着"迫近的敌意"的那种凶暴的特点。bode 意为"预示；为……的兆头"。

893. the glimpse of the steamboat：（野人们）一看到我们的汽船。

894. takes the form of apathy：以冷漠的形式表现。这里似乎呼应了马洛在海岸边的贸易站附近遇见往山顶运送土筐的黑人劳工的情形。那些劳工在苦难的重压之下，脸上全都是死一般的漠然，但是马洛对他们心存戒备，并没有和他们同行，而是躲开了他们。马洛知道，他们也许会"不在沉默中爆发，就在沉默中消亡"。马洛也因此认为，那些残酷役使着自己同类的殖民者都是"魔鬼"。

to grin[895], or even to revile me: but I believe they thought me gone mad—with fright, maybe. I delivered a regular lecture[896]. My dear boys, it was no good bothering. Keep a lookout? Well, you may guess I watched the fog for the signs of lifting[897] as a cat watches a mouse; but for anything else our eyes were of no more use to us than[898] if we had been buried miles deep[899] in a heap of cotton-wool. It felt like it[900], too—choking, warm, stifling. Besides, all I said, though it sounded extravagant, was absolutely true to fact. What we afterwards alluded to as an attack was really an attempt at repulse. The action was very far from being aggressive[901]—it was not even defensive, in the usual sense: it was undertaken under the stress of desperation, and in its essence was purely protective.

"It developed itself[902], I should say, two hours after the fog lifted, and its commencement[903] was at a spot, roughly speaking,

---

895. had no heart to grin：不敢（朝我）发笑。

896. delivered a regular lecture：一本正经地演说了一番。regular 在这里意为"端正的；一本正经的"。

897. for the signs of lifting：寻找（雾气）消散的迹象。

898. for anything...us than：这里的正常语序可能是"our eyes were of no more use to us than for anything else"，眼睛既不能用来闻味道，也不能用来听声音；现在眼睛也没法用来看了。那么它的作用就和它在别的方面一样完全等于零了（不能闻，不能听，又不能看，眼睛还能有什么用呢？）

899. been buried miles deep：被埋在几英里深（的棉花堆里）。这里是对浓重的雾气的夸张描述。

900. It felt like it：完整的形式是"the thick fog felt like a heap of cotton-wool"。

901. was very far from being aggressive：根本谈不上是什么攻击性的。

902. It developed itself：事情开始有了进展。

903. commencement：（事情的）开始；开端。这里指的是"转折点；转机"。

about a mile and a half below Kurtz's station. We had just floundered and flopped round a bend[904], when I saw an islet, a mere grassy hummock of bright green, in the middle of the stream. It was the only thing of the kind; but as we opened the reach more, I perceived it was the head of a long sand-bank[905], or rather of a chain of shallow patches[906] stretching down the middle of the river. They were discoloured[907], just awash, and the whole lot[908] was seen just under the water, exactly as a man's backbone is seen running down the middle of his back under the skin[909]. Now, as far as I did see[910], I could go to the right or to the left of this. I didn't know either channel[911], of course. The banks looked pretty well alike, the

---

904. floundered and flopped round a bend：费尽九牛二虎之力才绕过河湾。flounder 意为 "在困难或困境中挣扎"；flop 意为 "垮掉；瘫倒；（无力地）摆动"。

905. sand-bank：沙洲；在水中形成的由沙子积聚而成的浅滩或岛屿。

906. a chain of shallow patches：一长串小块的浅滩 / 沙洲。shallow patches 是 sand-bank 的同义复现。

907. discoloured：褪色的；颜色暗淡的。这里指的是水面下的沙洲，因为没在水中而显得颜色不那么鲜明的样子。

908. the whole lot：整个那一串沙洲。

909. is seen...under the skin：这里是以人的脊椎骨比喻河道中央的一连串沙洲，比喻十分生动形象。人的脊椎骨看上去正是在皮肤之下沿着后背中央一贯而下，就好像这里的一连串沙洲隐没在水下沿着河道中央一直延伸一样。

910. as far as I did see：这里基本上等同于 as far as I saw，可能是用 did 表达一种强调语气，即 "正如我当时所见；根据那时所看见的"。

911. didn't know either channel：无论哪一条河道我都不熟悉。由于那时非洲丛林和刚果河还是未开发的地方，马洛的整个航行都是在没有地图指引的条件下完成的，这是一件很不容易的事情。

depth appeared the same; but as I had been informed the station[912] was on the west side, I naturally headed for the western passage.

"No sooner had we fairly[913] entered it than I became aware it was much narrower than I had supposed. To the left of us there was the long uninterrupted shoal, and to the right a high, steep bank heavily overgrown with bushes. Above the bush the trees stood in serried ranks. The twigs overhung the current thickly, and from distance to distance a large limb of some tree projected rigidly over the stream. It was then well on in the afternoon, the face of the forest was gloomy, and a broad strip of shadow had already fallen on the water[914]. In this shadow we steamed up—very slowly, as you may imagine[915]. I sheered her well inshore—the water being deepest near the bank, as the sounding-pole informed me.

"One of my hungry and forbearing friends was sounding in the bows just below me. This steamboat was exactly like a decked scow. On the deck, there were two little teakwood houses, with doors and windows. The boiler was in the fore-end, and the machinery right astern. Over the whole there was a light roof, supported on stanchions. The funnel projected through

---

912. the station：这里指的是库尔茨的内陆贸易站。

913. fairly：这里可能是用来强调，我们刚一"完全"驶入那条河道。但是我觉得译文中也可以不必直接体现。

914. a broad...on the water：一片宽广的阴影已经投在了水面上。这里也是照应了上文所说的 well on in the afternoon。下午将近黄昏的时候，太阳低沉，物体的影子总是会被拉得很长。

915. as you may imagine：正如你所想象的（那样慢）。这里倒过来译为"你简直想象不到有多慢"。

that roof, and in front of the funnel a small cabin built of light planks served for a pilot-house. It contained a couch, two camp-stools, a loaded Martini-Henry leaning in one corner, a tiny table, and the steering-wheel. It had a wide door in front and a broad shutter at each side. All these were always thrown open, of course. I spent my days perched up there on the extreme fore-end of that roof, before the door. At night I slept, or tried to[916], on the couch. An athletic black belonging to some coast tribe and educated by my poor predecessor, was the helmsman. He sported a pair of brass earrings[917], wore a blue cloth wrapper from the waist to the ankles, and thought all the world of himself. He was the most unstable kind of fool[918] I had ever seen. He steered with no end of a swagger[919] while you were by; but if he lost sight of you, he became instantly the prey of an abject funk, and would let that cripple of a steamboat get the upper hand of him in a minute.

"I was looking down at the sounding-pole, and feeling much annoyed to see at each try a little more of it stick out of that

916. or tried to: 或者说是试图（睡觉）。这其实是说马洛晚上在那里根本睡不好。

917. sported a pair of brass earrings: 很夸张地戴着一对铜耳环。sport 在这里意为 "（引人注目地）穿戴；展示"。

918. the most unstable kind of fool: 最不靠谱的那种傻瓜。unstable 在这里指的是状态不稳定，让人不敢放心把事情交给他。

919. with no end of a swagger: 昂首挺胸，架势十足。swagger 意为 "神气十足；趾高气扬"，no end of 在小说里出现过好几次，这个表达带着点夸张的幽默，比较受到作者的偏爱。

river[920], when I saw my poleman give up on the business suddenly, and stretch himself flat on the deck, without even taking the trouble to haul his pole in. He kept hold on it though, and it trailed in the water. At the same time the fireman, whom I could also see below me, sat down abruptly before his furnace and ducked his head. I was amazed. Then I had to look at the river mighty quick, because there was a snag in the fairway. Sticks, little sticks, were flying about—thick: they were whizzing before my nose, dropping below me, striking behind me against my pilot-house. All this time the river, the shore, the woods, were very quiet—perfectly quiet. I could only hear the heavy splashing thump of the stern-wheel and the patter of these things. We cleared the snag clumsily. Arrows, by Jove! We were being shot at! I stepped in quickly to close the shutter on the landside. That fool-helmsman, his hands on the spokes, was lifting his knees high, stamping his feet, champing his mouth, like a reined-in horse. Confound him! And we were staggering within ten feet of the bank. I had to lean right out to swing the heavy shutter, and I saw a face amongst the leaves on the level with my own, looking at me very fierce and steady; and then suddenly, as though a veil had been removed from my eyes, I made out, deep in the tangled gloom, naked breasts, arms, legs, glaring eyes—the bush was swarming with human limbs in movement, glistening of bronze colour. The twigs shook, swayed, and rustled,

---

920. at each try...that river: 字面意思是"每探测一次，杆子露出水面的部分就会更长一点"，也就是说，"每测探一次水位就下降一点"。

the arrows flew out of them, and then the shutter came to[921]. 'Steer her straight,' I said to the helmsman. He held his head rigid, face forward; but his eyes rolled, he kept on lifting and setting down his feet gently, his mouth foamed a little. 'Keep quiet!' I said in a fury. I might just as well have ordered a tree not to sway in the wind[922]. I darted out. Below me there was a great scuffle of feet on the iron deck; confused exclamations; a voice screamed, 'Can you turn back?' I caught sight of a V-shaped ripple on the water ahead. What? Another snag! A fusillade burst out under my feet. The pilgrims had opened with their Winchesters, and were simply squirting lead into that bush. A deuce of a lot of smoke[923] came up and drove slowly forward. I swore at it. Now I couldn't see the ripple or the snag either. I stood in the doorway, peering, and the arrows came in swarms[924]. They might have been poisoned, but

---

921. came to：这个表达在前边也出现过，意思是"停船或抛锚"，而它的常见意思是"醒过来；恢复知觉"。the shutter came to 的意思可能是，百叶窗"恢复了原来的状态"或者是"落下了；落了下来"，也就是说百叶窗又被重新关上了。

922. I might...in the wind：这句话是一个带着幽默和无奈的类比，其中甚至还有点焦急和愤怒的口气。前文说过马洛认为黑人舵手是个不靠谱的傻瓜，这里则形象地展示了这一点。黑人在迫近的危险面前表现得十分紧张，操舵的动作也相当生硬。马洛觉得，"让这个压力之下的舵手不要紧张"，等同于"命令狂风中的树木不要摇动"，两者都是完全不可能的。我觉得作者的这一段描述生动形象，但也确实有把黑人"脸谱化"的嫌疑。

923. A deuce of a lot of smoke：一大片活见鬼的烟雾。a deuce of 上文中提到过，可能是用于强化语气。

924. I stood...came in swarms：我站在（驾驶室）门边，仔细地看着（烟雾下的河面和暗桩），而（与此同时）箭矢密集地袭来。peer 意为"凝视；费力地看"，came in swarms 意为"蜂拥而至"，化译为"暴雨般袭来"。

they looked as though they wouldn't kill a cat. The bush began to howl. Our wood-cutters raised a warlike whoop; the report of a rifle just at my back deafened me. I glanced over my shoulder, and the pilot-house was yet full of noise and smoke when I made a dash at the wheel. The fool-nigger had dropped everything[925], to throw the shutter open and let off that Martini-Henry. He stood before the wide opening, glaring, and I yelled at him to come back, while I straightened the sudden twist out of that steamboat. There was no room to turn[926] even if I had wanted to, the snag was somewhere very near ahead in that confounded smoke, there was no time to lose, so I just crowded her into the bank[927] — right into the bank, where I knew the water was deep.

"We tore[928] slowly along the overhanging bushes in a whirl of broken twigs and flying leaves[929]. The fusillade below stopped short, as I had foreseen it would when the squirts got empty. I threw my head back to a glinting whizz that traversed the pilot-house,

---

925. dropped everything：放下手头的一切。这里其实是说"黑人舵手丢下舵轮不管了（所以汽船由于无人驾驶，陷入了危险的境地）"。

926. There was no room to turn：没有回旋余地了。这里是说，由于前方的障碍物已经很近了，马洛的汽船已经没有掉头空间了。

927. crowded her into the bank：把她（指汽船）往岸边推挤 / 挤过去。crowd 在这里是动词，意为"推挤"。这个词用得很形象，因为岸边丛林密布，植被繁茂，汽船要努力贴近岸边，就好像"挤过去"一样。

928. tore：这里是 tear 的过去式，意为"撕开"，指的是前进的汽船一路劈开河岸边的茂密植被，沿着岸边行驶的样子。可以译为"我们的汽船缓缓地闯了过去"。

929. a whirl of broken twigs and flying leaves：译为"枝折叶落，四下纷扬"，a whirl of 意为"一阵旋风"，这里指的是"旋转飘落的样子"。

in at one shutter-hole and out at the other. Looking past that mad helmsman, who was shaking the empty rifle and yelling at the shore, I saw vague forms of men running bent double, leaping, gliding[930], distinct, incomplete, evanescent[931]. Something big appeared in the air before the shutter[932], the rifle went overboard, and the man stepped back swiftly, looked at me over his shoulder in an extraordinary, profound, familiar manner[933], and fell upon my feet. The side of his head hit the wheel twice[934], and the end of what appeared a long cane clattered round and knocked over a little camp-stool. It looked as though after wrenching that thing from somebody ashore[935] he had

---

930. running bent double, leaping, gliding：弓着身子奔跑，跳跃，健步如飞。注意小说中多次出现动词、名词或形容词罗列的写作手法，翻译的时候最好不要也相应地罗列词语，而是根据汉语习惯重新整合表达。

931. distinct, incomplete, evanescent：这些形容词修饰的是 vague forms of men，也就是说，那些人影先是清晰（离得远或者速度不快），然后模糊（速度加快），最后消失了（速度已经相当快）。evanescent 意为"容易消散的；逐渐消失的"。

932. Something big appeared in the air before the shutter："一个很大的东西凌空出现在百叶窗前面"。这里的 something big 指的是上面提到的飞奔的野人。他们几乎是一瞬间就扑到了汽船的驾驶室外面，并从敞开的百叶窗里投进一根长矛，杀死了马洛的黑人舵手。

933. in an extraordinary, profound, familiar manner：用一种不同寻常、深邃而又熟悉的表情 / 眼神。这里指的是舵手被刺中后不敢相信的样子。这里也同样需要处理词语罗列的情况。

934. hit the wheel twice：两次撞上舵轮，很有可能是撞上之后又反弹了一下。

935. wrenching that thing from somebody ashore：从岸上的什么人手里用力夺过了这个东西（指的是这根棍子，实际上是野人的长矛）。wrench 意为"猛拉；猛扭；挣脱；夺走"。实际上长矛并不是黑人舵手夺过来的，而是他被刺入的力道太猛，而且刺入太深拔不出来，看上去反而好像是舵手把长矛夺了进来一样。

lost his balance in the effort. The thin smoke had blown away, we were clear of the snag, and looking ahead I could see that in another hundred yards or so I would be free to sheer off, away from the bank; but my feet felt so very warm and wet that I had to look down. The man had rolled on his back and stared straight up at me; both his hands clutched that cane. It was the shaft of a spear that, either thrown or lunged through the opening[936], had caught him in the side, just below the ribs; the blade had gone in out of sight, after making a frightful gash; my shoes were full; a pool of blood lay very still, gleaming dark-red under the wheel; his eyes shone with an amazing lustre. The fusillade burst out again. He looked at me anxiously, gripping the spear like something precious[937], with an air of being afraid I would try to take it away from him. I had to make an effort to free my eyes from his gaze[938] and attend to the steering. With one hand I felt above my head for the line of the steam whistle, and jerked out screech after screech hurriedly. The tumult of angry and warlike yells was checked instantly, and then from the depths of the woods went out such a tremulous and prolonged wail of mournful fear and utter despair as may be imagined to follow the flight of the last hope from the

---

936. either thrown or lunged through the opening：要么是从窗口掷进来的，要么是从窗口戳进来的。lunge 意为"刺；戳"。

937. gripping the spear like something precious：好像握着一件什么宝物似的紧抓着那根长矛。这里是形容黑人舵手紧紧抓着长矛不肯放松的样子。

938. make an effort to free my eyes from his gaze：我费了好大劲儿才移开目光，不再和他一直瞪着我的双眼对视。

earth[939]. There was a great commotion in the bush; the shower of arrows stopped, a few dropping shots[940] rang out sharply—then silence, in which the languid beat of the stern-wheel came plainly to my ears. I put the helm hard a-starboard[941] at the moment when the pilgrim in pink pyjamas, very hot and agitated, appeared in the doorway. 'The manager sends me—' he began in an official tone, and stopped short. 'Good God!' he said, glaring at the wounded man.

"We two whites stood over him, and his lustrous and inquiring glance enveloped us both[942]. I declare it looked as though he would presently put to us some questions in an understandable language; but he died without uttering a sound, without moving a limb, without twitching a muscle. Only in the very last moment, as though in response to some sign[943] we could not see, to some whisper we could not hear, he frowned heavily, and that frown gave to his black death-mask an inconceivably sombre, brooding,

---

939. be imagined...from the earth：让人觉得是在失去了全世界的最后一缕希望之后（发出来的号叫）；或者是"追随着最后一缕希望而去"。flight 在这里意为"逃走；消失"。

940. dropping shots：（射出去之后）正在掉落的箭；或者是零零星星的（大家都停下了还只有几个人没停下）射出的箭，即"掉了队"的箭。

941. put the helm hard a-starboard：向右打满舵。hard a-starboard 意为"右满舵"，a-starboard 意为"向右舷"。

942. enveloped us both：他的目光包裹着我们，即他的目光（直勾勾的，呆滞的，散的，木的，充满不甘和困惑）同时望向我们两个人。这种濒死的眼神，曾在电影《绣春刀》结尾处被聂远精彩演绎过。

943. in response to some sign：回应着某个迹象／幻象。sign 意为"标志；迹象；符号；踪影"。

and menacing expression[944]. The lustre of inquiring glance faded swiftly into vacant glassiness[945]. 'Can you steer?' I asked the agent eagerly. He looked very dubious; but I made a grab at his arm, and he understood at once I meant him to steer whether or no[946]. To tell you the truth, I was morbidly anxious to change my shoes and socks. 'He is dead,' murmured the fellow, immensely impressed. 'No doubt about it,' said I, tugging like mad at the shoe-laces. 'And by the way, I suppose Mr. Kurtz is dead as well by this time.'

"For the moment that was the dominant thought[947]. There was a sense of extreme disappointment, as though I had found out I had been striving after something altogether without a substance[948]. I couldn't have been more disgusted if I had travelled all this way for the sole purpose of talking with Mr. Kurtz. Talking with...I flung one shoe overboard, and became aware that that was exactly what I had been looking forward to—a talk with Kurtz. I made

---

944. an inconceivabl...menacing expression：一种令人无法想象的阴郁而又狰狞的沉思的表情。inconceivably 意为"不可思议地"，menacing 意为"威胁的；险恶的；狰狞的"。

945. fade swiftly into vacant glassiness：（目光）很快黯淡了，变成了一片玻璃似的空茫。glassiness 意为"玻璃质；玻璃状"。

946. meant him to steer whether or no：无论如何他都必须（给我）掌舵。

947. the dominant thought：主导的想法。一是，这种想法当时在马洛头脑里占上风，是他最为相信的；二是，这种想法完全占据了马洛的头脑，他满脑子都在想着这件事。dominant 意为"占支配地位的；占优势的"。

948. something altogether without a substance：完全虚幻不实的东西；海市蜃楼；水月镜花；一团泡影。substance 意为"真实的、有形的物质"。

the strange discovery that I had never imagined him as doing, you know, but as discoursing. I didn't say to myself, 'Now I will never see him,' or 'Now I will never shake him by the hand,' but, 'Now I will never hear him.' The man presented himself as a voice[949]. Not of course that I did not connect him with some sort of action. Hadn't I been told in all the tones of jealousy and admiration that he had collected, bartered, swindled, or stolen more ivory than all the other agents together? That was not the point. The point was in his being a gifted creature[950], and that of all his gifts the one that stood out preeminently, that carried with it a sense of real presence, was his ability to talk, his words — the gift of expression, the bewildering, the illuminating, the most exalted and the most contemptible, the pulsating stream of light, or the deceitful flow from the heart of an impenetrable darkness.

"The other shoe went flying unto the devil-god of that river[951]. I thought, 'By Jove! it's all over. We are too late; he has vanished — the gift has vanished, by means of some spear, arrow, or club[952]. I will never hear that chap speak after all' — and my

---

949. presented himself as a voice：作为一个声音呈现他自己 / 而呈现出来。也就是说 "他是以一种声音的形式向我呈现的；他对我而言只不过是个声音"。

950. his being a gifted creature：他是一个有着天赋才华的人。his being 这种形式可以让句子充当介词的宾语。

951. flying unto the devil-god of that river：飞向河里的水神或者水鬼了。这里体现了马洛带着点自暴自弃或者由于过于激动而变得对什么都不再在乎的那种语气。devil-god 这里可能是指 "鬼或神"。

952. by means of some spear, arrow, or club：由于某根长矛、箭或者木棒。by means of 意为 "通过；借助"，表示通过某种方法、手段或工具而实现。

sorrow had a startling extravagance of emotion[953], even such as I had noticed in the howling sorrow of these savages in the bush. I couldn't have felt more of lonely desolation somehow, had I been robbed of[954] a belief or had missed my destiny in life[955].... Why do you sigh in this beastly way, somebody? Absurd? Well, absurd. Good Lord! mustn't a man ever—Here, give me some tobacco." ...

There was a pause of profound stillness[956], then a match flared, and Marlow's lean face appeared, worn, hollow, with downward folds and dropped eyelids, with an aspect of concentrated attention; and as he took vigorous draws[957] at his pipe, it seemed to retreat[958] and advance[959] out of the night in the regular flicker of tiny flame[960]. The match went out.

---

953. a startling extravagance of emotion：一种程度惊人、近乎失控的感情。extravagance 在这里意为"过分，过度"。

954. be robbed of：被剥夺，指某人的财物、权力或机会被他人非法夺走。

955. missed my destiny in life：在生命中错失了自己的（本来应该拥有的）命运，指的是"迷失了生活的目标""命运多舛""命运和某人开了个玩笑"等。

956. a pause of profound stillness：指的是马洛停下来之后，周围陷入了一片深沉的寂静。

957. took vigorous draws：用力地抽（烟）。vigorous 意为"强健的；有力的"，draw 在这里意为"抽（烟），吸（气）"。

958. retreat：原意是"撤退"，这里指的是（马洛的脸）隐入（黑暗）。

959. advance：原意是"前进"，这里指的是（马洛的脸从黑暗中）显现出来。

960. the regular flicker of tiny flame：微小的火焰（指的是烟头的火光）在有规律地闪烁。flicker 意为"闪烁；摇曳；闪现"。

"Absurd!" he cried. "This is the worst of trying to tell.... Here you all are, each moored with two good addresses[961], like a hulk with two anchors[962], a butcher round one corner, a policeman round another, excellent appetites, and temperature normal—you hear—normal from year's end to year's end. And you say, Absurd! Absurd be—exploded[963]! Absurd! My dear boys, what can you expect from a man who out of sheer nervousness had just flung overboard a pair of new shoes! Now I think of it, it is amazing I did not shed tears. I am, upon the whole, proud of my fortitude. I was cut to the quick[964] at the idea of having lost the inestimable privilege of listening to the gifted Kurtz. Of course I was wrong.

---

961. each moored with two good addresses：这里字面意思是说，（马洛的船员朋友们）都在两个安全 / 坚实 / 良好的地点上停泊。这句话的表述比较抽象，因此我根据自己的理解，将其展开翻译为"你们安安稳稳地坐在船上，整日往返于出发地和目的地之间，过着踏踏实实的日子"（这种展开来意译的方法，除非我认为在某种意义上有必要，否则一般不会采用）。比如说马洛讲这个故事的地点——奈利号，它从伦敦的港口出发，作为近海帆船，很可能其目的地只不过是英国的另一个港口城市。这样的航程相对来说很安全可控，出发地和目的地都是 good addresses；而马洛曾经去过的刚果河流域恰恰是"安全可控"的反义词。因此马洛觉得他的历险故事也许不会被那些根本没有离开过安全港湾的船员朋友所理解，例如有一个听者对他说"荒唐"。这令马洛十分不平。

962. a hulk with two anchors：一条装有两个锚的大船。一般来说大型船只会安装两个锚，甚至三个锚，目的是增加安全系数。两个锚可以有一个作为备用，另外为了防止海水腐蚀，很多时候都是两个锚轮流使用。这里是用装着两个锚的大船来比喻马洛的船员朋友们的生活又踏实又安全。

963. Be exploded：这里是一种加强语气的说法，意思是"去他妈的荒唐"。

964. I was cut to the quick：来自于 cut somebody to the quick，意为"戳到某人的痛处；刺痛某人的心"。quick 有一种"猛然传来的锐痛"的感觉。

The privilege was waiting for me. Oh, yes, I heard more than enough. And I was right, too. A voice. He was very little more than a voice. And I heard—him—it—this voice—other voices—all of them were so little more than voices—and the memory of that time itself lingers around me, impalpable, like a dying vibration of one immense jabber[965], silly, atrocious, sordid, savage, or simply mean, without any kind of sense. Voices, voices—even the girl herself—now—"

He was silent for a long time.

"I laid the ghost of his gifts at last with a lie[966]," he began, suddenly. "Girl! What? Did I mention a girl? Oh, she is out of it—completely. They—the women, I mean—are out of it—should be out of it. We must help them to stay in that beautiful world of their own, lest ours gets worse. Oh, she had to be out of it. You should have heard the disinterred body of Mr. Kurtz saying, 'My

---

965. a dying vibration of one immense jabber："一场七嘴八舌的巨大吵闹声之后渐渐低沉的余音"。dying 意为"渐渐消失的"，vibration 意为"震动；颤动"，jabber 意为"急促而无意义的话，无聊的话"。有种"生活是杂乱喧嚣且无意义的，而回忆就是这阵喧嚣的袅袅余音"的意味。

966. laid the ghost of his gifts at last with a lie：用一句谎言埋葬了他那天才的鬼魂。这里出自 lay somebody to rest，即"安葬；使安息；彻底解决"，意思是通过一句话或者一个仪式，使得死去的灵魂再也无牵无挂，从此彻底消失于世间。这里又是一次时间线的向后跳动，呼应的是小说最后的情节。马洛见到了库尔茨的未婚妻，由于不忍将库尔茨的真正遗言告诉她，马洛对她说"他最后呼喊着的，是你的名字"。这个谎言让库尔茨的未婚妻得到了宽慰，也让库尔茨从此得到了安息（马洛认为的）。顺便一提，R.I.P 也常见于葬礼，出自拉丁文"愿灵安息（Requiescat In Pace）"，其对应的英文是 Rest in Peace（逝者安息）。

Intended.' You would have perceived directly then how completely she was out of it. And the lofty frontal bone of Mr. Kurtz! They say the hair goes on growing sometimes, but this—ah—specimen[967], was impressively bald. The wilderness had patted him on the head, and, behold, it was like a ball—an ivory ball[968]; it had caressed him, and—lo!—he had withered; it had taken him, loved him, embraced him, got into his veins, consumed his flesh, and sealed his soul to its own[969] by the inconceivable ceremonies of some devilish initiation. He was its spoiled and pampered favourite. Ivory? I should think so. Heaps of it, stacks of it. The old mud shanty was bursting with it. You would think there was not a single tusk left either above or below the ground in the whole country. 'Mostly fossil,' the manager had remarked, disparagingly. It was no more fossil than I am[970]; but they call it

---

967. specimen：标本；样本。特指某一个观察对象。这里指的是库尔茨的额头。

968. an ivory ball：一个象牙球。用"象牙球"比喻库尔茨的头颅，外观上十分贴合，另外还暗示了库尔茨之所以变成这个样子，其原因正是象牙。是对于象牙的渴望让他走进了非洲丛林，并在这里染病死去。

969. sealed his soul to its own：把他的灵魂据为己有。seal 意为"封上；盖印"，这里有表示独占的意思。也就是说，库尔茨死在荒野里，埋骨于斯，最后他的血肉融入大地，也化作了荒野的一部分；他的灵魂从此就与荒野再也密不可分。

970. It was no more fossil than I am：（象牙）并不比我更像化石。因为马洛是个活生生的人，而库尔茨的那些象牙也都是新鲜采下的，因而他／它们绝非什么年深日久的化石。这里是马洛反驳经理的话。经理挖出这些被库尔茨埋入地下藏起来的象牙，抢走了本属于库尔茨的财富，还要洋洋得意地说风凉话，这令马洛看不下去。

fossil when it is dug up. It appears these niggers do bury the tusks sometimes—but evidently they couldn't bury this parcel deep enough to save the gifted Mr. Kurtz from his fate[971]. We filled the steamboat with it, and had to pile a lot on the deck. Thus he could see and enjoy as long as he could see, because the appreciation of this favour[972] had remained with him to the last. You should have heard him say, 'My ivory.' Oh, yes, I heard him. 'My Intended, my ivory, my station, my river, my—' everything belonged to him. It made me hold my breath in expectation of hearing the wilderness burst into a prodigious peal of laughter that would shake the fixed stars in their places[973]. Everything belonged to him—but that was a trifle. The thing was to know what he belonged to, how many powers of darkness claimed him for their own[974]. That was the reflection that made you creepy all over. It was impossible—it was not good for one either—trying to

---

971. save the gifted Mr. Kurtz from his fate：挽回天才的库尔茨先生的命运。这里是说，尽管部落里的黑人们把库尔茨的象牙藏了起来，但是由于藏得不够隐蔽，还是被经理发现并抢走了。库尔茨被经理欺压、掠夺的命运并没有得到挽回。

972. the appreciation of this favour：对于这些象牙的喜爱／欣赏。favour 在这里意为"喜爱的东西；（大自然的）馈赠"，即库尔茨弄到手的这些象牙。

973. shake the fixed stars in their places：把恒星从原本的轨道上震脱。这里是夸张手法，极言旷野的笑声之震撼。

974. claimed him for their own：宣称（库尔茨）归他们所有。这些争夺库尔茨的所有权的黑暗势力，具体层面可能是：殖民者；黑人部落的佣兵等。抽象层面可能是：旷野中潜伏着的死神；库尔茨内心的贪婪和残酷，等等。

imagine. He had taken a high seat amongst the devils of the land —
I mean literally. You can't understand. How could you? — with
solid pavement under your feet, surrounded by kind neighbours
ready to cheer you or to fall on you, stepping delicately between
the butcher and the policeman, in the holy terror of[975] scandal and
gallows and lunatic asylums — how can you imagine what
particular region of the first ages a man's untrammelled feet may
take him into by the way of solitude — utter solitude without a
policeman — by the way of silence — utter silence, where no
warning voice of a kind neighbour can be heard whispering of
public opinion? These little things make all the great difference[976].
When they are gone you must fall back upon your own innate
strength[977], upon your own capacity for faithfulness[978]. Of course

---

975. in the holy terror of：（自以为）神圣地对于（流言蜚语、绞刑架和疯人院）心怀恐惧。这里是说马洛的听众都是一些规规矩矩、道貌岸然、遵守文明社会运行法则的人。

976. These little things make all the great difference：正是这些小事造成了两者（文明与荒蛮）的天壤之别。

977. fall back upon your own innate strength：（人要是一旦失去了外部的约束，就只能）回去借助于自己天生的力量。这可能指的是人性。想想看，如果有一天法律和道德不复存在，那么作为底线来规约人的行为的，就只能是人自身的人性——限制自己的欲望；不可杀人；扶助弱小；等等。

978. your own capacity for faithfulness：你自己的坚持信念的能力。所谓"疾风知劲草"，在外部压力的考验下，往往才会看得出一个人能够在多大程度上坚持自己的信念。例如经典电影《烈火中永生》中的江姐，就证明了自己具有无比坚定的信念。但是也有很多人在外部条件的诱惑下轻易地放弃了自己的信念，例如为了高官厚禄而变节，为了掠夺财富而背弃自己原本善良的初衷，等等。

you may be too much of a fool to go wrong[979]——too dull even to know you are being assaulted by the powers of darkness[980]. I take it[981], no fool ever made a bargain for his soul with the devil; the fool is too much of a fool[982], or the devil too much of a devil[983]——I don't know which. Or you may be such a thunderingly exalted creature as to be altogether deaf and blind to anything but heavenly sights and sounds. Then the earth for you is only a standing place[984]——

---

979. be too much of a fool to go wrong：太傻了以至于连自己是否在犯错误都不知道 / 没能力去犯错误。如果猜测一下这句话的意思的话，比如说前文中提到的那个黑胡子壮汉，他的言行都十分残暴且愚蠢，对于这样本身就没有是非观、善恶观甚至连巴结经理往上爬都做不到的人，黑暗的势力根本不屑于让他加入（比如经理是殖民者的头领、库尔茨是丛林野人的头领），而且他也根本不知道自己究竟犯下了何等罪行（他残酷地把黑人劳工鞭打致死，但是完全意识不到这是杀人的罪行）。

980. being assaulted by the powers of darkness：正在被黑暗的势力攻击。这里可能指的是：在丛林中染病（被潜伏的死神攻击）；说谎和谋害他人（被卑鄙的魔鬼攻击）；掳掠象牙（被贪婪的魔鬼攻击）；屠杀黑人（被暴虐的魔鬼攻击）等等。所谓"被什么样的魔鬼攻击"，就是说原本清白的良心被黑暗的想法侵袭，最后完全倒向黑暗，从善良的人变成了魔鬼的一分子。

981. I take it：完整形式可能是 I take it that，意为"我认为；依我看；要我说"，表示对某事的理解或推测。

982. the fool is too much of a fool：傻瓜太过愚蠢。比如说像黑胡子壮汉那样的傻瓜，根本都意识不到世上有魔鬼的存在，当然不会主动与魔鬼做交易——因为他原本也没有一个聪明的头脑或者一颗有价值的良心。

983. the devil too much of a devil：魔鬼太精明。就好像《浮士德》中所描写的那样，魔鬼要做交易的话，必然是想要得到世人最宝贵、最珍重的东西，比如生命，良心，理想等等。魔鬼和经理做交易，用象牙换走了他做人的良心、道德和底线；魔鬼和库尔茨做交易，用象牙换走了他的生命和原本高尚的理想。

984. the earth for you is only a standing place：地球只不过是你的一个立足之地罢了。类似"超出红尘外，不在五行中"。但是这样超凡脱俗的人，实际上是并不存在的。

and whether to be like this is your loss or your gain I won't pretend to say[985]. But most of us are neither one nor the other[986]. The earth for us is a place to live in, where we must put up with sights, with sounds, with smells, too[987], by Jove!—breathe dead hippo, so to speak, and not be contaminated. And there, don't you see? Your strength comes in[988], the faith in your ability for the digging of unostentatious holes to bury the stuff in[989]—your power of devotion, not to yourself, but to an obscure, back-breaking business[990]. And

---

985. whether to be like this is your loss or your gain I won't pretend to say：我也不敢说这对你而言究竟是得是失。也就是说，如果一个人极其圣洁，完全是吸风饮露的存在，这样究竟好不好呢？作者也表示不敢评论。

986. most of us are neither one nor the other：我们绝大多数人既不是前者也不是后者。也就是说，我们既不是笨得无可救药的傻瓜，也不是高洁得不履凡尘的圣人。

987. put up with sights, with sounds, with smells, too：忍受那些景象（比如黑人劳工受苦的样子），那些声音（比如经理的爪牙喋喋不休的盘问），甚至还有那些气味（比如死河马肉的臭味）。

988. your strength comes in：你的力量开始起作用了。就是说，你要借助自己的人性和心中的信念，抵抗外界的因素对你的侵袭，尤其是魔鬼对你的诱惑。

989. the digging of unostentatious holes to bury the stuff in：挖一个不起眼的洞，把那些（不得不忍受的）东西统统埋进去。比如说，经理爪牙对马洛拉拢和威胁的那些话，马洛听到了，而且记住了，但是他不能让那些话污染自己的良心。他只能在心里默默挖一个洞把这些垃圾埋进去，不让它们烦扰自己。也就是说，"要尽量忘记它们"。

990. an obscure, back-breaking business：一项说不清道不明，但是非常累人的工作。译为"为了那无人知晓的事业鞠躬尽瘁"。这项事业，可能指的是马洛内心的目标，也就是要找到库尔茨，听他谈一番话，看看他到底能干出什么样的一番高尚事业。谁也不知道马洛内心深处的这个想法，而马洛也在船上拼命工作，为了实现目标而坚持不懈地努力。obscure 意为"难以说清楚的；模糊的；鲜为人知的；默默无闻的"，back-breaking 意为"累断腰的；使人筋疲力尽的"。

that's difficult enough. Mind, I am not trying to excuse or even explain—I am trying to account to myself for—for—Mr. Kurtz—for the shade of Mr. Kurtz. This initiated wraith from the back of Nowhere[991] honoured me with its amazing confidence[992] before it vanished altogether. This was because it could speak English to me. The original Kurtz[993] had been educated partly in England, and—as he was good enough to say himself—his sympathies were in the right place[994]. His mother was half-English[995], his father was half-French. All Europe contributed to the making of Kurtz[996]; and by and by I learned that, most appropriately, the International Society for the Suppression of Savage Customs had intrusted him with the making of a report, for its future guidance. And he had written it, too. I've seen it. I've read it. It was eloquent, vibrating with eloquence, but too high-

---

991. from the back of Nowhere：来自那个无名之地的深处。Nowhere 指的是库尔茨所在的那片丛林，那个"无名之地"。

992. honoured me with its amazing confidence：曾经以它（指的是库尔茨的幽魂，因为在马洛讲述故事的这个时候库尔茨已经死了）深深的信赖使我倍感荣幸。这里是说库尔茨临死的时候最信任的人是马洛，他把自己的一切都托付给了马洛，这让马洛感到荣幸。

993. the original Kurtz：原先的 / 最初的 / 早年的库尔茨。即"年轻时的库尔茨"。

994. his sympathies were in the right place：他的同情心总是用在正确的地方，即"他的同情总是与正义同在"。

995. half-English：半个英国人，即"有一半英国血统"。

996. contributed to the making of Kurtz：（全欧洲都在）致力于打造出这个叫作库尔茨的人。也就是说库尔茨身上汇聚了欧洲很多国家的血统。或者也可以理解为，他成长的足迹踏遍欧洲，很多国家的思想文化都影响了他。

strung, I think. Seventeen pages of close writing he had found time for! But this must have been before his — let us say — nerves, went wrong, and caused him to preside at certain midnight dances[997] ending with unspeakable rites, which — as far as I reluctantly[998] gathered from what I heard at various times — were offered up to him — do you understand? — to Mr. Kurtz himself. But it was a beautiful piece of writing. The opening paragraph, however, in the light of later information, strikes me now as ominous. He began with the argument that we whites, from the point of development we had arrived at, 'must necessarily appear to them [savages] in the nature of supernatural beings — we approach them with the might of a deity,' and so on, and so on. 'By the simple exercise of our will we can exert a power for good practically unbounded,' etc., etc. From that point he soared and took me with him[999]. The peroration was magnificent, though difficult to remember, you know. It gave me the notion of an exotic Immensity ruled by an august Benevolence. It made me tingle with enthusiasm. This was the unbounded power of eloquence — of words — of burning noble words. There were no practical hints to interrupt the magic current of phrases, unless a kind of note at the foot of the last page,

997. preside at certain midnight dances：主持一些夜半舞会。这里是说明库尔茨没有坚定的信念，很容易受到外界的诱惑。有的人因为仰慕他的才华而向他献上"午夜舞会"，他也并没有洁身自好，克制自己的欲望，而是欣然笑纳了。

998. reluctantly：不情愿地；不得不做的。这里是说尽管马洛不愿相信，但是他还是不得不承认，这些仪式都由库尔茨本人笑纳了。

999. he soared and took me with him：他带着我一起翱翔天际。这里是说库尔茨开始慷慨陈词，而马洛也全然被他吸引住了。

scrawled evidently much later, in an unsteady hand, may be regarded as the exposition of a method[1000]. It was very simple, and at the end of that moving appeal to every altruistic sentiment[1001] it blazed at you[1002], luminous and terrifying, like a flash of lightning in a serene sky: 'Exterminate all the brutes[1003]!' The curious part was that he had apparently forgotten all about that valuable postscriptum, because, later on, when he in a sense came to himself, he repeatedly entreated me to take good care of 'my pamphlet' (he called it), as it was sure to have in the future a good influence upon his career. I had full information about all these things, and, besides, as it turned out, I was to have the care of his

---

1000. the exposition of a method：方法说明；对于一种（实际操作的）方法的说明。即，库尔茨的大作文采灿烂，酣畅淋漓，可是除了这些高调的雄辩，并没有提出实际中运作的方法。只有最后加上的一句附记，似乎是在说明一种具体的实现方法。

1001. that moving appeal to every altruistic sentiment：对所有利他主义情怀的感人呼唤。altruistic 意为"利他主义的；无私的"，sentiment 意为"多愁善感；细腻的情感"。

1002. blaze at you：（强光）刺伤了你的眼睛。这里指的是这句附记的内容触目惊心，令人震骇。

1003. exterminate all the brutes：把这些畜生统统消灭掉。对于这句话中 brutes 的理解，由于马洛并不知道这是在何时写上去的，当时库尔茨处于何种状况下，因此我觉得有几种可能性。一是，brutes 指的是土著人。库尔茨先是大发利他主义的感慨，最后却竟要杀死所有的土著人，这确实令人震惊。二是，brutes 指的是白人殖民者。库尔茨目睹了殖民者在非洲的残暴行径，又无法改变他们，所以才选择离开经理的贸易站，以示与白人殖民者的决裂。后来他也确实曾下令攻击马洛的汽船，而且似乎还曾想杀死经理一行。三是，brutes 指的是库尔茨在夺取部落权力的时候遇到的土著中的反对者。后来库尔茨确实把反对者全部杀死，并将他们的头颅暴晒示众。但是不管 brutes 到底指的是什么人，可以确定的一点是，库尔茨的精神状态实在并不稳定。

memory. I've done enough for it to give me the indisputable right to lay it, if I choose, for an everlasting rest in the dustbin of progress[1004], amongst all the sweepings and, figuratively speaking, all the dead cats of civilization[1005]. But then, you see, I can't choose. He won't be forgotten. Whatever he was, he was not common. He had the power to charm or frighten rudimentary souls[1006] into an aggravated witch-dance[1007] in his honour; he could also fill the small souls of the pilgrims[1008] with bitter misgivings[1009]:

1004. an everlasting rest in the dustbin of progress：（让库尔茨）永远待在时代进步遗留下来的垃圾堆里，指的是让库尔茨的记忆随着时间的流逝而被人们彻底遗忘。如果马洛不为库尔茨发声，库尔茨确实将会随着时代的发展而彻底湮灭无闻。everlasting 意为"永远的"，dustbin 意为"垃圾箱"。

1005. all the dead cats of civilization：所有的"人类文明的死猫"。这是一个比喻，说的是如果马洛不发出自己的声音来保留下对库尔茨的记忆，那么时代进步所留下的垃圾堆（它们注定会被历史所遗忘）里，就会有三样东西：一是库尔茨先生；二是 all the sweepings，也就是其他一些没有价值的人或者事物；三是所有的"人类文明的死猫"。dead cats 的含义可能有："永远失去了开口的权利的人；再也无法为自己发声的人；沉默者"；"无用的弱小者"。英文中，人们有时会开玩笑地说"What do you do with a dead cat?"意思就是说死猫又小又没用，放着还碍事，你还能拿它们怎么办。这里可能指的是在西方强大的话语权压制之下那些命悬人手的沉默的弱小民族。这里似乎是作者借用殖民者的口吻进行反讽。

1006. charm or frighten rudimentary souls：（库尔茨）可以迷惑住或者震慑住那些蒙昧的土著人（初等的灵魂，意思是土著人的文明水准还徘徊在原始的年代）。

1007. an aggravated witch-dance：这里可能是指"狂热的巫祝之舞"。aggravated 意为"加重的；愈演愈烈的"，witch 意为"巫婆；巫师"。

1008. the small souls of the pilgrims：那些朝圣者们的渺小灵魂。朝圣者们没有崇高的理想，他们只知道孜孜求钱，蝇营狗苟，所以他们的灵魂只能用 small 来形容。

1009. misgiving：疑虑；担忧；不安。前文那个负责做砖的经理爪牙，就因为库尔茨的存在而瞻前顾后，惴惴不安。

he had one devoted friend[1010] at least, and he had conquered one soul in the world[1011] that was neither rudimentary nor tainted with self-seeking. No; I can't forget him, though I am not prepared to affirm[1012] the fellow was exactly worth the life we lost in getting to him[1013]. I missed my late helmsman awfully—I missed him even while his body was still lying in the pilot-house. Perhaps you will think it passing strange this regret for a savage who was no more account than a grain of sand in a black Sahara[1014]. Well, don't you see, he had done something, he had steered; for months I had him at my back—a help—an instrument. It was a kind of partnership. He steered for me—I had to look after him, I worried about his deficiencies, and thus a subtle bond had been created, of which I only became aware when it was suddenly broken. And the intimate profundity of that look he gave me when he received his hurt remains to this day in my memory—like a claim of distant kinship[1015]

1010. one devoted friend：一个忠诚的朋友。这里指的是马洛自己。马洛忠诚地信守了他对库尔茨的承诺。

1011. conquered one soul in the world：征服了这世上的一个灵魂。这里指的也是马洛自己。库尔茨崇高的理想和雄辩的才华令马洛深深折服。

1012. I am not prepared to affirm：我无法让自己去相信（为了找到库尔茨，真的就值得黑人舵手为此而死）。

1013. worth the life we lost in getting to him：如上，"为了找到库尔茨，真的就值得黑人舵手为此而死"。

1014. a grain of sand in a black Sahara：黑色撒哈拉（指众多黑人）中的一粒沙（指黑人舵手）。

1015. a claim of distant kinship：宣布（马洛和黑人舵手）在久远的年代里曾经血脉相连。kinship 意为"亲属关系"。

affirmed in a supreme moment[1016].

"Poor fool! If he had only left that shutter alone[1017]. He had no restraint, no restraint—just like Kurtz—a tree swayed by the wind[1018]. As soon as I had put on a dry pair of slippers, I dragged him out[1019], after first jerking the spear out of his side, which operation I confess I performed with my eyes shut tight. His heels leaped together over the little doorstep; his shoulders were pressed to my breast; I hugged him from behind desperately. Oh! he was heavy, heavy; heavier than any man on earth, I should imagine. Then without more ado I tipped him overboard. The current snatched him as though he had been a wisp of grass, and I saw the body roll over twice before I lost sight of it for ever. All the pilgrims and the manager were then congregated on the awning-deck about the pilot-house, chattering at each other like a flock

---

1016. affirmed in a supreme moment：在那个崇高的时刻（黑人舵手弥留之际）确认了（黑人和白人之间的血脉联系）。

1017. If he had only left that shutter alone：这里是虚拟条件句，意思是"他要是别管那扇百叶窗就好了"。马洛原本已经关上了窗，黑人舵手为了开枪射击打开了窗户，因而在子弹打光之后被岸上的黑人用长矛刺死。

1018. a tree swayed by the wind：任凭狂风摆布的树；只能随风东摇西摆的树。这里是说库尔茨和黑人舵手一样抵不住内心冲动的驱使，做出了不该做的危险的事。如果黑人舵手克制着自己不去打开窗户放枪，他就不会死；如果库尔茨克制着自己不去投入丛林的怀抱，他也不会死。但是当内心的想法翻腾不息的时候，他们都好像一棵小树那样，只能在狂风的驱使下东摇西摆，失去了自己坚定的立场。

1019. drag him out：把他拖出去。这里是马洛要把黑人舵手的尸体从驾驶室弄出去。

of excited magpies[1020], and there was a scandalized murmur at my heartless promptitude. What they wanted to keep that body hanging about for I can't guess. Embalm[1021] it, maybe. But I had also heard another, and a very ominous[1022], murmur on the deck below. My friends the wood-cutters were likewise scandalized, and with a better show of reason — though I admit that the reason itself was quite inadmissible[1023]. Oh, quite! I had made up my mind that if my late helmsman was to be eaten, the fishes alone should have him[1024]. He had been a very second-rate helmsman while alive, but now he was dead he might have become a first-class temptation[1025], and possibly cause some startling trouble[1026]. Besides, I was

---

1020. a flock of excited magpies：一群激动的喜鹊。英语中的"喜鹊"常用来比喻唠叨、饶舌、嚼舌根的人，而在中国文化里，喜鹊是一种吉祥的鸟，它的叫声能带来喜讯。中文里的"麻雀"才是和英文里的"喜鹊"较为对应的意象，因而这里似乎翻译成"一群激动的麻雀"更好些。

1021. embalm：涂香膏；防腐；使不朽。朝圣者们窃窃私语，说马洛立刻就把黑人舵手推下船去，毫无人性；而马洛在这里表示讽刺，尸体不推下船去，留在船上干什么？难道是要为它涂香膏、做防腐处理吗？这里也反映了马洛头脑清晰，行动力强，而朝圣者们不干实事，只会搬弄唇舌。

1022. ominous：不祥的；不怀好意的。这里是说黑人船员们不像朝圣者们那样，用什么"人性道德"来给马洛扣帽子，他们的诟病马洛的理由更让人毛骨悚然，因为他们觉得马洛推下船去的不是尸体，而是食物。

1023. inadmissible：不能被许可的。也就是说，尽管黑人船员更有理由抱怨马洛，但是马洛认为他们的理由是无法被容许的。

1024. the fishes alone should have him：只有鱼才能够吃它（人类不可以）。

1025. a first-class temptation：上等的诱惑。指的是新鲜的尸体可以作为食物。

1026. cause some startling trouble：惹出一场大乱子／轩然大波。食人从人道上是无法接受的，而且一旦开了先例，船上的那几个白人也可能陷入危机。startling 意为"令人吃惊的；不寻常的"。

anxious to take the wheel, the man in pink pyjamas showing himself a hopeless duffer at the business.

"This I did directly the simple funeral was over[1027]. We were going half-speed, keeping right in the middle of the stream, and I listened to the talk about me. They had given up Kurtz, they had given up the station; Kurtz was dead, and the station had been burnt[1028]—and so on—and so on. The red-haired pilgrim was beside himself with the thought that at least this poor Kurtz had been properly avenged. 'Say! We must have made a glorious slaughter of them[1029] in the bush. Eh? What do you think? Say?' He positively danced, the bloodthirsty little gingery beggar. And he had nearly fainted[1030] when he saw the wounded man! I could

---

1027. directly the simple funeral was over：那场简单的葬礼刚一结束。这里马洛把"推黑人舵手下船、白人和黑人船员一边围观一边议论着死去的舵手"说成"简单的葬礼"，似乎是在反衬其实这一切根本就称不上是什么葬礼。directly 引导时间状语从句（主句不一定非要倒装），表示主句和从句的动作时紧密相连的。主要在口语中使用，特别是在英国。比 as soon as 语气强些，但比 immediately 和 instantly 语气稍弱。

1028. burnt：被烧毁了。从这里可以看出，经理一行人其实根本就不想找到库尔茨。这趟救援只不过是他们出来转一圈装装样子，以便交差。他们自己能够安全回去才是最重要的。但是马洛确实真的一心想要找到库尔茨。

1029. made a glorious slaughter of them：把他们杀了个痛快。glorious 意为"光荣的；值得称道的"，在英式英语中通常用来表达人们对自己的某个行为的骄傲和自豪，例如 1688 年英国发生的一场资产阶级限制君权并建立议会制的革命，由于过程中没有流血冲突且结果十分令人满意，被英国人骄傲地称之为"光荣革命"，即 Glorious Revolution。这里朝圣者说"a glorious slaughter"，也反映出他对这场战斗洋洋得意的心态。但是下面马洛很快就用 glorious 这个词反将一军，对朝圣者进行了辛辣的讽刺。

1030. had nearly fainted：差点昏过去。这里反映出朝圣者色厉内荏的本质。faint 在这里意为"昏倒；晕厥"。

not help saying, 'You made a glorious lot of smoke[1031], anyhow.' I had seen, from the way the tops of the bushes rustled and flew[1032], that almost all the shots had gone too high. You can't hit anything unless you take aim and fire from the shoulder[1033]; but these chaps fired from the hip[1034] with their eyes shut. The retreat, I maintained—and I was right—was caused by the screeching of the steam whistle. Upon this[1035] they forgot Kurtz, and began to howl at me with indignant protests.

"The manager stood by the wheel murmuring confidentially about the necessity of getting well away down the river before dark at all events, when I saw in the distance a clearing on the riverside and the outlines of some sort of building. 'What's this?' I asked. He clapped his hands in wonder. 'The station!' he cried. I edged in at once, still going half-speed.

1031. a glorious lot of smoke：一团光荣的烟雾。这里是马洛借用朝圣者的句型来讽刺对方的话，因为他们拿着枪乱放一气，没什么杀伤力不说，放出来的烟雾还挡住了马洛观察水面的视线，差点让汽船被水里的暗桩开膛破肚。在马洛眼里，这伙人根本就是毫无用处，甚至全是在帮倒忙。

1032. rustled and flew：沙沙作响，枝叶乱飞。这都是朝圣者的子弹打出去之后的效果，子弹飘得太高，全都擦着树顶飞出去了。可见对隐蔽在丛林中的敌人是毫无作用的。

1033. fire from the shoulder：（把枪）架在肩膀上进行射击。保持瞄准、从肩膀上射击才是正确的姿势。

1034. fired from the hip：这里是说朝圣者们的射击姿势不正确，他们只是把枪拿在手里，从胯部（屁股）的高度把子弹射出去的。hip 意为"臀部；髋部"。

1035. upon this：听了这番话。意思是朝圣者们一听到马洛说"野人的撤退完全是因为汽笛的尖啸声"（顿时炸了锅）。

"Through my glasses[1036] I saw the slope of a hill interspersed with rare trees and perfectly free from undergrowth. A long decaying building on the summit was half buried in the high grass; the large holes in the peaked roof gaped black from afar; the jungle and the woods made a background. There was no enclosure or fence of any kind; but there had been one apparently, for near the house half-a-dozen slim posts remained in a row, roughly trimmed, and with their upper ends ornamented with round carved balls. The rails, or whatever there had been between, had disappeared. Of course the forest surrounded all that. The river-bank was clear, and on the waterside I saw a white man under a hat like a cart-wheel[1037] beckoning persistently with his whole arm[1038]. Examining[1039] the edge of the forest[1040] above and below[1041], I was almost certain I could see movements—human forms gliding here and there[1042]. I steamed past prudently, then stopped the engines and let her drift down. The man on the shore began to shout, urging us to land. 'We have been attacked,' screamed the manager. 'I know—

1036. through my glasses：透过望远镜。glasses 在这里指的是望远镜。

1037. cart-wheel：马车的车轮。"车轮那么大的帽子"确实够夸张的，结合下文"他的鼻子在脱皮"可以知道，一定是非洲的太阳太毒辣，晒得这个白人受不了，所以不得不用巨大的帽子来为自己遮阳。

1038. beckon persistently with his whole arm：不停地使劲挥舞胳膊向我们打招呼。beckon 意为"（招手）示意；召唤"。

1039. examine：检查；（用目光）搜索。

1040. the edge of the forest：树林的边缘。

1041. above and below：这里可能是指"从上到下／上上下下（仔细搜索）"。

1042. human forms gliding here and there：到处都有快速移动的人影。

I know. It's all right,' yelled back the other, as cheerful as you please[1043]. 'Come along. It's all right. I am glad.'

"His aspect reminded me of something I had seen—something funny I had seen somewhere. As I manoeuvred to get alongside, I was asking myself, 'What does this fellow look like?' Suddenly I got it. He looked like a harlequin. His clothes had been made of some stuff that was brown holland probably, but it was covered with patches all over, with bright patches, blue, red, and yellow—patches on the back, patches on the front, patches on elbows, on knees; coloured binding around his jacket, scarlet edging at the bottom of his trousers; and the sunshine made him look extremely gay and wonderfully neat withal, because you could see how beautifully all this patching had been done. A beardless, boyish face, very fair, no features to speak of, nose peeling, little blue eyes, smiles and frowns chasing each other over that open countenance[1044] like sunshine and shadow on a wind-swept plain[1045]. 'Look out, captain!' he cried; 'there's a snag lodged in[1046] here last night.' What! Another snag? I confess I

1043. as you please：随你喜欢。这里可能是表达岸边的白人欢乐程度之甚。

1044. chasing each other over that open countenance：（悲与喜）在那张纯真的脸上交替闪现。open 在这里可能指的是"真诚坦率；不隐藏，不作伪"。这也正和上文的 boyish（孩子气）相呼应。

1045. sunshine and shadow on a wind-swept plain：在风吹过的平原上交替出现的阴影和阳光；风云变幻。

1046. lodge in：打进去；嵌进去。这里指的是把树桩打进河里作为障碍物，以阻止汽船的行进。

swore shamefully[1047]. I had nearly holed my cripple[1048], to finish off that charming trip[1049]. The harlequin on the bank turned his little pug nose[1050] up to me. 'You English?' he asked, all smiles. 'Are you?' I shouted from the wheel. The smiles vanished, and he shook his head as if sorry for my disappointment. Then he brightened up. 'Never mind!' he cried encouragingly. 'Are we in time?' I asked. 'He is up there,' he replied, with a toss of the head up the hill, and becoming gloomy all of a sudden. His face was like the autumn sky, overcast one moment and bright the next[1051].

"When the manager, escorted by the pilgrims, all of them armed to the teeth, had gone to the house this chap came on board. 'I say, I don't like this. These natives are in the bush,' I said. He assured me earnestly it was all right. 'They are simple people,' he added; 'well, I am glad you came. It took me all my time to keep them off.' 'But you said it was all right,' I cried. 'Oh, they

---

1047. shamefully：不体面地。这里是说马洛惊怒之下忍不住冲口而出一些骂人话，有点"不顾形象"。想想马洛一路上千辛万苦，险象环生，终于才让汽船安全地来到了目的地；但是就在已经看到了岸边的时候，蓦然被告知前边还有一个树桩，而且还是被人打进去的！原来一路上那些要命的树桩都是被他们打进去的！马洛的心情可想而知。

1048. hole my cripple：把那条蹩脚的破船给捅上个窟窿。hole 在这里用作动词。

1049. finish off that charming trip：结束这一趟迷人的旅行。finish off 意为"完成；结束；了结"。

1050. pug nose：狮子鼻；蒜头鼻；翘鼻。这是一种鼻子短而上翘的形状，通常被认为是一种可爱的面部特征。pug 意为"哈巴狗；狮子鼻"。

1051. overcast one moment and bright the next：上一秒钟阴云密布，下一秒钟又雨过天晴。这里是形容俄国年轻人的神情变化很快。事实上，这个年轻人本身性格十分积极乐观，就像一个开心果，但是他是库尔茨的朋友，深知库尔茨病得很严重；一想到库尔茨的时候，他就会变得忧愁起来。

meant no harm,' he said; and as I stared he corrected himself, 'Not exactly.' Then vivaciously, 'My faith, your pilot-house wants a clean-up!' In the next breath he advised me to keep enough steam on the boiler to blow the whistle in case of any trouble. 'One good screech will do more for you than all your rifles. They are simple people,' he repeated. He rattled away at such a rate he quite overwhelmed[1052] me. He seemed to be trying to make up for lots of silence, and actually hinted, laughing, that such was the case. 'Don't you talk with Mr. Kurtz?' I said. 'You don't talk with that man—you listen to him,' he exclaimed with severe exaltation. 'But now—' He waved his arm, and in the twinkling of an eye was in the uttermost depths of despondency. In a moment he came up again with a jump, possessed himself of both my hands, shook them continuously, while he gabbled: 'Brother sailor...honour... pleasure...delight...introduce myself...Russian...son of an arch-priest...Government of Tambov[1053]...What? Tobacco! English tobacco; the excellent English tobacco! Now, that's brotherly. Smoke? Where's a sailor that does not smoke[1054]?"

1052. overwhelm：使不知所措，这里是说年轻人讲话滔滔不绝，简直要把马洛给淹没了，这让马洛来不及反应也插不进嘴。

1053. Government of Tambov：坦波夫政府。坦波夫是俄罗斯地名，坦波夫市是坦波夫州的首府，位于首都莫斯科东南 480 公里，茨纳河与斯图杰涅茨河交汇处。

1054. Where's a sailor that does not smoke：哪有不抽烟的水手。水手面对的是难以预测的危险环境和长期高强度的枯燥工作，因此抽烟和粗声大气地说话是他们的共同特征。真正的水手是坚强勇敢、不拘小节、极具男子气概的。他们的形象在 2000 年沃尔夫冈·彼得森导演的电影《完美风暴》中得到了很好的诠释。

"The pipe soothed him, and gradually I made out he had run away from school, had gone to sea in a Russian ship; ran away again; served some time in English ships; was now reconciled with the arch-priest. He made a point of that. 'But when one is young one must see things, gather experience, ideas; enlarge the mind.' 'Here!' I interrupted. 'You can never tell! Here I met Mr. Kurtz,' he said, youthfully solemn and reproachful. I held my tongue after that. It appears he had persuaded a Dutch trading-house on the coast to fit him out with stores and goods, and had started for the interior with a light heart and no more idea of what would happen to him than a baby[1055]. He had been wandering about that river for nearly two years alone, cut off from everybody and everything. 'I am not so young as I look. I am twenty-five,' he said. 'At first old Van Shuyten[1056] would tell me to go to the devil,' he narrated with keen enjoyment; 'but I stuck to him, and talked and talked, till at last he got afraid I would talk the hind-leg off his favourite dog[1057], so he gave me some cheap things and a few guns, and told me he hoped he would never see my face again. Good old Dutchman,

---

1055. no more...than a baby: (with) no more idea than a baby 意思是 "并不比一个婴儿考虑得更多"，即 "根本就没怎么考虑/想到"。这句话反映了俄国年轻人的乐观天性，他踏入了丛林的危险之地，却根本就不想想自己将会遇到什么危险。

1056. old Van Shuyten: 老范休顿，可能是上文提到的海边的荷兰贸易站的负责人。俄国年轻人为了去探险，向他索要武器和物资。

1057. talk the hind-leg off his favourite dog: 这里的老范休顿很有可能真的养了一只宠物狗/猎狗，所以俄国人才会这样说。这句话来自英语习语 talk the hind-leg off a dog/donkey/horse，意思是 "唠叨不休；滔滔不绝"。

Van Shuyten. I've sent him one small lot of ivory a year ago, so that he can't call me a little thief when I get back. I hope he got it. And for the rest I don't care. I had some wood stacked for you. That was my old house. Did you see?'

"I gave him Towson's book. He made as though he would kiss me, but restrained himself. 'The only book I had left, and I thought I had lost it,' he said, looking at it ecstatically. 'So many accidents happen to a man going about alone, you know. Canoes get upset sometimes—and sometimes you've got to clear out so quick when the people get angry.' He thumbed the pages. 'You made notes in Russian?' I asked. He nodded. 'I thought they were written in cipher,' I said. He laughed, then became serious. 'I had lots of trouble to keep these people off,' he said. 'Did they want to kill you?' I asked. 'Oh, no!' he cried, and checked himself. 'Why did they attack us?' I pursued. He hesitated, then said shamefacedly, 'They don't want him to go.' 'Don't they?' I said curiously. He nodded a nod full of mystery and wisdom[1058]. 'I tell you,' he cried, 'this man has enlarged my mind.' He opened his arms wide, staring at me with his little blue eyes that were perfectly round."

1058. nod a nod full of mystery and wisdom: 充满神秘和智慧地点了一下头。这里的"智慧"指的是知道别人所不知道的一些事情。

III

"I looked at him, lost in astonishment. There he was before me, in motley, as though he had absconded from a troupe of mimes, enthusiastic, fabulous. His very existence was improbable, inexplicable, and altogether bewildering. He was an insoluble problem. It was inconceivable how he had existed, how he had succeeded in getting so far, how he had managed to remain— why he did not instantly disappear. 'I went a little farther,' he said, 'then still a little farther—till I had gone so far that I don't know how I'll ever get back. Never mind. Plenty time. I can manage. You take Kurtz away quick—quick—I tell you.' The glamour of youth enveloped his parti-coloured rags, his destitution, his loneliness, the essential desolation of his futile wanderings. For months—for years—his life hadn't been worth a day's purchase[1059]; and there he was gallantly, thoughtlessly alive, to all appearances indestructible solely by the virtue of his few years and of his unreflecting audacity. I was seduced into something like admiration—like envy. Glamour urged him on, glamour kept him

---

1059. his life hadn't been worth a day's purchase："朝不保夕的日子；有今天没明天的日子"，也就是说他的生命始终处于一种危险的状态，稍有不慎就可能死在荒野里。或者也可以理解为，他过着极度贫困的日子。

unscathed. He surely wanted nothing from the wilderness but space to breathe in and to push on through[1060]. His need was to exist, and to move onwards at the greatest possible risk, and with a maximum of privation. If the absolutely pure, uncalculating, unpractical spirit of adventure had ever ruled a human being, it ruled this bepatched youth. I almost envied him the possession of this modest and clear flame. It seemed to have consumed all thought of self[1061] so completely, that even while he was talking to you, you forgot that it was he—the man before your eyes—who had gone through these things. I did not envy him his devotion to Kurtz, though. He had not meditated over it. It came to him[1062], and he accepted it with a sort of eager fatalism[1063]. I must say that to me it appeared about the most dangerous thing in every way he had come upon so far.

"They had come together unavoidably, like two ships becalmed near each other, and lay rubbing sides at last. I suppose Kurtz wanted an audience, because on a certain occasion, when encamped in the forest, they had talked all night, or more probably Kurtz had talked. 'We talked of everything,' he said, quite

---

1060. push on through：整句话是 "but space to push on through"，即 "只需要一个空间，让他能够不断前进"。push on 意为 "继续前进；坚持下去"，through 指的是 "穿过去；穿越那片 space（丛林；荒野）"。

1061. consume all thought of self：烧光了一切为自身打算的想法。这里是说俄国年轻人全身上下洋溢着青春的热情，他无私地帮助别人，几乎完全不曾为自己考虑什么。就好像 "自私的想法都已经被热情的火焰烧光了" 一样。

1062. It came to him：事情发生在他的身上；落到了他的头上。这里是说 "和库尔茨相遇" 这件事情发生在俄国人的身上了；他们两个就这样相遇了。

1063. a sort of eager fatalism：一种狂热的宿命感。也就是说俄国人觉得这是命中注定的，于是他就要热情地去拥抱这份命运（崇拜并帮助库尔茨）。

transported at the recollection. 'I forgot there was such a thing as sleep. The night did not seem to last an hour. Everything! Everything!...Of love, too.' 'Ah, he talked to you of love!' I said, much amused. 'It isn't what you think,' he cried, almost passionately. 'It was in general. He made me see things—things.'

"He threw his arms up. We were on deck at the time, and the headman of my wood-cutters, lounging near by, turned upon him his heavy and glittering eyes[1064]. I looked around, and I don't know why, but I assure you that never, never before, did this land, this river, this jungle, the very arch of this blazing sky[1065], appear to me so hopeless and so dark, so impenetrable to human thought[1066], so pitiless to human weakness[1067]. 'And, ever since, you have been with him, of course?' I said.

"On the contrary. It appears their intercourse[1068] had been

---

1064. his heavy and glittering eyes: 他那深沉疲顿，但仍炯炯有神的眼睛。heavy 在这里可能指的是人的眼神由于倦怠、饥饿等肉体的痛苦而变得深邃的样子。

1065. the very arch of this blazing sky: 那闪耀（着强烈而刺眼的日光）的天穹。arch 意为"拱顶；拱形物"。

1066. impenetrable to human thought: 以人类的思想（对自然造化）是揣摩不透的。

1067. pitiless to human weakness: 对人类的弱点（例如不吃饭就会饥饿，不休息就会疲倦，生老病死，七情六欲，喜怒哀乐等）毫不同情。这里是说即使有人正在经历着饥饿、苦役、疾病等等苦难，大自然也仍在以其既定的法则持续运行，并不会对任何人表现出半分同情。事实上何必苛求自然造化，即使人类之间，有时候悲喜也并不相通。

1068. their intercourse: 他们之间的沟通交流。指的是库尔茨和俄国人之间的联系。

very much broken by various causes. He had, as he informed me proudly, managed to nurse Kurtz through two illnesses (he alluded to it[1069] as you would to some risky feat[1070]), but as a rule Kurtz wandered alone, far in the depths of the forest. 'Very often coming to this station, I had to wait days and days before he would turn up,' he said. 'Ah, it was worth waiting for!—sometimes[1071].' 'What was he doing? exploring or what?' I asked. 'Oh, yes, of course;' he had discovered lots of villages, a lake, too—he did not know exactly in what direction; it was dangerous to inquire too much[1072]—

1069. allude to it：提到这件事。这里指的是俄国人讲述这件事的态度和口吻（又骄傲又兴奋，好像这就是什么了不起的英雄冒险故事一样）。

1070. as you would to some risky feat：这里省略了 allude，完整形式是 as you would (allude) to some risky feat，意思是"就好像你讲述英雄冒险故事时的口吻那样"。risky feat 意为"惊心动魄的丰功伟绩"，比如"王子历经艰险终于斩杀了恶魔从城堡中救回了公主"之类。这反映了俄国人头脑简单，善良单纯。

1071. it was worth waiting for!—sometimes：库尔茨还是值得等的——有时候是值得等的。这里是说俄国人期待见到库尔茨，可是即使在漫长的等待后终于见面了，他们之间的交流也并不总是很友好。库尔茨的精神状态不怎么稳定。但是毕竟也有坦诚友好的时候，因此俄国人说"有时候等待还是值得的"。

1072. it was dangerous to inquire too much：打听得太多是很危险的。在这里要注意 he 这个人称代词的指代对象，"他发现了很多村子，还有一个湖"，这里的"他"是独自在外探险的库尔茨；破折号后面的"他"就切换到"俄国人"了，意思是"那些村子和湖的具体方位，俄国人并不清楚；但是俄国人不敢向库尔茨打听太多，因为这样很危险——库尔茨可能会将他视为同样觊觎着象牙的竞争对手，从而对俄国人采取敌对行动"。破折号后面的"他"再次切换为"库尔茨"，意思是"虽然库尔茨发现了村子和湖，似乎是在做地理勘探，但是更多的时候库尔茨的探险还是为了搜寻象牙"。这里的指代对象的切换是很隐蔽的，译义中也不太能够明显提示读者，因此还是需要读者根据作者两次使用破折号的提示来细细体会。事实上，这里的两个破折号，其实就等于一对括号，用来插入俄国人为自己解释的一段话。

but mostly his expeditions had been for ivory. 'But he had no goods to trade with by that time,' I objected[1073]. 'There's a good lot of cartridges left even yet,' he answered, looking away[1074]. 'To speak plainly, he raided the country,' I said. He nodded. 'Not alone, surely!' He muttered something about the villages round that lake. 'Kurtz got the tribe to follow him, did he?' I suggested. He fidgeted a little. 'They adored him,' he said. The tone of these words was so extraordinary that I looked at him searchingly[1075]. It was curious to see his mingled eagerness and reluctance to speak of Kurtz. The man filled his life, occupied his thoughts, swayed his emotions. 'What can you expect?' he burst out; 'he came to them with thunder and lightning, you know—and they had never seen anything like it—and very terrible[1076]. He

---

1073. object：反对；反驳；质疑对方的说法。这里是马洛对俄国人的说法（库尔茨主要是出去找象牙的）表示质疑，马洛认为，库尔茨手里既然已经没有了货物（他自己切断了和总站的联系），那么即使找到象牙也无法换到自己手里，所以，说库尔茨是去丛林里勘探地形的，也比说是去找象牙的更能讲得通。

1074. looking away：移开了视线；别过了眼睛。讲话的时候眼睛不敢看着对方，这是一种心虚的表现，多半显示讲话人言不由衷，或者在故意隐瞒信息。

1075. The tone...him searchingly：他说这些话（They adored him 这句话）的语气很不自然，于是我就盯着他上下打量。这里是说俄国人讲话的态度明显让人感到他没完全说实话，于是马洛就盯着他看，用探究的目光施加压力，逼迫他说出实话来。extraordinary 意为"异乎寻常的；令人惊奇的"，这里指的是"有些异样的"，searchingly 意为"探究地；彻底地"。

1076. terrible：可怕的。这里是说库尔茨在土著人面前炫耀武力，而在土著人眼里，来复枪就是所谓的"雷霆闪电"，是神明一样可怕的力量。化译为"他们被吓坏了"。

could be very terrible. You can't judge Mr. Kurtz[1077] as you would an ordinary man. No, no, no! Now—just to give you an idea—I don't mind telling you, he wanted to shoot me, too, one day—but I don't judge him.' 'Shoot you!' I cried 'What for?' 'Well, I had a small lot of ivory the chief of that village near my house gave me. You see I used to shoot game for them. Well, he wanted it, and wouldn't hear reason[1078]. He declared he would shoot me unless I gave him the ivory and then cleared out of the country[1079], because he could do so, and had a fancy for it[1080], and there was nothing on earth to prevent him killing whom he jolly well pleased[1081].

1077. judge Mr. Kurtz：评判库尔茨先生。judge 在这里意为"评判；评价；批评"，更侧重于给人以负面评价。而且似乎还带点轻慢的意味，即"随随便便地评价"，好比说"这个人还行；那个人不咋地"。在俄国人看来，如果评价一个普通人，这样随随便便就给句评语倒也还说得过去；但是库尔茨先生有思想的非凡的人，他不是什么普通人，因而绝不能以这种轻忽的方式对他妄加评判。

1078. wouldn't hear reason：根本不听解释。这说明库尔茨对象牙的占有欲极强，只要是他的"地盘"上的象牙，无论如何他也要据为己有，即使别人是通过正常途径拥有的，他也要蛮横无理地抢到自己手里。他认为这里所有的象牙都只能属于他，这也呼应了前文中写过的："他就是茫茫荒原上的天之骄子了"；"一切都是属于他的"。库尔茨可能具有一种偏执人格，而且有点精神分裂。他是天使与恶魔、天才和疯子的混合体。

1079. clear out of the country：滚出这个地方。这里是说库尔茨不允许任何人在他的"地盘"上挑战他的权威，分享"他的"象牙，即使是知心朋友、救命恩人也不行。在他心里，象牙的重要性超过了一切。

1080. had a fancy for it：很喜欢这样做。这里是库尔茨威胁俄国人的话，意思是"不要以为我不敢／不会（开枪），事实上我很乐意（开上一枪，如果你还要拿走我的象牙的话）"。

1081. nothing on...well pleased：世上没有任何人／事能够阻挡得了他杀掉一个自己想杀的人。这里也是库尔茨的威胁，意思是"不要以为你在我生病的时候照顾过我，我就不会杀你"。

And it was true, too. I gave him the ivory. What did I care! But I didn't clear out. No, no. I couldn't leave him. I had to be careful, of course, till we got friendly again for a time. He had his second illness then. Afterwards I had to keep out of the way[1082]; but I didn't mind. He was living for the most part in those villages on the lake. When he came down to the river, sometimes he would take to me[1083], and sometimes it was better for me to be careful. This man suffered too much. He hated all this[1084], and somehow he couldn't get away. When I had a chance I begged him to try and leave while there was time; I offered to go back with him. And he would say yes, and then he would remain; go off on another ivory hunt[1085]; disappear for weeks; forget himself amongst these people[1086]—forget himself—you know.' 'Why! he's mad,' I

1082. keep out of the way: 避让；远离某人或某物，以免妨碍他人或让自己受到伤害。这里指的是俄国人从此接受了库尔茨的规矩，按照他划下的红线小心行事——再也不碰"他的"象牙了。这里并不是说俄国人躲着库尔茨，相反，他很希望能够尽量接近库尔茨，听他谈话。俄国人只要"远离象牙"就行了。

1083. take to me: 靠近我；接近我。这里可能有一种亲近的意味，但是是居高临下、带有一种压迫感和掌控感的亲近。就好像俄国人所说的，"你不能和他谈话；你只能听他谈话"。

1084. hated all this: 痛恨这一切。在上文中，马洛讲过罗马将军和罗马年轻人来到蒙昧时期的英国的故事，事实上也影射了很多现代殖民者来到非洲的心态。

1085. go off on another ivory hunt: 出发 / 动身开始了下一次的狩猎象牙之旅。go off 在这里意为"离开；动身"。

1086. forget himself amongst these people: 一来到那些人当中，他就浑然忘我了。指的是库尔茨先生一来到那些土人中间，他就仿佛已经不是一个具有学识、理想和道德的文明人了，他就会完全放纵自己原始的本性和阴暗的欲望，享受支配权力的快乐、享受土人对自己的崇拜，并不顾一切地狩猎象牙。

said. He protested indignantly[1087]. Mr. Kurtz couldn't be mad. If I had heard him talk, only two days ago, I wouldn't dare hint at such a thing[1088]....I had taken up my binoculars while we talked, and was looking at the shore, sweeping the limit of the forest at each side and at the back of the house. The consciousness of there being people in that bush, so silent, so quiet—as silent and quiet as the ruined house on the hill—made me uneasy. There was no sign on the face of nature of this amazing tale[1089] that was not so much told as suggested to me in desolate exclamations, completed by shrugs, in interrupted phrases, in hints ending in deep sighs[1090]. The woods were unmoved, like a mask—heavy, like the closed door of a prison—they looked with their air of hidden knowledge[1091], of patient expectation, of unapproachable silence. The Russian was explaining to me that it was only lately that Mr. Kurtz had come down to the river, bringing along with him all the fighting men of

---

1087. protest indignantly：愤慨地抗议。这说明俄国人很"护短"，他把库尔茨视为偶像，因而不允许马洛说库尔茨不好。

1088. dare hint at such a thing：竟敢暗示这样的事；竟敢说出这种话。这里是俄国人抗议马洛"竟敢判断说库尔茨已经疯了"。

1089. There was...amazing tale：这个故事惊心动魄，但是你从眼前的森林和河流的表面却看不出任何端倪。

1090. suggested to me...in deep sighs：通过凄凉的感叹暗示给我，以耸肩而结束，通过断断续续的话语，通过以深沉的叹息结束的暗示，来让我知道了这个故事的。这种可能属于无法直译的英文，应该在完全理解作者本意的基础上，对译文做出符合汉语行文习惯的调整和改进。

1091. their air of hidden knowledge：它们那而不言的神态。knowledge 在这里意为"知晓的事情"。很多故事，包括库尔茨的故事，都发生在丛林之中；丛林作为见证者，知晓所有人的秘密，但却闭口不言。

that lake tribe. He had been absent for several months—getting himself adored, I suppose—and had come down unexpectedly, with the intention to all appearance of making a raid either across the river or down stream. Evidently the appetite for more ivory had got the better of the—what shall I say?—less material aspirations. However he had got much worse suddenly. 'I heard he was lying helpless[1092], and so I came up—took my chance[1093],' said the Russian. 'Oh, he is bad, very bad.' I directed my glass to the house. There were no signs of life, but there was the ruined roof, the long mud wall peeping above the grass[1094], with three little square window-holes, no two of the same size[1095]; all this brought within reach of my hand, as it were. And then I made a brusque movement, and one of the remaining posts of that vanished fence[1096] leaped up in the field of my glass. You remember I told you I had been struck at the distance by

1092. lie helpless：（病）倒了没人照顾。这里应该不是"没人管"，可能那些土人会为他祈祷、驱魔之类，但是真正具有医疗性质的照顾和护理肯定是没有的。所以在俄国人看来那就是 helpless。

1093. took my chance：抓住我的机会（做某事）。这里可能是抓住这次机会，再劝劝库尔茨离开非洲。因为这里已经侵染了他的身心，他的身体染病了，他的精神也快要失常了。再留在这里，也许库尔茨就万劫不复了。

1094. peeping above the grass：因为墙上有几个窗洞，所以那面墙"就好像（一张人脸）从深草中探出头来张望似的"。这里也反衬出山顶的荒凉，"事实上是没有任何生命的迹象"。

1095. no two of the same size：没有两个窗洞是一样大的。这也反映了房屋的建造十分粗糙。

1096. the remaining posts of that vanished fence：那个已经消失不见了的篱笆残留下来的木桩。事实上，这个马洛猜想中的"篱笆"根本就不曾存在过，那些木桩当然也不是篱笆残留下来的。那本来就只是木桩而已——用来插人头威吓众人的木桩。

certain attempts at ornamentation, rather remarkable in the ruinous aspect of the place. Now I had suddenly a nearer view[1097], and its first result[1098] was to make me throw my head back as if before a blow[1099]. Then I went carefully from post to post with my glass, and I saw my mistake. These round knobs were not ornamental but symbolic[1100]; they were expressive[1101] and puzzling, striking and disturbing—food for thought and also for vultures[1102] if there had been any looking down from the sky; but at all events for such ants as were industrious enough to ascend the pole[1103]. They would have been even more impressive, those heads on the stakes, if their faces had not been turned to the house. Only one, the first I had made out, was facing my way. I was not so shocked as you may think. The start back I had given was really nothing but a movement of

---

1097. a nearer view：这里指的是望远镜给出了一幅更大的近景。

1098. its first result：（这幅近景）所造成的第一个结果。也就是说马洛一看到望远镜里的情景，就随之做出的一个动作——惊骇地向后一仰。

1099. make me throw my head back as if before a blow：把头往后一仰，好像在躲避迎面而来的一记拳击似的。中文中类似的表达是"吓得我差点扔掉了（手里的望远镜）"。

1100. not ornamental but symbolic：不是装饰性的（为了装饰房屋的圆球），而是象征性的（用来杀一儆百的人头）。

1101. expressive：极具表现力的 / 极具视觉冲击力的。也就是说任何人看到这一幕，都会心生恐惧——这正是库尔茨想要达到的效果。

1102. food for thought and also for vultures：food for thought 是抽象意义的，指的是那些人头会引发观者心中不停翻滚的种种想法；food for vultures 是具体层面的，它们确实是秃鹫喜欢的美食。vulture 意为"秃鹫；秃鹰"，一种食腐的鸟类。

1103. such ants...ascend the pole：那些足够勤恳，能够一直沿着桩子爬到顶上去的蚂蚁。

surprise. I had expected to see a knob of wood there, you know. I returned deliberately to the first I had seen—and there it was, black, dried, sunken, with closed eyelids—a head that seemed to sleep at the top of that pole, and, with the shrunken dry lips showing a narrow white line of the teeth, was smiling, too, smiling continuously at some endless and jocose dream of that eternal slumber[1104].

"I am not disclosing any trade secrets[1105]. In fact, the manager said afterwards that Mr. Kurtz's methods had ruined the district. I have no opinion on that point, but I want you clearly to understand that there was nothing exactly profitable in these heads being there. They only showed that Mr. Kurtz lacked restraint in the gratification of his various lusts, that there was something wanting in him—some small matter which, when the pressing need arose[1106], could not be found under his magnificent eloquence[1107]. Whether he knew

---

1104. smiling continuously...eternal slumber：在这永恒的睡眠中，不停地笑着一场无休止的滑稽的梦。这里是形容人头的面部表情仿佛在笑，也是作者借机表达对库尔茨残暴行为的讽刺和抨击。

1105. disclosing any trade secrets：泄露什么商业秘密。前文曾经写过，马洛签合同的时候被要求"不得泄露商业秘密"。这里似乎也说明了，之所以有这样的条款是因为公司的"商业秘密"太多了，而且这些黑暗的内幕，和公司在欧洲宣传的"文明进步的事业""使徒精神"完全背道而驰。这也是为什么马洛一开始就觉得"自己好像被卷入了某种阴谋"。

1106. the pressing need arose：迫切的需要出现（的时候），即"当他对某样东西产生贪念的时候"。

1107. magnificent eloquence：辞藻华丽的雄辩。这句话是说，当一个人产生贪欲的时候，他最需要的就是自制力；自制力算不上多么了不得的东西，但是有的时候确实非常重要——有的时候，一念间天堂，一念间地狱。但是库尔茨尽管可以雄辩滔滔，才华过人，但是他的言辞里从来没有出现过"自制力"这个词，他的头脑里也从来都没有"自制力"这个概念。

of this deficiency[1108] himself I can't say. I think the knowledge came to him at last[1109]—only at the very last[1110]. But the wilderness had found him out early[1111], and had taken on him a terrible vengeance[1112] for the fantastic invasion. I think it had whispered to him things about himself which he did not know, things of which he had no conception till he took counsel with this great solitude[1113]—and the whisper had proved irresistibly fascinating. It echoed loudly within him[1114] because he was hollow at the core[1115].... I put down the

---

1108. deficiency：缺乏；不足。即库尔茨"没有自制力"的缺点。

1109. the knowledge came to him at last：最后，这件事终于被他意识到了。即"库尔茨最终意识到，是没有自制力的这个缺点害死了自己"。

1110. only at the very last：但那已经是最后的时刻了。即，就算库尔茨意识到了这一点，也已经无济于事了，因为他的生命也即将结束了。

1111. had found him out early：（荒野）早就看透了他了，早就知道他的缺点了。

1112. take on him a terrible vengeance：对他进行了可怕的报复。这句话的正常语序是"take a terrible vengeance on him"，vengeance 意为"报仇；复仇"。

1113. took counsel with this great solitude：took counsel with 意为"与某人商量"，这里译为"与这巨大的荒凉世界对话"。solitude 意为"孤独；僻静"，是英语中具有抽象意义的词汇，译成中文最好采用与原文意思相对应的具体词汇。

1114. echoed loudly within him：在他的身体里用巨大的声音回响着。在这里意为"荒野诱惑的声音在他的头脑里不断回荡着"，即"荒野的诱惑让他无法忘怀，深受蛊惑"。

1115. he was hollow at the core：他整个人是个中空的了。前文说到过经理"是个中空的"，因为他的身体里已经没有了良心和道德；这里讲到库尔茨"是个中空的"，因为他的身体里已经没有了自制力。《黑暗之心》整部小说里充满了各种隐喻，可以从很多不同的角度去解读。艾略特读过康拉德的作品，而且从中深受启发。在他的《荒原》和《空心人》中也看得到《黑暗之心》的痕迹。

glass, and the head that had appeared near enough to be spoken to seemed at once to have leaped away from me into inaccessible distance.

"The admirer of Mr. Kurtz was a bit crestfallen[1116]. In a hurried, indistinct voice he began to assure me he had not dared to take these—say, symbols—down. He was not afraid of the natives; they would not stir till Mr. Kurtz gave the word. His ascendancy was extraordinary. The camps of these people surrounded the place, and the chiefs came every day to see him. They would crawl.... 'I don't want to know anything of the ceremonies used when approaching Mr. Kurtz,' I shouted. Curious, this feeling that[1117] came over me that such details would be more intolerable[1118] than those heads drying on the stakes under Mr. Kurtz's windows. After all, that was only a savage sight, while I seemed at one bound to have been transported into some lightless region of subtle horrors[1119], where pure, uncomplicated savagery was a positive relief, being something that had a right

---

1116. crestfallen：垂头丧气的；气馁的。这里是说，在库尔茨暴行的罪证面前，即使是他的崇拜者也无从推诿，无法替他辩驳。

1117. Curious, this feeling that：这句话的正常语序是 "This feeling that...is curious"。

1118. such details would be more intolerable：这些细节（比木桩上的人头）更令人难以忍受。因为人头象征着一种野蛮行径，毕竟比较简单直接；而拜谒仪式则象征着一种精神上的控制和堕落，这种精神侵蚀的影响将是长期和持久的，其破坏力相比简单地杀死几个人显然更大。

1119. some lightless region of subtle horrors：某个暗无天日、充斥着隐约的恐怖的地方。

to exist—obviously—in the sunshine. The young man looked at me with surprise. I suppose it did not occur to him that Mr. Kurtz was no idol of mine. He forgot I hadn't heard any of these splendid monologues on, what was it? on love, justice, conduct of life[1120]— or what not. If it had come to crawling before Mr. Kurtz, he crawled as much as[1121] the veriest savage of them all. I had no idea of the conditions, he said: these heads were the heads of rebels. I shocked him excessively by laughing. Rebels! What would be the next definition I was to hear? There had been enemies, criminals, workers—and these were rebels. Those rebellious heads looked very subdued to me on their sticks. 'You don't know how such a life tries a man like Kurtz[1122],' cried Kurtz's last disciple. 'Well, and you[1123]?' I said. 'I! I! I am a simple man. I have no great thoughts. I want nothing from anybody. How can you compare

---

1120. conduct of life：人生准则；如何端正品行；为人之道。or what not 的完整形式是 or these splendid monologues on what are not love, justice, conduct of life，反讽库尔茨先生的演讲之中既有着引人向上的力量，又充斥着许多黑暗卑鄙的谎言。

1121. crawled as much as：（俄国人在精神上）已经（和真正的野蛮人）一样完全匍匐了。

1122. tries a man like Kurtz：（那样的生活）淬炼出了像库尔茨这样的人。try 在这里意为"考验；磨炼"。

1123. Well, and you?：这句话是马洛对俄国人的一句讽刺，完整形式是 "Well, and such a life also tries a man like you?" 马洛不认同俄国人的话，他觉得俄国人在为库尔茨找借口。人的变化不能总是归因于外界因素。如果说，是艰苦的生活让库尔茨变成了贪婪残暴的人，那么同样过着艰苦生活的俄国人，难道也同样变得贪婪残暴了吗？显然并没有。因此俄国人为库尔茨做的辩解，在马洛的反问之下，瞬间变得苍白无力。

me to...?' His feelings were too much for speech, and suddenly he broke down. 'I don't understand,' he groaned. 'I've been doing my best to keep him alive, and that's enough. I had no hand in all this[1124]. I have no abilities. There hasn't been a drop of medicine or a mouthful of invalid food for months here. He was shamefully abandoned[1125]. A man like this, with such ideas. Shamefully! Shamefully! I—I—haven't slept for the last ten nights....'

"His voice lost itself in the calm of the evening. The long shadows of the forest had slipped downhill while we talked, had gone far beyond the ruined hovel, beyond the symbolic row of stakes. All this was in the gloom, while we down there were yet in the sunshine, and the stretch of the river abreast of the clearing glittered in a still and dazzling splendour, with a murky and overshadowed bend above and below. Not a living soul was seen on the shore. The bushes did not rustle.

"Suddenly round the corner of the house a group of men appeared, as though they had come up from the ground. They waded waist-deep in the grass, in a compact body, bearing an improvised stretcher in their midst. Instantly, in the emptiness of the landscape, a cry arose whose shrillness pierced the still air like a sharp arrow flying straight to the very heart of the land; and, as

---

1124. had no hand in all this: 没有参与这些事（指的是库尔茨的暴行）。下一句 I have no abilities 可能指的是俄国人只能眼睁睁地看着，却无力阻止库尔茨的种种作为。

1125. shamefully abandoned: 可耻地抛弃了。这里指的是（经理他们）抛弃库尔茨的行为很可耻。

if by enchantment, streams of human beings—of naked human beings—with spears in their hands, with bows, with shields, with wild glances and savage movements, were poured into the clearing[1126] by the dark-faced and pensive forest. The bushes shook, the grass swayed for a time, and then everything stood still in attentive immobility[1127].

"'Now, if he does not say the right thing to them we are all done for[1128],' said the Russian at my elbow. The knot of men with the stretcher had stopped, too, halfway to the steamer, as if petrified. I saw the man on the stretcher sit up, lank and with an uplifted arm, above the shoulders of the bearers. 'Let us hope that the man who can talk so well of love in general will find some particular reason to spare us[1129] this time,' I said. I resented bitterly the absurd danger of our situation, as if to be at the mercy

---

1126. poured into the clearing：倾倒在那片空地上。这里是一个比喻，"不断涌出来的野人好像是被那片阴郁的树林倾倒在河边的空地上一样"。

1127. stood still in attentive immobility：一动不动地站着。attentive 意为"专注的"，immobility 意为"固定；不动"。这里是形容野人们剑拔弩张，危机一触即发的样子。

1128. we are all done for：这里的完整形式可能是"we are all done for living"，意即"如果他不说几句正确的话（即帮着马洛他们说话），我们就别想活了"。done for living 在这里的意思是"就活着这件事而言，这就算结束了"，也就是"死定了"。

1129. find some particular reason to spare us：找出个具体的理由来饶我们一命。这句话是马洛的讽刺，他讽刺库尔茨总是擅长泛泛的空谈，什么"普遍之爱""崇高之爱"，而在当下却是需要他展示具体的爱心的时刻——饶这几个白人一命。马洛拭目以待，因为库尔茨接下来的行为就可以验证他之前那些动人的演讲究竟是真心还是假意。particular 意为"特定的；详细的"，spare 意为"饶恕；赦免"。

of that atrocious phantom[1130] had been a dishonouring necessity. I could not hear a sound, but through my glasses I saw the thin arm extended commandingly, the lower jaw moving[1131], the eyes of that apparition shining darkly far in its bony head that nodded with grotesque jerks. Kurtz—Kurtz—that means short in German—don't it? Well, the name was as true as everything else in his life—and death[1132]. He looked at least seven feet long. His covering had fallen off, and his body emerged from it pitiful and appalling as from a winding-sheet. I could see the cage of his ribs all astir, the bones of his arm waving. It was as though an animated image of death carved out of old ivory had been shaking its hand with menaces at a motionless crowd of men made of dark and glittering bronze. I saw him open his mouth wide—it gave him a weirdly voracious aspect, as though he had wanted to swallow all the air,

---

1130. to be at the mercy of that atrocious phantom：只能任由那个残暴的幽灵摆布。at the mercy of 意为"受制于；任凭支配"，atrocious 意为"凶恶的；残暴的"，phantom 意为"幽灵；鬼魂"，这里指的是"将死之人"。

1131. the lower jaw moving：下巴在动。这里指的是"库尔茨在说话"。

1132. the name...and death：这名字正如他生命中包括死亡在内的一切东西——只除了（他的身材）。因为库尔茨的生命很短暂，他拥有的东西（爱情，象牙，历险）也很短暂，它们都和"库尔茨"在德语中的意义（"短"）十分契合。但是他的身长可并不"短"，他身高 7 英尺，也就是 2.13 米。在作者的设定里，库尔茨身高两米多，确实是一个比较惊人的身高。作者的用意也许是在隐晦地告诉读者，库尔茨是一个"神化了的人物"。他曾有着崇高的理想和强大的能力，并以无比高大的形象接受着野人的服从、俄国人的崇拜和未婚妻的怀思，简直如同天神降世一般。在古埃及的壁画中，神和贵族的形象比普通人大得多，这是 power 的具象化。2016 年上映的美国电影《神战：权力之眼》中也可以看到神的身形远大于人的场景。

all the earth, all the men before him[1133]. A deep voice reached me faintly[1134]. He must have been shouting. He fell back[1135] suddenly. The stretcher shook as the bearers staggered forward again, and almost at the same time I noticed that the crowd of savages was vanishing without any perceptible movement of retreat, as if the forest that had ejected these beings so suddenly[1136] had drawn them in[1137] again as the breath is drawn in a long aspiration.

"Some of the pilgrims behind the stretcher carried his arms—two shot-guns, a heavy rifle, and a light revolver-carbine—the thunderbolts of that pitiful Jupiter. The manager bent over him murmuring as he walked beside his head. They laid him down in one of the little cabins—just a room for a bed place and a camp-stool or two, you know. We had brought his belated correspondence, and a lot of torn envelopes and open letters littered his bed. His hand roamed feebly amongst these papers. I

1133. swallow all...before him：把他面前所有的空气，所有的土地和所有的人全部吞下去。这里事实上可能是库尔茨因为病入膏肓而大口吸气，但是从马洛带着感情色彩的视角看来，这个吸气的动作象征了库尔茨无与伦比的贪婪。

1134. reached me faintly：我隐约听到。reach 在这里指的是"声音到达听者的耳朵"。

1135. fell back：倒了回去。这里可能是病弱的库尔茨在一通动作之后体力不支。

1136. eject these beings so suddenly：如此突然地把这些人吐出来。这里是把阴暗的森林比喻成某种"母体"，那些野人好像是被森林"吐出来"的。eject 意为"排出；射出"。

1137. draw them in：把他们一口气吸回去。这里指的是"野人们又回到了树林里"。

was struck by the fire of his eyes and the composed languor of his expression. It was not so much the exhaustion of disease[1138]. He did not seem in pain. This shadow[1139] looked satiated and calm, as though for the moment it had had its fill of all the emotions[1140].

"He rustled one of the letters, and looking straight in my face said, 'I am glad.' Somebody had been writing to him about me. These special recommendations were turning up again[1141]. The volume of tone[1142] he emitted without effort, almost without the trouble of moving his lips, amazed me. A voice! a voice! It was grave, profound, vibrating, while the man did not seem capable of a whisper. However, he had enough strength in him[1143] — factitious

---

1138. not so much the exhaustion of disease：并不怎么像是病后虚弱的样子。这里是说库尔茨沉静的样子并不是由于染病衰弱而导致的，而可能是他内心深处得到了解脱，或者想开了什么，因而目光明亮，神色平静。

1139. This shadow：这个影子；这个幽灵。指的是将死的库尔茨。因为病弱的库尔茨已经不是那个生龙活虎的库尔茨了，以前他能干很多事，而现在只能躺在床上奄奄待毙。和以前相比，现在这个躺在床上的人充其量只能算是"库尔茨的影子"。

1140. it had had its fill of all the emotions：它已经体验过全部的感情了。这里用 it，对应的是上文的 this shadow。fill 在这里意为"（某人的）需求总量；（容器的）最大容量"，指的是库尔茨一生中所能够体验的全部甘苦。

1141. These special...up again：这些推荐我的信又在这里出现了。这里是呼应前文的情节，经理爪牙在盘问马洛的时候，不小心提到他曾看过公司高管推荐马洛的信，而且支持马洛和支持库尔茨的是同一派（道德派）的人。马洛当时就意识到经理他们私拆公司的机密信件。现在这些信又出现在船上，说明写给库尔茨的那些信在他本人查看之前，早已被经理暗中拆阅过了。

1142. The volume of tone：这里指的是库尔茨说话的音量。

1143. had enough strength in him：在他的身上仍然有着足够强大的力量。这里指的是库尔茨仍然掌管着土人部落，他只要一句话就可以让土人进攻经理他们。

no doubt—to very nearly make an end of us, as you shall hear directly.

"The manager appeared silently in the doorway; I stepped out at once and he drew the curtain after me. The Russian, eyed curiously by the pilgrims, was staring at the shore. I followed the direction of his glance.

"Dark human shapes could be made out in the distance, flitting indistinctly against the gloomy border of the forest, and near the river two bronze figures, leaning on tall spears, stood in the sunlight under fantastic head-dresses of spotted skins, warlike and still in statuesque repose. And from right to left along the lighted shore moved a wild and gorgeous apparition of a woman[1144].

"She walked with measured steps, draped in striped and fringed cloths[1145], treading the earth proudly, with a slight jingle and flash of barbarous ornaments. She carried her head high[1146]; her hair was done in the shape of a helmet; she had brass leggings to

---

1144. moved a...of a woman：这里是倒装，把谓语 moved 提前了。gorgeous 意为"华丽的；美丽动人的"，apparition 意为"幽灵；幻影；离奇出现的东西"，这里可能是表达一种"河边怎么会出现这样一个美丽的土著女人"的惊讶语气；或者是，由于土著女人处于情人离她而去的极度悲伤中，看上去好像一条怨魂一样充满哀苦、失去了生气。

1145. draped in striped and fringed cloths：披着缀有条纹和流苏的长衣。"身披长衣"似乎是土著人中地位高者的象征。striped 意为"有条纹的；有斑纹的"，fringed 意为"加穗的；带边饰的；缀着流苏的"。

1146. carried her head high：高高地昂着头；举着头。这里所有的神态、动作、服饰，都在说明这个土著女人在部落里地位很高，可能是女首领，也可能是酋长的女儿，当然，更有可能是库尔茨的情人。这里有点类似印第安公主波卡洪塔斯爱上白人殖民者的故事。

the knee, brass wire gauntlets to the elbow, a crimson spot on her tawny cheek, innumerable necklaces of glass beads[1147] on her neck; bizarre things, charms, gifts of witch-men[1148], that hung about her, glittered and trembled at every step. She must have had the value of several elephant tusks upon her[1149]. She was savage and superb, wild-eyed and magnificent; there was something ominous and stately in her deliberate progress. And in the hush that had fallen suddenly upon[1150] the whole sorrowful land, the immense wilderness, the colossal body of the fecund and mysterious life seemed to look at her, pensive, as though it had been looking at the image of its own tenebrous and passionate soul[1151].

1147. glass beads：玻璃珠子。前文提到过，殖民者用于交换象牙的工业制品中就有玻璃珠子。这里我们看到了非洲人购买玻璃珠子的用途之一——作为地位较高者的装饰。

1148. gifts of witch-men：巫师献上的礼物。在这里，符咒（护身符）和巫师献上的礼物，很可能是这个土著女人为了祈祷库尔茨痊愈而挂在自己身上的。

1149. had the value of several elephant tusks upon her：身上挂着的这些东西具有好几根象牙的价值。这也说明土著女人拥有财富和地位。tusk 在这里和 ivory 同义。区别可能是，tusk 更侧重于指那些长在活着的大象身上的长牙，而 ivory 是已经从大象身上切割下来的象牙，是已经成了死物的象牙。

1150. the hush that had fallen suddenly upon：突然间降临下来的寂静。这里指的是土著女人的非凡气度摄住了旁观的人，让他们觉得天地之间也似乎一下子安静了，所有的目光都聚焦到她的身上了。hush 意为"寂静；鸦雀无声"。

1151. looking at...passionate soul：望着自己那同样艰晦而又热烈的形象。这里是说，"荒野"望着那个土著女人，就好像望着它自己一样，因为土著女人和荒野有着同样的灵魂——充满野性，喜怒难测，热烈深情。tenebrous 意为"阴暗的；晦涩的"，在这里指的是"不能轻易被人们所理解的"。这也是荒野和野人留给马洛他们的一种印象，马洛觉得荒野总是阴沉、平静、富有耐心，谁也不知道它在打算着什么企图，接下来带来的是福是祸。

"She came abreast of the steamer, stood still, and faced us. Her long shadow fell to <u>the water's edge</u>[1152]. Her face had a tragic and fierce aspect of wild sorrow and of dumb pain mingled with the fear of <u>some struggling, half-shaped resolve</u>[1153]. She stood looking at us without a stir, and like the wilderness itself, with an air of brooding over an inscrutable purpose. A whole minute passed, and then she made a step forward. There was a low jingle, a glint of yellow metal, a sway of fringed draperies, and she stopped as if her heart had failed her. The young fellow by my side <u>growled</u>[1154]. The pilgrims murmured at my back. She looked at us all as if <u>her life had depended upon the unswerving steadiness of her glance</u>[1155]. Suddenly she <u>opened her bared arms</u>[1156] and threw them up rigid above her head, as though in an uncontrollable desire to touch the sky, and at the same time <u>the swift shadows</u>[1157] darted

---

1152. the water's edge：水边。这里是说夕阳已经沉得很低，人的影子拖得很长，一直从地上拖到了河水边。

1153. some struggling, half-shaped resolve：挣扎犹豫的、半成形却又不坚定的决心。这里似乎无法直译，直译将会损失中文译本的文学性，这是两种语言的表达方式的差异造成的。所以我在这里选择根据作品的意境进行化译，孰得孰失，见仁见智。

1154. growl：咆哮；威胁性的吼叫。这里可能是因为语言不通，所以俄国人用吼声向她表示阻止和威胁。

1155. her life...her glance：她的生命全靠着这坚定不移的目光才得以维系。这里也似乎是化译为好。

1156. opened her bared arms：张开她赤裸的双臂。其实土著女人的手臂上还是挂着臂钏的，只是没有袖子。

1157. the swift shadows：迅速弥漫的阴影。这里指的是太阳落山，天黑得很快。

out on the earth, swept around on the river, gathering the steamer into a shadowy embrace. A formidable silence hung over the scene.

"She turned away slowly, walked on, following the bank, and passed into the bushes to the left. Once only her eyes gleamed back at us in the dusk of the thickets before she disappeared.

"'If she had offered to come aboard I really think I would have tried to shoot her,' said the man of patches[1158], nervously. 'I have been risking my life every day for the last fortnight to keep her out of the house. She got in one day and kicked up a row about those miserable rags I picked up in the storeroom to mend my clothes with. I wasn't decent[1159]. At least it must have been that, for she talked like a fury to Kurtz for an hour, pointing at me now and then. I don't understand the dialect of this tribe. Luckily for me[1160], I fancy Kurtz felt too ill that day to care[1161], or there would have been mischief. I don't understand.... No—it's too much for me[1162].

1158. the man of patches：那个满身补丁的人。指的是那个俄国年轻人。

1159. decent：在这里意为"规矩的；得体的；待人宽厚的"。这里是说俄国年轻人觉得自己不是个"被人骂了都不还嘴"的宽厚之人，也就是说如果土著女人找茬骂他，他绝不会宽宏大量地不还嘴、不记仇。

1160. Luckily for me：幸好；好在。这里是说幸好库尔茨没理会这件事。

1161. felt too ill that day to care：那天觉得太难受，因而没理会（他们的争吵）。

1162. I don't understand.... No—it's too much for me：这里呼应了俄国人之前说自己"是个头脑简单的人"，他眼中的世界很单纯，虽然事情往往比他想象的要更复杂。比如说这里这件事，有可能那个土著女人想要借机赶走俄国人。当然这并不是因为俄国人用了库房的碎布补衣服，真实原因可能是土著女人认为俄国人的那套照顾方法（其实比较科学）是没有用的，甚至可能会害死库尔茨，她觉得自己从巫师那里得来的护身符和各种符咒才管用，因此她想要让库尔茨赶走俄国人，转而用她的巫术来治好病。

Ah, well, it's all over now.'

"At this moment I heard Kurtz's deep voice behind the curtain: 'Save me!—save the ivory[1163], you mean. Don't tell me. Save me!Why, I've had to save you. You are interrupting my plans now[1164]. Sick! Sick! Not so sick as you would like to believe[1165]. Never mind. I'll carry my ideas out yet—I will return. I'll show you what can be done. You with your little peddling notions[1166]—you are interfering with me. I will return. I....'

"The manager came out. He did me the honour to[1167] take me under the arm and lead me aside. 'He is very low, very low[1168],'

1163. Save me!—save the ivory：这里是库尔茨讽刺经理的话，"与其说是救我，还不如说你是想救那些象牙"。

1164. Save me...my plans now：why 后面可能都是库尔茨引用经理的话，也就是经理给出的"必须救库尔茨"的冠冕堂皇的理由。因为经理说："我早就必须救你了（虽然被一连串的耽搁给拖到了今天）；而且（我是主张跟当地人和平交换象牙的，而你抢劫象牙的做法）现在已经破坏了我的计划"。

1165. Sick! Sick! Not so sick as you would like to believe：我对于这句话的理解是，第一个 Sick! 是库尔茨表示"经理的那些理由令人恶心"，第二个 Sick! 可能就转为带点双关了，从"恶心"往"疾病"的意思上过渡，Not so sick as 就已经完全是"疾病"的意思了，库尔茨说"我还没有病得如你所愿"，说明他对经理心里打的什么算盘是完全明白的。

1166. your little peddling notions：你的那些小算计；你那些到处兜售货物的蠢主意。peddling 意为"叫卖的；兜售的；小而琐碎的；鸡肠狗肚的"。这里无论库尔茨指的是"和经理开展业务的理念不合"，还是指的"经理故意拖延救援的阴谋算计"，总之都是体现了库尔茨对经理的敌对态度。经理善于伪装，总是暗地里使招数，而库尔茨比较直率，直接当面说破经理的想法。

1167. did me the honour to：赏脸（很亲密地拉着我）；给我荣幸／荣宠。

1168. He is very low, very low：这句话的重点是对于"low"的理解。这里可能是"情绪低落"或者"用心卑鄙、轻视别人"的意思。结合上文库尔茨对经理的一顿痛骂，经理这句话应该也带有自我分辩、顺便回敬库尔茨的意味，所以译为"他的状态很不好，他把别人都看得太坏了"。

he said. He considered it necessary to sigh, but neglected to be consistently sorrowful. 'We have done all we could for him—haven't we? But there is no disguising the fact, Mr. Kurtz has done more harm than good to the Company. He did not see the time was not ripe for vigorous action[1169]. Cautiously, cautiously—that's my principle. We must be cautious yet. The district is closed to us for a time[1170]. Deplorable! Upon the whole, the trade will suffer. I don't deny there is a remarkable quantity of ivory—mostly fossil[1171]. We must save it, at all events—but look how precarious the position is—and why? Because the method is unsound.' 'Do you,' said I, looking at the shore, 'call it "unsound method?"' 'Without doubt,' he exclaimed hotly. 'Don't you?' ... 'No method at all,' I murmured after a while. 'Exactly,' he exulted. 'I anticipated this. Shows a complete want of judgment. It is my duty to point it out in the proper quarter.' 'Oh,' said I, 'that fellow—what's his name?—the brickmaker, will make a readable report for you.' He appeared confounded for a moment. It seemed to me I had never breathed an atmosphere so vile, and I turned mentally to Kurtz for relief[1172]—positively for relief. 'Nevertheless I think Mr. Kurtz is a remarkable

---

1169. vigorous action：积极有力的行动。这里指的是与和平交易相对的武力掠取。

1170. The district is closed to us for a time：这片地区暂时对我们关闭了。即，"我们暂时没法在这里开展贸易了"。

1171. fossil：化石。这里指的是库尔茨埋入地下、又被经理挖掘出来的象牙。这些象牙很新鲜，只是因为是从地下被挖出来的，所以经理把它们叫作"化石"。

1172. turned mentally to Kurtz for relief：在精神上倒向了库尔茨，来寻求解脱（让自己的良心能够过得去）。

man,' I said with emphasis. He started, dropped on me a heavy glance, said very quietly, 'he was[1173],' and turned his back on me[1174]. My hour of favour was over[1175]; I found myself lumped along with Kurtz[1176] as a partisan of methods for which the time was not ripe: I was unsound! Ah! but it was something to have at least a choice of nightmares[1177].

"I had turned to the wilderness really[1178], not to Mr. Kurtz,

---

1173. he was：这里是经理在否定马洛的这句话 "Mr. Kurtz is a remarkable man"，把它改成了 "Mr. Kurtz was a remarkable man"，即，"库尔茨先生过去是个了不起的人物（但是现在已经不是了）"。

1174. turned his back on me：转过身去背对着我；不再理睬我。这说明马洛被经理划为异己分子了。

1175. My hour of favour was over：我得宠的时间就此结束了。

1176. lumped along with Kurtz：和库尔茨划为一党了。lump 在这里意为"把……归并在一起"。

1177. but it was...of nightmares：这句话的正常语序可能是 "but to have at least a choice of nightmares was something"，意思是"但是至少（敢于）从噩梦之中自己选择一个，这就很了不起"。即，摆在马洛面前有几个选择，一是和经理沆瀣一气，迫害和污蔑库尔茨；这样做可以保证马洛的个人利益，但是却污染了马洛清白的良心，这是一个"与魔鬼同行"的噩梦；二是选择和库尔茨站在一起，为库尔茨发出真实的声音。这样的话势必会得罪经理，马洛的经济利益和个人前途都将蒙受损失，这是一个"与魔鬼结仇"的噩梦。马洛选择了第二个噩梦，成了经理和所有朝圣者的敌人，被他们孤立起来。但是他保住了自己正直的操守和清白的良心。因此，这个选择算得上是"something"，是一个了不起的成就。

1178. turned to the wilderness really：其实（我是在精神上）投向了那片荒野（而不是真的投向了库尔茨）。所谓"在精神上投向某人"，意思是"支持某人；认为某人是正确的，是可以依靠的"。马洛面对着相互斗争的几方势力，其中对于经理（代表着绝对的恶），马洛的态度是绝对鄙视的；对于库尔茨（代表着善恶交织的矛盾体），马洛是同情、敬佩和批判交织的；对于荒野（无所谓善恶，是包容一切的存在），马洛是充满敬畏的。

who, I was ready to admit, was as good as buried[1179]. And for a moment it seemed to me as if I also were buried in a vast grave full of unspeakable secrets[1180]. I felt an intolerable weight oppressing my breast, the smell of the damp earth, the unseen presence of victorious corruption, the darkness of an impenetrable night....The Russian tapped me on the shoulder. I heard him mumbling and stammering something about 'brother seaman—couldn't conceal—knowledge of matters that would affect Mr. Kurtz's reputation[1181].' I waited. For him evidently Mr. Kurtz was not in his grave; I suspect that for him Mr. Kurtz was one of the immortals. 'Well!' said I at last, 'speak out. As it happens, I am Mr. Kurtz's friend—in a way.'

"He stated with a good deal of formality[1182] that had we not been 'of the same profession[1183],' he would have kept the matter

---

1179. as good as buried：（库尔茨）就和已经入土的人差不多了。也就是说，马洛觉得库尔茨已经病入膏肓，离死不远了。as good as 意为"差不多等于；事实上等于"。

1180. in a vast grave full of unspeakable secrets：装满了各种不可言说的秘密的巨大坟墓。这里指的是经理所编织的谎言和阴谋让马洛感到身边弥漫着一种坟墓般阴暗的氛围。unspeakable 意为"无以言表的；难以启齿的"。

1181. affect Mr. Kurtz's reputation：影响库尔茨先生的声誉。这里指的是"马洛的汽船遇袭是库尔茨下的命令"这件事。这件事如果让经理他们知道，他们一定会大做文章，甚至指证库尔茨"背叛了自己的身份"等等，让库尔茨名誉扫地。

1182. stated with a good deal of formality：一本正经地做了一大堆声明。这里是说因为俄国人觉得这件事事关重大，所以在讲出来之前，要反复声明，让马洛不要误会自己，同时认识到这件事情的重要性。

1183. of the same profession：从事同一职业；干同一行的。这里是说俄国人和马洛都是水手。

to himself without regard to consequences. 'He suspected there was an active ill-will towards him on the part of these white men that—' 'You are right,' I said, remembering a certain conversation I had overheard. 'The manager thinks you ought to be hanged.' He showed a concern at this intelligence which amused me at first. 'I had better get out of the way quietly,' he said earnestly. 'I can do no more for Kurtz now, and they would soon find some excuse. What's to stop them? There's a military post three hundred miles from here.' 'Well, upon my word,' said I, 'perhaps you had better go if you have any friends amongst the savages near by.' 'Plenty,' he said. 'They are simple people— and I <u>want nothing</u>[1184], you know.' He <u>stood biting his lip</u>[1185], then: 'I don't want any harm to happen to these whites here, but of course I was thinking of Mr. Kurtz's reputation—but you are a brother seaman and—' 'All right,' said I, after a time. 'Mr. Kurtz's reputation is safe with me.' I did not know <u>how truly</u>[1186] I spoke.

1184. I want nothing：我对他们从无索求。这句话出现了几次，似乎体现了作者的一种观点：如果两个民族想要和平相处，那就需要真诚、平等地交往，而不是强势一方对弱势一方大肆搜刮，横征暴敛——want something 是交不到真正的朋友的。

1185. stood biting his lip：咬着嘴唇站在那儿。这表现了俄国人还有点犹豫，但是已经下了决心（要告诉马洛）。

1186. how truly：到底有多么真。这句话如果从事前来看，那就是马洛为了催促俄国人赶紧讲出那个秘密而做的保证，其实他也不知道自己的话有几分真，那时还只是脱口而出一句催促的话罢了；如果从事后来看，马洛这句"safe with me"的保证，被他完全忠实地贯彻了，他成了库尔茨最值得托付一切后事的人，那么这句感叹就是"那时候我并不知道，我的这句保证是多么真实（地被实现了）！"但是这两个意思似乎无法同时体现在译文中。

"He informed me, lowering his voice, that it was Kurtz who had ordered the attack to be made on the steamer. 'He hated sometimes the idea of being taken away—and then again....But I don't understand these matters. I am a simple man. He thought it would scare you away—that you would give it up, thinking him dead. I could not stop him. Oh, I had an awful time of it this last month.' 'Very well,' I said. 'He is all right now.' 'Ye-e-es,' he muttered, not very convinced apparently[1187]. 'Thanks,' said I; 'I shall keep my eyes open.' 'But quiet-eh?' he urged[1188] anxiously. 'It would be awful for his reputation if anybody here—' I promised a complete discretion with great gravity. 'I have a canoe and three black fellows waiting not very far. I am off[1189]. Could you give me a few Martini-Henry cartridges?' I could, and did, with proper secrecy[1190]. He helped himself, with a wink at me, to a handful of my tobacco[1191].

1187. not very convinced apparently：显然并没有完全被说服。马洛安慰他说"库尔茨现在已经没事了"，也就是向俄国人保证库尔茨已经安全无虞了，但是俄国人显然并不太相信。因为他也看出来库尔茨和经理之间是有矛盾的。虽然他并不能理解其中到底是怎么回事，但是他能感觉到经理这里绝不是什么真正的"安全港湾"。

1188. urge：敦促；强烈要求。这里指的是"嘱咐"。

1189. I am off：我要走了 / 下班了 / 下线了。这里指的是俄国人要离开（汽船）了。

1190. with proper secrecy：适当的机密性。这里是说马洛私底下给了俄国人一些子弹，很小心地不让别人注意到。

1191. helped himself...my tobacco：正常语序是"helped himself to a handful of my tobacco with a wink at me"，这是运用插入语的一种情况。另外，文中出现的两种非正常语序还有：为表示强调而将谓语提前；为符合语法规则（例如虚拟条件句）而将 had 提前。help oneself to sth 意为"随意取用（转下页

'Between sailors[1192]—you know—good English tobacco.' At the door of the pilot-house he turned round—'I say, haven't you a pair of shoes you could spare[1193]?' He raised one leg. 'Look.' The soles[1194] were tied with knotted strings[1195] sandalwise[1196] under his bare feet. I rooted out an old pair[1197], at which he looked with admiration before tucking it under his left arm. One of his pockets (bright red) was bulging with cartridges, from the other (dark blue) peeped 'Towson's Inquiry[1198],' etc., etc. He seemed to think himself excellently well

---

（接上页）某物"，这里是说俄国人自己伸手到马洛的口袋里抓走了一把烟丝。wink 意为"眨眨眼；使个眼色"。这里俄国人朝马洛眨眼睛的潜台词可能是"我可是当过水手的人，知道英国烟是好东西。既然你有好东西，就分我一点呗"。

1192. Between sailors：这件事只有干过水手的才知道；这个秘密只有咱俩知道；咱们都是水手，所以交情自然别人好。这些理解我觉得都是可以的。译文中采用的是"英国烟到底有多么好，只有咱们当过水手的人才知道"。

1193. a pair of shoes you could spare：你能匀出来一双鞋子送给我吗。spare 在这里意为"抽出；匀出；分给"。

1194. sole：在这里意为"鞋底"。

1195. with knotted strings：用打着结 / 打满结的绳子。这说明俄国人连一根长一点的绳子都没有，还要把几根绳子打结连在一起才够长，可见他在物质上匮乏到了何等地步。这也更反衬出他在艰苦的生活中积极乐观的精神的可贵。

1196. sandalwise：sandal 意为"拖鞋"，sandalwise 意为"像拖鞋那样"。这里是说俄国人所谓的"鞋子"就是两个拖鞋一样的鞋底而已，用绳子系着不让它们掉下去。

1197. root out an old pair：翻找出来一双旧鞋。root out 意为"连根拔起；彻底扫荡"，这里指的是"翻了个底朝天"。这反映出马洛对待俄国人很真诚，为了帮助他是真的倾尽全力，毫无保留。

1198. peep 'Towson's Inquiry'：露出了《陶森的探索》(那本书)。peep 意为"窥视，偷看；隐现，微现"，这里指的是"(那本书从口袋里)露出头来(偷看着外面)；冒出来；露出来"，带着点拟人的味道，是一种十分形象的用法。

equipped[1199] for a renewed encounter with the wilderness. 'Ah! I'll never, never meet such a man again. You ought to have heard him recite poetry—his own, too, it was, he told me. Poetry!' He rolled his eyes at the recollection of these delights[1200]. 'Oh, he enlarged my mind!' 'Good-bye,' said I. He shook hands and vanished in the night. Sometimes I ask myself whether I had ever really seen him— whether it was possible to meet such a phenomenon! ...

"When I woke up shortly after midnight his warning came to my mind[1201] with its hint of danger that seemed, in the starred darkness, real enough to make me get up for the purpose of having a look round. On the hill a big fire burned, illuminating fitfully a crooked corner of the station-house. One of the agents with a picket of a few of our blacks[1202], armed for the purpose, was keeping guard over the ivory; but deep within the forest, red gleams that wavered, that seemed to sink and rise from the ground[1203] amongst

1199. excellently well equipped：装备相当精良。有了一把子弹、一把烟丝、一双鞋就算是"装备精良"，只能说俄国人实在具有乐观主义精神，令人感佩。

1200. roll his eyes at the recollection of these delights：一回想起那些愉快的往事，他连眼球都（激动到）颤动起来（即眼睛熠熠闪亮的样子，说明他对那些美好的记忆十分回味）。roll 意为"转动；摇晃"，recollection 意为"回忆；回忆起的事物（或景象）；往事"，delight 意为"高兴；愉悦"。这说明俄国人十分珍视他和库尔茨的友谊，并且为库尔茨的才华而倾倒。

1201. his warning came to my mind：我想到了他的警告。即俄国人警告马洛要小心，库尔茨可能还会对他们不利。

1202. our blacks：我们的黑人，指的是那些受雇于马洛公司的黑人。

1203. sink and rise from the ground：仿佛时而钻入地下，时而又从地底冒出来似的。我觉得这里也有两种理解，一是火苗本身忽隐忽现；二是周围的山上聚集了很多野人，他们的营火好像长蛇阵那样沿着山峦起伏，远远看去就像是一会儿隐没不见，一会儿又从山脚下冒出来，盘旋而上。但是这里似乎也不必如此深挖含义，理解成"火光在山峦间时隐时现"应该就可以了。

confused columnar shapes of intense blackness, showed <u>the exact position of the camp</u>[1204] where <u>Mr. Kurtz's adorers</u>[1205] were keeping their uneasy vigil. The monotonous beating of a big drum filled the air with muffled shocks and a lingering vibration. <u>A steady droning sound</u>[1206] of many men chanting each to himself some weird incantation came out from the black, flat wall of the woods as the humming of bees comes out of a hive, and had a strange narcotic effect upon my half-awake senses. I believe I dozed off leaning over the rail, till an abrupt burst of yells, <u>an overwhelming outbreak of a pent-up and mysterious frenzy</u>[1207], woke me up in a bewildered wonder. It was cut short all at once, and the low droning went on with <u>an effect of audible and soothing silence</u>[1208]. I glanced casually into the little cabin. <u>A light was burning within</u>[1209],

----

1204. the exact position of the camp：（红色的营火暴露了）野人们的营地的确切位置。

1205. Mr. Kurtz's adorers：库尔茨先生的崇拜者 / 信徒，指的是那些被他收服的部落的野人们。

1206. A steady droning sound：持续不断的嗡嗡声。droning 意为 "声音低沉单调的；发嗡嗡声的"。其中 drone 做动词意为 "嗡嗡叫；喋喋不休"，作名词还有另一个词义 "无人机"。想想无人机飞行的时候发出的那种嗡嗡声，真的十分形象。

1207. an overwhelming...mysterious frenzy：一种被压抑着的神秘狂怒的骤然爆发。overwhelming 意为 "（如同涨满的洪水一样）巨大的；压倒性的"，pent-up 意为 "被压抑的；幽闭的"。

1208. an effect of audible and soothing silence：一种能够起到抚慰效果的听得到的寂静。这里指的是野人们嗡嗡吟唱咒语的那种白噪声。

1209. A light was burning within：一盏灯正在屋里燃烧着。这里可能是煤油灯，因为虽然电灯早在 1879 年就被发明出来，但是直到 20 世纪初才得到普及。within 后面省略了 the little cabin。

but Mr. Kurtz was not there.

"I think I would have raised an outcry if I had believed my eyes. But I didn't believe them at first—the thing seemed so impossible. The fact is I was completely unnerved by a sheer blank fright, pure abstract terror, unconnected with any distinct shape of physical danger. What made this emotion so overpowering was—how shall I define it?—the moral shock I received, as if something altogether monstrous, intolerable to thought and odious to the soul, had been thrust upon me unexpectedly. This lasted of course the merest fraction of a second, and then the usual sense of commonplace, deadly danger, the possibility of a sudden onslaught and massacre, or something of the kind, which I saw impending, was positively welcome and composing. It pacified me, in fact, so much that I did not raise an alarm.

"There was an agent buttoned up inside an ulster and sleeping on a chair on deck within three feet of me. The yells had not awakened him; he snored very slightly; I left him to his slumbers and leaped ashore. I did not betray[1210] Mr. Kurtz—it was ordered[1211] I should never betray him—it was written I should be loyal to the nightmare

---

1210. betray: 背叛。这里马洛说自己没有背叛库尔茨。尽管他提防库尔茨，但是他信守了对俄国人的承诺，并没有告诉任何人库尔茨曾经差点杀掉他们，而且在库尔茨夜里逃走之后，选择了只身追踪，而没有告知船上的任何人。如果他告诉经理库尔茨逃走了并且带人追踪，那就意味着背叛——库尔茨勾结野人图谋不轨的罪名就有可能成立。

1211. it was ordered: 上天（内心的声音）命令我。实际上这种上天的声音（it）正是马洛心中朴素的善恶观、正直的良心。在关键时刻，马洛本能地认为自己应该帮助库尔茨，而不能和经理沆瀣一气。

of my choice[1212]. I was anxious to deal with this shadow by myself alone—and to this day I don't know why I was so jealous of sharing with any one the peculiar blackness of that experience.

"As soon as I got on the bank I saw a trail—a broad trail through the grass. I remember the exultation with which I said to myself, 'He can't walk—he is crawling on all-fours—I've got him.' The grass was wet with dew. I strode rapidly with clenched fists. I fancy I had some vague notion of falling upon him and giving him a drubbing. I don't know. I had some imbecile thoughts. The knitting old woman with the cat obtruded herself upon my memory as a most improper person to be sitting at the other end of such an affair[1213]. I saw a row of pilgrims squirting lead in the air out of Winchesters held to the hip. I thought I would never get back to the steamer, and imagined myself living alone and unarmed in the woods to an advanced age. Such silly things— you know. And I remember I confounded the beat of the drum with the beating of my heart, and was pleased at its calm regularity.

1212. be loyal to the nightmare of my choice：忠于我自己选择的那个噩梦。在经理拉拢马洛的时候，马洛面前有两个选择：投向库尔茨，保住自己的良心，但是失去与经理结盟所能获得的利益；投向经理，保住自己的利益，但是永远失去自己的良心。这两个选择都是噩梦。在马洛出言拒绝经理的拉拢之时，他就等于选择了"投向库尔茨、损失自身利益"的噩梦，他知道自己从此将被经理孤立和排斥，也许以后在公司都不会有前途了。但是他的决心不会改变，他会忠于自己的选择。

1213. sitting at the other end of such an affair：坐在这件事的另一端。这里是说编织黑毛线的老女人仿佛是一种预兆，她远远地坐在时空的另一端，却正预示了马洛今夜的结局——死在丛林里，或者永远被留在岸上，再也回不到文明世界。这里是马洛极度紧张之下的胡思乱想。

"I kept to the track though—then stopped to listen. The night was very clear; a dark blue space, sparkling with dew and starlight, in which black things stood very still. I thought I could see a kind of motion ahead of me. I was strangely cocksure of everything that night. I actually left the track and ran in a wide semicircle (I verily believe chuckling to myself) so as to get in front of that stir, of that motion I had seen—if indeed I had seen anything. I was circumventing Kurtz as though it had been a boyish game.

"I came upon him, and, if he had not heard me coming, I would have fallen over him, too, but he got up in time. He rose, unsteady, long, pale, indistinct, like a vapour exhaled by the earth, and swayed slightly, misty and silent before me; while at my back the fires loomed between the trees, and the murmur of many voices issued from the forest. I had cut him off cleverly; but when actually confronting him I seemed to come to my senses, I saw the danger in its right proportion. It was by no means over yet. Suppose he began to shout? Though he could hardly stand, there was still plenty of vigour in his voice. 'Go away—hide yourself,' he said, in that profound tone. It was very awful. I glanced back. We were within thirty yards from the nearest fire. A black figure stood up, strode on long black legs, waving long black arms, across the glow. It had horns—antelope horns, I think—on its head. Some sorcerer, some witch-man, no doubt: it looked fiendlike[1214] enough.

1214. fiendlike: 恶魔般的；邪恶的。这里体现了马洛对野人巫师的畏惧，因为现在形势对他很不利，如果库尔茨一声召唤，那些野人随时可能发现马洛并把他抓走。

'Do you know what you are doing?' I whispered. 'Perfectly,' he answered, raising his voice for that single word: it sounded to me far off and yet loud, like a hail through a speaking-trumpet. 'If he makes a row we are lost,' I thought to myself. This clearly was not a case for fisticuffs, even apart from the very natural aversion[1215] I had to beat that Shadow—this wandering and tormented thing. 'You will be lost,' I said—'utterly lost.'[1216] One gets sometimes such a flash of inspiration, you know. I did say the right thing, though indeed he could not have been more irretrievably lost[1217] than he was at this very moment, when the foundations of our intimacy were being laid[1218]—to endure—to endure—even to the

---

1215. the very natural aversion：很自然的反感／不情愿。这里指的是马洛本来也不愿意殴打库尔茨（这是由于马洛的善良和不忍心，因为库尔茨已经十分衰弱。另外的原因就是，殴打和吵嚷的声音必然会惊动不远处的野人，这对马洛是最不利的）。

1216. 'You will be lost,' I said—'utterly lost.'：既然由于"不忍"和"不能"这两个原因，马洛无法用暴力手段带库尔茨回去，那就只能用语言劝说了。马洛说的是，"（如果你现在回到野人中间的话）你就将会失去自我，彻底地失去自我"。也就是说，如果库尔茨不和马洛回去，而是选择回到丛林，他就将永远成为一个野人、一个暴君、一个叛徒、一个笑柄，从前那个有理想和抱负、作为公司贸易代理人的库尔茨，就将彻底消失于世间。甚至他的名字也将永远被钉在耻辱柱上，令他的未婚妻和远在欧洲的亲人蒙羞。虽然丛林对库尔茨极具诱惑，但是一时冲动的后果却是他不得不考虑的。

1217. he could not have been more irretrievably lost：他（那时其实）早就无可挽回地迷失自我／彻底堕落了。这里是说其实库尔茨早就铸成了不可挽回的大错。他掠夺象牙，发动战争，肆意杀人，独裁统治，每一件都是不可饶恕的罪行，他的灵魂早已得不到救赎了。

1218. the foundations of our intimacy were being laid：我们之间惺惺相惜的知己之情就此奠定了基础。这是说马洛一语点醒梦中人，他说的这一句话，让库尔茨知道马洛才是真正了解他的人。从此之后他们彼此信任，结下了终生的情谊（虽然在这不久之后库尔茨就死了）。

end—even beyond[1219].

"'I had immense plans,' he muttered irresolutely. 'Yes,' said I; 'but if you try to shout I'll smash your head with[1220]—' There was not a stick or a stone near. 'I will throttle you for good,' I corrected myself. 'I was on the threshold of great things,' he pleaded, in a voice of longing, with a wistfulness of tone that made my blood run cold[1221]. 'And now for this stupid scoundrel—' 'Your success in Europe is assured[1222] in any case,' I affirmed steadily[1223]. I did not want to have the throttling of him, you understand—and indeed it would have been very little use for any practical purpose. I tried to break the spell—the heavy, mute spell of the wilderness—that seemed to draw him to its pitiless

---

1219. beyond：这里是"超越了（生死的界限）"。在这份知己的情谊和永恒的承诺中，即使库尔茨死了，马洛也会继续忠诚于他们之间的约定；即使马洛也死了，他们的情谊也将永世流传，永不磨灭。

1220. smash your head with：用（木棍或石块）打碎你的头。这里是马洛对库尔茨的威胁，或者说是用坚决的话语帮他当机立断地下定决心，让他马上清醒过来，和马洛回到汽船上的文明世界中去（虽然文明世界有的时候会比丛林更加黑暗）。

1221. made my blood run cold：让我的血变冷了。这里的意思是，库尔茨回归丛林的渴望让马洛感到绝望和恐惧。

1222. is assured：有保障，放心好了。这里是马洛挽回库尔茨的再一次尝试。马洛用库尔茨在欧洲的名望来劝诱，目的是引起库尔茨对文明世界的留恋不舍，也让他有所顾忌。当然，马洛也兑现了他的承诺，他保守了库尔茨的黑暗秘密，也保住了库尔茨在文明世界的高大形象。

1223. affirmed steadily：坚定地断言；斩钉截铁地说。马洛在这场危机之中头脑清醒，立场坚定，他要拉回库尔茨，不让他迈出决定性的最后一步。在不能动手、只能用言语阻拦的情况下，马洛可谓绞尽了脑汁软硬兼施。他恳求道"这一去，你就不再是你了"；威胁说"如果你再走一步，我就弄死你"；劝诱说"只要你回来，你在欧洲还是个公认的成功人士"。马洛尽力了。

breast by the awakening of forgotten and brutal instincts, by the memory of gratified and monstrous passions. This alone, I was convinced, had driven him out to the edge of the forest, to the bush, towards the gleam of fires, the throb of drums, the drone of weird incantations; this alone had beguiled his unlawful soul beyond the bounds of permitted aspirations[1224]. And, don't you see, the terror of the position[1225] was not in being knocked on the head—though I had a very lively sense of that danger, too—but in this, that I had to deal with a being to whom I could not appeal in the name of anything high or low[1226]. I had, even like the niggers, to invoke him—himself—his own exalted and incredible degradation. There was nothing either above or below him[1227], and I knew it. He had kicked himself loose of the earth[1228]. Confound the man[1229]! he

---

1224. beguile his...permitted aspirations：引诱他那不知法度的灵魂超越了能够被允许的欲望的界限。beguile 意为"欺骗；诱骗"，unlawful 意为"不正当的；不合法的；不安分的"。

1225. the terror of the position：我当时所处的境地的可怕之处；我当时所面临的最大危险（是吃上一记闷棍；被野人抓走或打死等）。

1226. appeal in the name of anything high or low：以最高或最低的名义（向他）发出呼唤。最高即至善的上帝；最低即至恶的魔鬼。这里是说库尔茨早已看破一切，无论用上帝之名来感召，还是用魔鬼之名来恐吓，对他都毫无作用。in the name of 意为"以……的名义"。

1227. above or below him：没有比他更崇高的事物，也没有比他更堕落的事物；或者是，既没有头顶的天堂，也没有脚下的地狱。

1228. kick himself loose of the earth：一脚把大地给踢开了。这里是说库尔茨已经看透了一切，也割断了他和这个俗世的一切联系。

1229. Confound the man：这里是一句语气强烈的感叹，可以译成"这个可恶的家伙"，"这个混蛋"等，表示对库尔茨现状的惊异。

had kicked the very earth to pieces[1230]. He was alone, and I before him did not know whether I stood on the ground or floated in the air[1231]. I've been telling you what we said—repeating the phrases we pronounced[1232]—but what's the good? They were common everyday words—the familiar, vague sounds exchanged on every waking day of life. But what of that? They had behind them, to my mind, the terrific suggestiveness of words heard in dreams, of phrases spoken in nightmares. Soul! If anybody ever struggled with a soul, I am the man. And I wasn't arguing with a lunatic either. Believe me or not, his intelligence was perfectly clear—concentrated, it is true, upon himself with horrible intensity[1233], yet clear; and therein was my only chance—barring, of course, the killing him there and then[1234], which wasn't so good, on account of unavoidable noise. But his soul was mad. Being alone in the

---

1230. kicked the very earth to pieces: 把这片大地踢成了碎片。这里是说库尔茨已经完全脱离了他原先的世界，再也没有回头的余地了。

1231. float in the air: 飘浮在空中。马洛似乎觉得连自己也分不清自己究竟是不是还停留在原先那个世界里了，还是说自己也被库尔茨弄得不正常了。

1232. repeat the phrases we pronounced: （向你们）复述着一些我们说过的话语。这里的意思是，马洛觉得其实他和库尔茨具体说了什么话并不重要，重要的是库尔茨自己内心的激烈斗争。

1233. concentrated...horrible intensity: 事实上，他正在高度集中精神，心无旁骛地关注着他自己。这里指的是库尔茨正在专注地思考着自己的去留，准备做出选择。

1234. barring, of course, the killing him there and then: 在那个时间和地点，我当然是不能杀死他的。bar 在这里意为"排除"，即"在那里杀死库尔茨"的这个选项是完全被排除了的。

wilderness, it had looked within itself[1235], and, by heavens! I tell you, it had gone mad. I had—for my sins, I suppose—to go through the ordeal of looking into it myself. No eloquence could have been so withering to one's belief in mankind as his final burst of sincerity. He struggled with himself, too. I saw it—I heard it. I saw the inconceivable mystery of a soul that knew no restraint, no faith, and no fear, yet struggling blindly with itself. I kept my head pretty well; but when I had him at last stretched on the couch[1236], I wiped my forehead, while my legs shook under me as though I had carried half a ton on my back down that hill. And yet I had only supported him, his bony arm clasped round my neck—and he was not much heavier than a child.

"When next day we left at noon, the crowd, of whose presence behind the curtain of trees I had been acutely conscious all the time, flowed out of the woods again, filled the clearing, covered the slope with a mass of naked, breathing, quivering, bronze bodies. I steamed up a bit, then swung down stream, and two thousand eyes followed the evolutions of the splashing, thumping, fierce river-demon beating the water with its terrible tail and breathing black smoke into the air. In front of the first rank, along the river, three men, plastered with bright red earth from

---

1235. it had looked within itself：它（库尔茨的灵魂）已经看透了它自己。

1236. had him at last stretched on the couch：最后终于把他放在长椅上躺好。这说明马洛终于把库尔茨劝回来了。这个过程无人知晓，但是惊心动魄。库尔茨做出了他一生中也许是最后一个最重要的决定；马洛也是用自己的生命冒了一次险。

head to foot, strutted to and fro restlessly. When we came abreast again, they faced the river, stamped their feet, nodded their horned heads, swayed their scarlet bodies; they shook towards the fierce river-demon a bunch of black feathers, a mangy skin with a pendent tail—something that looked a dried gourd; they shouted periodically together strings of amazing words that resembled no sounds of human language; and the deep murmurs of the crowd, interrupted suddenly, were like the responses of some satanic litany.

"We had carried Kurtz into the pilot-house: there was more air there. Lying on the couch, he stared through the open shutter. There was an eddy in the mass of human bodies[1237], and the woman with helmeted head and tawny cheeks rushed out to the very brink of the stream. She put out her hands, shouted something, and all that wild mob took up the shout in a roaring chorus of articulated, rapid, breathless utterance.

"'Do you understand this?' I asked.

"He kept on looking out past me with fiery, longing eyes, with a mingled expression of wistfulness and hate. He made no answer, but I saw a smile, a smile of indefinable meaning, appear on his colourless lips that a moment after twitched convulsively. 'Do I not?' he said slowly, gasping, as if the words had been torn out of him[1238]

1237. an eddy in the mass of human bodies：在那群人中间掀起了一阵涡流。这里指的是那个土著女人分开人群走出来，所到之处，野人们纷纷给她让路。

1238. been torn out of him：从他（心里面）撕扯出来的。这里是说，库尔茨说这几个字的时候很艰难、很痛苦，似乎是心如刀绞地说出来的。可能是野人的吼叫（他们是在传达土著女人的话）有什么特殊的含义，或者让他回忆起了某种往事。

by a supernatural power.

"I pulled the string of the whistle, and I did this because I saw the pilgrims on deck getting out their rifles with an air of anticipating a jolly lark. At the sudden screech there was a movement of abject terror through that wedged mass of bodies. 'Don't! don't you frighten them away,' cried some one on deck disconsolately. I pulled the string time after time. They broke and ran, they leaped, they crouched, they swerved, they dodged the flying terror of the sound. The three red chaps had fallen flat, face down on the shore, as though they had been shot dead[1239]. Only the barbarous and superb woman did not so much as flinch, and stretched tragically her bare arms after us over the sombre and glittering river[1240].

"And then that imbecile crowd down on the deck started their little fun, and I could see nothing more for smoke.

"The brown current ran swiftly out of the heart of darkness, bearing us down towards the sea with twice the speed of[1241] our upward progress; and Kurtz's life was running swiftly, too,

---

1239. been shot dead：被（枪）打死。在这里，朝圣者们还没有开枪，所以他们的样子虽然好像中枪倒地似的，但其实只是他们自我保护的动作而已。

1240. over the sombre and glittering river：隔着那条阴冷地闪着波光的河流。这里也是将主观感情色彩带入客观事物的表现手法。每当殖民者作恶的时候，作者笔下作为目睹者的丛林、河流、荒野，就会呈现出一种仿佛是阴森森的神色，似乎在耐心地酝酿着什么企图。这是作者的一种警示，作恶者或早或晚，终将承受来自荒野的报复。

1241. twice the speed of：以（来时）两倍的速度。马洛的汽船来时逆流而上，缓慢无比；回去的时候顺流而下，速度很快。

ebbing, ebbing out of his heart into the sea of inexorable time[1242].
The manager was very placid, he had no vital anxieties now, he
took us both in[1243] with a comprehensive and satisfied glance: the
'affair' had come off as well as could be wished[1244]. I saw the
time approaching[1245] when I would be left alone of the party of
'unsound method.' The pilgrims looked upon me with disfavour.
I was, so to speak, numbered with the dead. It is strange how I
accepted this unforeseen partnership, this choice of nightmares
forced upon me in the tenebrous land invaded by these mean and
greedy phantoms.

"Kurtz discoursed. A voice! a voice! It rang deep to the very
last. It survived his strength to hide in the magnificent folds of
eloquence the barren darkness of his heart[1246]. Oh, he struggled! he

---

1242. the sea of inexorable time：无情的时间之海。这里是一个类比，载着
汽船急速冲向大海的水流，就好像库尔茨的生命之流一样；库尔茨的生命之
流正在迅速从他的心口流出，正如退潮的水急速流向时间的大海，然后永远
地消逝了。这里是说库尔茨的情况急转直下，已经命不久矣。另外，以奔流
向海的河水比喻时间流逝，中西皆然。孔子曾说过："逝者如斯夫，不舍昼
夜。"与康拉德在这里的比喻异曲同工。

1243. took us both in：这里是说经理扫过来一眼，把马洛和库尔茨两个人都
扫到了。

1244. the 'affair' had come off as well as could be wished：这件"事情"已经
如他所愿那样地了结了。马洛前面说过，他第一次见到经理的时候，经理曾
说"就打算三个月吧，三个月的时间，做这件事情还是够用的"。实际上经
理指的并不是"修汽船要三个月"，而是指"拖死库尔茨要三个月"。现在事
情的结局正如同经理的预期。come off 意为"成功；达到预期结果"。

1245. the time approaching：（库尔茨死去、马洛被孤立）的时间就快要到了。

1246. It survived...darkness of his heart：这句话的正常语序是"It survived his
strength to hide the barren darkness of his heart in the magnificent folds（转下页）

struggled! The wastes of his weary brain were haunted by shadowy images now—images of wealth and fame revolving obsequiously round his unextinguishable gift of noble and lofty expression. My Intended, my station, my career, my ideas—these were the subjects for the occasional utterances of elevated sentiments. The shade of the original Kurtz frequented the bedside of <u>the hollow sham</u>[1247], whose fate it was to be buried presently in the mould of primeval earth. But both the diabolic love and the unearthly hate of the mysteries it had penetrated <u>fought for the possession of</u>[1248] that soul satiated with primitive emotions, avid of lying fame, of sham distinction, of all the appearances of success and power.

"Sometimes he was contemptibly childish. He desired to have kings meet him at railway-stations on his return from some ghastly Nowhere, where he intended to accomplish great things. 'You show them you have in you something that is really profitable, and then there will be no limits to the recognition of your ability,' he would say. 'Of course you must take care of the motives—right motives—always.' The long reaches that were like one and the

---

（接上页）of eloquence", 句子主干是 "It (The voice) survived his strength", 意思是 "即使他已经没有了……的力量, 他仍有着这个声音"。survive 意为 "比……活得长; 挺得久"。而 "那种力量", 指的是把 "the barren darkness of his heart（他心中空虚的黑暗）" 掩藏（hide）在 "the magnificent folds of eloquence（雄辩的华丽外衣）" 之下的那种力量。

1247. the hollow sham: 那个空荡荡的赝品。这里指的是病榻上的库尔茨已经完全失去了原先的力量, 只能算是个 "赝品" 了。sham 意为 "假冒者"。

1248. fought for the possession of: 争着抢夺对（库尔茨的灵魂）的所有权。这里体现了库尔茨内心深处的极度矛盾。

same reach, monotonous bends that were exactly alike, slipped past
the steamer with their multitude of secular trees looking patiently
after this grimy fragment of another world[1249], the forerunner of
change, of conquest, of trade, of massacres, of blessings. I looked
ahead—piloting. 'Close the shutter,' said Kurtz suddenly one
day; 'I can't bear to look at this.' I did so. There was a silence.
'Oh, but I will wring your heart yet[1250]!' he cried at the invisible
wilderness.

"We broke down—as I had expected—and had to lie up
for repairs at the head of an island. This delay was the first thing
that shook Kurtz's confidence. One morning he gave me a packet
of papers and a photograph—the lot tied together with a shoe-
string. 'Keep this for me,' he said. 'This noxious fool' (meaning
the manager) 'is capable of prying into my boxes when I am not
looking.' In the afternoon I saw him. He was lying on his back
with closed eyes, and I withdrew quietly, but I heard him mutter,
'Live rightly, die, die...' I listened. There was nothing more. Was
he rehearsing some speech in his sleep, or was it a fragment of a
phrase from some newspaper article? He had been writing for the

---

1249. this grimy fragment of another world：来自另一个世界的肮脏碎片。这
里指的是出现在非洲原始世界的代表着工业文明的汽船。grimy 意为"肮脏
的；污秽的"。

1250. I will wring your heart yet：我还会重新掌控你的。wring your heart 意为
"把你的心脏握在手中拧绞"，通常比喻"令人肝肠寸断"，这里可能指的是
"把某人攥在手中；让某人臣服并乖乖听话"。也就是说，库尔茨还想要让那
片荒野臣服于他，在他的脚下震颤。

papers and meant to do so again, 'for the furthering of my ideas. It's a duty.'

"His was an impenetrable darkness. I looked at him as you peer down at a man who is lying at the bottom of a precipice where the sun never shines. But I had not much time to give him, because I was helping the engine-driver to take to pieces the leaky cylinders, to straighten a bent connecting-rod, and in other such matters. I lived in an infernal mess of[1251] rust, filings, nuts, bolts, spanners, hammers, ratchet-drills—things I abominate, because I don't get on with them. I tended the little forge we fortunately had aboard; I toiled wearily in a wretched scrap-heap—unless I had the shakes too bad to stand.

"One evening coming in with a candle I was startled to hear him say a little tremulously, 'I am lying here in the dark waiting for death.' The light was within a foot of his eyes. I forced myself to murmur, 'Oh, nonsense!' and stood over him as if transfixed.

"Anything approaching the change that came over his features I have never seen before, and hope never to see again. Oh, I wasn't touched. I was fascinated. It was as though a veil had been rent. I saw on that ivory face the expression of sombre pride, of ruthless power, of craven terror—of an intense and hopeless despair. Did he live his life again in every detail of desire, temptation, and surrender during that supreme moment of complete

---

1251. an infernal mess of: 一大堆乱七八糟的东西。infernal 在这里是加强语气的用词，但是马洛明显对这些修理工作深恶痛绝，所以"水深火热"的译法似乎也比较可取。

knowledge[1252]? He cried in a whisper at some image, at some vision—he cried out twice, a cry that was no more than a breath:

"'The horror! The horror!'[1253]

"I blew the candle out and left the cabin. The pilgrims were dining in the mess-room, and I took my place opposite the manager, who lifted his eyes to give me a questioning glance[1254], which I successfully ignored[1255]. He leaned back[1256], serene, with that peculiar smile of his sealing the unexpressed depths of his meanness. A continuous shower of small flies[1257] streamed upon

---

1252. that supreme moment of complete knowledge：那个大彻大悟的至高时刻。指的是死亡的一瞬间。supreme 意为"最高的；杰出的"，这里指的是"涉及死亡的"。complete knowledge 在这里指的是"看透一切；领悟一切"。

1253. 'The horror! The horror!'：1979 年马龙·白兰度主演的美国电影《现代启示录》，套用了《黑暗之心》的主要情节。影片讲述了越战期间，美军情报官员威尔德上尉奉命沿河而上，刺杀已经擅自脱离军队并在柬埔寨丛林里成为部落首领的库尔兹上校。库尔兹上校临死时，口中也轻声呼喊着"可怕！可怕啊！"这似乎是在对战争反人性的残酷本质进行揭露和批判。而《黑暗之心》中库尔茨所说的"可怕！可怕啊！"，则似乎是看透了人类的本性中所具有的黑暗面。但是如前所说，康拉德的文本往往是开放性的，可以对其进行多重解读。

1254. give me a questioning glance：给了我一个询问的眼神。这里是说经理用眼神向马洛询问"库尔茨现在是不是已经死了？"

1255. I successfully ignored：我成功地忽视掉了。这里是说马洛不露痕迹地装作没看见经理的询问的眼神。马洛不愿意从自己口中说出面前这个卑鄙的魔鬼最期待听到的消息。

1256. leaned back：往（椅子背上）一靠；往后一靠。这个动作表示经理看到马洛的反应已经心中有数，他知道，自己已经大获全胜了。

1257. A continuous shower of small flies：小苍蝇源源不断地好像雨点似的飞过来。作者擅长使用象征主义表现手法，这里的苍蝇和上文中会计师办公室里的苍蝇一样，都预示着有人死亡。shower 意为"阵雨；不断落下的一批东西"。

the lamp, upon the cloth, upon our hands and faces. Suddenly the manager's boy[1258] put his insolent black head in the doorway, and said in a tone of scathing contempt:

"'Mistah Kurtz—he dead.' [1259]

"All the pilgrims rushed out to see. I remained, and went on with my dinner. I believe I was considered brutally callous. However, I did not eat much. There was a lamp in there—light, don't you know—and outside it was so beastly, beastly dark. I went no more near the remarkable man who had pronounced a judgment upon the adventures of his soul on this earth. The voice was gone. What else had been there? But I am of course aware that next day the pilgrims buried something in a muddy hole[1260].

"And then they very nearly buried me.

"However, as you see, I did not go to join Kurtz there and

1258. the manager's boy：这里的意思不是"经理的男孩"。这里的 boy 指的是"errand boy"，即"听差；跟班；跑腿；供差遣的仆役；（黑社会大哥身边的）小弟"。上文提到过经理豢养了一个来自海边的黑人走狗做他的 errand boy，颐指气使地对待那些白人，以显示经理的权威。这里的 boy 就是那个黑人。

1259. 'Mistah Kurtz—he dead.'：'Mistah 似乎是一种发音不标准的法语，意为"先生"。这里可能是模拟黑人听差蹩脚的发音。康拉德的《黑暗之心》曾对著名现代派诗人、1948 年诺贝尔文学奖获得者托马斯·艾略特产生过巨大的影响，其诗作《空心人》的题记之一据说就是这句台词"库尔茨先生——他死啦"。但是或许是版本不同，我所见过的版本并没有这句题记。但是在艾略特与其好友埃兹拉·庞德的对话中可以看到，艾略特的著名诗歌《荒原》中，有着《黑暗之心》的影子，他曾有一段章节（后来被庞德删去）直接引用了库尔茨的故事。

1260. buried something in a muddy hole：把一样东西埋进了烂泥穴里。指的是朝圣者们把库尔茨的遗体挖坑埋葬了。muddy 意为"泥泞的；浑浊的"。

then[1261]. I did not. I remained to dream the nightmare out to the end[1262], and to show my loyalty to Kurtz[1263] once more. Destiny. My destiny! Droll thing life is[1264]—that mysterious arrangement of merciless logic[1265] for a futile purpose[1266]. The most you can

---

1261. join Kurtz there and then：在那时那地追随库尔茨而去。这里是说库尔茨死后，马洛感到唯一的光明已经熄灭，经理和朝圣者那些代表黑暗势力的魔鬼包围着他，让他感到压抑甚至窒息，就好像自己也被埋入了墓土一样。这是一种精神上的濒死感。但是马洛毕竟还要活着，为了完成他对库尔茨的承诺，他不能放任自己颓废萎靡，让自己的精神也随着库尔茨一同死去。他必须振作起来和经理他们斗争到底，让光明的火种不被黑暗彻底吞噬。

1262. dream the nightmare out to the end：把这个噩梦做到底。意思是马洛要和以经理为代表的黑暗势力斗争到底。

1263. show my loyalty to Kurtz：表达我对库尔茨的忠诚。这里一是说马洛要忠于他对库尔茨（还有俄国人）的承诺；二是说马洛决心要忠于自己清白的良心，库尔茨此时已经成了马洛心中的一个象征，象征着对理想和光明的憧憬。

1264. Droll thing life is：正常语序是"Life is (a) droll thing"，接下来的 that mysterious arrangement of merciless logic 可能是 droll thing 的同位语，省略了其中的谓语动词。这个句子的完整形式可能是"Life is a droll thing that mysterious arrangement of merciless logic has been done for a futile purpose"。droll 意为"滑稽的；可笑的"，这里是表达马洛对人生的一种强烈感叹，类似我们中国人常说的"世事无常"。

1265. mysterious arrangement of merciless logic：无情的逻辑做出的神秘安排。这里指的是环环相扣却又荒谬绝伦的命运。

1266. a futile purpose：徒劳的目的；毫无意义的目的。这里是说最后（事件的终局；人生的终局）你会发现一切的努力和得失皆为虚妄，如梦幻泡影，过眼云烟，终归寂灭。刘慈欣在《三体》系列最后一部中写道："一切终将逝去，只有死神永生"，读来令人警悟。但是死亡和结束也是生命循环的一部分，既然知道一切并非永恒，那么更应珍惜现在，在生之奋斗中追寻自我认同。

hope from it is <u>some knowledge of yourself</u>[1267]—that comes too late—<u>a crop of unextinguishable regrets</u>[1268]. I have wrestled with death. It is the most unexciting contest you can imagine. It takes place in an impalpable greyness, with nothing underfoot, with nothing around, without spectators, without clamour, without glory, without the great desire of victory, without the great fear of defeat, in a sickly atmosphere of tepid scepticism, without much belief in <u>your own right</u>[1269], and still less in that of your <u>adversary</u>[1270]. If such is the form of <u>ultimate wisdom</u>[1271], then life is a greater riddle than some of us think it to be. I was <u>within a hair's breadth</u>[1272] of the last opportunity for pronouncement, and I found with humiliation that <u>probably I would have nothing to</u>

1267. some knowledge of yourself：对于自己的一些了解和认识。人也是在和命运的不断斗争中慢慢认识到自己的品格和力量的。

1268. a crop of unextinguishable regrets：收获到的只是难以忘怀的悔恨。这里似乎是在感叹库尔茨的命运，他和命运抗争了搏斗了，最后失败了。也许在他生命的最后时刻他彻底地认清了他自己，但是一切都已无法挽回，空留余恨。unextinguishable 意为"无法扑灭的；不可磨灭的"。

1269. your own right：right 在这里可以理解为"权利"或"正当"，我选择后一种理解。

1270. adversary：敌手；对手。这句话的完整形式可能是"and still less belief in that kind of right of your adversary"，意为"更不怎么相信你的对手能代表多少正义"。

1271. ultimate wisdom：终极智慧。指最高层次的智慧，例如宇宙的本源、生命的意义等。这些智慧超越了常人的认知和理解。ultimate 意为"最终的；最根本的；终极的"。

1272. within a hair's breadth：间不容发；只差一点。这里是说马洛也曾距离死亡只有一线之隔（从而像库尔茨那样，真正得到了那个说出遗言的机会。那是唯一的机会，也是最后的机会）。

say[1273]. This is the reason why I affirm that Kurtz was a remarkable man. He had something to say. He said it. Since I had peeped over the edge[1274] myself, I understand better the meaning of his stare, that could not see the flame of the candle, but was wide enough to embrace the whole universe, piercing enough to penetrate all the hearts that beat in the darkness[1275]. He had summed up—he had judged. 'The horror!' He was a remarkable man. After all, this was the expression of some sort of belief; it had candour, it had conviction, it had a vibrating note of revolt[1276] in its whisper, it had the appalling face of a glimpsed truth—the strange commingling of desire and hate. And it is not my own extremity I remember best—a vision of greyness without form filled with physical pain, and a careless contempt for the evanescence of all things—even of this pain itself. No! It is his extremity that I seem to have

---

1273. probably I would have nothing to say: 也许我一个字都说不出来。这里是说，如果要马洛在他生命的最后一刻为自己的一生做一个总结，为这个世界下一个论断，也许他也想不出什么合适的话来说。留下一句深沉有力、令人警醒的遗言，也许并不是每个人都可以做得到的。

1274. peep over the edge: 窥视到那条边界另一边的景象。这里指的是马洛的濒死经历。闲话一句，康拉德本人据说曾在一次决斗中受了枪伤住院，也许"马洛"的濒死体验就来源于此。

1275. penetrate all the hearts that beat in the darkness: 看透所有在黑暗中跳动着的心。这里指的是库尔茨已经看透了人性中的黑暗。

1276. a vibrating note of revolt: 颤抖着的反叛的声音。vibrating 说明这颤抖的声音也许很微弱，因为库尔茨本将要油尽灯枯；但是这却是代表着反抗的最强音，对于人世间的黑暗和不公，库尔茨以无比坚定的立场说出了自己真实的看法。正如马洛所说，这句总结／判语，甚至可以称得上是一种"信念"。库尔茨认为"人世间的真相是可怕的"，他的意志无人能够撼动。

lived through[1277]. True, he had made that last stride[1278], he had stepped over the edge, while I had been permitted to draw back my hesitating foot[1279]. And perhaps in this is the whole difference[1280]; perhaps all the wisdom, and all truth, and all sincerity, are just compressed into that inappreciable moment of time in which we step over the threshold of the invisible. Perhaps! I like to think my summing-up would not have been a word of careless contempt[1281]. Better his cry—much better. It was an affirmation, a moral victory paid for by innumerable defeats, by abominable terrors, by abominable satisfactions. But it was a victory! That is why I have remained loyal to Kurtz[1282] to the last, and even beyond, when a long time after I heard once more, not his own voice, but the

---

1277. It is his extremity that I seem to have lived through：每个人的经历不同，马洛的濒死之时和库尔茨真正临死前的一刻，其体验和感悟肯定大不一样。为了理解库尔茨的那句论断，马洛必须让自己试着去体会库尔茨当时的境地和心情。

1278. made that last stride：迈出了最后的一步。stride 意为"大步；阔步"，这里有一种"昂然迈步，一去不返"的悲壮感。其实，任何一个生命从这个世界离去，都是一个哲学议题，都是一个崇高、悲壮的时刻。

1279. draw back my hesitating foot：收回了犹豫的脚步。这是说马洛在鬼门关前转了一遭，又回到了人间。be permitted 意为"获准"，这里的意思是"命运准许他重返人间"。

1280. perhaps in this is the whole difference：这句话的正常语序是 perhaps the whole difference is in this，意为"也许全部的区别就在于此"。

1281. a word of careless contempt：一句无谓的轻蔑之语。这里是说，如果一个人留在世上的最后一句话是 Oh my God 或者 Shit 之类，未免有些"轻如鸿毛"。一个真正有思想的人应当说出更深刻的话语。

1282. why I have remained loyal to Kurtz：我始终忠于库尔茨的原因。因为库尔茨的论断包含着真理。

echo of his magnificent eloquence <u>thrown to me from a soul</u>[1283] as translucently pure as a cliff of crystal.

"No, they did not bury me[1284], though there is a period of time which I remember mistily, <u>with a shuddering wonder</u>[1285], like a passage through <u>some inconceivable world that had no hope in it and no desire</u>[1286]. I found myself back in <u>the sepulchral city</u>[1287]

1283. thrown to me from a soul: 一个灵魂向我发出来的。这里的 a soul 可能就是指库尔茨，是饱含着理想主义的激情写下十七页报告的那时候的库尔茨。马洛在把库尔茨的手稿交付给记者的时候也许重温了库尔茨雄辩的文字，也感受到了那时的库尔茨清澈而又巍峨（年少纯真，充满了高尚的理想）的灵魂。

1284. No, they did not bury me: 是的，他们并没有埋葬我。这里的 No 我觉得最好翻译成"是的"。这句话其实是承接前一段的"那个时候，他们也几乎埋葬了我"，意思是马洛眼看着黑暗势力得到了胜利，他感慨万千，几乎意气消沉——"也好像一同被埋葬掉了"。但是，马洛知道自己不能消沉。他必须振作起来，和那个曾经高尚的库尔茨站在一起，与黑暗势力斗争到底。"是的，他们并没有埋葬我"的意思就是"马洛其实并没有一蹶不振。他并没有向黑暗低头、放弃斗争"。

1285. with a shuddering wonder: 带着一种不寒而栗的惊异。shuddering 意为"发抖的；战栗的"。这里是说，库尔茨死后，马洛度过了一段痛苦迷茫的日子。

1286. some inconceivable...no desire: 一个不可思议的世界，那里没有希望也没有欲求。这里也是在反映马洛在库尔茨死后的精神状态。库尔茨之死让马洛看透了这个世界，他似乎已经游离于一切之外，觉得整个世界已经变得空空荡荡，既没有什么吸引人欲望的东西，也不再有什么值得让人去不懈追寻的东西。

1287. the sepulchral city: 那个坟墓般的城市。也就是马洛公司总部所在地的那个法国城市（可能是巴黎）。顺便说一句，巴黎的地下 112 米深处是绵延 320 公里的"巴黎地下墓穴"，堆放着 18—19 世纪的 600 余具人类尸骨。除了普通人，拉伯雷、孟德斯鸠、拉瓦锡、罗伯斯庇尔等名人也埋骨于此。这里的石碑上刻着贺拉斯的警言："切记，每一天都是你的末日。"如果说"浪漫之都"同时也是一座"墓穴之城"，其实也并不为过。

resenting the sight of[1288] people hurrying through the streets to filch a little money from each other[1289], to devour their infamous cookery[1290], to gulp their unwholesome beer, to dream their insignificant and silly dreams. They trespassed upon my thoughts[1291]. They were intruders whose knowledge of life was to me an irritating pretence[1292], because I felt so sure they could not possibly know the things I knew[1293]. Their bearing, which was

---

1288. resenting the sight of：带着厌恶之情看着眼前的一幕（即普通人行色匆匆、尔虞我诈、为了一点利益争执不休的那种日常生活）。

1289. filch a little money from each other：从彼此身上骗取一点小钱；从彼此身上占点小便宜；彼此算计。filch 意为"窃取"。经济活动的本质是相互交换，人们都希望在交换中获取更多的利益，这本身无可厚非。只是马洛经历了丛林中的生死考验再回到这个普通人的世界，再看到那些斤斤计较着鸡毛蒜皮的凡夫俗子，实在是只能表示不屑。

1290. devour their infamous cookery：大嚼着那些醒齤的食物；饕餮着俗鄙的饭食。devour 意为"狼吞虎咽；吞吃；吞噬"，infamous 意为"臭名昭著的；无耻的；令人恶心的"，cookery 意为"烹饪；食物"，通常指比较精致的菜式，比如法国的"红酒蜗牛""鹅肝酱""鱼子酱"之类。但是 cookery 却用了 infamous 来形容。这种出人意料的措辞反映了马洛对欧洲餐桌上优雅进餐的情景（或者"鹅肝"之类的所谓美食）已经看不惯了。这也说明马洛从非洲回来之后性情变化很大，经历了思想上的洗礼和重生之后，他对文明世界的一些惯常之物的看法也变得和以前不一样。也许正应了马洛出发前那位法国老医生的话，"真正发生变化的地方，在头骨的里面呢"。

1291. trespassed upon my thoughts：马洛不能忍受这些庸俗的凡人，他们和马洛相处甚至只是出现在马洛面前，都让马洛感到自己的思想在被他们污染和践踏。trespass 意为"侵入；闯入；擅自进入"。

1292. whose knowledge...irritating pretence：在我看来，他们对生活的态度就是一种令人恼火的装腔作势。也就是说，他们自以为很了解人生，这种自命不凡的态度令马洛只想冷笑。irritating 意为"使人恼火的；激怒的"。

1293. they could not possibly know the things I knew：他们不可能知道我所知道的那些事情。因为那些普通人都没有去过真正荒蛮的世界，经历过文明间的碰撞，目睹过残暴的虐杀，思考过善恶、生死和宇宙等等真正宏大的命题。

simply the bearing of commonplace individuals going about their business in the assurance of perfect safety, was offensive to me like the outrageous flauntings of folly in the face of a danger it is unable to comprehend[1294]. I had no particular desire to enlighten them, but I had some difficulty in restraining myself from laughing in their faces so full of stupid importance. I daresay I was not very well at that time. I tottered about the streets—there were various affairs to settle—grinning bitterly at perfectly respectable persons. I admit my behaviour was inexcusable, but then my temperature was seldom normal[1295] in these days. My dear aunt's endeavours to 'nurse up my strength' seemed altogether beside the mark. It was not my strength that wanted nursing, it was my imagination that wanted soothing[1296].

1294. the outrageous...to comprehend: the outrageous flauntings of folly 意为"那些蠢人简直让马洛受不了的那一副洋洋得意的样子", in the face of a danger it is unable to comprehend 意为"面对着它所无法理解的危险", it 指代的是 folly, 是抽象名词"愚蠢", 译文中具象化为"蠢人; 蠢猪"。这句话的意思是, 那些蠢人蠢得令人发指, 他们面对着巨大的危险还全然不知, 因为他们的理解能力实在有限; 但是他们在超出他们理解范围的危险面前还做出种种得意炫耀的姿态, 这就简直让马洛完全看不下去了。outrageous 意为"无法容忍的", flaunting 意为"炫耀; 卖弄"。

1295. my temperature was seldom normal: 我的体温几乎没有正常过。这是说明库尔茨之死带来的打击仍然在影响着马洛。一个人如果情绪波动很大, 身体状况自然也会受到影响。

1296. it was my imagination that wanted soothing: 这里是强调句, 其特征是"去掉 it was 和 that 之后剩下的是一个完整的句子"。例如这句, 去掉上述部分剩下的是"my imagination wanted soothing", 主谓宾俱在。it was 和 that 之间的部分是强调部分, 这里强调的是"想象力", 即"不是我的身体需要将息, 而是我的想象力需要抚慰"。打个比方, 一个追星的人, 心里充满了对偶像的想象, 一张海报、一个报道都会是他渴望想要得到的, 因为他想要知道关于偶像的更多消息。在这里, 马洛通过形形色色的来访者口中（转下页）

I kept the bundle of papers[1297] given me by Kurtz, not knowing exactly what to do with it. His mother had died lately, watched over, as I was told, by his Intended. A clean-shaved man, with an official manner and wearing gold-rimmed spectacles, called on me one day and made inquiries, at first circuitous, afterwards suavely pressing, about what he was pleased to denominate certain 'documents.' I was not surprised, because I had had two rows with the manager on the subject out there[1298]. I had refused to give up the smallest scrap[1299] out of that package, and I took the same attitude with[1300] the spectacled man. He became darkly menacing at last, and with much heat argued that the Company had the right to every bit of information about its 'territories.' And said he, 'Mr. Kurtz's knowledge of unexplored regions must have

---

（接上页）得知的关于库尔茨的描述，也慢慢在脑海中拼凑起曾经那个在欧洲的库尔茨的形象，满足马洛的想象和好奇——库尔茨到底曾经是个什么样的人？马洛此时并不在乎自己身体如何、是否发烧什么的（这却是马洛姨妈关注的重点，所以说她 beside the mark），他只是想尽可能多地了解库尔茨的过往。soothe 意为"安慰；安抚；减轻；缓和（疼痛或焦虑等）"。

1297. the bundle of papers：一捆书信 / 文件。指的是库尔茨临死时交托给马洛的东西。

1298. out there：这里指的是"在非洲；在刚果河那边的时候"。也就是说，库尔茨刚过世没多久，也许还在汽船上的时候，经理就向马洛索要库尔茨交托给他的那些东西了。

1299. scrap：（纸、布等的）碎片；丝毫；一丁点。这里是说马洛保护着那些东西，连其中的一张纸片也拒绝交给经理。

1300. took the same attitude with：（马洛）对（这个眼镜男）也是完全一样的态度（拒绝交出哪怕一张纸片）。

been necessarily extensive and peculiar[1301]—owing to his great abilities and to the deplorable circumstances in which he had been placed[1302]: therefore—' I assured him Mr. Kurtz's knowledge, however extensive, did not bear upon the problems of commerce or administration. He invoked then the name of science. 'It would be an incalculable loss if,' etc., etc. I offered him the report on the 'Suppression of Savage Customs,' with the postscriptum torn off. He took it up eagerly, but ended by sniffing at it with an air of contempt. 'This is not what we had a right to expect,' he remarked. 'Expect nothing else[1303],' I said. 'There are only private letters.' He withdrew upon some threat of legal proceedings[1304], and I saw him no more; but another fellow, calling himself Kurtz's cousin, appeared two days later, and was anxious to hear all the details about his dear relative's last moments. Incidentally he gave me to understand that Kurtz had been essentially a great musician. 'There was the making of an immense success,' said the man, who was an organist, I believe, with lank grey hair flowing over a greasy coat-collar. I had no reason to doubt his statement; and to

---

1301. been necessarily extensive and peculiar：（库尔茨对那片荒野的了解）必然是全面而又独到的。

1302. the deplorable...been placed：（鉴于）他所身处的恶劣环境。库尔茨深入非洲丛林，这种"深入虎穴"的经历是其他欧洲人都没有的。deplorable 意为"恶劣的；糟透的"。

1303. Expect nothing else：这是马洛接着眼镜男的句型回的一句话，非常犀利。意思是"既然不要这个，那么其他的东西不好意思，一概欠奉"。

1304. withdrew upon...legal proceedings：嘴里一边威胁着说要走什么法律途径，一边离开了。这里表现了眼镜男终究没能得逞的悻悻的样子。

this day I am unable to say what was Kurtz's profession, whether he ever had any—which was the greatest of his talents. I had taken him for a painter who wrote for the papers, or else for a journalist who could paint—but even the cousin (who took snuff during the interview) could not tell me what he had been—exactly. He was a universal genius—on that point I agreed with the old chap, who thereupon blew his nose noisily into a large cotton handkerchief and withdrew in senile agitation, bearing off some family letters and memoranda without importance. Ultimately a journalist anxious to know something of the fate of his 'dear colleague' turned up. This visitor informed me Kurtz's proper sphere ought to have been politics 'on the popular side.' He had furry straight eyebrows, bristly hair cropped short, <u>an eyeglass on a broad ribbon</u>[1305], and, becoming expansive, confessed his opinion that Kurtz really couldn't write a bit— 'but heavens! how that man could talk. He electrified large meetings. He had faith—don't you see?—he had the faith. He could get himself to believe anything—anything. He would have been a splendid leader of an extreme party.' 'What party?' I asked. 'Any party,' answered the other. 'He was an—an—extremist.' Did I not think so? I assented. Did I know, he asked, with a sudden flash of curiosity,

---

1305. an eyeglass on a broad ribbon：用一条宽带子拴着眼镜。康拉德擅用外貌描写映射人物的品质。这里的记者也戴眼镜，但是和上文中的眼镜男在给人的感受上完全不同。这个记者"眉毛浓直、头发短硬，眼睛不修边幅"，给人一种正直、敬业的感觉；而上文的眼镜男"戴着金丝眼镜，胡须刮得很干净，态度温文尔雅"，给人一种"精明险诈，斯文败类"的感觉。

'what it was that had induced him to go out there?' 'Yes,' said I, and forthwith handed him the famous Report for publication, if he thought fit. He glanced through it hurriedly, mumbling all the time, judged 'it would do,' and took himself off with this plunder.

"Thus I was left at last with a slim packet of letters and the girl's portrait[1306]. She struck me as beautiful—I mean she had a beautiful expression. I know that the sunlight can be made to lie[1307], too, yet one felt that no manipulation of light and pose could have conveyed the delicate shade of truthfulness upon those features. She seemed ready to listen without mental reservation, without suspicion, without a thought for herself[1308]. I concluded I would go and give her back her portrait and those letters myself. Curiosity? Yes; and also some other feeling perhaps. All that had been Kurtz's[1309] had passed out of my hands[1310]: his soul, his body,

---

1306. the girl's portrait：那个姑娘的肖像。这里的 portrait 可以理解为"画像"，也可以理解为"照片"，但是我觉得更有可能是照片。照相术是 1839 年发明的，到康拉德写作本书的时候（1900 年左右）照相术已经比较成熟且已经普及开来，很多士兵都会随身携带恋人或妻子的照片。因此库尔茨也很可能是带着未婚妻的照片从欧洲来到非洲的。

1307. the sunlight can be made to lie：阳光可以被用来制造错觉。这里是说通过调整光线可以美化（或丑化）照片上的人像。lie 意为"说谎"，这里指的是制造假象，欺骗观者的眼睛。

1308. without a thought for herself：丝毫没有顾念她自己。这里说明库尔茨的未婚妻有一种自我牺牲的精神。

1309. All that had been Kurtz's：曾经属于库尔茨的一切。正如库尔茨在前文所说，"我的象牙，我的贸易站，我的河流"，等等。一切都曾经属于他。

1310. passed out of my hands：从我的手上交出去了。指的是马洛见证并参与了库尔茨人生的最后一段旅程。

his station, his plans, his ivory, his career[1311]. There remained only his memory and his Intended—and I wanted to give that up, too, to the past, in a way[1312]—to surrender[1313] personally all that remained of him with me to that oblivion[1314] which is the last word of our common fate[1315]. I don't defend myself. I had no clear perception of what it was I really wanted. Perhaps it was an impulse of unconscious loyalty, or the fulfilment of one of those ironic necessities that lurk in the facts of human existence. I don't know. I can't tell. But I went.

"I thought his memory was like the other memories of the dead that accumulate in every man's life[1316]—a vague impress on the brain of shadows that had fallen on it[1317] in their swift and final

---

1311. his soul...his career：库尔茨的遗言是马洛听到的，他的尸体是马洛看着埋葬的，马洛带着他最后一次离开了他的贸易站，在丛林的那个黑夜里终结了他东山再起的计划，驾船送走了他的象牙，为他的事业画上了句号。

1312. give that up, too, to the past, in a way：（把他的未婚妻和对于他的记忆）也以某种方式交付给"过去"。也就是说，马洛要把一切承诺中该做的事情都完成，然后彻底做一个了结——忘记库尔茨。

1313. surrender：这里的意思是"放手"，也就是"放开手，让关于库尔茨的一切都归于遗忘"。

1314. oblivion：遗忘；湮没；湮灭无存。

1315. the last word of our common fate：我们共同的命运的最后的那个词——oblivion。也就是人类命运的最后终结——被遗忘 / 湮灭无存。繁华落尽终归尘土，一切的一切，最后都是了无痕迹，仿佛不曾存在过。

1316. accumulate in every man's life：堆积在每个人的生命里的。每个人在他自己的生命跨度中，都会目睹其他很多人的离去。那些相继离去的背影将会层层叠叠地堆积在他的记忆里。

1317. shadows that had fallen on it：那些闯入 / 观映到脑海里的幽魂（指的是临终的人）。

passage[1318]; but before the high and ponderous door, between the tall houses of a street as still and decorous as a well-kept alley in a cemetery, I had a vision of him on the stretcher, opening his mouth voraciously, as if to devour all the earth with all its mankind. He lived then before me; he lived as much as he had ever lived—a shadow insatiable of splendid appearances, of frightful realities; a shadow darker than the shadow of the night, and draped nobly in the folds of a gorgeous eloquence. The vision seemed to enter the house with me—the stretcher, the phantom-bearers, the wild crowd of obedient worshippers, the gloom of the forests, the glitter of the reach between the murky bends, the beat of the drum, regular and muffled like the beating of a heart—the heart of a conquering darkness[1319]. It was a moment of triumph for the wilderness, an invading and vengeful rush which, it seemed to me, I would have to keep back alone for the salvation of another soul[1320]. And the memory of what I had

---

1318. their swift and final passage：它们（指的是那些幽魂 / 将死之人）最后停留在人间的一段短暂时刻。例如马洛所见到的在树荫下等死的黑人劳工，在汽船的舱房里期待着重返丛林、实际上却在等待着死亡降临的库尔茨等。

1319. a conquering darkness：征服了一切的黑暗。这里的黑暗可能指的是"死神；死亡"。只有死亡才能够征服一切。

1320. the salvation of another soul：为了拯救另一个灵魂。salvation 意为"拯救；解救"。这里的"另一个灵魂"指的是库尔茨的未婚妻。她已经承受了荒野的复仇——也就是失去库尔茨的痛苦，但是荒野还不打算放过她，如果她得知库尔茨真正的遗言，那将是又一次信念的覆灭。马洛尽管痛恨谎言，但是在此时却告诉她"库尔茨最后呼喊着的，是你的名字"，带给了库尔茨的未婚妻一丝苦难中的慰藉。荒野的这一次复仇，被马洛一个人全部承受了。他违背自己的天性说了谎；他再一次重温了库尔茨那句可怕的断言。但是他保护了库尔茨的未婚妻，没有让她受到来自荒野的再一次的伤害。

heard him say afar there[1321], with the horned shapes[1322] stirring at my back[1323], in the glow of fires, within the patient woods[1324], those broken phrases[1325] came back to me, were heard again in their ominous and terrifying simplicity[1326]. I remembered his abject pleading, his abject threats, the colossal scale of his vile desires, the meanness, the torment, the tempestuous anguish of his soul. And later on I seemed to see his collected languid manner, when he said one day, 'This lot of ivory now is really mine. The Company did not pay for it. I collected it myself at a very great personal risk. I am afraid they will try to claim it as theirs though. H'm. It is a difficult case. What do you think I ought to do—resist? Eh? I want no more than justice[1327].' ...He wanted no

---

1321. afar there：在那个遥远的地方。指的是非洲丛林。

1322. the horned shapes：头上戴着角的人影。指的是丛林里的土著部落的巫师。

1323. stir at my back：在我的背后活动着 / 蠢蠢欲动。这是那一夜马洛和库尔茨对峙时的情景。他们身后不远处就是土人部落，可以说是近在咫尺；马洛一旦被土人发现，可能就永远走不出那一夜的丛林了。这是马洛距离危险最近的时刻。stir 在这里译为"蠢蠢欲动"，表现了马洛内心深处的惊惧。

1324. the patient woods：富于忍耐的丛林。指的是殖民者尽可以在丛林中为所欲为，看似没有任何后果；但是丛林是富于忍耐和报复心的，它早晚会让入侵者尝到自己种下的苦果。

1325. those broken phrases：那些支离破碎。断断续续的句子 / 话语。指的是马洛和库尔茨那一夜的言语交锋。看似波澜不惊的普通话语，背后蕴藏着的却是一个灵魂的拯救与堕落，一个人生命最后时刻的抉择。当然同时也牵系着马洛的前途和性命。

1326. ominous and terrifying simplicity：不祥而又可怕的简洁。这里是说库尔茨的话语很简短，但是背后意蕴深刻，而且牵涉重大。稍有差池，所有人都会堕入深渊。

1327. want no more than justice：只不过想要个公道。justice 意为"公平；合理；公道"。

more than justice—no more than justice. I rang the bell before a mahogany door on the first floor, and while I waited he seemed to stare at me out of the glassy panel[1328]—stare with that wide and immense stare embracing, condemning, loathing all the universe. I seemed to hear the whispered cry, 'The horror! The horror!'

"The dusk was falling. I had to wait in a lofty drawing-room with three long windows from floor to ceiling that were like three luminous and bedraped columns. The bent gilt legs and backs of the furniture shone in indistinct curves. The tall marble fireplace had a cold and monumental whiteness. A grand piano stood massively in a corner; with dark gleams on the flat surfaces like a sombre and polished sarcophagus. A high door opened—closed. I rose.

"She came forward, all in black, with a pale head, floating towards me[1329] in the dusk. She was in mourning. It was more than a year since his death, more than a year since the news came; she seemed as though she would remember and mourn forever. She took both my hands in hers and murmured, 'I had heard you were coming.' I noticed she was not very young—I mean not girlish. She had a mature capacity for fidelity, for belief, for suffering. The room seemed to have grown darker, as if all the sad light

---

1328. stare at me out of the glassy panel: 从玻璃般光亮的门板里望着我。这里其实是马洛在不断回想着库尔茨，似乎从门板光亮的漆面里都看到了库尔茨的影子。

1329. float towards me: 向我飘了过来。这里用 float，一是说明当时环境昏暗，二是表现出库尔茨未婚妻沉浸在悲痛之中，身影飘忽的样子。

of the cloudy evening had taken refuge on her forehead. This fair hair, this pale visage, this pure brow, seemed surrounded by an ashy halo from which the dark eyes looked out at me. Their glance was guileless, profound, confident, and trustful. She carried her sorrowful head as though she were proud of that sorrow, as though she would say, 'I—I alone know how to mourn for him as he deserves.' But while we were still shaking hands, such a look of awful desolation came upon her face that I perceived she was one of those creatures that are not the play things of Time[1330]. For her he had died only yesterday. And, by Jove! the impression was so powerful that for me, too, he seemed to have died only yesterday—nay, this very minute. I saw her and him in the same instant of time—his death and her sorrow—I saw her sorrow in the very moment of his death. Do you understand? I saw them together—I heard them together. She had said, with a deep catch of the breath, 'I have survived' while my strained ears seemed to hear distinctly, mingled with her tone of despairing regret, the summing up whisper of his eternal condemnation. I asked myself what I was doing there, with a sensation of panic in my heart as though I had blundered into a place of cruel and absurd mysteries not fit for a human being to behold. She motioned me to a chair. We sat down. I laid the packet gently on the little table, and she put her hand over it.... 'You knew him well,' she murmured, after a

---

1330. the play things of Time：时间之神的玩物。这里指的是感情会随着时间流逝而变淡的那一类人。

moment of mourning silence.

"'Intimacy grows quickly out there,' I said. 'I knew him as well as it is possible for one man to know another.'

"'And you admired him,' she said. 'It was impossible to know him and not to admire him. Was it?'

"'He was a remarkable man,' I said, unsteadily. Then before the appealing fixity of her gaze, that seemed to watch for more words on my lips, I went on, 'It was impossible not to—'

"'Love him,' she finished eagerly, silencing me into an appalled dumbness[1331]. 'How true! how true! But when you think that no one knew him so well as I! I had all his noble confidence. I knew him best.'

"'You knew him best,' I repeated. And perhaps she did. But with every word spoken the room was growing darker, and only her forehead, smooth and white, remained illumined by the inextinguishable light of belief and love.

"'You were his friend,' she went on. 'His friend,' she repeated, a little louder. 'You must have been, if he had given you this, and sent you to me. I feel I can speak to you—and oh! I must speak. I want you—you who have heard his last words—to know I have been worthy of him.... It is not pride[1332].... Yes! I am proud

---

1331. an appalled dumbness：惊骇之下的沉默。这里可能是说她对库尔茨的爱超出了马洛能够想象的程度。

1332. It is not pride：这里是说，她认为自己配得上他，并不是出于一种对自己的骄傲自负。她似乎也是在说明自己并不是一个自视甚高，或者说有点傲慢的人，希望马洛不要因为她说自己"配得上他"而误会。

to know I understood him better than any one on earth — he told me so himself. And since his mother died I have had no one — no one — to — to — [1333],

"I listened. The darkness deepened. I was not even sure whether he had given me the right bundle. I rather suspect he wanted me to take care of another batch of his papers which, after his death, I saw the manager examining under the lamp[1334]. And the girl talked, easing her pain in the certitude of my sympathy; she talked as thirsty men drink. I had heard that her engagement with Kurtz had been disapproved by her people. He wasn't rich enough or something. And indeed I don't know whether he had not been a pauper all his life. He had given me some reason to infer that it was his impatience of comparative poverty[1335] that drove him out there.

"'...Who was not his friend who had heard him speak once?' she was saying. 'He drew men towards him by what was best in

---

1333. I have had no one — no one — to — to — ：这里 to 后面可能是省略了上文中的 speak。这句话承接的是上文中的 "I feel I can speak to you — and oh! I must speak." 也就是说，库尔茨的母亲去世后，他的未婚妻觉得"世上已经没有人能够听我诉说（我是有多么地懂他）了"，直到马洛作为库尔茨的朋友出现在她面前，她才又有了诉说的对象。

1334. examining under the lamp：在灯下细细翻阅 / 检查。examine 在这里意为"（仔细地）检查；审查"。这里说明她的不停诉说已经让马洛有点耐不住了，甚至有点分心走神，思绪都飘到别的事物上边了。对马洛来说，一个女人对爱人的绵绵思念并不是他能够一直专心听下去的话题。而对于库尔茨的未婚妻来说，在一个合适的听者面前倾诉自己的感情却是非常必要且无法停止的。这也许就是男女之间的某些差异。

1335. his impatience of comparative poverty：他对这种相对贫困的生活的无法忍耐。这里是说库尔茨已经受不了继续过着贫苦的生活了。impatience 意为"不耐烦；无耐心"。

them[1336].' She looked at me with intensity. 'It is the gift of the great,' she went on, and the sound of her low voice seemed to have the accompaniment of all the other sounds[1337], full of mystery, desolation, and sorrow, I had ever heard — the ripple of the river, the soughing of the trees swayed by the wind, the murmurs of the crowds, the faint ring of incomprehensible words cried from afar, the whisper of a voice[1338] speaking from beyond the threshold of an eternal darkness[1339]. 'But you have heard him! You know!' she cried.

"'Yes, I know,' I said with something like despair in my heart, but bowing my head before the faith that was in her[1340], before that great and saving illusion[1341] that shone with an unearthly glow

---

1336. what was best in them: 人们的天性中最闪光的部分；人们心中最美好的情感。这里也是 "把抽象译为具象"。

1337. have the accompaniment of all the other sounds: 有着其他很多声音来作为伴奏。这里指的是库尔茨未婚妻诉说的声音和马洛耳边（脑海里）缭绕着的其他声音交织在一起，就好像 "诉说的声音" 是主唱，"马洛脑海里的声音" 是伴奏一样。accompaniment 意为 "伴奏；伴随物"。

1338. the whisper of a voice: 那个语声的微弱耳语。这里的 a voice 指的是库尔茨的声音，the whisper 指的是库尔茨那两声微弱的呼喊，"可怕！可怕啊！" 这个耳语般的声音一直萦绕在马洛耳边。

1339. from beyond the threshold of an eternal darkness: 从永恒的黑暗的门槛的那一边传来。这里指的是 "从那边的死者世界传来的"，也就是已死的库尔茨曾经说过、到现在还一直让马洛难以忘怀的话。

1340. the faith that was in her: 她心中的信念。指的是她坚信库尔茨是个心地纯洁、正直高尚、才华卓越的人。

1341. great and saving illusion: 那个伟大的救赎者的幻象。指的是 "高尚的库尔茨" 的形象。

in the darkness[1342], in the triumphant darkness[1343] from which I could not have defended her—from which I could not even defend myself.

"'What a loss to me—to us!'—she corrected herself with beautiful generosity; then added in a murmur, 'To the world.' By the last gleams of twilight I could see the glitter of her eyes, full of tears—of tears that would not fall.

"'I have been very happy—very fortunate—very proud,' she went on. 'Too fortunate. Too happy for a little while. And now I am unhappy for—for life.'

"She stood up; her fair hair seemed to catch all the remaining light in a glimmer of gold. I rose, too.

"'And of all this,' she went on mournfully, 'of all his promise, and of all his greatness, of his generous mind, of his noble heart, nothing remains—nothing but a memory. You and I—'

"'We shall always remember him,' I said hastily.

"'No!' she cried. 'It is impossible that all this should be lost—that such a life should be sacrificed to leave nothing—but sorrow. You know what vast plans he had. I knew of them,

---

1342. shone with an unearthly glow in the darkness：在黑暗中闪耀着奇异 / 可怕的光芒。指的是 "高尚的库尔茨" 尽管光彩熠熠，但是马洛知道他的结局，他心中原本的纯洁高尚早已堕落成了贪婪而又残暴的累累罪孽。所以这光芒是奇异的、可怕的。

1343. the triumphant darkness：胜利的黑暗；战无不胜、压倒一切的黑暗。这里指的是在库尔茨的命运里，人性中的黑暗终究还是占了上风；黑暗最终支配了他，获得了胜利。

too—I could not perhaps understand—but others knew of them. Something must remain. His words, at least, have not died.'

"'His words will remain,' I said.

"'And his example,' she whispered to herself. 'Men looked up to him—his goodness shone in every act. His example—'

"'True,' I said; 'his example, too. Yes, his example. I forgot that.'

"'But I do not. I cannot—I cannot believe—not yet. I cannot believe that I shall never see him again, that nobody will see him again, never, never, never.

"She put out her arms as if after a retreating figure, stretching them back and with clasped pale hands across the fading and narrow sheen of the window. Never see him! I saw him clearly enough then. I shall see this eloquent phantom as long as I live, and I shall see her, too, a tragic and familiar Shade[1344], resembling in this gesture another one[1345], tragic also, and bedecked with powerless charms, stretching bare brown arms over the glitter of the infernal stream, the stream of darkness. She said suddenly very low, 'He died as he lived.'

"'His end,' said I, with dull anger stirring in me, 'was in

1344. a tragic and familiar Shade：一个悲伤的、似曾相识的身影。这里是说马洛以后也会常常回想起库尔茨的未婚妻这时的样子。之所以用 Shade，是因为她由于过度的悲伤失去了活力，整个人也仿佛是一个幽灵一般。

1345. resembling in this gesture another one：她的姿势很像是另一个（女人）。库尔茨未婚妻伸出双臂的样子，看在马洛眼里，和他心中另一个女人（那个野蛮而又高贵的土著女人）伸出双臂的悲哀形象重合了。

every way worthy of his life[1346].'

　　"'And I was not with him,' she murmured. My anger subsided before a feeling of infinite pity[1347].

　　"'Everything that could be done[1348]—' I mumbled.

　　"'Ah, but I believed in him more than any one on earth—more than his own mother, more than—himself. He needed me! Me! I would have treasured every sigh, every word, every sign, every glance.'

　　"I felt like a chill grip on my chest[1349]. 'Don't,' I said, in a muffled voice.

_____

1346. in every way worthy of his life：这里马洛说"库尔茨的结局完全对得住他这一生"，事实上是带有贬义的。但是由于英文的双关性，库尔茨的未婚妻肯定会误以为马洛是在附和她"虽死犹生"的那句无比怀恋的正面评价。这是因为在场的两人所思所想并不一样。马洛想到的是库尔茨对未婚妻的背叛，对那个非洲女人的抛弃，因此心中对于库尔茨的作为感到愤怒；很可能马洛还想到了库尔茨在非洲挑动战争、掠夺象牙所犯下的累累罪行，因而认为死亡对他而言才算得上一种赎罪。他心中对库尔茨的怒火无处发泄，又无法把真相告诉面前那个可怜的女人，所以说出了这句双关语。马洛说出这句话的时候，心中真正所想的也许是"库尔茨罪有应得 / 死得其所"。

1347. My anger subsided before a feeling of infinite pity：马洛之所以平息了对库尔茨的怒火，完全是出于对眼前这个女人的同情。她不知道真相，她是无辜的受害者，因此马洛不愿继续就这个话题说下去，以免伤害她的感情。

1348. Everything that could be done：这句话的完整形式是"Everything that could be done had been done for him"，意思是"我们能够为库尔茨做的事都为他做了"，即"我们已经尽力了"。这是对库尔茨未婚妻的一种安慰。

1349. I felt like a chill grip on my chest：马洛感到"心中一片冰凉"，这是他因为他感受到了现实的残酷和荒谬。库尔茨的未婚妻不知道真相，一直在心中怀念着一个无比崇高的理想化了的库尔茨，甚至一生都走不出对于库尔茨的完美想象和悲痛怀念，在知晓真正的库尔茨到底是个什么人的马洛看来，这无疑是一个巨大的悲剧。

"'Forgive me. I—I have mourned so long in silence—in silence....You were with him—to the last? I think of his loneliness[1350]. Nobody near to understand him as I would have understood. Perhaps no one to hear....'

"'To the very end,' I said, shakily. 'I heard his very last words....' I stopped in a fright.

"'Repeat them,' she murmured in a heart-broken tone. 'I want—I want—something—something—to—to live with.'

"I was on the point of crying at her, 'Don't you hear them?' The dusk was repeating them in a persistent whisper all around us, in a whisper that seemed to swell menacingly like the first whisper of a rising wind. 'The horror! The horror!'

"'His last word—to live with,' she insisted. 'Don't you understand I loved him—I loved him—I loved him!'

"I pulled myself together and spoke slowly.

"'The last word he pronounced was—your name[1351].'

1350. I think of his loneliness：库尔茨的未婚妻先是讲述自己是如何孤独地默默消化着心中的悲伤，然后话锋一转，想到库尔茨也是和她一样的孤独，在临死的时候身边没有一个理解他的人陪伴他。这在她看来是一种极大的遗憾，她认为两个心意相通的人被现实无情地隔绝两地，这是一件多么可哀的事。这里马洛未婚妻想象中的情境多少有点类似李清照《一剪梅》词中的"一种相思，两处闲愁"。

1351. The last word he pronounced was—your name：马洛在这里怀着巨大的矛盾和无奈，几乎是走投无路地，对库尔茨的未婚妻说出了这句谎言。他这样做的原因是为了给她一个心灵的慰藉，能够支撑她活下去，支撑她度过余生中漫长的怀念的岁月；但是马洛自己却为此承受了极度的心灵痛苦。马洛在前文中说过，"我厌恶谎言，因为谎言会让我嗅到死亡的味道"，意思可能是"我宁死也不愿说谎"；但是在这里他却被逼得不得不说出（转下页）

"I heard a light sigh and then my heart stood still, stopped dead short by an exulting and terrible cry, by the cry of inconceivable triumph and of unspeakable pain.

'I knew it—I was sure!' ...She knew. She was sure. I heard her weeping; she had hidden her face in her hands. It seemed to me that the house would collapse before I could escape, that the heavens would fall upon my head. But nothing happened. The heavens do not fall for such a trifle. Would they have fallen, I wonder, if I had rendered Kurtz that justice which was his due[1352]? Hadn't he said he wanted only justice? But I couldn't. I could not tell her. It would have been too dark—too dark altogether...."

（接上页）这句谎言，因为"为了拯救另一个不幸的灵魂，我唯有独自承受来自荒野的复仇"。库尔茨在非洲的种种作为是对那片土地的戕害，荒野也通过自己的方式夺去了他的性命，算是报了仇；但是荒野的复仇不仅在肉体上消灭了库尔茨，也在精神上摧残着库尔茨的未婚妻，所以马洛此时唯有挺身而出，用违背自己本心的谎言结成一道最后的屏障，竭力保护这个无辜的女人。

1352. rendered Kurtz that justice which was his due：马洛这句话有多重含义。他说："如果我把他应得的那些公道还给他，天是否还会塌下来？"在这里，库尔茨应得的公道是什么？也许"他出生入死才搞到手的、而公司没有付钱就拿走了的"那些象牙，这是以经理为代表的公司对库尔茨的不公正的欺骗和压榨——而拿回这笔钱几乎是不可能的，这是库尔茨"求而不得"的"公道"；但是 justice 除了"公平、公道"，还有"正义"的意思。如果库尔茨一定要寻求正义的彰显，那么除了公司亏欠他的财富，是不是他所杀过的人也要向他讨还公道？他所肆意破坏的荒野，他所辜负的两个女人，是不是也要向他讨还公道？在这个世上，到底什么是真相，什么是正义，什么是公平？还是说，这些光明的事物其实都是不存在的，唯有黑暗才是不可战胜的、永恒存在的？这些找不到答案的问题也许已经上升到了哲学的层面，这样的问题想得多了，就成了马洛心灵中的不可承受之重，甚至让他觉得"天似乎也会塌下来。"